The Roof of Voyaging

When Kupe, one of the great Polynesian voyagers, chases a huge octopus across the ocean, he discovers the strange and mysterious Land-of-Mists and rescues a man and a woman from the wild sea. He carries them back to the island of Raiatea where the pale strangers witness the momentous events that follow the death of the king and the struggle for succession.

But the gods are watching also, and when Prince Tangiia and his followers secretly flee the island in search of a new home, their intervention becomes inevitable.

The Princely Flower

Kieto's destiny, set in the heavens, is to conquer the Land-of-Mists, the mysterious island discovered by Kupe, one of the great Polynesian voyagers. But he knows it won't be easy: the wild native tribes, particularly the Scots and Picts, have two formidable advantages – iron and horses.

Land-of-Mists

It was always Keito's destiny to lead the Polynesian armies against the Celts and the Picts of the Land-of-Mists. And now the time has come. The Warriors are assembled, the boats are ready, and the gods are preparing for the confrontation. Only Seumas, the Celtic warrior taken from his homeland years before, speaks out against the great adventure. But Seumas is an old man now, embittered by the loss of his beloved wife, Dorcha.

Soon the mighty army is on the move, crossing the sea towards the unknown land, and Seumas and his son swell its numbers. They encounter storms, magic, monsters and tragedy even before they reach their destination – the cold, rainy land of muted colours that will decide their fate – and that of their gods.

Also by Garry Kilworth

Novels

In Solitary (1977)
The Night of Kadar (1978)
Split Second (1979)
Gemini God (1981)
A Theatre of Timesmiths (1984)
Abandonati (1988)
Cloudrock (1988)
The Voyage of the Vigilance (1988)
The Street (1988) (writing as Garry Douglas)
Hunter's Moon (1989)
Midnight's Sun (1990)
Frost Dancers: A Story of Hares (1992)
House of Tribes (1995)
A Midsummer's Nightmare (1996)
Shadow Hawk (1999)

Angel

1. Angel (1993)
2. Archangel (1994)

Navigator Kings

1. The Roof of Voyaging (1996)
2. The Princely Flower (1997)
3. Land-of-Mists (1998)

Collections

The Songbirds of Pain (1984)
In the Hollow of the Deep-Sea Wave (1989)
In the Country of Tattooed Men (1993)

Garry Kilworth

SF GATEWAY OMNIBUS

THE ROOF OF VOYAGING
THE PRINCELY FLOWER
LAND-OF-MISTS

GOLLANCZ

LONDON

First published in Great Britain in 2014 by
Gollancz
An imprint of the Orion Publishing Group
Orion House, 5 Upper St Martin's Lane,
London WC2H 9EA

An Hachette UK Company

A CIP catalogue record for this book is
available from the British Library

ISBN 978 0 575 11419 7

1 3 5 7 9 10 8 6 4 2

Typeset by Jouve (UK), Milton Keynes

Printed and bound by CPI Group (UK) Ltd, Croydon, CR0 4YY

The Orion Publishing Group's policy is to use papers
that are natural, renewable and recyclable products and
made from wood grown in sustainable forests. The logging
and manufacturing processes are expected to conform to
the environmental regulations of the country of origin.

www.orionbooks.co.uk
www.gollancz.co.uk

CONTENTS

ENTER THE SF GATEWAY . . .

Towards the end of 2011, in conjunction with the celebration of fifty years of coherent, continuous science fiction and fantasy publishing, Gollancz launched the SF Gateway.

Over a decade after launching the landmark SF Masterworks series, we realised that the realities of commercial publishing are such that even the Masterworks could only ever scratch the surface of an author's career. Vast troves of classic SF and fantasy were almost certainly destined never again to see print. Until very recently, this meant that anyone interested in reading any of those books would have been confined to scouring second-hand bookshops. The advent of digital publishing changed that paradigm for ever.

Embracing the future even as we honour the past, Gollancz launched the SF Gateway with a view to utilising the technology that now exists to make available, for the first time, the entire backlists of an incredibly wide range of classic and modern SF and fantasy authors. Our plan, at its simplest, was – and still is! – to use this technology to build on the success of the SF and Fantasy Masterworks series and to go even further.

The SF Gateway was designed to be the new home of classic science fiction and fantasy – the most comprehensive electronic library of classic SFF titles ever assembled. The programme has been extremely well received and we've been very happy with the results. So happy, in fact, that we've decided to complete the circle and return a selection of our titles to print, in these omnibus editions.

We hope you enjoy this selection. And we hope that you'll want to explore more of the classic SF and fantasy we have available. These are wonderful books you're holding in your hand, but you'll find much, much more … through the SF Gateway.

www.sfgateway.com

INTRODUCTION

from The Encyclopedia of Science Fiction

Garry Kilworth (Born 1941) is a UK author who began to publish SF and fantasy stories and novels in the mid-1970s on retiring after eighteen years' service as a cryptographer in the RAF; raised partly in Aden, he has travelled and worked in the Far East and the Pacific. He published his first SF story, 'Let's Go to Golgotha' with the *Sunday Times Weekly Review*, 15 December 1974, having won the associated competition, and some of his many stories have been assembled as *The Songbirds of Pain: Stories from the Inscape* (1984), *In the Country of Tattooed Men* (1993), *Hogfoot Right and Bird-Hands* (1993) and *Moby Jack and Other Tall Tales* (2006). During the first years of his career he focused primarily on SF, in novels notable for their combination of generic adventurousness and an identifiably English dubiety about the roots of human action; at points, the opportunities offered by the SF toolkit and his sense of reality may have clashed, though it might be suggested that, more often than not, sparks flew.

His first novel, *In Solitary* (1977), is set on an Earth whose few remaining humans have for over 400 years been dominated by birdlike Aliens, and deals with a human rebellion whose moral impact is ambiguous; *The Night of Kadar* (1978) places humans whose culture has an Islamic coloration and who are hatched from frozen embryos, on an Alien planet where they must attempt to understand their own nature; *Split Second* (1979) similarly incarcerates a contemporary human via Timeslip in the mind of a Cro-Magnon; *Gemini God* (1981) again uses aliens to reflect the human condition; and *A Theatre of Timesmiths* (1984) isolates a human society in an ice-enclosed urban Pocket Universe as Computers fail, and questions about the meaning of human life must be asked by a protagonist so isolated from this restricted environment that her Perception of that world becomes problematic; *Cloud-rock* (1988) pits brothers – Kilworth often evokes kinship intimacies in his work, of whatever category – against themselves and each other in a further pocket-universe setting; and *Abandonati* (1988), set in a desolate Near-Future London, reflects grittily upon the implications for the UK of the last decades of this century.

During this period, Kilworth had also published two landscape-dominated non-fantastic novels, *Witchwater Country* (1986) and *Spiral Winds* (1987); and at the end of the 1980s, in what turned out to be a lasting break with his

SF career, he began to publish primarily in other genres, beginning prominently with three expertly sustained animal fantasies: *Hunter's Moon: A Story of Foxes* (1989), *Midnight's Sun: A Story of Wolves* (1990) and *Frost Dancers: A Story of Hares* (1992), in all of which he scrutinized nonhuman terrestrial life with an unblinking eye. He also moved into contemporary Horror with *Angel* (1993) and its sequel, *Archangel* (1994). More impressively, he then published the Navigator Kings Trilogy, which is fantasy (see below). At the same time, he began publishing Young Adult tales in quantity, most of them fantasies, with about twenty-five titles released since 1990. Works of this sort became his main focus as a writer.

It may be that, as an SF author, Kilworth found himself incapable of ignoring his clearly realistic but ultimately dispiriting sense of the constrictions of the actual world. There is very little escape in Kilworth's SF, unlike his fantasy or his Young Adult work in general, and it is less widely read than it deserves. It is fortunate that, for his career, he was able to work out modes of storytelling that provide some escapes from prison. Unfortunately, though his very considerable skills have been exuberantly utilized for over two decades in these more liberating genres, the nagging feeling remains that fantasy and Young Adult's gain has been science fiction's loss.

With the publication here of the Navigator Kings Trilogy, assembling in one volume *The Roof of Voyaging* (1996), *The Princely Flower* (1997) and *Land-of-Mists* (1998), we have a welcome chance to encounter Kilworth at the very peak of his very considerable career. The long multi-generational tale is set in an Alternate World version of the South Pacific, here known as Oceania, and depicts a Polynesian culture similar to that which once exists in this world, except for literal existence, and intervention, of the Polynesian pantheon. Every sentence seems simple, but every sentence is lit from within. The Magic Realist richness of the tale only deepens when it is discovered that the Land-of-Mists is not (as we may have supposed) New Zealand but a version of Britain before the Anglo-Saxons came and exiled the early folk. The Navigator Kings glows and grows in the mind's eye. There is much of Kilworth to discover, but because of its sustained length and its joy, this is the crown jewel.

For a more detailed version of the above, see Garry Kilworth's author entry in *The Encyclopedia of Science Fiction*: http://sf-encyclopedia.com/entry/kilworth_garry

Some terms above are capitalised when they would not normally be so rendered; this indicates that the terms represent discrete entries in *The Encyclopedia of Science Fiction*.

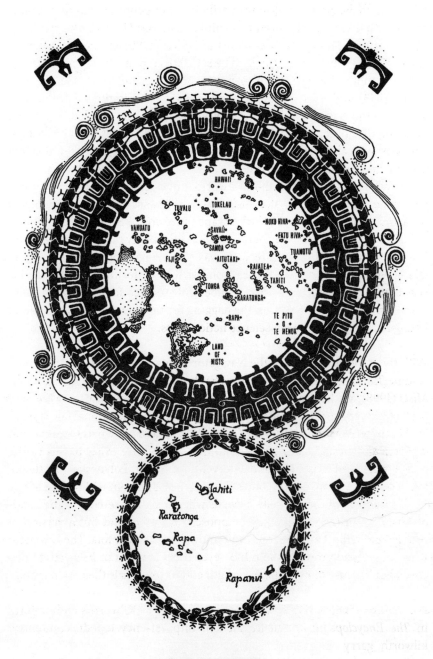

OCEANIA

AUTHOR'S NOTE

This is a work of fantasy fiction, based on the myths and legends of the Polynesian peoples and not an attempt to faithfully recreate the magnificent migrational voyages of those peoples. Other authors have done that, will do it again, far more accurately than I am able to do. This particular set of tales, within these pages, alters a piece of known geography, while hopefully retaining the internal logic of the story; my apologies to the country of New Zealand, which has changed places with Britain. (New Zealand and the Maori are not forgotten and appeared in Book II of The Navigator Kings). The gods of the Pacific region are many and diverse, some shared between many groups of islands, others specific to one set of islands or even to a single island. Their exact roles are confused and confusing, and no writer has yet managed to classify them to absolute clarity, though Jan Knappert's book is the best. Where possible I have used the universal Polynesian deities, but on rare occasion have used a god from a specific island or group for the purposes of the story. Since the spelling of Polynesian gods and the Polynesian names for such ranks as 'priest' varies between island groups, I have had to make a choice, for example *Tangaroa* (Maori) for the god of the sea and *Kahuna* (Hawaiian) for priest. In short, for purposes of homogeneity I have taken liberties with the names of gods and with language.

For the facts behind the fiction I am indebted to the following works: *The Polynesians* by Peter Bellwood (Thames and Hudson); *Nomads of the Wind* by Peter Crawford (BBC); *Polynesian Seafaring and Navigation* by Richard Feinberg (The Kent State University Press); *Ancient Tahitian Canoes* by Commandant P. Jourdain (Société des Oceanistes Paris Dossier); *Pacific Mythology* by Jan Knappert (HarperCollins); that inspiring work, *Polynesian Seafaring* by Edward Dodd (Nautical Publishing Company Limited); *Aristocrats of the South Seas* by Alexander Russell (Robert Hale); the brilliant *Myths and Legends of the Polynesians* by Johannes C. Andersen (Harrap); and finally the two articles published back to back that sparked my imagination and began the story for me way back before I had even published my first novel, *The Isles of the Pacific* by Kenneth P. Emory, and *Wind, Wave, Star and Bird* by David Lewis *(National Geographic* Vol. 146 No. 6 December 1974).

Also: *Myths and Legends of the Celtic Race* by T. W. Rolleston (Constable); *Dictionary of Celtic Mythology* by Peter Berresford Ellis (Constable); and *Celtic Gods Celtic Goddesses* by R. J. Stewart (Blandford).

Once again, and finally, grateful thanks to Wendy Leigh-James, the design artist who provided me with a map of Oceania decorated with Polynesian symbols and motifs and the various windflowers which decorated each of the ten separate parts of each volume.

PANTHEON OF THE GODS

Amai-te-rangi: Deity of the sky who angles for mortals on earth, pulling them up in baskets to devour them.

Ao: God of Clouds.

Apu Hau: A god of storms, God of the Fierce Squall.

Apu Matangi: A god of storms, God of the Howling Rain.

Ara Tiotio: God of the Whirlwind and Tornado.

Aremata-rorua and **Aremata-popoa:** 'Long-wave' and 'Shortwave', two demons of the sea who destroy mariners.

Atanua: Goddess of the Dawn.

Atea: God of Space.

Atua: Ancestor's spirit revered as a god.

Brighid: Celtic Goddess of smithcraft and metalwork.

Dakuwanga: Shark-God, eater of lost souls.

Dengei: Serpent-God, a judge in the Land of the Dead.

Hau Maringi: God of Mists and Fog.

Hine-keha, Hine-uri: The Moon-Goddess, wife of Marama the Moon-God, whose forms are Hina-keha (bright moon) and Hine-uri (dark moon).

Hine-nui-to-po: Goddess of the Night, of Darkness and Death. Hine is actually a universal goddess with many functions. She is represented with two heads, night and day. One of her functions is as patroness of arts and crafts. She loved *Tuna* the fish-man, out of whose head grew the first coconut.

Hine-te-ngaru-moana: Lady of the Ocean Waves. Hine in her fish form.

Hine-tu-whenua: Benevolent goddess of the wind who blows vessels to their destination.

Hua-hega: Mother of the trickster demi-god Maui.

Io: The Supreme Being, the 'Old One', greatest of the gods who dwells in the sky above the sky, in the highest of the twelve upper worlds.

Ira: Mother of the Stars.

Kahoali: Hawaiian God of Sorcerers.

Kukailimoku: Hawaiian God of War.

Kuku Lau: Goddess of Mirages.

Limu: Guardian of the Dead.

Lingadua: One-armed God of Drums.

Magantu: Great White Shark, a monster fish able to swallow a pahi canoe whole.

Manannan mac Lir: Celtic Sea God.

Maomao: Great Wind-God, father of the many storm-gods, including 'Howling Rainfall' and 'Fierce Squall'.

Marama: God of the Moon, husband of Hine-keha, Hine-uri.

Mareikura: Personal attendants of Io, the Old One. His 'angels'.

Marikoriko: First woman and divine ancestor, wife of Tiki. She was fashioned by the Goddess of Mirages out of the noonday heatwaves.

Maui: Great Oceanian trickster hero and demi-god. Maui was born to Taranga, who wrapped the child in her hair and gave him to the sea-fairies. Maui is responsible for many things, including the birth of the myriad of islands in Oceania, the coconut, and the length of the day, which was once too short until Maui beat Ra with a stick and forced him to travel across the sky more slowly.

Milu: Ruler of the Underworld.

Moko: Lizard-God.

Mueu: Goddess who gave bark-beating, to make tapa cloth, to the world. The stroke of her cloth-flail is death to a mortal.

Nangananga: Goddess of Punishment, who waits at the entrance to the Land of the Dead for bachelors.

Nareau: Spider-God.

Nganga: God of Sleet.

Oenghus mac in Og: Celtic Lord of Fatal Love.

Oro: God of War and Peace, commander of the warrior hordes of the spirit world. In peacetime he is 'Oro with the spear down' but in war he is 'killer of men'. Patron of the Arioi.

Paikea: God of Sea-Monsters.

Papa: Mother Earth, first woman, wife of Rangi.

Pele: Goddess of Fire and the Volcano.

Pere: Goddess of the Waters which Surround Islands.

Punga: God of Ugly Creatures.

Ra: Tama Nui-te-ra, the Sun-god.

Rangi: God of the Upper Sky, originally coupled to his wife Papa, the Goddess of the Earth, but separated by their children, mainly Tane the God of Forests whose trees push the couple apart and provide a space between the brown earth and blue sky, to make room for creatures to walk and fly.

Rehua: Star-God, son of Rangi and Papa, ancestor of the demigod Maui.

Ro: Demi-god, wife of the trickster demi-god Maui, who became tired of his mischief and left him to live in the netherworld.

Rongo: God of Agriculture, Fruits and Cultivated Plants. Along with Tane and Tu he forms the creative unity, the Trinity, equal in essence but each with distinctly different attributes. They are responsible for making Man, in the image of Tane, out of pieces of earth fetched by Rongo and shaped, using his spittle as mortar, by Tu the Constructor. When they breathed over him, Man came to life.

Rongo-ma-tane: God of the Sweet Potato, staple diet of Oceanians.

Rongo-mai: God of Comets and Whales.

Ro'o: Healer-God, whose curative chants were taught to men to help them drive out evil spirits which cause sickness.

Ruau-moko: Unborn God of Earthquakes, trapped in Papa's womb.

Samulayo: God of Death in Battle.

Tane: Son of Rangi the Sky God, and himself the God of artisans and boat builders. He is also the God of Light (especially to underwater swimmers because to skin divers light is where life is), the God of Artistic Beauty, the God of the Forest, and Lord of the Fairies. As Creator in one of his minor forms he is the God of Hope.

Tangaroa: God of the Ocean, who breathes only twice in 24 hours, thus creating the tides.

Taranis: Celtic God of Thunder.

Tawhaki: God of Thunder and Lightning. Tawhaki gives birth to Uira (lightning) out of his armpits. Tawhaki is also the God of Good Health, an artisan god particularly adept at building houses and plaiting decorative mats.

Tawhiri-atea: Storm-God, leveller of forests, wave-whipper.

Te Tuna: 'Long eel', a fish-god and vegetation-god. Tuna lived in a tidal pool near the beach and one day Hine went down to the pool to bathe. Tuna made love to her while she did so and they lived for some time on the ocean bed.

Tiki: Divine ancestor of all Oceanians who led his people in their fleet to the first islands of Oceania.

Tikokura: Wave-god of monstrous size whose enormous power and quick-flaring temper are to be greatly feared.

Tini Rau: Lord of the Fishes.

Tui Delai Gau: Mountain God who lives in a tree and sends his hands fishing for him when he grows hungry.

Tui Tofua: God of all the sharks.

Ua: Rain God, whose many sons and daughters, such as 'long rains' and 'short rains' are responsible for providing the earth with water.

Uira: Lightning (See Tawhaki).

Ulupoka: Minor god of evil, decapitated in a battle amongst the gods and whose head now rolls along beaches looking for victims.

Whatu: The God of Hail.

THE ROOF OF VOYAGING

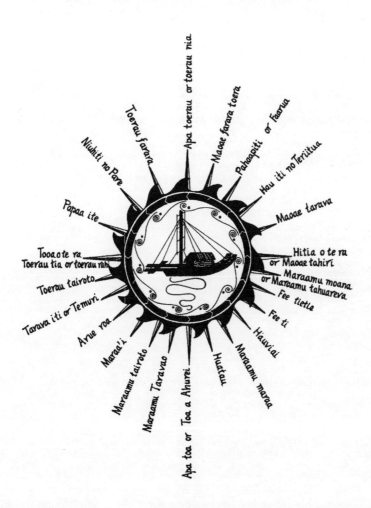

To Lisa and Bill Fedden

PART ONE

'Sail to the left of the setting sun'

1

The giant Head rolled along the beach, driven forward by a strong, cold sea-breeze.

Leaves rustled in the frangipani trees and white blossoms drifted down to the earth as the wind swept the Head beneath their branches. Fruit bats like prehistoric birds soared through the thickening dusk. Palm-rats, sensing the presence of evil, stiffened in their climb, panted quickly, and stared with small fearful eyes at the strange tracks left upon the coral sands.

On the face of the Head, twice the size of that of a mortal, was a look of intense purposefulness. The Head had smelled the presence of seafaring men on its shore. Mingling with the sea-bottom odour of drying weed, shellfish and crustaceans coming from the exposed reef, the thick cloying perfume of trumpet blooms, the sometimes unbelievable stench of rotting mud in the mango swamp, was the smell of groin sweat, oiled skin and hair, and stale breath.

There were exhausted seafarers, potential victims, who had fallen asleep in the land of the Head. One of these newcomers to the island was close to death and very ripe.

The Head's long black hair whipped the coral sand with its flails as it sped along.

Crabs scattered in panic out of its path.

The Head's lips were curled back in an expression of contempt, to reveal two rows of neat, even teeth. Its smoky eyes were smouldering with the desire for blood and flesh. The two broad nostrils were flared and cavernous.

The Head belonged to the god Ulupoka, severed in a great battle with the sky god, Rangi. Now it roamed the sands of certain islands, bringing disaster and disease to the earth, looking for men near to death to bite in their sleep to make certain of their demise. Once bitten by Ulupoka, either around the neck or the feet, the wound was fatal.

There was a beached double-hulled canoe above the waterline. Its Tiki, impotent on the shore, stared fixedly at the sky above the distant horizon. The pandanus sail was spread to dry between two chestnut trees near by. Perched on the prow of the boat, its feathers powdered with the pollen of orchids, was a barking pigeon, a bird whose call was not unlike the sound of a dog. The dust of dried lichens greyed the sides of the vessel, where it had been dragged over rocks to the top of the beach.

Not far from this boat the rolling Head of Ulupoka found Kupe and his six companions asleep in a make-shift hut beneath some giant ferns. Since they had fallen asleep a giant spider had woven a web with strands thick enough to catch a small bird in its nets across the entrance to their hut.

The Head bounced into the encampment and jumped into the hut, breaking the web and releasing its victim. It flew away, its high note waking the dying man. The sailor opened his eyes just as Ulupoka landed heavily on his chest. The Head bit the dying man deeply in the throat, swallowing his larynx so that he could not cry out. The only sound the mariner made was that similar to the single *gulp* of a tree frog.

It was enough to awaken the youngest member of the party, a boy of seven by the name of Kieto.

'Who's there?' cried the boy, in terror.

Ulupoka's Head, unwilling to be seen by a mortal, bounced out of the hut and into the swiftly descending night. When it was some distance from the Oceanians it let out a sound like that of a parrot burned by fire: a hideous laugh. The forest echoed with the noise and souls were chilled. Ulupoka rolled on, into the waters of the ocean, to cross the reefs to another island where there might be more dying men.

The spirit of the bitten man left his body and began the long walk along the path across the sea to the land of Milu, ruler of the dead. The dead man was rather resentful. Although he knew he had been dying, of heatstroke and exhaustion, he had been thinking very hard in his sleep about the meaning of life. Gradually, as he slept, the answer had come to him. He felt now it was bitterly ironic that he should come to know the meaning of life just at the point of his death.

'Just before Ulupoka bit me, I realised what it was all about,' he complained to Milu, who was waiting for him at the end of the purple path. 'And I died before I could tell anyone.'

Milu smiled. 'It's always the way,' he said.

After the boy's cry woke Kupe and his men, they found the dead mariner. In the light of torches lit from the embers of their small fire they saw he had torn open his own throat, with the nails of his fingers, in his terrible fever. The man had drunk sea water just before they had sighted land and they concluded this had driven him out of his mind. They took him out of the palm leaf hut and laid his tattooed corpse on the mosses under a nokonoko tree.

'We'll bury him tomorrow,' said Kupe. 'Rest now, my brave fishermen.'

'I had a nightmare,' complained the boy, Kieto. 'I dreamed a monster came into the hut. A great head without a body. Its eyes were like embers and its tongue was a giant centipede. Its hair was long and thick, like black weed. It grinned at me – a grisly grin, like a dead man's smile.'

'A monster?' cried one of the other seafarers, shuddering. 'Listen to the boy ...'

Kupe knew that his men would not stay on the island and get their much-needed rest if they believed a monster was on the loose. It was necessary that they replenished their store of drinking coconuts at least. Even if the boy was right – and young people were often more sensitive to these things than older men – it would be courting death by thirst to leave the island immediately.

'It was a *dream*,' he told Kieto and the others, 'nothing more. Since we have no kahuna with us to interpret the dream, then we can't be sure whether the omens are good or bad. Let's sleep on it tonight and discuss it in the morning. All dreams are clearer in the light from Ra's benevolent rays.'

There was a grumble of dissent from the fishermen, but they were very tired too and gradually sank back down onto their mats and into fitful sleeps. Kupe placed the torches around the hut, keeping his men within their circle. The gods, ancestor spirits and demons who shared the known world with men, there being no other place to inhabit, were all wary of fire.

The boy was still awake when Kupe went back into the hut.

'Are we safe?' asked the trembling Kieto.

'Yes, safe, safe,' replied Kupe.

The boy then fell instantly asleep, reassured absolutely by the leader of the expedition, the great navigator, Kupe.

It was a strange expedition, completely spontaneous, and one that would soon catch the imagination of all men and enter the legends of the Oceanians even as it was being carried out. Kupe had been fishing off the shore of his home island, Raiatea, when a giant octopus had stolen the bait from his hooks with its many arms. Enraged, Kupe had leapt from his small fishing canoe into an ocean-going vessel cruising near by. He had turned the crab-claw sail and given chase, at that time encouraged by the men already in the large canoe.

Following the ripples of the giant octopus they had been taken far away from Raiatea, until some of the men were concerned that they would never see their homeland again.

'Where's your seafaring spirit?' cried Kupe. 'Who knows what new islands we shall discover under the roof of voyaging? This octopus is obviously some kind of sea demon, sent by one of the gods, intent on leading us somewhere beyond our knowledge, for it never completely submerges and loses itself. Perhaps the Great Sea-God, Tangaroa, wishes to show us some new land we have never seen or heard of before? When I trap this great octopus and kill it, *then* I shall return to Raiatea and not before.'

Since they were ordinary fishermen and Kupe was of noble birth they did not argue, though one or two would have killed him if they thought they could get away with it. However, Kupe always kept his lei-o-mano, his dagger of kauila wood rimmed with sharks' teeth, stuck in his waistband. Kupe was a great warrior and the opportunities for catching him unawares were almost non-existent. Finally, his mana was almost as great as that of a king, so the fishermen did as they were told, day by day, night by night, ever sailing on into the unknown reaches of the Great Ocean ruled over by the god Tangaroa.

Kupe was confident in himself, for though Oceanian navigators might not know where they are going, they *always* know where they have been. He had memorised the way across the roof of the heavens, and across the many-islanded sea, to where they were now. His mariners would have done likewise. Even the boy, were he the last to survive, could find his way back home again. It was in their nature, in their instinct, to memory-map their path as they voyaged. What was more, on returning home they would describe their journeys so accurately to those who had never made the trip, the voyages could be repeated without them.

Kupe knew where he was from the shape of the waves, the star paths, the Long Shark At Dawn which was the rash of white stars across the roof of voyaging, the underwater volcanoes, the sea birds, the swell and the drift, the passing islands, the trade winds, and a thousand other things that were like signposts to him and his men. He could follow these markers back to Raiatea, possibly even *blind* when the breezes carrying the aromatic blends of islands and sea were in the right direction.

He could *smell* his way home.

At the same time he kept a record of his voyage on a piece of cord in the form of knots. The size, type and distances between the knots enabled him to recall certain sightings as well as to mark the distances between islands. This device was used by many Oceanic navigators and would be inherited by a named chosen legatee on the death of the navigator.

Tonight, the giant octopus had gone into an ocean trench, at least a league deep, and out of Kupe's reach. Kupe was sure however that they were not at the end of their journey, where he expected a battle with the ocean beast. He was being led to the creature's home waters, where the fight would be to the octopus's advantage.

Kupe had asked himself many times – *why?* Why was he following this creature at a whim? Kupe had suffered stolen bait before, from crabs and cuttlefish, lobsters and crowns-of-thorns. Why had he taken it into his head to chase after this particular beast?

It had to be the work of the gods. His fate was at the end of this voyage, one way or another. It would either be Kupe's destruction, or he was being given a precious gift. He had no idea what shape or form that gift would take. Perhaps the gods were leading him to a heavenly island?

The only other explanation was that Maui, the ancient trickster hero, was leading him on a fruitless voyage to nowhere. This was of course possible, but if the slight but powerful Maui had decided to play a game with you, you went along with it or you were destroyed. Kupe knew it was best to ignore that possibility and hope for a better.

When morning came, and the roof of voyaging with its islands of stars had gone from the sky, Kupe leapt to his feet.

As always he was first up. The torches had burned to the ground and were charred and cold. He used wood from a kaikomako tree to produce fire by friction, making a nest of coconut fibre to catch the smouldering sawdust. This he whirled about his head on a cord until it burst into flames. Soon he was cooking yams and bananas over the heat of a fire made with white driftwood from along the shoreline.

The parrots, fruit doves and parakeets were already shouting at one another. The frigate birds, bandits of the air, were wheeling above the ocean, ready to steal from more successful feathered anglers and each other. Shoals of tiny fish, like thousands of silver splinters, were arcing across the surface of the lagoon. It was a new and brilliant morning, with a softness to the puffed clouds lying on their blue bedding.

'Up, up,' he cried, allowing the smell of the food to waft over the sleeping men, to stupify them. 'Eat, my brave sailors, we must be on our way. The great octopus stirs out in the deeps, beyond the lagoon. The dark waters bubble. We must sail when he comes to the surface.'

The men rose, grumbling, rubbing the fine, white sand from their creased faces. Some of them went immediately to a pool to drink, while others simply sat and stared bleakly at the still blue surface of the lagoon, finding it difficult to suppress the desire to fish its bountiful waters.

The boy, Kieto, assisted Kupe with the cooking, eager to be of service. His nightmare was now forgotten in the brightness of the sunshine, when the fears of night had left with the departure of Hine, Goddess of Darkness and Death.

'Will we be going home soon?' Kieto asked of Kupe. 'Shall I see my father?'

For all his eagerness to follow the giant octopus, Kupe regretted one thing: that he had not cast the boy into the sea before leaving Raiatea, so that Kieto could have swum back to the reef or shore and would not now be on a dangerous voyage into the unknown. The octopus had left the scene so quickly though, there had been little time to think of such things.

'Soon,' he told the boy. 'I feel it in my bones. The journey will be over soon.'

Leaves rustled in the trees and the boy Kieto stared up at them.

'We have no ancestors here,' he remarked in a hushed voice. 'These ghosts are all strange to us, Kupe. They play in the trees and bushes like our own spirits, but we cannot offer them worship, for we do not know them.'

Kupe nodded. 'True, Kieto, but there are powerful gods with us on this voyage. The great Tangaroa will not let any harm come to you.'

'You are beloved of Tangaroa, are you not, Kupe?' said Kieto, his face shining with admiration.

'Perhaps I am,' smiled Kupe, touching the boy's hair. 'But I would rather have Maui for a friend than any other ancient hero, for he plays such mischief with those he does not love. Now let us eat, quickly, for the octopus stirs.'

The pandanus mat sail filled with wind and the light double-hulled canoe sped through the chopped waves. The seafarers were on a platform between hulls made from te itai trees, lashed together with hand-rolled fibres from the coconut husk. On this platform sat a palm leaf hut for shade. A bailer worked almost constantly on the hulls, as canoes always leaked water where the wood was sewn together and caulked with breadfruit sap.

'We are heading towards Apa toa,' cried Kupe. 'Keep the ocean swell to starboard.'

Apa toa was the name of a wind, not a place, for though they had no instruments or charts to follow, there was a windflower carved in the bows. The tattoo signs for twenty-three major and minor winds, with arrows pointing at the direction of their sources, were etched deeply into the wood, making the shape of a many-petalled circular bloom. The windflower was both aesthetic and practical; an artistic decoration which had a functional purpose.

Ahead of them, below the surface of the sea, swam the great dark shadow which was the octopus. The beast was languid in movement, but not slow. It took all Kupe's skill to keep up with the creature. Po, the man at the helm, struggled with the steering oar to keep the craft on a true course.

Kupe, as the navigator, was constantly searching the surface of the ocean and the skyline, even the clouds, for signs to remember. A light green colour on a cloudbase to one direction meant an island or even atoll, where the waters of a lagoon were reflecting on the sky. Frigate birds meant there was land somewhere near. He listened for the sound of reefs and watched the colour of the water change through many shades.

The double-hulled canoe Kupe was sailing belonged to the fisherman Po and it was Po's Tiki which stood on the deck of the vessel. The carved wooden idol was the eyes and ears of the crew. Since Po had hewn this Tiki it was to Po it spoke, inside his head, and it irritated Kupe that he was not directly in control of the entire boat. Po, however, did his best to please Kupe on all occasions, knowing that once the voyage was over he would be rewarded for his part in the expedition.

There was a bird cry from inside the deck hut and Kieto went in to feed their latest captive: a kula parrot from the islands they had just left. Kupe would have liked to have taken a breeding pair, since the bird had a breast of scarlet feathers. It would have made them all rich men, for red feathers were the currency of exchange on Raiatea and Borabora. However, the octopus had left just as they had caught their first kula and there had been a scramble to get on board the boat and head out to sea, leaving the riches behind them.

When the night came down again, Kupe was able to watch for the kave-inga, the path of stars which rose one after the other over the dark horizon. He knew their secret names, and those of the slower-wheeling fanakenga, or zenith stars which pointed down to particular islands in their wake.

When he had to sleep, Po took over the watch and the oar both, keeping the gleaming phosphorescent ripples made by the fleeing octopus in his sight.

After many weeks there came a time when the sea darkened quickly and large waves reared before them. The craft bravely fought through these, the men using their heavy oars rather than trusting to the sail. Eventually they came upon some high cliffs of an island too large to hold in the eye. It swept away on both sides of the craft to somewhere deep in the mists.

They followed the octopus down the length of this land, to its bottom, where the shore was wild and untamed. Here the wind was cold, the sea was cold, the skies grey. Sharp, hissing rain joined with stinging spray to rob the seafarers of energy, to fill them with a bleakness of spirit. The waves grew mountainous, with rushing peaks of white which touched the swirling grey-ness above, and sky and sea seemed one.

The sea and scouring rain had hewn the rocks of the coast into grotesque shapes and tall stacks. The wind had cut fissures in the rockface deep enough to swallow a man. There were pinnacles that towered like giant spears over the small craft and great boulders loomed suddenly as if vomited from coves just a few moments ago. It was a dark, forbidding place with ancient secrets moaning for release from a hundred-thousand caverns; with cryptic silences locked in fathomless caves.

'The giant beast has led us to a giant land,' said Kupe, in wonder. 'It is here we shall do battle.'

Indeed, as if the octopus had heard his words, it rose frothing to the sur-face and turned, coming towards the canoe at a monstrous speed. Its massive tentacles were pumping behind it, shooting it through the spume like a racing canoe powered by a hundred men. Its great eyes were wide with hat-red. Its beak chopped at the surface of the sea, in anticipation of crunching the bones of its determined adversary.

Po let out a cry and pulled hard on the steering oar, while the rowers beat the waves with their rowing oars. The hero Kupe stood on the front of the craft, awaiting the onslaught, his lei-o-mano in his strong right hand.

Po, with the help of the brave little Kieto, managed to turn the canoe at the last moment, and the octopus swept by the stern. A single tentacle flashed over the deck of the craft, snatching at the beast's enemy. Kupe's tattooed body was hauled over the side, caught in the suckers on that terrible limb.

'He's gone!' cried Po, to the other sailors, who let out a moan and started paddling away from the scene.

Kieto yelled, 'Don't leave him!'

They ignored the boy in their desperation to escape the giant. Their terror would not allow them to accept the thought that Kupe might win. All they wanted to do was put a great distance between themselves and the octopus, fearful that the creature might wreak more revenge upon the craft. Kupe and the octopus were lost behind a huge wave thrown back by the high cliffs of the land.

'Stop,' screamed the boy. 'He'll be left to drown in these grey seas ...'

Still the wide-eyed mariners, nightmares running like shadows over their faces, through their eyes, would not stop paddling. Kieto raced to the sail and heaved upon the line, half raising the pandanus mat in the full force of the wind. The craft lurched sideways, spilling one of the rowers into the sea. Luckily the man overboard clung to one of the trailing lines and managed to keep with the craft.

A mariner rushed for the boy, wielding a paddle club.

'You stupid young idiot!' shrieked the man. 'Don't make me kill you.'

Kieto stood his ground and would have been felled by the man, had not Po cried, 'Look!'

All eyes turned to where he was pointing and they saw a thrashing and foaming on the surface of the water. Tentacles were waving, whipping the waves, causing a boiling of the ocean. When the spray fell hissing around the craft and their vision was clear, they saw Kupe sitting astride the octopus's head, his legs wrapped around the enormous beak keeping it locked shut, his arm plunging repeatedly into the bulbous form. Once, twice, thrice ... then the hardwood dagger snapped, its shark-toothed point buried deep in the flesh of the octopus.

Po groaned, 'He's done for. The beast will take him down now, pulp him and feed on his rotting flesh.'

But even as Po spoke, and the creature began to dive, Kupe bit the octopus, sinking his teeth between the creature's eyes. He bit deep, seeking a vulnerable spot in the beast's brain. The pair of them disappeared down into the depths, leaving a trail of small bubbles in their wake.

This time the mariners waited in silence, not attempting to flee, their strength gone and their will tied securely to the man who had slipped down towards the home of Tangaroa. Mists were drifting over the edge of the nearby cliffs, spilling like slow liquid into the leaping waters of the ocean. They filled the cracks and caves along the high walls of rock with cold smoke and rolled over the colder surface of the sea.

Suddenly, up came the great Kupe, like a coconut released from submarine weeds, bobbing on the waves.

Kieto cheered. 'There he is! There he is! Kupe has won!'

Po let out a whoop, and was joined by his fellow mariners; it was the sound of relief rather than joy, yet the dripping Kupe, as he was hauled aboard, did not blame them. This was a selfish act he had carried out, this act of revenge. Yet he acknowledged to himself, if not to them, that he had no choice in the matter. He had been compelled by some inner spirit to make this journey and fight this fight. Now it was over. They could return to Raiatea, having found an immense island, perhaps more than an island, far beyond their own waters.

'I shall call this place "Land-of-Mists",' he told his mariners. 'If ever you are asked how to reach it, you must tell the inquirers to sail a little to the left of the setting sun at this time of the year. That will lead them to the Land-of-Mists as surely as the octopus led us.'

2

'We shall fashion a new sail when we reach one of the smaller islands,' Kupe told his crew, pointing to the crab-claw. 'In the weave shall be the shape of an octopus – a symbol of my triumph over the creature. But first, I wish to explore these coasts just a little before we begin to return to our homeland.'

Aware that they had entered a new ocean, new seas, the Oceanians felt insecure and a little afraid. This eerie, tall world was far removed from their own. It seemed less civilised, less understandable. Here there were strange winds, from unusual corners. Here the weather was ruled by unpredictable gods with moods sometimes savage, sometimes sullen, but rarely joyous. Here currents and tidal eddies seemed erratic and impetuous, changing at whim, following some mad god's directions.

At every turn the Raiateans expected horrible monsters to lurch from the caves, or rise dripping with seaweed from the depths. They sensed the area's differentness in their souls, knowing it to be a place quite unlike any Ocean-ian island. This was a piece of the earth which *should* have dropped away, into the chasm of nothingness beyond, but had somehow remained attached to the true world of the myriad islands of Oceania.

They sailed the waters for a few days, touching land once or twice, but warily. There were the lights of fires on the cliff tops at night, and on some of the smaller islands which were scattered some way up from the main body of land. In places the fires were so numerous Kupe felt there was a strong pres-ence, a great many inhabitants, on that rugged coast. He and his men would stand no chance in open battle against such a number.

'I wonder what dark gods they pray to here?' he murmured to his crew. 'This is indeed a place fit for demons.'

The Oceanians heard the beat of drums on the night air and the wailing of diabolical voices on the breeze.

The skies over the main island seemed always grey, with thick cloud blocking out the face of Ra. There was a great deal of rain, which washed down its own pathways on the cliffs, into the restless ocean. It was a brooding land, seeming to nurse resentment in its breast for some unknown ills perpetrated upon its crags and buttresses. A wild nature it had, with a savage spirit. Its warriors, Kupe was certain, would be just as fierce, just as brutal as the landscape on which they lived.

Then finally, as the crew were about to set off towards home, Kupe asked them to wait. He pointed to a cliff face.

'Look there,' said Kupe. 'A white figure.'

The men, on following his arm, saw a creature on the vertical granite, working its way from crevice to crevice.

'A demon, more like,' cried Po.

If it was a demon it was in the shape of a white-skinned, barefoot man in sea-washed ragged garments, a cloth bag slung over his shoulder. He was collecting birds from their cliffside nests as he went, fulmars which he first strangled then placed carefully in the bag. The man seemed strong and nimble as he swung from crack to crack on the sheer face of the grey rock, at a height of some fifty men. Sometimes he hung by only one hand, his feet dangling, his other hand engaged snatching the fulmars from their nests. Sometimes the birds wheeled about him, shrieking in his ears, furious at his murder and theft of their comrades. He was a white and grey ghost mobbed by smaller white and grey ghosts.

Kupe concluded that the man was very strong, to be able to bear his own weight so frequently with a single arm.

'See how he clings to the rock,' he murmured. 'And his movements are so dexterous.'

Still, the figure seemed confident, uncaring of the attacks by the birds, unimpressed by the drop into the deep ocean. If he fell, the sea would be sure to swallow him whole; Tangaroa would eat him. Even as they watched the waves clawed at the stone face, eager to rip the man from his perch. What amazed Kieto about the man was his long, flailing hair. Surely he was not a demon, but a hero from the past?

Po suddenly shouted, 'See – at the top of the cliff.'

They all stared upwards, to witness another figure, this one with black hair flying in the wind. The face was again of a whiteness they had never seen before, except in albino children, and this new figure was slight, less muscled. The arms were slim, the shoulders lean. Kupe thought it to be either a woman or a youth in a ragged shift.

When the wind blew the shift hard against the figure, emphasising the shape beneath, Kupe concluded it was a woman; the breasts were large, the waist slim, the hips wide.

This person screamed something down to the man collecting fulmars, her face contorted. There was either distress, or anger, or some other violent emotion evident in her gestures. Her hands seemed to claw at the air. Her body contorted as if she were struggling with an unseen assailant. At times her mouth opened to scream words incomprehensible to the Raiateans, while the high wind lashed at her, screaming back.

She disappeared for a moment, then reappeared with a large rock in her hands. She purposely threw the stone down on the man. It struck and bounced from crag to crag, knocking off further chunks of stone. The man managed to swing one-handed out of the path of the falling rocks, though the acrobatics left him dangling dangerously for a moment.

'A husband and wife battle, I think,' joked one of the mariners. 'Perhaps he has not been in her bed recently, but wandering a little amongst the beds of others?'

The men laughed at this, pleased to have some release from the tension.

The woman was railing at the man again, clawing at her breast as she did so. Spitting ugly words down upon the lone climber. She was clearly very distraught, as if the man were stealing her babies from those nests, rather than seabirds. Every so often she threw her arms high and shrieked at the dark, grey clouds, as if requesting assistance from the gods.

'This is no matrimonial dispute,' said Kupe. 'I really think she means to kill him.'

Indeed, as if to prove him right, the woman disappeared again and returned with a rock larger than the one she had thrown down on the man before. So heavy was this stone she appeared to have difficulty in lifting it. Buffeted by the strong winds at the top of the cliff, the woman heaved the massive stone over the edge, the effort pulling her forward.

The stone plunged through space, completely missing the bird-nester, to splash only half a man's length from the Oceanians' bows.

'Look out!' cried Po. 'The bitch nearly sank us.'

'See, she falls!' Kieto yelled.

The winds and the weight of the rock had caused her to overbalance and she followed in the wake of the stone she had cast down on the head of the man. She made no sound, but turned once in mid-air on her descent, her arms and legs stretched wide to form the shape of a star. The climber reached out for her as she passed, to grasp and save her, but her weight ripped him from the rock face too. Together they plummeted the whole way into the waters of the ocean, not far from the craft. It would only take a short while for the cold waters to drag them down, where they would be smashed by the waves against the cliff.

'Take them,' said Kupe.

The Raiateans paddled the canoe to where the two figures were struggling

21

in the waves. The man was dragged aboard first. Po struck him with a paddle to keep him quiet. Then the woman was hauled over the deck. She was only semi-conscious, from her great fall, and they tossed her in the palm leaf hut.

'Now, let us be on our way,' Kupe ordered. 'Steer to the right of the sun.'

When the man came round they were in calmer waters. Kupe had bound the man, hands and feet, so he would be no trouble to them. The woman was also bound with sennit cord, to stop her from jumping into the ocean, something she had already tried. So far the woman had remained silent, sullen and brooding, simply staring bleakly out over the passing waters at some unsee-able thing in the middle distance.

The man woke on his side, coughed seawater on to the deck, and then tried to lift his head to see his captors. Now that the sun had dried him, they saw his hair was thick and red upon his head, not dark as they had first thought. His face too was covered in coarse, reddish hair, so that only his eyes and nose were visible. His pale, freckled arms were also hairy.

Po said, 'He's got more hair than a hog.'

'*Is e Dia mo bhuachaill,*' he yelled into the face of Po.

Po leapt back with alacrity, his face taut.

'It's true, he *is* a demon,' Po cried. 'We must chop him into small pieces and throw him into the water before he chants again. Who knows what magic he can conjure with those strange speakings?'

Kieto said, 'I think he has the head of Ra. See how the red hair circles his white face ...'

The man then proceeded to pour such dark language forth from his lips, all of it seemingly directed at Po, who was in his line of sight. Po looked around frantically for a weapon, seized on a wahaika club, and was about to dash the man's brains out, when Kupe took hold of his arm.

'No! This man is my prisoner.'

'But he's not a man,' wailed Po. 'He's a creature of the darkness.'

'Then why hasn't he set himself free?' Kupe reasoned. 'If he's such a power-ful demon, why does he allow himself to be trussed like a chicken? No, this is a man, a very *strange* one, I'll grant you, but a man just the same. Look how bruised his white skin is – this is ordinary flesh.'

'*Cha ghabh mi tuille,*' shrieked the man.

Po shuddered, remembering the land where the mist dropped like veils from high stone walls and drifted over the cold face of the sea as if it were shrouding a monster beneath.

Kupe had not admitted it to his fellow seafarers but he was fascinated by the creatures they had caught. The woman seemed quite wild, like a creature born of a storm, and the man too was not civilised or refined in any way. Kupe had already formed a certain respect for the man, for though like Kupe the man had no tattoos on his face, there were several on his body. They were of a design Kupe did not understand – in fact the longer he stared at them the more they confused him, making him feel giddy and a little ill with their complex interweavings – but they were definitely a body decoration of some kind.

There were, unlike those tattoos on his own body, pictures of strange creatures on the man's skin. A shiver of fear went through the normally phlegmatic navigator when he looked at these illustrations. They were like no other animals he had ever seen before and he did not want to ask their names in case they were beasts from some damned place, some taboo land in an Otherworld, the names of which might turn an ordinary man's mind to dust.

In a calm moment, when the man was no longer frantically fighting his bonds, nor screaming at Po and trying to bite the terrified mariner's legs as he passed, Kupe sat by the sickly-pale creature and tried for information.

Kupe pointed to himself. 'Kupe,' he said.

The man's washed-blue eyes stared hard at Kupe and he shook his red mane petulantly.

Kupe repeated the gesture and the word several times. Then he pointed to his prisoner.

'Who are you?' he asked.

The man blinked those strange eyes, the colour of the sky near the horizon after rain.

Finally, the man said, 'Pict.'

Kupe pointed to the woman, who glared back.

'Who is she?'

The man gave the woman a tight, bitter little smile, before saying to Kupe, '*I so a' Scot bhean*.'

Kupe shook his head, indicating that he did not understand so many words strung together.

'Scot,' the man repeated. 'Scot *bhean*.'

The woman spat at him and turned her head away.

So it appeared their names were Pict and Scot, and that they hated each other with a terrible venom. Or at least the woman loathed the man. Kupe was not so sure that Pict hated Scot, for there was something wistful in the way that Pict's eyes rested on the form of the woman sometimes; almost as if the man deeply regretted the antipathy. Some secret lay between these two creatures which would not be resolved until Kupe and his crew taught them to speak properly, in the way real people should. He gave the task of teaching them to young Kieto, since they both appeared to prefer the child's company to that of any of the men.

'Will you teach them to talk?' asked Kupe of Kieto. 'I would appreciate your help.'

Kieto, who was afraid of the two white demons they had dragged from the sea, hesitated, but finally said, 'I can try, Prince Kupe.'

'Good,' Kupe smiled at the boy and ruffled his hair. 'One day I think you will become a great hero, Kieto.'

'Like you?' said the boy, in great pleasure. 'Just like you?'

'Perhaps greater,' laughed Kupe. 'I have only discovered a new land – you, I think, will conquer it.'

It was Kupe's intention to revisit the island where they had picked up the kula parrot, but on the way back a storm blew them off course and he understood that the gods did not wish him to become wealthy.

'Wealth spoils a man, in any case,' he told Po. 'It makes him suspicious of other men and it makes him mean and pointed. Don't you agree?'

'Yes,' said Po, sighing, 'but I think I would have enjoyed being spoiled.'

Kupe smiled and shook his head.

'You think you would.'

'I *know* I would,' said Po, refusing to be shaken.

At first, the deadly chill of the wind and evaporation of the seawater from the skin of the captives took their toll on the newcomers' strength. It was conditions such as these which had shaped the physical and mental nature of the hardy Oceanians over the centuries. Spray from the bows drenched every part of the canoe and drying a wet skin in a cold wind was an accepted fact of a mariner's life. Kupe's seamen were provided with a layer of insulating fat and stamina to help them.

The captives however were not used to being sodden much of the time. They sat miserably shivering and hugging themselves on the deck of the canoe, even on hot days, until their bodies readjusted a little and they were able to cope. Both were hardy individuals, used to a cold, wet climate, even if they usually spent much of their time in stone-and-turf crofts. They were not the kind of people to die in such circumstances, though many others might. They were too obstinately angry with each other, and with life in general, to allow the wet and cold to carry them off. A fatal blow to the head with a club wielded by one or the other, yes, but not a thing like exposure.

Kieto began teaching the man to speak like a real person, instead of a demon or ghost.

The man learned quickly, over the many weeks, there being all the time in the world and no distractions. The woman refused to learn at all, simply glowering every time Kieto tried to engage her attention. So it was that they spoke with the man first and took his side of the story as the truth.

His name was not Pict – that was his people – he was called Seumas, and the woman the Pict told them, from a different people called the Scots, was named Dorcha. Seumas had killed Gealach, the husband of Dorcha, in a fair fight over the possession of a weapon called a 'sword', which once the deed had been done and bitterly regretted by Seumas, he had flung into the sea in an attempt to expunge his guilt.

'A man's life is not worth a *sword*,' he told Kieto. 'I have wished Gealach back to life again a thousand times.'

'What is a sword?' asked Kieto.

'A long knife,' replied Seumas.

Kieto knew what a knife was: a lei-o-mano, or a spike of sharpened obsidian, or a sliver of shell with a wooden handle.

'How did you kill him?' asked Kieto, fascinated by tales of single combat.

The pale, faded eyes stared at the boy for a moment before replying, 'We fought on a hill at dawn, just as the world was waking. It was a long fight, for though Gealach was small, he was heavy-set and strong. Twice he almost broke my spine when he had me in a bear grip. On the third time I plunged a blade into his throat seven times. The blood spurted forth like a burn from a mountainside, staining the heather. He cursed me with his last gargled scream ... that's why I'm here today, I suppose – the result of Gealach's curse.'

Kupe, who had been listening, said, 'If that's so, why is the woman here? Was she cursed too?'

Seumas conceded that this was a mystery. He stared at the woman, sulking as usual under the deck hut.

'Perhaps she was unfaithful to him, at some time? Perhaps she was barren and could not bear him children? Perhaps she was cold in bed and kept her thighs tightly together when the passion was on him? Who knows. If I am here because I was cursed, then she too must have done something to displease a dying man whose oaths the gods take seriously.'

Kupe said, 'If a woman wishes to go with another man, then that is a matter for the priests to decide. If a woman cannot bear children, then another will bear them in her place and make a gift of them to her. If a woman has no wish to be penetrated, that is her right, and the man must either seek his gratification elsewhere, or find a cold stream to rid himself of his desire.'

Seumas stared at Kupe and a grim expression came over his face.

'Your people must be very different to mine. It is our right to kill the woman if she goes into another's bed. A barren woman, we believe, must have sinned and upset the gods at some time to be so cursed, and therefore it is *her* fault there are no offspring. If a husband wants his wife, she must give herself to him, or be taken in anger.'

'Indeed,' said Kupe, shaking his head sadly, 'we are from different worlds.'

That night the vessel passed the 'island with the stink of ghosts' putting fear into the hearts of the men as they passed on the outside of the reef, their eyes on the moonlit bleached bones of the dead, like broken coral, which were the beaches on the island with the stink of ghosts. Po asked the Tiki to take them away as quickly as possible, before the smell of the unhappy, dead spirits overwhelmed the crew and they were forced against their will to land on the island.

'What is that foul odour?' asked Seumas, but no one answered him for fear of arousing the rage of the island's castaway ghosts, and they slipped on under the stars to happier waters.

Next morning, on a calm sea, the Pict was being rubbed down with vegetable oil by Kieto. The Pict's pale complexion had turned a nasty red colour under the sun, even though he spent much of his time in the shade of the deck hut. The oil would help protect his delicate skin.

The woman too was beginning to darken a little, though she had been much more careful than the man to keep herself covered from the sun.

Seumas stared at the wooden statue on the deck as he was being massaged and asked Kieto, 'Who is that ugly brute Po seems to love so much?'

He nodded at the roughly hewn idol strapped to the front of the deck.

'That is Tiki,' whispered the boy. 'You must not call him ugly or he will take us out onto false waters, where we'll lose ourselves in darkness and all drown.'

'Really?' said Seumas. 'But what is it, this Tiki?'

'Tiki was our first ancestor, who led us out of the darkness into the light. Now he is still with us, in our wooden statues of him.'

Seumas stared at the idol. 'Well, he was surely an ugly bastard ...'

'Bastard?'

Seumas hesitated and then replied wryly, 'Someone born out of wedlock – if Tiki was the first, then he couldn't have had married parents could he? So, in a manner of speaking, he was a bastard orphan – with all due respect.'

Dorcha stirred in the hut. There were two men on the back of the craft, fishing for the day's meal. A small turtle already lay on the deck. The woman had been watching these two, but she turned now and stared at Seumas.

'I know of another bastard,' she said, darkly in the language of the Oceanians.

'Meaning me, I suppose?' said Seumas. 'I thought you couldn't speak their words.'

'I only had to listen while they were teaching you,' she sneered. 'You think you're so clever? I got it while you were still stumbling over that thick tongue of yours.'

She then ignored Seumas and turned to Kieto.

'Boy,' she said, her dark-stone eyes flashing, 'who is this Tiki? Is he the Adam of your people?'

Kieto was frightened of this savage woman who looked like a witch in her ragged dress, with her curly, matted, dark hair piled wild and thick about her head. Her face, beneath the tangle of hair, was pretty enough, though a little sharp and often quite dirty. And she ringed her eyes with the black of charcoal from the fire, making them look like deep pits within which were two glintering black jewels.

As the Pict had done before they made him bathe, she stank strongly of body odour and the peat turf of her homeland, with a few other unidentifiable smells besides. The toes of her feet, bound in leather strips, poked filthy and odorous from between the hide cladding. She resisted all attempts to wash her body, scratching and clawing at any man who laid a hand on her, as if cleanliness would weaken her in some way. Since the dirt was thick beneath her nails, not unnaturally the men were frightened of getting an infection from the wounds she inflicted.

'The Adam?' asked Kieto, nervously. 'What is the Adam?'

'Adam and Eve,' said the woman. 'Are you heathens too, like that bastard there?'

Seumas laughed. 'She's heard about a new religion,' he said. 'The worship of a man who was pegged through his hands and feet – nailed against a tree.'

'What's that?' asked Kupe, who had been busy with the sail, 'a man was pegged up on a tree? Surely, it must be the tree they worship then, not the man? The man was obviously a sacrifice to the tree, wasn't he?'

'That's my thinking, certainly,' said Seumas. 'This new religion has come from somewhere south of our land of Albainn, from the country of the Angles and Jutes. It started on one of the islands, so they tell me – a place called Lindisfarne – and there are people known as monks and priests involved. I would hang the lot.'

Dorcha gave Seumas a disgusted look and turned away, as if he were not worth the effort of an argument.

Kupe asked, 'What is your thinking then? About the gods?'

'Me? I might make a prayer to the sun for coming up in the morning, or to the moon for giving me a good hunt – perhaps to the mossy rock where I took my first girl, or a sacred tree from which I cut my first spear? – but I would not pray to a crucified man hanging from a tree. Let the flesh rot on him, and the corbies pick at his bones, he wouldn't get *my* words sprinkled on his spirit.'

'Heathen,' muttered Dorcha. 'Murdering heathen bastard – l hope *you* rot on a tree some day.'

'Heathen am I?' snarled Seumas. 'Don't I ask the Owl-god to watch over me at night and warn me of the coming of my enemies? Don't I call to the Hare-god or the Stag-god for speed when I run? Don't I yell for the Eagle-god when I fall on the kill? How can I be a heathen? I pray to more gods than you have fingers and toes. More than *one*, at any rate.

'And if I do hang on a tree, I don't want them to pray over *me* like they do to that creature of yours.'

'Don't worry, they won't – they'll just spit on the corpse.'

'Good. Make sure you're the first.'

'I want to be the one who puts you up there!' she said, whirling on him, her eyes flashing.

*

Kupe was steering the canoe in the direction of the wind Maoae farara toe-rau, which on the windflower was the first to the right of the top petal of the bloom. There was a thin layer of light grey ambergris on the surface of the sea, which had a pleasant smell in the noonday sun. Kupe had been explaining to Seumas that the waves had points in this part of the ocean and its colour was a deep grey-green, which put them in the region of an island known as the Conch.

'We are nearing our home island of Raiatea and will soon be amongst our people.'

Seumas nodded. It meant nothing to him. He was, now that the initial shock of his capture and his interest in his captors had waned a little, feeling very homesick. He wanted to be in the mountains and glens of Albainn, smelling the sweet turf, chasing the deer, feeling a chill wind on his skin and the dew beneath his feet. The ocean around him seemed endless, surely *was* infinite, and his life ahead of him eternal.

There was a woman he loved back there in Albainn, with a lithe pale body and a temper to match a wildcat's. Seumas had been about to be joined with her in tribal marriage when he had killed the Scot, thus delaying the wedding. The two spiral tattoos on his neck were symbols that he was betrothed and unavailable to other women. Po had told him that on Raiatea the men wore a flower called a frangipani bloom behind their left ear when they were similarly betrothed, but even Seumas could see that the flower could be switched to behind the bachelor ear in a sexual emergency. Now he had betrothal tattoos and yet he was still unmarried. No woman would take him seriously.

He stared gloomily out over the desert of water wondering if he would ever see his homeland again. Kupe had taken him, so the man himself had said, in order to familiarise the Oceanians with the ways of the Albannachs. Did Kupe really believe that Seumas was a traitor, that he would betray his people? Seumas had said as much to the great navigator.

'Not yet,' Kupe admitted, 'but by the time we need your help, you will be one of us.'

'I shall never be one of you,' replied Seumas, fiercely. 'I am a Pict first and an Albannach last, and there is no room for any other loyalties between those two.'

'So you say now,' smiled Kupe, infuriatingly. 'In any case, just by studying you and the woman, we can get a certain amount of information about your people – useful facts.'

Seumas had nodded grimly. 'If you're thinking of trying to conquer Albainn, forget it. The tribes there are full of fierce and brutal warriors, who would rather kill outsiders than each other, and they're quite fond of murder and pillage amongst their own kind, believe me. Scots, and my own people, the Picts. Clans who hate each other will join to fight a common enemy. In the land above us the Angles and Jutes have found that to their cost. They too are more than a match for you, being more advanced in the science of warfare than us. They have weapons the likes of which you have not even dreamed.'

'We shall conquer Albainn *and* the land of the Angles – what do you call it?'

'*They* call it Engaland. We call it *Cú-Tìr*.'

'What does that mean?'

Seumas smiled. 'Land of Dogs.'

Kupe nodded. 'We shall conquer that land – and yours.'

Seumas laughed. 'They are too many – and there are Irish on an island near Engaland.'

'We shall still conquer them also,' said Kupe, with remarkable if infuriating confidence.

Dorcha spoke now, from the shadows of the hut, where she was drinking coconut juice and eating sweet potato and breadfruit.

'The Pict is right – you will never conquer our tribes, nor those above us, the tribes of Engaland.'

'And why is that?'

'Iron,' she said, simply.

She had used the Gaelic word, not knowing the Oceanian equivalent.

Seumas saw what she meant and had to give her credit for her intelligence. Not until now had he actually realised that there was no metal on the boat, in the boat or about the Oceanian seafarers who crewed the craft. Their weapons were made of wood, teeth, shells and bone. There were wooden pegs and binding cord keeping the canoe together. They wore no copper amulets, nor bronze tores, nor golden earrings. It had been obvious to Dorcha and was now clear to Seumas, that the Oceanians did not know metal. It was outside their experience.

'The woman is right,' he said. 'You can't fight a war against the Albannachs and English tribes without iron weapons. You'd be cut down like wild wheat under sickles.'

'This *iron* is a superior material?' questioned Kupe.

'It is harder, tougher and more resilient than the hardest stone or flint, and you can sharpen it so finely you can cut a hog's hair in two lengthways.'

'It sounds lethal.'

'It makes a man ten times more powerful.'

'Well,' smiled Kupe, 'so at least we know about this iron, before we go into battle against it.'

Seumas's face fell. He knew that he and Dorcha had been duped by the smooth tongue of Kupe. It was exactly as the great navigator had told him just a short time ago – the Oceanians would learn much just from talking casually with their captives, without the full co-operation of the Pict and the Scot.

'Perhaps,' continued Kupe, 'you can show us how to make this iron prior to our departure for the Land-of-Mists, which is the name I have given your country.'

Seumas looked quickly at Dorcha, then said to Kupe, 'I wouldn't and I couldn't – you can't make iron out of nothing – you have to have ore.'

'You think we haven't got this ore?'

'I'm certain, or you would have found it and used it by now, just as we have. Anyway, it's as I say, we wouldn't show you how to use it, even if we could. You're talking about invading our land, our people. How can you expect us to assist you in that endeavour?'

'We're not going yet. Perhaps not in my lifetime. One day, when the time is right, when the gods decide we must go to the Land-of-Mists and conquer it. Then we shall go. But that's in the future. By then you will have children by one or more of our women, and Dorcha will have for a husband one of our men ...'

'A very brave one,' muttered Po, sitting sewing nearby. Kupe ignored this remark, while Dorcha glared at the mariner with black-rimmed eyes, causing him to twitch in embarrassment – and not a little fear of witchcraft.

'... and you will be Raiateans, both of you.'

'It still won't help you defeat men of iron,' Dorcha told Kupe. 'Even if we fall down and kiss your feet.'

'There are ways,' replied Kupe, his casual confidence confounding both the Albannachs. 'Alliances can be made, friends can be bought. The time will come.'

Kupe suddenly turned and sniffed the breeze.

'I smell land,' he said. 'The swell is taking us closer to an island. Look.'

He pointed to a far distant cloud on the base of which was a light green tinge.

'That's the reflection of a lagoon,' he told the two Albannachs. 'An atoll or an island. We shall soon be in Raiatean waters. Tiki has seen us home.'

'God bless him,' muttered Dorcha, but even Seumas didn't know whether or not she was being sarcastic.

3

Once he had become used to the idea of captivity, a condition which would have been abhorrent to him several weeks ago, Seumas was able to turn his mind to studying his captors.

There was much to admire in them. They seemed civilised and appeared to have a higher standard of living than his own people. There was a harmony between them which Seumas did not recognise at first, coming from a clan where discord was the prime mover and motivator of deeds.

The Picts lived in caves and hovels, while Kieto had described to him houses made of hardwood with elaborately carved doorposts and pillars, good thatched roofs which kept out the rain, and solid walls. Inside these houses it was neat and clean. There were no half-gnawed bones scattered over the bedspaces, as there were in Pict dwellings, nor the ashes of a dozen previous fires littering floors.

For food the Raiateans had a vast array of fruits and vegetables. Even on board the canoe there were taro roots, yams, coconuts, pandanus fruit, dried bananas, sweet potatoes and breadfruit. In separate gourds there were bread-fruit paste, hard poi and fresh water. There was no meat on board, but Kieto had told him that back on the island there were pigs, dogs and something called a chicken which was apparently a flightless domestic bird.

Most of the flesh the islanders ate however came from fish in the sea; a dozen varieties of reef fish, dorado, shark, barracuda and turtle kebabs.

In turn hundreds of varieties of shellfish were gathered from the coral, along with crabs, lobsters, cuttlefish and squid.

The Raiateans seemed to eat like kings.

The climate on Raiatea, and its near neighbour Borabora, was kinder than that of Albainn, being hot and sunny most of the time, with much rain at certain times of year.

Yet, there were things Seumas did not like about his captors.

They seemed arrogant beyond their measure, which to him was a great sin. A Pict was modest about his achievements and his prowess. Po would brag for hours about a shark he had caught with a magic stone. The bailers would laughingly challenge Seumas to keep up with their rhythmic bailing with half-coconut shells and laugh at him again when he had to stop because his arm felt like it was being wrenched from its socket. Even Kupe, the aloof navigator prince, informed Seumas proudly of his achievements as a warrior, saying he had never been beaten in single combat and describing how he had chased and killed the great octopus which had led him to Albainn.

They are too full of themselves, he thought. *They make too much of their skills and talents.*

Again, their physical appearance and manners were too feminine for a Pict. Even though they were a stocky race of creatures, their faces were too pretty, too unblemished. Seumas could not help feeling superior to them in manliness, though he was at a loss to explain how. Certainly their seaman-ship was second to none, their navigating skills nothing short of magical, their individual strengths astonishing. Yet, they were not *masculine* in the Pict sense. They moved too fluidly, walked too lightly on their feet, had too ready a smile and too soft a touch.

A Pict, or indeed Angle and Scot, held himself inside, did not reveal easily his ability at anything. A Pict had fortitude without display. A Pict hid his endurance and grit, his mettle, beneath a gruff but indifferent exterior. A Pict did not smile overmuch, nor fuss with foodstuffs, nor care very much where he shat. A Pict was stern and hard, hitting a man first then offering hospitality to the cripple later, after the man was disabled and pathetic. A Pict was a rock of a man, walking heavily on the earth, stepping aside for no one, bludgeoning those who dared to block his path.

A Pict was, in Seumas's opinion, more of a *man*.

Finally, he was contemptuous of the way they treated Dorcha, most of them being afraid of her, and others, Kupe especially, treating her like some kind of a *lady*. None of them seemed to smell or see the *womanliness* about her. None of them seemed in the least interested in bedding her. The smell of her drove Seumas crazy with sexual desire. He could not understand how his captors could stay away from such a woman. Once, her loose shift blew up above her waist, under which she had nothing, and Seumas almost choked on his passion.

If Dorcha had been a captive of *his* he would have taken her long before now (though almost certainly against her will). Seumas found the widow of the man he had killed immensely desirable. Seumas was glad his breeks were loose and full, for they often hid a penis stiffened to the point of being painful. His lust for her haunted his every waking moment, as he often caught sight of her white thighs while she slept under the deck hut on a windy afternoon, or the shape of her breasts disclosed by a wet shift that stuck to her skin. Sometimes he felt he would go mad because he knew he could not have her.

After the death of her husband Dorcha had only one thought in mind: to kill her husband's murderer. The desire for revenge flooded her every moment. She was desperate to see the Pict's blood splashing on the earth. She had pictures in her head, of him begging her for mercy, of her laughing at him, reminding him of how little mercy he had shown her husband, and then dashing out his brains with the laugh still ringing in his ears. These were wild thoughts, wild pictures, but they had sustained her through her grief and through the realisation of her poverty.

It was true she had loved her husband and desired the death of the Pict for emotional reasons, but she also had to avenge her husband's death in order to be accepted back once more into Scots society. The other women of the clan would not speak to her until she had righted the wrong, retrieved her family honour, shown the Picts that the Scots were a people with whom to be reckoned. Until that time she would have been an outcast, eating the roots of trees, begging for scraps from strangers, perhaps selling her body to wayfarers and travellers.

Had there been a man in the family, a father or brother, who could have carried out this deed on her behalf, she could have stepped back and been a spectator. But the clan had been massacred the previous year in a battle with a clan in the next glen and many of the menfolk were already dead. A murder was a murder, however, and a stain on a clan's honour.

On being captured by the Raiateans, something bad inside her had died. She still wanted to kill the Pict, but there was an indifference settling next to her desire for revenge. The world of Albainn seemed far away now, another life, and it was clear to her that the Oceanians were not going to harm her in any way. She had no doubt they could be ferocious in war, indeed whenever the necessity arose, but they did not seem to feel the need for constant aggression like her own people. They were not belligerent for the sake of it, had little scorn in them, and there was a gentleness about their spirit which she felt was a power of good.

In these waters she sensed the presence of strange gods, quite unlike those she had known in Albainn, or the new religion which was creeping into her homeland. More psychic than her fellow Albannach her spirit quickly tuned to the supernature of her new environment and she believed the stories Kieto told of ancestor ghosts, the spirits of ancient heroes and the tales of the creator gods of the sea, earth and sky.

Here, under this clear sky, the stars were brighter and more numerous. Recently, having come out of her sulks, Kieto had shown her the major constellations: The Bird's Body, The North Wing, The Bamboo, Small Face with Small Eyes, Adze, The Carrying Stick, Double Man, White Squirrelfish Stars, The Net, The Path Of Three and The Tongs. Her people had no names for these sets of stars, but a monk passing through her village from Lindisfarne, the same man who had brought the message of the new religion, had told her another list of names, like Sirius, Aries, Alpha and Beta Centauri, Southern Cross and Taurus. It was all so fascinating, so magical, and she wept for the knowledge that could be hers if someone would only pass it to her.

There was little homesickness in her, for the peat-fire hearth she had left behind, for the damp, stinking croft where her blankets rotted and her husband's empty stool stood ready to remind her of her widow status.

From what she had heard she was going to an island in the sun, whose name was Raiatea. A *heaven*. That sounded better than the place whence she had come, which once she had lost her man might be called 'Near Hell'. She was going to a place where food was in plenty; where there were hot, white sands and gentle breakers on beaches protected by something called a coral reef; where the women were held almost equal to the men; where colours were bright and days were long and warm with delicate breezes caressing the skin, where fruit could be picked from trees all year round and the only thing to fear was a tropical storm.

That sounded like a heaven to her.

As for the Pict, she now felt a little sorry for him, though this feeling was heavily diluted by her hate for him. He looked miserable and forlorn as he sat on the front of the canoe's deck, the spray flicking over his salt-stained ragged vest and breeks. Occasionally he would turn and look at her and she would see the lust in his eyes and feel contempt for him. He wanted her, she believed, not because he desired her for herself, but because she was the wife of his victim. He wanted complete victory, to conquer all. That was why he wanted her, though she doubted he understood that himself.

The Pict himself, she also realised, unlike her was longing for his home. But then the Pict had more back there than she had herself. He was a man, for one thing, and had a much higher status in life. He could do as he wished: beat his wife when he felt unhappy, kick his dog, hunt, kill a man for a sword or any other possession. He could get out of the hovel whenever he wanted to, and leave his woman to wash his filthy clothes, to cook his meals, to make his bed, to wait in patience with open legs ready for him to bury himself inside her. He was master back there, and she much the slave, and all that had changed when the two of them had been swept away into this other world of darker men with brighter souls.

Kieto was no longer so afraid of the woman with the strange smell and fish-belly skin. Kupe had instructed him to teach the woman and the man the legends and stories of real people, tales of larger-than-life heroes of the ancient world, like Maui; of great ancestors like Tiki; and of Great Gods like Tangaroa. Kieto began with the story of how the coconut came into being.

The goddess Hine, who has always been known for her appetite for men, fell in love with the gigantic Eel-man, Te Tuna. She lived at the bottom of the sea with him amongst the waving fronds of the sea bed plants. Eventually, however, Hine became bored with Te Tuna despite his great size in the region of passion, and she made an excuse to leave him.

'I need a new raiment,' she said. 'I shall visit the Nekaneka tribe, who are superb weavers.'

'As you wish, my dear,' said Te Tuna, not suspecting that she intended to stay away forever, 'but come back to your sea bed soon.'

With that, Hine left, but not to seek garments, for she could spin her own with great skill, but rather to look for a new man to satisfy her. She called first at the atoll of the Raru-vai-i-o, the Deep-penetrating-men, who were known throughout Oceania for their sexual prowess. Arriving in the early evening, when the skies were blood-red, at a time when the men were seeking their partners for the night, she stepped naked onto the coral shores. They asked her who she was, and she told them. She said she was a woman seeking a new great shaft of desire to fulfil her needs.

'Look to my dark triangle, you men of these fair isles, for it has a need to be cloven asunder!'

Now Hine is a goddess of amazing beauty, but her presence on the atoll terrified the tribesmen.

'You must not stop here, Hine,' they cried in fear, 'for we know the monster Eel-man to be a ferocious warrior. He will come here with his intimates and slay every one of us. You must look for your new lover elsewhere, for our fear makes us hang limp like a palm leaf in the rain.'

Feeling nothing but contempt for the Deep-penetrating tribe, she continued on her way to arrive at some islands where lived the men of the Peka tribe, or Loving-hug people, who were famous for their lingering embraces and sexual stamina.

'Will one of you take me to his bed?' cried Hine, in frustration, 'or are you frightened little men, like the Raru-vai-i-o tribe?'

'Let your desire carry you further,' shouted the Peka men, hiding in the bushes, 'otherwise Te Tuna will thrust himself amongst us as a blunt-nosed shark and cause us untold misery.'

Angrily, Hine left the Peka men and sought out the men of the Ever-erect tribe, whose sturdy staves were known throughout the watery world, but on hearing Hine's request they scuttled away and hid in damp caves, where for the first time in their lives they became flaccid and useless to women.

Fuming with discontent now, Hine went on her way, to arrive at last on the shores of the island where the demi-god Maui lived with his mother.

Now Maui's mother wanted grandchildren and she knew Hine to be a fertile goddess, so when she heard Hine's plaintive call, she encouraged her son to go out and invite the goddess to his home. Maui did as his mother bid and fell in love with Hine immediately, taking her to his bed that very night. Hine's sighs could be heard over half the ocean and all the other tribesmen emerged from their hiding places knowing she had at last found a lover who could satisfy her carnal needs.

The trouble was, the tribesmen were so relieved they took to mocking Te Tuna, telling him he was a cuckold. The great Eel-man, whose penis everyone believed to be the largest in the world, was at first unconcerned by their taunting, since he was not a creature who liked to roam far from his nest. He satisfied himself by sullying Hine's name, calling her a woman of no virtue. He told everyone she was hopeless as a paramour and had never satisfied him anyway and that he was glad to be rid of her.

Still they jeered at him, cried that what lay under his skirt was a small insignificant thing compared to that which was under Maui's, until finally he lost his temper and threatened to visit Maui's island to teach him a lesson.

'We'll see who has the biggest,' he cried. 'Mine is so large the elements go mad when they see it!'

Te Tuna then began a karakia chant, to assist him in his endeavour to destroy Maui, for nothing now would satisfy his fury but the total destruction of the little demi-god.

The tribesmen listened to the chant and then went to tell tales on the Eel-man, calling at Maui's island and informing him that Te Tuna was going to meet him in mortal combat, and that he should make himself ready for a contest.

'Pooh, I am not afraid of an *eel*,' said Maui. 'How big is he anyway?'

'Big?' the tribesmen cried, delightedly, 'he is *immense*.'

'Is he as erect and massive as that stone stack over there?' asked Maui, pointing to a tall needle of rock.

Fearing that Maui would shy away from the fight, they replied, 'More like a soft-wood tree.'

'What about the shape,' asked Maui. 'Is it straight?'

'More like a curved fern tree,' they answered.

'Ha!' sneered Maui. 'Then he'd better beware, because if I reveal what I have underneath my tapa bark skirt it will turn the weather insane.'

Nothing happened for a while, however, because Te Tuna was busy with his chants. As his power grew the skies became darker and darker, lightning flashed, and thunder rolled. The waves on the ocean grew large and crashed on the beaches of Maui's island and the other people of his tribe began to grow frightened.

'What if Te Tuna is not satisfied with destroying Maui,' they whispered amongst themselves, 'but wants to demolish the whole of our nation?'

They grumbled that men should not steal the wives of others, even if those wives should come to them first.

One terrible day, when the sky was black with worry, the Eel-man finally arrived on the shores of Maui's island and called him to come out and fight. Te Tuna had brought with him four very dangerous friends: Pup-vae-noa, or Mound-with-a-target; Porporo-tu-a-huaga, or Massive-testicles; Toke-a-kura, or Swollen-clitoris; and Maga-vai-i-e-rire, or Loop-that-strangles-man's-penis.

Te Tuna stood on the reef of Maui's island and took off his tapa bark kilt, revealing his monstrous eel. The ocean reeled at the sight and produced a tidal wave, which swept towards Maui's island and threatened to engulf it.

'Ha!' cried Maui, in triumph. 'I knew I was larger!'

With a sweeping gesture he tore off his own skirt and exposed a small man's most mighty weapon. It was twice the size of the Eel-man's and the sky gasped and swallowed the wind, the land shuddered and shrank, and the giant wave reversed itself immediately, rushing back and carrying off Te Tuna's friends.

The Eel-man himself was left at the mercy of Maui.

Now Maui is not a vindictive demi-god, but simply a cocky young half-deity. He is magnanimous in victory. He is always full of himself, but with good reason, having a thousand tricks at his fingertips. Once the two were clothed he extended a welcome to Te Tuna and asked him to spend the night on the island.

'Just because we have fought, and you have lost, does not mean that I should not offer you hospitality,' said Maui.

However, though the Eel-man accepted the invitation he had to spend several sleepless hours behind thin walls, listening to the moaning of Hine in the throes of ecstasy. Maui made love to Hine the whole night long. It was more than Te Tuna could stand.

'We must fight again,' he said savagely to Maui. 'This time the contest must be a little more fair.'

'What do you suggest?' asked the trickster god.

'We must each go inside the other's body, one at a time, and try to defeat one another.'

Maui agreed to this and said Te Tuna could go first.

The Eel-man began by chanting his karakia.

The enormous eel swims through the sea,
His strength is superlative,
His boldness and courage unbeatable.
The moray is majestic muscle, it fills the coral hole
*   with its menacing form.*

With that he disappeared into Maui's body and tried to destroy Maui from within, seeking out his heart to squeeze it until it burst. But the tricky Maui kept his heart on the move, changing it now with his liver, now with his kidneys, now with his pancreas, all of which slipped from Te Tuna's fingers, they being so slithery. Finally, Te Tuna's time was up and he had to emerge.

'Now it is my turn,' said Maui.

Now the feisty man begins to fight,
Entering with no fear or fright.
He is disdainful of the other's deed
Being sure to fulfil his own creed,
*   To win at any cost!*

With that, Maui entered the body of Te Tuna, who immediately began moving his heart around so that Maui could not grasp and crush it. Maui did not bother doing this because the tricky demi-god had swallowed a stem of mohio fern which made him expand to four times his normal size. Maui grew rapidly until he caused the mighty Eel-man to burst asunder. Te Tuna exploded like a plugged volcano, his flesh flying everywhere. Only his head remained intact, which Maui severed from his shoulders.

Maui threw the head on a rubbish tip, but his mother got hold of it and told Maui to bury it beside the house. Maui did so, underneath the window, then forgot all about it.

After the annual rains had been he noticed a shoot coming up from the ground where he had buried Te Tuna's head.

'That's a new one,' he murmured. 'What kind of plant is that?'

The shoot grew into a sapling, then a tall tree with feathery fronds at the top. At the point where the leaves grew, some sea-green oval shapes appeared. Maui's mother called them coconuts.

When Maui first picked one he found the juice very sweet. Later there was meat inside the kernel. Maui planted some more coconut palms. He took the leaves from the palms and used them to make a roof for his house. The trunks he employed as corner posts. Soon other men were doing the same, putting to use every part of the coconut palm. The gigantic Eel-man had become one of the most useful plants in the whole of Oceania. Maui sang:

> *This is the way we favour our foes:*
> *We do not throw them on the offal heap,*
> *Nor cast them into the ocean:*
> *We let them ripen anew*
> *In some more useful form to men.*
>
> *I am the trickster demi-god Maui*
> *Who swallowed a leaf, destroyed my foe:*
> *The dolt Te Tuna tried to undo me*
> *But cunning and cleverness overcomes*
> *⠀⠀⠀⠀anger, strength and boastful oaths.*
>
> *Such a dunce, Te Tuna, pompous eel!*

When the story was over, Seumas raised his eyebrows and looked at Dorcha. She ignored his attempt at conspiracy, so he said to Kieto with some prudishness, 'I don't think it's fitting that you should tell such stories in front of a woman.'

'And why not?' asked Dorcha, turning on him. 'You think women don't talk of such things?'

'I don't think they should,' he said, primly.

She snorted at him. 'You are a poor man, Seumas.'

He didn't know what she meant by that, but it left him feeling wretched.

At that moment the mariners on board the ocean-going canoe started yelling and jumping up and down. Seumas looked up to see what was the matter and discerned a white line of breakers in the distance. Beyond this were the still waters of a light-green lagoon, and from the middle of this placid lake rose an island, green and lush, with ragged peaks and crags veiled in mist.

The shape of the rocks was quite unlike those of Seumas's homeland, where the boulders and ridges had been worn smooth by the passing of time. The natural architecture here rose narrow and sinister out of deep clefts in the mountain and some twisted into hideous shapes as if clawing at passing clouds. Seumas was quite willing to believe there were gods amongst those ugly mizzle-shrouded peaks.

On the beach, from which the sail with the black octopus had been sighted, were laughing, waving people with flowers in their hair, around their necks, and even around their ankles and wrists.

'Raiatea,' cried Po in Seumas's ear. 'My homeland.'

Seumas nodded. 'Your homeland – but not mine.'

Po's Tiki received the crew's thanks for leading them homewards. Kupe reserved his main worship for Tangaroa, the god of the ocean. Tangaroa was greatly pleased with Kupe, who had followed the octopus sent by Tangaroa to lead the navigator prince to the shores of the Land-of-Mists. He received the sacrifice of turtles and sharks which Kupe cooked and ate in his honour, with due gratification. The god of the sea slept green and peaceful that night, in the knowledge of his success.

PART TWO

Most Sacred, Most Feared

1

The place is Tapu-tapu atia, 'Most Sacred, Most Feared', beneath the shadow of the ancient mountain. Low, tenebrous clouds seem to gather here, during the wet season, around high walls of rock dressed in old lichen and ancient mosses, coloured a darker green where they have absorbed the cold shadows into their damp garments. These clouds, with the forest behind and the clothed rock face in front, effectively enclose the area, making it a kind of capped glade rejected by the creatures of the island because of its isolation and lack of sunlight.

At the centre of Tapu-tapu atia stands the massive Investiture Stone, the four corners of which were once supported by the corpses of four men, the sacrificed guardians of the stone, though these are now dust and their spirits stand in their stead. Youths beloved of the tribe were brought godlike here, in earlier virtuous times, to the throb of drums and the chant of sacred fangu, and their skulls cloven with the edge of a priest's paddle club. Their goodness was shared among the living, went into the fertile land, the deep stone. Only the most beautiful, the most adored, deserved such an end.

'Most sacred, most feared' still has the smell of death clinging to the great stone, whose face is bare of any moss or lichen, and whose coldness emanates from within its heart to chill the air within the glade.

It was here, in this place – taboo when no ceremony was taking place and the priests were absent – where young men were given their adulthood, that the spy Manopa met with Prince Tangiia to impart his information.

Ra was just coming out of the night sea, into the sky god Rangi's territory, overpowering the 'Long Shark at Dawn', that flush of stars which sweeps across the roof of voyaging in a great rash of brilliant white.

Manopa stared around him at the whispering leaves; there were unseen ghosts abroad. There was only one world, shared by the quick and the dead alike. The spirits of the dead had to live on the same landscape as people of flesh and blood. Each did their best not to trespass on the domain of the other. Sometimes a clash was inevitable and ghosts, being the more sensitive of the two, were angered.

A wickerwork shark hung from the branch of breadfruit tree above Manopa's head, telling all that the fruit from these boughs belonged to the gods. Such fruit was mashed and stored in stone vaults, underground by priests. In time of famine this stored food might be blessed and distributed amongst the people. A king could eat it at any time, his mana being great.

The shark, hanging by a single thread, turned this way and that, as the wind changed direction. Manopa stared at this spinning, hollow fish and shivered. This silent valley was a gathering place for the sau of his ancestors. There would be malevolent demons as well as dark gods, in this place of blood. Manopa gripped a magic whalebone club in his right hand, hoping this would be enough to ward off any malignant spirits that might want to enter his body.

Tangiia, on the other hand, was more concerned with the living. His brother Tutapu's men were everywhere and while it was doubtful his brother would have him wilfully assassinated while their father was alive, there might be an overzealous warrior willing to take the law into his own hands, hoping for eventual favours from the future king.

'What news is there?' asked Tangiia. 'Is my brother still plotting against me?'

'The moment your father dies,' said Manopa, 'Tutapu intends to kill you and eat your roasted heart. He will not share the island with you, nor give you any part of what he considers to be his rightful inheritance – not Borabora, nor any of the smaller isles which come under your father's rule.'

Tangiia sighed. 'I would be quite willing to take a small piece of what my older brother considers to be all his own, but it seems the gods don't want me to remain on my home isle. If I'm to avoid bloodshed I must make preparations to leave Raiatea for good. Will you and your men come with me, Manopa?'

The broad-faced Manopa grinned. 'If I stay here your brother will eat *me* instead.' He became serious once more as a dark shadow fluttered through the forest near by; perhaps a bat returning to a cave; perhaps an ancestor-spirit looking for a live soul to devour. 'We must build some canoes, Prince Tangiia – at least three great pahi canoes – enough for two hundred people. I shall see to their secret construction on the far side of Raiatea. Your brother at present resides on Borabora, since he cannot stand to be near you, and we must hope he stays there until after we've gone.'

The young and handsome Tangiia, still only eighteen years of age, nodded his head.

'He's afraid I will attempt to assassinate him in his sleep. He's even had a wooden floor constructed around his bed which makes twittering sounds when someone walks on it. I'm told that when one treads on the planks the sound of birds warn him that someone is in the room. He's sure to remain on Borabora until he feels ready to attack me with his warriors. Now for our part, we must recruit others for a voyage into the unknown,' he said to Manopa. 'Perhaps Kupe will come with us?'

Manopa shook his head. 'Prince Kupe remains aloof from politics. He's a lone adventurer. His expeditions are spontaneous voyages, made on the spur of the moment without any real preparation. He would become bored with all the intrigue, the boat building, the provisioning of craft, the selection of greater and lesser navigators. Ask him to jump into a dugout and go within the moment, and you're more likely to get him as an ally – but he won't join a mass exodus. He hates crowds.'

'You're right, I wasn't thinking. What about his young protégé, Kieto? The boy is almost fourteen now. He went on the voyage which brought the other people to us.'

'Seumas and Dorcha? Yes, but Kieto was a child on that voyage – not more than seven or eight years.'

'Still, he learned much from Kupe, and has hardly been separated from the navigator since that time.'

Manopa nodded. 'True – and speaking of the goblin, why not take him too? He longs to leave this island.'

'Seumas wants to go home to this Land-of-Mists which Kupe found, not to another island, but you're right, he's a restless soul and he might be useful to us, if we meet some of his kind by accident.' The young prince hesitated, then said, 'I want to take Nau Ariki with me.'

Something cold, like an invisible clam shell, seemed to razor into Manopa's soul. He had been dreading these words from his young prince and friend. It was not enough that the youth was restless and ambitious, but he had to want the very female destined to marry his older brother.

'Nau Ariki is to be Tutapu's *wife*. You would be foolish to abduct her. The anger—'

'Perhaps she would come of her own accord?' interrupted Tangiia a little waspishly. 'Have you thought of that?'

'She is promised to your *brother*,' said Manopa. 'Hard as that may seem. Look, we share the same basket of food, you and I – we have done since children – I would not lie to you, Tangiia. The girl must go to your brother. She wouldn't thank you for taking her with you. It would make both of you unhappy.'

Tangiia was young and headstrong, deeply in love with Nau Ariki, and would not listen to good advice. He spoke almost feverishly of the young maiden, his eyes burning.

'I *must* have her with me – she is part of it all – don't you understand? Without her I would rather stay here and have my brains dashed out by my brother's club.'

Nothing Manopa said would alter Tangiia's mind about Nau Ariki. The youth was completely infatuated by the seventeen-year-old girl, who, Manopa admitted, was something of a rare beauty. Not only that, she had a spirit to match. There was that which was bright and open about her, which caught a man's attention the moment she spoke to him. This candid and unguarded disposition often hid the fact that Nau Atiki was highly intelligent. It was no wonder Tangiia was in love with the maiden: half the men on the island loved her.

'I must—' began Tangiia, but then both men heard the single *clack* and whirled towards the rainforest.

Manopa turned pale and gripped his whalebone club.

'Is it one of the Peerless Ones?' he whispered, meaning the forest fairies who often disguised themselves as birds and wrapped their forms in sunlight and moonlight to confuse mortals.

The sound came again, this time unmistakably seashells being rattled together. It was not fairies but some man or woman spying on the pair as they stood near the Great Stone.

Manopa was first to move, with Tangiia close behind him. The pair of them ran straight towards an area of thick bushes. A startled, frightened creature ran from the shrubs, like a deer, through the shafts of sunlight penetrating the canopy. The two men would never have caught up, so fast was their quarry on its feet, had the runner not tripped over a buttress root and gone sprawling, the shells tied in the long locks rattling.

The two men, one large and bole-chested, the other broad-shouldered and strong, caught up and stood over an exceptionally tall Raiatean with a pretty face.

'I didn't hear anything,' cried Boy-girl, hands out to ward off the blows. 'I heard nothing at all.'

Boy-girl curled up like a leech, making herself look very small and pathetic. Manopa's club was on the descent, when Tangiia caught his arm.

'No,' said the prince.

'But he *heard*,' hissed Manopa. 'He'll betray us. You can't trust a creature like this.'

'I won't tell anyone,' sobbed Boy-girl. 'Don't hurt me, please, Manopa. I'll be as silent as the sacred rock.'

'Stand up, Boy-girl,' said Tangiia.

Boy-girl climbed slowly to her feet. She stood in a bright pillar of sunlight and was at least a head taller than Tangiia, who was no dwarf himself. Boy-girl's body was extremely lean and supple, though not *thin* in the sense that no bones protruded. Her hair was decorated with dozens of pretty seashells, the bounty of the ocean, and it was these which had made the noise that gave her away. There were ribbons and flowers hanging from her locks too, and from her wrists and ankles. The colours of her bark-cloth skirt were brighter than those of the two men who confronted her and she had make-up around her eyes to enhance their beauty.

'Please don't hurt me,' she said, calmer now. 'I want to be one of you – go away with you.'

From an early age Boy-girl had shown a preference for feminine ways and once this had been seen to be a permanent part of his personality it had been encouraged, and he became *she* to all those except men like Manopa who was secretly afraid of her special powers. From time to time there were men who wanted to live their lives like women and Oceanians in general saw no harm in this behaviour; in fact the Boy-girls of the clans performed a special social function. There were warriors of the tribe who had no desire to be feminine, but who preferred sleeping with another man to lying with a woman. Boy-girls took these warriors to their breast and gave them comfort.

'We need people who are *useful* to us,' said Manopa with some contempt. 'Not silly-headed creatures.'

Boy-girl turned on the stocky, bluff warrior. 'I am so *useful* it would make your head *spin* to know the ways, you tragic man,' she cried. 'I can sing songs you've never heard before – I can make such music as you would think the sea was coursing through your veins—' Boy-girl was indeed very creative. '– but better than that, I can steal a man's mind.' She stared directly at the bulky warrior.

Manopa shuddered. He had witnessed this feat. Boy-girl could look into a man's eyes, whisper in his ear, and the man would start barking like a dog, believe he *was* a dog, and eat scraps from around the fire, yap at passers-by, and cock his leg up at a tree for a piss. Boy-girl had done this to a man who had insulted her. She had made a woman who had cast a slur on her act like a cockerel for many hours. Later, when Boy-girl had called the magic off, the dog-man and rooster-woman wondered why people were laughing at them when they passed, having no recollection of their time spent as animal and bird.

Manopa considered this a very dangerous skill, this magic passed down from some mischievous god, and he wanted no demonstration of it here.

'Take your eyes off me, damn you,' cried Manopa, turning his head away. 'You turn me into a dog and I'll tear your throat out, whatever Prince Tangiia says.'

Boy-girl giggled and rattled her shells.

Tangiia said seriously, 'Do you understand what a position you've put yourself in here, Boy-girl? If my brother gets to know of my plans, I am dead where I stand. It would be safer for us to kill you now.'

'Safer, but not wiser, my prince,' said Boy-girl. 'You wish to build some pahi canoes without Tutapu's knowledge, yet if he goes out on the waters in his canoe he may hear the hammering and chiselling, the adze's hewing out the trunks. I could whisper in his ear, get him and his basket-sharers to ignore such noises. No outsider can reach Tutapu without going through his bodyguards or his priests – he isolates himself from the rest of the people for fear of assassination.'

Tangiia looked up at Boy-girl doubtfully. 'Can you do that? Can you beguile a whole counsel of men? It doesn't seem possible.'

'If I can get them all together, I can do it.'

Manopa, who had been listening with some interest now, moved next to

Boy-girl, trying to ignore the sweet smell of the oil with which she bathed her body, saying, 'How can *you* get close to Tutapu?' he asked. 'How can you get access to the inner circle of his basket-sharers?'

Boy-girl smiled one of those smiles which normally infuriated Manopa.

'He likes me,' she said. 'He calls me to his bed.'

Manopa grunted and shook his head at Tangiia. 'This creature will betray us,' he warned. 'With pillow-talk.'

Before Tangiia could reply, Boy-girl snapped, '*Creature* yourself, hog's-body. If I could kill Tutapu now, I would – I *hate* the vile man. He's nasty to me, pinches me, hurts me and makes bruises after he's finished with me and starts feeling ugly with himself. He's a despicable man. But I'm not strong enough to murder him with my bare hands and I have to go to him naked. They even inspect my mouth before they let me in his hut, to make sure I have no needle to use as a weapon under my tongue. I wish I *could* kill him for you.'

'Why can't you do something with this magic of yours?' asked Manopa, grunting out the words.

'It's not that powerful,' admitted Boy-girl. 'I can't make a man kill himself or put himself in deadly danger. Believe me, I would have him dancing and singing over the clifftops if I could, onto the rocks below.'

'I wouldn't want you to,' Tangiia interrupted. 'I have no wish to kill my own brother, no matter how he feels about me. Show me the bruises, Boy-girl, where you've been hurt by my brother.'

Boy-girl let her skirt drop to her ankles and revealed her thighs. The smooth, silky skin was covered in ugly wheals. Even Manopa winced.

'He uses a piece of sharp bamboo sometimes,' said Boy-girl, 'in places I *can't* show you.'

'I believe you,' said Tangiia, sighing.

Though it was said he would make a good king over a nation, Tutapu had a reputation for cruelty towards individuals. There was something in his make-up, a vicious streak, which came out at odd times. Tutapu could also be extraordinarily generous and warmhearted when the mood was on him. While they had been growing up together, Tutapu had been a good older brother, teaching the younger Tangiia how to hunt and use weapons of war. Tutapu had also sung many songs to his sibling, patiently teaching Tangiia the words. It was only once they had reached manhood that the canker had entered Tutapu's heart.

'What do you want me to do?' asked Boy-girl, covering her male genitals, though not without a sly look at Manopa, to make sure he had been looking at her.

'If you can beguile my brother's basket-sharers, then I wish you to do so. Since you are committed to our cause you can also recruit one of the other people, Seumas. Your success in this will prove to me your loyalty and your worth, for if my brother finds out you have helped me in any way, he'll skewer your kidneys and barbecue them over a charcoal fire.'

'If he doesn't, I *will*,' grunted Manopa.

'You great hog,' giggled Boy-girl, 'you're so *strong*.'

On a remote beach on Raiatea the boat-building began some seven days later. The heavy work was to be carried out using almost exclusively one tool – the adze. The Raiatean adzes were mainly of basalt, though some of those for lighter work were fashioned out of a clam shell fixed to a haft. There were also stone axes, drills of sharks' teeth and bone needles. There were large scissors and chisels of human upper-arm bones, graters of coral and sanders of sting-ray skin. These tools were first placed in an open-air temple dedicated to Tangaroa, constructed near the building site, in order that the Great Sea-God, the creator, might impregnate them with his divine presence.

A priest invoked Tane with this fangu chant:

Go and take hold of the adze,
In the niche of the holy place.
Hold, that it be taken out enchanted
Made light that it may produce sparks
In doing its many tasks.

The awakening of the adze!
Let it travel a little seaward,
Present it, let it fight and attack:
Let the axe go against the spray
Inaugurating its flying girdle,
Awake for Tane
Great god of artisans!

Along with extraordinary ability the boat builders required a profound religious mentality to assist them in their task.

Then the work began with the cutting of the chosen trees. Ati wood for the keel and the planks of the hull. Hutu wood for the masts. Mara, from the breadfruit tree, for the oars.

There was a special hut constructed for the building of each pahi canoe, so that work on polishing the keel, the sides, and other pieces could take place while continuing the preparation of the rigging and sails, the former braided from nape fibres of the coconut shell, and the latter from dried pandanus leaves cut into ribbons and whipped together to form matting.

Once the parts had been shaped and smoothed the wood was covered with a protective coat of red clay and charcoal, then assembled: pegged and glued with utu sap, and lashed with sennit. Breadfruit sap and shark oil provided the caulking material, smeared over every part of the great canoe.

Fitted to the prow of each vessel was a small part taken from an ancient sacred canoe, to introduce the new canoe to Tangaroa and the minor gods of the ocean.

'*O what have I, O Tane,*' sang the boat builders while they worked, '*but sennit, the cord of the coconut, to hold thy cane, that she might go over long waves, and over short waves, to the near horizon, even to the far-off horizon, this sennit of thine, O Tane. Let it hold! Let it hold!*'

There would be more rituals once the boat was complete, for the launching and the consecrating of the boat once it stood in the water, drinking the waves.

On the deck of each vessel, once they were complete, would stand two masts and a couple of bamboo huts. The canoes would hold 60 to 70 passengers and a crew of 20, plus supplies for a month and baggage necessary to start a new life.

Io, the Old One, Father of the Gods, watched this activity below with some interest. He had heard Papa, the Earth-Goddess, and Rangi, the Sky-God, speaking about the coming events. There was already conflict between certain gods, not necessarily between Papa and her husband Rangi, but others who were concerned with the rights and wrongs of Tutapu's threat to kill his half-brother. These were Tangaroa, Maomao, Hine, Hau Maringi. Any friction on earth always had its counterpart amongst the gods. The truth was, the gods loved distractions, and mortals were always providing them with new amusements. They were bound to take sides in such issues. Io saw it as his task to maintain some sort of balance, a fairness, in these times.

Seumas, lying in the shade of the doorway of his hut, saw Boy-girl coming. He wondered whether to remain where he was, or walk down to the lagoon. Boy-girl always made him feel uncomfortable. He wanted to shake her by her shoulders and tell her to wipe her face, comb the shells out of her hair, and walk like a man. Boy-girl had always had a crush on Seumas which she did little to disguise in front of him. She even followed him up the cliffs sometimes, where he collected eggs, the frigate birds whirling about his head the way fulmars had done on the cliffs of his homeland of Albainn.

When she reached the hut, Boy-girl stared down at the bronzed, tattooed man and looked lovingly into his sea-washed blue eyes.

'I love your tattoos,' she murmured, reaching out to trace one with an elegant finger, 'all those swirls and circles.'

'What do you want?' growled Seumas, testily, knocking her hand away. 'I'm not in any mood for idle chat.'

Boy-girl squatted down and played with the hem of her bark-cloth skirt. Seumas was wearing a similar wraparound, made from the paper mulberry tree, his woollen garments having long since rotted away in the humidity of the tropics.

'I have to talk to you,' she said, 'about something important.'

'If it's about the fairies again, forget it – I'm not interested in meeting any of them.'

The last time Boy-girl had been to see Seumas, she had told him she had a fairy trapped in a cage of twigs in the forest, and would show it to him if he went with her. Seumas, quite rightly, believed it to be a ruse to get him into a solitary place where Boy-girl hoped to work her charms and not inconsiderable enchantments on the 'other person' to make him her lover, if only for a short while.

The temptation to see one of the Peerless Ones he had heard so much about was strong with Seumas, but not so strong that he was fool enough to accept Boy-girl's invitation on trust.

'It's not about my games, it's about Tangiia.' She lowered her voice. 'He's planning to leave the islands forever, along with his people. His brother, you know, is scheming to kill him once their father dies. Tangiia doesn't want to fight his brother – he would rather seek a Faraway Heaven.'

Seumas was vaguely aware of these affairs, from the whispers of the shell gatherers, when they combed the shallows of the lagoon at low tide looking for edible molluscs.

'What's all this to do with me?' he asked. 'I don't want to get mixed up in politics – it's more than my life's worth.'

'You could come with us. I'm going. So are Po, Keito and a number of others. It might take you closer to your homelands.'

Seumas glanced quickly into Boy-girl's brown eyes.

'You're going to the Land-of-Mists?'

Boy-girl shrugged. 'Possibly in that direction.'

'Too vague,' growled Seumas.

Seumas stared across at the hut where Dorcha lived with her two husbands, twin brothers who could not bear to be parted, even by marriage. One of the husbands, Ti-ti, was cooking some fish in an earth-oven. There were stones in the umu pit around which firewood had been burned, thus bringing the stones to a high heat. Fish wrapped in damp pandanus leaves had been laid on the stones to cook. The belly of each fish had been slit, the innards removed, and hot pebbles put in their place to ensure cooking right through the flesh. Ti-ti suddenly realised he was being observed and looked up, to scowl at Seumas.

'Don't look at me like that, man, or I'll stuff one of your hot cooking stones down your throat,' growled Seumas, under his breath.

Boy-girl giggled, aware like everyone else that Dorcha's husbands hated Seumas, and that the feeling was mutual. Everyone knew that Seumas was in love with Dorcha, and that Dorcha hated Seumas so much that she was not above flaunting herself in front of him to let him know what he was missing, thus infuriating her jealous husbands and rousing Seumas to such a pitch of choler he almost choked on his frustration.

When the two Albannachs had arrived on Raiatea Seumas had been stunned by the comeliness of the local women. What was more he was unusual enough to find himself much in demand amongst these lovely females. One after the other came to him in his hut over the first two or three years and he sated himself on sex that would have been unthinkable back in his homeland. A man *there* was lucky if he had one woman who remained passably pretty for a few years before the ague, fire smoke and childbirth in bad conditions took its toll on her looks.

Here there were astonishingly graceful and captivating beauties who actually enjoyed going with a man, seeming to get as much pleasure from it as he himself.

Yet, once he had been to bed with a dozen of them, it all began to pall. They were ravishing, exciting, but he was not in love with any of them. For the first time in his life he realised that to get the most out of the sexual act, there had to be a spiritual union, as well as a carnal one. His head had been full of fantasies before but when the fantasies became reality he came to the knowledge that it was necessary to love the person you were making love to, if there was to be a flight into absolute ecstasy.

So he had taken a wife, after Dorcha had taken in her husbands, the two brothers who fussed over her like mother hens. Mary, as he had called her, not liking many of the names they gave themselves, over which his tongue continually tripped, had been a sweet woman with a happy disposition six years younger than himself. She was not the most beautiful woman he could have chosen, but she was enough like the girl he had left behind in Albainn to make her interesting to him. In his way he had been very fond of her and they had been reasonably content, until she died in pain when some organ in the region of her stomach turned rotten and poisoned her blood.

Dorcha had visited him then, for the first time without rancour, and offered her sympathy.

However, her bitterness went so deep she could not help herself throwing a parting shot at him as she left him by the grave, saying, 'Now you know how it feels.'

Boy-girl, seeing how intently the glum Seumas was staring at Dorcha's hut, whispered, 'I can make her come with us.'

His head swivelled round and he stared into Boy-girl's eyes, then back again at Ti-ti.

'And,' added Boy-girl, 'we can leave those two behind.'

Seumas said nothing. He stared again at Boy-girl, then rose to his feet without a word and strolled slowly down to the lagoon, past the magnificent house of the father of Tangiia and Tutapu, with its carved wooden doorposts and its totems.

Inside the house an old man lay sick and dying. Seumas knew that once the king was dead, which could only be a matter of weeks, there would be civil war on the islands. He might try to remain aloof from the disturbance, but it was unlikely he would be allowed to. One or the other side would eventually demand his loyalty and he would have to choose between them.

If Tangiia left Raiatea and sought a new home, this would avert the immediate crisis it was true, but Seumas did not trust the self-indulgent and paranoid Tutapu, who saw a plot against his life under every leaf of the forest. There were good rulers and there were despots, and Seumas had no doubt which one Tutapu would turn out to be, when he took over.

Once on the white coral sands, which burned his feet in the noon sun, Seumas walked into the shallow waters of the lagoon, followed for a while by his pet dog, Dirk. When Dirk saw that his master was deep in thought and paying no attention to him, the hound left him and went back to sleep in the shade.

Seumas waded slowly out to the edge of the reef, keeping to the smooth coral paths winding amongst the many-coloured stags-horn and fan corals with their sharp edges and points.

There was much beauty in the waters of the lagoon, from the hundreds of gaudy and graceful reef fish and anemones, with lacy scarves for fins, to the hermit crabs in their stolen homes – fragile combs, polished cowries, frilled murexes – scuttling out of his way.

There was also a sinister side, with thick-bodied moray eels poking their narrow heads out of holes, octopuses dancing away like fleshy spiders, and the odd barracuda trapped inside the reef when the tide went out. There were stone fish, ugly as a heinous sin manifest, the dorsal fin of which was deadly poison and if trodden upon took your life within a day. There were whip-tailed sting-rays and huge, tentacled jellyfish as delicate and monstrous as the wedding veils of an ogre's bride.

The lagoon, the reef, was thriving with life and colour though, and Seumas never ceased to marvel at it. It helped him think, to walk through this wonderland of grotesque fish and many-hued coral with its fantastic forms.

He reached the edge of the reef where the waves reared high above his head, becoming thin and translucent green for a moment, before crashing down on the coral barrier and magically melting into the placid waters of the lagoon, though they were only a body-length away from where he stood.

Out there, in the deep ocean, were monsters. Sharks that could swallow

boats, giant squids that could crush canoes to pulp, swarms of deadly stinging translucent bells more numerous than wasps, killer whales, sea snakes
more venomous than any serpent found on land. There was one type of
tawny jellyfish that weighed as much as thirty men together and spread its
filaments as wide as an island.

Did he really want to travel where there was the possibility of meeting
such company?

'Well?' shrieked a voice over the boom of the surf. 'Are you coming?'

Seumas turned to see that the tall, willowy Boy-girl had followed him out
to the foaming gulleys where he liked to stand and meditate. She looked
unhappy. Boy-girl was not at home in the water, unlike most Raiateans, preferring dry land beneath her feet.

'I'm *thinking*,' he roared at her.

Miserably, Boy-girl found an exposed head of brain coral, the earthly symbol of Tangaroa himself, and stood upon it while Seumas made up his mind.
Eventually he turned to her and smiled.

'Why not? It'll be a great adventure, won't it? What have I got to lose?'

She smiled at him and clapped her hands. 'Wonderful – I shall tell Tangiia
today.'

'When is it to be – the departure?'

'When the pahi canoes are ready and the weather is right – we must have
a diversion – a storm or something.'

'We're going to leave in a *storm?*'

'Perhaps,' she smiled, wagging a long finger at him. 'We'll see. A big brave
man like you shouldn't be worried about such things. Shame on you. Are you
afraid of death?'

'I'm not afraid of dying, I'm afraid of the *boredom* of being dead,' he confessed. 'I'm afraid that there'll be nothing to do but lie in my grave staring
into an endless future. I hate being bored. It's agony for me to do nothing, or
to do something which makes the time drag and makes me wish it was over.
Some journeys are like that you know. Death must be like that.'

'Shame on you,' she said again, laughing.

Boy-girl then began wading back to the beach as if she were walking
through raw sewage.

Seumas turned to face the great expanse of ocean again, upon which once
more he was about to embark. There were small crab-claw sails out there
now: fishermen in their canoes. The sea was as much their home as the
island; they spent almost an equal amount of time on both. Yet there was
something about a major voyage which captured the imagination of everyone, even a landsman, a climber, an egg-gatherer and bird-strangler like
Seumas, who was more at ease on a sheer cliff than he was on the water.

He felt heroic at first and his spirit expanded inside him. Then he remembered what had been promised him and to what he had agreed, and his swollen soul shrank within his body again.

'Yes,' said Seumas to himself in Gaelic, thinking of his planned abduction of Dorcha, 'shame on me.'

After speaking with Seumas, Boy-girl went to where Kieto was fishing from the beach. Boy-girl and Kieto were friends, brought closer together by their mutual interest in the goblin, Seumas. When Seumas and Dorcha were first on the island there were few Oceanians who would engage them in conversation, or even pass them with a greeting. Most were afraid of the white-skinned savages who sometimes spoke with the tongues of demons, and others thought it best not to risk contamination.

Kieto, however, had come to regard Seumas and Dorcha with some affection, after their voyage over the great ocean together, and Boy-girl was obsessed with the strange beauty of the man. Sometimes the two Raiateans met to discuss the pair, though Boy-girl's interest was more with Seumas than with Dorcha.

'I have persuaded Seumas to come with us on the voyage,' said Boy-girl, sitting on the sands and watching the young Kieto whirl his net.

Kieto gave up his fishing and came and sat by Boy-girl.

'That's good,' said the boy. 'Is he pleased to come?'

Boy-girl shrugged. 'Not so pleased, but I think he will be, once we are out on the ocean.'

Kieto nodded, looking out at the toothed waves rearing and crashing on the reef. The ocean was like a wild beast, caged by the coral reef. Its great mouth was ever foaming; its jaws opening wide in its attempts to swallow the island; it rushed and gnashed and bit at the reef, trying to break through. The ocean, with its hard-edged light and big, brittle skies, was a beast which would never be tamed. You rode on its back and hoped you would survive the experience.

Kieto said, 'Yes – here he is just idling away his time, not really living. Seumas is a man made for adventure. He is like one of our heroes, waiting to prove himself. I think that out on the ocean he will wake, as if from a long sleep, and begin living the life he was meant to live.'

Boy-girl nodded. 'I remember how he was when he first came to us – angry at everyone, at everything. You could see the cruelty in him. He can be a cruel man. You could see the hardness like flint, in those blue eyes. And he hated us all then, especially me,' Boy-girl giggled. 'He hated my lovely decorations, my nice slim hands, my pretty face. He once yelled at me, "Is there a man underneath?" and I told him, "A bit of one – enough for *you*." He could be so confused. He didn't know how to treat me – or others. But there was a *fire* in him, which seems to have died now.

'The bitterness, and his idea of what a man should show of himself, conduct himself – how a man should act – has changed. He's mellowed. Now the fire is just a few glowing embers. It needs the ocean winds to make those embers flare into flame. Seumas will come alive again.'

Kieto nodded. 'Yes, much of the old Seumas is good – but not the Seumas who's afraid to show compassion or kindness. We don't want the unfeeling Seumas to return.'

Boy-girl nodded and smiled at Kieto. 'Don't worry, you and I will never let him become that silly man he once was, completely – we will draw out the bravehearted adventurer in him, direct him along a straighter path, and then he will not need those jaggedy edges he thought were so necessary to him when he first came to us.'

'He is not a man to control,' warned Kieto. 'If you try that, he'll kick against it.'

'I don't mean we shall control him, just steer him gently towards those things which make a man brave and honourable – once he knows the way, he will go there himself,' replied Boy-girl.

'I think there will be no need for us to do anything, once we get out there on the ocean's back,' said Kieto. 'I think Tangaroa's world will shape him into what he can be.'

Boy-girl nodded and replied, 'Perhaps you're right.'

2

'The king once went on a voyage himself,' explained Kieto, to Dorcha, 'as a young man. He was not much older than I am now when he left the island. There were two brothers older than him when he left and he thought he stood little chance of becoming king once his father died, so he believed he had nothing to lose.'

'But he must have come back,' Dorcha said, 'to be here now.'

'He was away on his travels for twenty years. By the time he returned his father and both his elder brothers were dead. The two young men had killed each other in battle, leaving the kingdom without a chief. As he stepped ashore there were warring factions, each claiming one of their own as the future king. He stated his own claim to the first people he met, proved he was the rightful heir, and demanded the kingdom.'

Dorcha was sitting inside the entrance to her hut, weaving some mats from dried grasses and strips of bark. She was almost as deft as the Raiatean woman at this particular craft and had added some artistic designs of her own to their decorative patterns. Kieto often came to teach her the history of his peoples, she being eager to learn.

'Had he not changed in twenty years?' she asked. 'Did they recognise him straight away?'

'Indeed, the ravages of his travels had taken its toll on his features. He had left Raiatea a young and handsome man, without a blemish on his body. Since that time he had been burned by the sun, bitten by a shark, had hungered and thirsted, all of which did much to change his appearance, as well as age filling out his body and stealing his youth.'

'I know,' cried Dorcha, 'they identified him by his tattoos!'

'No, he was too young to have tattoos when he left the island.'

Dorcha grumbled, 'Oh, come on then, you'll have to tell me how he proved his name – 1 can't guess.'

'What is it that we have, which you admire so much?' smiled Kieto.

Dorcha stopped her weaving and looked across at the youth.

'Why,' she said, 'your memory, of course. It's something you people have kept which we in Albainn have lost over the centuries. And the way you see things. I'm told you can remember every part of the journey to my old island, Kieto. It all looked the same to me – the waves, the sea, the stars ... every part of it. How did memory help the king?'

'He was able to recite the genealogy of his family, without a flaw, going back to the first ancestor.'

'And they accepted this as proof of his identity?'

'Of course,' said Kieto, 'any other man would have recited a *different* genealogy.'

'Of *course*', she smiled, but she knew Kieto missed the irony in her tone.

Kieto said, his voice much lower, 'Will you not come with us, with Tangiia, when he leaves the island?'

Dorcha shook her head. 'No, Kieto. I've found my home and here I'm staying, whoever is in charge. I've found a contentment here I never thought existed. You may all perish out there on the waves – or even before, if Tutapu discovers what you're up to. Everyone seems to know you're leaving except him – I don't understand why.'

'Boy-girl has bewitched him,' whispered Kieto.

'Well, it only takes one person disgruntled with Tangiia or any of you, to betray you.'

'No one can get near Tutapu except his basket-sharers, and they have had their ears shut by Boy-girl.'

Dorcha shook her head as she weaved. 'It's a very dangerous game and you'll be lucky to get away.'

Suddenly, the doorway darkened, and both the occupants of the hut looked up, startled to see a figure blocking it. Then Kieto heaved a sigh of relief, as he recognised who it was. Dorcha, however, snarled, 'Get out – you haven't been invited.'

Seumas remained where he was. 'I saw your two little flowers go off gathering molluscs for you, chattering like young girls. I need to talk to you.'

'Well, I don't wish to speak with you,' she said, turning over her weave and inspecting the back of it. 'Get out of my light.'

'Dorcha, for the sake of the gods,' he pleaded, 'it's been nearly eight years since I killed your husband in a fair fight – will you never forgive me?'

'*Never*,' she said, her eyes flashing hatred.

'It was a fair fight,' he repeated wearily, looking at Kieto, as if hoping for some support. 'If it had been me that had been killed, she would have forgotten it had ever taken place by now. I never took advantage, I never cheated. It was right under all the rules of single combat.'

'It left my husband dead,' Dorcha said, 'you can't expect me to forget that, ever.'

Seumas squatted down, still in the doorway, and stared at the mats on the floor beneath his feet.

'What can I do?' he asked, very quietly. 'How can I make you forgive me? I will do anything.'

'Go away,' she said.

'I am going away,' he replied, 'with Tangiia's fleet, when it sets sail. I want you to come with us. You may be in danger here, when Tutapu becomes king. He's not the most stable of men, and you're a foreigner here.'

'I'm staying,' she said, attentive to her work.

Seumas sat there for a very long time while Kieto stared at him, unwilling to get involved himself in this long-running feud between two people he both loved.

Finally, Seumas said, 'Boy-girl offered to make you come on the voyage ...'

Dorcha, dark and lovely in her twenty-seventh year, looked up sharply.

'You what? Why are you telling me this? You must have asked her to do it for you.'

He nodded. 'I can't do it. I've hurt you enough already. I thought I could do anything to get you, but I can't. I'm ashamed I even accepted Boy-girl's offer in the first place. I want you to come, but I want you to come *willingly*, without any magic from Boy-girl. It would be wrong ...'

'It would not only be wrong,' she said, her voice low and hoarse with fury, 'it would be your last unholy act against my person. Seumas, you must see this is best for both of us – you go, I stay, and when I'm out of your sight I'll go out of your mind, and we can forget each other for good.' She paused for a moment, then added, 'I promise, once you've gone, I'll think well of you again – I'll forgive you for murdering my man.'

'Very magnanimous of you,' he said, dully. 'You're prepared to forgive me, if I'm prepared to lose everything I ever wanted in life.'

She stared at him, feeling some pity in her heart for him at last.

'I'm not your *everything*, Seumas, believe me. If I gave myself to you now, you would be tired of me within a week. This is a great opportunity for both of us. We can start to live again, properly, without the constant reminder of each other. I think I shall be able to breathe easily once more.'

Seumas groaned and got to his feet. He left the hut without another word. Dorcha continued to stare at the place where he had crouched and finally shook herself.

'It's best this way,' she muttered, returning to her craft.

'Are you sure?' asked Kieto.

Dorcha slapped his leg playfully. 'Don't you start too, young man!'

Now the doorway darkened again, but this time it was Rian, Dorcha's other husband, standing there. In his right hand he had a basket of live shells. He put this down and reached for a patu club, propped against the doorpost.

Dorcha said sharply, 'What are you doing, Rian?'

Rian looked at her darkly. 'I saw him leave – *he's* been here – violated my home.'

'So, you're going to fight him?' she spat at her husband. 'Are you prepared to die?'

'I'm not going to die. I'm going to kill *him*.'

Rian was the better built of the two husband-brothers, having broad shoulders and a thick chest. His arms and shoulders were muscular. He had distinguished himself in battle when the Raiateans had been at war with the people of the Huahine Islands. There was a dramatic scar on his tattooed rib-cage from a lei-o-mano knife, the sharks' teeth having left the mark of lightning from his left nipple down to his naval.

'If you go out to kill someone, you must be prepared to die. Seumas has killed men in single combat too. He fought and killed my first husband over a piece of iron. You haven't seen him in battle mood. I would say he's at least your equal.'

Rian looked hesitant, but argued, 'Your first husband was a man like him – of the same land. Seumas doesn't look very strong to me—'

'If you think it's strength that wins fights, Rian,' interrupted the young Kieto, 'you have much to learn.'

Rian's eyes opened wide at this remark, coming from a youth who had not even been invested yet.

'A boy? Would you teach me how to fish?' cried Rian.

'Kieto's trying to make you see what you know is true yourself, Rian,' said Dorcha, 'only your pride and anger is blinding you. Seumas is a skilful warrior. It's true I didn't invite him into the hut, but he came here out of good will, and not to insult you. Please, put down your club.'

Rian stood for a moment, his jaw set, then his shoulders slumped a little and he replaced the club by the doorpost.

'If he comes here again,' said Rian, 'I'll splatter his brains on the coral. You be sure to tell him that, boy, when you see him next.'

Kieto knew when it was wise to remain silent.

Tutapu's kahuna, the priest Ragnu, was officiating at the kava-drinking ceremony. The stupefying drink was being mixed in a wooden bowl in the centre of Tupatu's council hut. Some time ago the women and children had chewed the peeled roots of the kava plant to a pulp and had spat the mush into the bowl, where it had been diluted and then put aside to ferment. Now it was ready to drink and simply required a fangu chant from the kahuna to give it full strength.

The prince himself sat cross-legged on his mat and brooded. Around the prince were gathered his basket-sharers; men who ate from the same basket as he did himself and therefore his closest companions, a small group like many other similar groups within the wider organisation of the clan. Even a lowly fisherman had his basket-sharers to assist him in times of trouble.

'Ragnu,' said Tutapu, 'how is the old man today?'

The kahuna looked up from his chanting and stirring to smile through the gaps in his teeth.

'He is well, my prince.'

Tutapu knew this was reverse news, to protect Tutapu from eavesdropping ghosts, and that he could be sure his father was sinking fast.

'Good, good,' he murmured.

His father was dying, yet the old man seemed to be hanging on to life with the tenaciousness of a limpet to a rock. Tutapu was fond of his father, in his way, but things were becoming difficult for Tutapu and until the king died nothing could be done about his brother Tangiia. The honourable thing was to wait until the king's death, then challenge Tangiia to single combat to the death. Tutapu believed his own skill as a warrior, coupled with the magic of Ragnu, would ensure his victory over his younger brother.

And if he was not victorious, well then, he would be dead and with his ancestors. One thing was certain, there could only be one king of the two islands of Borabora and Raiatea, and Tutapu meant to be that king. To leave his brother alive, even though Tangiia might swear loyalty to him, was too risky. One day Tangiia would be sure to let his ambition and jealousy rule his head and there would be insurrection. Better to sort it all out when their father died and have done with it.

It was especially difficult, because Tutapu did not hate his brother, indeed he had loved him strongly once. They had grown up together, played amongst the palms, gone fishing together, shared first experiences.

Tutapu would always recall with fondness the time they had climbed the mountain together and become lost in a labyrinth of hanging valleys. It had been Tangiia who had brought them through, with his fierce conviction that they would not die, that someone would find them. Indeed, this had spurred Tutapu into greater efforts to find a path out of the valleys, which he eventually did, and the pair of them were discovered by searchers leaving the maze of valleys.

The first cup of kava was placed in Tutapu's hands by Ragnu.

'Drink, my prince,' said the priest.

Tutapu motioned Ragnu to his side.

'Tell me what you saw today – at the marae,' he ordered the priest in a low voice.

The kahuna Ragnu was also a visionary, who had eyes in the future. Those eyes were not as clear as Tutapu would have liked them to be, for their view was foggy and vague since the mediator was Hau Maringi, the God of Mist. However, Ragnu was able to give some indication of future events. That day he had been to Most Sacred, Most Feared, to ask Hau Maringi to show him the future.

Tutapu was beloved of Hau Maringi. This was mainly because Hau Maringi hated Tangiia, the youth having slighted him once while out fishing by calling an oath because the mist descended just as the young prince had found a shoal of fish. Tangiia had lost sight of the shoal and swore violently at the mist for losing him his catch. Hau Maringi had never forgiven Tangiia for this insult.

Nevertheless, Hau Maringi had still demanded a human sacrifice, for the task of showing Ragnu what might be.

Ragnu was hesitant now that Tutapu had asked him the question. His news was not good and messengers sometimes paid a price for bad news.

'Come,' growled Tutapu to his kahuna, his eyes bloodshot. 'Tell me.'

Ragnu stared at the patterns on the prince's body, some like whirlpools on the breast, an elaborate comb-like tattoo across the upper chest, sea-wave lines around the shoulders, the backbone of a fish, running down the length of his sternum, its spines following the spread of the ribs on either side. He looked into these designs and felt himself drowning in them for a moment, felt himself gazing into the vortex of his master's body and experienced a giddy sensation. He forced out his answer.

'I saw the two islands in chaos,' murmured the priest. 'I saw people like wraiths in the mist, thin and hungry. It wasn't clear, but it seemed that there was the smell of decay in the air, the scent of death and disease.'

Tutapu sipped moodily at the intoxicating kava juice.

'What does this mean?' he asked.

Ragnu said quickly, 'Hau Maringi is showing us the future as it will be – if your brother lives.'

'You're sure of this?'

'No one can be *sure*, my prince,' said Ragnu, silkily, 'but I am *almost* certain.

How else could it be? If Tangiia is dead, and you alone rule the islands, there can only be harmony.'

Tutapu thought about this for a while and finally, to Ragnu's relief, he nodded. 'It seems to me that what you have seen is the chaos of a divided kingdom.'

'Quite so,' Ragnu said.

Tutapu nodded and dismissed the priest with a wave of his hand.

'Dancing,' he ordered.

A conch horn sounded and drums began to beat, rapidly, causing the blood of those who heard them to race in their veins. The drummers' hands were a blur, as they performed their art, the sound they made filling the night air. The crickets and tree frogs ceased to be heard as their cacophony was drowned.

Soon there were maidens gyrating before the prince, causing a stirring in his loins that would soon be dampened by the kava, once it took its hold on him. Only Boy-girl could make him feel anything while he was under the influence of kava, and Boy-girl was not on Borabora that evening.

Boy-girl had excused herself and asked that she be allowed to attend another feast, on Raiatea, a celebration to appease the ocean demons Aremata-Rorua and Aremata-popoa, the 'Long-wave' and 'Short-wave', whose immense power often took the lives of sailors and fishermen. Tutapu had reluctantly agreed to her absence, but was now beginning to regret his decision.

The dancing, feasting and drinking went on for several hours. To eat there was suckling pig, dog which had been fed only on fruit and vegetables since its birth and consequently its flesh tasted sweet and succulent, ovenbaked reef fish, all manner of spitted and roasted birds, taro, yam, sweet potato, breadfruit and banana. The prince liked a good show of food, even if he himself tasted its delights with a desultory tongue.

Finally, the prince's companions were quite drunk, though the prince himself remained coldly sober, his murderous thoughts chilling his brain and keeping the full effect of the kava at bay. At one point in the evening he sighed heavily and was asked by one of his friends, the man Nanato, why he was so sad.

'My brother ...' murmured Tutapu.

Nanato was very drunk and also very eager to please his prince, who allowed him to share the royal basket. Nanato was grateful for the privileges he received. Nanato unwisely allowed his gratitude to slip into his tongue.

'Leave your brother to me,' said Nanato, placing a hand on the prince's thigh.

Even as he spoke the words Nanato knew how foolish he was being, but the drink had blunted his reason and his emotion was running like a fast tide. The promise had been made in haste and now there was nothing Nanato could do but follow through with the deed. He experienced a sense of helplessness, as he realised that his statement – vague as it might have been – was eagerly grasped by the prince.

Tutapu stared at his companion hard. 'I do not wish to know what you

mean,' he said. 'If I'm without the knowledge of your intentions, I am innocent of any deed. The gods can't punish me for something I know nothing
about. However, if you should choose to please me in some way, there are
fifty red feathers in my treasure box which shall be yours.'

This was indeed a generous reward. Fifty red feathers would make Nanato
a rich man. With ten red feathers he could buy a pig, with twenty a canoe,
with thirty a beautiful woman.

'I leave you now,' he said to his prince, and climbed awkwardly to his feet,
to stagger to the door.

Once outside, the cool air struck Nanato in the face, sobering him a little.
There was a certain horror in his heart, for what he was about to do, but he
had robbed himself of any alternative. If he failed to kill Tangiia tonight,
Tutapu would have him put to death. Nanato, not surprisingly, did not want
to die, not yet, not for a foolish, drunken statement.

Now that the job had to be done, Nanato gave it his full consideration.

The choice of weapon was important. A club was too messy and not sure
enough. A knife was better than a club, but unless Nanato could catch Tangiia
in a deep sleep there might be a struggle. Nanato was not certain he could
beat Tangiia if it came to hand-to-hand fighting. A spear was too unwieldy. It
would be best, he decided, if Prince Tangiia were unaware of what was happening to him, and that meant subterfuge.

The safest way to kill the prince, Nanato came to the conclusion, would be
to use poison. He would poison the tip of a bone-hooked barracuda lure,
fixed to a wooden shank, and prick the prince's leg in the dark. The prince
would think he had been bitten by an insect, rub the spot, and go back to
sleep again. In his sleep his blood would thicken and by morning he would
be dead of heart seizure.

It was a good plan – for a drunkard.

The lure was found, the point poisoned, and Nanato then set out in his
canoe across the sea between Borabora and Raiatea.

Amai-te-rangi, a god who lived in the sky, was furious to learn from one of
the forest fairies of Borabora that a man was planning to kill a prince with a
fish hook.

'That's *my* prerogative,' the god grumbled. 'I am the fisher who angles for men!
This Nanato creature is stealing my mode of dealing out death to mortals.'

Amai-te-rangi delighted in lowering nets and lines from the sky and catching mortals, whisking them up to his home where he cooked and ate them.
Small, relatively insignificant gods like Amai-te-rangi guarded their methods
of catching men jealously, their techniques being all they had to make them
special amongst their contemporaries. That a man was about to kill another
man using a fish hook was disrespect to Amai-te-rangi.

Yet, there was little he could do about it himself, since it was night and he could not see the man in the canoe. If he dropped his lines, he might catch the man by chance, but it would be an uncertain thing. Amai-te-rangi sought the assistance of the Great Wind-God, Maomao, explaining the reason for his fury and asking for his brother's help.

Maomao said, 'I can understand your anger and would like to help, but if I blow at the moment, I might create a hurricane which would destroy more than a single man in a canoe. It would be better to ask the Great Rain-God Ua to drown the man in his canoe as he crosses the waters.'

Ua was not very sympathetic to Amai-te-rangi's request, since he had only recently created a deluge for another minor god, in another part of Oceania.

'I need some rest,' said Ua. 'Try someone else.'

Eventually, Ara Tiotio, the deity of the whirlwind, agreed to assist the injured fisher-god, and came screaming through the darkness to blow the terrified Nanato back to Borabora, shipwrecking the unfortunate man on the beach and sucking the remnants of his canoe up into the night sky, to be scattered later over a distant part of the ocean.

Honour was satisfied and Amai-te-rangi thanked Ara Tiotio, and went away to find a place to rest.

Nanato woke on the beach the next morning and staggered back to his hut. There he was found by others of Tutapu's basket-sharers and dragged before the prince. The prince, quite understandably, wanted to know if Nanato had anything of importance to tell him, now that the night was over.

'I – I was shipwrecked,' complained Nanato. 'I had no time to kill your brother.'

Tutapu raised his eyebrows. 'Kill my brother? What, before the death of our father? This is a monstrous crime you planned to commit. Have you no shame, no remorse? I ought to banish you from the islands!'

'But you *knew* I was going to murder Tangiia,' cried the hapless Nanato. 'We agreed—'

'I agreed to nothing,' said Tutapu, stiffly. 'It remains for me to pronounce your punishment.'

Tutapu, who had no wish to dispose of such a potentially willing assassin as Nanato, was about to give the man a relatively light sentence, when Ragnu whispered in his ear.

'We are in need of a good man,' murmured the priest, 'to pay Hau Maringi for his visions of the future.'

'Ah yes,' nodded Tutapu, a little disappointed by the intervention. 'Hau Maringi must be paid.'

'I must test Nanato for suitability.'

'Do so,' replied Tutapu.

This conversation took place out of the earshot of Nanato, who was taken by Ragnu to a quiet stone room in the temple.

'Now,' Ragnu said, after the terrified Nanato had been seated on the floor. 'I have a few questions.'

Nanato watched as the high priest squatted down opposite him and began chewing on a root.

After gathering his thoughts, the Ragnu asked, 'Have you ever done anything evil in your life?'

Nanato's panicking mind swept back over his past. He could, with all sincerity, deny any serious evil-doing. Had he murdered Prince Tangiia, of course, he would have been unable to give a negative answer. However, that deed had not taken place, thanks to the God of Whirlwinds.

'Not *really* bad. I – I've cheated a little when trading meat and fruit – but everyone does that, don't they?' he pleaded.

'Of course,' said Ragnu, in an understanding voice. 'No one expects you to be absolutely pure. If you were, you would be a god. Anything else?'

Happy that Ragnu was so compassionate, Nanato searched his mind for other small misdeeds.

'I once stole a canoe – but I took it back again.'

'When did you take it back?'

'Six months later. I thought the owner was going to die of an illness, but he recovered.'

'That seems to be all right. You simply *borrowed* the canoe, while he could not use it. You were actually making sure the canoe was maintained, otherwise it might have rotted away through misuse.'

'Yes – yes, that's it.'

Ragnu nodded and seemed to go off into another reverie. Nanato wanted to be told to go, to leave the temple and return to his hut. The question of banishment still hung in the air. In some ways banishment was worse than death, since a man might end up on a ghost-filled island in the middle of nowhere. He did not know what had passed between the priest and the future king, but he guessed his fate was in Ragnu's hands. He realised of course that he was being tested. Having answered all the questions to the obvious satisfaction of the high priest, he wanted now to be told he was free to leave.

'Have you – have you ever done anything *good* in your life?' asked Ragnu. 'I mean, something above the ordinary? Remember, you are in *my* temple. The gods will tell me if you are lying. Only the truth will serve you here.'

Again Nanato scoured his memory and came up with a true and happy answer.

'I once saved a woman from a shark. She was standing in the water when a shark took off her leg and would have eaten all of her if I hadn't jumped out of my dugout and beat it with my canoe paddle. She lived for three months afterwards. Unfortunately, her stump rotted and she died.'

'Still, you performed a courageous act – was this from the same canoe of which we spoke? The *borrowed* canoe?'

'I think it was,' said Nanato, eagerly. 'I'm *sure* it was.'

'Hmmm, so because you borrowed the canoe a woman had three extra months of life – and was not carried away to sea by a shark, but buried in a family grave?'

'That's true. That's true.'

Rangu nodded thoughtfully and after a while said, 'I think you are basically a *good* man, Nanato, and therefore a fit subject for a human sacrifice to the God of Mist and Fog, Hau Maringi. Have you anything more you wish to say?'

Nanato, who believed until now he had been defending himself against banishment, realised too late what were the reasons behind him being tested.

'I am unworthy!' he cried, desperately. 'Please – I am not good enough.'

'Let me be the judge of that,' murmured Ragnu, rising.

'The prince *loves* me,' sobbed Nanato.

'We could not sacrifice you otherwise.'

The terrified Nanato was bound hand and foot to a long pole and carried out on to Ragnu's marae.

Ragnu and his priests began the chants, the sacred fangu, and gradually the kahuna weaved his way towards the platform where the unfortunate Nanato lay.

As Ragnu raised the obsidian dagger, Nanato spoke.

'I am a loyal subject,' he said, helplessly. 'I have always loved Prince Tutapu.'

'That is as well,' whispered Ragnu, 'since you are being sacrificed for your goodness, not because you are evil.'

The dagger still poised, Ragnu looked up into the trees, which stirred with a gust of wind.

'Dakuwanga is there,' said the high priest, 'I sense it. He swims through the air, waiting for your sau to leave your body, so that he might swallow it and grow strong.'

'The Shark God?' cried Nanato. 'Please wait until he goes away – I want to go to Milu's land ...'

Ragnu was not unsympathetic to this request and waited until the leaves in the trees were still, then he plunged the ritual weapon down through Nanato's chest, the glassy-stone dagger crashing through the rib cage, to pierce the victim's heart. Blood fountained, covering the priests as well as the sacrifice. There was a shout of joy amongst them, for goodness and mercy had triumphed over evil – again.

The ritually slaughtered Nanato was left on the ahu platform decorated with skulls and carved wooden planks, just where a pig had been lying two days before.

Tutapu was made quite sad by his loss.

Hau Maringi was pleased with his gift.

3

Nau Ariki's affectionate name was 'Kula', after the bird brought back by Kupe from a strange island. She was the daughter of an ariki, or high chief, and his wife Papite who was captured in a war raid on Maupiti Island. The kula bird had a breast of red feathers, used as money, and was therefore considered very precious by the Oceanians. Nau Ariki was regarded as the most precious possession of the high chief of a fertile volcano region of Raiatea and hence her nickname.

That Kula was a healthy, beautiful woman did not make her exceptional, for there were many beautiful maidens amongst the hillside women. The air was cooler on the mountainside, the canopy of the rainforest more protective of the skin, and the water cleaner and clearer. What made her exceptional was her cleverness and her strong sense of duty. She was only seventeen, yet she saw the path of life clearly before her, which was marriage to Tutapu, once he became king.

Kula was bathing in a pool in the forest, with her companions and basket-sharers, girls of her village. They were laughing and ducking each other under the waterfall in water as green as the leaves on the bushes. They had a trick of flailing the surface with their long black hair, by flicking their heads, to keep their companions away. It was while Kula was performing this feat that she noticed a motion in the shrubs near by.

She stopped and called, 'Who's there?'

There was no answer and one of the younger girls cried, 'It's a ghost!'

A ripple of anxiety went through all the women, then a man stood up from behind the shrub and revealed himself.

'Prince Tangiia?' cried the seventeen-year-old Kula. 'What are you doing here, watching the girls bathing?'

Her voice chastised him gently. It was forbidden to gaze upon bathers, whatever their sex. Those maidens standing halfway out of the water turned their backs towards the man. Those on the banks of the pool wrapped their tapa skirts around the lower half of their bodies.

When he did not answer her question, Kula said, 'Have you come to court someone?' She looked around her at the other maidens. 'Who's the lucky girl desired by the handsome and bold Prince Tangiia? Hands up anyone who wants to marry a prince with the face and body of a young god?'

Several giggling maidens put up a hand, some of them thrusting two in the air, laughing shyly as they did so. Tangiia scowled, not pleased by this mocking, taking the frangipani flower from behind his ear and casting it to the ground. Kula realised she had gone too far.

'I'm sorry, you must expect a little teasing when there are girls all together. Did you wish to talk to anyone?'

'I – I wanted to talk to you,' said the young man.

'To *me*?' said Kula, in mock tones again, unable to help herself joshing this awkward young man. 'You need the permission of my grandfather for that.'

She was teasing him, for Kula's grandfather, like several venerated old men, was taboo to anyone outside her family. Only those directly related to him could go near and speak with the old man, his advice being a marketable commodity which could be sold by the family to others. Tangiia would have needed an intermediary to ask the grandfather's permission for anything and since the most available person to act as that go-between was Kula herself, she was creating a paradox for him.

'Do I?' he said, confused. 'How ...'

Kula laughed and rolled her eyes. 'Tangiia, you are *slow* sometimes.'

'I'm a warrior,' he said, stiffly, 'not a priest.'

'Warrior or priest,' she said, 'you're treading on a tree I planted yesterday.'

Tangiia moved his foot, awkwardly, aware that he had crushed a tiny sapling, just sprouting from its seed. The Princess Nau Ariki was a devotee of Rongo, God of Agriculture, Fruits and Cultivated Plants. She spent much of her time planting and growing things which would later yield a harvest. Her grandfather called her affectionately 'the gardener'.

'I'm sorry,' he said, clearly frustrated. 'I came to speak to you about marriage.'

She frowned. 'Marriage to your brother? Does he need an emissary now? I thought it was all settled.'

'I came to ask you to marry me,' said Tangiia in a choked voice.

'You?' Kula said, wondering if it was a joke. Was he teasing her back now, getting even? As she stared at his face she could see by his eyes that he was serious.

Kula felt a jolt of annoyance pass through her. Without another word she left the pool and picked up her skirt, wrapping it around her waist. Then she walked off into the rainforest, with Tangiia following her. When they were beyond the hearing distance of the other maidens, she turned on him in anger.

'How dare you ask such a question in front of my companions? You know I'm promised.'

'I haven't asked any question yet,' he replied, huffily. 'I simply told you what I came to speak to you about.'

They were in a glade where the shafts of sunlight broke through the canopy and illuminated the mosses and grasses of the forest floor. He tried to reach out to touch her, but she backed away. He sighed and plucked a leaf from a nearby bush, startling a monitor lizard resting beneath.

'You don't love me,' he stated.

Kula was a little confused by this remark. 'It's not a question of love. It's a question of *duty*. It's common knowledge that your father is on his death bed and that Tutapu is poised to become king. As king he will need a wife. He has chosen me to be that wife. My mother and father are very proud of the fact that I've been chosen. The death of an old king, one who has ruled wisely and without favour, always disturbs an island such as ours for a while. It's important that things settle down quickly – as his wife I can help Tutapu establish himself, be accepted as his father's replacement.'

By the time she had finished this speech, she had calmed a little, and was breathing more easily. The tension in the glade was high, not just because of him, but because of her too. She had feelings she did not want to admit to anyone, least of all Tangiia, and hopefully with a certain amount of effort not even to herself. She had been told, and believed, that once she was married to Tutapu she would forget all other men. Her situation would dictate her feelings to her and she would grow comfortable in her position as queen of the two islands.

'Then I am lost,' murmured Tangiia, hanging his head in despair. 'I must do what I must do.'

Thinking he meant suicide, Kula took hold of his hand for a moment.

'Oh, no,' she said, 'you must not harm yourself.'

It was traditional for young men to throw themselves off clifftops when they took their lives. Kula suddenly had a picture in her head, of Tangiia's smashed, broken body lying on the rocks, with the waves washing over it. It was an image that horrified her.

'You will find another wife, one better than me.'

'Never,' said Tangiia, his eyes burning hotly. 'I can never love another woman. How can you even think it?'

'Men do,' she replied, sadly, letting his hand fall. 'Some men can forget very easily.'

'I'm not one of those men.' He stared about him, at the rainforest. 'I'm not talking about killing myself anyway, I'm talking about going away from here, forever. These islands – I shall not be sorry to see them behind me.'

Kula nodded. 'There is a rumour you're leaving. It's a secret from your brother – to prevent war between you. I think it's very wise of you, and very noble. No good can come of a kingdom contested by two brothers.'

'And you don't care that I shall be gone,' he said, bitterly.

She wanted to tell him she cared very much, that she would weep for him, that she would always carry a special place in her heart for his memory, but she dared not.

Instead, she replied, 'I shall be sorry to see my husband's brother leave the islands where he was born.'

'Ha!' he cried and turned on his heel to stalk away, down the slopes, to his home near the shore.

Kula sighed deeply and walked slowly back to the pool where her basket-sharers, subdued by her absence, greeted her quietly. No longer did the green glade, with its sparkling waterfall and placid pool, seem beautiful to her. No longer were the waterplants and grasses fringing the bathing area a source of pleasure. The lustre had gone from the wet rocks, the glitter from the rivulets rushing downstream, the shimmer from the freshwater fish that played amongst them and nipped their toes. It was as if a storm cloud had moved over, and all fell in its dull shadow. Kula blamed Tangiia for this change in the atmosphere and tried to feel anger.

All she could feel was despair.

Her friends could tell Kula was troubled, but did not press her for the reasons. They each had their idea of what was bothering her. When Kula did not enter the water again, they began to get out and dry themselves. Finally, they were all ready, and walked with her along the paths to where their village was perched on the volcanic hillside.

Kula went to the hut of her grandfather and found him sitting outside. She took up a wooden bowl and began to serve him some banana porridge with her fingers. Since he was a tapu the old man was not allowed to touch food and had to be fed by others.

He saw that she was confused and unhappy and asked her why.

'Grandfather,' said Kula, 'why is life so complicated?'

He stared at her for a while, then said, 'You mean why are you in love with one man, yet must go to another?'

Her head came up and she stared into his rheumy but wise old eyes. 'Yes,' she said.

Her grandfather smiled at her and gave her a nose-kiss.

'Be assured,' he said, 'the gods will not let you do the wrong thing. If you are meant to marry the man you love, then the gods will ensure that happens, and if not – why then they will keep you from him. What is meant to be, will come.'

Her grandfather was a great storyteller amongst their people and to help her over her sadness she asked him to tell her a tale about love.

'Tell me a story about a love that was never meant to be,' she said, 'and so ended tragically.'

She believed a tale that reflected her own position might aid her in under-standing her own situation better. At her young and emotional age, to immerse herself in the sadness of another, an even more unfortunate lover than herself, helped to eclipse her own unhappiness. It was an indulgence.

Her grandfather obliged her, as she fed his toothless mouth the cold por-ridge, and he spoke between swallows.

'You remember the story of the Moon-Goddess, Lona, who fell in love with a mortal, a beautiful young man named Ai Kanaka, whose tattoos were the wonder of all who saw him? He was having his latest tattoo chiselled on to his thigh when the moon came out and Lona saw him. She fell instantly in love with him and wanted him by her, even though he was a mortal. The trouble was, he was too far away for her to reach from her moon-kingdom, and since he was a fisherman he never slept on a hill, always in his palm hut close to his canoe on the shore.

'Enlisting the forest fairies, she asked them to beguile Ai Kanaka. They clustered around his hut, as he sat outside roasting a fish. He saw the fairies in the light of the dying flames of his fire, staring at him from the shadows of the forest with large, beautiful eyes. Clearly he was the object of their interest and he played with the fire, poking it with a stick, and watching the Peerless Ones out of the corners of his eyes. When they did not go away, intrigued and fearful, Ai Kanaka finally spoke to them and asked them what they wanted with him. The fairies told him if he climbed the high mountain and stayed there until the dawn he would receive a magnificent reward.

'Ai Kanaka was not only afraid of the fairies, he was eager to learn what treasure would be his, so he climbed the ancient mountain and fell asleep between the roots of a tall tree.

'Since he was now close to her, Lona had not far to fly. Descending from the roof of voyaging on her wings that very night, she carried him off while he was asleep, into the White Kingdom of the Moon. There she ruled with Ai Kanaka at her side, and they were very happy for a while, but shortly after arriving Ai Kanaka died because he was an earthling.'

Kula's deep-brown eyes were damp with sorrow.

'How terribly sad,' she said. 'If I took a lover to my breast and he died, I should want to die too.'

'So did Lona,' replied her grandfather, 'but she had a duty to do – to light the earth and ocean with her purity.'

'Of course,' nodded Kula. 'Her duty.'

In a small corner of Raiatea preparations for an exodus were moving quickly ahead.

The three pahi canoes were almost finished now and were receiving their final coating of vegetable and shark oils to keep the water out of the stitched hulls. They were magnificent craft, especially now their rigging was almost complete, and the sails of woven leaves were in place, two to each vessel. Shaped like the crab claw which gave them their name, the sails were dedicated to the Wind-God Maomao, who was pleased to bless them. A pahi was built to run before the wind, but was also extremely manoeuvrable for its size.

The pahi themselves were double-hulled canoes with a deck between, two masts – one fore, one aft – and twin huts side by side on the deck. Their length was that of fourteen men, head to toe, lying on the sand. Their speed was that of a fast-walking or trotting man along a hard-packed beach.

Most of the men who were to sail these craft had not yet been on a long voyage. Many had sailed to nearby islands in smaller boats, even as far as Tahiti, using the shunting method of changing tack: picking up the mast bodily, with the flapping sail still attached, and placing it in a different position on the deck. These great pahi sails could not be so managed, and thus the rigging and manner of changing course was completely different, a supervised operation under a deck officer who bellowed instructions to the sailors as they worked the rigging.

Moreover, this voyage across a vast tract of ocean was a venture into the unknown. Mankind has always feared the unknown and the Raiateans were no different from other peoples. There was a sense of dread in many a breast. They imagined, dreamed at night, of a multitude of disasters which might befall them, which *could* befall them.

There would be encounters, surely, with great ocean monsters. There would be storms, great winds, currents that would take them off their course, monstrous waves, fast seas, strange tides, swells, waterspouts, whirlpools, hunger, thirst, and a thousand other unforeseen catastrophes to surmount. They would, at times, be lost on a vast ocean of water, not knowing which way to go, though the old king had been a magnificent navigator worthy of his rank, and he had passed these skills on to his two sons. It did not matter, the sailors told each other, that Tangiia had never made such a voyage; memory was the key to knowledge and an Oceanian's memory was superb.

Their courage was bolstered by their faith in Prince Tangiia, who, once he left these shores, would be their new king. Tangiia, with the help of other navigators of lesser rank: the blind old man, Kaho, who used his son Po'oi as his eyes; the star watchers: those who knew the directions of the te lapa, the streaks of subsea light; the feelers of the swells that lifted the stern of the boat; the bird watchers; the good listeners who could hear reefs from a long way off; the smellers who could scent land from afar. All these, and others, would assist their king in finding a path across the sea to a Faraway Heaven where Tangiia could rule his people in peace.

Yet, it did take *immense* courage to contemplate leaving their homeland. All they had, all they had ever known, was invested in these islands. To leave them behind was to die and hope to be born again. And *only* hope, for nothing was certain.

The alternative was to stay and face a civil war, with brother killing brother, and the land polluted with bitterness and a desire for revenge which would take generations to clean.

While the pahi canoes were being finished the loading of provisions began. Caged rats, dogs, chickens, pigs. Water in gourds. Breadfruit paste, pandanus fruit, green bananas, yam, taro, sweet potatoes, dried akule fish, arrowroot flour, dried skipjack and tuna, sugar-cane, hard poi, and most important of all, coconuts at all different stages, from hard meat coconuts, to soft meat coconuts, to drinking coconuts.

They took also seeds and roots to plant when they arrived at the new island, which were stored on the vessels, in case there was no paper mulberry there, or (Rongo forbid) no coconut palms from which to take fibres for cordage, posts for huts and bridges, leaves for roofs and basketwork, and shells for containers. Without the coconut palm they would be desperately poor and possibly even perish.

The provisions they took were enough to last the voyagers at least a month, perhaps twice as long with severe rationing.

Then there was the ceremony of the launching.

It was deemed a shame amongst the boat builders that no recent war had left the islands with enemy bodies, which could be placed between the log rollers when launching the canoes, to ensure a sacred entry into the ocean for their craft.

'In my grandfather's day,' said one master artisan, 'they put *live* captives under the keels at the launching, but people are only concerned about naval architecture these days – they care nothing for the religious side of things.'

This was not quite true, for their operations were regulated by clearly defined rites during the building of a pahi, the artisans themselves members of a caste and working under the guidance of a high priest.

Manopa hardly ever left the site, overseeing things in a nervous and upsetting way for the boat builders, who worked best when left to their own devices. No instruments or drawn plans were used; the boats like their dwellings were vernacular architecture. There were men amongst the artisans whose job it was to measure by judgement, and whose eye was to be trusted for length, shape and size.

Manopa constantly interfered in this exercise, by suggesting that a curve was slightly out of true, or a plank a shade too long. He was invariably wrong, there being nothing the matter with the eye of the artisan, and everything the matter with Manopa's perception of the length, breadth and height of sections of the craft. Still, he continued to insist on his own judgement, which had little skill or experience behind it, and slowed the building to a point where the artisans complained to Tangiia. Tangiia took Manopa aside.

'Look, I know you're doing your best here, Manopa, but you have to leave these people to do their work in their own way.'

'Who's been complaining about me?' demanded Manopa, glaring around him at the boat builders.

'I'm not going to tell you – it's not important. You are a warrior, a captain, good in battle. I need you here on the site in case it's discovered and you have to defend it, but you must not interfere with the work.'

Manopa was hurt. 'I've built boats before. I'm as good as the next man at building boats—'

'Small craft, like a vaa or pu hoe, with an outrigger, but not a great pahi. You are not qualified to judge in these matters, Manopa, and I am asking you as a friend to leave these people alone. We *must* get the canoes finished soon.'

Manopa dropped his head, feeling something of a failure. It was in him, as in many men, to wish to be good at *all* things. He needed to be the father figure, to whom all men of all professions came for advice. It was difficult for him to admit to himself that there were others who knew better.

'The trouble with every one of us,' said Tangiia, 'is that we can all build a small canoe, every man and boy amongst us. We all have our little tool kits: the adze, augers, drills and abrasers. Our grandfathers give them to us when we are young and we treasure them before handing them on to our grandchildren. Because of that every man thinks he can build a pahi.

'It's not true, my friend. The pahi requires special talents. It has to be exactly right. Think of the strength needed for such a voyage – the durability needed to cope with monstrous waves of great power and long days of constant movement of planks, ropes, hulls, for storms and other adverse weather conditions. A pahi doesn't just need to carry nearly a hundred people, it needs to withstand the pressures and strains of a mighty ocean, day in, day out, for months.'

'But a small canoe ...'

'A small canoe gets beached every few hours, the binding cords tightened when necessary, the repairs done on time. A small canoe only has to cope with lagoons and coastal waters. There's no comparison between a small canoe and a pahi. A man has to be close to the gods to build a pahi – he has to be pure artisan, through and through, with no warrior or fisherman inside him to interfere with his mental calculations. Do you understand – you're not less of a man because of that, Manopa. I wouldn't try to tell them how to do it myself.'

'You wouldn't?'

'A boy of eighteen? Why should I know what has taken men more than a lifetime to learn?'

Manopa's brow furrowed at this remark. 'How can it take them more than a lifetime? They only live one life.'

'The knowledge is in their bones, in their blood, passed down to them from their forefathers. They have a natural skill we could not learn in a thousand years, you and I. Yet put them in battle beside us, and see who kills the most foe.'

Manopa's bole-chest swelled. 'Ah, yes – see then who has the skill!'

Manopa then took on the task of supervising the loading of weapons and other artifacts aboard the three pahi canoes.

Into one of the twin huts on each pahi deck went patu, kotiate and wahaika hand clubs of whalebone and stone, spears with tanged obsidian points, harpoons, lure shanks of schist and serpentine, fish hooks, adzes, knives of stone, hardwood and fishbone, and finally, slings.

The handling of weapons was a job for which the boat builders considered Manopa to be much better suited.

It was late evening and the king's house was in semi-darkness, with only a small fire to light the room. His thin, frail body lay on a bed of leaves, the eyes open and staring at the rosewood ceiling. A ceremonial cloth was draped over his loins, to hide the shrivelled remains of what had once been a man.

In his time the king had been a giant, with muscles that stood proud of his heavy frame. In those days his oiled, tattooed body had been the envy of many of his male subjects and the desire of many of the female islanders. The hands that wielded club and knife so deftly in battle had been known to crush limestone to powder. His strength had been legendary, his feet nimble, his navigating skills equal only to the great Kupe.

Now the skin that bore the tattoos was wrinkled and grey, the muscles wasted, the cheeks hollow and gaunt. Bones protruded from every part of his anatomy. There were dark rings around his eyes. His thin, grey hair was spread around his head like a fan, giving him the look of a frightened animal. Indeed he *was* frightened – by his impending death – and the gnarled fingers clawed feebly at the earth beside him.

He had almost come to believe himself immortal. Like many before him and many that would follow him he had begun to confuse absolute power amongst mortals with heavenly power. It had come to seem ridiculous to him that a man whose whole being and presence, whose nail parings, hair, dirty washing water and very shit was considered to be sacred and had to be buried with ceremony in a holy place, would take the path of a normal man and eventually die. 'Surely,' he had told himself as an old but fit and healthy man, 'I shall live forever?'

There had been three queens, but now they were all dead. A sister as old as himself now cared for him, night and day, washing his body, feeding him, administering medicinal herbs and potions left by the king's personal kahuna.

Tangiia hated to see his father brought so low, this man who was so full of mana, whose very shadow was taboo to commoners. Only family, high priests and royal personages could touch the king or stand in his shade. Any food which passed the old man's lips immediately became taboo to others. There were trees which belonged only to the king, amongst them a type of banana tree which bore fruit only once in its life. There were canoes which only the king and his priests could touch. There were caves, and waterfalls, and stones which had to be avoided by all others but the king. The wicker-leaf sharks hung by cords to warn others of the taboo nature of these objects and places.

'Father?' said Tangiia, kneeling by the old man and taking his hand.

The eyes swivelled as the king looked into his son's face.

'It would have been better,' said the king in a voice like dry leaves rustling, 'to have died in battle.'

'But who would have killed you?' asked Tangiia. 'None could beat you.'

'True, true,' said the old man, with a wisp of a smile flitting across his face. 'I was too skilful for them all – none could touch me.'

He sighed, the phlegm rattling in his throat. His sister brought him a bowl into which he spat a red-green fluid. Tangiia looked away.

'Not a pleasant sight,' said the king, 'to watch an old man die.'

'You are afraid, Father?'

The old man turned bleak eyes on his son again.

'Yes – but I would say that to no one but you. Your brother would laugh at me – the Great King afraid of a thing that comes to all men and women in the end – it would amuse him. His soul is harder than your own. But he is not cruel, he simply lacks compassion. He will make a good king.'

'So will I, Father – even though I do not have the heart of a shark.'

The king tried to sit up, shaking his head, but fell back on the bed again.

His sister said, 'You are upsetting him.'

Tangiia replied, 'I have to tell him something – leave us, please.'

She hesitated but Tangiia glared at her. 'Go!'

After a few more moments she left the house, picking up an empty water gourd on the way out.

'There must be only one king of the two islands,' croaked the old man. 'You must serve your half-brother. Otherwise there will be bloodshed – a divided kingdom. The valleys will ring with the lament of the mourners, the hills with the cries of the dying. A red tide will run across the sea.'

'As the son of my father and his third wife, I would serve the son of my father and his second wife, but he would have me killed if I tried. He is too suspicious of me, knowing that some of the people prefer me to him. I shall be king, Father, but of a new land. I plan to seek a Faraway Heaven.'

The old man stared at his second son and the light of old remembrances came to his eyes.

'You are leaving? A voyage?'

'Yes, Father. I-I-have come to say goodbye, for I must leave before ...'

'I should be more willing to go to Hine-nui-te-po, the Goddess of Darkness and Death, whom even the great Maui could not defeat, if I knew my kingdom was safe from strife.'

'Be assured it will be so, Father, and when you meet the cunning, intrepid Maui, be so kind as to ask him to watch over me on my voyage across the ocean.'

Maui now dwelt in the Land of the Dead, being the first man on earth to die as he tried to pass through Hine-nui-te-po without her knowledge while she slept, when a songbird woke her and she discovered Maui's presence inside her.

'I shall do as you ask, my son,' said the king. 'A man alone on a voyage ...'

'I'm not going alone, Father, I'm taking three pahi canoes full of people with me.'

The old man's brow furrowed again.

'Will that not anger your brother Tutapu?'

'I can't be held responsible for my brother's emotions, Father. I must do what I feel is right. And I can't make such a voyage alone – I am not *you*, I don't have your self-sufficiency – I need people around me. I should go mad on my own. In any case, what is a king of an island without people, but a lost dreamer, a man of wickerwork and leaves? My brother will have the two islands and if he is not satisfied with that, then I believe the gods will be angry with *him*, for his greed.'

The old king sighed again, the wind fluttering through his parched lips like a dry breeze through a breadfruit tree.

'I am making a lone voyage again – the voyage we all have to make alone, even you.'

'Yes, Father.'

The king rolled on to his side, the effort obviously painful for him. He reached out and touched his son's head, tracing the youth's tattoos with one of his fingers. Then he fell back again and returned to lying on his back.

'You are a handsome boy,' said the old man. 'You look like I looked when I was young.'

'Not so handsome, Father.'

The old man nodded. 'And what about the goblins, what will they do when you leave?'

The king meant Seumas and Dorcha, who were often compared to tapua, mountain goblins, not because of their size but because of their white skin. When Kupe brought back his two captives several years before, the old king had thought about sacrificing them to the gods, being convinced by his high priest that such creatures were not human and therefore had to be destroyed.

Only the fact that Seumas had tattoos had saved both him and Dorcha from ritual execution, the king being convinced that he was a mortal like any other, to have to prove his manhood by suffering the dangerous and painful operation of having tattoos chiselled into his skin.

'One is coming with me, the other is staying – the woman wishes to remain here.'

The king nodded slightly. 'Does the Seumas still have eyes in the back of his head?'

He was referring to the way in which Seumas rowed a dinghy he had once made, with his back facing the direction in which the boat was travelling. This method had so upset the people of Raiatea that Seumas had destroyed the boat, for fear someone was going to accuse him of being a supernatural fiend.

'Not any longer, Father.'

'Good, good. He might be of use to you, the goblin, if you meet any demons. He speaks with their tongue, you know, for I have heard the harsh sound myself. He talks with his dog too – I swear they understand each other. To feed a dog on meat and give it a name! I never was quite sure I had done right, to allow the goblin to survive. Once, I remember, he fashioned a living monster from a dead pig's hide, with bamboosticks for legs. An evil, wailing thing.'

The old man shuddered even now at the thought, before continuing.

'His fingers danced down one of the creature's legs, while he blew into the hollow end, and the sound of the dead pig came out, screaming for its life back. I tell you, king or no king, it put the fear of demons into me ...'

'I remember that time,' said Tangiia, 'when he brought the pig back to life. I was a young boy. It *terrified* me, that monster he made out of skin and twigs.'

The king coughed and spat into his wooden bowl. 'We burned the monster on a fire – the pig with no eyes, ears or mouth, which could shriek like a tortured parrot – and we nearly burned the goblin along with it. He promised not to bring back to life any more of his deviant beasts, so I allowed him to live. Now he is to go with you, on your voyage. But what of the other?'

'She has her two husbands.'

The king grunted as he tried to imagine what it would be like making love to a mountain goblin. His head became full of hillside waterfalls and dense greenery, of mossy beds, buttress-rooted trees reaching high into the roof of voyaging, and dark caves full of bats. He rather envied the twin brothers, Ti-ti and Rian, finding out what it was like between the legs of a woman whose skin was so fair. Yet, on the other hand, she had a temper like a rooster on fire. Perhaps the experience would not be as interesting as it was awful?

A cough rattled in his chest once again and the old man let his tired eyes rest once more on his younger son.

'So, we must say goodbye now?'

'Yes, Father, I leave tomorrow at dawn.'

There was a wetness in the king's eyes, which he tried to wipe away with a feeble hand.

'Take me with you?' he said, almost like a baby.

'Father, you know …'

At that moment the king sat up with a jerk, as if someone had kicked him in the back, and he stared around the hut.

'Sister?' he called, with fear in his voice.

The old woman came trotting back inside and on seeing the king's face let out a cry herself.

'He's going!' she said.

Tangiia took hold of the frail body and tried to force it down again on to the bed of leaves, but it was as if his father's bones were locked. It was impossible to move him. The king's eyes rolled in his head, his twitching lips let forth a hissing noise, and then he keeled over sideways.

The king's sister put a finger to the old man's lips, held it there for a moment, and then withdrew it.

'He is with Hine-nui-te-po,' she murmured, and then suddenly started to let out a mourner's wail.

Tangiia quickly reached out and staunched the sound which came from her mouth with his hand.

'NO!' he said. 'No one must know the king is dead – not before I leave the island.'

'You're leaving?' the old woman questioned.

The prince nodded, quickly. 'My brother will move against me if I stay.'

The king's sister was silent for a moment, then she said, 'We will pretend he is asleep. You must go as soon as you can – may the gods be with you.'

Tangiia left his father's body and went quickly to the house of the Farseeing-virgin, Kikamana. He quickly informed her of what had passed and asked her what were the signs. Kikamana looked through the doorway at the darkening sky.

'Maomao is coming,' she said, 'in his biggest cloak of feathers – perhaps before another dawn.'

Tangiia stared at the sky, but could see nothing untoward. Still, Kikamana was seldom wrong about these things. Her visions were unsurpassed, even by Boy-girl. A hurricane was coming. Well, it might be a blessing in disguise. If they could beat the wind, it would prevent any early chase by Tutapu, should he feel so inclined.

'We start as soon as it gets dark,' warned Tangiia.

Next he went to one of the novice priests who had been in charge of the boat building, not running because that would have attracted attention, but strolling and calling greetings on the way to friends and neighbours.

Manopa was still at the site and he saw by Tangiia's face that something had happened.

'What is it?' he asked. 'Tutapu?'

'No, it's my father, the king ...'

The prince told them what had happened and of his plans to leave the island that night.

He said to the priest, 'We shall need a god with us, besides the Tikis already on the vessels, to help guide us through our troubles. Many of the statues at Most Sacred, Most Feared are of hardwood and too heavy to take on board. Take some men when darkness falls and steal me an effigy of the Great God of the Sea, Tangaroa – and place it on the deck of my canoe.'

'Steal a god?' cried the priest, a little shaken. 'What if it curses me?'

'Tangaroa will not curse the priest of Tangiia,' said the prince with impressive confidence. 'Go!'

The priest waited no more, but called men to his side, then set off towards Tapu-tapu atia, where there were statues of gods sprouting from the rainforest floor as if growing from the grass and moss of that sacrosanct ground.

'Manopa, you begin gathering the people together, but be discreet. Start with Boy-girl. Tell her I need her here immediately.'

'At once,' replied his lieutenant, too loyal to voice again his misgivings about the task for which he knew Boy-girl was required.

Tangiia stared at the roof of voyaging. Already the signs of evening were moving over the sky as Ra turned the clouds to the scarlet of precious feathers. A short time later he saw Boy-girl dancing along the sands towards him.

'Now for Kula,' murmured the prince.

Tangiia's men approached the enormous Investiture Stone at Most Sacred, Most Feared with great trepidation. They were aware of the living part of the stone; the spirits of the men who belonged to the dust of the corpses beneath the four corners of the stone. They were aware that the four guardians, now themselves revered ancestors who required human sacrifices from time to time, would not approve of the removal of Tangaroa's image from the shadow of the ancient mountain.

The glade pulsed with silence, its stone heart filling the night with a dreadful, heavy stillness.

Even the priest, new to his profession, felt the terror clutch at his heart.

Around the great stone, which reached like a primordial tree towards the roof of voyaging, stood many wooden statues half-buried in the ground. They thrust themselves from the moss like rotten molars in an old man's mouth, their features covered with lichen and often crawling with insects. The eyes of the idols were not blind though, having spiritual sight, and the men who had come to steal one of them could feel those eyes boring into them, out of the darkness of this hallowed, awesome hollow.

'Go softly, go softly,' warned the priest, staring about him, unable to see very much except vague shapes in the gloom of the glade. There was a belt of human skulls around the nearest idol, which because of its height and position the priest guessed to be the Goddess of Darkness and Death. Since the priest was a young man, a neophyte, he did not know the glade as well as one of the elders amongst the kahunas, and was having difficulty in orientating himself. His unease over what he was doing did not help matters.

There was a moon, but Tapu-tapu atia was under a rock hang, beneath a canopy of vines and aged trees, and they could *feel* darkness around them. It was like being enveloped in a soft, damp blanket. The men frequently trod on the planted bones of their ancestors, or tripped over a leaf-twig effigy; they were dizzy with misgivings and apprehension.

The priest offered up prayers to the more powerful ancestors, while his four companions stumbled around in the dense gloom, feeling for the statue of Tangaroa the Great Sea-God. The priest could feel the sponginess of the moss beneath his feet and half expected the forest floor to open and take him down for violating the sanctity of this place belonging to heroes, dead spirits and gods.

One of the men placed his hands on an image. He ran his hands over the head of the carving, wanting it to be the right statue, eager to be gone from the place of Most Sacred, Most Feared.

'Here it is,' he whispered, quickly. 'This one feels like Tangaroa – this must be the idol Prince Tangiia meant—'

Then he gave out a strangled cry, like a bird caught in a noose, and fell to the floor in a fit. He thrashed around amongst the leaves and twigs, filling the hearts of his companions with horror. One of the other men ran away, gasping for breath as he did so, his feet drumming on the forest floor, his fear overcoming him.

A second man had the presence of mind to fall on his unfortunate companion having the fit, and push a stick between his jaws, to stop him from biting off or swallowing his own tongue and choking himself.

'The demons are in him,' said the priest, softly. 'He must have unclean hands. One of you take the statue ...'

'Not me,' said a man, quickly, 'I may have unclean hands too.'

The priest knew that there was very little time, so he pushed through the group of men himself, felt around on the forest floor for the wooden statue, and eventually found it.

'Help me,' he snarled to the nearest man, and began rocking the wooden totem backwards and forwards.

There was a moment's hesitation, then someone came to his aid. They frantically pushed the statue backwards and forwards, to loosen it in the turf.

It seemed that either the totem itself had grown roots, or it was caught amongst the network of tree roots which ran beneath the rainforest floor. Even when it was as wobbly as a child's first tooth, it refused to be wrenched from the ground. Two men broke some vines from nearby trees and wrapped them round the wooden idol to pull in the dark, while a third used a broken branch to lever beneath the stubborn god. Finally, it was eased out of its hole, the smell of its rotten base filling the glade. Insects flowed from the hole and up the arms of the men, who let go of the god and brushed them away quickly.

Then the image was hoisted on to shoulders and borne off at a rapid pace through the rainforest. The man having the fit was slung across the back of another and he too was carried from the dreadful place, gibbering as he was bounced along. The one who had run away was waiting for them in some agitation on the edge of the forest and he mumbled his apologies for allowing fear to overcome him, before helping with the sick man.

The idol was taken quickly to the vessel in which Tangiia himself would sail and laid inside one of the deck huts, ready for erection once the journey began. The young priest, now feeling quite pleased with himself, rolled the idol on to its back, knowing it was irreverent to leave it face down on the deck. The mossy features of the totem were now visible to him, in a shaft of moonlight, and he recoiled in horror.

The image they had taken from the glade was not of Tangaroa after all, but some obscure god which the young priest did not even recognise, its features were so worn and pitted with the passing of time. It was obviously a great god in a minor form, whose special powers were unknown to the neophyte.

There was no time to go back to Tapu-tapu atia, and in any case the priest was too shaken to make a second journey. It was better to deal with Prince Tangiia's anger later than to repeat what had already been a terrible experience. It must be, he told himself by way of excuse, that this is the god we need on the voyage, otherwise why would it be here now?

He quickly covered the totem with palm leaves and went out of the hut into the fresh air.

This, the prince's canoe, had already been launched and was bobbing gently on the waves in the lagoon. The wind was rising steadily as men, women and children were herded on board. On the beach the other two canoes were being dragged over the log rollers towards the water, the launching parties eager to get away from the islands before the hurricane arrived.

Men and women were all helping with the launch, while others were tending to the livestock: the dogs, pigs and birds. There was a sense of quiet urgency about the exodus.

People sniffed the air as they worked, taking in the last draught of the fragrance of blossoms and the scent of vegetation they would have for a long while. This was the smell of their homeland, which they would have to leave behind. Already many of them were beginning to feel homesick. They stared into the darkness, visualising the volcanic mountainous hinterland, knowing that the next landfall they might see would not have familiar contours. They would have to memorise new maps of their surroundings, new pathways, new trees. Old friends – the pool in the forest glade, the waterfall, the great silk cotton tree by the ledge – all these would be far behind them.

More importantly, they would have to find fresh maps of the coastal waters of their new homeland. Around Raiatea and Borabora they knew where to find hiding squid, shoals of bonito, prawns, shellfish, crabs, the whole bounty of their immediate surrounding waters. In their future island they would be lost for a while, fishing in fallow waters, running lines for a harvest that was not there, spearing flashes of light.

So their last scent of Raiatea was important to them; a moment to treasure, to be able to recall at a later time.

The wind became brisk and began blowing a coconut husk along the beach as if it were Ulupoka's Head.

4

A traitor lit a fire high on the slopes of the Raiatean mountain. The light from its flames was visible from Borabora and on seeing the glow from this particular crag, another man ran through the forests of Borabora, towards the house of Prince Tutapu. His excitement was such that on reaching the house he ran straight past the unprepared guards and into the room where the prince slept. The sound of birds filled the bed chamber and Tutapu leapt instantly to his feet, a club in one hand and a knife in the other. His face was creased in fury.

'Ha! An assassin!'

He struck out with the club, catching the runner on the shoulder, felling him to the floor. A crunch of bone had preceded the man's fall and he screamed in agony. Tutapu was about to deliver a death blow when the man shrieked, 'Prince – I'm the messenger, from the mountain!'

Tutapu's hand was stayed as he peered through the dimness of the room at the man. The two guards ran in from outside and stood over the messenger, their spears raised ready for the order to kill. Tutapu rubbed his sleepy face with his hand.

'What? Why do you come charging in here at this time? Are you insane? You deserve to die.'

'The light from the signal fire – Raiatea – your father is dead!' cried the unfortunate man.

Tutapu stood for a moment in the stillness of the room, while he absorbed this information, then he walked briskly towards the door, the twittering of songbirds following his every footstep.

'Warriors!' he yelled. 'Awake, awake! Sound the alarm! Make ready the war canoes. The king is dead.'

A moment later there was the sound of a conch horn blowing in the night air. A great hollow-logged drum which had been patiently gathering silence and dust, now released its deep sounds. Warriors leapt from their beds and ran down to the beaches. The prince himself was already donning his feathered war headdress and selecting his favourite weapons, a large spear, the head of which was made from obsidian, and a flattened club with a tapered edge which could slice the top off a man's skull at a single stroke.

Tutapu was a formidable fighter who had killed many enemies in battle and now he was going to kill his brother.

Smaller drums were sounding now, from the front of the war canoes, where stood the wooden effigies of Oro the War-God. Tonight Oro had on his war face and his spear was raised in wrath. Accompanying their fierce and brutal father on this expedition were smaller goddesses: Oro's three daughters, Axe-eye, Head-eater and Escape-from-a-Hundred-Stones. Two of the daughters faced the flanks, the other one looked behind, in the opposite direction to her father.

The daughters would help protect the warriors from sneak side and rear attacks, while Oro was in the forefront of the battle with his bloodthirsty warriors, wreaking havoc.

Five war canoes were launched and the fleet set out towards Raiatea, the drums pounding.

On Raiatea the faint sound of the distant war drums was heard floating over the ocean. Men and women froze into statues; children began crying. There was a suppressed panic felt in every breast. Tangiia was a good young prince who would make a fine king, but none of his people believed he was a match for his older brother, who had already been tried and tested in war and was known to be a vicious but superlative warrior.

A calm voice suddenly sounded from the midst of the launching parties on the beach.

It was that of Kikamana, the Farseeing-virgin.

'Do not fear the spears of Prince Tutapu, people of Prince Tangiia – the gods are with *us* tonight. I have appealed to one of the goddesses, who has promised her help.'

This information had an immediate calming effect on the launching parties. The splendid figure of Kikamana in her robe of white feathers, her arms lifted in supplication to the night, her hair flowing like black water in the wind, was enough to fill the hearts of the people with trust. They continued in their work of moving the mighty canoes into the lagoon.

Tangiia himself was assisting with the launching when Boy-girl appeared out of the rainforest edge. She was leading a young woman gently by the hand. When she came close Tangiia was relieved and happy to see that the woman was indeed his beloved Kula. The eyes of the princess had a glazed look and with a motion of her hand, Boy-girl indicated to Tangiia that he must not speak to the maiden. He watched, as did many of his followers, as Boy-girl led the mesmerised Kula past the launching parties and on to a canoe. It was not the pahi which Tangiia himself would command. Tangiia wisely decided he would not need to confront Kula until she was used to the idea that she had been abducted against her will.

Seumas, who had witnessed this scene, was suddenly sorry he had not taken Boy-girl's offer to do the same with Dorcha.

'You've got *your* woman then,' he said to Tangiia, hardly failing to disguise the envy in his tone.

Tangiia nodded and sighed. 'Yes, I have her – but can I hold her?'

Seumas realised the prince was right. Certainly if Dorcha had been tricked on board, she would still not have submitted to him once the spell wore off. He would have been in no better a situation than the one he had experienced on Raiatea for the past several years. It was probably better to make a clean break and forget the Celt woman, put her out of his mind forever.

Seumas went back to assisting with the launching.

Finally, all three canoes were on the water.

'That way, that way!' raged Tutapu, pointing with his spear. 'Are you blind? Can't you see where Raiatea lies?'

The sailors managing the boat were at a loss. In front of them was the island of Raiatea, a dark, hunched giant rising from a darker sea, yet the prince was pointing away from this piece of land, towards an empty horizon.

'Turn the vessel, turn the vessel,' shrieked Tutapu. 'Are you all traitors? You want my brother to become king, is that it? Well, this is the way I treat traitors!'

With these words Tutapu struck the nearest man with his paddle club, cleaving his skull. The sailor flopped half over the edge of the canoe, his limp arms trailing in the water. Tutapu kicked savagely at the body, sending it over the side, where it would no doubt make a meal for the sharks and barracuda, ever active in this stretch of water.

On seeing this act, the other sailors immediately changed tack, heading in the direction towards which their prince was pointing. If Tutapu wanted them to go out into open sea, then that's where they would go, land or no land.

Ragnu, in command of another war canoe, called across the water to Prince Tutapu, asking him where he was going.

'To kill my brother,' yelled Tutapu. 'Are you against me too, high priest?'

Ragnu, who like all priests was an unrecognised half-brother to both Tutapu and Tangiia, assumed that Tutapu had seen something out of his own vision, such as a flotilla fleeing from Raiatea. The high priest ordered the other war canoes to follow that of Tutapu's, whose constant harping at his men had taken them at least seventeen boat lengths in front of the fleet. Ragnu kept his eyes open for signs of the refugees seen by his prince, so that he might be amongst the first to board their boats. Ragnu was looking forward to taking the life of his half-sister Kikamana, the Farseeing-virgin, whose powers fired his jealousy and anger.

The wind was picking out the waves now, pinching their tops and drawing them to high points. One of Maomao's sons, Howling Rainfall, came sweeping in from the Arue Roa direction on the windflower. The rain soaked the mat sails and slowed the fleet until the rowers were ordered to increase their pace.

Ragnu looked at the sky, dark and swirling with high clouds, and knew Maomao was coming himself.

'The Big Wind,' he murmured.

It was then he began praying to Hau Maringi, the God of Mists and Fog, their ally in this battle against Tangiia.

Hau Maringi came at Ragnu's bidding and enveloped the fleet of Prince Tangiia, swallowing the canoes so they rested deep inside Hau Maringi's gullet, a place of eternal greyness, where even Tane could not penetrate with any force.

Inside the body of Hau Maringi, Prince Tangiia's people began to panic, running this way and that over the decks, trying to raise the sails by feel, telling each other they would be able to get through the Eater-of-boats, the coral reef, by sound rather than by sight. Hau Maringi thickened himself, until even sounds were muted and the crashing of the waves on the reef had strange echoes which confused the listeners, causing them more anguish.

But Hau Maringi was no match for most other gods, and one of Maomao's sons arrived, the vanguard preceding the Great Wind-God's own arrival, to blow Hau Maringi into an empty quarter of Oceania, where he fumed coldly, resting on an ocean without vessels.

Once the fog had been blown far out to sea, the great pahi canoes with all their livestock, crew and passengers on board, began to head out towards the reef. It was a scene of colour and noise that was witnessed from the beach by those who had chosen to remain behind. The hasty but brave departure was now in progress. The open ocean, with its unknown perils, its vast empty regions, awaited them.

The hindmost to leave the lagoon shore was Tangiia's vessel, now named *The Scudding Cloud*. Seumas was one of the last men aboard, accompanied by his pet hound, Dirk. The dog watched Seumas, to satisfy itself that it was all right to be on this floating island, then settled down on some bedding. Seumas stared at the shoreline, then made a decision.

Seumas cried to Kieto, 'Hold on to Dirk, for me, lad!' and leapt from the deck into the water, then he ran across the shell-covered beach towards Dorcha's hut.

Dorcha was standing beneath a palm, watching the fleet leave the island. Rian and Ti-ti were standing with her. Seumas saw her and went to her. Rian stepped forward, a heavy club bearing the war face of Oro in his hand. There were honed whales' teeth protruding from the head of the club, and carved spikes from the upper part of the haft. It was Rian's intention to see one of these sharp projections buried in Seumas's temple.

'Hine-nui-te-po has given you to me,' said Rian, triumphantly. 'Now you will go to *her* bed.'

Dorcha cried, 'No, Rian!'

The warrior turned on her. 'Be quiet, woman – this is for us to settle. You wanted him dead, now I'm going to give you your wish. Later you will thank me.'

He turned back to Seumas and began swinging his club, aiming first for Seumas's head. The Pict ducked and weaved, as skilful in his footwork as any Raiatean warrior. Rian then began attacking his body, hoping for a blow which would put paid to the lithe movements of his adversary, so that he could then step in and crush his skull.

Seumas arched his body as the club swept past his midriff. Out of his waistband the Pict finally drew a knife made from a sliver of a large clamshell with a hardwood handle. The blade had been whetted, sharpened to a fine edge. When Rian moved in again, the wide sweep of the club exposing his body, Seumas threw the knife.

Rian gave a grunt as the shell-blade pierced his abdomen and dangled there, like a fish that sunk its teeth into his belly-fat and refused to let go. When he looked down at his wound, Seumas launched a drop-kick at his opponent. Struck in the throat by the Pict's heels, Rian went flying backwards and lay on the ground gargling, his club abandoned.

'Seumas!' yelled Tangiia from the craft. 'We're casting off – *now*'

The blood was roaring in the Pict's ears. He snatched up the club and stood over the wounded Rian, making ready to deal a death blow to the man's head. The club went up.

A shout came from Dorcha. 'Seumas – no!'

Seumas paused. He had already killed a husband of this woman and she hated him for it. Now he was about to repeat what was in her eyes a terrible crime. The knife wound in Rian's stomach was not mortal, the shell-blade being too light to throw effectively. It had not penetrated deeply. Seumas let the club fall to the ground. Ti-ti rushed forward with a cry and fell on his knees, to cradle his twin brother's head in his arms.

Seumas looked towards the lagoon and saw that *The Scudding Cloud* was halfway to the inner reef.

'Dorcha?' he said, in a pleading tone. 'Come with me – please?'

She seemed about to move towards him, just a slight gesture, then her mouth set firmly.

'No – get out of here, go away. I shall be happy never to see you again.'

'Dorcha?'

There was another shout from the canoe as it picked up speed, heading for the gap in the reef.

'Go!' she screamed, her black eyes glistening.

Seumas sighed heavily and turned to run down the sands to the water. He dived into the lagoon and swam swiftly towards the canoe. He could see Kieto, straining to hold back an anxious Dirk, who stood on the back of the canoe's platform deck, barking across the lagoon.

A line was dropped overboard, which trailed the boat, and eventually, just as the craft was passing through the gap in the reef, he caught hold of the end of this cord. He was dragged over a patch of coral, which scratched him severely, then they hauled him on board. His hound, Dirk, came to him and licked his face and shoulders, wagging its tail, pleased that it had not been abandoned as it had feared.

Seumas just lay on the deck, gasping.

Tangiia said, 'Kieto, find some herbs to put on these scratches before they fester.' Then to Seumas, 'You were nearly left behind – and all because of a goblin.'

Seumas went up on to his elbows. 'I'm a goblin too,' he said.

'Yes, a very foolish one,' Kieto intervened. 'Now hold still while I staunch the blood ...'

Seumas did as he was told, his eyes on the beach. The dawn was just coming up. Ra was shaking his fiery head, getting rid of the sleep, before rising from his bed. In the first few rays to penetrate the morning air Seumas could see Dorcha standing on the sands. She was perfectly still, illuminated by a ray of light that had cut through the rain clouds. Her ferocious beauty tore a hole in his heart. He watched her until she became a small, cloaked figure, like a dark fairy, then saw her raise a pale hand and give a single wave.

He waved back, solemnly, wondering if he had finally been forgiven for his trespasses.

By the time Tutapu finally realised he had been tricked by Kuku Lau, the Goddess of Mirages, the war flotilla was far out at sea, in the opposite direction to that taken by Tangiia's fleet. So real had Kuku Lau's false 'Raiatea' seemed, that Tutapu had almost stepped ashore, on to what was most certainly a wave of water. Only a change in the light had stopped him from leaping on to a non-existent beach.

'A mirage!' he cried in anguish. 'I should have listened to you, Ragnu.'

By now the rest of the flotilla had caught up with the leading war canoe and they were all locked together with their paddles, waiting for the king's orders.

The wind was becoming dangerously high now, the waves rearing and crashing into each other, churning the ocean to a milky white. Spume from the tops of the combers lashed the bodies and faces of the warriors, soaking and chilling them as the temperature dropped. The spray was so fine, it was like mist that blew constantly into their eyes, stinging them, blinding them with its salt. A strange sky with a hard light at its core had grown around the flotilla and almost every man there was aware that calamity would befall them if they did not get to some safe haven before Maomao swept down upon them from his faraway country.

Tutapu ordered his rowers to turn towards the real Raiatea, knowing they would be lucky to make the lagoon without loss of life. A Big Wind was most certainly coming and Maomao could not be appeased with mere words. A sacrifice was necessary, of a pig or dog; something to show Maomao that he was not taken for granted. It needed to be a temple ceremony in a marae, not just a quick effort out here on the ocean, or even on a beach.

They rode the whitecaps back towards Raiatea, with Tutapu constantly asking his men if they could see the island too. His confidence had been severely shaken by Kuku Lau's tricks. He realised how easily even a minor goddess could toy with an ordinary man, even if that man was a king.

By the time the flotilla reached the outer reef, the waves were giant rollers with high twisting peaks. War canoes were not fashioned for bad weather conditions, like the great ocean-going canoes, but for the quick strike. A 'long wave' from Aremata-rorua caught one of the war canoes broadside and capsized it, sending men tumbling into the mountainous waters. Several were swept away, their cries for help lost on the wind. Others struggled to hold on to the rest of the canoes, or managed to ride over the reef on a high wave of surf, and then strike out across the lagoon for the shore. Stone weapons sank to the bottom of the sea; wooden ones floated away into the lashing waves.

When the canoes reached the beach they were hastily drawn up the sands and then men ran for the safety of some caves. There was no time for sacrifices to Maomao, only to crawl away into a rock hole, where the wind could not reach.

Tutapu's precious headdress was torn from him and whisked away by

Maomao to some trove where the Wind-God kept all the treasures he robbed from mortals.

However, the king managed to reach the caves before the full force of the hurricane began to sideswipe Raiatea. One of the last men to reach the caves was almost inside when a whole palm tree snapped at the root and flew through the air to hit him like a mighty spear full in the chest, carrying his corpse away on its point, its haft flighted with feathery palm leaves.

Inside the caves were huddled other inhabitants of the island, bemoaning the loss of the old king and pondering on the damage the hurricane would cause to crops, houses, canoes and livestock. Also inside the cave were the most precious of the last of these: pigs, fowl and packs of dogs, all sitting quietly, stunned into immobility and silence by the awesome furore of the god who had deigned to pay them a visit.

'When this is over,' growled Tutapu, 'I shall seek out my half-brother and slay him.'

One of the Raiateans shook her head. 'They're gone,' she said.

Tutapu was perplexed. 'Gone? Who's gone? Where?'

'Prince Tangiia and over two hundred people. They left in the dawn. There were three pahi, each carrying about seventy passengers.'

Tutapu's eyes narrowed. 'Run away, has he? Am I the only one here who did not know he was planning this escape? How has he managed to build canoes without me being told? These people who have gone were your neighbours. You must have seen them gathering stores together, making preparations.'

One old man said, 'We tried to tell you – at least we tried to tell your basket-sharers. They listened, told us they would inform you, but obviously never did. Even Ragnu was told many times of the planned exodus by our spies—'

'Liar!' hissed Ragnu, gripping a club. 'I was told nothing.'

The old creature, who was a fisherman and whose salt-encrusted skin had white wrinkles, chuckled offensively. It seemed that this aged but sagacious servant of the king was too elderly to be afraid of death, which was extremely close at hand, and continued divulging previous secrets.

'You *were* told, but you didn't *hear*!' said the old man, his face crinkling with a wry smile. 'Boy-girl put a spell on all Prince Tutapu's basket-sharers, so they would nod their heads when being told of the escape, then immediately forget what had been imparted to them. Even when you were told what Boy-girl was doing, you still didn't hear what was being said.'

Ragnu stared at the old savant and searched his own mind for fragments of the truth.

In the end he nodded. He said to Tutapu, 'I think he's right – we were bewitched by Boy-girl.'

Tutapu spat into a corner of the cave. 'So, my brother has fled? So be it. No blood need be shed. He has more good sense than I gave him credit for, and less ambition than I believed he was nurturing. I hope he finds a home somewhere a long way from Raiatea and Borabora, so we may never need to meet again. I can no longer stand the sight of him.'

The high priest added, 'These islands were becoming too crowded as well. Taking two hundred or so islanders with him has done us a favour, my king. Fewer mouths to feed, more land to occupy. And the old king's house is yours at last.'

Tutapu felt a warm satisfaction spread through his limbs and torso.

'Yes, good. I shall live in my father's house with Nau Ariki as my bride ...'

'Ah,' said the old man, who seemed suspiciously close to enjoying himself, 'I don't think so.'

Tutapu frowned. 'What don't you think?'

'That Nau Ariki, the one they call Kula, will be your bride.'

Ragnu snorted and said imperiously, 'You foolish old man – have you not heard that the princess has already agreed to marry King Tutapu?'

'I heard that, yes,' the old man's throat rattled with catarrh, 'but it won't happen.'

'Why won't it happen?' asked Tutapu, gradually coming to the realisation that others knew more about everything than he did himself.

'Because Princess Kula has gone with Tangiia.'

Tutapu leapt instantly to his feet and was about to rush out through the cave doorway, where the storm howled and screamed, calling for further victims.

Ragnu clutched his king's ankle and forced him to sit down, at the risk of having his own head caved by a club.

'You can't go out there now, my king. Wait until the storm dies down. Then we'll catch up with Tangiia.'

Tutapu's impatience to get at his half-brother and throttle him with his own loin cloth held for the moment.

The hurricane actually took three days to subside, by which time Tangiia and his canoes could have been anywhere in the world. Just because he had set off in a certain direction, did not mean he was keeping to it. Tutapu left the cave with a terrible fervour in his breast. Not only had he been robbed of his brother's death, but of his own bride! Eventually, someone would have to pay for those crimes. Now was not the time though, for there was much work to be done, an island kingdom to restore to its former glory. A prince might go flitting off after his dreams, but a king had responsibilities.

'One day,' he told Ragnu, 'I shall find that brother of mine and make him swallow dirt by the handful.'

'I shall be the one to force his mouth open, with my dagger,' snarled Ragnu. 'You must know too that our spy has gone with Tangiia's fleet.'

'For our purposes, or for his?'

'Our man is still for you, my king. A bird arrived back at its nest today, flying from the Hitia ote ra direction on the windflower – when Tangiia finds a new home, I expect our spy will return to us and tell us where your brother has gone.'

'In the meantime,' mused Tutapu, 'we shall know my brother's where-abouts from the birds?'

'His direction, at least. And there will be signs left by our spy, on the route they take. It will not be difficult to follow him, if we ever wish it.'

King Tutapu said, 'But not at this time. Now is the time to make the islands my own. They still have my father's colours running through them. I need to concentrate on this.'

The high priest, who also had no desire to be riding the waves while there were islands to rule, quickly agreed that this was the time to rebuild, not chase after errant princes.

Raiatea had been devastated by the hurricane and Maomao had left noth-ing but a broken land in his wake. They could not curse Maomao, for he might return and make them pay, so they went about clearing the mess with heavy hearts. There were huts to restore, canoes to carve, crops to replant, shattered trees to clear, totems of gods to right.

For food they used the coconuts that had been blown from the palms and the shellfish cast up on the beaches by the storm. The work began, with King Tutapu presiding over his people.

A royal funeral took place after the initial clearance had been completed, since ancestors had to be given due ceremony.

The former king was given a magnificent burial on a sand-bar at the mouth of a small river, thus on land but close to water, and in his grave were placed water-gourds, necklaces, sharks' teeth, adzes, tattooing needles of dogs' teeth, candle-nut soot for tattoo pigment in bone containers, harpoons, drilled eggshells of many colours and tanged spear heads. These gifts to his father from Tutapu were greatly appreciated by the spirit of the old man, who went to his rest clutching a carving of a canoe in one bony hand and a model house in the other.

There were many songs sung in praise of the old king, which echoed through the high green valleys.

He had been a great warrior and would be a loss to his people, the songs said, but now he was with his ancestors who feasted on the flesh of sacrificed men and turtles, and was happy to take his place in the world of spirits.

There was one huge feast in which pigs were roasted, sharks were baked, and for which many kinds of fruits and nuts were gathered.

There was dancing and singing, the shadows of ancestors joining the living at the fires. Each family's atua was present at the feast and treated with great awe and respect. Heroic deeds were re-enacted, the masked dancers *becoming* the heroes of yesteryear, slaying sea monsters, defeating powerful enemies and eating their hearts and livers, hunting the great wild boar-like creature, Puata, who walks on hind legs, talks like a human, is incredibly strong and eats people.

When the feasting and dancing was over, the people crawled away exhausted. The new king had not failed in his duties towards them or to his father and ancestors and they felt grateful for that. It seemed that now Tutapu's half-brother had gone from the islands, he was a changed man, and destined to become one of the great chieftains of the kingdom.

Dorcha had for the first time, like many of the islanders, witnessed the funeral of a dead king and the inauguration of a new king, and was fascinated by both. Tutapu sent for her the day after his father's funeral and thanked her for not joining in the exodus.

'They told me you would have me executed,' she said, 'in their efforts to make me go with them.'

'Why should I do that? You have proved to be a loyal and trustworthy subject. You will be rewarded for that.'

She stepped forward to take his hands, to thank him, but he recoiled from her quickly.

'I'm king now,' he warned her. 'I've moved closer to the gods – one step away from divine. My person is sacred. I am – taboo. If you touch me you may die from the divine power which fills my body. Even now my mana is filling the void in this room.'

'Oh,' she faltered, 'of course.'

His face took on an expression of petulance.

'It's very awkward. I used to be surrounded by basket-sharers, but they can no longer touch my basket. If a fruit I eat has lain next to one they eat, then they become sick. Only the priests can come close to me now, since their own sacredness protects them from my mana – only they can prepare the food for me. It's very troublesome.'

'One of the hazards of being king, I suppose.'

He sighed as if he bore the burdens of the world upon his shoulders.

He sent her a small pig and a necklace of rare shells, which she in turn thanked him for graciously, pleasing him the more. Dorcha felt valued once again and had Seumas returned to the islands at that moment she might have spat in his eye and told him what she thought of him and his Prince Tangiia, who had taken little notice of her except to call her a goblin.

With her two husbands fawning on her, and the new king pleased with her, Dorcha was almost a princess in her own right. In her old land of Albainn she had been a drudge and a skivvy, valued it had to be admitted, by her husband in his way, in the way of Celt males, but treated as less worthy than a good hunting dog. Dorcha had left a son behind, whose birth had been a difficult one and had left her with damage to those female organs that facilitate the bringing forth of children. If she had not died in childbirth attempting to produce another son, she would have faded into an early old age, creased and dried by constant cooking over a peat fire, disregarded by her son and gradually rejected by her husband in bed.

Here, she was loved and cherished.

It was true there was little *passion* in her life, but was passion a necessary ingredient to happiness? When she really thought about it, passion was a destructive thing in itself, creating tension and cravings that were not always fulfilled. She was, she decided, better off without passion. She only had to think about Seumas to remember how passion could eat away at a soul and destroy a person from within.

King Tutapu oversaw the rebuilding of his kingdom, sparing little thought for his younger brother, now out on the ocean somewhere, trying to find a new home. There was, strangely, little rancour in his breast either, which even he found surprising, given how much he had hated his brother.

One day, however, King Tutapu discovered a small imperfection, a defect in his new kingdom. He was lying on his mat with one of his many cousin-concubines. She had stroked him with her soft hands until his penis was a budded, hardwood shoot. He was just gently prising her knees apart, to find the garden of his pleasure in which to plant his ripe cutting, when Ragnu came running to him, to tell him that a god had been stolen from Tapu-tapu atia, probably by Tangiia's men.

'Which god?' asked Tutapu, the anger building in his breast again. 'One of the Great Gods?'

'No, a lesser god – one hardly ever noticed.'

'Yes?' said Tutapu, impatiently.

Ragnu replied, 'The God of Hope.'

PART THREE

The Long Shark at Dawn

1

Now that Tangiia had left the island, he too was a king, of the people he carried on his three pahi canoes. However, he was a king without an island and his mana was not yet strong enough to warrant a full taboo. Kikamana told him he would not move closer to the gods until he owned his own land, with its own particular set of gods, and until then he would not need to regard himself as truly sacred.

He was relieved to hear this, since it would have been difficult to live in the limited space on board canoe with almost a hundred people, and not touch and be touched by someone every so often, especially since he was the navigator and needed to be constantly moving around the craft, taking sightings, knotting his cord-device, memorising features. Priests could have screened him, but he had not enough of those to surround his royal person.

Had he great mana it would have been very dangerous for his people, whom he wanted to protect. To touch someone with great mana was like being hit by a bolt of lightning; such could result in the death of the commoner, whose body was not strong enough to resist the charge.

Tangiia's fleet was blown by the hurricane's edge off its intended course, which was due Apa toa on the windflower, and instead he went in the same direction as Hitia ote ra. Fortunately the full force of the big wind passed them by, but they were caught on the periphery and pushed out into a region of the ocean which, after three days' sailing, became strangely still and calm. Kikamana told Tangiia this was because the hurricane Maomao had sent, to prevent Tutapu from following the fleet, was a gift that had to be balanced by a period of no wind.

'All gifts from the gods have their price,' she told him. 'We must wait until Maomao sees fit to send us the Goddess Hine-tu-whenua, to speed us on our way.'

They drifted along on a deep, wide current, having little choice in the matter since their paddles made little impression on the fast flow of warm water. Tangiia used the time to recheck their stores and make sure every man and woman knew their task on board the vessels.

It was Tangiia's intention to set Tangaroa up on the deck of *The Scudding Cloud*, behind his Tiki, so that the Great God of the Sea would have a view over the Tiki's shoulders at the ocean path ahead and help guide the ancestor to a new home.

'What's this?' cried Tangiia, on uncovering the totem taken from Most Sacred, Most Feared. 'This isn't Tangaroa.'

Kikamana was called.

'It's one of Tane's children,' she explained. 'It's the God of Hope.'

The young priest who had stolen the god was on board the third canoe and out of Tangiia's reach at the time, or he might have suffered a terrible punishment. Tangiia was at first incensed that his men had brought the wrong god, but then Kikamana told him to stop and think.

'What better god could we have with us than the God of Hope?' she said. 'Hope is the one thing we need to sustain us during our ordeals ahead. I see many trials in front of us, before we eventually reach a Faraway Heaven. We shall need to call on spiritual stamina to see us through, and this god can help us keep our hope alive, through these bad times.'

Tangiia was a young man and it was hard to quell his anger, but eventually he saw the wisdom in the Farseeing-virgin's words. He pardoned the young priest and his men, sending a white cowrie shell to the man to show him that he was forgiven. The fleet continued on its way in harmony once more.

The Scudding Cloud took the lead. Immediately behind the prince's canoe was *The Royal Palm* captained by Manopa, followed by *The Volcano Flower*, with Po in command. Po had risen in rank because of his famous voyage with Kupe and was now a highly respected ocean-going captain whose navigating skills were sought after by those who wished to cross leagues of water.

Kieto helped Tangiia with his daily duties during the lull, while Seumas, to take his mind off Dorcha, had agreed to have a new tattoo. This was an extremely dangerous and painful process which would allow little room in the mind of the victim for thoughts of unrequited love.

The tattoo was to be administered by Tangiia's second priest, Makka-te, since Kikamana would have nothing to do with touching the bodies of men.

Dirk took as much interest in seeing the tattoo kit laid out as did Seumas himself: the dog and boar teeth needles fixed to bamboo shafts, and the leaf-pouches full of the soot from burnt candle-nuts. Dirk sniffed at the soot and then sneezed, making Seumas laugh, even though he did not feel in the least bit merry.

'You crazy hound,' he said, ruffling the hair on the dog's neck. 'You might have guessed it would tickle your nostrils.'

Dirk had been the only pet dog in the kingdom of Raiatea and Borabora and this was his status on board the three pahi. All other dogs were vegetarians and bred for the table; they were domestic livestock. Some Oceanians had been quite tickled when they saw how Seumas trained his hound, treated it as if it had some sort of intelligence. Many were scornful of this peculiar handling of an animal normally destined for a pot roast.

They were amused that Dirk slept at the foot of Seumas's bed, followed him everywhere, and protected the Pict against hostility from others.

One might as well, they told him, take a chicken for a wife.

Once, someone from another valley had caught Dirk in a net-trap in the rainforest. Thinking he was a stray, the man was about to slit his throat and barbecue him on an open fire, when Seumas appeared and struck the man.

When questioned about this extraordinary behaviour, not to say breaking of the law, Seumas told the chiefs who were judging him that a Pict would die for his dog, if necessary, for the hound would certainly give up his life for his master.

'But it's just a *dog*,' argued the judges, as if they were speaking about a lizard.

'This is not just a dog, it's *my* dog,' answered Seumas. 'I'm his owner and it's up to me to care for him. Besides,' he said, adopting a more practical approach, 'I feed him meat. He wouldn't taste good spitted and roasted.'

'You give the dog *meat*?' they said, looking at one another, giving up the argument. 'Valuable meat?'

'The dog brings *me* meat. He helps me hunt, fetches wild birds. He's my companion, and a damn good one.'

They fined him a pig and told him not to attack another man in favour of his hound, or he would be punished more severely the next time. They saw him pat the dog's head as he walked away from the temple courtyard, and the dog licked his hand, nuzzling the palm. Then at a snap of the Pict's finger the hound fell into step at his heel. The judges shrugged at each other, as if to say who can fathom the mind of a mountain goblin who makes friends with creatures whose destiny it is to be eaten?

This was also the opinion of the priest Makke-te.

'The dog is stupid,' said Makka-te, a male virgin in his forties.

'Not *stupid*,' replied Seumas, 'just curious.'

He felt like arguing more hotly with the priest, whose attitude irritated him, but wisely refrained when he considered what the man was about to perform. Makka-te could make the operation as painful as he wished, without Seumas adding to any natural sadistic tendencies the priest might or might not have. Dirk might be stupid, but Seumas was not.

Seumas was no longer wild and hirsute, as he had been when first captured, but shaven and hairless almost to the crown of his head, where a long, thick plait sprouted out of a bed of red hair no bigger than the top of a sliced coconut shell.

The Pict sat cross-legged on the deck, his head tilted back slightly, while Makka-te began the pin-prick hammerings on his chest, making a tiny path of dark pigment. Seumas had asked for two hornbill beaks, one either side of his collar bones. Almost as soon as Makka-te started piercing him, he began wishing he had asked for much smaller songbird beaks instead. The pain drilled into his head making his brain reel.

The women, weaving baskets, gutting fish, and carrying out various other tasks around him, watched with interest the mountain goblin being tattooed. Children too, gathered in a circle around this event full of curiosity, there being little to keep their interest over the many slow hours on the water. Some were attached to safety lines, the little ones, while older brothers and sisters roamed free. They had seen men tattooed before, of course, but never the goblin. Anything that happened to the goblin was of interest. Even the mariners who should have been paying attention to their tasks, glanced occasionally towards the tattooist and his victim.

Those on other canoes stared wistfully across the divide, unable to get any closer to the proceedings. To swim, even over a short distance, was dangerous, the currents being swift and deliberate. A dugout canoe travelled between the three pahi when necessary, but this boat only took one or two men.

Seumas's pale skin and hard flat muscular body had been an object of attention amongst the Raiateans and Boraborans since he first arrived on the islands. They would touch his shoulder or chest as he passed them, not necessarily for sexual reasons, though this was not unknown, but because of the fine texture and translucent nature of his skin. Some found it a little repulsive, like a lizard's belly, while others wanted to stroke him as if he were made of soft fabric.

'See how stark it looks,' said one woman, as if Seumas were not there. 'Like the markings on a white cone shell.'

'I think he's very brave,' said a young woman who was known to be infatuated with Seumas. 'I think he's a great warrior!'

Seumas turned to smile at this young maiden – whose high cheek-bones and full lips had often tempted him – but had his head sharply twisted back again by Makka-te, who was like an impatient barber and not at all impressed by a wandering target.

Thinking about the girl, with her supple waist and tightly rounded bottom, Seumas remembered Princess Nau Ariki, who was on board *The Volcano Flower*. Tangiia had not yet dared face her, though her oaths and curses on waking, and finding herself a captive of a man going nowhere, had been sharp and loud enough to penetrate the roof of voyaging to its heart.

Kula had tried to throw herself to the sharks and Seumas was also reminded of Dorcha and her utter determination never to be touched by the Pict. Now Tangiia was having a taste of the bitter fruit swallowed by Seumas himself over the past decade.

There! And he had been determined himself, not to think of the Celt woman with her long legs and wild hair!

'Ow!' he grumbled, as a particularly white-hot pain went through his skull and pierced his brain. 'Watch it ...'

But Makka-te was having none of this moaning.

'Are you a warrior or a pig?' he asked, pleasantly.

'A warrior,' growled Seumas.

'Then be silent like a warrior instead of squealing like a stuck sow.'

I'll give you stuck sow, my fine, pretty priest, thought Seumas, I'll puncture your arrogance the first chance I get, once this thing is done!

The tattooing process had begun in the late afternoon, which slipped swiftly into evening, there being no twilight in that part of the ocean. Kieto played the nose flute for him; beguiling tunes to take his mind off the pain. When the stars came out Seumas, lying on his back now, recognised the star group known to the Oceanians as White Squirrelfish, and another called Te rakau tapu, or The Sacred Timber. He liked the way Raiateans saw shapes in the star patterns, and gave them names.

Right across the heavens washed a swathe of milky white which was Mango-roa-i-ata, The Long Shark At Dawn, flung there by Maui who had caught it while fishing for islands in the creation. It was this rash of stars towards which the currents took them, into unknown waters, towards unknown islands.

Life on board a pahi was essentially ruled by the sea. The classic intervals of night and day were spliced together then cut into three equal slices, regardless of light and dark. If a storm ensued then everyone worked, never mind whose shift it was when the storm arrived. The motion of the sea dictated motion of the body.

Seumas had been born with the sea around him, on Albainn, but he would never be as close to the ocean as these people who had captured him. From the moment a boy or girl was old enough to understand what was being said to them, an Oceanian heard stories about the rigours and exhilaration of life at sea. When a child first learned to walk it would be wading in the waters of the lagoon, looking for shellfish, playing on the coral sands, the sea always in its ears, always in its sight.

The rhythms of the tides were in an Oceanian's blood, the coursing of the currents in an Oceanian's arteries. The wide bowl of the roof of voyaging, with its horizons all round, was almost always above his or her head, so little time was spent inside a hut. On land the clean warm air of the days and the balmy soft air of the nights were their blankets, while at sea the wind and spray shaped them into a hardy people, fit to travel over the great ocean which was as much their home as the islands that dotted its surface in their thousands.

When a child was due to go on its first fishing trip it would undergo a rite of passage, whereby it would be wrapped in a bark-cloth skirt and painted with turmeric dye. On return from the trip the youngster would be washed with aromatic leaves and fed on taro pudding. At not much older the child would be making model canoes, of all types, in preparation for the time when it would become a builder of full-sized vessels. And always the sound of the ocean, always the sight of waves, filled their waking days and sleeping nights. The importance of the sea was impressed upon them from birth.

Seumas had seen them learn the wave patterns on the open ocean, and gather knowledge of the star paths from their seniors, and he knew he could never match these people in their affinity with the great waters. They were part of their world and he was an addition to it, surely grafted perhaps, but not an original branch. He could not match their ear for a change in the wind, nor the feel of their hand for a hidden ocean swell, nor their eye for an alteration in the wave patterns or a cloud on the horizon. He would always be an inferior on the pahi, though he knew he could match most men in single combat.

The pain from the tattooing process became excruciating and it was all Seumas could do to stop from crying out. Makka-te noticed this and asked for men to hold Seumas down, one to each limb. Seumas was about to protest, but the tattooist said, 'This is normal – there is no shame attached,' so he allowed himself to be pinioned. Makka-te began chanting now to the rhythm of his tattooing, using a variety of needles made from fish, human and bird bones. A comb was repeatedly hammered into the flesh using a heavy wooden stick.

As Makka-te's assistant was rubbing in some more soot from the burnt candle-nuts, Kieto came to Seumas.

'Shall I play some more tunes on my nose flute for you?' asked the youth.

It would help distract him from his agony. Seumas nodded and said, 'Yes – play me a song, Kieto.'

Mercifully, the process was finished by midnight and Seumas was left alone with his wounds and his pain.

The following morning his skin was inflamed and extremely sore to the touch. There was a red weal all around the wounded area, raised like an earth rampart. By noon the skin was swollen and puffy. He felt giddy and sick, and was going hot and cold in turns. Kieto made him lie down in the shade of one of the huts, where the youth began crushing some stems from a bunch of green bananas.

'What are you doing?' asked Seumas, faintly. 'Is that a poultice?'

'Yes,' replied Kieto. 'It'll help take down the swelling. My grandmother did one for me, when I had my first tattoo.'

'This is not my first tattoo.'

'It's your first tattoo from a Raiatean priest – you should do as I say.'

The balm helped to relieve the soreness and swelling, and later Kieto administered some medicine from the nono tree, which was even more effective in healing the wound.

'Many people die from tattooing,' Kieto told Seumas, cheerfully. 'Beauty is not a thing the gods give easily to a man. You know how the first tattoo came to man?'

'No,' groaned Seumas, 'but I've got a feeling I'm going to be told, while I lie here helpless to defend my ears.'

'Well,' said Kieto, 'there was a prince named Tamanui who had a beautiful wife called Rukutia, but she ran away to another prince, whose name was Koropanga. She sent a message to Tamanui saying she had left him because she found him unattractive. You know what Tamanui did then?'

'I know what I would have done,' growled Seumas. 'Take my club and bash Koropanga's head in – then drag Rukutia back to my hut and—'

'No, nothing like that,' interrupted Kieto. 'He changed himself into a white egret with magic and flew up to his ancestors on the mountaintop to ask their advice. They told him they would paint his body, just as they painted themselves, and Tamanui let them. Unfortunately, once he was back in his own body and went swimming, the colours all washed off.'

'And I thought this was going to be a nice short story, so I could get some rest,' Seumas moaned. 'Get on with it.'

'Well, the prince went back again to his ancestors and asked them the *real* secret of their beauty. They told him that he had to have his body tattooed, but they warned him he might die of pain or sickness.'

'Thank you for reminding me again.'

'That's all right – anyway,' said the guileless youth, 'they cut long gashes in Tamanui's body and filled the wounds with a mysterious dye, which when his body healed would make him a beautiful man. Tamanui passed out once or twice, but he lived, and when he could walk again he went looking for his wife, who saw him from a long way off and asked out loud, "Who is that wonderful creature with the body of a god?" "It is I," said Tamanui, and Rukutia ran to him and loved him.'

'Did he beat her for being unfaithful?'

'Why, no, because it was *his* fault, for being so ugly before the tattoos.'

'I would have beaten her,' said Seumas, emphatically, taking great satisfaction in this thought, which helped relieve his pain. In his mind was a picture of a white-skinned, dark-eyed woman with long legs and wild hair submitting to his harsh treatment. 'I would have thrashed her soundly.'

'Then she would have slit your throat with a lei-o-mano while you slept,' replied Keito, with sound common sense.

'It might even be worth that,' sighed the love-sick Pict, 'to hear her begging for mercy – just once.'

'Who?' asked Keito, grinning.

'Why, Dorc—' began Seumas, breaking off the word just in time and then saying quickly, 'this Rukuwhatsit woman … damn you boy, do you have to chatter all day? Get about your business, will you, and leave a man in peace?'

A long-voyaging sea bird landed near Seumas and was immediately chased away by an excited Dirk.

'Leave the bird alone,' moaned Seumas. 'Can't you see it's exhausted, dog? It needs to rest.'

Kieto said, 'That's a funny thing for you to say – when I first saw you, you were *strangling* birds.'

'I was doing it for a reason, not just for fun.'

'Tell me the reason,' asked Kieto.

'Then will you leave me in peace?'

'If you like,' smiled the boy.

Seumas explained, 'We caught the fulmars not for food, but for their oil. If I hadn't strangled the birds as I caught them, they would have been sick and the contents of their stomach would have been lost to me. It was necessary to wring their necks before they could disgorge the oil.'

'Ah, that explains it.'

'Now will you go?'

Kieto did as he was asked and left Seumas recovering from his ordeal, with Dirk lying beside him and licking his face occasionally, bewildered as to why his master was not up and walking around the deck.

On the evening of the third day Seumas was over the worst of his fever and was able to sit up. The ordinary fisherfolk had not been very successful in the waters through which the canoes drifted, and so Aputua, the chief of the shark-callers, studied the shape of the clouds in the other ocean above. Finally, he declared it a good and proper stretch of water for a shark hunt and ordered the shark-callers of all three vessels to listen to his commands.

'We must feed our people,' he told them. 'Go and find your threshing devices.'

Seumas was fascinated by this ceremony, which he had not witnessed before. He asked Kieto to explain things as they went along. Kieto began by telling him that because grey reef sharks had been plentiful around the islands, there had been no need for the shark-callers on Raiatea to work their magic.

'Watch this,' Seumas told Dirk. 'You might learn how to get your supper to jump out of the sea.'

Dirk was duly attentive, though it seemed he was not sure exactly what was expected of him.

Firstly, Aputua blew softly on a conch horn. The sound drifted out over the still evening waters. Others began blowing conches then, but with gentle notes. It was an enticing sound, alluring even to Seumas, whose ear was not musical.

Kieto whispered to Seumas, 'They are calling in the sharks to the area, but they must do it softly in case Magantu, the Great White Shark, hears the call and comes to swallow our canoes.'

Seumas watched the shark-callers line up, kneeling on the front of the deck. They then beat the water with their decorated paddles to attract sharks, which would be noosed with sennit cord, or speared with harpoons, and dragged on board. When the sharks failed to come, Kikamana threw magic stones into the water, which the sharks would swallow and then would be unable to prevent themselves from ignoring the shark-callers.

The shark-callers continued to thrash the water, while singing magic songs in the evening air.

Finally, there was suppressed excitement amongst them and Seumas looked over the edge of the vessel to see, in the light of the dropping sun, deep shadows and running streaks of darkness in the water below. Then the first great snout broke the surface, the jaws opened wide revealing a mass of teeth, and then slammed shut on painted paddle, taking a huge chunk out of the wood. A noose was dropped and then a harpoon struck and the snapping, writhing shark was dragged on to the deck.

Then another, and another.

The water frothed with grey shapes, red-and-white mouths, and dark, glinting eyes. It seemed the more sharks that were caught, the more eager were their comrades to join the landed harvest. Madness prevailed amongst the victims, who flung themselves at the threshing devices in a frenzy of excitement, as if to ignore the general lunacy would be to miss an invaluable experience, never mind that experience was death.

The shark-callers were yelling instructions to each other, doing their best to keep out of the way of those who had caught a shark and were trying to subdue it with clubs, yet at the same time wishing to catch their own fish. It appeared to be pandemonium, though in fact there was an underlying sense of order to the proceedings.

Before Seumas could grab Dirk's ruff, the dog rushed forward barking and snapping himself, dangerously close to the first shark that had been hauled on to the deck. Dirk thought he could tackle the flip-flopping, jack-knifing creature, but in fact he was in danger of losing his head.

'Heel, Dirk!' yelled Seumas. 'NOW!'

The dog continued to bark, but glanced over his shoulder at his master, and on the second bidding returned to Seumas's side, growling softly in the back of his throat. Seumas clipped the dog's rump with the flat of his hand.

'Come on the first call,' said Seumas. 'Not the second, you ill-trained beast.'

'Who trained him?' asked Kieto.

'Some fool soft on hounds,' answered Seumas.

When the shark-calling was over, the catch was skinned and cleaned. The raw flesh was cut and smoked over a small, stone-hearth fire on the deck of *The Scudding Cloud*. Fuel was precious, so the meat was cut into thin strips which would cook quickly and easily over the flames from the coconut fibres.

The meal was tough, but nutritious.

*

One hot night, while the crew were listless and inattentive, the pahi passed a small island. Kikamana had warned Tangiia that they were not to stop at this place. She told the king there were no provisions there and that it was a place like 'the island with the stink of ghosts' – an unhealthy piece of dirt.

Tangiia accepted what his high priestess had to say, without questioning her. She was the authority on mystical matters. He had limited knowledge of the supernatural landscapes and seascapes of Oceania, through which they had to slide from time to time, and he simply accepted her word. She had told him what the island was, and to whom it belonged, and he had nodded and shuddered, before going to his rest.

Seumas was not sleeping, but standing by the mast, staring at the forbidden island as they passed. There were dark shapes like large birds or fruit bats skimming the air above the island, their flight patterns tight and strangely limited. They swept and dived, swept and dived, as if trapped inside some invisible vessel that enclosed the whole landscape. They seemed to Seumas to be some kind of predatorial creatures, raptors perhaps, that sought small prey in the air.

The island itself looked quite scanty. He surmised that a man could walk around such an island in an hour. It was thickly wooded though, looking like a bristly hog's back on the darkness of the ocean. As Seumas watched he thought he saw a shape, running very fast along the sands of the beach – but then it was gone, into the thickets, if it was ever there at all.

Kikamana, the Farseeing-virgin, was standing near by, also unable to sleep for reasons of her own.

'Did you see that?' asked Seumas, pointing. 'Is there someone on that place?'

'Yes, there is,' she replied. 'That's why I want us to pass it quickly.'

She stared around her, at the night sky. There were swirling clouds running over the face of the moon; dark veils made of fine black hair. The surface of the sea was like liquid ebony, noiseless as flowing oil. These were strange hours on stretches of transcendental ocean where the delicate balance between the unnatural and natural world could be tipped either way by a word or a gesture, and a nightmare might begin.

At that moment a freak wave, perhaps Aremata-popoa, rose out of the soundless sea and swept towards the last pahi in the chain, *The Royal Palm*. A child of ten years or so had risen from her sleeping mat, to parch her thirst with coconut water, when the wave hit the canoe aft. The crew quickly clutched at fixings, holding on to the boat, but the young girl was carried off on the crest of the wave, towards the small island.

'That child!' cried Seumas.

'Oh no,' groaned Kikamana. 'Why can't he let just one fleet go by without claiming a victim?'

After this enigmatic remark Tangiia was woken immediately and told what had happened.

'I must go to the island,' said Kikamana, firmly. 'I must get the child before anything happens.'

'I will go with you,' said the king. 'We'll take Po and Manopa, and—'

'No, I must go alone,' replied Kikamana. 'He would slaughter you all. That's what he wants, to gather a crowd of people on his island, then to massacre them for his larder.'

Tangiia shook his head. 'You can't go alone – you must take some of your priestesses with you. They can help protect you.'

Kikamana shook her head, as sea anchors were dropped into the water and the dugout canoe was made ready for her.

'I shall take Seumas,' she said. 'His strangeness will confuse Matuku.'

By this time the two other pahi had come up alongside and had linked to *The Scudding Cloud*. Manopa and Po were informed that Kikamana and Seumas were going to the island. They nodded gravely and made a sacred sign in the air.

'Now just a moment—' began Seumas, who had not been consulted on his willingness to risk his life but before he properly knew what was happening, he was bundled into the dugout canoe and it was launched. He barely had time to snatch up a weapon, a patu club, in his right hand and a flaming brand in his left. Then he found himself being paddled over the oily waters towards the spit of land. It bristled in the moonlight, as if expecting its visitors.

'Who's on that island?' asked Seumas, fitting the brand to a socket and dropping the club. He took up a paddle to help with the rowing. 'Who's Matuku?'

Kikamana didn't answer. She simply picked up the weapon Seumas had brought and dropped it overboard.

'Wha—? What did you do that for?' cried Seumas. 'Now I'm defenceless. We're both without arms.'

'We cannot kill Matuku,' she stated simply.

'You'd be surprised who I can kill,' growled Seumas. 'There's not many men I can't fell in single combat.'

'I mean, we *mustn't* kill him, or we will put the whole fleet at risk – Matuku is a demi-god.'

At that point the canoe reached the beach and Seumas had no time to ask more questions.

At first it seemed to Seumas that the island was silent. Then he heard the crying of the child. It came from the middle of the clump of trees. Between the sobs of the child there was another less obvious noise, a kind of swishing in the air above the trees. He guessed this was the noise of the birds or bats he had seen from the craft.

'Come,' said Kikamana.

Seumas followed her in great trepidation. The stink of evil was on this place; he could smell it in the air. The grasses and weeds seemed to clutch at his ankles. The roots of the trees deliberately attempted to trip him.

He discovered to his horror that the earth beneath his soles was crawling with insects – he could not avoid treading on them, squashing them by the hundred. Ants, beetles, millipedes and other insects flowed over his feet, biting him, nipping his skin, stinging him. Spiders with bright eyes stared from the foliage; thousands of them on one bush alone. In the poor light from the torch he was not able to identify many creatures specifically, but he knew they were unnaturally multitudinous and gathered in unusual groupings. There were savage flesh-eating insects next to mild plant-eating creatures.

The milling insects formed a band around the forest, like a protective barrier.

As they went through the rainforest, the leaves brushed their skin, and Seumas was aware of a new disquieting presence.

'Beasties,' he muttered in disgust, shuddering in revulsion as he noticed a clutch of long dark bulging shapes on the arm carrying the torch.

When he shone the brand down by his torso and on his legs, he could see dozens of them, scattered over his body. There were many more on the priestess, even on her neck and cheeks. Seumas felt his stomach turning liquidly over.

'Oh good grief,' he moaned. 'Kikamana, we're covered in bloodsuckers.'

'Forget the leeches,' she said. 'Don't pick or knock them off or they'll leave their heads under your skin. They will rot and poison your blood. We'll get them off later.'

'Don't tell me how to deal with *bloodsuckers*,' he growled, taking refuge from his repugnance in mild anger. 'I know how to deal with the beasties all right.'

Finally, they came to a clearing, in the middle of which a white cage structure soared almost as high as the tallest trees. So grand was it, in size and arrangement, that Seumas might have called it a palace. It was complicated in design, having several layers of meshed bars, which swept crisscrossing upwards into hollow keeps and towers. The surrounding trees had grown around and through the corners of the structure, so that it was firmly embedded in their individual trunks, part of their galled growth, bolting the massive cage securely to the earth. Hot winds blew through the network, causing a low moaning noise, not unlike the sound of pain.

Seumas could tell at once that it was fashioned of bones, human bones by the look of them. He recognised thigh bones and shin bones and skulls employed as locking blocks and keystones. They were fused together in a tight formation, so that a man could not pass his hand between the bars. Inside the cage sat the child, sitting on the dirt. She was crying softly.

'Great God of the Sky,' said Seumas, forgetting his leeches instantly, 'what have we here?'

'Matuku's palace,' replied Kikamana. 'And there are his toys, strung to the towers.'

Seumas stared up into the starry night and saw the birds and bats again, but they were tied fast to the bone palace, skimming around the heavens each on a long length of sennit string.

'Kites,' he said, recognising them at last and laughing softly. 'They're bloody kites.'

He was able to reach up and pull one in. It was indeed a kite, made of banana leaf stretched over a cross-frame. A very simple design: the sort a Pict might make for his son out of animal skin and sticks, the sort of kite that Seumas had played with as a boy, on the cliffs of Albainn.

'You know these magical creatures?' asked the girl in the cage, wiping away her tears.

'They're not *creatures*,' said Seumas. 'They're just bits of leaf and string.'

'But Matuku has made them *live* – they fly through the night and day – his sea-ancestors taught him how to breathe movement into an ordinary leaf.'

'Rubbish,' snapped Seumas, shortly. 'I may be a savage and a barbarian, but I know my kites.' He turned to Kikamana. 'Look, we've got to get the girl out of there.'

With Kikamana's help Seumas managed to snap off a large bough from a tree. The pair of them then tried to prise open the human-bone bars of the cage with this lever. There seemed to be no visible door to the palace. And the bones were so welded together that it seemed impossible to enter, unless they had some instrument to smash their way in. Seumas looked around the area for a large rock, but found nothing of any weight. It seemed the island was simply soil on a hidden mushroom of coral.

At that moment there was a crashing from the undergrowth and a figure appeared.

The figure stopped at the edge of the clearing. It was a naked man, but taller again by half than a normal man. There was long matted hair falling from his head, and thick hair on his chest and limbs. When he opened his mouth his teeth were sharply pointed. The man began to move forward.

Kikamana said softly, 'Speak to him – in your own tongue.'

Seumas cried, *'Ciod e a tba ort? Na biodh eagal ort.'*

The monstrous man stopped dead and his eyes grew round. He regarded Seumas with some awe. Seumas followed up his advantage and pointed to the bone palace, then waved the broken bough in the air before the creature's face.

'Bi cho math agus an dorus fhosdgladh.'

Matuku let out a cry of alarm and then fled back into the trees.

'You frightened him with your club,' said Kikamana. 'Now we'll lose him.'

'Not if I have anything to do with it,' Seumas said. 'This island's not big enough to hide on.'

He raced after Matuku with the branch still in his hand, chasing the great man through the forest tracks to the beach, over the river of insects, collecting more leeches on the way. There he saw Matuku run into the water until the creature was out of his depth and sank from sight. The giant man remained completely submerged, while Seumas waited on the beach. After a while it became apparent to Seumas that Matuku was not going to reappear. The big man with the pointed teeth had drowned after all. Seumas looked backwards and forwards along the beach, thinking the creature might have swum under water and emerged elsewhere, but there were no footprints in the sand.

Returning to Kikamana, the Pict said, 'The man must be dead – he went into the sea and didn't come out.'

Kikamana shook her head. 'Matuku can walk along the bottom of the ocean bed – it's one of the tricks his sea-ancestors taught him. I told you he is a demi-god – the son of a mortal woman and Tawhaki, God of Thunder and Lightning. He's a cannibal of ruthless character, eating raw human flesh from his living victims. He likes children because their meat is soft and sweet. What did you say to him – in your own language?'

'I said, "What ails thee? Be not afraid."'

'And the second time?'

'I asked him to be so kind as to show me the door – to the cage.'

Kikamana sighed.

Seumas asked, 'Will he be back?'

'I think he will – out of curiosity.'

The girl was still sniffling in the cage. She said, 'I want to go to my mummy – I want my mummy.'

'And you shall soon, child,' said Kikamana. 'Be patient now.'

Seumas waved the branch. 'Let's trap him in a net and I'll threaten to brain him unless he opens the cage?'

'We cannot harm him, or even threaten him – Tawhaki will destroy the fleet. To threaten to kill a son of one of the gods, no matter how despicable he is, would be to ensure our own doom. We must persuade him to open the hidden door without intimidating him or hurting him in any way.'

'An eater of *babies?*'

Kikamana shrugged. 'Would you rather the fleet was torn apart by lightning?'

Even as he spoke the words, Matuku came crashing out of the under-growth and pinioned Seumas's arms to his sides, forcing him to drop the branch. Matuku shrieked in delight at having caught the white demon so easily. He spat over Seumas's shoulder, into the face of Kikamana, who stood passively watching the Pict being slowly crushed to death. She stepped back, murmuring a karakia trying to protect Seumas with one of her magic chants. It worked for a few moments, then Matuku shook his head and squeezed hard. A rib cracked in Seumas's chest, then another. Kikamana, on hearing sounds, spoke at last, just as Seumas's head was reeling with red smoky pain.

Kikamana said quickly, 'If you kill the demon, he won't show you how to make a special kite.'

'Ahhh!' cried Matuku. 'Kite. Kite.'

The pressure was relieved for a moment.

Seumas groaned, 'What kite?'

'You must know another kind of kite,' muttered Kikamana. 'You said those are simple ones, he has there. Make him a more complicated one.'

'I – I Don't know – I can't remember.'

'Kite!' shouted Matuku, letting Seumas fall to the ground. 'Make Matuku kite!'

'I – can't,' wheezed Seumas, finding it difficult to breathe through the pain of his broken ribs.

'Think!' flashed Kikamana.

She turned to Matuku. 'Let us have the child – we will make you a wonderful kite.'

Then to Seumas, 'Well?'

'Perhaps – I once met a wandering seller – we call them pedlars – he showed me a picture of a box-kite – a big square kite ...'

'Make one, now.'

Matuku stood by, grinning wildly, his eyes shining with insane delight.

'Big kite! New Kite! Yes, yes.'

'I – I shall need some animal skin, some hide,' said Seumas, 'and some bamboo sticks – sennit string.'

Matuku rushed off, back into the rainforest.

While the creature was gone, Kikamana bound up Seumas's ribs with strips of tapa-bark cloth torn from her own gown.

'You'll be all right,' she murmured.

'I'm glad you think so,' replied Seumas, patting his padded chest. 'It still bloody hurts.'

'It's better than a crushed heart.'

Seumas smiled, grimly, 'That was crushed long ago – by someone with hardly any strength at all.'

Kikamana was aware of the sadness in his voice and touched his cheek with her fingertips.

'Even that might mend, one day.'

Matuku returned with all the kite parts, including some large pieces of thinly stretched hide and a sharp-edged razor shell. There were markings on the hide, drawings of a kind, which showed up under the flickering lights, but Seumas was too intent on considering his mental plans for the kite to bother too much with these. Seumas made a few more fire brands and arranged them in a circle around a mossy bank. Then he set about cutting the skins, at the same time instructing Kikamana on how to tie together the struts which would form the cage for the kite. He drew designs for her in the dust, showing her what the finished kite should look like.

'We're going to have to help each other here,' said Seumas, 'because I've never actually seen one made. I've just heard about it from the lips of another – seen a picture.'

Kikamana's intelligence was not lacking in any respect and she soon had a box-kite cage in progress. She prayed that Tangiia would not launch any kind of attack on the island, now that the pair of them had been gone for quite a long time. While the torches flickered away, under the eyes of both Matuku and his young prisoner, the kite took shape. Seumas asked for tree sap to seal the skin along the edges of the box, which Matuku seemed to find with remarkable alacrity, even in the darkness of the forest. It occurred to Seumas that the monster knew every corner, every tiny fraction, on this small island where he had been imprisoned by his father.

There!' cried Seumas, as the dawn was reaching with grey-blue fingers over the sky. 'The box-kite!'

He handed the toy to Matuku, who took it with surprising gentleness into his hands and stroked it lovingly. Then Matuku produced a ball of sennit wound around a short stick from a hidey-hole in a tree. He tied one end of the string to the kite and then ran off along a rainforest path, to the beach. The other two followed him quickly, Kikamana praying out loud that the kite would actually work, that the wind would carry it.

'Maomao,' she said, 'Great God of the Winds – *make* this toy fly, if only for a short while ...'

'Oh ye of little faith,' Seumas remarked, looking down into the beautiful priestess's eyes. 'It'll fly.'

And he was right. The kite lifted into the air with ease.

Matuku ran along the beach, his tall supple frame rippling with excitement, his laugh sounding over the waters, reaching the ears of those on the pahi canoes. They would be able to see, in the morn's light, that Seumas and Kikamana were alive and well. They might well be wondering what Seumas and Kikamana were doing, flying kites on the beach, when they were supposed to be freeing a little girl from captivity, but Kikamana hoped Tangiia would exercise patience, and trust her.

Matuku let out the string until the kite was a small oblong shape high above the island.

'Cloud!' he cried, delightedly. 'Up there, up there!'

He anchored it to a piece of coral jutting from the sands.

Kikamana said, 'And now, Matuku, your side of the bargain – you must release the child.'

Matuku suddenly looked sullen.

'Here we go,' muttered Seumas. 'The revoking.'

The Pict was convinced that the flesh-eating demi-god was now going to go back on his word.

From the sky, however, came a rumble like the growling in the back of a dog's throat. Matuku looked up, alarm in his eyes. There were no dark clouds in the heavens, from which the thunder might have come.

'Your father,' stated Kikamana. 'He does not think well of those who break their promises.'

Matuku stared at her, then after a few moments began walking the path to the palace of bones. Kikamana and Seumas followed him, once again passing over the insect barrier. By this time Seumas had been bitten and stung so many times he was almost immune to the pain.

While they watched, Matuku fiddled in a particular spot on the cage, pushing and pulling tiny needles of bone – a toe-bone here, a finger-bone there – slipping one backwards, another forwards, in an intricate series of movements. The locking device was like some strange puzzlebox of inter-locking strips of wood, the kind that pedlars might sell to impressed peasants in the villages of Albainn. Finally the cage door swung open and its captive was released into the arms of Kikamana.

'I swear that door was invisible,' said Seumas, rubbing his sore ribs. 'Could *you* see it?'

'No,' admitted the priestess. 'Now let's get this girl back to her mother.'

'Yes, I want my mummy,' sniffed the child.

Seumas turned to look at Matuku, who nodded, his eyes still shining.

'Good kite,' said the demi-god. 'Fly good.'

In the dugout on the way back to the pahi, Seumas let Kikamana and the girl do the paddling. He concentrated on burning off his leeches with a glowing twig, then doing the same for Kikamana. At a touch from the red-hot end, the leeches curled up, rearing their heads and tails and releasing their victim. The bites and stings from the insects would be treated with medicinal herbs, later in the day.

'Will these ribs mend soon?' he asked.

'They'll be fine in a few weeks,' said the kahuna. 'Just rest for a while.'

'Not much chance to do else,' grumbled the Pict. 'One thing though – it's a good job that hide Matuku brought us was cured to such a thinness. Any-thing thicker and the kite might have been too heavy to lift off the sand.'

Kikamana stared into his eyes. 'It hadn't been cured to a thinness – it was like that already.'

Seumas looked puzzled. 'I think you're wrong,' he said. 'What kind of ani-mal would produce a pelt that thin?'

'That wasn't what you'd call a *pelt*,' replied Kikamana, calmly. 'It was human skin. Matuku always skins his victims before he eats the flesh from their bones. He keeps the cured skins flapping from a hidden tree.'

Seumas winced and stared at the box-kite, flying high above the beach, tugged at by the monster's hand.

'*Human* skin,' he said. 'That's disgusting.'

He looked at his own hands, remembering how easy it had been to slice the hide and cut it into shape, remembering the markings he had seen which of course he now realised were tattoos. Some dead person, some unfortunate shipwrecked mariner, was now flying over the island, looking down on his own interlocking bones, hovering over the creature who had skinned him alive, who yet held him captive on the end of a piece of string, tugging him into jerky motion.

That was something to think about, while the ribs mended in Seumas's chest.

As they passed the other two pahi, Seumas saw the wistful face of Boy-girl, peering from behind the mast. Boy-girl gave him a plaintive wave. Safe on a separate vessel, Seumas waved back. Seumas had insisted that he be put on a different pahi to the desperate Boy-girl, otherwise his life would have been made a misery, unable to get away from Boy-girl's pestering.

'Come and see me?' cried Boy-girl, as the dugout passed.

'Soon,' Seumas lied. 'In a while.'

2

Twenty days after they had visited Matuku's island, during which one woman gave birth, one man died of natural causes, and a child fell overboard and was attacked by a shark, they were still drifting. They managed to save the child's life, but the whole left side of her body was paralysed.

The shark was duly caught and a ritual punishment took place whereby the shark had a line tied to its tail and was dragged backwards through the water until it was almost dead. Then a stinging jellyfish was caught and rammed down the shark's throat, which eventually swelled. The shark was then cut into small pieces and the less edible parts fed to boobies. Poetic justice for a predator who sometimes carried out sneak attacks and devoured exhausted booby birds resting on the water.

Several days after this event Tangiia sighted a circular cloud on the horizon and knew it to be one of those sky formations which clung to the peaks of mountains. He marked the cloud on his cord-device, which was growing quite lengthy and was strung with knots of many shapes and sizes.

'Keep a sharp eye out for signs of land,' he told his lesser navigators.

Then some white birds were seen, beautiful creatures with long red tail-feathers, that seemed to paint the sky with their bodies. Sometimes they even flew backwards in their elegant dance. The Raiateans had seen nothing like them before. They were clearly birds which remained in the area of land.

Tangiia kept watch, noticing some rips in the sea to the sun side of the canoe, and having his rowers move clear of them. Some seaweed was found and given to the blind Kaho, who felt its texture.

'I have heard of some islands which, on Raiatea, were supposedly in the direction of Ra. Dancing white birds and coarse weed is to be found there. What is the colour of the water, my son?' asked Kaho of Po'oi.

The child replied, 'The colour of an unripe coconut.'

'Ahh.' The old man smiled sightlessly. 'This is indeed the place of which I have heard. We must be careful in these waters. There are hostile peoples here.'

Tangiia thanked the old man.

The very next day they heard the sound of reefs on the wind and finally, at noon, approached an island with a lush green mountain rising from its centre. It was a sultry, morbid-looking place where thick vegetation came right down over the beach to touch the sea. The Raiateans could see mangrove swamps in some of the coves, the trees standing on tall exposed roots, as if ready to run with spidery legs away from the tide. Finally, the vessels came across a stretch of sand which reached like a spit out into the sea. Here they moored the canoes.

'We must take on some fresh water,' said Tangiia, with a sense of foreboding warning him not to linger. 'It's not an island I would wish us to populate.'

A six-man exploratory party was organised to seek for fresh water, while others gathered drinking coconuts, and anything else they could find, from the shoreline.

Manopa led the six-man expedition. Included within its numbers were the young priest who had stolen the God of Hope, Po and Seumas. Seumas's cracked ribs had almost healed now and he was back to his normal state of fitness.

King Tangiia remained with the pahi canoes, though he expressed a desire to go with the exploratory party. Kikamana told him his place was with his people and that now he was king he had a duty to protect his person from harm.

'If anything happens to the party, we must cast off and sail away – and you must be with us. Despite your youth, you are our king and you must suppress your adventurous nature at times like this. Without our king, we should be lost in an unknown ocean without reason for being there.'

Boy-girl, who had been travelling on *The Volcano Flower*, agreed with the priestess.

'You should stay here with us, to protect the women and children with the rest of your warriors.'

Sighing heavily, Tangiia agreed, knowing that while the canoes were moored together he would have to face the onslaught of Princess Kula's wrath, from which the open waters had protected him until this moment. Indeed, he could see her smouldering form stepping on to the sand spit at the very moment he was speaking with Kikamana. The princess began striding purposefully towards the new king, who uttered faltering apologies to his high priestess, before walking quickly along the spit and down to the shoreline, where he hoped to escape for a while in the near environs of dense jungle.

At that moment, unnoticed by others, a bird was released from a cage on one of the pahi. It was mobbed by local frigate birds as it climbed into the sky and on hearing the commotion Tangiia glanced up. He saw the frigates attacking a stranger in their midst, but then shrugged and took his attention from the scene, as the bird climbed higher and out of danger.

Frigates were always attacking some poor feathered creature, robbing it of food, or simply harassing it because it was in their territory. The incident was instantly forgotten. There were important issues at stake and it was as well not to be diverted by the vagaries of the natural world.

If King Tangiia had kept watching, he would have noticed that the bird flew away over the ocean in the very direction from which the fleet had come, and thus he might possibly have saved himself future grief.

Manopa led his small party, each carrying a number of empty gourds, into the interior. They were only lightly armed and hoped to rely on flight if attacked by any warlike peoples. No sight nor smell of smoke was detected, however, and Manopa had hopes this piece of land was uninhabited.

It was hot and humid under the canopy of leaves, and insects stuck irritatingly to sweaty bodies as the party cut their way through the vegetation with bone knives. The air was heavy and difficult to breathe. Sometimes the stink was unbelievably powerful when it rose from a mangrove swamp where gas bubbles burst, releasing an ancient organic stench into the enclosed atmosphere. Fiddler crabs scuttled amongst the tidal reaches of the swamps and reptiles hung from thick, dark-green leaves over the swilling, brackish waters. It was a place where Moko, the Lizard-God, might scatter his green, living jewels.

Apart from the obvious physical unattractiveness of their surroundings the young priest told them he could sense spirits in the foliage all around them.

'Dwarves too,' he murmured, with a shiver. 'I can feel the Lipsipsip around us ...'

Po groaned and Seumas asked him what was the matter.

'Lipsipsip,' said Po, glancing behind him. 'They are small demons who live in rotting trees and black stones. Spirit people, who devour you if you offend them.'

'How does one offend these creatures?' asked Seumas, whose own country of Albainn was overrun with dwarves and giants, living as they did in deep caves and high on the hillside crags.

'Just by being here, if one is a stranger.'

'Quiet,' said the more pragmatic Manopa. 'Do you want to tell the whole island where we are?'

Manopa led his party towards the most likely area where a stream would fall from the mountain and cut its way through the undergrowth to the sea. They worked hard with their long bone knives, chopping away at tangles of vines and thick-stemmed, succulent plants that spread under the canopy. Finally, they were rewarded with the sound of cascading water.

'This way,' grunted Manopa, leading them into a clearing.

A thin waterfall dropped from a cliff as a silver flail and lost itself in a natural, mossy drain hole to an underground stream. Seumas stared around the glade, which was clearly man-made, in apprehension. He saw, on an otherwise smooth stump, the carved face of a god eating a lizard. The head and front legs of the lizard were poking between the god's lips like a swollen tongue. The carving's eyes were round and large, its nose long, and broad at the tip, its lips thick and brutish.

It was the head of the lizard that made Seumas shudder; it had the face of a terrified man.

'Who's that?' whispered Seumas to Po.

Po stared and shook his head, indicating that he didn't know, and did not *want* to know.

Behind the carving were painted totems, each about the size of a man's arm, projecting at all angles from the turf. There were animals and birds, as well as faces and skulls, carved on the totems. Dirty, bark-cloth rags hung from the mouths of some of the chiselled features, like frozen vomit. Spikes pierced the eyes of the carvings. In some cases the lips had been drawn back to reveal long, squared teeth. The tongue of one wooden human face was as long as a man's intestines, and ran over the scrubby ground and down the throat of a totem, like a ribbon snake crawling into a hole.

Manopa's group were now quite terrified. They had clearly stumbled on to a sacred waterfall. It was a dreadful place, where the horror of awful deeds was almost tangible and could be tasted in the foul air. Each man expected that any moment a loathsome, drooling monster would spring from behind a stone. At that moment Po let out a yell.

'Arrrhhh!'

He dropped the gourds he was carrying and lifted his club to defend himself as a dense fern parted to reveal a man.

The stranger also jumped back and levelled his spear. He stuck out his tongue and went into a crouched stance. The yell of a war cry left his throat.

Manopa took hold of him from behind and motioned for him to lower his weapon. Po did as he was bid.

The wary stranger came forward, still crouched, followed by a number of other men in single file. If Manopa's group were going to attack, now was the time to do it, but they had been shocked by the encounter, and had lost the initiative. Manopa did not know how many of the local warriors there were in the vicinity and whether or not they were surrounded. The only method to employ here was hit and run, but their path back to the sea might have been closed behind them.

Manopa studied the natives with a practised eye.

They were tattooed, but with symbols not used by the intruders. Unlike the Raiateans, who regarded facial tattoos as distasteful, these warriors had bars tattooed across their noses and cheeks. In their features they were much like the Raiateans, though their heads were shaved except for two twisted horns of hair which projected from their scalps. Their stature was in fact somewhat stockier and shorter than that of the intruders.

Gradually more and more men came into the clearing and surrounded Manopa's party. They were all heavily armed and seemed by their demeanour and their bodily decorations to be outfitted for war. It would have been suicide to attempt to fight this many warriors in the tightness of the glade. Manopa waited for an opening speech from the natives, before committing his men to any course of action. He was not afraid to fight, but he wanted to give his men the best chance.

'Why have you come here?' asked one of the natives, who from his head-dress appeared to be a chief of some kind. 'What are you doing?'

He spoke with a peculiar accent in a dialect used by all voyaging Oceanians; almost a separate language in itself. It was the tongue employed by mariners to communicate with each other when they met on the high seas, or in situations such as this, where strangers arrive on an island. It was a limited language, but adequate for its purpose.

'We touch nothing here,' said Manopa. 'We have not touched the water.'

'Water taboo,' snapped the chief.

Manopa said quickly, 'Yes, we understand.'

All the while they were carrying out this brief exchange, Manopa was aware that the natives were creeping around behind his group, in order to stare at something, and that those at the front were craning their necks to look over the shoulders of his own party. It took him a few moments to realise that the object of their interest was Seumas, who stood between the young priest and another man. Manopa and his men were so used to the strangeness of Seumas's skin, hair and eyes, that they quite forgot how odd it might seem to an outsider.

'Not albino,' said the chief, staring hard at Seumas. 'What is it?'

Manopa was quick to seize the moment.

'A demon we caught in a trap. We trained him to fight for us. His eyes are made of blue shells. On the parts of his body where no sun has shone his skin is pure white.'

Seumas caught the drift of what was occurring here.

'*Tha e cho geal ris an t-sneachdj*,' he said, telling them in the language of demons that it was as white as snow.

The chief's eyelids narrowed, he stepped back quickly, and the circle around the hapless group suddenly widened.

'He is a *demon?*'

'*Our* demon,' said Manopa.

The chief, who now felt it was required of him as the bravest member of his war party, went forward cautiously and touched Seumas on the chest with tentative fingers, which he quickly withdrew. Seumas stood quite still, allowing himself to be appraised and studied, from head to foot. His gingery-red plait he knew was a shocking colour to the Oceanians, and he had frightened many with his light-blue penetrating eyes. The chief seemed mesmerised by him.

Finally, the chief said, 'You eat with us,' and took the path by which he had entered the glade.

It seemed that Manopa and his band were expected to follow. Native warriors blocked the way back to the sea, so Manopa motioned for his small band to do as they had been told.

They were led into the interior and up the side of a mountain, to a flat shelf which was almost a plateau, except for the fact that it was overshadowed by a great curving hooked rock which rose behind the shelf and swept over it. Seumas noted that there was only one path up the steep ascent, which followed a narrow ridge over which they had to cross single file. On either side of the ridge, the width of a man's shoulders, the world dropped away to deep valleys below.

The village on the plateau was a fortress: almost impossible to attack. Seumas surreptitiously searched the landscape for ways of escape and it seemed that if the ridge was well guarded that action would be virtually impossible too.

The group were the object of much interest as they entered a large village of stone huts roofed with palm leaves. Sullen-faced women and children came out to stare at them as they passed, but there were no sounds of greeting or welcome; simply a ponderous silence. Seumas came under special scrutiny; some of the children hid behind their mothers as the party approached with him. Dogs came running from the village edge, barking and snapping at the strangers. One of them worried Manopa's heels until he kicked it and sent it yipping into a pack which was less bold and had kept its distance.

They were taken to a large, rectangular ceremonial area with a stone floor inside which were several platforms of stone at different levels and around which were houses of differing size and height. They were asked to sit in the middle of this rectangle, a temple which Seumas gathered was called a *tohua* in the local dialect. Drink was brought to them.

Gradually the temple began to fill with warriors, sitting around Manopa's group, until there were at least two to three hundred in and around the stone structure. Seumas had judged from the size of the village that there were more men somewhere else. There were houses to support at least two thousand people on the plateau and clearly not all of the warriors were present; the bulk of the fighting men were somewhere else. Perhaps out in their war canoes, fighting another local island, but more likely down on the shoreline, attacking the Raiateans.

'What is the name of this island?' asked Manopa of the chief, who could not take his eyes from Seumas.

'Nuku Hiva,' replied the chief, refusing to avert his gaze. 'You sell your demon to me? I give you many women, many shells, many red feathers.'

Seumas glanced at Manopa, who stared back stony-eyed.

'Yes,' he said at last, 'I'll think of a good price.'

'Good,' smiled the chief, showing an even row of teeth. 'Come the night – we eat. Tomorrow you tell me price. Now you want a woman for each man?'

Manopa's face set into a grim smile. 'Yes – good.'

Seumas knew the tactics, had used them himself in the clan wars. They were to be wined and dined and sapped of strength by lovemaking before being slaughtered. Feed your enemy, get him drunk, drain him physically, put him off his guard, then when he falls into an exhausted sleep, cut his throat.

Seumas wondered about the trading business, and decided the chief possibly had a perverted sense of honour which required that he offer to *buy* a demon rather than take it immediately by force. No doubt he felt it might be unlucky to simply massacre a group of men and then take their demon as spoils of war. A demon was something unusual and with unusual creatures you trod warily, careful not to upset any obscure gods, or break any cryptic taboos. At least the offer had been made and if the seller was not alive to take advantage of the deal then that was hardly the fault of the buyer.

'Good,' repeated the chief. He called something in his own dialect. Some wooden platters and giant clamshells of nuts and fruit were brought, and laid before him. The chief and his basket-sharers took their pick of the edibles, then offered some to Manopa's men, who also partook of the food.

After they had eaten, naked maidens were ushered from one of the stone houses. From their looks and demeanour they were of a different tribe, possibly from another island. Seumas guessed they were captives taken in a raid on some neighbours. They looked frightened and bewildered.

Each of Manopa's group was assigned a woman, until only Seumas was left alone. A nude mature female of thirty or so was pushed forward, in front of him. She was slightly overweight, but with pleasant features.

The local chief said something which Seumas did not catch and he turned to look at Po.

Po grunted, 'An enemy chief's wife – you're being honoured. Her husband is required for another ceremony.'

Seumas nodded, not knowing what Po meant about the husband. The captured wife or daughter of an enemy chief was a prize not lightly given.

The woman looked terrified and Seumas could well understand why. Apart from being used as an object to help subdue some strangers from across the ocean, she was about to be handed over to a tattooed, white demon from hell. Perhaps his cock would be made of fire? Or his loins covered in fish hooks which would hold her to him forever? Or his breath perfumed with the fragrance of deadly poisonous flowers?

Seumas turned away from her.

Po grabbed his arm and hissed in Raiatean dialect, 'You have to do it – they will kill us where we stand if we don't accept their gifts.'

'I'll take a few of them with me,' snarled Seumas, looking directly at the chief.

Po said, 'Yes, they don't want that – they want to soften us up first – but give us a chance. Do what they want until we get the opportunity to escape.'

Seumas turned back to the chief's wife. Already the other Raiateans were lying with the young women on woven mats, observed silently by two hundred or so native warriors. Seumas dropped his loin cloth to show the frightened female he was not made of fire underneath, and that there were no hidden traps beneath the bark-cloth. She stared at his loins, then after a few moments, lay down for him on the mats covering the stone floor.

When he took her in his arms she was trembling violently with fear. He stroked her hair for a few moments under the direct scrutiny of the local chief, whose face wore a puzzled frown. Seumas knew he was supposed to take the woman dispassionately, without any show of affection, but he could not do it. He had to at least show he was going to be gentle to calm her terror if he could. He could feel her heart pounding against his ribs and when it quietened a little, he lay on his back and allowed her to penetrate herself, so that she could control the act.

She was still shaking when he entered her and her musty breath told him she was close to tears. Seumas soothed her with little sounds as she moved above him. He had not intended to reach orgasm, hoping for her sake to fake it, but in the end could not help himself and clung to her for a moment, holding her close to his chest. Then it was over.

She took herself away, obviously relieved that the ordeal had not been as

terrible as she had imagined, and he watched her walk with a dignified posture towards the stone house whence she and her fellow captives had come.

The chief laughed delightedly and turned and threw a ripe fruit at the
woman, striking her on the buttocks, splattering the tops of her legs, and up
her back, with yellow juices and flesh. She paused in her stride to wipe her legs,
then without turning around continued on her journey. The warriors around
her jeered and poked her with sticks, until she finally left the courtyard.

In that moment Seumas hated the chief. It took all his reserves of spiritual
strength to stop himself leaping on the grinning man and throttling him with
bare hands.

The darkness came a little while after that and fires were lit around the
temple. Seumas could sense a certain excitement in the air. Shortly after this
he could smell the delicious aroma of roasting pork and realised that a feast
was about to take place. Looking out towards the fires, he could see that there
were carcasses being turned on spits over glowing charcoal. Kava was brought
to them in coconut shells. Seumas noticed that Manopa and his men drank
slowly and he did likewise, hoping the food would come soon or he would be
drunk very quickly.

The evening air was redolent in and around the temple and it was difficult
not to feel comfortable. The cicadas stopped buzzing and the crickets came
out, the night choir replacing the day with hardly a pause between. Torches
were lit and placed all around the tohua, bringing shadows to life. Warriors
moved from place to place, carrying wooden platters and bowls.

Finally the meat was brought. It smelled delicious and despite his situation,
Seumas began to salivate. He had not eaten since mid-morning and his gastric
juices were swirling in his stomach, trying to deal with the raw alcohol.

'Good,' he said, as a long haunch was placed before him. 'Food at last.'

Po gave him a sidelong glance, but said nothing.

There were no drums, or nose flutes, nor any kind of accompanying music,
which Seumas felt was eerie. He guessed it was probably because the missing
warriors from this community were down on the shoreline getting ready to
attack the fleet from the cover of the forest. They would not want their
enemies warned that the island was heavily inhabited.

Seumas could see Tangiia in his mind's eye, staring at the jungle's edge
from the deck of *The Scudding Cloud*, wondering what had happened to his
exploratory party, trying to decide whether he was going to cast off once the
morning came around, or send in a search party.

'Eat!' cried the chief.

His warriors needed no second bidding and they immediately sank their
teeth into the roasted flesh.

Just as Seumas was about to bite his haunch a woman brought him a leaf-
plate with two round objects on it. Seumas knew immediately they were the

testicles of the slaughtered beast. He had eaten all parts of sheep, goats and pigs before and was not squeamish about any part of an animal, be it brains, eyes or even intenstines. So long as it was well cooked, he would eat it, and thank the gods with a satisfied belch.

'You are being honoured again,' said Po. 'You must salute our host.'

Seumas looked towards the chief, braced himself, then smiled and rubbed his stomach. The chief grinned back through a mouthful of food. Seumas ate the two oval pieces of meat, finding them a little crunchy. He guessed they had come from a suckling pig, since they were quite small. The chief let out a delighted yell and picked up what looked like a plate of two eyeballs and a heart. These he proceeded to eat himself.

'The final insult,' said Po, under his breath.

'What?' asked Seumas, starting on his haunch.

'To eat the eyes and heart of a rival chief. Now the dead man can't join his ancestors.'

Seumas looked doubtfully at the long haunch of crispy, reddish-brown meat in his hand.

'This?' he said.

'His forearm.' Po nudged Seumas and pointed towards the cooking fires.

There, spitted and turning over the fierce heat from the charcoal, were three bodies. Seumas stared hard at the one closest to him, lit only by the glow from the fire, and realised it was not a pig as he had thought at first glance. A pig does not have a tongue that can be extended to curl around the spit like a snake around a stick.

It was – he could see it now – an eyeless and literally gutless man. A man whose hands were trussed around the back of his neck, and the elbows tied at the front, so that his arms resembled chicken wings. His legs were straight however and tied at the ankles. The cavity where his stomach, intestines, liver and lungs had been, was stuffed to overflowing with wild herbs. In place of his eyes were sweet potatoes. The hair on his head and body had been singed to tight, crisp curls.

Seumas could see that the hardwood spit went through the middle of the ankle bonds, entered the anus and disappeared into the torso, and reappeared out of the mouth. A man never had so straight a back as that man who turned on the spit over the charcoal fire.

'In the name of the gods,' he whispered. 'Did he feel anything or was he dead before …?'

'Before they cooked him? Probably he was dead – killed in battle. In any case they would have sucked his brains through a straw stuck into the eye socket. It's traditional.'

'Traditional?' breathed Seumas, wonderingly, as if this was a custom preserved for its quaintness. 'Tradition is it?'

The meat on the spit was a roasted-red colour, brittle crackling on the out-side, and revealing soft blisters where the skin had split and the flesh was bursting through. Under the fire, which rested on raised volcanic rocks, was a long wooden tray like a short dugout canoe. The natural fats dripped con-tinually from the roasting man, down sizzling into the fire, some of it flowing between the rocks and reaching the tray. A large pool of liquid human lard swam in the bottom of the tray into which women regularly dipped ladles to baste the meat in its own juices.

Seumas stopped chewing. The meat which had begun to warm him from within and had started to make him feel more at ease, now turned to cold clay in his stomach. He could feel the fatty fluids trickling through him, leak-ing into his veins, into every corner of his body, seducing him. This was the arm of a *man* like himself. Human flesh from a human bone. Meat destined for a burial mound, stolen from the mouths of worms.

Another thought struck him. 'What about – just now?'

Po shook his head.

'You took his wife and then you ate his balls – if you ever meet him in the Otherworld I should run away, very fast.'

Seumas felt like vomiting. This was the husband of the woman he had made love to, just a short while ago, this meal. He had just eaten the bollocks of a great chief. Perhaps not so great, if he was beaten in battle? Whatever, he wished he could spit them into the face of that other chief, sitting there with a grin on his greasy chops and his mouth full of another man's eyes. It was not only an insult to the dead man, it was also an insult to a Pict, to trick him into eating human flesh.

'On the other hand,' said Po with a tasteless touch of humour, 'a castrated ghost might not be much of a warrior.'

'I feel sick,' said Seumas.

'Eat,' muttered Po. 'You have to keep up your strength.'

Implicit in that remark was the warning not to *overeat*, for they would have to make their bid for freedom that night, and overindulgence meant lethargy. Seumas did not need to be warned about eating too much human flesh. Every swallow of meat made his stomach heave. It went down like grave earth.

'You are guests of Nuku Hiva people this night,' announced the local chief, smiling. 'You stay here, yes.'

It was not a question.

Dakuwanga the shark-god swam through the ether in the spirit world around the feasting mortals. Passing through rocks and trees, under the earth, in the waters of the streams, through mountains, along valleys, Dakuwanga searched for morsels and tidbits, fragments of a human soul. His wide crescent mouth below the blunt nose was ever open, while his tiny, empty-looking eyes searched amongst the shadows for souls on their way to Milu's Cave in the Land of the Dead. Ten thousand souls had passed through Dakuwanga's gullet.

While the mortals were feeding on the cooked human flesh of their enemies, the shark-god was busy hunting down and devouring their spirits, growing strong on their sau. Dakuwanga's energy came from the spiritual potency of the sacrificed victims of cannibals. A chief's soul was better than a warrior's, but the spirit of a kahuna was the choicest dish of all. Dakuwanga, however, was the scavanger of the spirit world and would eat any wisp of a human soul lost in shadowland.

Tangaroa watched the activities of Dakuwanga with some contempt. The Great Sea-God had little time for minor gods, even with eternity on his hands. His interest was purely as an observer. Unlike Maomao, the Great Wind-God, and Hau Maringi, the God of Mist and Fog, Tangaroa had not yet chosen sides between King Tutapu and King Tangiia. However, it had to be said that he was inclined to favour Tutapu, since Tangiia had blundered in his efforts to take an idol of Tangaroa with him on his long voyage. The Great Sea-God had not made up his mind whether or not he had been insulted.

For the present, he preferred to wait and see what mettle was in the blood of these two brothers; once he had made up his mind to support one or the other, or neither, then perhaps he would intervene and sweep aside minor gods such as Dakuwanga – or perhaps not.

Tangaroa, by his very nature, was a fickle god.

3

'The gods have deserted us,' moaned Po, as the group sat on the edge of the plateau on the side furthest from the ridge by which they entered the village.

Even as he spoke though, Hine the Moon-Goddess, came sailing out from behind a cloud and began to cross the roof of voyaging. Tonight she was Hine-keha, her bright form, as opposed to Hine-uri, her dark, invisible state. She illuminated the plateau with her radiance, revealing to the captives how hopeless was their position on the mountain.

There was a sheer drop of a thousand feet before them, and behind them two hundred warriors lay sprawled over the village grounds. Sometime in the night, when it was certain all the visitors were asleep, a death squad would rise up from amongst those warriors and quickly dispatch the visitors, sending them on their way to a grateful Milu.

Seumas stared out into the blackness.

'What are we going to do, Manopa?' he asked the gloomy leader of the expedition.

The big man put his head in his hands. Manopa was a good warrior, an exceptional fighter, and he was an intelligent man – but he was no lateral thinker. His plans and schemes were always straightforward, based on experience and knowledge of other well-tried plans and schemes. He had no answer for a highly unusual situation, except to attack his captors head on and try to reach the ridge without being cut down, a task he knew to be impossible, given the number of enemies out there.

'I don't know,' he admitted. Then he asked hopefully, 'Has anyone else got any ideas?'

No one answered. Po looked around him in panic.

'Someone must have a plan,' he said. 'Someone's got to have a plan.'

Silence. And more silence. Then Seumas stirred.

'I have,' he said, 'but it won't save you lot.'

Manopa said, 'You don't need to save yourself – they're going to let you live anyway, *demon*.'

'What sort of life would it be and for how long?' snorted Seumas. 'They'll put me in a cage until they need me, and when they realise I can't do magic, they'll spit me and roast me, like that poor bastard we ate tonight.'

Po frowned. 'How would you save yourself then?'

Seumas pointed to the edge of the plateau. 'I could climb down there and probably collect birds' eggs on the way.'

Manopa snorted. 'You couldn't climb down a face that sheer – you'd drop off before you got twenty feet.'

The Raiateans could shin up palm trees, scramble up steep tracks, balance on aerial walkways, but they were not good at straight rock-climbing on sheer faces, having little need for such skills on their home island.

Po contradicted his leader. 'He's right, Manopa. He can do it. When we found him, in the Land-of-Mists, he was climbing a cliff face just as sharp as this one. He was collecting wild seabirds from their nests, and the birds were attacking him too.'

'He fell off, didn't he?' snapped Manopa.

'No,' Po corrected Manopa, 'the woman Dorcha fell and *he* tried to catch her as she passed him. She broke his hold with her weight. I think he *could* climb down there.'

'Easily,' Seumas said.

'Well, then, save yourself,' muttered Manopa. The other men agreed, telling him to go quickly, while there was time. Seumas shook his head.

'I have a better idea – one which might save us all – if you have the courage for it.'

Po said, 'Tell us, quickly.'

'Well, it means you following me, putting your hands where my hands have been, copying my body movements, putting your feet in the cracks where my feet have been. If you follow me exactly, you should be able to make the climb.'

Po nodded, enthusiastically. 'I'm willing to chance it. If I fall it can't be any worse than having my skull crushed like a coconut and then being toasted.'

Manopa sighed and shook his head. 'There's a problem you haven't fore-seen, goblin. You have to go down the cliff face first, with us following. How can we watch for your hand and foot holds, without falling off? It's impossible.'

'That's why we go up, instead of down.'

Manopa, Po and the other men looked up, to see the great hook of rock curving above the plateau, casting its black, wicked-looking shadow over the village. It was like some great fishing lure of the gods, Maui's perhaps, when he angled in the great empty ocean at the beginning of time, using his own blood for bait, and pulled up Oceania's islands, one by one.

'Up?' repeated Manopa, puzzled.

'Yes, up. If we throw a loin cloth over the edge here, so that it catches on a shrub down below, they'll think we climbed down. They'll go charging off over the ridge to reach the bottom of the cliff before we do. Then we'll come down and fight our way through whoever's been left here.'

One of the other men nodded. 'He's right, if we go up we can watch where he puts his hands and feet.'

'But we've got to come down again,' grumbled Manopa, short-sightedly. 'How do we get down? Fall?'

'We use some of those vines up on the crest, to lower ourselves,' Seumas said. 'We can't lower ourselves down a thousand-foot cliff, but we can from a hundred or so feet. Are you for it, or not?'

Manopa took one last look at the climb and said, 'Let's go.'

They waited until Hine-keha went behind another cloud and the captives could not easily be seen from the village. Then Manopa took off his loin cloth and threw it over the edge of the cliff. It floated out and disappeared into the blackness. 'Acchhh,' he said, disgustedly. He then snatched another man's garment and knotted a stone in its corner, before dropping it very carefully on to a shrub some ten feet below the lip. 'That should do it,' he said. 'Now climb, goblin.'

Seumas began scaling the curve of the hook. He put to good use the shrubs and other vegetation, including vines that ran down the steep face. He was wary of relying *too* much on the roots and stems of bushes, for though they clung tenaciously to the surface of the cliff, there was often not a great deal of surface soil and their grip did not allow for the weight of a man. At first he went too quickly for Po, directly behind him, even though he felt he was climbing at an extremely slow pace. His head was a little groggy still, from the effects of the kava juice, but he was not drunk. The knowledge that death was only a small misjudgment away was a sobering influence on him, as it must have been on all the climbers there.

Each man followed the movements of the man before him and in this way the group ascended the massive crag. The path of the climb took Seumas not only upwards, but to the side of the great hook as well, until the party were actually over a drop which fell into the fathomless valley below. He had no choice, for the lay of the climb was in that direction.

As the fickle gods would have it, the wind for which they had been waiting many days now, sprang to life while they were desperately clinging to a piece of rock.

The man behind Po was the young priest who had stolen the God of Hope. He was no climber at all and made the mistake of looking down, when he should have been concentrating on watching where Po put his hand. In consequence, he chose the wrong hold, which crumbled under his grip. He fell out and backwards, into the void, clipping the naked Manopa behind the ear with his heel as he passed.

Manopa managed to hold on, but the falling man dropped away out of sight, only the faintest sound coming back to the group when his body hit the bottom. To his eternal credit the ill-fated Raiatean priest did not cry out on his descent to his death, knowing that to do so might mean the discovery of the climbers.

Po, trembling with fright, had to touch Seumas on the ankle to signal a stop. Po needed to recover his composure. For a few moments the shaken fisherman flattened himself against the rock, feeling giddy and shivering from head to toe, wishing he were on flat ground. The others below him did the same, glad for a respite, horrified when they thought of their position as insects halfway up one of the walls of the world.

Po then felt a tap on his head and knew he had to go on. He gritted his teeth and, looking up, continued the climb. Eventually, after what seemed more than a lifetime, the group reached a narrow ledge. There they huddled, waiting for events to unfold below them.

Seumas went on, further up, to collect a vine growing from the summit of the hook. He would have to dig it out by the roots with his bare hands, having no knife with him. He found a flat stone to use as a shovel and hacked away as quietly as he could at the base of the vine, finally loosening it enough to be able to wrench it free from its moorings.

There was a shout from below, which woke Seumas with a start. He had been dozing, his head against another man's shoulder. Their absence had been detected by the warriors sent to kill them. Men were running around with flaming torches now, looking in all the crevices, inside hollows, behind boulders. Then the loin cloth was found and the discovery was greeted with great excitement. Several lighted brands were thrown over the cliff, in order to look down below. One of the warriors stated that he thought he could see a body down in the valley.

There was a general call to arms then, with warriors rousing each other from their beds. Looking over the edge of the hook, Seumas could see the chief directing operations, sending his troops out to search for the missing guests. When the area of the plateau revealed nothing, the warriors began flowing along the ridge, their torches streaming like living fire balls.

The chief remained in the village, with a dozen or so of his men, while the rest of them crossed the ridge.

Seumas wrapped the end of the vine around a rock and held it there with his own hands.

'Down,' he murmured to Manopa.

The first man shinned down the vine until he was level with the plateau but still over the big drop, then he kicked out sideways, swinging himself like a pendulum, until he was over the lip of the plateau, when he let go and rolled. One by one the Raiateans went safely down the long vine, until there was only Manopa to go.

'I'm very heavy,' he warned.

'The rock's taking the strain,' said Seumas.

Manopa began climbing down the vine when Seumas suddenly noticed that the constant swinging had frayed the vine. It was too late to stop Manopa, who was almost at the bottom.

'God of Vines, whoever the hell you are,' growled Seumas, 'Don't let this one break ...'

He held his breath as the bulky Manopa began kicking awkwardly at a projection, trying to get himself within reach of the plateau. The other men were holding hands, so that one of them was reaching out over the lip, trying to catch Manopa as he struggled to get to them. Manopa spun precariously on the end of the vine, his face white with fear and exertion. He managed to stop the spin, but was still dangling helplessly.

Seumas took the vine in both hands, below the frayed part, and began swinging the man below. It took every ounce of strength in his body, but gradually the swings became longer and longer, until finally Po managed to grab Manopa's hand in a double-wrist grip. Manopa instantly and rather stupidly let go of the vine and almost dragged Po to his death. The chain of men held, however, and at last Manopa crawled over the lip of the plateau and lay panting in the dust.

The whole drama had been enacted in complete silence.

After a short rest, to allow the strength back into his arms, Seumas scuttled down to join the group.

'I prayed to the God of Vines for him,' he whispered to Po.

'What God of Vines?' asked Po. 'There isn't one.'

'Well, there should be – you've got a god for everything else – even breadfruit.'

The group, now depleted by one, crept off the rock shelf and back into the village. They armed themselves with whatever they could find: rocks, hunks of firewood, a fishing net, an adze left outside a hut. The remainder of the local warriors were gathered in the tohua, sitting on the temple floor, no doubt awaiting news from the world below the plateau. Manopa and his men attacked quickly and silently, throwing the net over the greater part of the assembly and proceeding to club them senseless while they fought with the folds.

A warrior not caught by the net came at Seumas shouting oaths and wielding a wahaika club. Seumas flung a stone, catching the man in the throat, then followed up with a kick to the groin. The warrior was very strong and stayed on his feet, while Seumas grappled with him for possession of the club. Had he been fighting a normal man, the warrior might have won the struggle, but he paused to stare into Seumas's face, and realised his eyes were locked with those of a demon. The thought froze his muscles for a few moments, long enough for Seumas to wrest the club from his hand and strike him down.

With the wahaika club in his fist, Seumas began laying about him in a frenzy of blood lust. The madness of hand-to-hand combat was again upon him. There was only one way to survive in the midst of a battle, hacking it out amongst desperate bodies, and that was to fight in a demented and frenetic manner, to throw all sanity to the winds, to go berserk and put the fear of death in those enemies around you. To strike a man with madness in your eyes, and strike him again and again and again, until his legs went from under him and he disappeared from sight, down amongst the legs of hale warriors, to the ground below.

It had been a long while since Seumas had been in a battle, even a skirmish, and it recalled those times in his youth when clan met clan on Albainn's highlands, leaving the burns plugged with bloody corpses and the air reeking with the sweet smell of putrid flesh. Then there had been men with him, wearing the same cloth, bearing the same tattoos, yelling the same war cries. Then there had been the aroma of peat hags in his nostrils, a cold wind rif-fling his wolfskin cloak. Then there had been the prospect of a roast goat and hot mead to follow, sitting around the fire with men of his own stamp, his own culture, petting the dogs and scraping the gore from deerskin boots.

Now, at his side was another warrior, Manopa, who might have been his highland brother, blood of his blood, helping him to protect their family and glen from invading hordes of wild coastal tribes. Manopa was, Seumas quickly learned, a brilliant hand-to-hand fighter. The pair of them felled five warriors between them, while Po and the others dispatched and wounded the remainder, all except for one, the enemy chief.

The chief was a savage and skilful warrior, who though he had not claimed any lives from the group, had seriously wounded one man, and had damaged Po's left shoulder with a blow of his nokonoko kotiate club. The club was big and heavy, difficult to wield in a tight space, and the chief was now retreating into a corner of the courtyard.

Women now emerged from the houses near by and began wailing when they saw the dead bodies on the stone flags of the temple. Some of them rushed towards the group, stooping to pick up stones to throw. The chief, who was now in danger of being felled, took this opportunity to turn and run towards the ridge.

'Leave him to me,' said Manopa, picking up a javelin.

'No,' growled Seumas, snatching the weapon, 'that bastard humiliated me. He's mine.'

Seumas took three long strides and launched the javelin through the moonlit air. It flew silently towards the running man, falling short by several lengths. Manopa grunted.

'Now it's my turn,' he said, finding a feather-fletched spear amongst the array of weapons on the ground.

Manopa took a much longer run and the spear left his hand and hissed through the night. It arced beautifully, gracefully sweeping down towards its running target. The barbed point struck the fleeing chief just below the left shoulder blade and penetrated right through his body.

The chief turned with a surprised look on his face. His nokonoko-wood club, with its ugly, bas-relief carving of Oro on its head, dropped from his fingers. He glanced down, at the foot or so of spearpoint protruding from his chest, as if wondering what it was doing there. Then he looked up with an annoyed expression at Manopa, as if about to chastise a child for doing something naughty. Finally his muscles sagged and he slipped sideways and fell down the mountain slope, the spear catching on a rock halfway to the bottom and snapping in two pieces.

'Good throw,' said Seumas, grudgingly. 'I missed my footing, otherwise ...'

Manopa said, disparagingly, 'Yes, otherwise you would have got him – we all know that.'

The stones from the angry women were raining down on them now, some of them as large as eggs, and there was a serious danger of injury.

'Let's get out of here,' said Po, who was supporting the wounded man. 'Now.'

Manopa took the limp man from Po and slung him over his broad right shoulder. Then he ran towards the ridge, as if carrying a sack of feathers. Seumas followed, wondering again at the strength of Tangiia's second-in-command, admiring it, envying it. Manopa was a good man to have if you were outnumbered in battle.

As Seumas joined the other men on the ridge, and began running across it, again he was mindful of the battles in the highlands of Albainn: the hasty retreats, the running advances, the speedy movements from glen to mountain to glen. Even now, crossing this ridge, he recalled the scents of the heather and pine, though the night air was actually carrying much more cloying perfumes of frangipani and flowering ginger.

In the light from Hine-kena's brilliant sails, the group found their way down the mountain tracks to the waterfall. There they rested and drank, unconcerned for the moment by the sacred nature of the pool, or the consequences of annoying a local Tiki. The gourds they had dropped that afternoon were still lying on the grasses around the glade and they gathered these up and filled them under the falls.

Then they collected their weapons, slung the full, roped-together gourds around their necks, and set off down the last track to the shoreline below. They moved warily now, knowing there were many enemy warriors in the forest.

They reached the beach without meeting any local warriors, where Manopa divested himself of his load. To their dismay the pahi canoes were moored beyond the reef now, probably using sea anchors. Tangiia had either already had a tussle with the islanders, or he was being extra cautious.

'The able men have to swim out there and tell them we have a wounded man back here on the beach,' said Manopa. 'I'll stay with him.'

Seumas said, 'No, I should be the one to stay with him – you're all better swimmers than I am.'

Manopa stared Seumas in the eyes, then nodded and said, 'You're right.'

Without another word Manopa slipped into the water, Po and the last fit man following, and they quietly swam out into the lagoon. When they were halfway to the pahi there was a shout from the rainforest. They could be seen in the moonlight. Seumas hunched down in the foliage with the wounded man, who was still unconscious, and made ready to put a hand over the man's mouth in case he came round and made a noise doing so.

A war canoe was launched from farther around the bay. Seumas could see the island's warriors in their war finery: the feathered helmets, the cloaks, the effigies of Oro held up high by yelling priests, the decorated war clubs.

Manopa and the others were striking out for the pahi now, and it looked as if they would reach it before the war canoe caught up with them. More war canoes were launched and the drums started pounding. By the time Manopa was pulling himself up on to the deck of *The Scudding Cloud*, there were thirty war canoes heading towards the Raiatean fleet and more being launched all the time. The Raiateans would be overwhelmed if they did not put to sea, which Seumas was both glad and unhappy to see them do.

The crab-claw sails were raised in the wind, men got behind their paddles, and the large ocean-going canoes pulled away from the islands, heading out into the deep ocean. The war canoes were much smaller vessels and they had little hope of catching the Raiateans. Soon the large crab-claws dipped down over the moonlit horizon. The war canoes drifted to a standstill, turned slowly, and came back to the island, the drums still beating and the warriors still primed for a battle which was now out of reach.

When the war canoes reached the shore, the excited warriors leapt from them and into the rainforest, running off the pent-up energy which they had been storing for the fight. They were high on adrenaline and this vigour had to be expended in some way, now there was to be no killing.

There would be both relief and frustration in each of them. One half of their emotions would be telling them it was a good thing, they did not have to die for their king; the other half would be disappointed that they had not been given the chance to prove their worth to these intruders who had dared to step foot on their sacred isle without so much as a gift for their king.

Seumas remained hidden under the foliage that overlapped the shoreline like a fringe. There was a green tunnel there, between bank and water's edge, and it was this that hid the two men from sight. Seumas hugged the wounded man, praying he would not start raving in his illness.

Soon, however, it did not matter how much noise they made because on the plateau above a frenzy of hedonistic dancing began, with the drums thundering under the roof of voyaging, and whistles and flutes screaming into the night. There would be triumphant feasting in the villages, a loud mourning for the dead, an overindulgence in just about all bodily pleasures. The warriors had driven off an invasion force and they would be full of self-congratulations and arrogance.

The wounded man, whose name was Wakana, came to consciousness at last in Seumas's arms.

'Where are the others?' he asked, looking up into Seumas's face. 'Where are *we*?'

'We're on the beach,' Seumas replied. 'Manopa and the others had to swim for the canoes – the whole fleet was chased over the horizon. I'm afraid we've been abandoned.'

Wakana was a young virgin whom Seumas had seen treading the fermented breadfruit in the pulping enclosures on Raiatea. Apart from this rather unexceptional skill performed only by those young men whose purity was unquestioned, Seumas knew nothing about the youth. He did not even know if the boy could swim; there were one or two Oceanians who could not.

'We've got to get out of here,' Seumas told him. 'How about stealing one of those war canoes moored out in the lagoon? Can you swim that far?'

Wakana looked at him in disgust. 'Of course I can swim!' he began to get to his feet, then reeled over, clearly still giddy from his head wound.

'You can swim,' muttered Seumas, 'but can you *walk?*'

The boy passed out again for a few minutes and Seumas laid him down on the sand and crept along the green tunnel, wondering if he could steal a canoe by himself. He couldn't see any guards from where he was crawling, but that didn't mean there weren't any. They might be posted further up the hill. However, their attention would not be fully on their job, he knew, because of the noise coming from the villages.

Then, when he was a short way from where he had left Wakana, he heard the soft plashing of a paddle. At first he thought he might be hearing waves on the shore, or some animal or fish in the shallows, but when he concentrated he could fit a definite rhythm to sounds. They were indeed paddle strokes.

Seumas was certain there was a war canoe sneaking along the shore.

He lay flat on his stomach and regulated his breathing. Hermit crabs scuttled over his body. The ripples from the lagoon reached out, stroking his prone form. The *thump, thump, thump,* of the drums up in the village vibrated through him. He turned very slowly and began crawling back, returning head first along the tunnel of vegetation, to where he had left Wakana. When he reached the spot where he had left the youth, he found it empty. Wakana's body was gone.

Had the boy woken and, finding himself alone, crawled off somewhere else?

Or, the more likely thing was, given that Seumas had heard a canoe, he had been discovered and hauled away.

The sound of the paddles again, dipping softly into the warm shallows of the lagoon.

Seumas found his club in the sand and made ready to use it. If he was going to die he was not going to die *easily*. He shuddered as he thought that in perhaps a few hours time he might be a meal for laughing warriors, who would pick through the flesh between his toes with their teeth, swallow his eyes whole with relish, and suck the cooked brains from his upturned skull through straws. It was an ugly thought that made his heart race with revulsion, as he wondered whether his degraded spirit would be aware of what was happening to his body, and if he would have to be a silent witness to his own defilement.

'Goblin?'

A quiet voice drifted to him from the water.

'Goblin? Are you there?'

Seumas parted the leaves of the tunnel to see Manopa sitting in a small dugout canoe. Hunched near him, was Wakana. Relief swept through the Pict. Manopa had returned for him.

'Here!' he hissed, then slipped into the water and waded out to the canoe.

'Quickly,' Manopa said.

Seumas climbed into the dugout and soon they were shooting towards the open sea.

Manopa kept his eyes on a kaveinga, a star path, which Seumas knew would lead them to where the fleet was moored with sea anchors. Wakana was still in no condition to paddle, but Seumas did his bit, driving the dugout through the water, letting Manopa fathom the way. Finally they came to a place where there was a sweet fragrance in the air; a wide pool of silvery-grey ambergris lay on the ocean, glinting in the moonlight. In the middle of this waxy substance lay the three pahi canoes.

King Tangiia was there on the deck of *The Scudding Cloud* and he helped to drag the groggy Wakana on to the deck. The boy was then taken off by Princess Kula, presumably to be administered medicine of some kind. Manopa and Seumas climbed out of the dugout unassisted, then the small canoe was taken on board the large one. Dirk was there to greet Seumas. The dog accepted a heavy pat as an acknowledgement and whined with pleasure.

Tangiia came forward and slapped Manopa on the shoulders.

'Good – no wounds?'

'None,' grunted Manopa. 'Now I must take command of my vessel.'

'You're exhausted,' said Seumas, who was just about all in himself. 'Rest first, then drink with me. You saved my life – I have to give you my bond.'

'Give it to someone else, goblin,' growled Manopa. 'I went back for the boy, not for you.'

Seumas stared at the big warrior and then said, 'It doesn't matter – you came back. I need to thank you. You have to give me that chance to pledge my life to you.'

'Go pledge it to the fish,' said Manopa.

Tangiia's captain then walked over the deck, to the far hull where *The Royal Palm* was lashed alongside. Soon Manopa had ordered his pahi untied from Tangiia's and the two vessels drifted apart. Seumas looked bleakly at Tangiia.

'He doesn't mean it,' said the navigator king.

'Yes he does.'

Tangiia shrugged. 'All right, he does – but he would have still come back for you, if Wakana had been with you or not. He would have gone back for a pet bird.'

'That's a comforting thought,' said Seumas, drily. He promised himself that he would pay Manopa back in full, at the earliest opportunity, so that he would not feel beholden to the chief for longer than necessary. It was humiliating to be saved and then rejected by the saviour. Manopa had risked his life for a goblin; well then the goblin would do the same, when the time came, and their lines could diverge again.

Seumas nodded to where Kula was ministering to Wakana.

'I see you have your friend on board,' he smiled.

Tangiia shot a look at the Pict, to ascertain whether or not he was being mocked, and when he was satisfied the remark was purely conversational, he said, 'That's another story, my friend, for a long, hot day. In the meantime, I understand you proved yourself out there. Manopa says you saved all their lives, with your climb up the rock. You owe him nothing.'

'It's true I saved them all,' said Seumas, considering this remark. 'Without my climbing skills every single man of us would have been murdered. I'm surprised Manopa gave me credit, and I thank him for it, but the other thing is a one-to-one. I helped the group I was part of to survive, while he alone came back to lift me from the beach. I do owe him.'

'If you do, you do – but don't lose any sleep over it. We all owe something to someone. By the way, Boy-girl's been weeping. She thought you were dead.'

Seumas groaned. 'Does she know I'm safe now?'

'I signalled *The Volcano Flower* to that effect.'

The conversation ended there, for Tangiia's navigational talents were needed by his helmsman. The king went aft to issue instructions, while Seumas sank into a deep sleep on the deck, his dreams uncomfortably damp, as Dirk lay beside him licking the salt sweat from his tattooed body and growling at anyone who came near his resting master.

PART FOUR

Isle of Rapacious Women

1

The Great Wind-God Maomao and the Great Sea-God Tangaroa had never been on good terms with one another. One of the reasons for this was because, by his very nature, Maomao found it necessary to stride about on his brother's back, and even flay him on occasion. These were circumstances under which Tangaroa felt humiliated and which infuriated him. There was no means by which Tangaroa could get his own back; the sea cannot punish the wind in any way. So any small opportunity for crossing his brother was swiftly seized by the Great Sea-God.

Maui, that puffed-up ancient hero of the Oceanian race, had been chattering in the Land of the Dead, about King Tangiia.

'He reminds me of myself,' said hero Maui, 'I was once a great voyager of the oceans, unafraid of men or gods, sailing into the unknown in my canoe. I prevailed because I was cunning and courageous, unconcerned by what the gods might fling at me, taking all in my stride on my passage through life ...'

Tangaroa, who had little time for Maui whose trick of fishing-up islands had robbed the Great Sea-God of some of his territory, listened to this prattle with growing interest. Tangaroa was aware that King Tangiia was receiving support from the Great Wind-God and he saw a way of getting some of his own back, by appearing to support Maomao, but subtly putting obstacles in the course of the Raiatean fleet. After all, Tangiia had made no sacrifices to Tangaroa, even preferring to take a minor god, the God of Hope, as the fleet's guardian, rather than Tangaroa himself.

As for the atua Maui, Tangaroa had never forgiven the ancient hero for catching the sun, Ra, in a net of ropes and beating him with a stick. Maui had been displeased by the shortness of the hours of light and at first had tried to net Ra in some dry ropes, which the fiery body easily burned through. The next time Maui used a trick of wetting the ropes with seawater and this time Ra had been entangled and was soundly thrashed by Maui. 'Why do you flog Tama Nui-te-ra?' cried the sun, using the full name given to him by Rangi. 'What have I done to you?'

Maui said, 'Nothing, but you must promise to go more slowly over the sky to lengthen our days.' Ra agreed, but forever bore a grudge against Tangaroa for allowing Maui to use his water to wet the net of ropes, a thing Tangaroa had been unable to prevent, not having much control over the precocious Maui.

So, all things taken into consideration, Tangaroa was not inclined to help Tangiia, and in fact was on the side of Tutapu and Hau Maringi, Lord of the Mist and Fog. While Maomao was sending Tangiia's fleet a brisk wind to blow him to the island of Tahiti, Tangaroa sent an adaro to the fleet, to draw it off its present true course.

King Tangiia was on deck one morning when the waves were rolling hills that swept under the pahi. He could see the sails of the other two canoes rising and falling behind his own vessel, disappearing on occasion into a wide trough, then rising up again to tower above him on the crest of a tall wave. The people on their decks were like busy ants, continually adjusting and readjusting the sheets.

Tangiia was running before the wind Maraamu-tairoto on the windflower, trusting to Maomao to fill the crab-claw sails and push the fleet in the direction of its true destiny. He had been noting the star paths and had fixed the present position of the craft under a fanakenga star. Then the dawn had come up and washed Rangi's face clean of kaveinga and fanakenga.

Around the king the crew and passengers were busy at their early morning tasks: the ever-present, always-busy bailers were rhythmically shovelling water from the hulls; the women were baking yams, cutting breadfruit, grating coconut, preparing the breakfast; the children were waking from a good sleep, salt-encrusted, bleary-eyed; the fisher-folk were preparing hooks with bait to trail alongside the craft; the navigators were noting the currents, the temperature of the water with their hands, the direction of the wind, the shape of the waves, the flight paths of different birds of the air.

Tangiia's mind was not on his people however, nor on navigation, but on the fact that Kula refused to speak to him, now that she had chastised him bitterly for abducting her and robbing his brother of his bride-to-be.

He stared down at himself, wondering why Kula did not love him. His body, he saw, was beautiful. The muscles were not too pronounced as to be knotted, but were like flat stones under his soft, brown skin. His hair he knew to be smooth and touchable, hanging like a black curtain around his broad shoulders. His feet and hands were well proportioned, both in themselves and relative to his torso and limbs. His face was pleasant to view, having no ugly blemishes or prominent features, such as a large nose. His eyes, he had been told, were like liquefied mud of the deepest brown.

And as well as all these handsome characteristics, he was a king!

Why, any other woman would have sold her father to cannibals if it meant marrying such a youth.

'Perhaps it's my own self she does not like?' he sighed. 'My disposition and qualities of spirit?'

'What's that?' asked Kikamana, standing near to him.

Tangiia suddenly turned and looked at the Farseeing-virgin, an idea coming into his young head.

'Kikamana,' he said, 'has there been any instance where a woman has not loved a man, or indeed the other way around, yet the unloved has managed to turn the love of the unlover?'

'There is a story of a boy who invented a love potion,' confirmed Kikamana. 'He made the concoction from aromatic leaves and it boiled over and some fell into the mouth of his sleeping cousin. When she woke she went rushing down to the surf in which he was swimming and insisted he make love to her. They were both found dead in the cave of Bokairawata with the herb of mint growing all around them.'

'Is mint one of the ingredients of the love potion – do you know the other ingredients?' asked Tangiia, eagerly.

'Yes,' replied his high priestess, 'but we don't have them on board.'

'The very next island we see, I shall stop and pick the necessary aromatic leaves for you. But this must be our secret, Kikamana, as I'm sure you know who I shall want to drink the potion.'

Kikamana said she did, but warned Tangiia that meddling with such things as love potions and love spells nearly always ended in a disaster of some kind. Tangiia was desperate though. He had to have the princess. His heart ached for her, his loins ached for her, his head ached for her. If she continued to reject him, he told Kikamana, he might even have to end his own life, for he was so sunk in spirits as to contemplate suicide.

Not long after this Tangiia was staring moodily at the kava-dark sea, tired from lack of sleep and dispirited by his lack of progress with Princess Kula. It was early morning, the watch were tired and inattentive. Because they were running before the wind there was little to do except gaze at the sea and sky. Tangiia had his eyes fixed on a patch of ocean just in front of the craft. A ripple appeared, like a sea rip, and then something dark mingled with churning foam. There was a shape of a being the colour of seaweed, moving in an arc.

Tangiia watched as a creature broke the surface, rolling like a whale, though this was a much smaller beast. His eyes opened wide, for though the wavetops were misty with flying spray and occasionally frothed white, thus impairing his vision, it seemed to him that the creature was a man. A man, but not like any other the king had seen. The swimmer seemed less fish than human, but it owned definite features which suited aquatic conditions more than life on land.

Tangiia walked to the bows of the canoe to take a keener look.

The man-shaped creature had tailfins on his feet, quite visible to Tangiia when they broke the surface, and there were slits like gills on the back of his head, behind his ears. There was a shark's fin on his back, cutting the water whenever he slid across the surface, and on his head was a projection like the spike of a swordfish or narwhal. The man-fish turned on his back, pointed in a direction at a sharp angle to the course taken by the pahi, and seemed to beckon Tangiia to follow him.

The king found his voice at last.

'Look at that!' he cried. 'Can you see?'

His shout seemed to frighten the creature, which dived deeper immediately.

The helmsman turned the vessel, crying, 'Is it a log? Are we about to strike something?'

'No, no,' cried Tangiia, excitedly, pointing at the empty ocean, which flicked and danced before his eyes. 'There was a creature like a man! A man-fish!'

The mariner, who was an old seafarer, was familiar with Kuku Lau's tricks and thought the king was seeing things.

'Perhaps it was a dugong?' said the helmsman. 'They look very much like women, if you just catch a fleeting glance.'

The other members of the watch began to gather around the king now, as well as adults and children waking from their sleep. They all stared at the spot where Tangiia was pointing, seeing nothing but the waves. Then a fin broke the surface and some people shouted, 'There! There!'

'A porpoise,' said one of the mariners. 'Haven't you see a porpoise before?'

'That was not the beast I saw,' cried the king, angrily. 'I saw another creature, a man-fish I tell you.' He described what he had seen.

Makka-te came forward then. 'What you have described,' he told Tangiia, 'is an adaro – a creature of the gods.'

Tangiia was in a fever of excitement now. 'We must go after this marvellous beast. It asked me to follow it and went that way ...'

Tangiia pointed a direction about three counts on the windflower away from the present direction of the breeze.

Kikamana, who had now come forward, said, 'Is this wise, to change our course, King Tangiia? Maomao has sent us this wind. It has the blessing of Hine-tu-whenua. We should stay on our present course and not become diverted by strange sights that may prove to be nothing more than a fleck in your eye.'

'It was not a fleck in my eye, it was a wonderful creature. If you had seen it, you would agree with me. It is my decision that we follow this man-fish. I'm sure we're being shown the true path for our vessels. Signal to Manopa and Po that we're changing course ... there! There it is again!'

As the king pointed to the adaro, which had again briefly broken the surface, all the attention had been on him. When the heads turned, the man-fish was almost gone again, only the tip of his back-fin visible, and the flick of one fin from his feet.

'I saw *something*,' said Makka-te. 'Perhaps a shark?'

'It was the *adaro*,' cried Tangiia, frustrated almost beyond endurance. Then in a firm voice which brooked no opposition, he added, 'I want a watch kept in the bows with eyes for that creature alone. Every sighting must be reported to me in detail. I will prove to everyone here that I'm not mad – the man-fish is out there and we're going to follow it.'

Seumas was awake by this time and he watched in worried puzzlement as *The Scudding Cloud* altered course. He rose from his rest with Dirk at his heels, to speak with Kikamana, the Far-seeing virgin.

'It seems to me,' said Seumas, 'the king was out of his head for a while. Has he been drinking seawater?' They both stared at Tangiia, whose eyes were still fixed on the surface of the water ahead. 'I mean, he wasn't exactly raving, but he wasn't far off either. Does he know what he's doing?'

'He is the navigator,' Kikamana said. 'We must trust to his judgement for the time being, until he's proved to be wrong. At least this has taken his mind off his problem with Princess Kula.'

'Where is she?'

'Still tending the wounds of that young virgin who was wounded at Nuku Hiva Island.'

Seumas raised his eyebrows. 'She hasn't fallen for him – the youth I mean?'

Kikamana shook her head. 'No, I'm sure she hasn't. She still sees her place as being with Tutapu. I think she believes King Tutapu will follow us and take her home to Raiatea. Until that happens, or something convinces her that Tutapu is not coming for her, she'll remain a virgin herself.'

The night was sultry. The crab-claw sail puffed and died, puffed and died, as if it were gently breathing. The wind had dropped to a series of delicate cross-breezes. Tangiia caught a scent of something in the air, very faint, and needed confirmation. He called for Kaho, the Blind Navigator, and asked him if he could smell land.

Kaho sniffed the air and said that he could. 'Though in what direction it lies, I can't tell. The wind is dancing this way and that, tonight.'

'Fetch me a young pig,' Tangiia said to Po'oi, as always standing by ready to assist his sightless father. 'But keep things quiet. I don't want the whole vessel roused.'

Seumas, on hearing this, rose from his bed and went to stand with Tangiia. The king was much calmer now than he had been two mornings ago when he claimed to have spotted the adaro. Since then Tangiia kept telling others he was constantly sighting the wonderful man-fish, but no one else on board caught any more than a glimpse of fin breaking the surface of the sea, or a tip of a sawfish or swordfish horn.

However, Tangiia was no longer feverish, but very composed and deliberate in his efforts to stalk the creature he claimed was an adaro.

'Something new happening?' asked Seumas, quietly.

'There's an island out there somewhere,' Tangiia replied. 'I'm just about to find out in which direction it lies.'

Tangiia then ordered the sails to be lowered and the duty watch to take to the paddles. One of the crew signalled with a flaming torch to the following pahi that they were changing course. He received an acknowledgement.

At that moment Po'oi arrived with the pig, which Tangiia immediately picked up and tossed into the water. The animal made a splash, bobbed to the surface, and began swimming away from the vessel.

'Follow the pig,' Tangiia murmured to his helmsman. He then explained to Seumas, 'A pig's sense of smell is superior to ours – it will always swim towards the nearest land.'

'A costly navigational aid,' said Seumas.

'Not at all. When we land on the island the pig will be there and it'll only be a matter of retrieving it. You still have a lot to learn, Seumas, about us Oceanians.'

'I can believe that.'

A while after following the swimming pig, whose snout remained like a short breathing-tube above the surface, Seumas could hear breakers on a reef or beach. Tangiia ordered soundings to be taken, until the shallowness of the water was such that they could go no further. He then commanded that the sea anchors be dropped. Then he lowered a dugout into the water and indicated that Kikamana should join him in it. She obeyed without question, and Seumas had the feeling that she knew what all this was about.

'Don't you want to take some warriors?' asked Seumas, as the dugout began to push off. 'There may be hostile people on that island. Remember Nuku Hiva?'

'This island is too small to support people,' said Tangiia. 'We're going for some … fruit.'

'How do you know it's too small? You haven't seen it.'

Tangiia shook his head. 'I told you, you have a lot to learn. I have someone else's memory of this place,' he gestured at the ocean. 'Kupe has been here. He once told me about this part of the ocean – I can recognise features in the waves, the swell, and the sound of that reef. Do you hear it? All reefs sound different, Seumas. Islands have their own particular aroma too. I heard the sound of a bird – a particular bird. This is an island Kupe told me about, when I was twelve years of age. Anyway, there are no fires.'

'We didn't see fires on Nuku Hiva.'

'That was different.' With this unsatisfactory explanation left hanging in the air, the young king pushed off from the side of *The Scudding Cloud* with his paddle and soon all Seumas could see was the dark water all around.

The darkness swiftly gave way to the morning light and soon a flat island, not much more than a vegetated sandbar, appeared out of the grey dawn. The three pahi were anchored in pale-green water not far from the slow spread of the beach. By the time the whole fleet was awake, Tangiia and Kikamana were back, the dugout laden with coconuts and fruits, the pig sitting snugly in the bows and not at all put out by his trip.

After Tangiia had taken the opportunity to speak with his other two captains the dugout was taken on board again. They set sail before the sun became too hot. The wind was still not as strong as it had been until Tangiia had seen the adaro, but it was enough to sideswipe the vessels and keep them moving over the water, *The Scudding Cloud* still obsessively following in the wake of the marvellous man-fish which Tangiia said he saw from time to time.

Kieto had told Seumas that an adaro, apart from swimming in *water*, could also travel through the sky by crossing over rainbows.

'If they become angry with you,' he told the sceptical Pict, 'they shoot poisonous flying fish at you.'

'I'll remember not to anger one,' replied Seumas.

Later the Albannach went to King Tangiia and said, 'You didn't go to that island just for fruit – you could have sent some men and women for that – why did you go?'

Tangiia, who was squatting on the front of the deck, transfixed as usual, indicated that Seumas should sit beside him. The Pict, covered from ankles to shoulders in bark-cloth to protect his skin from the sun, his face shining with vegetable oil, squatted down easily next to the royal Raiatean. There was, as always a fine spray lifting from the water and drenching the deck of *The Scudding Cloud*, wetting everything at leg-level.

Tangiia whispered, 'I tell you this on pain of death if you betray me ...'

Seumas nodded, wondering if he was about to be privy to some terrible state secret and whether he actually wanted to know.

'Seumas, my friend,' hissed Tangiia, not taking his eyes from the sea, 'Kikamana and I have gathered magic herbs from that island.' He turned and gave Seumas a strange smile. 'Soon the Princess Kula will be begging me to make love to her – *begging* – once she has drunk the love potion Kikamana is mixing. See – see the man-fish break the surface ...' he ended, crying softly in preoccupied wonder.

'A giant turtle,' Seumas said. 'I saw a turtle. Listen, do you think it will work, this potion? Will she come to her senses and realise she is really in love with you after all? Is it fool-proof?'

Seumas had immediately thought of Dorcha and was kicking himself for not speaking with the Far-seeing virgin about such things. Perhaps she could have helped him win Dorcha, while they were still on Raiatea? Perhaps there was love for him in the Celt's breast which only needed awakening?

'Of course it will work. It *must* work. I must have that woman.'

Seumas sighed, heavily. 'I know how you feel.'

'Of course,' mused Tangiia, 'I shan't keep her in that condition – it would be wrong – so we collected the aromatic leaves to make a medicine which will counteract the effects of the love potion, once the Princess has given herself to me.'

'You intend to bring her out of her love trance?'

'Yes, once it is too late for her to go back on her commitment to me.'

Seumas raised his sandy-coloured eyebrows in surprise. All at once he felt distaste for the king's methods. To help someone fall in love with you was one thing. That was like wearing a sweet-smelling oil on your hair, washing your body in perfumed water and putting on fine clothes, in order to influence their judgement, make them reconsider your attractiveness. But then if that love could be taken away, just as easily, it was not the awakening of something dormant, already there, but the injection of a false emotion in the subject's breast. Seumas was not sure that he approved of this at all. His views on women and love had changed radically since he had arrived on the heavenly island of Raiatea. He had grown more tender in his thoughts, less savage in his ways.

'That's all very tricky. It sounds a little like getting someone drunk on kava and raping them to me ...'

The young king looked at him angrily. 'You think I'm immoral, doing this? What choice do I have? She hates me. I can't stand it.'

'I know, I know,' said Seumas, softly. 'Believe me, I understand. For years now I have been going through the same thing. But this is very drastic.'

'If you tell a soul, I shall have you beheaded,' snapped Tangiia, his eyes hot with temper.

Seumas rose from his sitting position and stood over the young king.

'I shall tell no one. I simply ask you to consider what you're doing. I wouldn't do it.'

'You are not me – wait – there – there – did you see? You must have seen? Out there, in the crook of the wave. He beckoned. We must go on – go on ...'

Seumas, thinking that they were now being guided by a madman, left the king staring ahead of the craft. Their navigator king's brains had been addled by some malevolent god, intent on leading the fleet to the edge of the world and watching them drop over into nothingness. The Pict thought there might be a mutiny on board soon, if the king did not come to his senses. There were already whisperings amongst the crew. He would have to keep an ear open himself, for he was considered close to the king, and when royal power was brought down, those standing next to it were often felled alongside.

It was difficult for Kikamana, on the great platform between the two hulls, to exercise the rights of a high priestess which made her profession worthwhile. Kikamana did not like people – or rather, did not like *crowds* – and on her home island she would be mostly alone in her temple. Her natural inclination was towards solitude and prayers, meditation and musings, during which time she considered deeply the workings of the universe, its symbols and its signs.

In her younger years Kikamana had learned, from older priests and priestesses, the fangu chants and songs which were important memory aids, carrying knowledge and power in their lines. She knew the weather and its patterns as well as any senior mariner, was aware of the shapes of the clouds and the temperatures of the wind which created squalls, or full-blooded storms, or dead calm. The landscapes and seascapes of her world were imprinted upon her mind like maps. Even among people renowned for the strength of their memory, she had phenomenal powers of recall. Inside her head were myriads of pictures with infinite detail, individual scenes she might only have seen but once in her life.

She was born the daughter of a weaver whose first three husbands died before she was twenty-four. One went to a shark, another fell from a coconut tree and broke his neck, the third died of a mysterious illness which made him first balloon like a puffer fish, then peel like an overripe fruit. Kikamana's mother took these deaths philosophically, but the priests at the time pronounced her taboo, thinking the gods did not intend for her to have a husband. Henceforth no man would go with her for fear of meeting a premature death. This aspect of affairs too formed part of her philosophy and her daughter was ambitiously raised in the belief that a man was not necessary to a woman's happiness and in fact might be more of a hindrance to a definite career. Since Kikamana later felt a natural inclination towards abstinence, this suited both mother and child.

Kikamana's mother was a religious woman who spent a great deal of time with her daughter, giving her the benefit of those stories which filled her head.

'Woman was the *first*,' she told Kikamana, 'for without a woman a man could not be formed. The god Rongo went abroad and fetched some pieces of clay and rock and these he gave to the god Tu, who made them into the shape of a woman using his spittle as mortar to keep the pieces together. The finished object was then handed to Tane who breathed warm air on the image, investing it with *spirit* and *breath-of-life*. The figure imbibed that life, a faint exhalation was heard, then a shudder went through the earth-formed female as the mortal spirit settled its home in her. Then at last the maid-of-clay opened her eyes, stood up, and was proclaimed – woman!'

Kikamana grew up in the belief that she was special and that her destiny was to be great and wise. She took this idea seriously, never doubting her mother for a moment. When she was fifteen and a man asked her to be his wife, she told him, 'I am saving myself for Maui.' This was very close to blasphemy, since Maui was almost a god.

'But Maui is in the land of the dead,' said the unhappy suitor.

'Precisely,' replied Kikamana.

At sixteen Kikamana went off to live in the mountains for ten years, where she found a cave and fasted. There her visions and dreams became real scenes and places. There were times when her visions manifested themselves and stayed with her for days, talking with her, passing knowledge to her. And other times when her dreams opened up and allowed her to walk inside them, gathering spiritual strength from their mana.

When the ten years were over Kikamana went down the mountain and rejoined the Raiatean community, where her powers soon became apparent and she was given one of the royal babies to watch over like a nurse. The child, Prince Tangiia, grew to manhood under her guidance. When he was fourteen Tangiia asked Kikamana to marry him, as many men had done before because she was so beautiful in spirit as well as body. She had told him to wait four years and ask her again. He promised her fiercely he would not forget to do it, that he would count the days, the moments, until he reached the age of eighteen years.

On his eighteenth birthday, just a short time ago, he had come to her in tears. He told her his honour was in shreds, his heart was broken and his spirit was torn.

'I cannot ask you to marry me, Kikamana, for I have seen a girl I love with all my soul.'

'And she is not me?' the mature Kikamana had said, smiling and stroking his head, teasing him.

'Why, no – she is a young maiden, a princess.'

'Then I release you from your promise.'

Tangiia had kissed her feet and left the temple with the tears still shining in his eyes and a smile on his lips.

He loved her, he told her later, as a brother, which he was, she being his half-sister.

He never again mentioned sexual love to her, until he asked her to make him a potion for Kula.

While Kikamana was at her prayers in the corner of one of the two huts, Seumas came to her and indicated that he would like to speak. Kikamana had not had a great deal to do with the Pict, since he never visited the temple on the island, as most Raiateans did, and seemed to avoid her at ceremonial feasts and other occasions. She had the feeling he was a little afraid of her, much like many other men, except he had an excuse. He was a newcomer and therefore wary of all priests of what was to him an alien religion full of strange gods whose names he had not learned as a toddler and whose ways were foreign.

Seumas sat opposite her in the darkness of the hut.

'There is a problem,' he whispered to her, for there were others in the vicinity. 'It's to do with the king.'

She appraised the pale, rugged man whose tattoos of beasts she had never seen in Oceania were symbols of his wildness. A long, thin rat, which was not a rat, chased an animal with tall ears and powerful back legs across his abdomen. There was a sharp-faced dog-creature on one shoulder and a larger, more hairy dog-creature on the other. Then there were the many symbols, curious curls, oddly shaped keys, that formed patterns over the flat muscles of his chest, around his decorated nipples.

His hair was like dry grass reddened under the sun. His muscular frame was lean, tall and compact. An angular face, becoming creased by the weathering of sun and salt water, held two sharp blue eyes that interested her more than any of his other features. She read a certain honesty in them. It was not the honesty of her own society, was not shaped by the same mind or culture. But nevertheless it was a trait to be respected as something he believed in and strove to keep pure; it was that aspect of him which was to be admired. He could also be, she thought, a loyal man if he found the right leader, the right ruler to follow.

Finally, his hands were touching hands, full of meaning, full of gravity. There was not a great deal of grace about him, when compared to an Oceanian, but his hands were graceful – gentle, tender, yet: firm and strong.

'Are you asking me to commit treason?' she asked.

The eyes became worried, as if a misunderstanding had occurred.

'No, nothing of that kind. Simply to find the king again – the *real* king – before he becomes too lost to reach.'

'And where is he now?'

Seumas said, 'Deep down, inside himself.'

She liked this kind of talk. He sparred well. He had a certain intelligence. It was more interesting than talk of fishing, or weather, or discussing blocked bowels with overweight men, and sickly babies with fussy mothers. She had underestimated this man in the past.

'What are these,' she asked, pointing to his tattoos, one at a time. 'Tell me their names.'

He looked down at himself in surprise. 'No one has asked me that before – I think they believed it to be unlucky. You're not worried that I might really be a demon? Maybe when I tell you what they are, you'll be under my spell?'

'I'm the sorcerer,' she said, wryly, 'not you.'

He laughed. 'Getting above myself, eh?' He pointed to each shoulder in turn. 'This is called *fox* and this one here is a *wolf* – they're dog-like creatures. The fox is small but cunning, the wolf is strong and savage. I like to think I have something of both of them in me, like any respectable Pict.'

'You are a Pict?'

'That's my race.'

She nodded thoughtfully. 'And the scene on your belly?'

'Well, this long, lean chap is a *stoat* – he changes the colour of his coat in winter and becomes the *ermine*. Here, he's chasing a creature called a *hare*. He'll never catch him, because hares can run too fast, but he never stops trying. It's the dogged hunter after the uncatchable prey. A man running after a deer will never catch his quarry on foot – even if he is the fastest runner of his tribe – but there are secrets of the mind that will help the hunter bring down the deer.'

Finally, amongst the swirls and whorls which formed the designs on his chest, she pointed to one.

'And this?'

He looked down and then up again, smiling, and she knew she had been astute.

'That's one of the secrets of the mind.'

'What do you call it?'

'Them – they're really two separate parts of the same weapon, though the way they're drawn here it seems like they're one single thing – they're called a bow and an arrow.'

'And how do they work?'

He smiled again. 'That's another secret.'

'There's one creature you still haven't told me about – perhaps it's because you can't see it yourself. It's on your back. A wonderful-looking beast—'

'A *horse*,' he said, simply.

'It has a powerful, muscular body.'

'The ownership of one of these creatures will make a man a king, whether he's born of royal blood or not.'

'One can *own* a horse – like a dog?'

The Pict stood up and held his hand level with his own shoulder.

'The height of a horse would reach at least to here,' he said.

Despite herself, Kikamana was surprised. The dimensions of the beast on Seumas's back were impressive. If one could own such a creature, perhaps it was useful in war, to bite and tear at one's foes, or kick with its hard-looking feet? Or flay the skin off a man's back with that tail? Perhaps it could be trained to stamp enemies into the dirt. It certainly had terrible eyes in that long head, cavernous nostrils for snorting fire, and whips along its neck.

'I suppose,' she said, 'this *horse* is another secret.'

'Of course,' he said, smiling and sitting down again.

'Like this *iron* you once spoke of?'

'Like *iron*.'

She said, 'You seem to have so many secrets your head must be ready to burst.'

He laughed. 'Me? I'm a poor, simple man, an ignorant peasant of a man. Someone else discovered the secret of the bow, of iron, of the horse, not me. I merely make use of the thoughts in another man's head, when the opportunity arises.'

'It seems to me that you can't have the horse or iron in our world, but you could make a bow and arrow.'

'Does it seem like that to you?' mused Seumas. 'Well then, that's how it is, isn't it? But I'm not going to show one of you how to make them. I still have old loyalties to consider. One day you people will return to Albainn, or the Land-of-Mists as your Kupe called it, and you'll want to conquer my people. If I tell you my secrets, then you'll know as much as your enemies, who are my cousins and brothers, my aunts and uncles, and sisters. Why, that would be *treachery*, Kikamana. Treason of the worst kind.'

She nodded and laughed. He really was an interesting man. Not a demon, but a man. One day she might have to use her powers to find keys to those secrets of his. But for now, it hardly mattered. They were not necessary to her.

'You came to see me,' she reminded him, 'about the king.'

His face took on a worried frown. 'I understand from him that there's a plot to make Kula fall in love with him – using some potion made from herbs.'

'He told you this?'

'Yes,' said Seumas, 'in an unguarded moment.'

'And?'

'I want to know if you approve of this plot, or whether you're simply carrying out the king's orders.'

Kikamana sighed and pulled her bark-cloth wrap more closely around her.

'My honest opinion is that it'll lead to more sorrow for King Tangiia in the end.'

Seumas nodded, as if this was the answer he had expected.

'I also understand,' he said, 'that you have another potion, which has the opposite effect?'

'The corrective. Yes, I can brew that too.'

Seumas leaned forward, close to her ear. Kikamana felt a certain distaste at having a man's lips so close to her face, but she realised he was merely trying to impart something. She listened intently.

'Why don't you,' whispered Seumas, 'just give this – corrective – to the king? Pretend to give Kula the love-juice, but instead give her something harmless. Tell the king he needs to take the potion too, but give him the corrective.'

'And the purpose of this?'

'To make the king fall out of love with Kula. Once he doesn't love her, it won't matter that we've tricked him, will it. She'll mean nothing more to him than a pig's orphan.'

Kikamana raised her eyebrows. 'You have a strange way of describing emotions.'

The Farseeing-virgin sat for a while and thought over this scheme from the Pict and it seemed to her to be the answer to several problems. Her integrity as a high priestess would have been stretched to the limits, if she had been party to the enslavement of a lovely young woman. As it was, Seumas's plan offered the king escape from his misery, and Kikamana herself an ethical way out of her dilemma. The king would no longer be entranced by Kula, captive to her charms, but free to concentrate upon the main task of navigating. He had for too long been brooding, his heart full of longing, his head spinning with the very real torture of unrequited love. Once freed from his obsession, the whole community would benefit.

'Excellent,' she told Seumas. 'An excellent plan.'

'Good,' breathed Seumas. 'I hoped it was.'

Kikamana said, 'Leave everything to me, but let me ask you, have you been this close to a king before?'

'Never – I told you, I'm a peasant – a bird-collector, a lowly warrior.'

'Well, you seem to have taken to court intrigue as if you were born for it.'

Seumas smiled, saying, 'You must think there's no limit to my talents. By the way, you can give some of that potion to me – the stuff that makes you fall out of love.'

Kikamana frowned a little, then said, 'Ahh, the dark-eyed Celt. Are you still pining?'

'I shall always pine,' replied Seumas, grimly. 'Though *pining* is not the word I would use. I still have hopes that one day she will come chasing after me.' He grinned, sheepishly.

'There's always hope,' replied Kikamana. 'After all, we carry the God of Hope with us, here on this very pahi.'

'By accident.'

'Accident or design, it matters not – he is with us and will watch over us, for we revere his image.'

He stood up then, and left the hut, walking out into the bright sunshine. Kikamana could see him afterwards, standing on the bows of the canoe, his legs entangled in the rainbows produced by the fine spray, his head somewhere in the clouds. Their conversation had given her a great deal of respect for the Pict. She hoped there would be more talks.

King Tangiia was by the mast, surveying the roof of voyaging with a critical eye. It seemed that a squall was about to descend upon the fleet. The wind was strong, the waves increasing in size and strength. Maomao was about to give Tangaroa another whipping. Tangiia had been following a te lapa streak at the same time as urging his rowers to catch up with the marvellous man-fish who was still drawing the fleet off its chosen course. The king had made some nets in which he hoped to catch the weird creature and study it at close hand.

Behind *The Scudding Cloud*, the other two pahi were visible, keeping in sight-contact with one another. All six crab-claw sails were straining at the seams in the rising wind. Children were huddled in the huts, protected from the flying spume by the bodies of their mothers. All able-bodied men stood by, ready to handle the sheets, if the sails had to be rolled up suddenly to reduce the area exposed to the wind.

During Tangiia's visit to the other canoes, while they were moored by the sandspit island, both captains had argued strongly with Tangiia on the folly of pursuing the adaro, but Tangiia would listen to neither of them. It seemed he was bewitched by the creature and would lead the fleet to its doom rather than give up the chase.

Near to the mast, just inside the doorway of one of the huts, sat Princess Kula. When Tangiia cast a casual glance her way, she glared at him, wasting no opportunity to let him know she hated him. She was shocked and surprised when his returning look was one of indifference. Normally his expression would either be one of piteous unhappiness, or one of defiant determination to win her in the end. In either one she read of his forlorn hope of love from her.

The look that he had just given her, however, appeared to indicate that he couldn't care less whether she loved or hated him. It was as if she were *nothing* to him.

Kula was puzzled. She knew that all she should feel was relief, that the young man was over her at last. She tried to tell herself how glad she was that he would not bother her any longer with those wistful stares, or with his whispered entreaties. No more would she need to scorn him, turn her shoulder to his advances, curl her lip in contempt whenever he tried to accost her. It was a *good* thing, wasn't it?

Yet she felt puzzled. What had happened to change him so abruptly? Young men, and indeed young women, could not switch from love to indifference in a moment. Was he faking his feelings, trying to make her think he had gone cold on her? Yes, that must be it. She would test this theory.

Kula stood up and adjusted her skirt. Her clothing was damp and clung to her trim figure, emphasising the firmness of her breasts and the gentle curve of her hips. She stepped out on to the deck and looked up, pretending to examine the weather. Then she turned to Tangiia and said in an offhand tone, 'I suppose you will manage to beat the squall to calmer water?'

He hardly looked at her, replying, 'It would be best if you returned to the hut.'

'Why – are you afraid for my safety?' she asked, haughtily.

He turned and looked at her with empty, cold eyes. 'Your personal safety is your own concern, not mine. I have the fleet to consider. I can't be bothered with individuals.'

Again she was shocked by the complete lack of regard in his expression. This was not acting! He really was more concerned with his duty than he was with her well-being. In the past he had whispered that he would die for her, kill for her, destroy the fleet and all its passengers and crew if she willed it. Now it seemed he could not care less whether she was swept overboard by a freak wave and sank to oblivion!

'Thank you for your advice,' she snapped. 'I'm well able to take care of myself.'

'Stop bothering me with your chatter, woman. Get in the hut with the others. I'm trying to outrun a storm here.'

He turned away from her and began issuing orders to his crew. Despite her indignation at his summary dismissal, she was impressed as always by his seamanship. He seemed to have the situation completely under control. There was a strong air of authority about him that went beyond his age and his rank of navigator king and was inherent in him as a man. She returned to her place in the hut, while the mariners dashed around the deck, loosening sennit sheets, tightening stays, rolling up the crab-claw sail. While they worked, the seafarers chanted a song to the great god Maomao:

'O wind from the top of the world!
Sprung from the chasm
Carrying the scudding clouds over untravelled horizons.
Great wind of Maomao,
Made manifest in the waves of the ocean,
fleeing before the fury of your roar
whose tempestuous blast
swells the rushing tumult of the sea ...'

The women too had their duties, in trying to keep the pandanus flour dry, the pigs from stealing the almonds and chestnuts, the breadfruit and coconuts from rolling away, the sugar-cane from being stolen by the children, the gourds from breaking, vegetarian dogs from making too much noise, and the mountain apples from shrinking in the saltwater spray.

Of the nearly one hundred people on board *The Scudding Cloud* there were few who had nothing to do once a storm threatened.

2

How the Great Wind-God loved playing with his whips! He lashed the back of Tangaroa with his flails until the Great Sea-God's skin rose in giant blisters, to burst and flow in all directions, the white momentary scars running with the rush of fluid. And Tangaroa's tears of anger and pain were evident in the clouds of spray and spume, only to be whisked away by the mighty blast created by Maomao's flogging.

Maomao's great winds opened the heavens for two other terrible storm-gods to enter: Apu Matangi, feared by all mariners, God of the Howling Rain, and his equally vicious brother Apu Hau, God of the Fierce Squall.

The Raiatean fleet were caught on the edge of this storm, which Maomao intended as a warning. The Great Wind-God was annoyed with King Tangiia for allowing himself to become entranced by the adaro. Maomao knew that men were fickle, inquisitive creatures, weak of flesh and spirit, and the gods could play with them as a child played with toys. It grieved Maomao that he had to remind his fledglings that their task was not to become sidetracked by wondrous sights, but to seek a new Faraway Heaven, somewhere on the wide world of the ocean.

To those on board the three pahi canoes, the wind and the sea had become one entity, inseparable. The air was white with spray which lashed at the mat sails, shaking them as if they were the branches of a tree. The masts creaked and threatened to snap and go flying out into the darkness. It was day, but it was night, and the canoes were flung between the wavetops like coconuts tossed from hand to hand at harvest time.

The Raiateans wailed and cried to their gods, begging for mercy, thinking they were all about to drown, while the crews fought with lines and paddles, trying to keep the canoes heading into waves that changed direction with almost every sweep of water. There were mountains where there had been plains, immense troughs that fell to the centre of the earth.

At times the vessels were almost vertical, falling down a sheer wall of water. It seemed at those times that they must plunge bows-first into the heart of the ocean and continue down to be buried under the massive deluge which had overwhelmed them.

At other times they clawed their way up precipitous slopes like a man tries to climb a cliff of loose scree. It seemed on occasion that the wave up which they were ascending would curl over and enfold them in its bosom, loving them to their deaths. Then miraculously the wave would flatten, the hump of water would run under their hulls, lifting the pahi high above the world, and then another mighty trough would appear before them, and they would stare down into its maw and once again feel that they were about to disappear into the salivating mouth of the Great Sea-God Tangaroa, who was displeased with them.

How flimsy their majestic pahi canoes seemed to them now, the pegs loosening in the hulls and flying free, the lashings on the logs squealing and shrieking like live creatures, the timbers grinding and grating and trying to change places. Those fixtures which had taken ten men to tighten, using capstans of rope, rock and pole, were now easily unfastened with the twists and turns of the crazy flood.

Here and there the currents met with such fierce opposition to one another that vortexes appeared, swirling in dizzying rings which turned to hollow cones. The crews fought as if they were mad, to keep clear of the sudden maelstroms that came and went like the furious ghosts of ancestors. Sometimes the vessels were caught and carried, racing, around the lip of one of these giant whirlpools, until terrified men and women dug in their paddles and fought against the suction with wide, wild eyes and frantic arms until they managed to pull themselves free.

For a day and a half they were battered and beaten, exhausted beyond sleep, until they finally emerged from the side of the storm into a place of calm.

It was in this tranquil state that Kikamana consulted with Rangi, through the medium of her ancestors and confirmed what she and Boy-girl had suspected for a long time, even before landing on Nuku Hiva. Rangi the Great Sky-God sees all things under his roof of voyaging, for nothing is lost from his gaze except those trapped inside Hau Maringi's fogs and mists.

Kikamana learned that the fleet was being stalked; someone was in pursuit. Her atua would give her no names, for the ancestors and gods will not provide such details, but a great flotilla of canoes decked out for war followed in their wake, an angry and violent admiral at their head.

When she spoke with Makka-te about this, he pronounced her knowledge unsafe.

'One cannot trust one's atua's *completely*,' he said. 'Ancestor spirits are inclined to exaggerate. Perhaps there are but one or two vessels following us? I shouldn't alarm the king unduly. It will only make him anxious.'

At first Kikamana saw the sense in this advice. If the king was worried about a pursuer it might impair his ability to navigate. It was enough to find his way across the vast ocean and to contend with the elements and gods, let alone concern himself with a hunter. Yet, in the end, her conscience would not let her withhold the information. Knowledge passed to her from their ancestors was not meant to be kept secret, otherwise it would never have been given in the first place.

Kikamana held a meeting with King Tangiia and Makka-te.

'Someone is after us – they hunt us over the seas. I had a dream before we came to Nuku Hiva that there was a dark cloud tracking our wake across the ocean. I spoke with Makka-te about this, but he said we should not alarm you until we were sure.'

Makke-te nodded thoughtfully. A naturally reserved and private person, he was a priest whose feelings were never wholly evident. He was, however, respected for his gravity and impartiality.

'Well,' continued Kikamana, 'now I am sure.'

'Who is it?' asked Tangiia.

Kikamana shook her head, but Makka-te said, 'We can guess who it is – the man so blinded with hatred for you, he cannot see straight ...'

Tangiia said, 'My brother?'

'Who else?' muttered Makka-te, grimly.

It was a green ocean into which the adaro had led their navigator king, with a curious green light to the sky. Rangi and Tangaroa were wearing similar verdant cloaks. It was a still place, with barely a breath of wind blowing. The fish there were lazy and seemed not to care if they were caught or went free.

Their torpid forms floated to the surface, dull in their lethargy. Their eyes did not shine, but were filmy and grey. Their scales were lacklustre too, barely reflecting the greenness of the sea and sky around them.

Weed floated in great clumps, going nowhere, becoming entangled with the paddles, slowing the fleet to a standstill at times. There was ribbon sea-weed, and the blistered variety, but worst of all was the blanket weed, thin strands that had multiplied to become an impenetrable mass of green slime. It almost seemed to crawl up the gunwales, like an animate creature, in an attempt to overwhelm the canoes.

In the patches where there was no weed, flotillas of listless jellyfish hung in the water, trailing their frills and streamers in a desultory fashion. They pulsated sluggishly in the hot day as if gathering their strength for some long journey, and when a hapless fish glided into their path only then did their tentacles drift out and sting the creature to death, afterwards to hold the corpse in a loose embrace, waiting for it to rot.

'I don't like this place,' said Kula to Kikamana. 'It has an air of decay about it.'

'It is a place we should leave as soon as possible!' agreed the priestess.

They meandered languidly in this green, slumberous world, until they came upon an exposed reef without an island, part of an underwater ridge that ran like a whale's dorsal fin along a stretch of ocean. On this lonely place the waves beat slowly and with deep, resonant tones, as if drumming against a vane of coral-tipped rock that went down a thousand fathoms.

Here the women and men seafarers disembarked to collect their preferred diet of shellfish which had been denied them on the voyage, since it was necessary to eat such fare on the day of the gathering.

Using bone hooks to feel under the ledges, for fear of being bitten by fish or stung by the waving fronds of pretty anemones, they collected the boun-teous harvest of the reef: the gastropods – strawberry tops, green helmets, harps, conches, mermaids' combs, violet snails, textile cones, murexes, shiny olives, white cowries, spires and variegated screws; the bi-valves – frog shells, clams, scallops, thorny oysters; and finally, the stickers – the abalones, lim-pets, barnacles.

The treasures of the reef, which the Raiateans had done without on their voyage so far, were eagerly garnered like glittering jewels, their colours, shapes and patterns unmatched by any other set of animate creatures over the whole and copious earth. The shells themselves would become orna-ments, or containers, after the molluscs had gone for sustenance. The harvesting in itself was a time full of excitement and chatter, even in such a place of strange light and sonorous sound.

After the feasting was over they set off again and in the evening of that same day came upon an island.

There was no reef encircling the island, which had the same torpid atmosphere about it as the sea in which it rested. In the centre of the island was an arrogant volcano with an open mouth, breathing sulphur gases into the atmosphere. The smell of these gases mingled with the heavy, cloying perfume of orchids and wafted across the bay inducing a heavy-lidded sleepiness on the Raiateans. Thick-winged birds circled on high thermals, like the dark souls of forgotten precursors.

The Raiateans felt drugged and insensible, unable to think straight.

King Tangiia said, 'This time *I* shall take some men ashore and gather provisions.'

'Is that wise?' asked Kikamana. 'We know nothing about this place. Why not let Manopa go, or Po? They did well enough on Nuku Hiva.'

'Yes, that's why it's my turn,' said the young man. Then in an extraordinary outburst, cried, 'Why does that woman keep looking at me like that? Get her out of my sight.'

He was referring to Princess Kula, who turned and went away of her own accord, her face a scene of misery.

At noon the men were collected, the dugouts lowered into the water, and their king joined them. They paddled towards the shore and landed on the beach without mishap. Immediately, they began gathering coconuts from the palms along the beach. Then the search began of the hinterland for yam, taro, sweet potato, breadfruit, plantain and banana. This was unusually easy. All were found in abundance, much to the surprise of Tangiia.

The dugouts, with two-man crews, ferried the goods back to the pahi canoes standing offshore. When it appeared that enough had been gathered, Tangiia then took his men further inland, to the base of the volcano, where the rich soil made the vegetation thick and lush. It was coming on evening and the greenness had changed to a rosy glow, partly due to the sunset, and partly due to the red hotness of the volcano's mouth.

Here an unbearable weariness came upon the party and they sank to the mossy floor of the rainforest and fell into a slumber. All except Tangiia, who, though fatigued, forced himself to stay awake in case they were attacked by hostile natives.

When the women came, Tangiia was not sure if he had fallen into a dream. They were the most beautiful creatures he had ever laid eyes on. Had he been of a sound spirit he would have been instantly aroused as the naked women silently lay down beside his men, one or two to each.

'Men,' whispered Tangiia, hoarsely, 'keep your senses – don't be bewitched ...'

One of these wondrous females came to him, smiling, her breath smelling of sugar, her hair of sweet-scented oils. Her eyes were unfathomable, as deep and rich as the roof of voyaging at night. Her skin was dusty-dark, soft as frangipani petals. Her parted lips were wet with tonguing, desire evident in their trembling. There were shadows on her lovely face, where the high cheekbones met her eyes.

She bent down to him and pressed her bosom against his chest, wrapping her thighs around his right leg. He could feel the hard nipples rasping against his skin. The mound between her legs was as soft and as yielding as a ripe fruit.

On the mossy bank below him, Tangiia witnessed his men, now awake, making love to the women in their arms. There was a raw, revived energy in them as they struggled with the effort of carnal enjoyment. However, each man soon came to the point of ecstasy, but once his orgasm was over, another woman came to him and aroused him again, beginning the passion all over again, from start to finish. The men seemed unable to resist the onslaught of these gentle but persistent maidens, who were insatiable in their sexual appetites.

Again and again the men performed, becoming more and more exhausted with each encounter. Yet still the women continued with their whispered supplications for love, love and yet more love. The men groaned and begged to be left alone, but each new orgasm brought a fresh companion, and the cycle seemed endless.

As Tangiia stared down upon this unreal scene he felt powerless to stop it. It was true that he himself was able to resist the charms of these lovely females, but he felt so drugged by the languid atmosphere he could make no move to assist his men. One by one the women came to him too, to stroke his body, whisper unintelligible words into his ear, and attempt to mount him even though he had no erection.

Finally, he managed to scream at the top of his voice and with his lei-o-mano he slashed at the woman crawling over his body, desperately trying to arouse him.

The blade seemed to pass through her form, though she leapt to her feet and ran into the rainforest. Her fleeing gave Tangiia the strength he needed to get up. Once standing he charged down the incline to the glade where his men were in the last throes of love. The women scattered before his attack, disappearing like wraiths into the undergrowth. Tangiia quickly gathered his men together, to lead them back to the shore.

Two men were already dead, their bodies drained of their lifeforce, while the others could barely stagger back to the shoreline. There they quickly boarded the dugouts and paddled back to the pahi canoes.

'Make sail immediately!' Tangiia cried, then went to see the priestess Kikamana.

He explained to Kikamana what had happened and asked if she had an explanation.

'There is an island,' she told him, 'called Kaitalugi, where shipwrecked seafarers are washed up on to the beach. There they are seized and raped by a crowd of naked women. Once a woman has had one man, the next one will take him, until the men finally die of exhaustion.'

'This must be that island,' said Tangiia, fiercely. 'The man-fish led us here.'

'You were bewitched by the adaro,' agreed Kikamana.

'Now these monstrous females have killed two of my men!'

Kikamana's eyes turned hard and she shook her head. 'If they are monstrous, it's because men have made them so. These women were banished from their home islands, set adrift in open boats and left to die. The Great Sea-God led them to this island, just as he has led us, to give them a home.

'Now the injured sau of those women seek justice and revenge for their maltreatment. They have the power of enchantment, the power to bewitch men. They wait for shipwrecked seafarers, who are unable to resist them, manifest themselves in human form, and rape the men to exhaustion and death. I myself do not blame them – their grievances were many ...'

Tangiia asked, 'What did they do to deserve banishment?'

'Refused a man intercourse, cried "rape" when they were being taken against their will, ran away from violent husbands.'

'But these are not crimes.'

'They were on some islands, in some places, at one time or another. Perhaps there are still islands where the woman has no rights and is treated worse than a dog? Considering all things,' Kikamana added, 'the men die a painless death – you could say they kill themselves. Poetically.'

Tangiia hung his head for a moment, then said, 'I've come to my senses at last. We must sail with the wind, let Maomao take us to our destiny ...' He paused to incline his head towards the entrance to the deck hut, which had darkened with a form. Seumas had entered, his dog at his heel. After a moment of silence Tangiia continued, '... what I don't understand, is how I was able to resist those women, while my men succumbed?'

'I gave you a drug, just before the storm – don't you remember?'

'I remember you gave me a *drink*,' said Tangiia. 'You gave one to Princess Kula, at the same time.'

'Hers was a harmless concoction.'

'And mine?'

'A potion to enable you to resist love, in all its forms.'

Tangiia frowned again. 'Why would you give me a potion like that, without my permission?'

'You were besotted – with – with the *adaro*. I believed the concoction would cure you of your obsession.'

Tangiia nodded, thoughtfully, 'I see – yes, that makes sense – but now I want you to give me something to counter the drug. It bothers me, this tampering with my emotions, my feelings. Next time, you should persuade me, not give it to me without my consent. You could have poisoned me.'

'I shall remember that, King Tangiia.'

After the king had left the hut, Seumas came forward and placed a hand on Kikamana's shoulder, staring into her eyes.

'I could have sworn you told a lie there, high priestess, but of course for a person with your views on morality, that's impossible. I must have been mistaken.'

Kikamana gave him back the stare with full measure.

'Be reassured, you *are* mistaken.'

'Yes, yes, I thought I was. Come on, Dirk, let's get out on deck, I think the captain's come to his senses at last. We're heading back on our true course again. Come on, boy, don't dawdle in the presence of a great lady.'

Dirk barked, loudly, looking from the lady to the man and back again, aware that something was amusing his master, but being a dog, was never going to know what it was.

3

Boy-girl's obsession with Seumas had begun the day she saw him stagger from Po's canoe after the great Kupe's magnificent voyage of discovery. A man with a pure white skin! He was ugly to her, yet he was beautiful. She was both repulsed and attracted to him, and this is where fascination begins. There was a desire to touch, but a fear of touch.

Boy-girl had been fourteen at the time, running around decorated with shells and flowers, but naked. Already tall and willowly, though thin rather than slender at this age, her movements were not as artistically feminine as they were to become. She was still, at fourteen, quite gauche.

'Horrid,' she said, as he passed her, his wobbly legs still unused to the firmness of the ground. 'Horrid demon.'

The demon turned, his salt-white, salt-encrusted skin blinding her with its brilliance in the bright tropical sun. His red hair fell around his shoulders like the. long feathers of a precious bird. Hawk-faced, hard-mouthed, he turned his terrible eyes upon her.

When she stared into those eyes, she saw they were an eerie, washed blue and deeply penetrating. Those eyes saw deep into Boy-girl's soul, searched every corner of her being, and she was chilled by a strange fear.

Boy-girl let out a gasp and stepped backwards.

A savage sound came from the demon's mouth as he snarled at her, making her back away even further.

Then Boy-girl realised there were two of them – two white demons – and she stared in wonder. But Seumas was the one who had caught her eye first and he became the object of her obsession. From that point on she wanted to be near him, around him, as often as she could get away with it. Other Raiateans scorned her for it, laughed at her, because they saw only in Seumas a strong man weakened by his obvious displays of masculinity, a man desperate to be seen as a man. Someone who had continually to prove himself tough and uncompromising must, they said, be at heart a very poor specimen of a human being.

But Boy-girl looked deeper than her fellow islanders, having a sharper intellect than most and a wisdom born of the ruthless, detached study of people, and saw the real compassionate strength beneath the weak show of hardness.

When she was older, and her sexual appetites were much stronger, she wanted Seumas with every fibre of her being. Her fantasies were always of him and though she eventually learned to control her obsession there were times when she thought she would go mad with desire.

For his part, Seumas felt his contempt for these islanders was fully justified since he had met this creature – clearly a male – covered in feminine trinkets and wiggling its bottom as it walked. His disgust for what he considered unwholesome girlishness had been effectively deepened by this meeting. On the other hand, he had developed a lasting respect for Kupe and Po, but as navigators and seamen, not as men. He still felt he could beat any one of them in single combat.

Seumas was given an abandoned hut which he was told was his own, unless he wanted to build another. Since he had no idea how to go about building a dwelling out of local materials he repaired the one he had been given and hoped it would not fall down before he had learned the native crafts. He was told he had the same rights as any other islander, though he was never to go off in an ocean voyager without a Raiatean on board.

Dorcha was given a hut close by, but she soon moved when she learned that she and Seumas were to be near neighbours. Dorcha built a teak and coconut hut with a pandanus leaf roof. She seemed to pick up in a week what it took Seumas to learn in several months.

At first the islanders stayed away from both of them – all except Kieto and Boy-girl – but gradually they grew less fearful and then they came to satisfy their curiosity. Seumas barked at them, but they got used to this, and soon one of the young women was sleeping with him.

Boy-girl ambushed this woman, savagely pulling her hair, and tried to claw out her eyes.

Boy-girl was brought before the council and told to stop this kind of thing or she would be banished to an uninhabited island. Boy-girl complied with the ruling, but wept bitter tears into her rolled-mat pillow that night.

Seumas said to Kieto one day, 'I think I am stronger than any of your men – they look too smooth and fat to be good warriors. I think I could beat any man here.'

Kieto, unused to bragging, replied, 'If you think that, you must be right. No one has seen you fight, Seumas, so I must take you at your word.'

After this Seumas began strutting around the island, making people step aside for him on narrow mountain paths, growling at anyone who stared too long.

'I could tear your face from your skull,' he would cry. 'I could blind you with one blow with my fist.'

Not because they were afraid of him, but because they were not familiar with this kind of boast, they looked at him nervously and then hurried on. He began to think of himself as invincible. Men who believe themselves invulnerable actually become overawed by their own power and very often take to bullying. Seumas became a bully.

One day he met a man named Manopa on a jungle path and expected the other to step aside.

'Out of the way, moron,' snarled Seumas.

When Manopa did not relinquish the path, Seumas tried to shoulder past the broad man.

Manopa, short but solid, remained firm.

Enraged, Seumas swung a fist at Manopa's head.

Manopa gave him the hiding of his life.

Seumas crawled back to his hut where Kieto was waiting for him.

'What happened to you?' asked the boy. 'Did you meet a terrible demon?'

'I met a man called Manopa,' mumbled Seumas through thick lips and bloodied gums. 'He must be the best fighter on the whole damned island.'

Kieto said, 'He's a *good* warrior, but there are others who are better. Kupe, who is close to the gods, can beat him of course, and Tutapu, and possibly even ...' and Kieto continued with a list of names that made Seumas wince.

'You mean to say,' said the Pict, 'that he's not that unusual?'

'He's a chief and a very good warrior, but there are many of those on the islands.'

'Just that?'

'Yes.'

From that point on, Seumas began gradually to revise his assessment of the natives. He realised they did not have to prove themselves men every hour of the day, because they were secure in the knowledge that they *were* men.

The night he was beaten, Kieto tended his bruises with local medicine, but Seumas was in a poor condition. One blue-black bruise extended over the whole of his left side and was agony to the touch. In the middle of the night, he felt Kieto rubbing balm into this wound, and was relieved to find that the fire went out of it almost immediately and he was able to sleep.

When Seumas woke the next morning, he found Boy-girl curled up alongside him.

He rolled away, alarmed. 'Wha – What are you doing here, creature?'

Boy-girl opened her eyes sleepily and smiled at him.

'I came to help you – I have mended your hurt side.'

'You slept with me!' cried Seumas, appalled.

'Yes, but you didn't do anything,' said Boy-girl, in a voice that revealed a mixture of annoyance and wistfulness. She was now seventeen and sexually active. 'You were hurt too much to do anything.'

'I don't like boys,' cried Seumas. 'I wouldn't have done anything if I was hale.'

Boy-girl smiled and rattled her shells. 'You never know,' she sighed, 'you might change your mind ...'

As soon as he was well enough, Seumas built a door to his hut, with a bar on the inside, so that he could lock it.

In those early days Kieto used to take him hunting for birds with a slingshot. One day Boy-girl asked to come too.

'We're going hunting, not dancing,' said Seumas, disparagingly. 'Those shells would frighten away an army of birds.'

'I always leave my jewels at home,' said Boy-girl.

Despite Seumas's protests, Boy-girl did come with them that day. The three of them went up into the rainforests to explore the deep valleys between volcanic hills. There it was lush and green and full of life. It seemed the world of the hinterland was thick-stemmed juicy plants, diaphanous mists drifting on the moist air, sudden waterfalls, and lightning streams that cracked down through rock and leaf-mould earth.

Under the canopy, inside the green world, Seumas remarked, 'This is indeed a wonderful land – it's not *my* land, but it's like a good woman – moist and warm and beautiful.'

Boy-girl grunted.

Kieto said, 'This *is* your land now, Seumas. You will become part of it, just as we are.'

Seumas looked at the boy, now in his tenth year. Already Kieto was showing signs of leadership. The other boys of his age, even some of the older ones, looked up to him. He was asked to take them on fishing expeditions or hunting birds. He would organise these trips with care and attention to detail, making sure every member of the party had a part to play, ensuring the best possibility for a good catch or a fine hunt. Seumas had heard what Kupe had once said, that one day Kieto would lead the invasion force on Albainn.

'You will want my help, when you attack the Land-of-Mists, young man –

you shall not have it, no matter how hard you try to make me one of your own.'

Boy-girl smiled sweetly. 'Oh, you will be one of us, Seumas, there's no fighting *that*.'

Seumas began to get angry. 'I say I will not! I have my own mind, I own my own soul. I say I shall never be traitor to my kind. Nothing will turn me into a betrayer.'

Kieto said, 'You will never be traitor to your own kind because *we* will be your people. It is us you will not betray – those others, on your old island – they are not your people any more.'

He said it with such conviction that Seumas almost went into a fury and struck the boy. However, he kept his temper and stared at these two young people, both utterly confident that he would not remain an Albannach at heart, but would become an Oceanian, a nomad of the wind, before the time came to attack the land of his forefathers.

'We shall see,' he growled at last. 'You'll see that I'm right. You are children. You have no concept of what's in a grown man's heart. When you're as old as I am, then you will know how impossible it is that I could betray my people. But one thing you will never completely know or understand – the fierce pride of the Pict, the pride that he has of his homeland, of his clan, of his birthplace. It is steadfast.'

Boy-girl said seriously, 'That may be so, Seumas, but you might not be able to help yourself changing. You're like a taro root taken from one island and planted on another. At first you refuse to flourish, because the new soil is not like your old earth, even though it might be richer – yet, you *will* grow, because the need to survive, the need to live, is strong.'

'I shall *grow*, but not as an islander.'

'Your soul will mellow in our heaven, Seumas, and you will be grafted to us.'

This disconcerted Seumas so much, he decided to change the subject.

'I want no more arguments – let's get on with the hunt. Boy-girl, what are you doing here anyway? You should be back on the beach collecting pretty shells ...'

At that moment a large bird flew overhead. With astonishing speed Boy-girl whirled her slingshot and let fly, striking the bird on the breast. It fell from the sky, almost at their feet. Seumas was amazed by her skill. He stared up at the heavens, then down at the dead wildfowl.

'I made a mistake,' Seumas said, 'unless that was a lucky shot?'

'It wasn't a lucky shot,' Kieto answered him. 'Boy-girl is one of the best slingshots on the island.'

Boy-girl smiled warmly at Seumas.

'You are mistaken about a lot of things, my lovely demon, but don't worry, all will be revealed in time.'

'Don't you try any magic on me,' warned Seumas, panicking a little. 'Don't you do that, or I swear I'll treat you like I used to treat fulmars. I'll wring your skinny neck.'

Boy-girl gave him another sweet smile.

'I mean it!' said Seumas.

Boy-girl pouted. 'Oh, you silly creature, of course I won't make you do anything you don't want to – where would be the fun in that? Anyway, I didn't mean *that*. The trouble with you, Seumas, is you're obsessed with sex …'

Seumas learned a lot that afternoon, hunting with the two people who loved him most on this strange island in this strange ocean. He learned that there was more to Boy-girl than just a pretty face. She was not empty-headed, but intelligent, incisive and an excellent hunter. He was beginning to respect and fear her. Kieto, too, he had discovered was astonishingly single-minded. The youth was not as sharp and deep as Boy-girl, but he was constant to his path. Yes, Seumas believed that one day Kieto would invade Albainn – whether he would conquer it was another matter, but Seumas was determined that nothing, nothing he as a Pict had to offer would be given willingly.

On the way back to their village, bloody birds strung about their necks like pendants, Seumas was taken by his hands, one on either side – Kieto held his right hand, Boy-girl his left. He did not pull away, recognising the simple friendship and honour that was being bestowed upon him as an outsider. It felt uncomfortable, the silky palm of Boy-girl especially, but he bore it, knowing to remove his hand now would be a horrible insult and would do irreparable damage to their relationships.

'One thing is certain,' he said, 'you pair, young as you are, have given me friendship, even though others have laughed at you for it. A Pict never forgets something as valuable as that – I am in your debt. From now on, your enemies are my enemies. I would die, or kill, for you both.'

He said it half in jest, but they all knew that underneath, Seumas was serious.

PART FIVE

The Relentless Pursuer

1

It was night.

Out on the ocean, approaching the island of Fatu Hiva, were three thousand lights from flaming torches. They illuminated the darkness like giant candles as they floated slowly towards the Bay of Virgins. The natives of Fatu Hiva were gathered on the beaches, watching the massed flames draw ever closer, knowing that each one of the brands was held by the hand of a warrior. A foreign fleet had arrived at their island and seeing the number of lights on the vessels which approached, they knew they could not match the invasion. Their chief waited in trepidation for the storming of his island, knowing resistance was useless against such a powerful force.

One of the island's fishermen had been out on open waters during the day and had seen a fleet of tipairua canoes, some thirty in number, all with black sails, heading towards his home island. The canoes had a war-like appearance with their fast v-shaped hulls and had alarmed him. He had fled back to the island as fast as he could, arriving just as dusk was settling. He informed his chief of what he had seen and the whole tribe went down to the beach in despair, to await the arrival of this awesome flotilla.

The lights off-shore were as numerous as fireflies and the local chief knew they had been lit for a purpose and were meant to intimidate him. Indeed, as he waited in agitation, he *felt* very intimidated. A smaller fleet of five hundred, or perhaps even a thousand warriors, would have had him armed to the teeth and waiting with fury in his breast. But the scale and size of this attack was unprecedented and he felt powerless to offer an opposition. His courage had turned to pork jelly.

So, he waited, with gifts of food, carvings, precious shells, red feathers, turtle shells, etched gourds and other treasures at his feet, ready to buy the lives of himself and his islanders.

The chief had removed a necklace of human teeth, taken from enemies, which he usually wore around his throat. The stick crowned with a human skull, normally shaken in defiance at strangers to the island, was hidden under a mat. His war helmet, of feathers on a frame of human skin, was still on its pole just inside the door of his house.

He made himself look as small as possible, stooping and hunching his shoulders, appearing thoroughly pathetic. He had smeared fire-soot on his tattoos, to hide those which proclaimed him a great warrior, afraid of no man. He had brought his three fat wives and their younger children, to show that he was a family man, and not inclined towards war.

Two of the prettiest girls in the tribe flanked him; they were his oldest daughters. He would hand them over without a murmur if necessary. Dishonour before death, in such circumstances.

The fleet moored outside the reef and a small outrigger canoe was launched to come gliding over the reef in a movement timed with the rhythm of the waves. Crossing a reef either way, and landing or launching in beach surf, was the most dangerous part of boatmen's manoeuvres, especially when the reef and beach were unknown to the mariners. Islanders ran into the surf, eager to help beach the outrigger and its crew, anxious to accommodate the foreign admiral.

Men and women on the beach began a song of welcome to the strangers, and a dance which proclaimed that the island was peaceful towards the newcomers. Garlands were brought forward and placed around the necks of the suspicious outlanders.

The crew of the outrigger were armed for war, but when they encountered no resistance and made certain no treachery was intended they signalled the tipairua that all was well. A second outrigger was launched and the fleet's admiral soon stepped out of the surf and on to the beach to confront the local chief, who could see at once by the feathered helmet of the arrogant-looking newcomer that he was in the presence of a great king. He made gestures of obeisance, waved his hand over the array of gifts, nodded smilingly towards his daughters.

'I am King Tutapu of Raiatea and Borabora,' said the stranger in haughty tones. He used the language of seafarers. 'I have some questions to ask of you.'

'Please,' said the chief, 'you are welcome at my fire. Come and rest. There is food and drink ...'

Canoes of warriors from the fleet were being ferried down to the beach now and the gifts were being loaded into the outriggers and shipped out to the tipairua canoes. King Tutapu, surrounded as always by his attendant priests who were also his bodyguards, followed the local chief up to the village, where there was a huge fire with several suckling pigs roasting on spits and many bowls of fruit and vegetables surrounding it.

The king was seated comfortably on a wooden stool and offered a drink of kava juice. One of his priests had first to perform a short ceremony over the kava, to make it worthy of a king and his mana. This ritual seemed to irritate the king a little, since it delayed the quenching of his thirst.

His retinue of priests noticed this and got to work on the rest of the food within a reach of the king. A roasted, impaled wild bird, stuffed with herbs, honey and ants' eggs, was purified for his consumption and placed at his right elbow. A dish of dried beetles, quails' eggs, sea worms and boiled crabs was placed at his left elbow. In front of him were laid platters of cooked turtle's flesh garnished with berries and beans.

The chief sat at the stranger's right hand, while his two lovely daughters, still unsure of their fate and looking frightened and glum, sat on the left side. One played fretfully with a necklace of shells around her slim throat, while the other was anxiously biting her bottom lip. Dancers began swaying around the fire, singing songs of peace and goodwill towards all men.

The king's lesser retainers were arriving now and seating themselves around the fire, waited on by local people. The chief was alarmed to see that one of these newcomers was a woman with a white skin and wild black hair. She looked to the chief very much like a vis – a creature which scratched out the eyes of victims with its long nails and then lapped the blood which flowed from the sockets. In fact the chief looked upwards quickly, at the night sky, to see if the vis was accompanied by its constant companion, a flying corpse still wrapped in its mat and known throughout Oceania as a balepa. Certainly this creature *shined* in the firelight, which was one of the things which gave the vis away to human onlookers.

'What are you staring at?' asked Tutapu. 'My goblin?'

'Ah,' replied the chief, much relieved, 'a tapua? I thought she was something else.'

Once Tutapu had eaten and drunk sufficiently the chief asked him tentatively, 'Er, to what do we owe the honour of this visit from the King of Raiatea and Borabora?'

Tutapu turned a dour face on the chief. 'I'm looking for my brother,' he said.

'Your brother?' laughed the chief nervously. 'What makes you think he might be here?'

'My brother is Prince Tangiia, who left our islands with three pahi canoes and a god belonging to me. The theft of that god has caused me much anguish and loss of prosperity. He stole from Raiatea's Most Sacred, Most Feared, the God of Hope. An island cannot live without hope – it moves into decline, decays and falls apart. Its people have no heart, no spirit, to face the future. It rots from within.

'My brother also stole my future bride. I mean to kill my brother and retrieve my possessions.

'On board my brother's fleet is one of my own men – a spy – who has been releasing homing birds at regular intervals. I have been following the flight path of these birds, sailing my fleet in the direction whence they came. That path leads me to your island.'

'Not to *here*, King Tutapu, surely?' said the chief, falteringly. 'I – I well – we have seen no other fleet.'

Tutapu stared at the chief disconcertingly. The chief became agitated by this look, knowing by it that his life was in the balance. It behove him to do something. The only thing he could think of was to stand up and make an announcement.

'People of my island,' he cried. 'Listen to me. This great king ...' he smiled obsequiously at his guest, 'Tutapu by name, has come in search of a robber, his own brother, a man of foul ways. Is there anyone here who can help the king? The brother, curse his repulsive name, is voyaging in three great pahi canoes and is believed to be in this part of the ocean.'

The chief anxiously searched the faces of his people in the firelight to see if anything had registered.

No one spoke.

The chief had visions of his village being razed to the ground, the men all clubbed to death, and himself (along with the tender babies) spitted and roasted alive, while all the females and young boys were raped. He could offer his services to the invader king of course, in return for his own life, but there was no room on the canoes for the whole village. He kept this idea in abeyance, until he was sure that none of his people had seen or heard of anything to do with the matter.

'Anyone at all?' he cried, desperately.

Of course, he might be able to kill the king in single combat, but how would that help him? And somehow, looking at the tall, disdainful warrior-king, the chief had an idea that it would not be an easy thing to subdue this man.

'Anything?' he cried, plaintively.

His men all looked down at the earth. His women shuffled on the soles of their feet. Not a sound came from them.

Why doesn't one of you stand up and tell a lie? thought the chief, angrily, wishing he had done so the moment King Tutapu had put the question to him. *Pretend, make up a story about three pahi canoes with savage crews who sank a cousin's fishing boat. Fabricate a tale. Are you all so stupid?*

No one spoke.

'I think ...' began the chief, wondering whether a quick smash at the stranger's skull with his patu club, then a glorious last battle, which would almost certainly lead to his defeat and death, might not be the best option after all.

However, the decision was taken away from him by a cry in the night.

'I have seen these three pahi canoes!'

The chief whirled. 'Who spoke?'

'Me! Polahiki, here – in the captive's hut!'

At the back of the village was a small, strong hut built of hardwood. It had no windows. There was a heavy log roof and a thick trapdoor without a handle. It was only three feet high, so that any man of normal height kept inside the hut would have to be on his knees the whole while, yet it seemed too short for a human inhabitant to lie full length within its walls. The whole structure was smeared on the outside with dogshit. Dead, rotting rats hung from the eaves. There was a slit through which a slim container of water or food could be passed. Through the slit, crawling with cockroaches and ants where slops had been spilt and had dried, poked some fingers with dirty broken nails. Blowflies crept over the fingers and in and out of the crack.

The smell of the hut and its unwashed inhabitant was nauseating.

'The prisoner,' said the chief, relieved. 'We took him on the last raid.'

'You raided another island?' questioned Tutapu. 'Which island was that?'

'No, no – they raided *us*, great king. They attacked a village on the far side of Fatu Hiva, taking the inhabitants away, carrying them back to Nuku Hiva. That's where those men come from. The Nuku Hivans are a war-crazy people, O king, unlike us who strive for peace and harmony.' He smiled silkily at the unmoved Tutapu. 'We arrived at the raided village just before dawn to find these two fiends, these dregs of a since-departed war fleet, still remaining, looting and pillaging graves. We took them prisoner, to hold them as hostages. One of them has since died, of, er, *neglect* and zealous overseeing, if you understand me.'

'Bring the speaker here,' ordered Tutapu.

The man from Nuku Hiva was brought before Tutapu and forced to his knees. He would have actually gone down on his knees quite willingly, if they had let him. He smiled through the pigshit that had dried on his face, flung there by angry villagers when he had run the gauntlet. A huge hut spider was caught in the tangle of his hair and struggled there, trying to free its hairy legs. He seemed not only unconcerned but actually oblivious of this arachnid.

There were bruises and lacerations all over the fisherman's body and his left arm hung limp, as if broken below the elbow. He knew he was in the presence of a great warlord and the right answers to the questions might bring him his freedom.

'You have seen these three pahi canoes?' he was asked.

'Not personally, O great one, but when I arrived back at Nuku Hiva after a few days' fishing out on the open sea, one of our chiefs lay dead and several of his bodyguard were also dead – killed by seafarers who had called at Nuku Hiva the day before I arrived home.'

'Were there any names? Can you tell me a name? You go free if I hear a certain name.'

The man picked at the hardened pig dung on his cheek.

'No, O great king, but I have something just as good as a name, something just as sure. Can I bargain with you, O Royal One? What is on offer here, may I ask?'

Polahiki was procrastinating, playing accepted local games, but he had misjudged his audience.

An angry Tutapu leapt to his feet and raised his kotiate club.

'Tell me guickly, before I smash your skull!'

'A demon, great king,' gabbled the terrified fisherman, hand up to protect his head. 'A demon as white as that one over there by the fire,' he pointed. 'Only it was a male tapua – a white demon who spoke strange harsh words – words from the Otherworld. This tapua killed one of our chiefs. He fought like a demon would fight – with high screeching yells and strange movements – not like a warrior from Oceania at all, but like a madman from the Underworld. Does this answer your question? Do not kill me, O king. I'm not worth the effort of washing the blood and hair from your club.'

Tutapu slowly lowered his weapon, staring at the man in front of him as if ascertaining whether or not he was telling the truth. Finally, he nodded, briskly.

'Clean this creature and put him on my tipairua,' ordered the king. 'Men, eat and drink your fill, then load the canoes with provisions. Dorcha, come here. Talk to me while we walk back to the shore. I want your opinion.'

The grateful Nuku Hivan fisherman was led away, knowing he would live, even if he had to sail with a foreign fleet.

The local chief heaved a sigh of relief, glad to be out of the spotlight at last. His daughters were whisked away into the rainforest, ordered not to return until the great fleet had left the shores. The chief then set about trying to preserve as much of his produce and goods as possible, by whispering to his villagers as he passed them, telling them to hide some of their breadfruit, taro, pandanus flour and other provisions in covered pits in the rainforest, so that they would have something to eat once the invading forces had gone from the island.

The Great Sea-God showed his favour towards the flotilla of tipairua canoes by giving them a favourable current to follow in the direction of the fleet of three pahi canoes. Tangaroa was not especially fond of Hau Maringi, the God of Mists and Fog, whose prejudiced efforts on behalf of King Tutapu were forever being thwarted by the Great Wind-God. On the other hand, Kuku Lau's mirages, in favour of Tangiia, were becoming less effective because of Tutapu's knowledge of her partisanship.

On the whole the gods did not like to be witnessed interfering in human affairs, but tended to do things on the sly. Io, the Father of the Gods, could be unusually harsh towards a god, great or not, who showed partiality and prejudice towards individual mortals. Meddling in earthly matters was considered to be rather beneath a god's or goddess's full attention. A casual adjustment here and there during an idle moment was acceptable, but a full-blooded interest might lead to more serious consequences.

There had been wars amongst the gods before. Their jealousy of each other's powers was legendary. Their imperious tempers were always close to the surface. Human conflicts might easily overspill into a divine war, if the gods took the affairs of humankind too seriously. So they pretended superficial interest and worked their ways through cunning.

After Tangiia had left the shores of Raiatea for ever, Tutapu had been willing to let him go, even after the discovery that a god had been stolen. It was true that Tangiia was a thief and a kidnapper, having abducted Princess Kula, but Tutapu was ready to swallow these insults if it meant that he did not have to kill his brother and slaughter a large proportion of his subjects in order to become king of the two islands.

However, following Tangiia's departure something seemed to go wrong with life on Borabora and Raiatea. It was not that disasters arrived to destroy the islands in the shape of winds or waves, or disease or famine, or stronger invading forces, but somehow the *life* seemed to go out of the islands.

There was the dull pall of depression hanging over the community which never seemed to dissipate. Everyone was listless, apathetic, and little work was done. Crops were planted in a desultory fashion, simply stuck in the ground without the usual rotting fish often buried with the shoot or root to fertilise it and help it to flourish. Little hunting was done, hardly any fishing, no gathering. People sat about their huts and moped, remarking that life was one long boring day after another and that death was beginning to look attractive.

'What's happened here?' asked the frustrated Tutapu of his high priest Ragnu. 'Why all this lethargy, this indolence?'

Ragnu had the answer ready. 'Your brother took the God of Hope with him, my king. Without hope we cannot survive. Without hope we shall languish and die. No one can live without hope – not for ever.'

Tutapu had brooded on this and came to see the truth in Ragnu's words. The God of Hope might be a minor god but he was absolutely essential to the well-being of the islands' peoples. No one could survive long without hope; eventually despair would engulf them and wither them away.

'Can we not carve a God of Hope?' he asked Ragnu.

The high priest's answer was plain. 'We already have one – the fact that it is out on the ocean is an unhappy circumstance for the people of these islands. There are not *two* Gods of Hope, only one.'

So Tutapu ordered the building of a mighty flotilla of ocean-going canoes, but with a war aspect to their design. These were the thirty tipairua canoes, each of which would carry a hundred people. In order to build them Tutapu had to deforest the island of Borabora and this caused him great anguish. He blamed his brother for the devastation of his favourite island and swore that instead of placing a rotting fish at the roots of each new sapling, as it was planted, he would put the decomposing corpse of a man, one for every new tree.

The king sent for Dorcha, who was ushered into his presence.

'I am going to pursue my brother across the great ocean,' said Tutapu. 'We have to recapture the God of Hope. I shall destroy my brother and then return here, to these islands. I intend to kill every one who went with him on that voyage and you have often expressed the desire to extract some sort of revenge on Seumas, who I understand was instrumental in your first husband's death? You may come with me on my expedition and fulfil that desire.'

Dorcha hesitated for a few moments, then replied, 'Good – I shall make ready.'

'Will you take your two husbands with you?'

Of late the twins had been quarrelsome and bad-tempered. Dorcha had been considering leaving the hut and finding herself a new home. The twins did little but squabble with each other over petty issues like who left an item where, and whose turn it was to do a chore, and Dorcha was thoroughly fed up with them. In fact she was sick to death of living with men and had decided to do without them. Until now she had deliberately avoided becoming pregnant, making her husbands wear a root skin over their penises when they made love to her.

Now she was regretting that, for a child would be a good companion for a woman alone.

The reason Dorcha had agreed to go with the expedition was not because she still desired Seumas's death, but because life had lost its meaning after he had left the islands. It had been a mistake to let him go alone, for when he was around she had some target at which to direct the anger that simmered in her breast. Tormenting Seumas had become one of her reasons for living, so she now believed, and since he was no longer there an emptiness had begun to grow within her. She could account for the feeling inside her no other way. Why else would she feel bereft? Why else was she experiencing a feeling of loss, if not for the joy of inflicting suffering on the hated Pict?

'I would prefer it if my two husbands didn't come,' Dorcha told King Tutapu. 'They bicker too much.'

The king agreed with this decision. In his opinion twins brought bad luck upon a voyage. This had been contended by his grandfather and he had no reason to disbelieve it. The twins would stay behind on the islands, when the flotilla sailed.

Once the tipairua canoes were built, and equipped with mat crab-claw sails stained black to symbolise the gravity of the expedition, Tutapu appointed his cousin Haari as regent and set sail. In his heart he carried no hatred, but a determination to destroy his wayward brother. He intended to hunt Tangiia down and slay him, thus to recover the God of Hope and end all contention to Tutapu's kingly authority.

Tutapu felt he had justice on his side, only occasionally recalling that it had been his own threats which had chased Tangiia from the islands in the first place.

Tutapu's course was apa toa on the windflower.

The king was, like his brother, a good navigator, having been taught by the same tutor, their father. Tutapu was especially good at short-haul navigation and always knew when the flotilla was close to islands. His keen eyes were able to detect *reflected waves*, which were of a barely discernible different shape to ordinary waves on the open waters.

Reflected waves are those waves caused by rebounding off an island or reef, rather than simply the product of wind and currents. By calculating their direction it was possible for a navigator to determine the location of an island or atoll.

Also, Tutapu was a great bird watcher. He knew those species of bird which slept ashore at night and fed on fish out in the open ocean during the day. In the early morning the birds flew out to the fishing shoals and when night came they returned to their island nests. Thus they were land-finding for a keen-eyed navigator, who could follow their direction.

Dorcha asked him one day to teach her the names of the birds which helped him find land.

'The makitopaa, mauakena, katoko, ngao and rakiia,' replied Tutapu without hesitation. 'But you would have difficulty in recognising which was which, when they are high in the air and have the sun behind them. They are all booby and noddy birds. We do not use for example the frigate bird, ropaa uvea, or the nanae, the sooty tern. These are unreliable.'

'What about that one up there,' Dorcha pointed to a white bird with a long, slim, red tail, which seemed to dance backwards in the sky. 'It's very beautiful.'

The bird was as elegant and lovely as a heavenly spirit. Its white trailing feathers wafted the air with such grace that Dorcha believed it was nothing less than the soul of a goddess, made manifest in the warm currents of the air and the torn lacy spindrift of high lazy waves. It was delicately fashioned from sea spume, light and airy as a cloud, and it danced in the blue sky with entrancing movements, bewitching the watcher. Dorcha felt her own soul dancing with the bird, using a light zephyr as a trapeze, floating between earth and ocean on angel's wings.

'I don't know the name of this bird – it must be local to these islands,' replied Tutapu.

A partially washed Polahiki, with badly cropped hair and crooked teeth, was sitting not far away on the deck, waiting to be called officially into the presence of the king. His scrawny body had been oiled, to protect the king's nose from its usual offensive odour, and the fisherman had been given a new, long, bark-cloth skirt which gave him a strangely stiff carriage when he walked, as if he was unused to clothes. The only tattoos he bore were around the lips of his mouth, making it look larger and grimmer than a normal mouth. His broken arm, which had set badly at an angle, had been rebroken by a kahuna and placed in wooden splints.

Polahiki said, 'I know this bird. It is called toake, the tropic bird, and we hold it sacred.'

Dorcha was fascinated by the man's mouth, which resembled the orifice of a large fish, opening and closing in the manner of such fish when they lay gasping on the deck.

'Do you use it to find land?' asked Tutapu.

'Some of us do, others say it is not reliable,' replied the fisherman grinning. 'Last night by the fire you saw the maidens dance the courtship dance of the toake bird.'

'I wasn't watching,' replied Tutapu. 'I was more interested in obtaining information.'

At that moment the helmsman called for the king's assistance in determining the angle of the vessel's wake to the canoe's path through the ocean, a necessary exercise in order to find the extent of the craft's leeway drift. The task called for a well-trained eye and a delicate, correcting touch on the steering oar.

Dorcha was about to enter one of the deck huts, when Polahiki spoke to her again.

'What are you?'

Dorcha was stepping carefully amongst men and women who were seated on the deck weaving fishing nets. She turned and stared at the gnarled fisherman, then returned to his side. Having lived amongst the Raiateans and Boraborans for so long now, their interest dulled by familiarity, she was surprised by someone who found her an object of curiosity.

'What do you mean, what am I? I'm a woman.'

Polahiki reached out and touched her leg, which she withdrew sharply.

He said, 'I've never seen a creature like you before. You must be made by magic. Who made you?'

His gaunt face was looking up at her expectantly, as if he thought he was about to hear some secret of the universe.

'Who made me?' she laughed. 'My mother made me.'

'And your father?'

'Well, he had a little to do with it, but not much. I'm told my mother met him on the road to the southern lowlands and they spent the night in the heather. Apart from a brief coupling, it was my mother who did all the making.'

'Ahh, and was she of the same paleness of skin?'

'Just the same,' smiled Dorcha. 'Except that she was more beautiful than me.'

'I'm very glad for her sake,' said Polahiki, 'because you are quite ugly.'

Stung by this, Dorcha said, 'I know I'm not young any more – I shall be thirty in a few years – still I have a good face and a good body. I'm not yet a crone.'

'I know nothing of your age, but you have an ugly skin – and those marks around your cheeks and nose – what are they?'

Dorcha touched her face. 'Freckles? Some men like them.'

'Not me,' shuddered the scrawny fisherman. 'I think they're hideous. You look like a lizard that's losing its scales. Is the white demon who killed one of our chiefs – is he your brother? Were you spawned by the same lizard-woman?'

'No – that is, I wasn't spawned by a lizard. I'm a person just like you.'

Polahiki shook his head violently. 'Oh, no, you're not like me – I'm a real mortal. I may rob graves and corpses, but at least I'm true flesh and bone.'

Dorcha said, 'I find *you* quite repulsive too. You look like a man of sticks. You have no meat on you.'

'Me?' cried the fisherman. 'How can you insult me, you pasty sow? The reason I'm thin is so that my fingers can get into small places, reach into graves without digging too much. Anyway, it helps when you get captured by foes.'

Dorcha had decided it was best to ignore the man's insults, since they seemed to get worse when she chastised him.

'How does it help?'

'Why,' he grinned, his teeth long pegs in his narrow jaw, 'who would want to roast and eat me? A chicken would make a better meal. A rat would be tastier.'

She nodded. 'I see what you mean.'

'I shall make myself useful to this king of yours. It seems he is about to have a battle with his brother? There'll be a few corpses around afterwards, I expect. Eh?'

'It's not a prospect for joy,' she chided him.

'Oh yes it is – plenty of bodies to rob of their necklaces and bracelets. Many weapons to gather. Plenty of stones and precious shells. An abundance of red feathers to pluck from the helmets of the fallen warriors. There'll be a singing in my heart after the fight. And the beauty of it is, you see,' he said in a confidential manner, as if imparting trade secrets, 'it doesn't matter who wins and who loses. Just so long as the fight is bloody and leaves plenty of carcasses.'

'You're disgusting,' said Dorcha.

'Yes and I want to be rich as well.'

She left the gloating fisherman and stepped again through the squatting people on the deck, trying to keep her feet clear of the nets which were growing in size and number. Inside the deck hut Dorcha sat next to a young girl of fourteen who had become her constant companion on the voyage. The girl's name was Elo and her mother had died shortly after the fleet had set out from Raiatea. Her father was a bailer and had little time for her, so Dorcha had partly adopted the young person.

'Have you cut the yams like I asked?' said Dorcha, sitting next to the girl.

'Yes,' said Elo, turning a smiling face on to Dorcha, melting the Celt's heart. 'Just as you asked.'

'Good,' smiled Dorcha, hugging Elo. 'The wind is picking up and these waves are making me a little woozy. Do you have a story to tell me, to take my mind off the sea?' Dorcha was actually feeling fine, but she knew that Elo liked to be of use. She lay with her back against a stack of pandanus flour leaf-packs.

'Last time I told you a story about Hine-keha, the Moon-Goddess,' replied the girl, 'but this time I have a tale of Maui.'

'Oh, Maui,' groaned Dorcha. 'Is there no end to stories of Maui?'

Elo laughed. 'No, there are many – listen, this is the story of when Maui was named Maui-of-the-many-devices …'

In the days when 'fire' was the sole property of Mahuika, a witch and one of the mothers of the ancient clans, Maui used to eat his fish raw. One day he decided he was tired of this tasteless food and made up his mind to get fire for his people, so they could roast their fish and make it more appetising. Mahuika was a terrible ogress, however, and ate men whole. It was said of her, 'She devours human beings as swiftly as her fire devours kindling.' A celestial chicken guarded her hearth and warned her of any attempt to steal her fire from its grate.

Maui however was not called Maui-of-the-many-devices for nothing! Even though Hua-hega refused to tell Maui where Mahuika lived he managed to find her house. Mahuika was truly horrible in appearance, but the courageous, small-statured Maui showed little fear. She ran at him with her mouth open, ready to eat him, but Maui cried, 'Look who I am! Your grandson Maui. I have come to pay you a visit.'

Mahuika stopped short and began to ask him questions about his background and where he came from. Finally, he asked her to give him some fire. Since her fingernails were made of fire, she pulled one out of her hand and gave it to him. He ran back to his canoe, but the fire burned his palms and he let it fall into his wooden canoe. It burned through the bottom and dropped into the sea, which of course put it out.

Maui had to return to Mahuika and ask her for another nail. This happened many times until the old woman lost patience with him and screamed, 'Have my hearth!'

Maui was immediately ringed by walls of flame from which it was impossible to pass through without being burned. In order to escape, Maui changed himself into a hawk, but even then the flames singed his feathers as he tried to pass over them.

This is why the hawk has reddish-brown feathers today.

Maui then changed into a fish and dropped into the ocean, but the fire was making the water boil and he had to leap out on to an island.

The island, called Whakaari, began to burn and is still burning to this very day.

Maui then called on the Gods of Rain, Sleet and Hail – Ua, Nganga and Whatu – to extinguish the fire. Only these three gods working together managed to put out the flames.

Mahuika was almost drowned in the flood they produced between them, but managed to throw her fire into the branches of a kaikomako tree, where it remained burning.

The kaikomako tree's wood is still used to make people's fires: the long-headed flames of Mahuika's hearth fire are trapped inside and released when the wood is rubbed vigorously against another wood.

No one knows what happened to the celestial chicken, but many believe Maui cut kindling from the kaikomako tree that very day and ate the bird for his supper. It was his first cooked meal. It was so tasty that thereafter he preferred roasted fish and meat to raw food and passed this on to his people.

Now that his brother's fleet had deviated from a straight course, the homing birds released by the traitor would not be seen by King Tutapu. It behove the king to listen to his high priest, Ragnu, and follow that man's inclinations. Ragnu informed his king that the Great Sea-God was showing them their path, with his ocean currents, and Tutapu had no choice but to follow where he was being led, trusting in Ragnu's judgement.

After many days sailing they entered a part of the ocean where the skies were stretched tightly like a light-blue skin over the roof of voyaging. The wind was slight but gusty and there was a chop on the surface of the sea. The current was strong enough to travel without sail, but the mats remained on the mast, swinging this way and that in changeable breezes. Tutapu wanted to waste no power in reaching his goal.

One evening the vessels, strung out like a snake with a line between each one in this relative calm, passed slowly by a distant island. The island consisted almost entirely of a single mountain with a flat top whose silhouette showed stark against the red sky. Men and women gathered in silence to stare at the island, while Ragnu performed a sacred dance and sprinkled the evening air with chanting and songs. One of his young priests played a nose flute, but no drums were sounded.

Dorcha asked Elo, 'What is that island? Why are people staring at it with such awe?'

'It's the drum of Lingadua.'

'Who is Lingadua?'

Elo said, 'Why, he's the God of Drums, of course – he only has one arm, but when he beats his drum the world shakes. His drumskin is made from the Great Earth-Goddess Papa's hymen, stolen from her while she was in her first ecstatic embrace with the Great Sky-God Rangi. We must not sound our own drums here, or the one-armed Lingadua will steal their voices …'

Darkness came swiftly as Ra fell into the sea, but before they were out of sight of Drum Island, Whatu the God of Hail sent down a shower out of Rangi's domain. Hailstones the size of pebbles came raining out of the sky, hammering against the tipairua canoes, driving through the roofs of the huts. Inside the huts were Tutapu's war drums and the hailstones pounded on the stretched hides of the drums, and on the hollow log-drums, and the sound reverberated over the ocean.

People themselves were struck down by the hailstones and hunched there becoming bruised and battered. Out on the ocean the water was hissing and pockmarked. The world was a white blur for some time as the hard sky shattered and fell on the unsuspecting Oceanians. Then finally the shower stopped just as abruptly as it had begun.

On all the decks of the canoes people began to rise, helping each other to their feet. Gourds had been shattered by the force of the hail and their liquid contents were flowing over the canoes. The leaf-roofed huts had been almost stripped of their covering. Hailstones still lay in layers on flat surfaces and heaped in natural pockets.

Ragnu was grim. 'Our drums have sounded within the province of Lingadua. If he heard them, he'll be angry. He'll steal the voices from our war drums and we'll be at a disadvantage when we next go to fight.'

'It wasn't our fault. We didn't beat the drums ourselves,' said King Tutapu.

'How is Lingadua to know that? He's an irritable god and doesn't stop to think before he acts. I'm sure we'll have trouble from him in the future.

'In any case, we know which side Whatu, the God of Hail, has taken in this conflict. He must favour your half-brother, Tangiia.'

King Tutapu rapped his knuckles on the nearest drum and it resounded through the hut.

'It seems he's left them with their voices,' he said.

Ragnu was doubtful. 'We'll see,' he said.

There were holes in the mat sails which had to be repaired and the decks were swept clear of the melting hailstones. Gradually life settled back into its normal routine. A new shift came on. Bailers toiled at their never-ending task, the steersman handled his steering oar, the look-out woman's keen eyes scoured the ocean ahead for any floating objects.

King Tutapu followed a star path which led to a constellation called Small Face with Small Eyes, and on through the Running Beast, the largest magellanic cloud of the roof of voyaging. He took these sightings not to find the way to where they were going, but to remember where they had been.

It was the natural duty of every Oceanian navigator, king or commoner, mentally to chart the great ocean on which they voyaged. Only in this way were memory maps assembled, to be passed on to descendants, so that journeys could be retaken and perhaps extended, to stretch the limits of known seascapes and oceanic knowledge available to seafarers.

One day perhaps the great-great-grandchild of King Tutapu would return again to Lingadua's drum.

The king went to his rest after midnight, that time of the dead pulse, when all things stand still for a moment.

He was woken from a bad dream by three beats on a drum.

Pulling a cloak of feathers around himself for warmth, he hurried out on deck, to find all was peaceful and still.

'Did you hear anything?' he asked of the deck watch.

'Some distant thunder,' said one man. 'Too far away to concern us.'

Tutapu stared out, into the darkness.

'Three claps of thunder?'

'It may have been three,' answered the man, casually. 'I didn't keep a tally.'

'Next time be more attentive,' snapped Tutapu, 'or you may be counting severed fingers.'

The man swallowed hard and stared with white, frightened eyes.

'Get back to your duties,' Tutapu growled. 'Keep a sharp watch – that means ears as well as eyes.'

He went back to his own hut and spent a restless night. The next morning he was woken to be told three fit men had died in the small hours. The cause seemed to be heart failure.

'Each one has a bruise on his chest, above his heart,' Ragnu told Tutapu, 'as if he has been struck by a heavy club.'

'Or a drum stick wielded by a one-armed god,' muttered Tutapu. 'Is this punishment, or is it merely a warning? The deaths of seamen is no penalty for a king. I have the feeling I'm going to be disciplined further, when the time comes.'

Ragnu could not disagree with his king and suggested a human sacrifice to try to appease Lingadua.

'That would probably be the best thing,' said Tutapu, 'though I have a feeling we might be too late.'

A young male virgin was chosen and brought to the front of the king's canoe. He was bound with sennit cord, hand and foot, and placed on an improvised ritual platform made of wood. A garland of leaves was placed around his head.

The youth's eyes were wide with fear, until Ragnu sat and talked to him, telling the young man he would become a great spirit in the sky, an atua, and that one day men would worship him and treat him with more respect than a mere king. Ragnu then gave the youth of bowl of porridge, in which there were secret spices known only to the priests, and the youth became docile and willing.

'The gods and our ancestors are hungry for sau,' cried Ragnu, in the ceremony that took place under the roof of voyaging. 'Here is food for the Lord of the Drum, Lingadua, whom we have displeased!'

So saying Ragnu slit the youth's throat with an obsidian dagger. The body fell forward and the scarlet blood splashed forth, staining the deck. It flowed over the stern of the craft, into the water, leaving a widening red wake. Foam became red froth until the surf spread and died.

The dying boy lay there, oiled, muscled, beautiful, his tattoos still fresh, his eyelids fluttering like butterflies. The gods had given him a superb body and they had taken it back before age had withered the flesh and time had corrupted the spirit. Indeed, the young man had been chosen for his almost perfect form.

There was chanting then, as the body drained of fluid. The youth's mother was distressed. She had already lost one son to the sea, the boy having fallen from the masthead and broken his neck at the beginning of the voyage. Friends comforted her, telling her that she had yet a third son who needed her love.

Nevertheless, she slipped quietly overboard later that night, surrendering herself to the embrace of Tangaroa.

Dorcha had witnessed the whole affair, indeed had seen many like it since coming to Oceania. In her homeland of Albainn the men were savage and would fight at a moment's notice, tear out an eye, or sever a limb. There was a kind of terrible fury bubbling inside an Albannach's brain, which overflowed when some delicate trigger was touched. They were like wolves, those men of her homeland, instinctively attacking in the subconscious knowledge that he who does not strike first might not live long enough to strike at all. It was defensive.

This calm deliberate taking of life, however, was not within her experience. She had heard horrible stories of sacrifices down where the Angles and Jutes lived. There, it was said, human victims were burned alive in wicker effigies. Giant basket-men were stuffed with dry hay and straw, then screaming people were crammed inside the cages and set alight. Holy men called

Druids were said to be responsible for this heinous rite; priests carrying out a spring time festival, a sacrifice to the fertility gods of flower buds and bird eggs.

But she herself had not witnessed such ghastly sights and the sacrifice of young men and women affected her deeply.

'You do not approve?' King Tutapu said to her, as she stared at the young man's body in the moonlight. 'Others forget him quickly, but you remain here.'

'It is not up to me to approve or disapprove of a king's command – I simply do not see it as necessary.'

'The individual is not important,' explained Tutapu. 'The community as a whole, everyone, must be protected against the impulsive wrath of fickle gods. This man has given his life for the many. It is a brave and wonderful thing to be able to sacrifice oneself for the benefit of the population. I hope I may be given the opportunity one day.'

She stared into his eyes and saw that he meant every word he said.

Dorcha had come on this expedition, not because she still harboured a grudge against Seumas, though her quarrel with him was still as hot and troublesome to her. She had come because she had been dissatisfied with her life back on Raiatea. Some inner voice had been urging her to strike camp, move on, seek a new home. This was in itself rather fickle, since she had told Seumas – and meant it at the time – that she wanted to settle down and live a comfortable life on the two islands.

Yet people do not stay the same, she told herself. They change constantly. It reminded her that one should not use the word 'always' or the word 'never', since they formed promises which must eventually be broken, unless the person who made them was fashioned of stone or wood – or straw.

2

Tutapu woke that night from a deep sleep. The air was hot and humid. Not a fly was stirring, the livestock was still, no man was abroad. He rose from his mat and went out on to deck to find all his crew asleep, even the helmsmen and bailers. The duty watch was nowhere to be seen. Bodies lay everywhere in a seemingly fathomless torpor. They were draped over rigging, sail mats, gourds and fishing nets. A woman lay on her side using her fat little boy, who was also in a drugged sleep, as her pillow. A man hung over a steering oar, as if he were a piece of washing drying in the moonlight.

It was as if a goddess had passed her hand over the boat, her hands dispensing sleep dust.

'Is anyone awake?' called the king, his voice deadened by the stillness of the night. 'Who watches over my canoe?'

No one answered.

He failed to rouse them with his call and was loath to touch them because he was taboo.

Strangely enough, the only movement came from the corpse of the sacrificed youth, still half hanging over the end of the canoe, his limp arms trailing in the water, his cut throat gaping like the open mouth of a giant frog. The ripples of the boat's wake made the youth's body roll gently from side to side, as if he were about to stand up and announce his return.

King Tutapu stared out over the kava-coloured sea. There was a sluggish calm that weighed oppressively on the night. The boat floated on this languid water as if carrying a cargo of opiate dreams. It slid slowly and silently, a vessel in slumber. Above him the stars were like glistening heavy stones imbedded in a dull sky. Between the boat and the stars the clammy air seemed to hold as much moisture as the sea itself.

The other twenty-nine tipairua drifted on behind. He could see them in the moonlight, like hard shadows on the ocean. They seemed to have no life in them, as if they were simply bark following bark naturally along a captivating current. No sailors steered them, nor even stirred on their boards. They were just driftwood which happened to resemble canoes, running in the track of the king's own vessel, caught by the same rivers of warm surface water, sliding over the heavy ocean.

Then, when he looked out over the bows, he saw a path of deep purple appear on the surface of the sea. The path led to a cave which had opened itself in the waters, a cave which led downwards into a nether land.

Tutapu now guessed what was happening. He had been murdered in his sleep by one of his subjects. Or his heart had stopped in the night, without warning.

But then he heard a voice, coming from the cave.

'*Tutapu, come to me.*'

The voice was like the sound of the wind blowing through the husk of a coconut. Or the rustling of dry grasses on a hill. Or the whisper that lives in an empty seashell.

Yet he knew at once it was the voice of his father, calling to him from the Land of the Dead. '*Come to me,*' repeated his father. '*Son, I must speak with you. Do not be afraid. Come. Bring no weapons. Eat nothing. Bring one of your babies.*'

But Tutapu *was* afraid. A man might be fearless in battle and the most dangerous exploit hold no terrors for him, yet when he is faced by the gaping maw that is a tunnel to the Land of the Dead, he feels such fear it almost strangles him.

Yet, he knew that he had to go – he was *compelled* to go. He would have rather not gone, for there were horrors there which he knew would leave a canker on his soul. He was going to see the dead, the empty ones, in their own foul habitat. They were not coming to his house, a terrible enough event; he was going down into theirs. He was taking the path walked just a short time ago by the sau of the sacrificed youth. Would he now have to meet this boy, perhaps pass him on the way to the underworld, the living being quicker of foot? Would the boy be angry with him? Perhaps even attempt revenge for an early death?

'I must get it over with,' he murmured to himself. 'If I must go, I shall go now.'

Tutapu picked up a club, but then remembered the last three commands of his father. It was hard not to take a weapon with him. He felt secure with the club in his hand. Yet he had been told to take nothing except a baby.

A child was sleeping nearby, close to his mother, one of the king's cousins and his concubine. Tutapu dropped the club and reached for the boy. When he held him in his arms, he stirred. Tutapu took little interest in the children born to his concubines, since they were not recognised as his sons. The boy would, if he lived to grow to adulthood, become a vestal priest and serve one of his half-brothers, a *true* son of king and queen. Just as Ragnu was an unrecognised half-brother to both himself and Tangiia, and Kikamana was their half-sister. The priests of the people needed to have some royal blood in their veins, in order to be immune from the taboo king's mana.

Tutapu studied the infant's smooth complexion, his half-open mouth, his chubby limbs and round little belly. Tutapu was not an ogre and he knew the mother would be heartbroken to find her child gone in the morning. Sentiment welled in his breast as he stared down at the beautiful child. In the end he knew he could not take the boy with him. Instead he took from the boy's arms a bark-cloth rag doll. The child stirred in his sleep, but did not wake. Tutapu put the infant back by his mother's side and stepped over the edge of the canoe on to the water.

Once on the purple path he walked down into the open mouth of the cave.

Milu stood there, at the opening to Te Reinga, but he spoke not a word to Tutapu, since the king was a living spirit.

The old king's voice came to Tutapu, in his head.

'Speak not to the God of the Dead. Look not into his eyes.'

Tutapu did as he was told, passing the beautiful pale form of Milu wrapped in his cloak of white and lilac flower petals without glancing up, though he was sorely tempted to do so.

The sea was spongy under the king's feet, yet firm enough to hold his weight. Once below the surface of the water the walls of the cave turned to crystal, with veins of coloured stone running through it. He could hear the sound of his own footsteps on the floor of the cave, as if he were walking on the hard hollow crust of a baked mudflat.

He did indeed pass the youth, who neither turned his head to look, nor spoke a word. The boy did not appear as happy as Tutapu might have expected. He had, after all, been chosen for the beauty of his body and his spirit, and it had been expected that he would remain in that perfect form for all eternity. Instead, the young man looked as if he were made of dingy sand, blown gently down a hillside; a swirling cloud of mournful dust, broadcasting such sadness it enveloped Tutapu as he passed and greyed his heart. Tutapu might have choked on the youth's misery, had he not hurried on down the tunnel, out of reach.

When he reached the end of the tunnel, the Land of the Dead lay before him, vast and unearthly. It was a place of blacks and greys, a land of moving shadows and shades. The ground was covered in sharp stones and jutting rocks, and nowhere was there any colour. It looked impossible to cross.

A man stood at the end of a valley, decorated for war.

The figure's tattoos stood out in relief – strong and heroic in nature. There was a magnificent helmet on his head, of many feathers, though none of any bright hue. In his right hand he held a patu club and in his left a shield. Though the man's frame was thin and wasted, there was about him an enormous aura of strength.

Tutapu recognised the figure as being that of his father.

Stepping out of the end of the tunnel, Tutapu was startled to see a giant naked goddess blocking his way. She was in fact at the exit to many tunnels, from many areas in the living world, squatting there, her vagina like a massive cave itself, surrounded by bramble bushes with wicked thorns. Into this living cave she fed the shattered bodies of men.

Newly dead people were coming out of the many tunnels. Some were immediately snatched up by the monstrous goddess, as tall as ten palm trees, and covered with nails and teeth. She dashed those she picked up against rocks, smashing their skulls and breaking every bone in them. Their broken bodies were pushed, limp and shattered, up inside her womb.

When her eyes rested on him, Tutapu reached automatically for his club as he prepared to defend himself. His hand found nothing and the goddess merely gave him a gruesome sharp-toothed smile. He knew then that if he had produced a weapon, she would have crushed him instantly.

'You are not one of the dead,' she said. 'You have no business here.'

'Who are you?' he asked her boldly. 'What *is* your grisly business?'

'I am Nangananga,' she cried, her long black hair flowing down her body and stretching like a bridal train. 'Goddess of Punishment. My business is with men who lived their whole lives without taking a wife. Bachelors are the curse of mankind.'

'It seems a harsh punishment for choosing to remain single,' said Tutapu. 'Why, even now a youth is on his way to this land whom I sacrificed to the gods. Is this to be his reward?'

'I am only interested in men past marriageable age, not in young virgins such as your victim. My task is to punish those who might have added to the strength of the people, by bringing forth progeny. Return to your canoe, King Tutapu, I have my work to attend to. You keep me from it with your chatter ...'

'I come to speak with my father.'

'Give me one of your children,' she demanded. 'I must eat one of your babies, or you cannot pass by me.'

It seemed to him that he would not hear his father's words, that he must return to the canoe. It was hard, considering his father was within sight. To be so close to his father, yet not be able to hear his words ...

He remembered the infant's rag doll.

'Here,' he cried, whipping it out of his waistband. 'Take my child.'

Nangananga snatched at the doll and without inspecting it she swallowed it whole.

'Pass, then,' she said. 'Quickly.'

With that the giant goddess, whose pendulous breasts swung this way and that with such force when she moved, they shattered obsidian rocks to slivers, turned away from him. Her hands, with their long talons, reached out and snatched an elderly man as he left the exit of a tunnel. She dashed his skull against a stone, smashed his bones to splinters.

To his horror Tutapu saw that the victim was not senseless, but was still aware, his eyes rolling in his pulped head, groans issuing from his gaping mouth.

'I must take me a wife as soon as possible,' muttered Tutapu, moving on. 'I must catch up with my brother and marry Kula before I come to this place.'

Tutapu was met by his mother, who said nothing to him, but crooked a finger and walked ahead, leading him through the maze of whetted and barbed rocks. He followed her, silently, wondering at her form. Instinctively he knew that even if he questioned her, she would not answer him.

Crossing Te Reinga, the Land of the Dead, Tutapu was aware of a great thirst, accompanied by ravenous hunger. There were inviting fresh-water streams running between the rocks and the food of the dead, ngaro, was distributed like guano over the rocks. He might have drunk from one of the streams, or eaten some of the ngaro, had not his father's voice rung in his head.

'*Eat nothing, drink nothing, for if you do you will have to remain in the place where you now walk.*'

Tutapu's father waited at the edge of a seething ocean, between sheer rocks, standing on the last Stepping Stone, a jetty. Not far from him stood his first wife, who had waited for him and led him through the bleak boulder-strewn landscape to the jetty for the canoe to carry all dead souls. His third wife, the mother of Tangiia, was there also. And now his second wife, Tutapu's mother, joined them.

There was indeed a boat there waiting, ready to take the old king across the sea to the silent village of Nabangatai, the place of invisible souls. Since he had been a warrior in life, he would have to fight with Samulayo, God of Death in Battle. Win or lose, Tutapu's father would then go before the Serpent-God, Dengei, who would interrogate and judge him according to his deeds. Tutapu knew all this, from the stories told by priests.

'Son,' said the old king, splendid in his battle attire and wearing his war face, 'I have not much time, so I must tell you now what you must do. You must turn your flotilla round and return to your home islands. Forget your brother, who has fled your wrath. Let him make his own kingdom, away from yours, in a new Faraway Heaven.'

Tutapu felt a flare of fury in his breast, despite the awe in which he held his warrior father's spirit.

'You could have told me this without me having to travel to the Land of the Dead. It has not been a journey without perils. You sent me commands, why not tell me about my brother?'

'Because you would not have taken my words seriously. I wanted you to know how grave is your situation. To do that, I needed you here, where I can look into your eyes.'

Tutapu tried not to look into his father's face.

'But Tangiia has done me a great wrong. He has stolen one of my gods and has abducted my bride-to-be. How can I let him get away with these crimes?'

'He is your brother.'

'*Half*-brother,' corrected Tutapu.

'Yet you are both my true sons. If you persist in your venture, one of you must join me here. When I was alive that did not seem a terrible thing, but now I'm dead I am aware of the waste of such a young life. You are two kings, you can both be great in your own spheres, but you must remain apart.'

'I'm sorry, Father, but I must destroy my brother, before he destroys me. I must recapture the God of Hope, marry the woman who was intended to be my wife, and right those wrongs perpetrated by Tangiia.'

The old king sighed. 'On your own head be it, then – but remember, it might be you who falls in battle.'

Tutapu said, 'I think not, Father – and in any case, I am willing to risk it.'

'Have pity on a dead king's son.'

'No,' said Tutapu, determinedly. 'It is impossible for me to feel pity for Tangiia.'

'I meant you,' said the old king.

'I need no pity, I need *revenge*.'

His words echoed around the Land of the Dead and the old king saw that he meant them, and that he was wasting his time.

'Then go,' said the old man, turning away to step into the sombre, stately canoe, whose decorating long black feathers made it appear like some giant scavenging bird, resting on the murky waters. 'Go now.'

The canoe pulled away, its invisible crew hauling on the sheets, raising the feathery crab-claw sail. The great bark was covered in dark effigies of gods unknown to living men. There were black banners that might have been the souls of the damned flapping from the mast and stays. In the place above the Land of the Dead, which would have been the sky in the real world, the clouds gathered like vultures. Tutapu watched his father go with great sadness in his breast. He had been a good father, a good king, and now he was nothing but a shadow.

Tutapu turned and retraced his steps through the boulder-strewn land to the mouth of the cave, where Nangananga worked tirelessly at weeding out the bachelors from the married souls and burying the former for ever in her womb.

When Tutapu stepped out of the cave, on to the sea of the real world, the purple path was gone. The sea became real water and he shouted in alarm as he began to sink. A shout went up from the canoe, which he recognised as Ragnu's voice.

'The king has been sleepwalking! He drowns!'

An ordinary man, one of the fisherfolk, reached out with an arm and clutched the king's hand, hauling him aboard.

Tutapu lay there, exhausted and dripping, while Ragnu came to him and stood over him.

'I saw you sleepwalking, my lord. You stepped out into the night as if you were going on a stroll. I was too late to prevent you from going over the side.'

Tutapu sighed. 'I have been on a journey.'

'In your dreams?'

'A momentous journey.'

He looked around him, for the mother and child, then remembered he had forbidden children under the useful age of twelve to be present on this voyage.

'My own dreams disobey my commands,' he murmured to himself, 'then cause me to forget I ever made them.'

The king went into the hut to dry himself, since there was a chill wind that night. He thought about his father's words and though he wanted to find room for them in his heart, he could not do it. His kingly breast was too full of other things to allow such feelings inside. It was in his destiny that he should find his brother and take his revenge.

'Perhaps the old man was trying to protect his younger son?' said Tutapu to himself. 'Perhaps I was not his concern at all, but Tangiia, my faithless brother, was his real interest?'

With this jealous thought in mind he fell into an uneasy sleep for the second time that night.

The fisherman who had saved the king, instinctively reaching out a hand to a drowning man, realised afterwards he had touched a taboo person. The man fell ill a little time later, wasted away, and died. King Tutapu was told of the man's death and asked, 'Was he married?'

'Yes, my lord,' said his priest.

'Good, then we need mourn his loss of life, but not his death, for he is safe.'

With this enigmatic statement puzzling his brain, the priest went to the man's relatives to try to comfort them.

PART SIX

The Time of the Green Lizard

1

After they had left that heavy, dream-like part of the world to which Tanga-roa's adaro had led them, King Tangiia's fleet set sail in a stiff, clean wind. They traversed the ocean, following Tooa-o-te-ra on the windflower, almost retracing their voyage to Nuku Hiva in the opposite direction. Kikamana told Tangiia they would come perilously close to Raiatea if they continued their present course, so the king ordered a slight change of direction, and headed for Tahiti.

The king himself had never been to this island, not more than a few days sailing from Raiatea, but several of his men had touched its shores. These men spoke of a people friendly to the Raiateans living on an island rich in resources. They were not certain of their reception, given that this was a fleet of three large canoes and not a fishing vessel of a few men, but they felt reasonably confident they would not be attacked without preliminary negotiations taking place.

At the end of twelve days' sailing, Tangiia could see a lagoon reflecting on the cloud base. This stretch of the voyage had seen the birth of three babies, the death of one old woman and the disappearance during the night of a young, healthy, male bailer.

The vanishing of the young man was put down to Amaite-rangi, the god who fished for people from his home in the sky. Someone said they even saw the line being whisked back up to the clouds, with something wriggling on the end of it.

While Tangiia was adding knots to the mnemonic cord-device, Kaho the blind navigator, the Feeler-of-the-sea, put his hand in the water. After a short while Kaho announced that there were many islands in the vicinity.

'The water is warmer here – this is a calm place – we are approaching Tahiti.'

A particular swell, unfelt by others, which Kaho had discerned by the motion of the boat to be dead astern until now, had changed its course. This swell had its origins thousands of miles away in the upper trade winds, beyond the equator. It had gone down like a sea serpent diving to a depth to where its coldness was no longer distinguished by the blind old man, and warmer, surface currents had taken its place.

That evening there was a minor tragedy. No one lost their life but when the shark-callers were beating the water, a great white shark hid amongst smaller cousins milling around the canoes. It rose suddenly, catching the shark-callers unawares, and took a man's leg with its crescent mouth. The leg was severed at the knee and the man pumped blood into the water, sending the other sharks crazy with excitement.

The wound was cauterised quickly and medicine used to sedate the victim. There were many injuries amongst the shark-callers, and some amongst other professions too. A body lost various parts during its journey through life – an eye taken out, a hand or an arm severed, a foot or a leg lost – the Oceanians did not consider this to be a major tragedy. If the victim lived, the body adjusted, and if the old job called for four limbs, two good eyes and perfect hearing, why, then the injured person took up another line of work, which did not require them.

Since it was too dangerous that evening to carry on fishing for sharks, the creatures being maddened by the blood in the water, and snapping at every shadow, the people used another method of fishing. They smeared some paste made from hotu nuts on a coral club which they then dangled in the water. The fish who came to investigate this substance were stunned by it, then when they floated to the surface were lifted from the water.

The following morning an island came into view. Its mountains were a fantastic labyrinth of pinnacles and gorges, with eerie windows in the myriad peaks of rock. It seemed a place where spirits dwelt high up in these mysteri-ous, jagged forests forming a fairy kingdom at the top of the island. Strange wisps of cloud encircled irregular igneous vanes of stone and every peak was like a claw, and every uncanny claw covered in tiny beaks of rock. A land which had swallowed birds. This was the taboo island Moorea, an island close to Tahiti.

'This is a sacred place,' Tangiia said, emphatically. 'We will not land here.'

They sailed on to the greater island, Tahiti. This place too was volcanic, but the mountains were less ghostly and covered in green rainforest. There were beaches beyond the reef, where people could be seen washing clothes, gath-ering shellfish, chattering and laughing together. On seeing the fleet these people pointed and gestured, some of them running up the beach to inform others that there were visitors to the island.

Tangiia moored the pahi canoes just inside the reef and waited for a recep-tion committee to come out to meet them.

Seumas stood on the bows, not at all convinced that the Tahitians were friendly, and when a war canoe was launched a little while later, this con-firmed his fears.

'Here they come!' he called to Tangiia. 'Are we going to have to fight?'

Tangiia came forward and stared at the oncoming war canoe. It was a mas-sive craft, longer than the pahi canoes by at least another third. There were no sails, but Seumas counted 144 paddlers, 8 steering oarsmen, and many warriors on the large elevated combat platform in the bows, surrounding a nobleman in war feathers. There were at least 300 people on board the canoe. Even the paddlers sitting on the gunwales were armed and ready to leap into action. There was packed muscle-power on that craft, strong fit warriors who had not been wearied by months at sea and a restricted diet.

The prow of the magnificent craft swept upwards in two great v-shaped curves. There were totems rising from the hulls, covered in elaborate carvings, some of which had coloured banners flowing from their heads. The royal personage, encircled by his priest-bodyguards, had a tall helmet whose edging feathers spread like a large fan above his head. Around his neck was a decorated u-shaped collar, also fringed with precious feathers, though smaller than those which bordered the helmet.

Standing beside the nobleman was an important kahuna wearing a helmet shaped like a fish head, the mouth open and revealing rows of sharp teeth. A frill hung from the back of this strange headgear, protecting the priest's neck from the sun. In his hand the kahuna held an engraved hardwood staff.

'Do we fight?' asked Seumas, agitated. 'Are we just going to stand here?'

Kikamana said, 'Don't be so impatient for bloodshed, Seumas. If they were serious about fighting they would have sent a dozen war canoes, not one. This is more in the nature of a royal barge ...'

The canoe finally came up alongside and warriors leapt from the combat platform on to the deck of the king's pahi.

There was a lot of yelling and thigh-slapping, rolling of eyes and tongue-showing, until finally the man wearing the royal helmet stepped on board the pahi and introduced himself to King Tangiia as the son of the King of Tahiti. He invited Tangiia to return with him to the island in the war canoe.

Despite Seumas's misgivings, Tangiia accepted.

Once the king had stepped on board the war canoe, outriggers with excited young women and men came shooting over the breakers to the reef. Barely touching the surf their light canoes seemed to fly like birds. They came with garlands and sweetmeats, fruit and juices to drink. They sang to the seafarers who had come to their island, helping to steer the three great pahi canoes over the safest part of the reef, throwing the hibiscus blooms on to the decks.

By the time Tangiia reached the beach he could see why these people had no need to put on a greater show of strength than just one war canoe. There were a great many of them; too many to concern themselves with subduing a small fleet carrying well under three hundred souls. King Tangiia took an escort of men and women, the most attractive of his people, to meet the king of this wealthy and well-populated island. Crowds had amassed now, along the sands, of men, women, children and dogs.

'I am King Tangiia,' said the navigator proudly to his host, 'and these are my people. We have fled the islands of Raiatea and Borabora, where my father ruled but is now dead. My brother has proclaimed himself king of those islands, but is fearful of my presence. Therefore I am bound for unknown parts of our ocean, to find a Faraway Heaven for my people.'

The King of Tahiti, surrounded by his retainers, nodded gravely.

'I am King Kopu, the Morning Star. Welcome to my island. I knew your father, young man. He was a wise and good ruler. Your brother Tutapu is also known to me and I respect his strength of purpose. You are young. You have the mark of the adventurer on your face. You have done the right thing, by removing this threat to your brother's authority, whether the danger of usurpation is real or not.

'Now,' he proclaimed, 'there will be a feast. You must tell me of your adventures on the great ocean.'

King Morning Star, a fat man twice as large as Tangiia, was then carried at shoulder level on a decorated platform by twelve youths, three on each corner pole. They led the procession, with Tangiia walking beside his host, back to a village at the foot of a great mountain. There the fat king clapped his hands and ordered meats, fruits, vegetables, fish and shellfish to be brought to the cooking fires. Dancing began again with the most beautiful maidens Tangiia had ever seen, swaying and singing, while the drums beat and the flutes trilled.

The heady fragrance of blossoms mingled with the smell of rained-upon earth and drifted down from high mossy valleys, where clouds of waterfall spray drifted as ghosts, keeping the rock towers green with furze and fern. Bird-song was in every narrow cleft, every hollow, echoing around rock walls which soared to the clouds, gathering light on their ascent. Petals floated down from tall spires of stone, to the rainforest far below, delicate fingernails of alpine flowers.

'Feasting, love, laughter!' the cry went up.

Mats were brought covered in designs which Tangiia was told were made by cutting stencils from broad leaves, the artisans amongst the Raiateans noting this new technique for decorating their wares for future use. Palm leaves were placed over the heads of the visitors, protecting them from the sun. Fresh clear water was brought from sparkling waterfalls which fell from the mountains of this beautiful island. It was obvious to the Raiateans that the land was bountiful and this was a rich and prosperous place which had known little strife and much harmony.

Sacred kava drink was brought and shared only between the two royal personages present.

King Morning Star noticed the one white body amongst the many brown and asked King Tangiia for an explanation.

'This is a captive of Kupe the Navigator, from a faroff place known as the Land-of-Mists. He is a free man and now sails as one of us. Do you wish to speak with him?'

'He is not a supernatural creature?'

'No,' said Tangiia.

'How disappointing, but indeed, he seems quite exotic nonetheless,' King Morning Star said, staring at Seumas as the Pict walked amongst the bowls of fruit, his dog at his heels. 'I shall talk with him later. Does he speak the tongue of seafarers?'

'Now he does, but he also has a darker tongue, of which we have not entirely been able to cure him.'

'I should tear it out at the roots with tongs!'

Tangiia smiled. 'Unfortunately that would rob him of his new tongue too and I must say I like talking with him. He has interesting ideas and can throw a different light on problems that need to be solved. His method of thinking is unusual.'

'Quite. I'm not surprised,' said Morning Star, 'and he seems to have a peculiarly strong attachment to his livestock. Does he think it will be stolen?'

The Tahitian king meant Dirk, and again Tangiia explained that in the Land-of-Mists men used dogs for hunting and treated them like human beings, a fact which astonished Morning Star so much that he wobbled on his stool, his fat body shaking.

'You mean they don't *eat* their puppies?'

'They feed their dogs meat, which makes the flesh of the animals unpalatable.'

'Incredible,' said the Tahitian king, shaking his head in wonderment. 'How fortunate for us that we live in a civilised part of the great ocean, and not in this strange land where skins are pale as fish bellies and dogs are raised as children.'

Tangiia made a mental note to pass that one on to Seumas later, when the Pict was getting above himself.

Ra finished his slow journey over the face of his father, Rangi, and Hine-nui-te-po urged Hine-keha to come out of hiding and show her bright visage to Papa.

During one unguarded moment Tangiia caught sight of Kula, sitting on the far side of the fire talking to a neighbour. He could see her face through the high flames, appearing and disappearing as the fire waxed and waned. Fiery sparks flew between them as the bark of the firewood peeled and rose on the hot air. Kula's head then turned and her eyes met his through the wavering longheaded flames. He read something in her sad-eyed stare which caused his heart to beat with excitement.

Turning to King Morning Star, Tangiia said, 'I must speak with that woman over there – she is Princess Nau Ariki.'

The king looked surprised but nodded.

Tangiia stood up and walked to the shadows of some huts. He stood there and waited. After a short while Kula rose and joined him. She came to him and stood before him.

There were flowers behind her ears and garlands decorating her throat. Her hair had a silver sheen to it which took his breath away; its blackness was deeper than the darkest night out on the great ocean, yet bearing the flush of shining white stars that made the Long Shark at Dawn. Her small pointed breasts with their dark nipples, below the streamers which flowed like waterfalls from her collar bones, rose and fell slowly, as she regarded him in silence. She was as beautiful as any goddess, or fairy, or mermaid. She might have been born amongst the lovely shells of the ocean, a princess of the coral kingdoms below the water-line.

Tangiia wished to crush her in an embrace; he longed to enjoy her softness, her sweet-smelling skin. He wanted to lick the sea-salt from her eyelids. He needed to kiss her eyebrows, her high-boned cheeks. He wanted their sensitive noses to caress one another. He desired her long legs to be entwined about his waist, his spear buried deep in her secret mossy target, her tongue searching his ear like a warm, wet snake, her two pointed breasts attacking his own with their sharp tips. He wanted to *possess* her body, utterly, completely, with profound tenderness and with an unruly passion.

'I love you,' she said, breaking the silence.

He could not believe what he had heard. He croaked hoarsely, 'You – you love me?' His mouth felt as dry and hot as a bone left lying in the sun. His stomach was an empty glade where leaves fluttered in strong breezes. His heart was fired clay on which the feet of running men pounded.

'Yes,' she said, fiercely. 'I had a duty, but that duty can never be fulfilled now. It's time to forget our old life, isn't it? Time to begin a new one.'

She seemed like a predator circling a prey, closing in gradually, coming near for the pounce – yet she had not moved in person, only in mind and spirit.

'Kula,' said Tangiia, caught unawares by the burning intensity of her words, 'are you sure? I thought you hated me – I thought ...'

'Of course I hate you. I hate you as much as I love you. Sometimes I could drive a dagger through your heart,' she said, ferociously. 'Yet,' her eyes turned liquid, 'there are times when I just want to lie with you in the dust and let our bodies pound together, rhythmically, making the sound that women make early in the morning pummelling the grain with their poles in the hollow stones, creating clouds of fine powder ...'

'Will you be my wife?'

'I shall be your princess, your slave, your mistress and your queen. I shall be all women to you, and you shall want no other. I *demand* you take no other. I can endure no companions on my husband's love mat. No other woman shall sport the patterns of its weave on her buttocks. I alone must carry the badge of my husband's lovemaking.

'If all this is understood, then I am yours.'

Tangiia's soul soared to the roof of voyaging, where Oro's Body, the brightest star in the sky, shone hard and bright.

The king took her hand and led her back to the firelight. There the dancing and feasting had continued, but on seeing Tangiia and Kula hand-in-hand, word passed quickly and the people of Raiatea rose almost as a single unit and turned towards them.

King Morning Star, who was not fully aware of what was happening, feared that a sudden subversive attack was about to take place, that the Raiateans had risen at a previously given signal and were about to fall upon their hosts.

'Ware the intruders!' he cried.

Tahitian warriors leapt to their feet, snatching up their weapons, ready to do battle. The whole atmosphere was tense with speculation and suspicion, until Kikamana, the Far-seeing virgin, stretched her arms and said, 'Tahitians – you have nothing to fear! Our king has found himself a bride.'

At that moment Tangiia lifted the hand he was holding and presented Kula to his people.

'Behold,' he cried, 'my queen!'

A mighty cheer went up from Tangiia's people.

The King of Tahiti stared solemnly for a moment at this extraordinary sight, then he began laughing, his whole body shaking with the effort, the fat on his belly and breasts wobbling, his jowls rippling, his bottom jiggling. On seeing him laugh, his people laughed too, and waved their weapons in the air not in anger but in delight. Then the Raiateans were moved to laughter, until the whole place echoed with the sound of mirth and merriment – and none were as happy as Tangiia and Kula.

'There's going to be a wedding!' cried Morning Star, laughing. 'We're going to have a marriage.'

It was the Time of the Green Lizard, a time of calm and peace. In periods when the weather was fine, the sea was tranquil, the colour of the light was misty-blue and soft as a moth's wing, then the Great Sea-God Tangaroa would change himself into a green lizard and bask on a rock in the sun.

Tangiia consulted with Makka-te and Kikamana, the Farseeing-virgin, and both agreed it was safe to rest a while in Tahiti, since the portents showed their pursuer to be several months behind them, lost somewhere on the great ocean. Since Kula was about to become his bride and queen, Tangiia felt it was right to consult her also, on their future. She too believed that a period of relaxation would do the Raiateans no harm.

Kula said, 'We must refresh the energy of our people, or their spirits will shrivel inside them, and they will not be able to go on. Our wedding will also be good for them. It will add cohesion to your rule – much strength and vigour results from the merging of a royal couple. It can only be good for us.'

King Morning Star insisted that the bride should have a new house for her wedding night and men were sent into the rainforest to cut hardwood posts for the uprights, bamboo poles to line the walls horizontally, and reed thatch for the roof. The splicers set to work on the binding ropes; the carvers prepared the upright posts, turning history and legend into tangible form; the wood masons cut the joining pegs, the rafters and beams, the blocks and pins, the frames.

While the craftsmen joiners worked their art, kahunas appealed to the spirits of ancestors, asking them to favour the young couple with their good will, not to demand human sacrifice on such a happy occasion, and to bless the house with their presence whenever it pleased them.

'You're a lucky man,' sighed Seumas, speaking to Tangiia. 'The woman of your dreams – it doesn't happen to many of us.'

Seumas was sitting on a log, at the edge of the rainforest, Dirk lying at his feet. The dog had one lazy eye open, but was clearly enjoying a noon-day doze. Tangiia had paused to talk with Seumas as he passed by.

'Yes,' replied the young king, but he answered with uncertainty in his voice.

It was clear to Seumas that now the deed was about to take place, Tangiia was going through that time most young men experience just before their wedding, when they begin to wonder if they've done the right thing. Marriage brings responsibilities on top of those already in hand, and what was more it meant that another person had to be consulted over most decisions. 'I'll go fishing today and just idle away a watery noon,' became, 'Is it all right to go fishing?' Freedom, in the sense that one could do exactly as one liked with one's time, was gone for both parties. There was a call on that time, for family duties, and later, 'Is it all right to go fishing?' would become, 'Shall I take the children off your hands for a while?' Even kings of Oceania had family responsibilities.

All this, Seumas knew, was going through Tangiia's mind. It wasn't that the youth did not love his betrothed – he loved her to distraction – but he was panicking a little about what he was taking on. Life would never be the same again. It would not be as lonely and miserably insecure, but it would not be as free and easy either. And what was more, it was supposed to be *for ever*. Any mistake was an eternal one. It was no wonder he felt like bolting into the rainforest and hiding there until it had all blown over.

'You don't look like a man who has just won the prize of a lifetime,' said Seumas.

Tangiia shrugged. 'I'm – scared.'

'Of what?'

'That things won't go right – afterwards.'

'You have to *make* them go right, work at it – that's what it's all about.'

Tangiia snorted, 'How would you know – you're not married.'

202

'No, but I have been. And I've thought about marrying Dorcha a million times and I know that marriage to her would be hell in some ways. She's a very fiery woman. She can be an unmanageable one. I would be exchanging the hell of loneliness for the hell of the battleground – but, by the power of the Oceanian gods, I'd do it tomorrow if I could.'

'You wouldn't feel like running away,' said Tangiia, sourly, 'no, not you.'

'Maybe,' Seumas said, 'but look, you think you're scared. What about Kula? She's feeling all those things you're feeling – and on top of that she's probably worried about the first night of the marriage bed. Don't forget she's a virgin. How would you like a stranger to ram a stiff fleshy part of their body into a place you've never had anything put before?'

'I'm not a stranger.'

'You are to her body. How does she know you won't become one of those violent husbands who beat their wives in secret? She's got to take that chance, too. No, my friend, it's *she* who should be afraid, not you. Hers is the bigger risk.'

Tangiia nodded gravely and sighed. 'I suppose you're right, but like Dorcha she's a very spirited woman too. Do you really think it will be a battleground? Will we have to fight with one another for supremacy in the family house?'

'Not if you listen to her with as much attention as you would listen to another man, respect her intelligence and judgement, don't take her for granted, be sensitive to her needs, trust her, and remember to be tender.

'And just think, a spirited, intelligent woman is the ultimate prize – would you want to be bored out of your brains for the rest of your life with drivel and small talk? What kind of a man would want that? Only one who wishes to dominate his partner because he's dominated by his fellow men.'

Tangiia grinned. 'You would make a fine husband, Seumas.'

Seumas grinned back. 'No, I'm just good at passing on advice to others. In fact I'm just a barbarian. I used to treat women like dogs. That advice was given to me by one of your own people – Kupe – when we first met. Kupe is a very wise man – it's good advice, when you think about it. If you respect the woman you love, then you respect yourself, because *you* chose her, no one else, and your judgement's at fault if afterwards all you want to do is stay out of her sight.'

'Seumas,' said Tangiia, solemnly, 'you must share my basket with me and others, before my wedding.'

This was a great honour for the man they called 'the mountain goblin' and Seumas was struck mute for a moment. Finally he managed to speak.

'Accept the thanks of a Pict,' he said. 'I've done nothing to deserve it, but I'm grateful you should consider me worthy.'

King Tangiia shook his head and smiled. 'And bring that hound with you, if you have to.' He nodded towards the dozing Dirk, who had not moved a muscle in the last hour.

Dirk immediately lifted his head, cocked an ear, and then looked from one man to the other.

'I swear,' said Tangiia, amazed, 'that dog knows every word we speak.'

'Every word,' smiled Seumas, patting Dirk's head.

Kula was indeed feeling as if she wanted to run into the rainforest and keep on running until she met the sea again, but not necessarily for the reasons Seumas had put to Tangiia. Kula was convinced that she was doing the wrong thing, according to her duty to her father and the gods, and that she was being selfish in giving in to her own passion. She wanted Tangiia, but felt she was wrong to want him and to submit to that desire.

It was late evening, the surf was booming along the reef creating a distant backdrop of sound, and the crickets were vying with the tree frogs in choral competition. Fruit bats rustled their drumskin wings at the top of palms. There was the occasional thud of a coconut falling from a tree top to earth, a constant danger to strollers when the fruit was ripe.

Kula was sitting on the shore just above where the waves were rippling amongst the coconut husks and dead, brown palm leaves that littered the beach. Hermit crabs scuttled under the arch created by her legs, wearing the various shells taken from dead molluscs. She stared at the place where redness had given way to darkness lit with bright islands of light.

'I'm not strong,' she said when praying to her favourite goddess Hine-keha. 'My will is weak.'

Hine-keha, the Bright Lady, had loved many, including a mortal who found her amongst some kelp in her dead phase, as Hine-uri, the Indigo Lady, after she had been floating in the sea. The handsome young man was a prince named Rupe. She took on human shape as he parted the seaweed which had entangled her form. Thinking she was a maiden who had fallen into the sea and almost drowned he lifted her from amongst the flotsam and jetsam and pressed her to his bosom to give her some warmth. They fell in love and she bore him a child, Tuhuruhuru.

'You know about love,' Kula said softly. 'Your duty is to love your husband Marama, but yet you have turned from that duty to love other gods and even mortals, so please do not judge me harshly for turning from my duty ...'

Kula was feeling vulnerable. She was racked with homesickness, wondering who was feeding her grandfather, and what the rest of her family were doing right at that moment. All her old basket-sharers, the girls who used to accompany her to the pool under the waterfall, were back on the islands. She had made new friends of course, new maidens who shared her food with her, and one in particular – a girl named Lolina. Still, she missed her old basket-sharers, and her parents and grandfather, and her sisters.

'Are you finished yet?' called Lolina.

'Yes, I'm coming,' replied Kula, enjoying the warm breezes which blew from the direction in which lay her old home. At that moment a silvery fish-shape leapt from the waters of the lagoon, into the moonlight, and entered the waters again with barely a light splash. It seemed to Kula that this was a sign which told her she was doing the right thing, at least by Hine.

'Hine-te-ngaru-moana!' breathed Kula. 'Lady of the Ocean Waves, I'm sure it was you!'

'What?' called Lolina.

'Nothing, nothing ...'

Kula went to join her friend and together they ran barefoot over the grass to where others were waiting to greet them. Baskets of fruit and roasted fish, with breadfruit and plantains, were brought to the group. Then the maidens began to eat and chatter at the same time. One of them told Kula she was so lucky '... he's such a handsome man, the king.'

'Not so much a man,' replied Kula, 'more of a youth.'

'But he's the *king*. His manhood is conferred by his rank. A youth can't be king.'

'So you say,' Kula answered, taking some breadfruit, 'but I say differently. What's more he's a youth who has injured me, my family and former intended husband.'

Lolina looked puzzled by this remark.

'Aren't you in love with him then?'

Kula looked her friend directly in the eyes. 'Of course I am, but he must be punished all the same, for abducting me – if not by the gods, then I must be the instrument. The honour of my family is at stake, which means my *own* honour, since I'm part of that family. I will not let anyone, even someone I love, stamp my honour into the dust. Not without punishment.'

The other maidens were aghast at this speech.

One cried, 'You will be his wife. You must go to him in humility and love, not with vengeance in your heart.'

'I go with love and a desire for justice,' said Kula, simply.

'What will you do?' asked Lolina, fearfully, thinking her friend the princess quite capable of taking up a patu club and braining her new husband during their first coupling, while he was helplessly in the throes of ecstasy.

'I shall withhold my virginity until we find a Faraway Heaven.'

The anxiety of the maidens turned to horror at these words. They felt sure the king would kill his new wife, if she refused to give him her body. Either that or he would abandon her and find a lover, which would be so humiliating she would have to kill herself.

'But what – what if he insists?' asked the terrified Lolina.

'You mean if he rapes me? I hope he does,' Kula said, calmly. 'Then his suffering will be more intense and will only need to be over a short time period. We won't have to wait then, until we reach a new island. He's not the kind of man who could rape a woman, especially the woman he loves, and not feel terrible guilt. I'll goad that guilt with sharp words, until he can't stand it any longer. Once he's paid for abducting me, then we'll be free to live a long and happy life together, unmarred by his bad deeds of the past.'

'If you live that long,' groaned Lolina.

'True,' smiled Kula, 'if he doesn't kill me in a fit of rage.' She became thoughtful for a moment, before adding, 'I hope he doesn't for his sake – he'd never forgive himself.'

At the time Kula was sharing her basket with her maidens, Tangiia was doing the same, with his companions. The special guests at this basket-sharing were Boy-girl whose new lover, Ranata, was a friend of the king, and Seumas. Also present was Makke-te, Aputua the leader of the shark-callers, Kaho the Feeler-of-the-sea, Po, Manopa and one or two others of lesser rank.

Boy-girl had the peculiar and distinct status of being eligible to share baskets with both men and women. She was clearly enjoying herself at this gathering, until the king asked her a question.

'Kikamana says a dark force is coming this way. Can you confirm this?'

Boy-girl nodded. 'There is something beyond the horizon, racing across the waves towards us.'

Tangiia asked the question Boy-girl was dreading.

'What is it?'

'I don't know,' admitted Boy-girl. 'I can't even tell if it's human, demon or god-like. Its identity is being protected by magic. All I can see is a dark cloud hiding a nefarious presence – and the cloud is rushing this way. Perhaps it's a monster sent by your enemies?'

Since Tangiia only had one enemy that he knew of this information was a little redundant.

Tangiia grumbled, 'What's the use of having Farseeing priests, if they can't tell you anything.'

Boy-girl said, 'I'm not a priest ...'

'Don't split hairs with me,' Tangiia growled.

Manopa said, 'Come – this is a social gathering, my king – let's not quarrel here.'

Manopa was able to use such strong words with Tangiia because of his high rank and age. He was the rock on which Tangiia stood. Manopa was steadfast, loyal and true, and his physical strength and mental control made him a formidable foe and a stalwart friend.

Manopa was not an intellectual, like Boy-girl, but he thought things through with great thoroughness and made decisions based on evidence and hard facts.

Where there were none of these, he used his experience and reasoning powers, and the mariners under his command respected him immensely, knowing that in the event of something terrible happening – like a great storm – Manopa would remain calm and in possession of his faculties. He would see them through the greatest adversities with a calm, authoritative voice and not the slightest show of unease or lack of confidence.

Manopa's figure standing firmly on the deck of his pahi, almost as if he were carved from the woodwork, issuing commands while the waves loured above the vessel and crashed around its hulls, inspired great efforts from his sailors. It instilled complete confidence in him.

Not a man easily swayed by emotions, Manopa was one of three husbands married to the same woman. He found his duties not irksome but demanding, and he only had a certain amount of time to give to a wife. A wife with one husband was always waiting for her man to return to the fireplace, to the bed, or to the meal table. Manopa gave of his all to his work, before even considering returning to his home and his bed. His present wife enjoyed the status of being connected with Manopa, but did not fret and whine if her husband, being only one of three, was only around a short part of the time.

'Pass me a mango,' said Po to Manopa.

Po was quite unlike Manopa, which was strange considering they were of the same rank and did the same job, that of captaining a pahi. Po had four wives, was as thin as a shadow, and his sense of humour was what kept his men at their posts during a crisis. During the recent storm, he had bellowed at the wind and the waves, 'Is that you, Tangaroa? All right, do your worst – punish us puny seafarers for some imagined insult – see if we care. Is *that* the worst you can do? That wave was hardly even worthy to be called mountainous. Surely you can produce a bigger one than that? Oh, wait – yes – I take it back. I see one coming on the horizon – my god, it's monstrous – it'll swamp us for sure ...'

The sailors would all raise their heads in anxiety, to witness a piddling little wave coming towards them, and realise their captain was being sarcastic. They would chuckle at Po's ranting and raving, which would spread to the women and children, and no matter how much the storm tossed their frail craft, they would be jollying each other along and giggling at Po's antics.

Po threw a piece of mango to Dirk, sitting beside his master.

Dirk looked at the chunk of fruit as if he had been offered a bat's turd.

'What's the matter with your dog, Seumas? That's good food I've given him. The other dogs would be fighting over that by now, if I'd thrown it to them.'

'You know he doesn't eat fruit,' snapped Seumas. 'If you want to feed him, give him a scrap of meat.'

Po reached into the basket and pulled out a chunk of meat which he then tossed to Dirk. Tangiia looked at Po disapprovingly, but Po just winked at his king. As a reliable captain and second navigator he could get away with almost as much as Manopa. The dog leapt on the cooked flesh and began to devour it with gusto. Po sniggered.

'What's so funny?' asked Seumas.

Po said with a snicker, 'That's his mother.'

Seumas shot a look at the piece of meat and then realised he was being teased. Dirk's mother must have been killed and eaten long ago.

'Are you calling my dog a cannibal?' he asked Po, in a soft threatening voice. 'Nobody insults my dog.'

Even Po was surprised by the quiet menace in Seumas's voice.

'What's wrong with being a cannibal?' he asked, pleasantly. 'Every man here has eaten human flesh at some time, even you.'

'I'm talking about you insulting my dog.'

The whole party had suddenly gone still. No one chewed or swallowed their food. All eyes were on Po and Seumas. Everyone knew Seumas was a awesome fighter in single combat. Po had seen him in action several times and had no wish to meet him hand-to-hand over the sensibilities of an animal which should have formed part of the pot roast.

Po said nervously, 'Oh, come on, Seumas, it's not one of your children – it's just a dog.'

Tangiia made things worse for Po. 'Dirk is like a child to Seumas – like one of his own sons.'

Seumas stared hard at Po, while the captain fidgeted with his food for a moment.

Finally Po burst out with, 'Oh, all right – I apologise, Seumas. I'm not going to fall out with you over livestock.'

'Not to me,' said Seumas, evenly. 'To Dirk.'

'To the dog? Oh, listen – look Seumas, the dog – after all – well then, dog, I'm sorry. There.'

'Say, "I'm sorry, *Dirk*." That's his name. He doesn't like being called "dog".'

'But he is a *dog*,' expostulated Po. 'He might not be a walking pork chop, but he is a blasted dog after all ...'

'Right, that's it – sic 'im, Dirk.'

Dirk instantly left the meat and stood up, his nape hairs bristling, his teeth frighteningly bared. There was a growl beginning in the back of his throat, which curled there, rolling slowly out of his mouth. His eyes showed their whites.

Po said quietly in a high voice, 'Seumas ...'

'All right, boy, sit,' said Seumas casually, going back to his eating.

Dirk settled again with his meat, while the other men returned to their food, chattering amongst themselves. Po sat there sweating for a moment, breathing quickly, his eyes upon his shaking hands. When he looked up again, everyone was staring at him and grinning broadly. Even Seumas.

He suddenly realised what was going on.

'It was a joke,' he said. 'A rotten joke. That wasn't funny, you know. I thought for a moment – Seumas, that wasn't funny. I almost crapped myself ...' Then he saw the funny side of it himself and began laughing, along with the others. So many times he had been the teaser, the one who mocked and heckled, and now he had been on the other end. It was quite funny. He showed them he could take a joke, by laughing with them, but he swore to himself he would get even with his friend Seumas. If it took him the rest of his life he would get even.

The tall, willowly Boy-girl, with her hair dangling with ribbons and shells said, 'Tell your dog to attack me, Seumas.'

Seumas said, 'No, I don't want him to hurt you.'

Boy-girl smiled. 'He won't hurt me – just tell him ...'

Seumas shrugged, then turned to Dirk and said, 'Kill,' pointing at Boy-girl.

The dog left the ground with hunched shoulders as if it had been kicked into the air, its eyes flashing, its mouth salivating and the jaws clashing together. The men around Boy-girl, including her new lover, vacated the area instantly. Boy-girl simply sat there, waiting, until the dog was an arm's length away, then she turned and stared into his eyes.

Dirk immediately came to a halt. He then went down on his haunches, still staring at Boy-girl, his tongue lolling out of the side of his mouth. Then, at a whisper from Boy-girl, he lay his head on his front paws, and regarded her with limp eyes.

'What a nice dog,' she said, reaching out to stroke the animal. 'What makes you so afraid of it, Po?'

'I'm not a bloody magician, that's what,' answered Po with his usual bluntness. 'He would have eaten me.'

Seumas was astonished at the speed with which Boy-girl was able to subdue Dirk. When he called the dog, it remained where it was, annoying him. He whistled and called again. Still no response. Boy-girl said something and finally Dirk stood up and went back to Seumas, its face registering the fact that it knew it had displeased its master.

'It took me a year to train this dog as a killer,' said Seumas, peevishly, 'and you turn him back into a puppy within a minute.'

Boy-girl smiled sweetly. 'He knows you love me, that's why he's nice to me,' she said.

Boy-girl's new lover shot Seumas a look of jealous hatred.

I don't need this, thought Seumas. It's bad enough having Boy-girl pressing herself against me at any opportunity, without having to look over my shoulder for jealous lovers coming out of the dark with a knife in their hand.

'Boy-girl, you know that's not true. I only like *real* women. Tell your new friend that we're just good chums.'

'We're just good chums,' said Boy-girl to her lover, but in a tone which implied that there was more to it than that. 'Seumas only likes *real* women.'

Seumas shook his head, ruefully, wondering whether he would ever manage to shake the tenacious Boy-girl from his life.

2

On the night of the wedding the airy spirits who inhabited the sky were in a happy mood. As always, they were playing ball games with superb dexterity amongst the clouds. The spirits of the sky were fair of skin, which made them an ancient race of beings, related to the ancestors of the Oceanians.

There were other spirits, less cheerful, in lost villages in the earth, in the water, in all the elements, spirits known to men as the 'gloomy ghosts' because they have no knowledge of fire and they eat their food raw. Once two fishermen stumbled on such a village and were told that they could eat with the spirits but if they laughed they would be killed. They were forced to swallow raw whale meat, even though they had found driftwood on the beach and had carried it under their arms to dry it. After the men left, they never laughed again.

And in the forest the bird-spirits recalled the time they had built the first canoe for the hero Rata, while the woods echoed with their songs.

A royal wedding was a cause for celebration amongst the spirit world, as well as amongst mortals.

King Morning Star was nothing if not generous and the food for the wedding feast was supplied in plenty.

There were sixty different kinds of yam, baked and roasted sweet potatoes, suckling pigs smeared with honey and roasted over slow fires, pit stews of dog and wild bird meat, fermented breadfruit, chickens stuffed with coconut and banana, Tahitian chestnuts, wild birds' eggs, crispy ants and beetles.

Then there were the seafare dishes, which outweighed the meat by far, consisting of sharks' roe, barracuda, squid, cuttlefish, an abundance of shell-fish, reef fish, eels in thick sauces, turtle-meat kebabs, turtle eggs, sea weeds of various kinds, crabs and lobsters, anemones and skipjack.

The fires were lit, the dancing began. The bride and groom sat one on either side of the Tahitian priest who was to perform the marriage ceremony. Flowers, bamboo and streamers, and decorated mats were everywhere, on the ground, adorning the houses and huts. Wooden personal gods marched out of the houses and stood in yards. Totems were dusted and set in the ground. Ahu had been raised for the sacrifices, though Tangiia had stipulated there were to be no human sacrifices at his wedding, only those of animals.

There were blooms in people's hair – Seumas and his dog were both decked in frangipani blossoms.

'You look very pretty,' Kikamana said to Seumas.

Po added, 'You'd better stay out of Boy-girl's way, or you'll wake up from the kava drink tomorrow to find yourself married to her.'

Boy-girl herself looked stunningly beautiful in a tapa cloth dyed red. She was so tall and elegant she towered over most of the Tahitians, yet her carriage was perfect. She refused to stoop to listen or speak to those below her height and her deportment was to be envied.

The bride and groom were quiet and serious, not looking at each other, possibly feeling quite shy.

King Morning Star was his usual jolly self, ordering food to be put in his mouth, calling for a particular dance, drinking enough kava juice to kill an ordinary man.

Seumas ignored Po's advice and drank kava juice until it ran down his chin and chest. Halfway through the evening he jumped up and began dancing, much to the consternation of Dirk, who kept running through people's legs in an effort to keep pace with his master. The dog could not understand what was happening.

Sometime in the late evening the marriage ceremony took place, but by that hour Seumas was so drunk things began to get a little fuzzy and uncoordinated. The dancing picked up in pace and Seumas especially felt his feet hopping in a furious manner, determined as he was to keep up with those lithe figures around him, to whom dancing was a natural expression of joy.

The drums were beaten with such skill and speed it made Seumas giddy to look upon the musicians. The trilling of flutes filled the air, patterned the night. Seumas's soul had trouble keeping up with his body, as he jumped and leapt and swayed and kicked.

Towards the end of the night, he found himself dancing opposite a bright-eyed girl whose features were so shiny and delicate they might have been fashioned from fragile seashells. She smiled at Seumas, as she swayed before him, her slender arms waving like fronds, her slim, beautiful legs peeking through the grass skirt, tantalising him. She was beauty in absolute and Seumas danced with his mouth agape, wondering how he could have missed seeing such a wonderful maiden before now.

However, when he happened to glance around him, it seemed that there were many more like her – dainty, ethereal creatures with small, heart-shaped faces. Their hair was like black rain falling over their sweet, pale features. It seemed to Seumas that if he touched one of them with a fingertip, they would bruise like ripe fruit. The maiden dancing with him kept smiling gently, a smile he was sure was an invitation.

'Do you want to go somewhere?' he asked, huskily, his feet still jigging with the dance.

She nodded, slightly, still wearing her serene smile.

'Just a bit more of the dancing first, eh?' he cried, quickening his pace, feeling quite elated at this conquest. 'Just to wear off the drink a little.'

The girl took his hand in her own and he marvelled at how tiny it was. She tugged at him, trying to draw him in amongst the rocks at the edge of the rainforest, but he still had not danced his full measure, and laughingly pulled her back again, into the cavorting throng. Her bright eyes looked at him questioningly, and he said, 'Just a few more steps.'

Finally, he had exhausted his energy and she was able to lead him to a soft, mossy bank between two great boulders. There she lay on her side, inviting him down with her. He was only slightly astonished to see she was completely naked, realising he was so drunk his powers of observance were practically nil. Her small, pale body hardly made an impression in the spongy moss, so slight and weightless she seemed.

He lay down with her, puzzled at the haze that surrounded her in the way that a bright mist often encircles the moon. Her breath was like that of perfume breathed from flowers. Eyes he had seen only in distant dreams shone from the petal-soft complexion, the need in them strong and evident.

Dirk crept around the boulders and lay not far away, sensing he was not welcome at this meeting of two humans.

Seumas took her head in his hands, cupping it like a sweet apple to be savoured, and bent to kiss her.

Her lips had the tang of wild fruit and her tongue tasted of honey. He kissed down her face to the bare shoulders, as intricately formed as that of a bird. When he reached her breasts, quivering with passion, he stopped – then opened his lips as if to drink, before taking one of them inside his mouth whole, so small and sweet were they. Her legs parted and the perfumed breath came faster and faster.

'Oh, my darlin' lovely girl,' he moaned. 'Thank you for choosing a rough man like me.'

The first rays of the dawn parted the air above the two great boulders, as Ra's shafts began to penetrate the day. Rangi's domain was swiftly overtaken, the light chasing away the darkness into unknown regions. Seumas tore away his loin cloth and drove upwards with his hardened penis –

– only to find himself stabbing at empty air.

'Wha—?' He looked down to see a shape dissolving into the moss. Where the maiden had been was nothing but mist. She had disappeared with the dawn and he was making love to twigs and leaves – to Papa, the Great Earth-Goddess.

The shock, on top of the massive amount of kava juice he had drunk, caused him to pass out.

Seumas spent the best part of the morning lying naked on the lichen-covered rocks. When he woke the sun was beating down on his head, punishing him for his overindulgence. Dirk was lying beside him, one eye open.

Seumas rose and staggered off to find the water hole, drinking down great draughts of the cool liquid when he found it and cursing himself for being so weak willed. Then, as he was splashing his head, he remembered the maiden he had almost made love to at dawn. Had it been a dream? Perhaps kava juice, taken in vast quantities, produced false images in his brain, made him see things that were not there.

Po arrived at the pool then, and he too splashed his face with cold water.

Po said, 'Did you see the tipairu?'

Seumas, lying full-length at the edge of the pool with his face half in the water, looked up dripping.

'Who?'

'The fairies,' said Po, excitedly. 'The Unequalled Ones, they came down to the dancing last night – very late – when they knew no one would pay much attention to them.'

'Were they ...?'and Seumas described his maiden.

'That's them,' said Po. 'Beautiful creatures. They live in the high pools and hanging gardens up in the mountains – I was told by the villagers last night. It seems they don't always come down, but they did for us.'

Seumas said, more to himself in wonder than to Po, 'I almost made love to a fairy.'

'You what?' laughed Po.

'She vanished into mist, when the dawn came.'

'Sure,' said Po, mockingly. 'A fairy fell in love with a grisly old mountain goblin, yet not a single beautiful young warrior could get an Unequalled One into the forest on her own? Please, don't insult my common sense, Seumas. Go and joke with someone else.'

'I tell you I did,' said Seumas angrily. Then he became quietly anguished, his voice full of regret. 'I tell you she took me to a mossy bank and – I kissed her breasts, her small, sweet breasts – they tasted of – of rose petals – and she almost gave herself to me – she almost ... it was a matter of a few moments. If the sun had been a second later, I would have had her. Maybe it was my fair skin? They had pale fair skins too. If I'd just had a little more time – the sun – and I'm *not* old – I'm not even thirty yet.'

'That's *old* when there are handsome youths of eighteen and nineteen around, with not a blemish between them. Look, I'm not saying you didn't have a woman. You probably picked up one of the Tahitian wives – they're a pretty free lot on this island – but I shouldn't tell her husband if I were you. It always helps to keep it quiet afterwards. Don't brag about your secret liaisons, Seumas – it isn't manly.'

'*It was a damn fairy*,' shouted Seumas, thereby making a sharp pain go through his head, as if a wooden stake had been hammered between his eyes. '*I could have had her, if Ra hadn't come between us.*'

'Have it your own way,' sighed Po. 'Never mind you were too drunk to see straight. Just keep away from the kava juice in future, or you'll have fairy children to look after, as well as a stupid dog.

'And if you did abduct a fairy from the fire dancing,' said Po, admonishing him sternly, 'then I would have expected the gods to stop you raping her. She would have destroyed you with her mana. No wonder Ra rose early this morning. It was to prevent you from violating one of his fairies and to save your worthless goblin hide. If he hadn't, you would have been a smoking piece of meat now, struck down by lightning of your own seeking.

'The lust of some men,' added Po with a fatherly shake of his head, 'often astounds me.'

'That's rich, coming from you,' Seamus snarled.

'I never meddle with the fairies,' replied Po, haughtily. 'I've got more sense than *that.*'

With that the captain got up and walked away from the pool, leaving Seumas wondering whether the kava juice really had been responsible for his night apparitions.

Tangiia emerged from his house the morning after the wedding with an angry look on his face. Manopa, on seeing the king, knew immediately that all had not gone well in the marriage bed and put it down to a sexual failure. After all, both parties in the marriage were virgins. Perhaps Tangiia had been over-excited and had brought forth his seed too early? Perhaps he had been too anxious and had not been able to achieve an erection? Maybe the bride was too terrified to let him enter her? These were not uncommon problems on the first night.

'Well, what are you standing around for?' growled Tangiia, storming past his second-in-command. 'Haven't you got any work to do? It's this place! It encourages idleness.'

The king went off into the rainforest, presumably to find the pool where he could wash.

'Definitely,' Manopa muttered to himself. 'No doubt about it – a personal failure.'

Around the village men and women were emerging from their huts and houses, bleary-eyed and hung over after the feasting and drinking at the wedding. Children, always the first to be up, were running around playing games.

The older ones were already doing their chores, lighting fires, pounding seeds, fetching fresh water. The women came out next, rubbing their faces, calling to the children to come and eat, or to do this or that, taking swipes at cockroaches with a handy log. Finally the men staggered out, bad-tempered, scratching their heads or their genitals, or both, many of them with full bladders or bowels, or both, heading towards the nearest clump of bushes.

Manopa noticed Po, down by the shore, talking to some returning night fishermen who had gone out after the wedding. There were always some who took advantage of the fact that others were over-indulging, using the opportunity to fish in grounds not strictly their own. He called to Po.

'Come here, will you?'

Po glanced across, frowned, and said a few more words to a fisherman, before walking slowly across the warming sands, over the under-tree grasses, to where Manopa stood.

'What is it?' asked Po. 'What's the crisis now?'

Manopa told him about the king.

'Well, what do you want *me* to do about it?' asked Po. 'Service the queen?'

Manopa glowered. He didn't like foul-mouthed talk, like Po and his fishermen friends. Besides, talk like that, about the queen, was not only tasteless, it was treason. If Tangiia had heard Po he would have been felled by a club in an instant. Po knew it too. His expression told Manopa that Tangiia's number three knew he had gone too far with that remark.

'I'll pretend I didn't hear that,' Manopa said, pompously. 'What I want you to do is have a little discussion with our king. You know the kind of thing I mean? Tell him it can happen to anyone, whatever it is that's bothering him. Tell him it's quite normal for a young man, a virgin, for things to – things not to work as one expects them to, especially after a wedding where the drink flowed so freely. Give him a fatherly talk about first nights ...'

'Me? Why don't you do it?'

'You're older than I am – more of a father figure – and you're better at these things than me. I'm a bit too blunt – I don't have your – your social skills.'

Po flicked his head irritably as if to say, oh sure, me again.

After a while he said, 'Oh, all right – but you'd better be within call. If he goes to bash my head in, I want you close by to stop him. An ordinary man doesn't take kindly to advice about his sex life, let alone a king.'

'It depends how it's done,' said Manopa. 'I'm sure you can find the right way and the right words. If I may make a suggestion, get him on his own by the bathing pool and start talking about yourself, when you were first – well, when you married your first wife, as a young man ...'

Po stiffened. 'Nothing went wrong on *my* wedding night, I'll have you know. I was as hard as a totem and I gave her what for at least six times. She was begging ...'

'Yes, yes,' snapped Manopa, losing his patience, 'no one's interested in your sexual prowess. *Pretend* can't you? Make it all up.'

'I'm not telling *anyone* that I had trouble on my first wedding night. I'd be the brunt of all the mariners' jokes. My status as a captain would be worth nothing.'

Manopa regarded the tall, skinny captain with exasperation.

'Why can't you do something to help your king?' he said. 'Why do you have to turn a simple chore into a massive problem?'

'If it's so simple,' snapped Po, 'why don't you do it?'

'Because – because I can't be as *subtle* as you.'

Po nodded. 'That's true.'

At that moment a dripping King Tangiia passed by them, flinging words over his shoulder.

'Still standing around, Manopa? I see you've passed this bad habit on to Po. Idleness is not a good friend.'

Po glanced at the king and then looked back at Manopa.

'Remember,' hissed Manopa, 'subtlety.'

Po nodded, then yelled after Tangiia, 'Couldn't you get it up then?'

Tangiia stopped in his tracks, his back still facing the two men. Manopa felt like sinking into the sand. His heart had shrivelled in his chest to the size of a dried nut kernel. He stared at Po in horror, knowing that Po was going to tell Tangiia that he, Manopa, had told him the king had failed to make love to his bride on the night of the wedding. He was going to die.

'Why are you doing this to me?' he squeaked at Po. 'Do you hate me so much?'

Po waved some fingers in Manopa's face, as if to say, don't worry, I have the situation well in hand.

Tangiia came back, his face stricken with misery.

'What did you say?' he asked Po, in a quiet voice.

'I was just telling Manopa here that you were a real man after all. He's not so far away from us, after all, I said, even though he's a king.'

'What are you talking about?' asked Tangiia.

'You know, not being able to do it, on your first night. It happens to everyone, even Manopa here – strapping fellow that he is. Why,' he smiled, 'it's almost a tradition amongst us virulent types. It's because we're so eager, so rampant.' He made a gesture with his fist and forearm.

'You mean virile,' muttered Manopa.

'Yes, that's what I mean.'

Tangiia looked from one captain to the other, slowly, then said in a very tight voice, 'I understand you're trying to allay any concerns you believe I might have, but my marriage bed is my own business. But I'll tell you this –

there's nothing wrong with my potency. It has nothing to do with me, you understand? Now I don't want to have to talk about this again – ever.'

He turned away and marched back to his house.

Manopa looked disgustedly at Po. 'Virulent?' he said, shaking his head.

Po shrugged. 'You're better with words than me.'

Tahiti was a land of pleasure at that time, with King Morning Star at its head. Corpulent, amiable and fun-loving, the king was as close to a hedonist as a man could get. He had seventeen wives, all of them pretty, some of them fat. There were feast days by the score, throughout the year. The king had revived as many old customs as there were gods to support them; so long as those customs involved either food, drink or sex, with dancing and music in between, he would make it a law.

Morning Star's favourite god was Rongo-ma-tane, the God of the Sweet Potato, a food he devoured in vast quantities. He would have made the sweet potato taboo to everyone but kings, if such an action would not have resulted in famine. As it was, most men and women were careful not to be seen by their king to be eating the vegetable, let alone wasting it.

Rongo-mai was another god to whom the king paid special deference, since he was God of Comets. Because the king was one of the stars in the heavens, he paid particular attention to this region of the world, and he loved falling stars and comets. His special treat was to lie on his back outside his house, looking up to the roof of voyaging, and watching the stars, counting meteors until he fell asleep. Then his priests would carefully lift him on the specially strengthened mats and carry him indoors.

Much as this idle pleasure suited Manopa, he saw his own king being sucked into a life of indolence. The Raiateans were beginning to make themselves too much at home. Some were building their own fishing canoes instead of borrowing a Tahitian outrigger. Others married local men and women, thus giving themselves a stake in the kingdom. Some took on posts which were unpopular amongst the Tahitians, like being responsible for the clearance of the beaches near the village.

Manopa went to see Tangiia in his house. The king had been brooding ever since his wedding night. Kula was there, making supper for the two of them. It seemed like a nice domestic scene. Kula was welcoming, showing Manopa to his mat, offering him a drink. There was a lightness to her voice which was absent from that of the king's. Tangiia watched after his wife, as she moved about the room, his eyes on her every moment. His expression was not angry, nor even sullen, but a little vacant, as if he were somewhere else.

Manopa got to work.

'I've sent for Kikamana. We must have a discussion, the three of us.'

'What about?' asked Tangiia, picking at the weave in the mat on which he was sitting.

'We must leave this place, we've been here almost six months,' said Manopa.

'What's wrong with it?' asked Tangiia, desultorily.

'What's wrong with it? There's nothing wrong with it, except that it's only a spit away from your brother's kingdom. Sooner or later there'll be mariners from Raiatea or Borabora visiting these islands and they'll carry word back to your brother. It's not safe here. We have to move on.'

'In a little while.'

'But our pahi are gathering barnacles and weed on their hulls out there. The sails are rotting with lack of use.'

'Get some men to drag them out of the water – scrape their bottoms. Make some new pandanus sails.'

Manopa said, 'That's not the point—'

At this moment Kikamana arrived.

Manopa said to Kikamana, 'Tell the king what you told me earlier – about the dark force.'

Kikamana nodded. 'King Tangiia,' she said, 'we must leave these shores. I believe your brother is very close now, leading a flotilla of tipairua canoes. My dreams are full of black sails and blood-red seas. We must go on. Our destiny is not here, but on some island we have not yet known.'

Tangiia paid attention now.

'If Tutapu is out on the high seas, who's guarding the islands of Raiatea and Borabora?'

'We can't go back there,' Manopa said. 'Eventually Tutapu will head towards home and he'll find you there and slaughter us all. If we leave now we have a chance of getting far away – of losing ourselves amongst the islands and reefs at the bottom of the world.'

Kikamana said, 'Manopa is right. Your place is on a new island with a new nation.'

'We're getting fat and lazy here,' complained Manopa. 'Look at our people. They were hardy mariners a few months ago, now all they do is look forward to the next festival day. The time of the green lizard is on us. We know Tangaroa favours your brother – the Great Sea-God is making life so easy for us with these fine days, this good weather, on this beautiful island – and it *is* a beautiful island – we don't want to leave.

'The problem is, it's not *our* island. When Tutapu gets here, how do you know Morning Star won't side with *him*? He's the older brother, the one entitled to the kingdom.'

'What does my new wife say?' asked Tangiia, testily.

Kula glanced over at the intent group and shrugged her shoulders.

'It's not my decision,' she said.

'You're the queen, aren't you?' Tangiia answered back.

'I – I haven't yet got used to that fact. It will take me some time before I feel able to offer you helpful advice. Until then, you rule by yourself, you must do it on your own.'

'Like a lot of other things around here,' muttered Tangiia, and Manopa gave his king a startled look.

'Well,' continued Tangiia, 'domestic quarrels apart, I suppose you're right. We should continue our voyage. Tangaroa deliberately allowed us to reach Tahiti because it's so tantalisingly near our old home. He's made it a haven of rest and beauty for us. Well, he'll beguile us no longer with his tricks. I'll bet he'll have the waves crashing on the shoreline within an hour, trying to stop us from getting away.'

Manopa stood up, relieved that the king had come to his senses at last.

'I'll start to make preparations at once.'

Kikamana also got to her feet, her long-flowing tapa robes rustling against the mats.

'It's the right decision,' she said.

She too left the house.

Tangiia turned to his wife. 'So that's why you've been holding out. You knew Tutapu was on his way and you've been saving yourself for him.'

She lifted her eyes and stared at him defiantly.

'If that's what you want to think.'

'What else should I think?' he said, heatedly.

'You should think that your wife has her reasons for restraint at this time, that she would never have married you unless she loved you, that she had no way of knowing that your brother was pursuing you, and that you should be thinking about becoming a man in your own right.'

She left him, standing there, and went out with a gourd to fetch some water from the stream.

After a moment he called softly after her, 'How can I become a man, if you keep rejecting me?'

The fleet left Tahiti on a fine morning bearing delicate wisps of cloud like streamers in Rangi's sky. There were dancers on the beaches to say farewell to Tangiia, Kula and the rest of the courageous seafarers, once more embarking on a voyage into the unknown. On the beaches too were the Raiateans remaining behind, most of them with mixed feelings. They had found a new home, it was true, but their comrades were going on to more adventures. Adventure too has its appeal and many would regret they stayed behind to wonder at the fate of their former king and the bold families who accompanied him.

All along the shoreline were huge rocks, half buried in the sand. There were unnoticed symbols on the rocks which dotted the shoreline. Such scratches could have been made accidentally, by the spears of fishermen, or sea creatures, but in fact had been left by the traitor amongst Tangiia's people. They were secret marks left for a pursuer. Marks which would be recognised by that pursuer or his kahuna.

PART SEVEN

Cave of the Poukai

1

'Even when the stars are not visible, the shape of the waves will tell you which of the three seas you are in, be it the darkest of nights,' said Kaho, the blind navigator. 'One need never be so lost that one doesn't know in which part of the great ocean one is sailing.'

Seumas shook his head. 'They all seem the same to me – at least, big ones and little ones, but the shape? They don't have any shape, do they? Not a regular shape.'

They were standing on the deck of *The Scudding Cloud*. Kaho, his head tilted a little, was obviously enjoying the feel of the sea wind on his face. He sniffed deeply, inhaling the ozone, filling his lungs with pure air. Seumas knew what the Feeler-of-the-sea was experiencing. Tahiti had been a beautiful island, but the smells of people living together, of cooking, sewage, animal dung, and rotting waste, pervaded every corner of the village. Out here on the ocean, the atmosphere was untainted by any odour from humankind.

'Oh, when you've lived as close to the ocean as we have, using it as a second home, treating it as an extension of the land, then you can recognise shapes in the unshapely.'

Seumas said, 'But even if you know which corner of the world you're in – those *corners* are pretty big stretches of water.'

'Most of the ocean's currents follow the prevailing winds,' explained the expert Kaho. 'It doesn't take long to know and understand the mean set of the seas, and information can be passed on through generations. But it would take more than a lifetime for an outsider to learn these things, so give up any ambition you may have to be a navigator.'

'There's no such ambition in my breast,' said Seumas, emphatically. 'I just like to talk with you.'

He stared out over the sea, a deep green colour under the lowering clouds. There was a brisk blow lifting the wave-tops, feathering their tips. Sheets and lines were flapping on the craft, slapping against wood.

'In my old country,' Seumas added, remembering, 'the ships always hug the coastline. We don't make long voyages like you people – the open sea is too full of dangers.'

'You should learn to trust to wave, wind and star, like the Oceanians,' said Kaho, before going off to rest.

'I trust the elements,' said Seumas to Dirk, 'as far as I could throw a pahi. And as for these gods of yours …'

They were now sailing in the direction of Papaa-ite on the windflower, following one of the trades. They had left Tahiti six days previously. Some of the people had elected to stay behind and live on Tahiti, about thirty in number. These were mostly men and women who had married Tahitians.

Assisted by Kieto, Tangiia was standing by one of the masts, knotting his cord-device, charting their progress. Tangiia was now wisely running before the wind, trusting to Maomao. He had promised himself and others that he would not be diverted by any tricks used by Tangaroa.

Kikamana, who had dream-knowledge of the gods through the sau of atua and Tiki, told Tangiia that Tangaroa was peeved rather than angry with the navigator king, for bringing the wrong god on the voyage. It was not so much the refugee Raiateans whom Tangaroa was trying to spite, it was Maomao the Great Sea-God. This was actually a quarrel between the gods, a jealous tiff between the supernatural beings who shared the world with humans.

Tangaroa could of course, if he wished, crush the expedition with one mighty tidal wave, and be done with it. Instead, he wanted to use the refugees to tease the Great Wind-God, to annoy Maomao by thwarting their plans. At the same time, Kikamana was told by her atua and informants, Tangaroa and Maomao were on the surface pleasant to one another. Io, the Supreme Being, would have it no other way. Io always expected harmony between the gods and goddesses and rather than upset the Old One, the most ancient of the gods, the supernatural inhabitants of earth, sky and sea maintained outwardly congenial relationships.

Tangaroa, who had indeed appeared as the Green Lizard to the island of Tahiti, thus bringing about the good weather and encouraging laziness and procrastination amongst the Raiateans, now brought a reef of spirits up from the depths of the ocean, to cause Tangiia's fleet of pahi to be diverted. This eater-of-canoes was brought just to the surface of the water, where it could be seen by the navigator king as rips in the ocean. Maomao, rushing by, would not notice the new reef, right out in the middle of the ocean, so far from land.

Tangaroa was hoping to alter Tangiia's course by the merest fraction. What began as a fraction often developed into a major change of direction the farther one sailed. In this way Tangaroa planned on leading the fleet to another of those parts of the ocean where the line between the real and the unreal was to be crossed, where the languid noons lulled wayward seafarers into a dreamy-weary state of mind.

Here the mariners' brains would fill with smoke under a hot sun and calm sea. Their judgement would be blunted by their inability to tell the substantial from the illusory, and they would be lost in their own imaginary world where anything could happen.

The navigator king saw the rips on the surface of the ocean and immediately changed tack to avoid them. However, the coral reef was a good deal longer than Tangiia had at first guessed and he had to circumnavigate the whole ridge, thus altering his so-far steady course across a broad sea.

At midday, three days later, the weather turned humid and hot. The sails were still full, the wind still blew, but the ocean remained as flat as a mountain pool. People sought the shade, finding the sweltering sky too much to bear.

There was a sound like the buzzing of insects in the air, though no such creatures could be seen. Fresh vegetables and fruit tasted dry and fibrous on the tongue. Bark became crisp and curled away from bare wood. Drinking water became warm in the gourds and failed to quench the thirst.

In the ocean itself, there were knots of sea-snakes floating on the dull, oily surface, as if they had become accidentally entangled and were doomed to die struggling with one another until the last gasp.

This energy-draining weather lasted many, many days, until finally land came into sight, like a dark mouth on the horizon. In the hard-edged light of the afternoon, it gleamed dully, its heat-waves rising like fronds from its dense stone. It was a long low island with a squat central ridge. The ridge was bare rock at the top, melting into jungle beneath.

There was the cloying perfume of blooms in the air, making it difficult to breathe.

In the natural harbour there was no reef and the remains of palms, without their tops, projected from the sea offshore. It seemed the ocean had reclaimed some of the land. The trees were black and rotten for the most part, but Tangiia found a stump strong enough to which he could moor his drifting pahi.

He then called to *The Volcano Flower* and *The Royal Palm* to moor up alongside *The Scudding Cloud*. The sound of his voice was leaden in the dull, heavy atmosphere. His call was returned stolidly by the other two captains.

Manopa came on board, followed by Po. Kikamana and Boy-girl attended the conference of the captains, joined by Kula, who exercised one of her privileges as queen. Opinion was divided fairly evenly. Manopa, Kikamana and Kula were for leaving the area immediately. The Farseeing-virgin said the portents were bad. On the other hand, although Boy-girl agreed with Kikamana about the portents, she felt that the crews, including the captains, could do with a few days' rest before setting sail again.

'Everyone is weary,' said Boy-girl. 'If none of us goes ashore, I feel we can risk sheltering in this harbour for a short while.'

Kikamana nodded. 'Boy-girl's right. If we do stay, the island should be forbidden territory, to all crew and passengers on the pahi. Not even the captains should put a foot on those sands. Not even a kahuna like myself must touch solid earth.'

'I shall feel uneasy even out here,' said Kula, shuddering when she looked at the island. 'There's something very sinister about this place.'

So it was settled that no one should go ashore and that the crews would rest for two days before the fleet continued on its journey.

'Seumas, Seumas, the boy's gone.'

'Wha – what's the matter?' asked Seumas waking from a deep, uncomfortable sleep.

His mouth was dry, he badly wanted a piss, and his brain felt sluggish and ponderous.

He looked up to see Po standing over him.

'Kieto, the boy. That fool dog of yours suddenly took it into its head to flop in the water and swim to the island. The boy saw it go – he took a dugout and went after it.'

'Dirk? Kieto?' He rubbed his drooping head. 'What did the hound do that for? He's never left my side without an order before. You know that.' Seumas looked over the inert water at the island. Nothing seemed to be moving there, not even the wind.

'We'll have to go after him.'

Po said, 'Tangiia gave an order than no one was to set foot on the island.'

'Where is Tangiia?'

'Asleep. They're all asleep, except for one or two fishermen. I can't wake the king or Manopa.'

Seumas said, 'It's this place. How come you didn't fall asleep like the rest of us?'

Po lifted his head and showed Seumas his nostrils.

'I stuffed some herbs up my nose, because I didn't like those tree blossom smells, wafting over from the island – I prefer the stink of fish to the tricky smell of perfume. Whenever I catch a whiff of flower fragrance, I end up getting married again. That's how I got my three wives, letting myself be charmed by an overpowering scent.

'And in my opinion that perfume in the air is what's sending people to sleep. So I'm breathing the tang of cooking herbs, not the fumes from that island. I thought some of us should stay awake. You should try it too. Kula has.'

He gave Seumas a handful of damp herb leaves. Seumas duly blocked his nostrils with some of them.

'Kula's awake?'

'She did the same as me, when she saw what I was doing.'

'Well,' said Seumas, rising to his feet, 'it's up to us then. Are you with me?'

Po nodded. 'I'll round up all those people I can wake. Some are more soundly asleep than others. Then we'll go and look for the boy.'

'And my dog.'

Po rolled his eyes to heaven.

Kula helped the captain of *The Volcano Flower* to stuff herbs in the nostrils of other men and women and eventually there were enough awake to form a search party.

'I don't want anyone asleep over *there*,' warned Po, pointing to the island. 'We don't want to be looking for you too.'

'They'll be all right,' said Kula. 'I hope there's some fresh cool water on that island. All the water here on deck is warm, from lying in the sun.'

They took two dugouts, one with Po, two fishermen and two other women – the other carrying Seumas, two mariners and Kula. When they got to the beach they pulled the canoes up above the high-tide mark and decided to split the search party into two separate groups, one going left, the other going right.

'You walk along the beach that way, and we'll go the other,' said Po. 'When we meet up, on the other shore, we'll take a path each inland. I just hope that jungle was too dense for that stupid dog of yours and they've stuck to the shore.'

Seumas didn't argue with the captain. He and Kula and the two mariners began to walk along the beach, calling for both Kieto and Dirk.

The foliage was a tangled mass at the top of the beach, rolling like a dark green wave. All along the shore were dead shells, bleached coral and white driftwood. Sometimes this litter was so deep it was difficult to walk. They trudged on, seeing no living creatures on that usually busy margin where land met sea – no crabs, no mudskippers, no myriad of insects.

'Kieto? Kieto?' Kula called in a clear, lyrical tone that she hoped would carry.

'Dirk?' cried Seumas, in a sharp voice. 'Here, boy – here. Come, Dirk. Dirk? Dirk?'

Occasionally Seumas would stop to whistle, while the two mariners put their hands over their ears, hating the shrillness of the sound. The whistle seemed to hit the heavy, humid air like a fast bird hitting a wall. It carried no further than did their shouts, which also fell to earth like dead birds and were lost in the crammed flora of the island.

At one point they found human bones, picked clean by some unseen creature. The backbone was scattered over a wide area, little sockets that had come unhinged. The leg-bones and armbones were missing, but the ribcage was still there, with the skull inexplicably imprisoned within it, staring out through the bars. It was as if the head had locked itself inside the cage, to escape from something ghastly on the outside.

'Wait,' said Kula. 'I hear something!'

They listened hard and indeed there were some shrill cries, coming from the hinterland.

Seumas said, 'Come on.' He gripped his obsidian-edged club in his right hand and began hacking a path through the jungle. Kula and the two mariners did the same. To their surprise, the deeper they went, the less dense became the growth, until finally they found a stream beside which were some prints, both boy's and dog's.

'Good,' said Seumas, 'we're on the right track.'

They followed the stream until they came to a clearing where a rock face, half hidden by vines and foliage, appeared as a backdrop. Out in the clearing was a huge totem, a living tree carved in antiquity, which soared upwards in a multitude of faces and forms to a small crop of green at its head. The figures on its trunk and along its branches had been so cleverly wrought, there was always bark flowing between them to allow the sap a continuous path, thus ensuring the life of the tree.

Growth had distorted the images on the massive totem, still resplendent with buttress roots, the middle of each vane standing as tall as Seumas. Organs – lips, eyes, noses, genitals – bulged from the carved faces and loins of the ugly figures. Staring at the twisted, warped features made Seumas feel giddy and ill, so horrifying were they. It was as if the tree-totem had deliberately grown galls and knots in places to emphasise gross parts of the now unrecognisable faces.

A hole in the trunk had become a hideous mouth with curled lips around it. A fat gall was now a bulbous nose, with cavernous nostrils beneath. Knots formed crazed eyes, veined and staring fixedly. A thick, stunted branch had grown to an ugly phallus, thrusting wildly at the sky.

And there were thousands of such faces, such torsos, from the roots to the topmost branch of the tree.

Around the base of the tree, all the undergrowth was dead, covered by a blinding-white crust of bird lime. And all down one side of the tree too, this bird lime ran like a frozen river, down from the phallus-branch which had obviously been used as a perch by a multitude of birds. Pure white faces on one side, brown on the other, all forming part of the same tree-totem. A totem whose eyes could see in every conceivable direction at once. A totem from the top of which the world could be viewed.

'Horrible,' said Kula, shuddering.

Spirits fluttered amongst its leaves, registering disapproval at her words.

'Yes, but look between the roots,' said Seumas.

Kula did so and saw that there were two living figures curled up asleep between the vanes of two buttress roots.

The party went to the foot of the giant tree and tried to wake both Kieto and Dirk.

'If they're so sound asleep,' said Kula, 'who was it that called?'

Seumas had no answer to this question.

Neither boy nor dog could be stirred, so one of the mariners lifted Kieto on to his back, using the youth's arms to hold him there. Seumas heaved his dog up on to his tattooed shoulders, draping him around them like a scarf, gripping the hound's paws to keep him secure.

'Let's get out of here,' said Kula, 'before we find out who carved this monstrosity.'

'They must be dead, those people,' said one of the mariners, a man called Pungarehu. 'The faces look so old.'

'Not up there,' Kula said, pointing. 'Look, the higher the figure, the cleaner the wood. Up near the top they are quite fresh ...'

Seumas added, 'They must be some climbers, to get up there and manage to carve faces so high off the ground.'

At that moment the sky darkened as it seemed that a cloud came sweeping low over the top of the cliff. The whole glade went cold as the area around the massive totem was thrown into the shade. It was more than the cold produced by a drop in temperature; it struck a deep, nefarious chill at the core of every soul present. Something wicked was casting that shadow, a fiend with a heart of pure obsidian.

Seumas looked up and his curiosity turned to a feeling of terror as he witnessed the arrival of a giant raptor, with claws and hooked beak large enough to grip a man. Just one of its great wings was enough to blacken the sun. The terrible bird of prey began circling the glade at an incredible speed, in small tight sweeps. Its piercing eyes were on the group below, as if preparing to stoop for a meal. Seumas had no doubt this was the creature which used the phallus branch as its perch.

Suddenly a shriek loud and shrill enough to skewer the brain began to fill the glade as the monster gave throat to its fury. The sound rose still higher, and yet even higher. Seumas's eyes watered as the scream penetrated his skull, threatening to shatter the fragile vessel which held his brain into a thousand small pieces. The giant bird of prey continued to wheel over the glade at a tremendous speed.

'The poukai!' cried Kula, her hands over her ears.

The group were strung out across the glade. Seumas and Kula were leading. Kula grabbed Seumas's arm and pulled him towards the trees at the edge of the clearing. Seumas, the dog a dead weight on his shoulders, followed willingly. Pungarehu, carrying Kieto, also turned towards the tree line. The last man however was closer to the totem and in a panic he dashed for the shelter of the buttress roots, waving his arms about his head as if to ward off the dreadful talons of the monster bird.

This waving action of the mariner's must have attracted the bird's attention, because he was chosen as its victim. It dropped from the sky like a rock, falling on the hapless mariner and snatching him from the ground before he reached the totem-tree. Seumas, now in the trees, witnessed the sickening sight of the mariner being carried wriggling and screaming, to the top of the cliff. There the bird took him in its enormous bill and shook him silly before smashing his head against the rocks. The waving arms and legs went limp and floppy.

'Oh no,' whispered Kula.

The poukai first picked out the eyes with the point of its beak, stuck its bill into the mariner's mouth and pulled out his tongue like a long, red worm, jerking it three times to tear it from its roots. Then the hideous freak pecked open the stomach of the lolling corpse and pulled out intestines like grey string, stabbing at the liver and other lights, eating the man from the inside out.

Blood and brains dribbled down the face of the cliff into some swamp water at the foot, as the body of the mariner was jerked this way and that in the bird's efforts to pick its bones clean. Every so often the bird's great head would look up from its task and stare around, as if watching for enemies.

When it had partially eaten its victim, the poukai flew to the totem-tree. There it found a suitable perch at the top of the tree and began to chisel at the trunk like a woodpecker, as if drilling for grubs beneath the bark. After a while it became apparent that it was hewing a face in the wood.

The face was recognisable.

'It's *him* – my sailing companion,' cried Pungarehu, as the features of the dead mariner began to take shape on the bole of the tree. 'It's carving my friend's face.'

The bird looked down at the source of this sound and let out a loud, echoing *cark* – a mocking tone.

'We must leave,' said Seumas.

The group took the path through the jungle, back to the pahi, before the death mask was finished. Kula helped Pungarehu carry Kieto, so that they could jog a little. They reached the two dugouts and cast off almost on the run. Po's dugout remained on the shore, testifying that he and his party were still walking somewhere on the island. Hopefully they had stuck to the beach as planned and could be picked up easily.

Seumas paddled as if he had mechanical arms, desperate to reach the pahi before the bird should decide to follow them. Even before they were two boat lengths from the ocean-going canoes, he was shouting, 'Everybody up! Everybody awake? We must leave here now. Tangiia, Manopa – everyone on your feet. Get the sails up. Call the paddlers ...'

People moaned in their slumber, one or two stirred and went up on to their elbows, weary and overblown with too much sleep and too little rest. Tangiia began to wake now, as Seumas leapt aboard. The king sat up, his face creased, sleep dust in the corners of his eyes. 'What's happening?' he mumbled.

'A giant bird!' cried Seumas helping the others carry the two bodies on board. 'The poukai, Kula calls it.'

'The poukai?' the king reached for a gourd and splashed water on his face. 'Oh, I remember the tales—'

'Here,' said Kula, going to him. 'Stuff this in your nose – everyone, fill your nostrils with damp herbs.'

'We have to get away from here,' Seumas babbled to Tangiia, his voice just a shade away from hysterical. 'You haven't seen this creature – it's a monster. Come on, get up, you lazy tics, on your feet.' He slapped a few backs. 'Get up and raise the sails, get to the paddles …'

He began kicking at the sailors in earnest. Most of them were still snoring deeply, lying on the bare deck, oblivious of the danger they were in. They rolled over, some staying asleep, others complaining in thick voices about being woken. One man lying in a hut took a swing with his fist at Seumas's ankle, angry at being disturbed, thinking Seumas wanted to steal his comfortable nest of sennit ropes and pandanus leaves.

'Are they dead?' asked Tangiia, unable to help himself yawning. 'The boy and the dog?'

'No, they're alive,' replied Kula. 'They're just asleep.'

Suddenly, Tangiia frowned. 'The poukai,' he murmured. Then more angrily to Seumas, he said, 'You risked my wife's life, taking her over there. It was forbidden.'

'The boy Kieto went after the dog without telling anyone. He was probably afraid we wouldn't go and fetch the hound. We had to go and get him back,' said Kula. 'There were only a few of us awake. Po is still over there, with four others. This is no time to be blaming people for doing what they had to do. Best get the sails up and go round the island to pick up the lost party before they're attacked.'

'Seumas and Po should have known better than to take you,' the king said loudly and persistently.

'They didn't take me – I went of my own free will. I'm not a pretty bird to be kept in a cage. I go as I please.'

Tangiia took this without a change of expression, then he rubbed his face again in irritation.

'What's making me so *weary?*' he grumbled. 'I can't think straight like this. I just feel so drowsy.'

'It's the perfume from the blossoms on the island's trees – push some more herbs up your nose. We have to get on, quickly, or that monster will pick us off the decks like insects.'

'Yes,' cried Seumas. 'We have to find Po and then get out into the deep ocean as quickly as we can.'

At that moment one man, an ordinary sailor, stepped forward and stood in front of Seumas.

'No,' he said. 'That bird is a menace to mariners and seafarers – we must rid the island of the creature.'

Seumas saw he was faced by the sailor named Pungarehu who had carried Kieto back from the island.

'What? Are you mad?' yelled Seumas. 'Nothing would make me go back there. Nothing.' He shuddered, violently.

Seumas had been truly shaken by his encounter with the monster. Never before had he witnessed such a scene as the attack on the dead mariner and he knew he would see that hideous head with its long curving beak, its glittering eyes, in his nightmares. Even now he could see the stubby red tongue of the bird deep in its throat, as the huge bill yawked wide in that ugly scream of triumph and fury.

Pit Seumas against a mortal foe, be he dwarf or giant or ordinary man, and Seumas would stand and fight. But against this brute bird he felt nothing but terrified revulsion. All those years on the cliffs, stealing fulmars from their nests, had come back to haunt him. This was retribution, this great feathered fiend, this bird-god come to claw out his guts, pick out his eyes, hook out his heart, for the theft of helpless birds on the cliffs of Albainn.

'We must go,' he muttered, shaking badly.

Pungarehu said softly, 'We must kill the bird. It is our duty as mariners. This poukai preys on our kind.'

Seumas turned half-crazed eyes on the sailor.

'And how do you propose to do that?' he cried.

King Tangiia was fully awake now and came and stood beside Seumas.

'Yes,' asked the king, but calmly. 'How?'

'I shall brain the creature with a stone axe,' replied Pungarehu. 'One of the large axes stored in the first deck hut. Seumas still has a squealing pig he made many years ago – he can make it screech to attract the poukai. We need to get the bird in a place with trees, so that it cannot easily take to the air.'

Tangiia frowned. 'The screaming pig Seumas made was burned – I saw it go on the fire myself.'

'Then he has made another one,' said the dogged Pungarehu. 'There are several mariners who know he has one – we've seen it in the second hut, wrapped in tapa-bark cloth. He brought it on board one night before we sailed from Raiatea. We were curious and had a look. It's there all right – the shape of an octopus with stiff legs and a body made from pigskin.'

Tangiia turned to Seumas. 'Is this true – you brought another of your living-dead pigs with us?'

'It's not *alive* in any way,' snorted Seumas. 'It's a musical instrument like a flute ...'

'It makes a noise like a pig in pain, not like a flute,' argued the king. 'It makes a noise like a boar being castrated with a blunt stone knife.'

'It's *not* alive,' insisted Seumas. 'I never brought anything back to life. I'm not a sorcerer. The noise it makes is beautiful to the ear of a Pict or Scot – you just don't appreciate the sound. I like to play.'

'Then you must play for Pungarehu,' said the king, firmly. 'You must make your pig squeal for him. See if the poukai monster appreciates your music. See if you can beguile it with your mountain goblin's flute.'

'No – no – I can't. Not that. It's like a terrible dream. I can't do it. I can't.'

Tangiia whispered in his ear, 'Are you a *warrior?* I was beginning to think you were like us. But you seem to have grown cowardly. Are all Albannachs cowards like you?'

'But this is different,' hissed Seumas. 'This bird has come for *me*. I know it.'

'All the more reason to kill it then.'

'Yes, but – someone else. I can't play. Look, my hands are trembling.' He held out his quaking hands for inspection. 'My fingers won't find the right holes on the chanter.'

'Will it matter?' asked Tangiia with a touch of sarcastic humour. 'Who can tell the difference?'

'I can,' hissed Seumas, his fierce pride in his clan's marshal tune making him rise to the challenge.

'Then make your fingers obey you.'

Only a little more persuasion was needed, for Seumas was growing in confidence all the while. He had been badly frightened on the island, but he told himself now that he could only die once, and he had thwarted death several times in his younger years. He should have died when he fell off the cliff into the sea, but Kupe plucked him from his grave. He should have died on Nuku Hiva, but somehow he had survived. There were many other, earlier times. If anyone should have died before now, it was him.

'I hope I don't run,' he said to Pungarehu, 'when I see that bird again.'

'You better hope I don't run,' said Pungarehu. *'You're* the bait.'

They both touched the God of Hope for luck before leaving the ship and paddling over to the island. Seumas had his bagpipes with him. Pungarehu had his great stone axe, a monstrous weapon that was used to fell hardwood trees. It had a haft as thick as a man's wrist and an obsidian head, chipped to a sharp edge, bound to the haft with sennit cord.

They beached the canoe and retraced their steps to the jungle clearing. Seumas was almost hoping that the great bird had gone and flown away somewhere, but it was still at the top of the cliff, picking at the carcass of the mariner. The plan was to stay within the trees, which were sparse but would hamper the bird's flight. Seumas made ready with his bagpipes, while Pungarehu positioned himself in the lower branches of a tree.

Seumas blew up the pigskin bag, and then began playing, his fingers dancing nimbly along the chanter.

It was a pibroch he played, a martial dirge, and even before the first few notes wailed over the glade, the bird left its perch and began to wheel.

Once again the fear knotted itself in Seumas's windpipe. It was all he could do to find air to fill the bag. If Pungarehu had not been with him he would have surely run away.

As he played, Seumas stared unbelievingly as the wind rushed through the bird's feathers creating a sound almost equalling that of the bagpipes in volume. The tail of the bird was shaped like an arrowhead, with long side streamers. These whipped the treetops as the poukai swooped and dived, trying to find a way in to the creature who was making all the noise. Shadows flickered over the two men as the bird cut through the shafts of sunlight above the forest. Seumas felt like a highland hare, about to be taken by a golden eagle; to be ripped open while he was still alive and feeling pain, and his eyes and tongue pecked out.

Come on! his mind yelled. *Get it over with.*

The poukai then let out one of its ugly screams, completely drowning the pibroch. It landed swiftly on the turf of the clearing and came running into the rainforest, half as tall as the trees. Its pace was phenomenal and at last the Pict's nerve broke. Seumas spat out the mouthpiece and turned to run for cover, as the monster weaved amongst the trunks, heading straight for him as fleet as any highland stag.

Seumas turned once, to look over his shoulder, and saw a large bright pair of eyes bearing down on him from the darkness in the canopy of the rainforest. The small knot of fear in his throat became a large twisted clout. He was going to die, he was sure of it. That hooked beak was about stab him in the back and pierce his lungs on the way through.

'Ahhhghh! Pungarehu?' he cried. 'Where are you?'

Had the Oceanian already taken to his heels? Seumas wouldn't have blamed him. He would hate him with his dying breath, and curse his progeny, but he wouldn't blame him.

The ground was a snake pit of tree roots. Seumas's foot caught in one of these and he fell headlong forwards. He hit the earth with a thump, winding him. He rolled on to his back and held the bagpipes up in front of his face in a vain attempt to protect his eyes.

'NO!' he yelled.

The poukai's beak jabbed and pierced the pigskin bag, forcing air through the pipes.

'Whhhheeeeeeeyyyy,' went the pipes, nasally.

A moment later Pungarehu dropped from his hiding place in the tree, on to the bird's back. The mariner swung his axe and shouted, 'Here, monster, up here!' for all the world as if he were calling a dog to his side.

The shocked poukai half opened its wings, forgetting that flight in the rainforest, however few trees, was impossible. The poukai began to run, with Pungarehu standing between its wings, a foot on each joint. It seemed as if the poukai was preparing to take off as it weaved amongst the trees, its wing tips brushing the scattered trunks.

Now, Seumas inwardly cried, *hit the bastard now!*

As if he could read the Pict's thoughts, the mariner swung the great axe at the bird. The monster sensed a blow coming and averted its head, but the wily Oceanian was not aiming at the poukai's skull – he was striking at the left wing.

The stone axe struck the creature squarely on the leading edge of its wing, shattering the bone.

The poukai screamed. It began to drag its dead wing, unable to close it now. Its run turned into a circular movement as it realised it was trapped in a ring of trees. The vicious head came up and over its shoulder, as the poukai attempted to peck Pungarehu from its back. Its great beak clacked as it tried to bite Pungarehu, but it had not the room to twist itself half-circle and snatch him with its bill.

Using the follow-through motion of the axe to form an impetus for the next blow, Pungarehu now swung right and broke the other wing, leaving the giant bird screeching in rage and pain, trailing both its wings.

It tried to escape Pungarehu's murderous stone axe, by running back to the glade, but it had lost its equilibrium and its broken right wing caught a tree, sending the monster crashing to the ground. The brave Pungarehu then stepped forward on to the neck and battered the poukai to death, splitting its skull with the edge of the axe and letting the brains bubble forth.

The poukai gave one last pathetic *cark* and died. Its great, soft body, still full of warmth, lay jammed between the trees, the branches brushing its back in the wind. Pungarehu jumped down from the bird and plucked as a trophy a giant primary feather from the trailing edge of the wing. The feather was as tall as a pahi mast and would make a sail in itself.

Seumas came forward and slapped the mariner on the back.

'You did it! That was a great feat. They'll make up songs about this, Pungarehu – and I hope you get all the credit. I panicked there, at the end.'

'I was scared too,' admitted the seaman, smiling. 'My blood was racing like a young river.'

'You kept a cool head and got the job done.'

'To tell the truth,' said the abashed mariner, 'I lost my nose plug and went into a drowsy sleep up there in the branches. It was the wail of your dead pig which woke me. If I had not heard it cry, you would now be carrion.'

Seumas stared at his companion and felt a cold sweat trickling down the hollow of his back.

'You fell asleep?' he said, quietly.

'Yes.'

'Then the God of Pigs must indeed have been watching over us,' breathed Seumas.

Pungarehu grinned broadly at the humour and rested his tired arms on the handle of his axe.

'You are indeed an Oceanian, Seumas,' smiled Pungarehu. 'Only we can joke about such serious matters.'

'Oh, no,' argued Seumas, 'Albannachs are good at that too.'

One who was not too happy with Pungarehu was the Great Wind-God Maomao, until now a friend of the fleet. The birds of the air were Maomao's children; they played in his warm currents and caressed his brow with fine, soft feathers. They filled the atmosphere with their nursery cries and made patterns of their flight to amuse the Great Wind-God.

'This nobody Pungarehu must one day pay for killing the king of the birds,' said Maomao to Papa the Great Earth-Goddess. 'He has slaughtered one of my children, not for meat or feathers, but simply because it was there.'

'It killed and ate his friend,' Papa reminded the fickle god. 'Men are emotional creatures – passionate about friends and family.'

Maomao was only slightly mollified by Papa's speech defending the actions of Pungarehu and never quite forgot the wrong the mariner had inflicted on the wind-god.

After the death of the poukai, Po and his band met them in the forest, having circumnavigated the island. Together the whole band of men and women climbed the cliff behind the totem, at the top of which they discovered a cave. In the entrance and deep inside the cave were piles of human bones and skulls. Sorting through the skeletons they found many necklaces, bracelets and amulets, belonging to the victims of the poukai.

They returned with these to the glade and hung them on the great live totem as a symbol of respect and deference to the ghosts of the cave and clearing.

While they did this, Pungarehu carved one last death image on the trunk, that of the poukai itself.

The party returned in triumph to the bay of the dead palm trees, where the pahi were moored. There they were greeted by King Tangiia, to whom Pungarehu gave the feather as a tribute, and wild celebrations followed. That night they sailed away from the island and this time Tangaroa was better pleased, having struck at his old rival Maomao, by having his own favourite people kill his favourite bird. It satisfied the Great Sea-God's appetite for revenge for a while.

PART EIGHT

Out of Tawhaki's Armpits

1

The name of lightning is Uira.

He is given life by the God of Thunder and Lightning, Tawhaki, not through a womb as with a mortal woman, but out of his armpits. Tawhaki *is* thunder, but to bring lightning Tawhaki spreads forth his arms and calls for the long jagged strips of blinding light, and flat pulses of brightness, that arc Uira.

Uira fell in furious mood on the flotilla of tipairua canoes three days out of Fatu Hiva. It was not that Uira was angry with King Tutapu, or that he was taking sides in the fight. What brought Uira down from the skies were the sixty masts, bearing the sixty black sails, of the thirty tipairua.

Uira always sought out masts which stood high above Tangaroa's ocean, and sixty of them at once was just too easy not to miss. Uira the feller of trees brought down seven of the sixty masts, rigging and sails too, causing havoc on the decks of the tipairua.

Following this onslaught, Maomao sent Hau-iti-no-teriitua on the wind-flower, to blow against the flotilla. An angry King Tutapu found he had to beat against the wind, all the way from Fatu Hiva, so then the king struck out towards Maraamu-tairoto on the windflower and reached the island of Rapa, almost at the bottom edge of the ocean, only to be told by Ragnu that the Great God Tangaroa had come to him as a sea snake at sunset and informed him that King Tangiia was now in Tahiti.

'Tahiti?' snarled Tutapu. 'What's my half-brother doing? Trying to get back to Raiatea and steal my islands?'

Tutapu set sail again towards Torau-farara on the windflower, only to find once again that he was beating against the gale.

The king refused to stop at any island, so anxious was he to catch his brother before he left Tahiti. The fisher folk had to put trolling lines in the sea, to feed the hungry thousands on the move. There was famine on the tipairua, and after a few months scurvy had begun to take a strong hold amongst the seafarers. Polahiki, the fisherman picked up on Fatu Hiva, complained bitterly to Dorcha that he was being misused.

'I'm not one of you people,' he complained. 'Why should I starve or catch some disease, just because your king wants to kill his brother?'

Dorcha looked in distaste at the lice-infested fisherman.

'You probably brought more diseases on board with you than anyone else here.'

The grimy, black-toothed Polahiki said he resented such a remark, coming from a mountain goblin's mouth.

One day, when the wind was in the wrong direction, Tutapu caught the drift of one of Polahiki's complaints. The king was pacing the deck at the time, trying to concentrate on his navigating, wanting to curse Maomao for obstructing him, but fearful of arousing more anger from the Great Wind-God. The whining he heard from Polahiki irritated him.

'Hurl that man overboard,' he ordered two of his sailors.

Polahiki heard the command and threw himself on the deck, clinging with his gnarled fingers on to Dorcha's ankles.

'No! No!' he shrieked. 'I'm sorry, my lord. Please, for the love of the gods – don't drown me. I'm not worthy – I'm not worthy – I'm not worthy …'

They ripped his hands away from Dorcha's flesh, where the nails had penetrated, causing her great pain. There were deep scratches where the fisherman's fingers had been. Then they heaved the struggling, shrieking man above their heads.

Polahiki then gripped one of the masts as they passed it and refused to release. He screamed and cursed them when they hit his fingers with a log. He bit one of the mariners savagely on the wrist as the log struck his hand.

Polahiki then clutched at one man's hair, and when his fingers were prised open, at another man's hair, until finally one of them held him while the other broke the fingers of his right hand, four at once.

He screamed in pain.

They then broke his left wrist.

To give him his due, Polahiki was obdurate to the point of insanity. He wrapped his legs around the neck of one of the mariners, locking his ankles. It took two more mariners to prise those legs open, with a thick bamboo pole, and by that time the man in the neck-lock was almost dead.

Tutapu watched all this in irritated amazement.

Finally, four men had one limb each and they tossed the wriggling, shrieking Polahiki into the air. He landed in the sea with a splash and disappeared from view.

A little later the fisher folk on the stern announced that Polahiki had caught hold of one of the trolling lines and was being dragged along by the canoe.

'Cut it loose,' snapped the king. 'He's slowing me up. Get rid of him *now*. If I hear that man's name again, I'll burn out the eyes of the person that's used it.'

The fisher folk did as they were told, but Polahiki kept grabbing other trolling lines, careless of the hooks that must have been penetrating his flesh. Finally, they managed to lose him and he was left thrashing in the sea – only to be picked up by another tipairua in the wake of the king's canoe, who probably believed that Polahiki had simply fallen overboard.

Dorcha washed her wounds in sea water, hoping they would not become infected. She thought it was entirely possible due to the filthy state of Polahiki's nails, that she would get some demon in her blood. She could see the culprit far behind, picking fish hooks from his arms with his teeth.

'I hope they tear you!' she yelled.

Then she felt bad about it. The poor man had broken bones, torn flesh, and lungs full of water. It was a miracle he was still alive. Dorcha was to find however that Polahiki was a born survivor. Even while on board the king's canoe, fit and healthy men had been dropping to the deck of fever and illness, while Polahiki's scrawny, sickly-looking frame seemed to resist every demon malady or injury known to humankind.

It was night and the stars had crystallised in the sky.

'I've heard enough stories about Maui,' said Dorcha, 'tell me a story about a woman.'

'I can tell you another story about how the first woman came to the world,' said Elo sweetly.

Dorcha sighed. 'That will do for a start.'

'In this story the first woman was made by the Goddess of Mirages ...'

'A goddess making a woman – we do things for ourselves, that's a *good* start.'

Little Elo frowned and said sternly, 'Please don't interrupt, Dorcha, while I'm telling the story.'

'I'm sorry, I'm sorry – go on,' replied Dorcha, suitably chastised.

'The Goddess of Mirages shaped the first woman from the heat waves of the midday sun, that time of day when mirages usually appear. This first woman was given a name. She was called Marikoriko and she married Tiki the first man—'

'Didn't have a lot of choice, did she?' interrupted Dorcha, tartly.

Elo put her head to one side and tightened her lips.

'Sorry, sorry – go on.'

'Well, Marikoriko and Tiki had the first child ever born on earth, who was a girl baby—'

'Another girl! Excellent! – sorry, sorry. I'm just wondering what we needed men for after this. Go on.'

'This first child was called "Lady of the Early Gentle Floating Shadows". Rainclouds appeared in the sky when she was born and these filled the rivers, but not so that they flooded, so that they flowed calm and serene, providing water for the people to drink ...'

'When the people came along of course, because at first there was just Marikoriko, Tiki and their baby girl.'

'Yes, later the people came, but before that the First Child asked for light in the world and morning broke.'

Elo smiled sweetly and fell silent.

Dorcha looked at the girl and then said, 'Yes – what about the story?'

'That *is* the story,' said Elo.

'That's it?' cried Dorcha, incredulously. 'That's all of it? What about the story where a woman saves the world?'

Elo frowned again. 'I don't know of any story like that.'

Dorcha stared at the girl, then at the sky, then at the sea, and said finally, 'I do. Or at least, I know one who tried.'

'Tell it to me then.'

Dorcha said, 'There was once, in the far corner of my island, a Celtic princess, who was raped by invaders when her father died. The invaders from across the seas stole her kingdom and sacked the holy places, murdering the Celtic priests and warriors who tried to stop them. When the princess complained she and her sister were savagely whipped and raped.

'So the princess gathered together many of her own warriors and led them against the invaders. The invaders were very strong people and their warriors were many, but the princess was a great fighter and she and her people killed thousands of the invaders, driving them out of her kingdom.

'Two great battles she fought and won, then on the third she was defeated by sheer weight of numbers – she died defiantly spitting in the face of her enemies.'

Elo's eyes were wide with wonder at this tale.

'She sounds a truly remarkable lady, this princess of your race.'

Dorcha nodded. 'She was.'

'What was her name?' asked Elo.

'Her name was Boudicca.'

Elo repeated the name slowly, having trouble with the pronunciation.

King Tutapu, who had been standing by the mast knotting his cord-device, overheard this story, and said, 'I am interested in this Boudicca of yours – you say she defeated a superior force of warriors? To do this she must have had something which the invaders did not have – not because she was a woman, but because a small force always needs an edge, to conquer a large force. The gods were with her, I suppose?'

'And the goddesses.'

'And her people were very angry,' he added, 'while the invaders had only their greed to inspire them?'

'Just so,' answered Dorcha.

Tutapu said, 'You would like to be such a woman? To fight like a man?'

'Not like a man, like a warrior queen. I don't like the work men leave to women.'

Tutapu shrugged. 'What else can you do?'

Dorcha stared into the king's eyes. They were standing just a short distance from one another. She knew she could not touch him, for he was taboo and she had not been given protection by the kahuna, but just at that moment Tutapu was very attractive to her. He had a regal stance, he radiated power, and he was extremely handsome.

She said, 'I've been watching you, listening to you speak with your helmsmen. I've watched you with your knotted cord-device, noticed your sightings and heard your soundings. I would like to be a navigator too.'

Elo gave out a little gasp, but the king smiled.

'Have you discovered any of my secrets?' he asked.

'Yes. I can recognise many of the kaveinga stars, and the fanakenga stars.'

He nodded to the roof of voyaging. 'Find me the Taro.'

She looked up and then pointed out a group of stars. 'That's it there, with its stem and leaves.'

'Very good,' he said, raising his eyebrows. 'And the Adze?'

'There – handle and blade.'

'The Octopus Tentacle?'

'There.'

'I'm impressed,' he said, 'and I'm sure you know many more of my secrets, but those that are most important take a long time to learn, like the names and directions of the swells, the shape of waves, the long- and short-flighted birds, the te lapa ...'

'I'm learning all the time.'

He questioned her for a long time as the tipairua glided through the night. She could tell he was fascinated by her correct answers to all he asked. When, on rare occasions, she did not know the answer, she told him so bluntly and he then relieved her of her ignorance. Finally he nodded thoughtfully and asked her one more question.

He held up his cord-device. 'And this – can you do this and map our way across the world?'

'That might take me years to learn, but I have this.'

She reached into her blanket smugly and produced a kind of a rectangular frame as long as her arm and half as wide. There were strips of split bamboo criss-crossing it haphazardly. Some of the strips were bent into a curve, others were straight. There seemed to be no order or reason to the irregular network of strips but dotted about, again seemingly at random, were small cowrie shells stuck to the bamboo.

King Tutapu looked surprised. 'What is that?'

'It's a similar thing to your knotted cord-device. See, the whole thing is the great ocean and the slivers of bamboo criss-crossing it are journeys made by great navigators. The cowrie shells are stars. See, this one is Tiuriuri, the Evening Star, and this one Te Tino A Manu ...'

King Tutapu did not take the device from her, because he was afraid his mana might harm her, but he went close and studied the bamboo chart, nodding thoughtfully.

'Yes, yes – I see how it might work. Who taught you this device?'

'Polahiki,' she smiled.

The king screwed up his face in distaste. 'That filthy creature?'

'He's a seafarer, for all his dirt – and he is from a different people, who have different ways.'

The king grunted, unconvinced it seemed.

He said no more for a while. Dorcha put her bamboo chart away and she and Elo chattered. Then Elo fell asleep on the deck. Dorcha too was tired and was about to lie down, when King Tutapu said, 'From tomorrow you will help me navigate. I want you to keep a record of our voyages, just as I do with my cord-device. Do not show it to me, unless I ask you to, otherwise we shall influence each other's recording. Ragnu will be told to raise your status to that of priestess. You are not a virgin, so you cannot hold high office, but there are priestesses with special duties who are not maidens.'

'But I am not your kin – the priestesses share your father with you ...'

'You are sufficiently different from an ordinary person to warrant holding office.'

'If you say so.'

'I say so, goblin.'

She looked at him, startled. 'Shall I do it?'

'I command it,' replied Tutapu.

Dorcha was silent for a moment, realising she had won a great victory. She was to be a priestess – and no common man was allowed to assist the king in his navigating. It was an *awesome* victory. She would have a useful job that was nothing to do with cooking, cleaning or gathering. She was to be a hunter at last – a hunter of secret signs in the night, a hunter of shapes and colours in the day, a hunter of *passage*.

'Thank you,' she said humbly.

Tutapu waved the thanks away with his hand.

'It is deserved.'

Maomao, having heard about Tangaroa's tricks which had led King Tangiia's fleet first to the Isle of the Rapacious Women, then to the Island of the Poukai Bird, decided it was time to do the same to the flotilla of tipairua.

Maomao blew the thirty ships with their black sails in the direction of a certain island where dwelt a giant called Flaming Teeth, whose fangs were fiery logs which flared and spat sparks when he breathed in and out.

Flaming Teeth loved the taste of charred human flesh and spent his days looking out to sea, hoping for a shipwreck on the shores of his island. When a log the size of a great tree trunk burned down to a stump in his mouth, Flaming Teeth would reach in with long thin fingers and pluck it out, pushing a new log into the empty socket.

Tutapu, impatient to find his brother, did not want to land on the island. He ordered his men to fight against the strong wind, to paddle as hard as they could. Finally, with his men exhausted, King Tutapu had to concede defeat. The helmsmen could do nothing to prevent the ships from being driven towards the beach, so fierce and unrelenting was the wind.

However, the Great Wind-God's timing was wrong, because when the flotilla was blown hard up against the shore of the island it was night and the giant's teeth were plainly visible, as he slept on the side of a mountain. Sparks flew up in brilliant showers, above the rainforest. The sky was lit up by the tall flames, hiding the stars beneath their light.

Although the wind was pushing the flotilla up against the shore, on the island itself the air was strangely calm, as if the island were enclosed in a great bubble. The air was muggy and dense like the atmosphere of a sweltering swampland.

Tutapu gathered together eighty of his strongest men and went ashore quietly, hoping to surprise the giant, but the crickets saw the men – all armed with huge rocks wrapped in sennet netting so that they could swing them like clubs – and called to the giant to wake up and defend himself. The pitch of a cricket's song is high enough to penetrate any other sound, including the furnace roar of Flaming Teeth's mouth.

Flaming Teeth, whose arms were as long as his whole body, and whose hands rested next to his feet while he slept on his back, sat up. Only half awake he asked the crickets if they had called him. The flames roared out, scorching the treetops, as he called out his enquiry.

The crickets all answered at once, in a confusing chorus.

'Of course we called you,' they said. 'What's the matter with you? Do you want to be struck down in your sleep?'

One of the giant's long spidery arms bent, the elbow near his knee joint, as a hand came up to scratch his scalp with its straggly, lank hair.

'What?' he cried, flames roaring forth. 'What say?'

The crickets asked him again if he wanted to die, and this time his other hand came up to scratch at his wispy pate.

'What say?' he flared. 'What say?'

At that moment Ragnu instructed his men to whistle and trill like birds, to scare the crickets into silence.

The crickets, surprised to hear birds singing at night, were struck dumb immediately. They did not want to give away their positions in the grasses to birds who might come, seek them out, and eat them. Eventually, when the crickets failed to answer him for a third time, the giant lay down to sleep again, thinking he had dreamt that the crickets had been calling him.

Ragnu said to King Tutapu, 'It seems we have a very stupid giant here, who scratches his head in frustration, every time he's asked a question. But it's not possible to confuse him in this way, because the heat from his mouth, and the roaring noise of the fire, doesn't allow men to get close enough for him to hear what is being said to him.'

Tutapu thought for a while and formed a plan, sending some of his men back to the tipairua. While they were gone he told other mariners to tie logs to the giant's hands with sennit cord, being careful not to wake him. Eventually the ones who had been back to the canoes returned bringing with them whole pig skins filled with sea water. These had been smeared on the outside with precious, sweet-smelling honey.

'Now,' whispered King Tutapu, 'we must get up level with his head.'

They passed the great giant on either side, carrying their large pigskin water containers on two-man poles. All around them, the forest was singed and charred where the giant had accidentally set fire to the undergrowth with his burning incisors and molars. The forests, hillsides and valleys were empty of human life and most large animals. Long ago the giant had eaten all the pigs and dogs of the island, and then started on the humans. The terrified people had run away to hide in the caves in the hillside, but Flaming Teeth easily winkled them out with the use of his long thin arms.

When Tutapu's seafarers reached a height level with the giant's head, but at a safe distance from the terrible flames, they made catapults out of springy saplings.

The giant's teeth flared and roared with each breath taken, the flames reaching higher than the treetops. It was impossible to get close to him, so intense was the heat from his fiery jaws. His mouth was a furnace which withered all the grasses around it and men were beaten back by the scorching flames to a place behind some rocks. Even there the giant's sweltering breath made it difficult for them not to swoon.

At a signal the mariners in the forest began to catapult the pig-sized water containers into the giant's mouth.

Flaming Teeth, thinking in his sleep that he was eating something tasty and sweet, chewed on the honey-covered pouches of water and punctured them. Salt water poured into his mouth, dousing the flames on his teeth with a hissing and fizzing. The giant then sat up, choking and spluttering, his mouth pouring steam and smoke in equal quantities. Without the fire the giant's island was plunged into pitch blackness. Never before had Flaming Teeth been subjected to the darkness.

'What's happened?' he cried. 'Why can't I see? Am I blind? Why is my mouth so wet? Why is it salty? Where are my precious flames? Who is on the island of Flaming Teeth, whose friend is Maomao the Great Wind-God?'

He ground his charcoal teeth together and huge damp splinters of charred wood sprayed forth.

'Who asks all these questions?' cried Tutapu. 'What is your name?'

Flaming Teeth immediately reached up to scratch his head at this question. He struck himself a brutal blow on his own skull with the log tied to his wrist. A yell of pain escaped his lips.

'Answer me quickly,' Tutapu cried, 'are you indeed blind?'

This time the other hand came up and struck the giant a blow on the other side of his head.

'Ahhhhggghhhh!' he screamed. 'Who strikes me?'

'Who strikes you indeed?' called Tutapu. 'Tell me his name and I'll kill him with my club.'

The giant's hand came up again, to scratch his skull, and he struck himself yet again, a terrible blow which made the forest ring with its echoes, wailing in anguish as he did so, crying to the gods to help him fight off his invisible opponent.

'Someone is attacking me in my blindness,' cried Flaming Teeth. 'A monster with thousands of shining eyes.'

He meant the stars, which he had never seen before, his fire having been so bright it overpowered their light.

Tutapu was relentless with his questions, asking one after the other, until finally the giant had beaten himself senseless. Tutapu's men then went forward. They built a platform on stilts, on which they raised a huge rock. This they let fall on the giant's skull, smashing it, and killing him stone dead.

They left the giant's body on the hillside, it being too heavy to move. Maomao blew through the giant's wispy hair and moaned across the great caves that were his nostrils. Maomao was not pleased that one of his adopted children had been slaughtered by King Tutapu, but Io spoke to him and told him he should recognise that it was he who had forced the king to land on the island and that it was partly his own fault.

Maomao had no option but to agree with the Father of Gods and gave Tutapu a fair wind to Tahiti.

Tutapu gathered stores and provisions and set sail once more for Tahiti, where he hoped to find his half-brother.

It was a clear, warm day with gentle breezes lifting the palm leaves like unseen hands. Up on the slopes of the Tahitian mountains a lookout spotted a line of black dots on the horizon. He called down to a runner, who went straight to the king's basket-sharers and informed them of what had been seen. The basket-sharers spoke briefly to the king's high priest. The high priest went into the king's house with the news.

King Morning Star, indolent and lazy in times of peace, was no slouch when it came to protecting his precious homeland. He immediately ordered the launching of a hundred and fifty war canoes. By the time Tutapu's mighty flotilla approached the reef, Morning Star's force was lined up ready for battle, with Morning Star himself in the front line.

Tangiia's force of three pahi had been of little concern to Tahiti, but three thousand warriors in canoes decked for war and bearing sinister black sails was a definite threat.

Drums sounded in the bay as the two fleets approached each other. There was much noise as the warriors sang out their battle songs, asking Oro the Great War-God to grant them victory in the coming battle. A single flush of spears left the leading Tahitian canoe, killing one of Tutapu's men and wounding a woman, before the Raiatean and Boraboran king held up his arms.

'Peace!' called Ragnu, across the water, to the head Tahitian kahuna.

'Peace,' agreed the high priest, after conferring with King Morning Star.

Tutapu signalled that he wished to step on to the Tahitian king's canoe and speak with King Morning Star, as the two great armadas faced each other uneasily in the wide bay.

Safe passage was granted and Tutapu, resplendent in his war helmet and carrying his club and lei-o-mano, leapt from his canoe on to that of the Tahitian king. He greeted King Morning Star with respect and then asked him if Tangiia was present. They spoke formally, with evident reserve and pride.

'Ah,' said Morning Star, 'the Relentless Pursuer. You are King Tutapu, who desires the death of your half-brother?'

'I am that man,' said Tutapu.

'And if I say Tangiia is with my warriors in the bay?'

'Then I shall do my utmost to destroy your fleet, though I die in the enterprise,' said Tutapu. 'I must have his life, for he stole one of my gods and will ever be a threat to me.'

King Morning Star nodded, his great cheeks quivering.

'You would wish me to give him up to you then?'

'Yes.'

'That I cannot do, because he is no longer with us – he left the island some days ago.'

The disappointment showed clearly on Tutapu's face, but he raised his head and said, 'Then I have no quarrel with you.'

King Morning Star nodded gravely and said, 'No, but you were prepared to attack my island, to take a guest from my hands by force, and therefore I refuse to allow you to land and gather provisions. You will sail away from my island now, or face my warriors in a sea battle which you will surely lose.'

Tutapu glared angrily at the Tahitian king, but he reminded himself that it was Tangiia he wanted, not a war with Tahiti. Such a war might be prolonged for generations and ruin both peoples with the waste that war brings. He looked around him, prior to returning to his tipairua.

'I see amongst your warriors and rowers, people from Raiatea,' he said. 'These are traitors to my lands.'

'They are Tahitians now,' Morning Star told him. 'They have married into my family.'

'Your family?'

'All my people are my family.'

Tutapu muttered, 'I see.'

Morning Star said on their parting, 'I have no quarrel with you, King Tutapu. I recognise your right to kingship of your islands and I respect that right deeply. You are the oldest son of my great friend, your father, and I have no wish to interfere in your quarrel. If you had come to me in vessels decked for peace, instead of war, I should have welcomed you with all the ceremony due to a king.

'But you came prepared for war, if not with your brother, with anyone who stood in the way of your brother. Your father would not have done this – he would have changed his sails, the posture of his canoes, the attire of his men, and he would have worn not his war helmet, but flowers in his hair. You have much to learn, Tutapu, about kingship.'

'Perhaps I have,' said Tutapu, wisely. 'Kingship is new to me. Perhaps the passing years will give me more wisdom. But my men are weary. Would it be too much to ask that we remain anchored here for a few hours, while they rest?'

'This request is granted.'

Tutapu returned to his tipairua in thoughtfulness, rather than in anger. He was still upset by his reception, but he had to admit to himself that he had not chosen the wisest method of approach. The Tahitian king was right about that, he had much to learn, but the lessons were coming thick and fast.

When he reached his vessel, he said to Ragnu, 'I would like to slaughter every Raiatean on that island.'

Ragnu gripped his club and said, 'Let us do it.'

Tutapu shook his head. 'No, no. There's no sense in depleting our warriors by fighting a war with the Tahitians for a few grubby traitors. It's Tangiia I want. What we must do is speak with one of those traitors and find out which direction Tangiia took, so that we can follow him.'

'Our spy must surely have left signs for us?'

'True, but any such signs will be on the island – if we cannot wander on Tahiti at our leisure, then we have little chance of coming across them.'

Ragnu said, 'There'll be Tahitian sentries on the beaches, watching us like hungry sharks. But one man might be able to slip through.'

'Who?' asked Tutapu.

'I'll go myself,' said Ragnu.

'If you are not back within a stipulated time,' warned Tutapu, 'I shall have to leave without you.'

'Understood,' replied the high priest.

When evening came Ra and Hine-keha passed each other in the sky without a sign.

As the daylight faded and the moonlight waxed Tutapu shouted orders to his crews, already briefed, to make ready to sail, commands that could be heard from the beaches of Tahiti. While the activity, designed to look speedy and efficient but actually just another delaying tactic, was in progress Ragnu slipped into the water and swam quietly parallel to the reef. When he reached a place where the sentries were thin on the ground, he swam ashore and crept up the beach into the rainforest.

From there he made his way back to the loose-knit cluster of several villages, where most people were still outside their houses and huts gawping at the foreign flotilla, watching as the sailors ran around the decks, hauling on ropes, tightening rigging, raising sails.

Ragnu moved around unobtrusively in the moonlight, searching features, until he found a familiar face.

He went back to the darkness on the edge of the rainforest and called the man's name.

'Over here,' he hissed.

The man looked back, frowning, clearly puzzled.

'What is it? Who's that?'

Ragnu didn't answer. He simply waited, hoping the man's curiosity would get the better of him. It was a successful ruse and eventually the Raiatean ambled over to him, saying, 'Who is it? What is it you want? I want to see Tutapu leave.'

When he was close enough, Ragnu grabbed the man by the throat and dragged him into the bushes. There he proceeded to strangle the man, having had the advantage of surprise, until the man's eyes bugged and he was clearly only seconds away from death. Only then did Ragnu release him.

'Uhhhhhh,' moaned the man, once he had recovered his breath.

'Wha – you – you tried to kill me ...' He rubbed his throat which carried the marks of Ragnu's strong fingers.

Ragnu pulled a kotiate club from his loin cloth and threatened the man with it.

'One word from you, to warn your friends, and I'll smash your skull. Now, I want to know some things from you! If you fail to give them to me, I'll send a kabu to you in the night and you'll die of fear. Have you seen the faces of men who die of fear? The terror makes them open their mouths so wide their jaws become unhinged. Their eyes jump out of their sockets on to their cheeks. Their nostrils bleed ...'

The man, whose face was hidden by shadow, said nothing. He was still clearly very weak from the ordeal of his strangling. He was kneeling on the ground. Ragnu was behind him gripping and stretching him by his long hair, bolt upright, while at the same time standing on his ankles. In his right hand Ragnu held the kotiate club, ready to strike if the man should utter a sound loud enough to alert the Tahitians.

It was a delicate balance. The kahuna did not want to alarm Morning Star's warriors and cause a major incident, perhaps leading to war. At the same time he had to get the information he wanted from this man.

'Tell me!' hissed Ragnu.

At that moment Ragnu felt the man tense and knew he was going to shout for help. A sound came out of the man's mouth which was abruptly cut short as Ragnu decapitated him with the edge of the kotiate club. Ragnu was disgusted in himself, for having chosen a man prepared to die rather than give him the intelligence he needed. He tossed the head into the forest where it landed with a thump similar to that of a coconut falling from a palm.

The noise the man had made had not been enough to alert the people watching the boats. One woman glanced behind, but when Ragnu made a thrashing sound in the bushes, similar to the sound made by a large lizard when it scrambled through dead leaves, she turned back and said something to her neighbour, who giggled.

Ragnu's problem was now time. Tutapu could not delay the departure for much longer and Ragnu realised he would have to get back to the tipairua right away. Cursing, he made his way to the beach, dreading his next meeting with King Tutapu. Once on the beach it occurred to him that perhaps one of the sentries might be a Raiatean and he could club the man senseless and take him back to the tipairua with him. Once he had someone on board the king's canoe they could set sail and torture the man at their leisure, being almost certain to obtain what they wanted.

Ragnu slipped behind a rock and peered over it at three sentries standing together, chattering and pointing occasionally at the foreign flotilla of canoes.

None of these three men looked familiar, but as Ragnu stared at them, he noticed something on the rock itself which showed faintly in the moonlight from Hine-keha's bright face.

It was a mark scratched into the stone surface by someone Ragnu knew well – King Tutapu's spy.

It was a cryptic symbol for papaa-iti on the windflower.

'Got you!' murmured Ragnu, in triumph.

The high priest then crept away from the three sentries and found a place on the beach where he could wriggle down to the water like a turtle without being seen. Once in the warm waters of the great lagoon he swam out towards the tipairua, only to see with consternation that they had already begun sailing away. When Ragnu reached the reef, the last tipairua was riding the surf over the dead, white top-coral.

Tangaroa had witnessed Ragnu's failure to get back to the flotilla in time and sent Aremata-rorua, the long-wave, to assist him. Aremata-rorua, normally feared by mariners, rose up in the lagoon and swept towards the reef. On his way the long-wave gathered Ragnu on its foaming crest and bore him over the dangerously sharp coral, into the ocean beyond.

Aremata-rorua continued his surge out into the deep ocean, until he reached the flotilla of canoes with their ominous black sails. There he petered out.

Ragnu was helped on board the last canoe, which then broke line and took the high priest to Tutapu's tipairua. One of the king's lovers, a young man of extraordinary beauty, was surprised to see Ragnu boarding the canoe and called to his lord that Ragnu was saved. Tutapu emerged from a deck hut. He had evidently been weeping and Ragnu was touched by the fact that he had been so missed by his king.

'Papaa-iti,' Ragnu said.

Tutapu's eyes opened a little wider, then he called to his helmsman.

'Papaa-iti, on the windflower!'

Once he had received an acknowledgement King Tutapu motioned for Ragnu to follow him into his hut. There was a girl in the hut, another of the king's paramours. The king continued to enjoy the bodies of both men and women, so long as they were young and sweet, or were special, like Boy-girl.

Tutapu's sexual appetites were not particularly strong or unusual, but they were definite. The king admired loveliness, in all its forms, for beauty – like sad music from flutes – made him cry. Beautiful youths and girls were invested with exceptional temporary powers by the head kahuna, to protect them against the king's mana. Thus, taboo to all other commoners, the king was able to satisfy his lust without harming his lovers.

The girl left the hut once she saw Ragnu entering.

Ragnu recounted his adventures on the island.

'They'll discover the beheaded corpse of course, if they haven't already done so – but who's to say it was not a local murder. No one saw me go ashore or return to this canoe. Even if the Tahitian king suspects something, there's little he can do to prove it, even to himself.'

King Tutapu said, 'You've done well. I shall reward you when we reach our home islands.'

'Your satisfaction is reward enough,' murmured Ragnu.

2

One day, five years after Seumas had arrived on Raiatea, Kieto had come running to him.

'Quickly, Seumas – it's Boy-girl. She's fallen over a cliff!'

To his eternal shame the first emotion that passed through Seumas's breast was a feeling of relief. At last he would cease to be pestered by the creature. Almost immediately however, he felt a sense of shame, and made brief enquiries.

'Is she dead?'

'No, she's caught on a ledge halfway down. There's a huge drop into a gulley below her. If someone doesn't climb down to her with a rope, she'll die.'

'Someone? Me, I suppose.'

Kieto looked at the Pict and shrugged. 'You're the best climber on the island.'

Seumas quickly gathered some sennit ropes from the corner of his hut and followed Kieto out into the sunshine, saying, 'I suppose I should feel flattered. What was she doing on the cliffs anyway?'

'Collecting birds' eggs.'

'Trying to steal their feathers, more like. All right, lead the way. I'm right behind you.'

Kieto took off at a run with Seumas on his heels, into the rainforest at the edge of the beach. They ran along jungle paths, up steep slopes, until they reached the tops of some cliffs on the east side of the island. Kieto went to the edge immediately and looked down. Seumas followed him.

There was Boy-girl, a good way below, with the sea birds swooping and diving around her. She looked like a wounded bird herself, with her ribbons flying. Clutching a pinnacle of rock that jutted from the cliff, she had since fallen a short way further down from the ledge which had first borne her weight. Far below was the greenery of the rainforest, with rocks piercing the canopy like white knives. A heavy mist clung to the tops of the trees and wound around the points of stone.

'Hold on, Boy-girl, I'm coming down,' yelled Seumas.

Boy-girl's frightened features looked up at him.

'Hurry,' she whispered into the wind. 'My arms are getting tired.'

Seumas tied a rope around the base of a tree and then began abseiling down the rockface, past shrubs laden with nests, until he reached Boy-girl. She stretched out an arm for him, but he held off for a moment. This was an opportunity not to be missed. Seumas would never have another like it.

'Boy-girl,' he said, 'I'm going to save you – but you must first promise me you won't bother me so much.'

'Wha – what do you mean?' shrieked the terrified Boy-girl. 'Get me up there.'

'Not until you promise,' said Seumas, firmly. 'I don't mind us talking once in a while, but I won't be pestered any more. I'd rather see you fall.'

Kieto, who could hear everything that was going on below him, called out, 'Seumas – *please.*'

'No, not until she promises.'

Tears began to stream down Boy-girl's face.

'I'd rather die,' she squealed. 'I'll let go *now*. Here, I'm letting go – and it'll be your fault.'

But she didn't let go, and Seumas waited patiently, inwardly ready to grab her if her arms gave way, but outwardly indifferent to her fate. Their eyes were locked and for all Boy-girl could see, Seumas was ready to let her die.

'All you have to do is promise,' he said. 'Then you can have the rope ...'

Boy-girl sobbed for a minute, then nodded.

'All right,' she said. 'I won't pester you so much.'

'You won't pester me at all.'

'I'll try not to.'

Seumas realised this was as much as he was going to get out of her and finally reached across and put the rope in her hands.

'I can't climb up,' she whispered. 'I'm too tired.'

Bridging himself between two rocks, Seumas freed his own hands to tie her wrists together. Then he looped her arms around his neck and began climbing upwards. When he was part the way up he realised Boy-girl, pressing hard against his back, had an erection.

'Boy-girl, stop that!' he snarled.

'I can't help it,' she whined. Then she sniggered.

'By the gods, if you're doing all this on purpose, I'll kill you,' muttered Seumas.

He reached the top of the cliff and then dumped her unceremoniously on the ground. Kieto was still looking shocked.

'You were going to let her fall,' he said.

'I wouldn't have done that,' Seumas grunted. 'I was ready to catch her. But I got my promise.' He looked at Boy-girl, who was lying on her back, recovering from her ordeal. 'You did promise, you know. No more bothering me.'

Boy-girl looked away. 'I know.'

Kieto walked Seumas back to his hut.

On the way, Kieto said, 'Thank you for coming, Seumas.'

'Don't mention it. It was an opportunity I couldn't ignore. At last I'll get a little peace.'

'Is that all you can think of?'

'Yes, Kieto, it is. If you were me you'd know how it feels to be chased from morning until night. I feel trapped all the time, here on this island, with someone who won't leave me alone.'

'Oh.'

A little while later, just before they parted, Kieto said to Seumas, 'You know, Dorcha said exactly those same words – the words you just spoke to me – not a day ago.'

After he had gone Seumas sat down in the darkness of his hut and mused. So Dorcha thought him a pest, did she? He was doing to her, what Boy-girl was doing to him. Was she then as repulsed as he was, concerning physical contact? Did she want him to avoid her completely? If that was the way she felt about him, why, she would have her wish. He was not a man to force himself upon anyone. She could go to hell, for all he cared. He needed neither sight nor sound of her.

And so, for a while, he managed to keep out of Dorcha's way, and not see her. But his hunger for her eventually overcame his sense of pride and shame, and he found himself peeking through bushes, going to the stream for water at certain times of day, hoping for a glance of her, or hoping to hear the sound of her voice on the warm air. Once, she caught him hiding behind a tree, watching her go by, and she remonstrated with him angrily.

'Don't you think I need some privacy?'

'I thought I was giving you plenty,' he told her miserably. 'I've hardly followed you once this past twenty days.'

'I'm supposed to thank you for that?'

So things returned to normal after a while. And though Boy-girl kept to her promise, more or less, for longer than Seumas kept to his, she too began to run into him more frequently, bothering him. In the end Seumas gave up worrying, both about Boy-girl and whether Dorcha was angry with him. He followed Dorcha, Boy-girl followed him, and little changed over the years until the time came for the great expedition.

PART NINE

The Tree of Many Branches

1

'This is a story about Maui,' said Kieto.

'Who else?' smiled Seumas, lying in the midday heat, stroking Dirk with one hand and shading his eyes with the other. 'Go on, what did he do now?'

'Well, when the world was fresh and new, all the winds were wild and blew in every direction, all at once, creating great turmoil and disasters. It was impossible to use a sail on a canoe. So one day Maui fought with the winds. He wrestled them until they submitted – and so he brought them under control.

'Tua-Uo-Loa promised to blow in one direction only – up from the bottom edge of Oceania. And Matuu from the top of Oceania, in the opposite direction. Furthermore, they agreed that only one of them should blow at any one time, unless the God Apu Hau released them from this rule for a short while.

'Mata Upolu, who blows from the left side of Oceania, and Tonga from the bottom left, were also subdued.

'Each of these winds has its own shape and strength, and its own particular ways, which I will describe to you if you wish.'

'I can do without it – go on with the story. Did any of the winds survive this drubbing by Maui? Any of them tell him to go peddle his clay pots elsewhere?'

Kieto shook his head solemnly. 'No – but Maui took pity on the gentle breeze, Fisaga, which was allowed to roam free.'

'A generous fellow, Maui.'

At that moment there was a shout that land had been seen and everyone stood up and stared. On the starboard side of the canoes great fountains of water could be seen gushing up into the sky with regularity. They appeared to be geysers, with gaps between the spouts. It was a while before the word went round that this was the sea, rushing in beneath a shelf of rock with holes in it. The force of the wave sent tall columns of water hissing through the holes like a forest of waterspouts, only to change to spray and mist a few moments later, carried away by the wind.

'What a sight,' said Seumas.

These were rugged islands where the landscape rose steeply from the shoreline. This was a high kingdom, where the fringing reefs were built on volcanic rock. Here moved the god Ruau-moko, who was still inside his mother Papa's womb, struggling to be born. The one god who never would be given birth, but was destined for ever to kick and roll inside his mother, causing the houses of men to tumble on the earth, and the trees to fall, and the rocks to split and rattle down the mountains. Ruau-moko made massive cracks in the earth, trying to open his mother's womb and escape, but none of them were ever wide enough to let him out. They passed one island that Kieto recognised.

Kieto said, 'I think I know this land, from my voyage with Kupe – it's the island of Savaii.'

'Will we stop here?'

Kieto shook his head. 'I do not think so – there are many people who live here already. They have no use for more.'

Before they sailed away from the region, Tangiia ordered sacrifices to be made, and chants to be sung. This was the land of Kai-n-tiku-aba, the sacred tree, which at one time grew on the back of the Father of the Gods, but was broken off by a destructive man called Koura-abi. Until then the whole population of the earth had dwelt under the tree's shade, but once it had been broken they turned to violence and war, and through conflict were gradually scattered over the whole vastness of the world, and they learned the meaning of sorrow.

The three pahi then headed in the same direction as Hauviai on the wind-flower. On the way they saw a fisherman, whom Tangiia took on board and questioned, asking him if he knew of any uninhabited islands in the region. The fisherman, who was from Savaii and clearly nervous, told Tangiia that he believed there were islands in line with Hauviai which had no people on them.

'Who told you this?' asked Tangiia.

'One of our great navigators, King Karika,' said the Savaiian fisherman. 'He has been wandering the ocean in search of a new land and the Great Sea-God Tangaroa has told him in a dream of a beautiful island in the direction you are voyaging.'

'I too have been voyaging a long time and my people are weary,' Tangiia said. 'It shall be a case of who gets to this island first – and I intend it to be me.'

With that King Tangiia ordered full sail. The fisherman was set adrift in his own canoe again and the fleet sped across the waves towards their destination. On the way they met a great storm, where Tangaroa and Maomao, each wanting their favourites to reach the uninhabited island first, had a furious struggle with each other.

Tangiia in his haste to reach the island before Karika refused to allow his men to take in sail and at the height of the storm, one of the pahi was swamped by a great tidal wave from Apu Matangi, God of Storms and the

Howling Rain, aroused to action by the struggling of his fellow gods on this wild stretch of the great ocean.

The Volcano Flower, Po's pahi, was smashed and sank. Tangiia at last took in sail and turned about to save as many souls as he could, as did Manopa with *The Royal Palm*. They managed to rescue many of the people, though at least a third were drowned, but more importantly the great canoe was lost.

Po was among those rescued and he grieved for the loss of his vessel and his passengers and crew. He attached all blame for the loss to himself, though others told him he had done all he could to keep *The Volcano Flower* afloat. None could charge him with a mistake in judgement, though such an error would have been understandable during so fierce a storm.

Men, women and children were shared between the two surviving canoes, but space was cramped and food and water was scarce. Tangiia beat himself about the head and chest, until he was stopped by Makka-te and Kikamana. He wailed that he was responsible for the deaths of his people and no one contradicted him for kings too have to learn to take responsibility for their actions. That evening he finally made an appeasing sacrifice to the Great Sea-God, Tangaroa, who forgave him for his previous indiscretions and accepted him to his bosom.

'Milu,' cried Tangiia, into the dying breath of the storm, 'look after my people for me – treat them well – for it is I who should be walking the purple path to your kingdom, not they.'

The two pahi continued on their journey, following the navigational signs the Savaiian fisherman had given them. The weather became fair, with a fresh wind that blew them swiftly over a rippling sea, a sea on which that wind chased fleeting shadows and evanescent patches of light.

There was a feeling on board the two canoes that they were at last heading towards their destination. A quietness settled on the Raiateans. Makka-te did some tattooing, for young men who had passed the age; Seumas groomed his dog and made it a rattan collar, into which was woven coloured strands of bark-cloth; Tangiia stood by the mast most days, staring at the horizon, looking for that shade of light green on the bottom cloud which signalled an atoll or island; Po and Kula comforted grieving relatives of those drowned souls: Aputua the shark-caller busied himself making lures; Kikamana the Farseeing-virgin remained aloof, staying inside one of the deck huts; Kaho the blind Feeler-of-the-sea tested the waters continually for a change in temperature, while keeping his son Po'oi amused with tales of great voyages, his memory map perfect in every detail.

One night they passed a conical island which glowed red at its top, but Kikamana told Tangiia this was not the island they sought and to keep on course.

Kaho came to Tangiia one morning to inform him that the temperature of the water had changed dramatically.

'Could this be the volcano island we passed?' asked Tangiia.

'No,' said Kaho, 'the currents are coming from the wrong direction for that.'

Tangiia kept a close watch on the surface of the sea that day and noted seaweed and driftwood.

Towards evening a lookout sighted a large voyager craft sailing parallel to them.

Tangiia climbed the mast and studied the vessel, which was taking the same line as the two pahi. It was under full sail and seemed to be keeping pace with Tangiia's canoes. Tangiia slipped back down the mast.

'More sail,' he ordered his crew. 'Bailers, I want you to work much harder. Get rid of every drop of surplus water, it's only extra weight. Po, organise some people and throw overboard anything we don't need from now on. Kula, signal our intentions to Manopa – we must outrun that canoe over there. It has to be Karika. We must beat him to the island.'

The bailers worked frantically, shovelling the water from the two hulls with their half-coconuts, changing shifts more often so that rested men and women could take over from the weary workers. Po went through the craft, section by section, tossing overboard anything that was of sentimental value only, or obsolete so far as the voyage was concerned. Manopa, when he received Kula's signals, began doing the same.

Tangiia knelt down before Tiki, imploring his ancestor to help him in his endeavours. He asked Maomao for more wind, to give him more speed, though by now the other craft was close enough to receive the same wind. He begged Tangaroa to open a smooth channel for him, without him having to battle against strong eddies and currents, having the swell behind him. The God of Hope was brought out into the sunshine, to inspire the crew and passengers with confidence in their undertaking.

The gods seemed to be with Tangiia, for he was granted all he asked, but the strange canoe seemed also to receive such assistance, because it kept pace with *The Scudding Cloud*. Kikamana was asked to pray to Whatu, the God of Hail, to pelt the other craft with huge hailstones, and to Tawhaki, to strike down the captain of that vessel with Uira, but no answer was received from either god. Kikamana told Tangiia that the gods had decided it was to be a contest between the two men only – himself and Karika – and that the gods were betting on the outcome, urging on their favourite, but would not intervene.

'A race, is it?' said the Raiatean king. 'Then let it be so!'

Tangiia used every ounce of his seamanship to get speed out of his pahi. Trawl lines were taken in. The rigging was tightened until it hummed, the masts bent like bamboo stems in a high wind. The wind then sang through stays and sheets. The high, curved bowsprits were like hungry mouths eating waves, flecks of foam flying from their jaws.

The deck huts were taken down and stacked flat. The cargo was distributed over the deck platform. All those not working were told to lie prone, to lower their wind resistance.

Gradually the Raiatean craft began to outstrip the Savaiian vessel, nosing ahead.

'Ha, ha!' cried Tangiia. 'Now we shall see who has the best canoe, who is the best captain!'

Seumas cried, 'She's changing sails – for bigger ones by the look.'

Indeed, the other vessel had raised a large red crab-claw sail on the port side and was doing the same on the starboard side.

Despite the size of the vessels they were now skipping over the wave tops. They hardly seemed to touch the surface of the water. Spume flew from the bows of the pahi. It hissed along, with the wind pushing hard. *The Royal Palm* was left behind, to follow as best as it could. The two racing vessels danced ahead, first one easing in front, then the other.

Tangiia had never before been at such a high speed. It seemed to him that they were racing for the edge of the world. It appeared to him that they were bound for disaster. If they should touch so much as a small floating log with their bows, there would be a catastrophe. Any small object like a coconut in the water would go through the hull like a catapulted rock through a taut banana leaf.

'The island!' screamed Po, through the wind. 'Port side.'

There indeed was an island. It rose out of the sea like a great green whale. Even from this distance Tangiia could see that it was indeed a Faraway Heaven. Its lush jungled interior had a mountain ridge dominating it. Around the edge of the island, shaped like a jellyfish, was a coral reef. The closer they came to this reef they could see it was tight in places, up against the shore, and looser in others. But nowhere did it reach right out into the ocean like some island reefs. It had a beautiful turquoise lagoon studded with smaller islands. Puffs of clouds decorated the high, dark-green peaks.

It was a perfect island, not too low like some atolls, vulnerable to tidal waves.

Not too high like others, and so drawing too much rain.

Perfect.

'My island,' screamed Tangiia, waving his fist at the other canoe. 'Keep away from my island!'

A man standing by the mast on the other vessel waved a weapon in the air. Tangiia knew that this must be the famous Savaiian captain, Karika. His exploits were known throughout Oceania. He was a great navigator in his own right and it seemed he had chosen the same time to look for a new island as Tangiia, or had been spurred on to do so by the gods. If the gods were responsible, they were cruel in their sport, to match two such men against each other over so important a prize.

The reef drew nearer and still the two vessels were neck and neck. Neither waited for a good wave to cross the coral teeth that could have ripped their canoes to pieces, they simply hoped for a crest to coincide with their landing. As it was, both craft slid over the reef without damage, and raced for the shallows.

Once close to the beach the craft had to be slowed.

Tangiia ran the length of the deck and dived into the water. Cheered by his people, he swam, striking out for the beach. Karika did the same, his people also giving voice. If there had been nothing between the vessels, there was now nothing between the men, for they swam stroke for stroke, neither gaining on the other, neither falling back. Tangiia's lungs were bursting, his muscles screamed at him, but he dug deep into his reserves of stamina, knowing that all depended on him winning.

The two swimmers reached their depth at the same time, struggled through the water, up through the surf, and reached the warm sands of the island simultaneously.

It was a dead heat.

They both fell on their backs, gasping for breath, sucking down air.

Wild birds whirled above them, as if anticipating what was to come next.

When the strength returned to his body Tangiia leapt to his feet, whipping out the shark-toothed lei-o-mano from his waistband.

Karika, seeing he was in danger, did the same.

They circled one another, warily.

'My island!' growled Karika.

'Mine,' said Tangiia. 'I have sailed too long and far to give it up to you.'

'My people have voyaged for many, many months.'

'My people have battled with the elements, fought with monsters, defied the gods to be here.'

'Mine too,' shouted Karika. 'They have suffered too long to be turned back to the sea now.'

'Go away,' said Tangiia, slashing at his opponent, 'find another island.'

'This is my island,' cried Karika, dodging the blow and thrusting at his antagonist. 'You find another one.'

Out in the lagoon a skirmish was taking place between the two vessels. Spears were flying through the air. Warriors from *The Scudding Cloud* had taken to dugouts and were trying to board the other vessel. Some of Karika's warriors had done likewise and were trying to find a way to climb on the deck of *The Scudding Cloud*.

The two would-be kings of the as-yet-unnamed island jabbed and slashed, trying to find an opening through each other's guards, each hoping Oro, the God of War, was favouring him alone.

Suddenly, out of the mêlée in the lagoon came a terrible scream. Tangiia looked up quickly to see Po, standing on the deck of *The Scudding Cloud*, a spear through his chest. The point of the spear had entered through his breast bone and exited between his shoulder blades. Blood gushed along the shaft as the captain of the sunken *Volcano Flower* staggered forward, his eyes wide with pain and fear.

'Tangiia!' he called. 'I'm – I'm—'

Po tottered to the edge of the deck, then fell headlong into the water, the haft of the spear sticking into the sand at the bottom of the lagoon and holding up the body in a grotesque fashion, like a skewered sacrifice.

Po was dead.

Tangiia dropped his guard, so distracted was he by Po's cry.

At that moment Karika could have plunged his dagger into his adversary's soft stomach and ripped it open like the belly of a fish, but for some reason he held back, stayed his hand.

All fighting had ceased on the canoes with the horrible shout let out by the dying Po. Tangiia let his arm fall by his side. Karika did the same. The two men just stood there, staring out at the body which wafted back and forth in the ripples from the waves.

Blood stained the waters in an ever-increasing circle. If there were any sharks in the lagoon, they would soon be in the area. Feelings of alarm swept through Tangiia. It was one thing to lose warriors fighting an enemy, quite another to have them torn to shreds by ravenous sharks.

'Get out of the water,' yelled Tangiia, to some men and women who had either jumped or fallen overboard in the struggle. 'Get on the canoes!'

'Quickly!' cried Karika, in tune with his adversary's thoughts of danger.

Those in the water recognised the peril they were in and thrashed back to the canoes, to be helped aboard by those already on deck. Karika's people were assisting Tangiia's people on board their craft and the same was happening around *The Scudding Cloud*. Soon enough there were fins cutting the water, around the body of Po. Hammerheads! The corpse too, was hauled on board. Dugouts were launched and the crews and passengers of both vessels began ferrying themselves to the beach.

Once on the beach the two sides separated again and faced each other on the sands. There were wounded amongst them, from the skirmish. One of Tangiia's men was bleeding from a shoulder wound. Another was pouring blood from behind his ear, where he had been struck by a club. A young woman had a broken wrist. There were similar injuries amongst Karika's people.

Tangiia and Karika were foremost, their weapons still drawn.

'What shall we do about this,' asked Tangiia. 'I want no more of my people to die.'

'Nor do I wish any more deaths on my people – they have suffered enough

265

already. We lost a canoe out on the ocean – Magantu, the Great White Shark, bit through one of the hulls and swallowed three bailers whole.'

'We also lost a pahi!' exclaimed Tangiia. 'My people have died of fevers, of violent weather, of treatment from hostiles, of encounters with monsters and demons.'

'Mine too.'

Karika was silent for a moment, then said, 'Single combat then, between us. Whoever wins takes the island and the loser's people leave. Agreed?'

Kikamana now stepped forward, between the two men.

'This is unnecessary,' she said. 'The island is big enough for both peoples.'

Tangiia shook his head. 'This has to be.'

Seumas, his patu club in his right hand, called to the king of the Raiateans, 'Listen to your high priestess.'

'It is not your place, to speak at such a time,' interrupted Makka-te, angrily.

'No,' said Seumas, 'but I'm doing it anyway. I have been on the same voyage as you, I have some say in how it ends. This is a good island. All together, Raiateans, Savaiians, we are few. It can support us and many generations to come, without any hardship. I say listen to Kikamana.'

'Yes,' cried Kieto.

'Be quiet, boy,' snapped Makka-te. 'This is a decision for a king, not for goblins or boys.'

Kikamana said. 'Why not share the island? Why not rule this land together?'

Tangiia turned to Kaho, the blind, old Feeler-of-the-sea.

'What do you say, my old friend?'

'Kikamana is right,' said Kaho, lifting his blind face to the breeze, 'the land smells rich enough for us all.'

At that moment a conch horn sounded and drums began to beat a martial rhythm. *The Royal Palm* had now arrived in the lagoon with Manopa standing on the deck. His warriors were armed and ready for war. A statue of Oro, roughly hewn during the long voyages, was lashed to the mast. Manopa had on his war helmet and his war cloak of yellow and red feathers, which fluttered in the wind. He looked truly formidable. The Raiateans had the edge now, commanding positions both on the beach and out in the lagoon. It no longer needed to be single combat; Tangiia's forces were twice those of Karika's.

Tangiia turned to study his opponent, a young man like himself with a fine physique. He could see that adventure on the high seas had shaped Karika's character much in the same manner as it had shaped that of Tangiia himself. Karika seemed a modest sort of man, with a strong sense of honour. He could have slain Tangiia very easily just a few moments before, when Po had distracted his king, but he stayed his hand. Tangiia was sure there were many similarities between the two of them. They might even grow to like each other.

'I would agree to a trial on that basis,' said Tangiia. 'Six months to see if it works.'

Karika stared at his opponent and nodded slowly.

'It is better we both live a little longer, certainly, and enjoy some time on this beautiful island. I would agree to a six-month trial, after which if it does not work out, we draw lots and the loser takes his people and leaves.'

Thus it was agreed between the Savaiians and the Raiateans that they share the island, perhaps for six months, perhaps for ever.

That evening Karika and Tangiia drank kava together on the sands of their new home. They talked for many hours. It was a good meeting, since they found they had much in common.

When Tangiia asked Kula what she thought about the arrangement, she said, 'When you can resolve differences as important as this one without resorting to violence, then I believe you have truly become a king.'

Po's sau walked the purple path to the place where Milu stood waiting for him. Po was a voyager, a man whose life had been entwined with that of an ocean which *was* the history of the Oceanian peoples. There were many deeds against his name, many journeys, many storms. He was a hero. Milu bowed his head slightly as Po approached him, acknowledging Po's status.

Po returned the gesture and then stared beyond the God of the Dead, into Death's kingdom. It was a solemn place, but not without its grandeur. There was a certain opulence in the use of mother-of-pearl for its pathways, in its dark, shiny obsidian walls and black waterfalls dropping down infinite chasms. It was not a comfortable place, but there was a kind of restfulness about the dimness of the light. It shone like those dark-blue, dully polished shells found in the deepest part of the ocean.

Moreover, Po had nothing to fear from Nangananga, having three wives to guarantee his safety. Since they were all three alive it would be his dead mother waiting for him, ready to guide him over the sharp rocks and through the maze of boulders. In the Land of the Dead it is the women who are supreme, with their strong wisdom, their deep intelligence, and their understanding of emotion. It is a place where infinity and eternity mingle and there is time to ponder the puzzles of the world. The men there are lost for a time, having to come to terms with their spiritual feelings, while the women have already spent a lifetime doing just that and are already prepared for death.

The boat of dead souls would be waiting for Po, its black feathers whispering sacred fangu.

Po moved forward as Milu stood aside to let him pass.

Po hesitated on the threshold and turning to Milu began, 'The sad thing is—'

'– you discovered the secret of life, just as the spear entered your chest and dispatched you here,' finished Milu.

'How did you know?' asked Po, surprised.

'It's always the way,' sighed Milu.

The island was indeed a place worth the voyage.

A strong person could walk around it in a day, but it had flat fertile land which flowed inwards for a good way, then climbed upwards into craggy but green heights.

Tiki was given thanks, as was Maomao and all the other gods who had assisted them on their great voyage, even Tangaroa who had at last been appeased by the Raiatean king.

The separate cargoes of tubers, roots, shoots and cuttings, from all three canoes, were ferried ashore and planted. These were their most precious possessions, for they would provide the new island people with their food over the coming decades.

There was fish in the lagoon, and shellfish in the coral beds, and pig and dog – even the ever-present rat was there to provide meat in times of famine – but fruit and vegetables had been developed over a long period of their history.

The cuttings and roots they had planted would keep them and their children healthy and fit for such trials as the gods and an uncertain future might throw in their way. Pens were built for the stock, land was marked and shared out in equal lots for all families, single men and single women. Huts were built for the commoners and houses for the royal families. Posts were carved, ahu made for sacrifices to the gods, temples were constructed with marae, gods were sculpted from local stone.

Po was buried with due ceremony on the slopes of the island, in sight of the lagoon. There were sacrifices to him, of chickens and pigs. Many mourned his passing, especially Kieto, who regarded him almost as a second father.

Canoe building began in earnest then of váa and pu hoe canoes, both outrigged vessels. These were craft with u-shaped hulls having a capacity from two to six – one man would have difficulty in managing the boat – used for fishing in a lagoon or close to a reef. The hull of one of these craft was hollowed from a single tree, with straight sides and a vertical stem. The slightly raised stern formed a platform behind, from which the fisherman threw his net or line.

People also began work on váa motu, larger outrigged canoes for crossing short stretches of open ocean. This craft had a tall mast supported by bamboo poles and a stay attached to the stern. A bouquet of feathers or leaves would crown the mast before a sailing, a symbol of peace to other mariners. On the end of the boom, fixed freely at the base of the mast, was a plume of delicate trailing feathers to assist the helmsman in finding the direction of the wind. A huge paddle called the hoe fa'atere was used to steer the craft.

On the seventh day Tangiia and Karika were inaugurated as the first kings of the island. They were to govern together for the first six months and if all was well, thereafter until one of them died. It would be the dead man's eldest son who would rule after both kings had gone, thus protecting the kings from each other. They might kill themselves to ensure their line, but they could not murder their co-ruler to make it so.

If the eldest son of the first-dead king was deemed unsuitable, because of mental illness or some other restricting factor of his birth, or if he had no wish to rule, a completely new king was to be chosen by the high priestess from the virgin males of the island. The selection was to be made at random from the fittest, most intelligent of the candidates; this to be determined by a series of tests run by the priests. This would help to protect the lives of newly born royal babies from ambitious members of either imperial family.

Tangiia's royal house was not yet constructed and he and Kula were spending the nights in a hut away from the huts of their people. Now that Tangiia had been invested as king of an island, he was taboo, and had to take the precautions necessary to prevent ordinary people from receiving a lethal charge of his mana.

On the evening of the eighth day he lay on his mat as usual, weary from the day's work, when Kula quietly lay down beside him.

He was surprised. Ever since the night of their wedding on Tahiti she had slept on her own mat, at a respectable distance from him.

'Do you wish me to sleep elsewhere?' he asked.

'No,' she whispered, shrugging her skirt from her, 'I want you to hold me.'

He took her in his arms and very soon they were making love for the first time. Tangiia felt he was in a dream as his beloved moved with him, murmuring her pleasure in his ear, giving him all he had ever desired from a woman. After they had both satisfied one another, they cried in each other's arms.

Early in the morning, before the parrots had woken and begun strutting their perches in the trees, Tangiia leaned over and said to her, 'Why now?'

'Because I promised my father I would not give myself to anyone but a king – you, my lord, were only a king in name, but now you are a king in land and people.'

'I see,' he said. 'And this is why you gave yourself to me at this time?'

'That, and because I have found during the voyages, and when you confronted Karika, that you are truly a man of great courage and honour, capable of compassion, tender and loving, and all the things I wanted in a man. You have many faults of course ...'

'I do?' he queried, frowning.

'Yes,' she smiled, putting her fingers to his lips, 'but I forgive you for them.'

He was quiet for a moment and then laughed.

'Thank you, and I forgive *you*.'

'For what?' she asked, archly.

'For bewitching me with your beauty.'

They laughed together, just as the first parrot started shrieking at his neighbours, waking the rest of the world.

2

There were no very young children on Tutapu's expeditionary force, only males and females over the age of twelve. The king had warned his people that any babies born on the voyage would be thrown overboard. However, among such a large number of people there will always be men and women who fall in love and cannot wait to consummate that love. Consequently three couples, the women pregnant, had already taken dugouts in the middle of the night and set themselves adrift, willing to face death rather than watch their child thrown to the sharks.

Yet Tutapu was not regarded as a bad king, or even a particularly harsh ruler. Many kings would not have bothered to warn the people of the consequences of their actions and would have killed the babies anyway. Many kings would have taken time out to hunt down and punish the perpetrators for stealing a dugout. Tutapu was simply single-minded, obsessive, in his desire to find his half-brother and execute him. Any obstacle, however small, in the way of that goal was dealt with ruthlessly. Babies were a distraction – they required constant attention – and Tutapu wanted his people to be as single-minded as himself in the endeavour.

Unlike Tangiia and Karika, Tutapu had lost none of his vessels. At the time the other two new kings were at the initial stages of building their new kingdom, Tutapu was on course for the island of Savaii. A lookout called to say a dugout with two people had been sighted off the starboard bow. The couple were recognised as the last pair to steal away in the night, presumably because the woman was pregnant. It seemed that fast currents had carried the lighter vessel ahead of the flotilla, but now the trade winds had given the latter speed enough to catch up with the smaller craft.

As the tipairua drew closer to the dugout it was apparent that the couple were close to death. By the look of them they were dying of thirst, there being little enough room to carry drinking coconuts or gourds on a dugout.

'Shall we pick them up?' asked the helmsman.

'Sail past,' ordered Tutapu.

Dorcha, on hearing this, said, 'But they're almost gone – they won't make it to an island.'

'They should have thought of that when they stole one of my dugouts and crept away like thieves in the night.'

Dorcha watched as the thirty tipairua with their black sails ignored the dugout, which went drifting through the squadron of vessels. Those on board the tipairua knew better than to look at the dying couple. It was as if there was nothing there but a floating log, to be avoided in order to prevent collision, but not to be studied intently.

The dying woman, recognising a relative, feebly raised her hand above the gunwales of the dugout, but her cousin ignored the wave, knowing he was under the eyes of the king.

To Dorcha it was a harrowing sight and though she had seen some callous acts in her time, this one sickened her beyond endurance.

'We must stop,' she said. 'This is not a good thing to do – wayfarers in trouble in my homeland are always given assistance. Anyone who refuses to help a traveller dying of hunger or thirst is dealt with harshly, if not in this life, then in the next.'

King Tutapu raised his eyebrows and said, 'You mean, even a king stops to assist a beggar?'

'No, that's not what I mean – and of course there are brigands who would rob a corpse, let alone a dying man – but most people see the sense in aiding a person in trouble. It might be *you* next time.'

Tutapu shook his head, adamantly. 'These are not wayfarers we have come across by accident, these are people who disobeyed my commands. *I* am not likely to steal away from my own tipairua, so it could not possibly be me. Another king would have ploughed through the dugout, drowning the occupants.'

'Perhaps even that would have been kinder,' said Dorcha.

Tutapu folded his arms and looked at her for a moment, then he ordered his signaller to send the last tipairua in the flotilla back to the dugout.

'Tell the captain to sink the canoe.'

'You mean, take the couple on board first, don't you?' prompted Dorcha, anxiously.

'No,' Tutapu replied, turning cold eyes on Dorcha, 'I mean to drown them. You yourself has said this would be better than leaving them to die of thirst. So be it. This is your doing and you shall take the responsibility. They shall have a quick death and let no one say Tutapu is not a magnanimous ruler, capable of compassion.'

Dorcha was stunned by this act of cruelty, but she said no more, knowing that she could not move Tutapu. He was an obdurate man whose mission he saw as too important to be delayed even a moment by disobedient subjects.

The couple had wronged him, had even now distracted him from his purpose, and so the Relentless Pursuer would have none of them. They had ordered their own execution the night they had made love without taking precautions and had conceived a child.

And so it was done. The dugout was sunk. The couple were drowned.

And it seemed to Dorcha that no one thought the worse of the king for his actions. Was it just that a king's deeds were above reproach because of his god-like status? Or did the people really approve of his actions? All that time she had spent with these Oceanians, and still she did not know them.

Nor did they know her, for shortly afterwards the king came to her and asked her about the course they were maintaining, and whether she believed it to be correct according to her bamboo-and-shell device. It was clear from his manner that he expected she would have forgotten all about the execution. It was obvious he thought she had engaged in a minor disagreement with him and had lost the argument, and there was an end to the trivial matter; that no bad feeling existed between them.

On the contrary, Dorcha was still appalled by what had occurred, and could not conceive of things ever being the same between her and the king again. She had seen human sacrifices performed by willing young men and women, she had seen harsh punishment meted out to malefactors for misdemeanours, she had witnessed judgements she considered poor, but had accepted all these as part of a culture she had no influence over.

It would have been so easy, however, for Tutapu to take the dying couple on board one of his craft. It would have been the act of a noble heart and mind. Had he done so, she would have respected him as a great man of honour.

Now, she despised him.

Yet she was alone in that feeling.

Even Elo would not speak against the king.

Tutapu's flotilla reached Savaii, where he learned that Tangiia had gone in search of an island which was also being sought by a Savaiian voyager, Karika. A fisherman had seen Tangiia's pahi and had taken the news back to Savaii that a battle was about to take place over the contested island. Both voyagers knew in which direction the island lay, it was just a matter of who reached it first, and if that king could hold on to it in the face of an invasion.

Tutapu cried to Tangaroa, 'Don't let him die by another hand – it must be my weapon that takes his life. Mine is just retribution for stealing the hope from my kingdom. If he should be killed, surely it would be best done by the brother who loved him once, who grew with him to manhood, who turned his hand against his flesh and blood only when a kingdom was threatened.

'You know that brothers must be sacrificed for kingdoms, that kin must be put aside for kingship, that thieves and robbers must be brought to book, though they be tied by family bonds to their prosecutors. Save his head for my club, his heart for my dagger, that he may die by one who has loved him, rather than by an enemy who despises him. Grant me this, O Great Sea-God!'

Dorcha's feelings for King Tutapu were confused and ambivalent. She both admired and detested him. He was a brilliant captain and navigator, and possibly even a great king, but his greatness was dominated by petty fears and jealousies, and his concerns motivated by selfish dreams. He wanted perfection for himself and his islands, and when he saw that such flawlessness was not there, he looked for someone to blame. His eyes had settled on his only brother.

He was also, she thought sadly, lacking in compassion. There was a coldness which filled him that left no room inside his heart for mercy. A momentary gain towards his goal was more important than the lives of a dozen commoners. His ambition was indeed blind to all but its own ends.

Yet he was not a man utterly convinced of the rightness of his actions; his feelings were in conflict with themselves.

Dorcha could see the torment Tutapu was going through, now that he was closing in on his brother. She recognised that the king of Raiatea and Borabora did indeed bear a fraternal love for Tangiia, but through circumstance felt compelled to hunt him down and kill him for the sake of peace of mind. While Tangiia lived Tutapu felt he could never be secure in his kingdom, that one day Tangiia might launch an expeditionary force against him and wrest the heaven of Raiatea from his grasp.

'He stole one of my gods,' Tutapu kept repeating, when he felt the need to justify the chase.

'And your future bride,' Dorcha reminded him, quietly.

'Yes,' he agreed, distantly, 'and Kula.'

The flotilla sped over the ocean, following Hauviai on the windflower. Maomao stayed behind them, as if helping them towards their destination. There were no more forced diversions to strange islands. It was as if the gods too had become single-minded in their efforts to bring the two brothers together in mortal combat.

One morning Dorcha was awakened by the shout of a lookout, telling everyone within earshot that land had been sighted.

She stared in the direction at which the lookout was pointing and saw a dark hump-backed whale in the distance.

'The island,' said Dorcha, suddenly coming to terms with her own reasons for this voyage. 'Seumas is there.'

'Have you come to hurt him, Dorcha?' asked Elo. 'Have you come to remind him of what he did to you?'

'I keep changing my mind,' replied the confused Celt. 'My husband's ghost tells me one thing and my heart, another.'

'Then why did you come? Why did you join the king's expedition?'

Angrily, Dorcha snapped, 'I don't know.'

'I'm sorry, Dorcha. I won't ask again.'

Dorcha, remorseful, turned and hugged the head of the girl to her breast.

'I'm sorry too, Elo. Who knows why I came? Dark reasons, good reasons? A mixture of both? Perhaps I've come to make my peace with Seumas?'

Elo said wisely for her years, 'That would be the best thing.'

PART TEN

The New Heaven

1

Thirty tipairua bearing black sails were seen on the horizon by the lookouts on the mountain.

The news was quickly relayed to the two kings, sitting in the marae of a new temple, in the process of being built for Rangi, Hine and Papa. One such temple had already been constructed for Maomao and Tangaroa. There would be another to Tane and Rongo. The mountain itself, where stood a needle rock, was reserved wholly for Io, the 'Old One', the Father of the Gods. There would be smaller places sacred to Ra, Hau Naringi, Kuku Lau and Ua. Neither king had seen the need to raise a temple to Oro, not this early in their reign on their new heavenly island.

The kings, minor chiefs, priests and their retinues gathered at the marae outside Tangiia's house, within earshot of Kula, who had been preparing tapa-bark cloth for dyeing, but who had stopped work like everyone else to listen.

'An invasion force,' said Karika, 'but who?'

Kikamana provided the answer.

'It is Tangiia's brother. His feather-banner flutters from the masthead of the leading tipairua. He has followed us here from Raiatea. I warned of his coming. My dreams have been full of his warriors' shadows.'

Tangiia sighed. 'Is it really Tutapu?'

Kikamana said nothing more, knowing the question was rhetorical in nature.

'Thirty vessels,' said Karika. 'If they're full, it means we have to face three thousand warriors.'

'Not *we*,' said Tangiia, placing a hand on the other's arm, 'that's my brother out there. This is my war, not yours.'

Karika clasped his fellow king's hand.

'We rule this island together – any threat to its peace is a threat to us both – *I* am your brother now. We will fight side by side. My warriors are your warriors – they are all *our* people. I would have expected no less from you.'

Tangiia sighed. 'Tutapu's men will lay waste to the whole island. He has a reputation in war, of slaughtering a conquered enemy. I loved him once, but he has grown into strangeness. I believe too, that he is a better warrior than me.'

'If we die,' Karika insisted, 'we die together.'

Tangiia nodded. 'In that case, prepare our men for war – we shall meet

Tutapu on the beaches. The advantage will be with us, since his warriors can be engaged as they try to leap from their canoes into the surf. Manopa, Seumas, you will lead half my warriors, Makka-te and Kikamana the other half.'

'Where shall you be?' asked Seumas.

'I shall be at your head of course, but I want to be free to concentrate on a personal battle with my brother. Once one of us dies, the battle will be over. Karika, I expect you to deploy your warriors in the way you know best.'

'They can go under the command of your officers. I shall fight by your side, to ensure you have a fair combat with your brother. He will be sure to have his own bodyguards.'

Tangiia nodded. 'Yes, no doubt he will. Now, where are those officers? Manopa? There, good – and Seumas too. Kikamana of course ... where is Makka-te?'

At that moment Makka-te was dragged across the courtyard by two young priests. He was trussed hand and foot, and looked sullen and defiant.

'What's this?' cried the young king.

'Some sentries caught him signalling to the enemy fleet,' said one of the priests. 'Since the sentries were commoners and couldn't touch him, they sent for us.'

Tangiia stared unbelievingly at Makka-te. 'You – a traitor?' he said softly.

Makka-te looked into the face of his king and sneered. 'Traitor to whom? My loyalties have always been with your brother. I joined your expedition knowing in my heart that he would never let you alone. It was impossible for him. With you alive he would have never felt safe. Now, thanks to me, he has caught up with you.'

One of the priests cried, 'He's been releasing birds to show Tutapu the way. He left a symbol on a rock at Tahiti, to point the direction on the windflower. Everywhere we have been he has left signs for Tutapu to follow.'

Tangiia paced up and down in front of Makka-te, stopping every so often to stare at him. In the end he said, 'Can you see into the future, priest?'

Makka-te smiled grimly and nodded. 'I see you roasting one who would have been your half-brother, had it not been that his mother was a king's concubine.'

'You think I should roast you?'

'I think you *will*.'

Tangiia shook his head. 'Take him down to the shore line,' he told Makka-te's captors, 'untie him and throw him into the water. He can swim out to my brother's canoes. I want no more of him.'

The other priests were aghast. 'Aren't you going to execute him?'

'No,' replied the king. 'This meeting between my brother and me was inevitable – it had to be. Makka-te has helped to bring that about sooner, rather than later. He has chosen his side in this battle, let him go to it.'

Makka-te looked puzzled, clearly expecting some sort of trick. Was Tangiia going to strike him down as they marched him away? Was there some hidden code in his words to his priests that meant they were to cut his throat on the way down to the beach? It didn't seem possible that Tangiia would let him go, a self-confessed traitor, a spy in his midst.

'Now,' cried Tangiia, striding out, 'we must arm for the fight. Sound the war conch!' he ordered a priest. 'I shall dress for the battle. Kikamana, prepare the marae for sacrifices to the gods. We can ill afford to slaughter livestock at the moment, just when we are beginning our life on this island and our breeding stock is low, but we must bring ourselves to their attention.'

At that moment a messenger came running, to fall at the feet of King Tangiia.

'King Tangiia,' cried the man, 'your wife—'

'What about my wife?' said Tangiia, whirling on the man.

'She – she has swum out with Makka-te to the tipairua in the bay. She has gone to your brother.'

Tangiia turned quickly to see that the spot where Kula had been sitting, mixing the dyes, was empty.

He let out a long cry of anguish.

Kula reached the tipairua before Makka-te, being a better swimmer than the middle-aged man. She climbed, dripping, on to the deck. Her wet hair was plastered against her scalp. There were droplets of water clinging to her breasts which glistened with colours in the bright sunlight. Her dusky skin was unblemished and smooth. She looked truly beautiful.

She faced a King Tutapu dressed and armed for war.

'You have no need to fight,' she said. 'I have come to you.'

King Tutapu stared hard and puzzled at the woman before him, then his expression changed as recognition came to him.

'*Kula,*' he said. 'Forgive me – I have not seen you for so many years – not since my father brought you to show to me when you were fourteen.'

Makka-te was hauled on board. King Tutapu went to him immediately. 'You revealed yourself to him? I told you to remain amongst them.'

'They found me out,' said Makka-te, struggling for breath. 'I didn't reveal myself – I was discovered.'

'What are their numbers?'

'Male warriors? Fewer than three hundred, but many of the women are prepared to fight.'

'Three hundred?' queried Tutapu, frowning.

'Tangiia has made an ally. Karika, the Savaiian. They rule the island together.'

'And Karika is prepared to fight with him?'

Makka-te said, ironically, 'They are closer than brothers.'

Kula ran forward and clasped the tall, muscled king around the knees.

'You have no need to fight, I am here now. I shall be your wife—'

Makka-te sneered. 'She is already the wife of Tangiia. They married in Tahiti. She has been on his love-mat since that time and is no longer a maiden.'

Tutapu shrugged, pacing the deck. 'What do I care for maidens? Does experience make them worse lovers, or better? Virgins make terrible wives for men with strong, healthy appetites. If I want a virgin I can take one, any time I choose. I am the king. My father promised me Kula for my wife. My wife she shall be.'

Kula spat triumphantly at Makka-te's feet and then let out a cry of relief.

'Let's sail away now, then – away to Raiatea and Borabora? Leave Tangiia to his island,' she cried.

Tutapu turned and looked at her. Ragnu was staring at Kula with interest written on his features. Near by, Dorcha was also watching the scene with concern in her eyes. Everyone present, except Kula and perhaps Makka-te, knew in advance what the answer would be from the king.

The king said, 'He still has the god he stole from me.'

Kula blinked, then shook her head, saying, 'But it's only an idol – a minor god, hardly significant.'

'He has robbed me of Hope,' cried the king loudly. 'My brother has taken away my joy. How can I live without hope?'

'But surely,' said Kula, now on her feet, 'this is just a feeling, *inside* you? It's all in the mind. You can have another God of Hope carved. Tane is with us all, in his many forms – isn't that so, priest?' She appealed to Ragnu.

Tutapu did not even let his head kahuna reply.

'Tangiia must die,' said the king. 'I must wipe out the insult of his theft. How else can the sacred be cleansed, except with blood? It has to be.'

'Then what did I come to you for?' wailed the distraught queen of the island. 'He will be grieving my loss. He will be full of anguish at my going.'

Tutapu raised his eyebrows. 'Do you care?'

'I *love* him,' cried Kula. 'I should be by his side. I came to you because it was my duty to do so. I came to prevent any bloodshed.'

'Then you're a fool,' snapped Tutapu.

Kula turned and collapsed into Dorcha's arms. Dorcha held her, stroked her brow.

'Nothing can stop the fight,' said the Celt, softly and sympathetically. 'Tutapu is determined.'

Dorcha might have used the word 'obsessed' for it would have been a more accurate one.

The king then ignored Kula in order to lay out his battle plans. 'Ragnu, make ready for the attack! It seems my brother is preparing for an assault on dry land, since he hasn't launched his pahi. That does him credit. Three pahi against thirty tipairua are poor odds for a sea battle. He'll stand a better chance against us, when we're struggling on foot through the surf to get on to the beach.'

'In that case, shouldn't we wait?' asked Ragnu. 'He'll have to come out to us eventually, if he sees we're not going to storm the island? We can blockade the fishing. Without fish they'll eventually run out of food.'

'I can't wait that long. We'll lose more men, but still the odds are heavily in our favour. I will lead five tipairua into the shallows as a frontal spearhead. This should draw all Tangiia's forces to that point on the shoreline. Then you will lead the right wing and Hioiutu the left wing, each of ten tipairua. Five tipairua will remain by the reef, as a rear guard and to prevent any of the enemy from escaping in boats. You will await my drummer's signal to attack the flanks.'

'What will be the signal?' asked Ragnu.

'Seven rapid beats on the drum.'

Tangiia's men were arranged in a crescent all round the bay. Sacrifices had been made to the Great War-God, Oro, to ask him to fight on the side of the island-ers. No one on the beach held out much hope that the war god would stand in their ranks however, for being the God of War, Oro was usually a friend of the strong and an enemy of the weak. Tutapu would be making the same sacrifices and asking for the same support. It seemed likely that Oro, given his lust for death and destruction, would favour the side most likely to win.

Nevertheless there were totems to Oro planted all along the sands, and priests carried Oro sticks carved into visages and bore Oro images made of feathers above their heads. They chanted their battle hymn to the stamp of feet on hard earth. The voices were full of hope, but there was dread among them, facing such fearful odds.

Oro, Great War-God, give us your strength!
Let the enemy be consumed in the huge fire,
Where you, Great War-God, throw the evil demons
You have vanquished, to smoke and burn.

Oro, Great War-God, let your three daughters,
Axe-eye, Head-eater and Escape-from-a-hundred-stones,
Be with us in the coming fight.
Let them slay our enemies by the thousand.

Oro, Great War-God, send your son,
Faithful Friend, to keep our courage high.
Oro, Great War-God, come yourself
And kill as many of our foes as please you!

The chant rang out over the sands.

On the tipairua, similar chants were in progress.

Tangiia was full of sorrow. His wife had deserted him and had gone over to the enemy. She had lied to him when she told him she loved him. If he survived the battle he promised himself he would cut her throat the moment he saw her, to stop her lying tongue from beguiling him again. She deserved no mercy. She was worse than the traitor in his camp.

Karika stood on his right side, a stranger not so long ago, now a friend willing to die for him. Karika carried a patu club and a canoe-breaker – a lump of volcanic rock lashed with sennit, with which to smash the hulls of canoes. The canoe-breaker could also be a fearsome weapon in hand-to-hand fighting. It was heavy and required time to swing, but it mashed to pulp any enemy head it met in the way of its arc.

On Tangiia's left was Seumas, a strange weapon in his hand – a wooden shaft bent into a curve and tied in place by a piece of taut sennit cord. Into the cord Seumas had fitted a tiny spear of thin bamboo, just as long as his arm. It was fletched with feathers at the notched end, while a sharp obsidian point weighted the other end. Seumas had shown he could fire the spear, which he called an 'arrow', a great distance when he drew back on the weapon he called a 'bow'. He told Tangiia he had not wanted to show the Oceanians this weapon, but since the odds against Tangiia's force were so great, he had to use it.

On Seumas's back was his set of bagpipes.

Dirk was at his side.

Midway down the bay on Seumas's wing was Manopa, a steady, solid, formidable figure amongst the ranks of warriors.

Kikamana in her long flowing cloak of feathers and leaves was on the other wing, with her force of thirty virgins, strong maidens with supple limbs. Kikamana was plying her magic, laying about her protective spells, and sending invisible darts of sickness and disease towards her foes. Kikamana called on demons and fairies alike, to join the fray.

Even the tall, willowy Boy-girl was there, shells in her locks, her tattered ribbons flying in the breeze. In her right hand was her deadly slingshot. In her left, a lucky charm, a puppy's foot fitted to a short stick. She wore poisonous flowers in her garments today, for their potency, and for their dark beauty, to put fear into the enemies she faced. She knew if she could look into a foe's eyes, that foe could be turned to an unwitting friend for the duration of the battle.

Tangiia stared along the line of warriors, either side of him. They looked colourful and fierce, their tattooed muscles rippling in the sunlight, their faces twisted and ugly with savage intent. They danced their war dances, their thigh slaps and projected tongues defying the enemy. The chiefs' war helmets fluttered in the wind. They all appeared to be full of heart for the coming fight, unafraid, indomitable.

Yet he knew they were really hollow, his men, and the belief amongst them was that they were all going to die.

'Come!' he called them. 'Be brave! You are fine warriors, fine fighting men and women. You must have the faith in yourselves, that I have in you. I know you will conquer today and the mighty foe will fall like severed flowers.'

A ragged cheer answered these words, vacuous and uninspired.

Just then, a lookout called from the top of a palm.

'Someone comes in a váa motu canoe – two people! They ride the reef. I think it is Kupe. Kupe comes to us!'

Tangiia stared at the place where the lookout was pointing and, sure enough, there was Kupe, standing at the mast while another, smaller man managed the rudder paddle. Kupe waved. He swept down in his little canoe, past Tutapu's tipairua squadron, and across the lagoon. When the váa motu approached the beach, the other man was hidden by the boom and the sail, and when Kupe dropped the sail, this man was nowhere to be seen. All that could be said of him was that he had been short of stature and his loin cloth had hung low.

Kupe leapt from the canoe, on to the strand.

A vigorous cheer went up from the warriors all along the shoreline. Kupe had come! Kupe, the great voyager and warrior, slayer of the giant octopus, had come to join the new islanders in their fight against an oppressor.

Tangiia ran forward and rubbed noses with Kupe.

'My friend,' said the king. 'How did you know where to come?'

Kupe smiled. 'Why, you saw my companion?'

'Yes, but I didn't know him – who was he?'

Kupe grinned more broadly and shouted for all to hear. 'That was the mighty Maui, come from the bosom of Hine-nui-te-po, Great Goddess of the Night and Death, to fill your warriors with bravery and heart. Maui is with you in the coming fight! Maui guided my canoe to these shores, to give you support against your brother. Tutapu should never have come here.'

The word was quickly passed along the line of warriors – Maui was with them. They might not have Oro in their ranks, but Maui the Trickster, Maui of a Thousand Devices, Maui who outwitted Te Tuna and his friends was with them today, Maui the Sun-beater, Maui of the Friendly Fire, Maui who Fished Islands. Their hearts swelled with courage, their hands grew stronger and they squared their shoulders and stood tall.

'Maui is with us!' the cry rang out. 'The day is ours!'

Kupe, older but still strong, hefted up a spear and took his place between Seumas and Tangiia.

'Where is my friend, Po?' he asked, looking down the line of warriors. 'I hoped to see him before the battle.'

'Gone,' replied Seumas. 'Killed in skirmish.'

'By whom?'

'By those who are now our friends.'

Kupe nodded, wisely. 'Then Po will be mourned by me, but not avenged.'

The squadron of five tipairua swept forward, detaching itself from the flotilla, just as dark clouds rolled over the sky like carrion crows. The prows were carved idols of Oro, their mouths sneering, revealing pointed teeth, the eyes hidden beneath heavy brows. Banners fluttered from the totems on the decks, warriors chanted songs of death, King Tutapu called for victory.

Tangiia, thinking that his brother had decided to establish a beach-head, called his warriors to his side. Using the waves, the squadron of tipairua rushed towards the sands. When they reached the shallows, Tutapu and his warriors leapt from their canoes and waded through the surf to engage Tangiia's warriors. Stinging jellyfish, sent by an unknown god, attacked Tutapu's warriors, hindering their rush to the beach.

The drummer, left on board, had instructions to give seven rapid beats on the drum, once the fighting started. At that moment however, Ua, the Rain God, brought forth a deluge. Lingadua, the One-armed God of Drums, had not forgotten what he imagined was an insult from King Tutapu of Raiatea and Borabora, and it was he who had persuaded Ua to drench the island.

The sodden drum skin was muted by the rain, sound would not carry far, and Ragnu leading the rest of the flotilla did not hear the seven-beat signal. Hau Maringi came down cloaked in mist, to hide Tutapu's warriors until they made the beach-head, but Ua's rain drove away the mist, dispelling it.

When Tutapu looked back, through the dark driving rain, Kuku Lau, the Goddess of Mirages, made him see the shadowy silhouettes of his flotilla, bearing down on Tangiia's flanks. He believed the battle was going according to his plan.

Moko, the Lizard-God, who saw that the intervention by the gods was uneven, came to the aid of Tutapu. He sent large lizards down from the sides of the mountain, to tangle the legs of Tangiia's warriors. Those of King Tangiia's people who were not in the fight, however – the old men and women and young children – rushed forward and began pulling the lizards out of the mêlée by their tails and whirling them back into the forest.

The Great Gods – Tangaroa and Maomao – did not become involved in the actual battle. Their squabble with one another was in a state of truce and the affairs of men were but events of mild interest to them beside their own majesty.

The rain stopped and Ra swept from behind a cloud to fill the day with brilliance.

Tangiia's men, unhampered by any attack on their flanks, drove into Tutapu's troops as they emerged from the surf. The invaders began to fall, clustered together as they were and hampered by the stinging jellyfish. They fought desperately to get from the boats to the shore. The cries of dying and wounded men filled the air.

Dakuwanga swam through the ether above the island, hungrily swallowing the sau of the dead as they left their bodies on the battlefield, tearing pieces from the spirits of fallen warriors as if they were carrion. The Shark-God would be bloated with food by the end of the day. A war was the greedy Dukawanga's happiest time: a time to be glutted on rich souls.

Kupe and Karika fought either side of Tangiia, as the young king battled to reach his half-brother, surrounded by veteran warriors.

One of Tutapu's spearmen, who had made the beach without injury, rushed along the sand and was about to hurl his spear at King Tangiia, when an arrow struck him in the chest, bringing him to his knees. Seumas the bowman was sending his missiles into the enemy troops, who panicked not knowing where these small spears were coming from. With a quiver full of shafts, Seumas was able to pick his target and protect individuals on his own side without joining in the tangle of struggling warriors.

When his arrows were spent, Seumas slipped his bagpipes from his shoulder and began playing a martial tune. His own people were now used to the terrible wailing sound they had first heard coming from the island of the giant bird. The sounds were like the screams of a god gone mad. Tutapu's troops were again thrown into a panic, thinking that Tangiia had forces of supernatural creatures fighting for him.

The word went down the line of the invaders – there were *demons* to conquer, as well as mortals – and fear swept through the attackers.

A warrior of Tutapu's forces, demented by the noise, rushed towards Seumas swinging a basalt axe, desperate to get rid of the sound that was addling his brains. When he was just over an arm's length from the Pict, his axe flailing the air, Dirk leapt at him. The man froze in horror as the mad-eyed hound buried its teeth in his side and hung there, twisting and turning like a shark gripping the belly of a whale.

The man fell to the ground where he was knocked cold by a blow from Seumas's foot. The Pict warrior did not even pause for breath as he continued his playing.

In his place on the beach, the great and magnificent Kupe, god-like in his presence and bearing, an utterly fearless champion, wielded his father's whalebone club with such calm and casual ferocity no enemy dare approach him after a while. They stood around him in a ring, their eyes revealing their admiration and fear, their bravery only growing as their numbers increased, until there were so many they could have swarmed over him like ants, yet still not one of them gave the signal, so overawed were they by Kupe's power and skill, by his charismatic composure.

Finally, a giant of a man cried, 'Are we all cowards to be afraid of Kupe? He is but a navigator, a man of the sea – he is but a *man* after all is said and done. So he slayed the giant octopus! I have killed many octopuses in my time, many monsters of the ocean. I will destroy the great Kupe with one thrust of my spear, then sever his head with my paddle club …'

So saying the big man stepped forward, only to be struck down by a lightning blow from the mighty Kupe, his skull cloven to the shoulders, his legs buckling under the force of the blow.

At this action they indeed tried to swarm over the splendid Kupe, only to find his club flailing amongst them, cutting them down like cane in a field, turning men to stubble, until even the most heroic amongst them, hungry for glory, turned and ran, leaving dead comrades littering the sand, and blood seeping down the strand to the wavelets of the lagoon. Finally, Kupe stood alone, amongst the corpses of his would-be killers, his teak-coloured skin shining with oil, his long hair flying.

Now that the rain had cleared, Ragnu saw that his king was in difficulties and guessed something had gone wrong with the signal they had arranged. He ordered the twenty tipairua to sail to the beach and join with the fighting. However, the wind had dropped to zero and they had to paddle the heavy canoes.

Maomao was not taking part in the battle; he had simply paused in his work to watch the outcome.

Tangaroa too, had ceased to make waves and was studying the fight with great interest, so the lagoon was quite calm.

At last Tangiia and Tutapu came face to face on the sands. Tutapu, resplendent in his helmet of red feathers fringed by grey feathers, looked fearsome. Around his neck dangled a corded, wrapped pendant, a representation of Oro. In his hands he held a club two thirds the height of a man, its honed edges bristling with whales' teeth.

A double-pointed obsidian dagger, the hilt in the centre of two blades, was stuck in the waistband of his loin cloth.

Tangiia had a short patu club and his lei-o-mano.

'At last, little brother,' cried Tutapu. 'You are within reach of my hand.'

At that moment the burly Manopa rushed out of Tangiia's ranks of warriors, shouting, 'Leave Tutapu to me!'

Before Tangiia could stop him, Manopa swung his kotiate club at Tutapu's head. Tutapu neatly sidestepped and swept his own club sideways, low and swift. Manopa's left leg took the blow and broke at the knee. With a cry of agony, Manopa fell to the ground. Tutapu raised his mighty club above his head. He brought it down on Manopa's skull. There was the sound of a coconut cracking open. Manopa was dead.

Stepping over the body, Tutapu swung again, this time at Tangiia's right shoulder. Tangiia was swifter, striking at his brother's wrist. The patu club reached its mark first. Slightly off-target it snapped four of Tutapu's fingers against the haft of the great club. Tutapu's blow hit Tangiia's shoulder. With a gashed and gushing upper arm he flew sideways on to the sand.

Tutapu dropped the club, his left hand now useless. He armed himself with his double-bladed stone dagger. As he leaned over Tangiia to strike him in the face with the point, Tangiia whipped out his lei-o-mano. The young king slashed down the inside of Tutapu's thigh. The flesh tore with the sharks' teeth opening a hideous wound. Blood rushed forth, unstaunched.

Tutapu had to reach down to Tangiia. This gave the younger brother an advantage. Tangiia slashed at the tendons behind his brother's right ankle. Severing these with one grating slice caused Tutapu to scream in agony and fall down beside his brother. Tutapu's body fell across Tangiia's arm, sending the lei-o-mano flying from the younger brother's grasp.

Tangiia was now unarmed.

Tutapu still had his stone dagger and rolling over he stabbed at Tangiia. The obsidian blade went through the fleshy muscle on the side of Tangiia's throat, pinning his neck to the ground. Although nothing vital had been pierced, Tangiia had effectively been nailed to the floor.

Tutapu however, had no other weapon to use, unless he withdrew the stone blade from his brother's neck. He sat on Tangiia's abdomen and leaned with his forearm across Tangiia's windpipe, trying to stem his flow of air.

The faces of the two men were very close at this point. They stared into each other's eyes. At one time they had loved each other, these two brothers, but now circumstances of power had replaced that love; not with hate, but with fear. They feared each other and so one of them had to die. It seemed like it would be Tangiia as the young man's eyes glazed over. His brain began to spin and the light started to fade.

The survival instinct in Tangiia must have been stronger than his mind. He reached up and laced the fingers of both hands behind Tutapu's neck. It was almost a gesture of filial affection. Then he pulled his brother's head sharply down towards his shoulder. It drove the second upright blade of the obsidian dagger through Tutapu's right eye.

Tutapu stiffened and then convulsed for a moment. He gave a final sigh. Then the pressure on Tangiia's throat was relieved. The two brothers were locked there, in one another's embrace, joined together by the double-bladed dagger, one blade pinning Tangiia to the earth, the other blade pointing upwards through Tutapu's eye socket into his brain.

Boy-girl came running over.

'King Tangiia!'

She lifted Tutapu from on top of Tangiia. Then she wrenched the dagger from the neck of her king. Tangiia sat up and marvelled that he was still alive. There was a feeling of exultation in his breast mingling with a deep sadness and a sense of failure and loss. He had killed his only brother. A few paces away, his good friend and basket-sharer Manopa lay dead on the earth. It was not a day to feel triumphant.

'Thank you, Boy-girl,' he croaked, his fingers on his neck-wound stemming the blood.

Boy-girl stood over her king, a spear in her hand, ready to defend him against other enemy warriors.

It was unnecessary.

A groan had gone through the invaders when they saw their king fall dead. They began running back to their tipairua canoes resting in the lapping wavelets just off the beach. A major psychological blow had been dealt them. They had believed Tutapu to be invincible, beloved of the gods, and now he was carrion. They had not the heart to fight on.

Ragnu's arrival at the shore coincided with the rush back to the boats and he shrieked at the warriors to turn and fight.

'Tutapu is dead,' they cried, ignoring his orders. 'Our king is no more!'

Ragnu cried, 'Fight for me! Avenge your king's death.'

But the warriors had no stomach for it. The fight had not been about land, or protecting their families against an enemy, it had been about a quarrel between two brothers. Now one of those brothers was dead. There was no need for any more fighting. There was no need for any more deaths. The warriors called to Ragnu to take them away, back to their homeland.

Ragnu knew his forces were still vastly superior in numbers to the defending troops on the island, but he also knew that his men needed a reason to fight. They had not loved Tutapu enough to feel the bitter need for revenge. He was a king who could be replaced without too much sorrow wasted on him. Not a *bad* king, but not a liked one either. Just another king.

Resentfully, Ragnu turned his tipairua and headed away with his squadron of twenty vessels, back towards the reef.

Tangiia, freed from his position on the sands, called to Karika to help him.

'I must go out there!' he said.

Karika assisted Tangiia, whose shoulder wound was more painful than the pierced neck, down to Kupe's canoe. The two kings then sailed out to the tipairua. Standing a spear's throw off, Tangiia called to Ragnu.

'You will need to replenish your provisions, if you are not all to die of hunger and thirst.'

'What do you suggest?' growled Ragnu, standing at the mast of his tipairua.

'Give me Kula and your men can come ashore, unarmed, and collect as much food and water as you need. You can bury your dead too. They will need friends to put them in the earth.'

Ragnu stared around him at his disillusioned warriors, knowing that if he set sail without provisions, there would soon be a mutiny amongst his crews.

'You can have her,' he called back to Tangiia, 'but can I trust you?'

'I am Karika,' cried that man. 'I have no quarrel with you, kahuna. I will guarantee the safety of your men.'

Eventually, Ragnu nodded. 'She comes to you now,' he said.

Kula was put in a dugout canoe and she paddled towards Tangiia and Karika.

Tangiia drew his lei-o-mano, but Karika gripped his arm and said, 'Wait until you hear what she has to say.'

'I need no further proof,' said Tangiia, grimly.

'You will not do this thing,' Karika insisted. 'If I have to break your arm to stop you.'

Tangiia stared at his co-ruler and saw that Karika was very serious. The young man, full of heat and jealousy, handed the knife over to his friend, saying, 'You hold the weapon. I cannot trust myself.'

When Kula reached the side of the váa motu, she looked up with sad, dark eyes. 'You won?' she said. 'He's dead?'

'Yes, are you sorry?' answered Tangiia, bitterly.

'I'm sorry that Tutapu is dead, but happy you are alive. I went to him to try to stop him, but he wanted your death more than he wanted me.'

'You offered yourself to save me?'

'He refused to accept.'

Tangiia stared at her with hurt in his eyes. 'Can I believe you?' he whispered.

'I love you,' she said, simply. 'If you don't know that, then you're truly lost.'

Tangiia hung his head and wept.

'I'm sorry,' he said. 'You should not have gone.'

'I know that now.'

Karika helped her aboard the váa motu and she immediately began fussing over her husband's wounds, much to his inner comfort. They sailed back to the shore, now lined with triumphant warriors, old men and women and children.

A mighty cheer went up as Tangiia and Kula stepped on shore. For Karika too, there were salutations. Boy-girl was leaping up and down in a kind of wild dance, her coloured ribbons flying in the wind. Seumas was hugging Dirk. Kikamana was already starting a sacred fire to Oro, to thank him for the victory over a superior enemy. Kieto was striding around, smiling, a young man having had his first taste of battle. Kaho was on his knees, his son Pooi beside him, offering prayers.

The dead were then gathered in and mourning for lost loved ones began.

Not the least of those grieved over was Tutapu by his brother.

Manopa was buried with great ceremony, alongside Po, mourned by his king and friend.

After the funeral of Manopa, Kieto had a few words with Boy-girl.

'Well, Boy-girl, we have come a long way from our ancestral island.

Remember we once sat on the beach and talked about Seumas – how the voyage would change him?'

They both looked towards Seumas, standing quietly on his own, physically away from the group, yet spiritually part of it, a self-possessed man, at peace within – a strong and able adventurer, resting between exploits.

Boy-girl said, 'He has conquered Seumas, as well as the ocean – he has no need to test himself, prove himself any more. His worth as a man has increased ten-fold. There is mercy and kindness in his eyes, instead of anger.' Boy-girl sighed deeply. 'It makes him that much more desirable.'

'You know that can never be,' said Kieto.

'I know, I know – just dreams,' replied Boy-girl.

Kieto said, 'I too need Seumas, but for a wider purpose – not yet, but one day in the future. The wise Kupe has prophesied my part in making our nation great. When the day comes for me to lead the Oceanians in the conquest of the Land-of-Mists, I will need Seumas as my advisor. It will be hard for him, for though he is now almost all Oceanian, a small part of him will still be Pict.'

'Perhaps you are wrong, Kieto, perhaps only a small part of him is Ocean-ian, and the greater part, hidden from our eyes, is Pict?'

'In that case,' said Kieto, 'we shall become enemies – but I hope he will remain my brother, not my enemy.'

Boy-girl nodded. 'We must both wish for that end, Kieto.'

Ragnu's men and some women were allowed to come ashore to gather provi-sions for their voyage back to Raiatea. Tutapu's cousin Haari would be waiting there for news of the expedition. Ragnu said he intended to confirm Haari as king. Tangiia, recalling Haari's disposition and common sense, thought the man would make an excellent ruler. Haari was not young, being a man in his early sixties, but so much the better. The fire might have gone from his veins, but he was a wise and stable man.

The enemy was watched night and day, until they were preparing to leave, in case Ragnu tried a sneak attack. They still had the warriors to overwhelm the island, but those warriors were obviously not in the mood for further fighting, for Ragnu's force stayed out beyond the reef.

The day of the flotilla's departure, a dugout with two people on board detached itself from a tipairua.

It was paddled towards the shore.

On being informed by Kieto that Dorcha was in the small canoe, Seumas went down to the shore. He stood waiting for her to arrive. Dirk was by his side and could sense his master's nervousness, because he whined softly and kept looking up at Seumas as if hoping for a change in his master's mood.

As he waited Seumas thought over the past years spent in Oceania with its various peoples. In the beginning he had despised the Oceanians, for their arrogance, for their apparent feminine ways, for many things. In the beginning he had resented most dreadfully his capture and forced exile. Since that time however, he had revised his opinion of the Raiateans, had made many deep friendships and strong ties. He had come to regard their mild manners and gentleness in the normal course of day-to-day living as more manly than the rough manners and aggressive nature of his own people, for he knew that when the time came for fierceness and courage, they were no more lacking than one of his Pict cousins. They borrowed the better nature of women for their daily dealings with one another and brought forth the pugnacious manliness within them for their battles.

He certainly missed the wild shores and rugged landscape of his homeland, it was true, but he had also come to love the cobalt-blue seascapes and jewel-green islands of Oceania. His whole existence was now plagued by ambivalent feelings. Yet he knew his life had been thus far an *interesting* one. He had seen things no Albannach had seen, except one other, who had shared those years with him, if not by his side, within his sight and hearing. He had experienced things of which no other Pict had dreamed. He was a man full of great stories, part of them, entwined within their multitudinous meshes. In truth, he would not have changed those experiences for a long and common life in the mountains and glens of his homeland, much as he loved his croft in the purple heathered hills of Albainn; much as he loved his clan and their fierce and glorious ways; much as he missed the white winters when the deer ran swiftly over the powdered landscape and the wolf bayed over a kill.

He thought back to his childhood, amongst the aromatic pines, running through different forests than those of Oceania. A barefoot Pict boy with an iron dagger, bow and a quiver of arrows. A hard little boy, inured to the freezing winds, careless of cliffs and their dangers, wolf-eyed, bitter-lipped, ruddy-cheeked. These were distant memories, of times when he wore ermine and foxskin coats; followed spoor over iron-hard earth, of hare and grouse. He remembered the time when he peeked through a chink in a neighbour's croft wall at a young woman changing her clothes and discovered another iron dagger between his legs – he recalled vividly how he was stunned by the sight of the dark furry creature between *her* legs and how the sight of it made his heart beat rapidly and his skin prickle with shock. And memories of stalking martens under a hard-edged, cold, stark moon; of wrestling in the rushing burns with his cousins; of being beaten by his father for crying tears when his pet ptarmigan was killed and roasted during a famine.

Such far-off memories, almost unbelievable.

Now he waited to learn the outcome of his fate in love.

When the canoe reached the shore, Dorcha stepped out and on to the beach.

Seumas said gruffly, using Gaelic because there was a stranger present, '*Thoir dhomh freagairt, caileag?*'

'What do I want? Wouldn't you like to know, *gille?*'

She called him *boy*, because he had discourteously called her *girl* and not *woman*.

'It's about time you learned some manners,' she said, haughtily, standing before him and lifting her chin.

'*Ciod e tha ort?*' he retorted, asking what ailed her.

She visibly softened and replied, this time in Gaelic, for she suddenly became shy, '*Tha gradh agam ort-sa.*'

Seumas stared at her, unable to believe his ears. What she had said, literally translated, was, 'Love is at me, on you.' In plain Oceanian, 'I love you.' Suspicion still lurked in his brain though. He wondered if she were playing tricks with him, a cruel joke.

'What do you mean, you love me?'

'It's been a long voyage. I set out looking for you because I thought I missed tormenting you. When we arrived here and I saw you standing on the beach with that damn dog by your side, I realised that what I missed, was simply *you*, yourself.'

The man with Dorcha was looking at them with wide eyes. Seumas noticed he was a filthy individual, with scabs and sores, an arm in a splint, and either his body or his ragged loin cloth smelled like stagnant swamp water. The man beached the canoe and began walking away from them, towards the huts. He moved swiftly, glancing behind him every so often.

Seumas was too overwhelmed by Dorcha's words to take any notice of the man's strange behaviour.

'Me?' he said to Dorcha. 'What about your dead husband?'

Her face went hard. 'I can never forgive you for that – but I love you anyway. It happens.'

'By heaven, I could take you now, on the sands,' he groaned, fearful that such a promise would be whisked away from him by some heartless god.

'You will not – you will wait until a respectable time.'

He said, 'You – you won't change your mind? You will become my wife? I – I need you, Dorcha, with me – always. I mean, for ever.'

'I shall grow ugly,' she said. 'If all you want is my body, you will be disappointed in me one day.'

He stared into her dark pupils, set in the pale face below the wild tangle of black hair. Already there were crow's feet at the corners of her eyes and mouth, yet her long face had such stately beauty in it he could not imagine a time when he would not see her as he saw her now. There was an inner glow to Dorcha that a thousand years could not dim.

'Never. It's *you* I love. There will always be beauty behind the signs of age –

because there is beauty *in* you. That doesn't mean I can't wait to make love to you.'

'I shall become your wife,' she confirmed, smiling.

He took her in his arms and hugged her close, kissing the salt from her face, much to the consternation of Dirk. His heart was full. She was his at last.

She whispered in his ear, 'This is a heavenly island, isn't it? What are they going to call it?'

'They are calling it *Rarotonga*,' he told her. 'And you're right, it will be our paradise.'

'Ours,' she said, smiling, and she took his hand and led him towards the rainforest.

Boy-girl, standing in the shadows, sadly watched them go.

Tangiia and Kula were in intimate embrace when a man threw himself into the doorway of their hut, landing on his knees.

'My lord!' cried the man dramatically, whose foul breath filled the hut almost immediately. 'Hear me!'

Kula drew back, revolted by the stench billowing from the man's body. Tangiia, startled by this intrusion, snatched up a patu club in haste, thinking there was an attack. He studied the creature blocking his doorway with distaste.

The man had blackened teeth and was covered in dirt of some indefinable nature. Tangiia would not have been surprised to learn that the grime had been acquired while the man slept, by choice, with pigs and chickens on the tipairua. Unkempt, matted locks hung from the man's scalp, which itself appeared to be flaking in large scales. The man's nose was running with mucus into some lip sores, around which there were black rims.

'Is it Ragnu?' asked Tangiia. 'Is he coming again?'

'No, my lord,' cried the man. 'He has left on the tide – but those two mountain goblins. I heard them on the beach. They speak with the tongues of foul demons.'

Tangiia relaxed, leaning on his club.

'What two goblins? Seumas is here alone.'

'Ahh,' smiled the man, greasily, revealing the gaps between his rotten teeth, 'the goblin woman has come too.'

'Dorcha is here?'

'The very same.'

'To kill Seumas?'

'They speak of love,' said the man earnestly, 'in that vile language they use. I mean, sometimes they speak with real words, other times they hiss and screech at each other in the ugly words of fiends and monsters of darkness.'

Tangiia glanced quickly at Kula, giving her an expression of mild surprise. 'Love?'

'Yes, my lord,' said the man, 'I thought you ought to know, considering that if they fornicate, there will soon be horrid little demons all over this lovely island – I hear they can spawn a thousand at a time, these profane creatures.'

'Talking of odious creatures,' said Kula. 'Who are you?'

The man smiled greasily. 'I am proud to be called Polahiki, O queen – a humble fisherman of no certain abode.' His face turned to a grim mask. 'I was wrongly captured by that brigand Tutapu, who called himself a king, but was nothing but a ship rat without fleas—'

'My brother, you mean?' said Tangiia.

Polahiki smiled uncertainly. 'A very fine brother, I'm sure, but a terrible king.'

'Wrong again, mongrel,' said Tangiia. 'He was a fine king, but a terrible brother.'

'That's what I meant,' Polahiki said hastily. 'I get my words mixed up sometimes – it's because I've been tortured, by – by that very fine king we mentioned.' He held up his splinted arm and showed Tangiia some crooked fingers.

Tangiia called for a priest, who came at the run and showed by his expression that he was horrified to find Polahiki in the doorway of the king's house.

Tangiia said, 'Take this creature and give him a bath.'

Polahiki looked panic-stricken. 'My lord?'

Tangiia narrowed his eyes. 'Let me show you that my brother's tortures were nothing beside mine. You will be scrubbed with hairy gourds until you shine. Your head will be shaved. Your lice will be slaughtered by the hundred thousand. That loin cloth will be burned. You will be, in short, horribly cleansed. Take him away. I don't want to see him until I recognise skin. And pull out the rest of those teeth. If we can't do anything about his flatulence, we can certainly make a difference at the other orifice. Not another word. Go.'

When Polahiki had been dragged from their sight, Kula turned to him smiling. 'You will make a good king,' she said. 'And Rarotonga a good home for our people.'

'Karika and I will rule as well as we can,' replied Tangiia. 'Now, where were we ...?'

Kula stepped out of her skirt.

'Here?' she said, laughing.

'Exactly,' he replied.

THE PRINCELY FLOWER

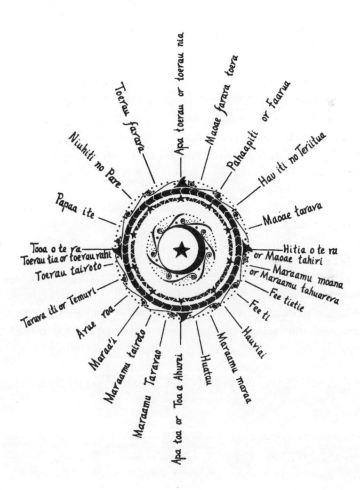

For Grace and John Chidlow

PART ONE

The leaping place of souls

1

The Earthquake-God Ruau-moko turned unexpectedly in his mother's womb and woke Tikokura, who rose up out of a gentle ocean to form a giant angry face of water which swept over the surface towards a defenceless atoll.

The mouth of the Tikokura's face was a massive maw filled with white, foam-flecked teeth. The hidden eyes were sightless, blinded by fury, buried beneath heavy lids of water. The hair on the head of the wave was spindrift, terrible in its aspect, which trailed behind the broad expanse of Tikokura's brow.

On the beaches of the atoll, a ring of six islands, the fishermen and shell-fish gatherers saw the tidal wave coming. Since the atoll was not more than six feet above sea level they knew that many, if not all of them, were about to drown.

'Tikokura's coming!' one of the women screamed. 'Save my children! Save my children!'

Birds flew up from the trees and beaches in a blast which momentarily filled the sky with black dots.

'I'm an old man, I can't run,' cried a white-hair in despair. 'Help me! Sons, daughters, help me!'

No one came to the elderly father's assistance, nor that of the unfortunate mother, for there was nothing anyone could do, there was nowhere to run.

Some islanders were immediately resigned to the idea of death: as inhabit-ants of a low sandy atoll on which life was hard, where work filled almost every waking hour, and disasters were common, they were an unhappy group of people hammered into a dulled state of acceptance by misery, constant labour and deprivation.

A few, however, scuttled away for the palm trees, hoping to climb high enough to be out of the reach of Tikokura. They dropped their nets, without which they would probably die of starvation anyway, and ran for the scrubby patches of palm trees which were all but the only vegetation on the isles. In these few that unquenchable spark known as the will-to-live drove out all common sense and had them mindlessly attempting to cling on to their empty and worthless existence.

One or two, those lucky enough to own canoes, took to the boats.

No one questioned: *why?* Tikokura was a minor but unpredictable god, cap-able of destructive fury for no reason at all. His breast was full of bitterness; he preferred *hate* over all other emotions; he killed for the love of killing.

One young man already in an ocean-going canoe, a seafaring warrior, a stranger merely touching the shores of the atoll briefly in order to replenish his water supplies, immediately turned his canoe and, unlike the islanders themselves, raced directly into the maw of the wave.

Those who saw this action were astounded. They wanted to call to the youth, warn him of the terrible consequences of his actions, turn him from his course. The warrior stood at his mast, however, a determined expression in his blue eyes, ready to do battle with the god of sudden waves.

He was a tall fair-skinned youth, out of whose partly shaven head pro-truded two dark-red twisted horns of hair in the fashion of the Hivans. Indeed, the three solid bars tattooed across the bridge of his nose, making his battle expression one of the fiercest in Oceania, also proclaimed him to be of the Hivan-peopled islands. In his right hand he held a barbed spear, which he brandished in the face of the oncoming god.

'Tikokura,' screamed the youth. 'My name is Kumiki, a warrior of Nuku Hiva. These useless people have no temples, or I would have sacrificed a pig or dog to you …'

The wave rushed onwards, seemingly unaffected by these words.

'Let me ride over your head, Tikokura,' pleaded Kumiki, 'for you have no quarrel with me. I'm not one of these miserable wretches who scrape an existence from your back. I'm Kumiki the Hivan, on a life-long quest to kill my own father. I must live until my father lies at my feet, the blood gushing forth from his throat, staining the coral of his home isle. Spare me until that moment – *then* take my life, if you must.'

Tikokura heard these words and knew then who was Kumiki's father. He sympathised with the youth's mission, for he had little love of his own people, let alone those from an alien place. The wave-god's hate for mankind would be better served by allowing this one Hivan warrior to live, so that the youth could cause an untold misery and upheaval amongst a distant island group. The boy was a weapon, a spear in flight, and for the sake of bitterness it was better not to knock him aside, but to let him fly onwards to his target.

Kumiki saw the wave part before him, allowing him a narrow passage over calm waters between tumultuous seas. Once his canoe was through and he was safe the gap closed and the wave continued on its relentless path towards the hapless atoll. When it hit the outer reef it thundered over the coral bed, drumming the island from a distance and causing climbers to be shaken from the palms like insects. They fell screaming to their deaths. Coconuts followed, raining on their twisted forms, pounding their bruised bodies into the coral dust.

Tikokura swept at last over the beaches and the islands, taking with him men, women and children, the force of his momentum gathering them up as a flood collects twigs. Flimsy huts disintegrated, fires were quenched in a brief hiss of steam, precious nets disappeared. The tops of palm trees, some bearing clinging mortals, were snapped like broom heads and washed away to unknown shores. Fishermen's boats were overturned, spilling out their occupants, who were instantly lost in the crashing, whirlwind foam of the breakers which tossed and tumbled over the small islands, grasping, crushing, destroying everything and anything which had been made or planted by human hand.

When the spilling torrent had finally rushed on, towards the horizon, the water left in its wake drained from the atoll, leaving the group of islands above the surface again.

Kumiki saw figures descending from the strongest and tallest of the palms, a few survivors climbing down to the wet coral dust, to stand and stare bleakly at the devastation that lay before their eyes. Everything they had ever owned had been torn from their grasp in a matter of moments. Their means of livelihood – their nets, their canoes, their scant crops – were all gone. All that was left were the flat islands themselves.

For the next few months, perhaps years, they would be scrabbling about in the lagoon searching for those shellfish which had not been ripped off rocks and carried away. They would be living on limpets and clams, seaweed and roots, fighting over the sparse numbers of coconuts, their only source of fresh drink since they had no wells. They would dwindle in numbers to eventually disappear completely as a people, until more exiles from the high islands began to land and populate the flat, uninteresting atoll – and the next wave came.

Kumiki turned his canoe in the direction of Arue roa on the windflower.

On his home isle of Nuku Hiva the eighteen-year-old Kumiki had left the girl who he hoped would one day be his wife. Her name was Miro and he loved her deeply. They had already made love in the sand and surf of the Hivan beaches, with others of their own age, since promiscuity and sexual licence among the unmarried was perfectly acceptable to Oceanians.

Once they were married, however, adultery was punishable by death, and she would be his alone to love and cherish.

It would not have been fair to have married her before he left, for he might never be able to return to Nuku Hiva. The sea might swallow him, the gods might take him, or a man might kill him, making the return trip impossible. Also, he had left her free to love whom she pleased, in a casual way, extracting only the promise that she would not marry another unless he, Kumiki, failed to return home within five years.

When Kumiki had asked for her promise, Miro had said, 'I shall never marry another – instead, if you do not return, I shall go to the leaping place of souls and end my life – for I know if you do not come back to me you must be dead.'

'Do not kill yourself,' he told her, knowing she meant to throw herself over the cliff where spurned and lost lovers ended their lives, 'for you can learn to love again.'

'Without you sharing my mat, dear Kumiki, I shall not want to live.'

This had disturbed Kumiki greatly. He did not want such a beautiful thing as the love between him and Miro to be stained with blood. It was enough they had loved for the short time given them until now. Still, he had every intention of returning to her, and no intention at all of allowing Tikokura to snatch his life, even after he had killed his father, despite what he had promised the wave-god in a moment of rashness.

Kumiki brooded on images of his father's death, once the pictures had re-entered his head.

The death of his birth-right father.

A brief inspection of Kumiki's skin would tell anyone that he was not of pure Hivan descent. From a distance he had sometimes been mistaken by strangers for an albino, or perhaps one of the Peerless Ones, the fair-skinned, fair-haired fairies of the mountains. Then, when he came closer and they noticed his hair, they changed their minds to believe him a goblin or demon. It was only when he was close enough to speak to them, and they recognised his tattoos, that they knew him to be a Hivan warrior from a princely family. A youth of noble lineage.

Kumiki had fair skin – fairer even than the pale Tongan, Samoan and Tahitian princes – and dark-reddish hair. Although adopted by a chief, his real father it might be thought was a supernatural creature. Yet Kumiki had been told a story which proved his real father nothing but a man – a man not from Oceania but from a land discovered by Kupe the Raiatean. A place called Land-of-Mists, where all men had white skins and blue eyes.

Kumiki's adopted father had told him that his real father had invaded their island with a band of warriors from Raiatea and had, in the course of that invasion, raped an innocent woman, who later died giving birth to Kumiki himself. Kumiki was the product of a savage outsider, a wild creature with none of the finer instincts of an Oceanian, no strong code of honour, no generosity of spirit.

The man known as Seumas possessed none of the traits which made men proud of themselves. He had not conducted himself with dignity after raiding Nuku Hiva, but had taken a woman by force in the troubled heat of the battle. This Seumas had not been able to control his basic urges at a time when he should have been glorifying Oro, the God of War, not slaking his lust in the dirt with a terrified woman.

Kumiki had been incensed when he heard what the boastful savage Seumas had done to his mother, even though it had resulted in his own birth. There and then he had resolved to seek out this foreign monster and kill him, first letting him know why he was going to die, then crushing his skull with a club. It was then Kumiki's intention to eat the head of Seumas, to steal his mana, and chew on his eyes and heart to humiliate him utterly.

Kumiki sighed as the wind drove the spray against his face, now set in the direction of Rarotonga.

'I can almost taste his brains,' whispered the youth, with longing in his voice. 'I can almost savour his eyes on my tongue at this very moment.'

There was a long way to go yet, however. Kumiki was no great navigator, no Kupe or Hiro, or even Karika. He was a youth who until the age of seventeen had sailed only in home waters. But sea-farers had come to his island, and he had talked long and hard with them, learning the ways of the open ocean, discovering the name and location of his enemy, gleaning the secrets of navigation on the high seas.

He had gathered together knowledge of the setting and rising stars in the roof of voyaging, the fanakenga and kaveinga; of waves, their sizes and shapes; of swells, rips, currents; of different types of wind; of seaweed and birds; of important cloud formations; of sounds and smells of distant land; of the colour of different running seas.

Still, he had no experience and would probably become lost at times. It would be enough to survive, *eventually* to track down his prey, murder him in cold blood, and laugh at those who tried to stop him.

It was all Kumiki could ask of his Tiki, the First Ancestor of all men, sitting now on the front of his ocean-going canoe. It was all he could wish of the demi-god Maui, the trickster whose body was held in thrall by the Hine-nui-te-po Goddess of Death, but whose spirit still roamed the world. It was all he could request of Tawhaki, the Great God of Thunder and Lightning, of whom Kumiki wished to be a personal favourite.

'I shall leave his body to be picked clean by the reef fish,' snarled the horn-haired Hivan youth, the three solid bars of his tattoo twisting into a ferocious expression as he thought about his quarry. 'I shall throw his liver to the frigate birds and watch them tear it to pieces as they fight over the shreds.'

These juvenile and immature chants by the warrior, into the teeth of the wind, helped him maintain his courage in the face of the long, dangerous and arduous voyage. He was not cutting new pathways through the ocean, but following a memorised pattern of the swells, clouds, islands, reefs, rips and other navigational signs, given him by adventurers who had traversed the same route before him and had returned to pass on their knowledge. His fury at his real father helped him to overcome his fears of being lost, or of meeting monsters, or of being swallowed by gods.

'I hate him for his nothing-family!'

This was the main reason why Kumiki loathed his real father: because Seumas had left him no family line, no ancestors to revere. A community worshipped the gods, but an individual worshipped the spirits of his ancestors. Kumiki had no ancestors to look up to, to love and fear, to thank in times of plenty, of whom to beg forgiveness and food in times of want. Kumiki had no long genealogy to trot out in front of severe and intractable temple priests, no thousand names, no layers of generations which would make him proud. His name stopped with his blood-father, who had no *real* name, no name which meant 'son of the moon' or 'strong as a spear' but was just a jumble of worthless letters which when put together was pronounced 'Seumas'. There were of course ancestors on his mother's side, but these were so much less powerful.

'I'm coming for you, Seumas,' screamed Kumiki, his muscles rippling over the tautness of his chest as his hate fought to get out. 'I'm coming to eat your head, you lizard's tongue, you sperm of stone fish, you festering dog's intestines – I'm coming to tear the heart from under your ribs!'

And the words were swept away, over the vast reaches of the ocean, lost in a thousand miles of watery world, seeking the ear of the man they had once called 'the goblin'.

In the distance, a thousand miles away, a volcano erupted, spewing its red-and-white hot molten lava into the atmosphere in an immense spectacular pyrotechnical display. Kumiki took this breathtaking sight as a sign that Pele the Goddess of Fire and Volcano was on his side. The youth felt buoyed by the sight of redness covering the sky. This artificial sunset was Pele's stamp of approval on his mission.

Rarotonga has only two seasons: Winter and Breadfruit. This was the Breadfruit season, a time of plenty.

Two thousand miles away from the voyaging youth, unaware that he had a son in the world, Seumas sat on his mat and contemplated his past. He was now in his early fifties, as was his wife Dorcha, and the pair were childless. Yet, that fact apart, they were not unhappy.

He had been happy on Rarotonga, an island which he had helped to find, and win. The two kings who ruled jointly had found a tribe in the interior, the remnants of an ancient race of people known as the Menehuna.

The Menehuna were wonderful masons and builders. It was the fairer-skinned Menehuna who had built the Toi's Road, which circled the island, and who had constructed the magnificent temple called Arai-te-tonga.

Over the years Seumas the Pict had gathered much mana unto himself. The young Oceanians regarded him as one of themselves, a distinguished citizen and warrior, full of honour.

It was true, too, that he looked very much like any other elder Rarotongan. Tattoos covered much of his torso, his arms and legs. His skin had been burned by the sun and stars into a rich mahogany colour. His pride and joy, his fiery hair, once plaited by Dorcha into a long red pigtail, had changed its hue. He was now an Oceanian in appearance as well as manner. Only his blue eyes gave any hint of his real origins.

'Seumas, don't sit in the sun too long,' warned Dorcha, her own black hair now streaked with white, 'you'll get one of your headaches.'

'Don't fuss over me, woman,' he grumbled. 'I like it here in the doorway.'

There was a dog named Dirk near his feet. All his dogs had been called Dirk, from the first faithful hound that he had owned in the country of Albainn, to this whelp that stared at him now, its brown eyes full of sorrow at having to laze away the day instead of running along the beaches with his master.

The shadows of day lengthened quickly, as they always do close to the equator, and soon it was dark. The sky above became a soft black imbedded with masses of bright stars. Hine-keha, the Moon Goddess, began smiling down on the island.

Dorcha had a fire going in the middle of the house, its smoke curling out through a hole in the roof, and Seumas went in and sat beside it.

While Seumas was serving them both the red snapper he had caught, cooked by Dorcha in a coconut sauce and garnished with a delicate seaweed, someone entered by the window.

'Hello, Kieto,' smiled Dorcha, 'you saw the smoke of our fire?'

Kieto's entrance by the window, instead of the door, was a gentle reminder that he was higher in rank than either of the house's occupants.

Kieto laughed. 'Since both Seumas and I are basket-sharers anyway, your rebuke has very little sting.'

Kieto was now a sturdy man in his mid-thirties, a strong warrior prince, the adopted son of Tangiia.

Kieto said, as he sat on the mat and was offered some fish, 'I've asked Boy-girl to join us. We need to talk about war, Seumas. The time is getting close.'

Shortly afterwards, the tall willowy figure of Boy-girl appeared in the doorway.

'At least someone comes in by the right entrance,' said Dorcha, with a side-long glance at Kieto.

Boy-girl smiled at her hostess. The lean smooth Boy-girl had been born the seventh son of a family without girls and had been raised as a woman and as such she had great mana. Like Dorcha, Boy-girl was steeped in the occult.

'Come, Lei-o-mano,' said Boy-girl to a cockerel who followed her, 'heel, boy.'

Seumas growled, but said nothing.

This was Boy-girl's idea of a joke, to copy Seumas by training a rooster like a dog and have it follow her everywhere, even naming it after the Oceanian dagger.

The cockerel trotted in, running between Boy-girl's legs, and began pecking at unseen bits of food around the hearth, much to the consternation of

Dirk, who kept looking at his master, then back at the bird, as if wondering when Seumas was going to toss this arrogant creature out into the night.

Boy-girl sat down between the two men, her decorative shells rattling as she did so.

Seumas shook his head as he stared at Boy-girl. 'Who would believe you're almost as old as me – you don't look as though you've added a year since we've been on Rarotonga.'

Boy-girl laughed, delighted at the compliment.

'Now,' said Kieto, 'to business. You have heard that the old king, Haari, is dying?'

What had once been an arduous and terrible journey, from Raiatea to Rarotonga, was now a flourishing shipping route. Consequently, news travelled between the islands too, keeping everyone informed.

Dorcha had now sat down and she said, 'I have heard this.'

'Well,' continued Kieto, 'one of the princes on the island is using the king's death as an excuse to form an expedition to find another island. He has no elder brother chasing him away, but he feels the island has grown too populous.'

'You're talking of Ru,' interrupted Seumas.

Kieto nodded. 'Prince Ru has persuaded his brothers and their wives to go with him in search of an island which he has seen in a vision. He knows the star in the roof of voyaging under which the island rests, and he proclaims that once he has seen it he will discover his new home. He has selected twenty royal maidens for his crew. These virgins have been chosen for virtue, strength and beauty – as the Great Sea-God Tangaroa has ordered in Ru's vision – and their purity and strength will ensure a safe voyage for the seafarers.'

Dorcha said, 'Yes, but what is all this to do with us?'

'You know my destiny, Dorcha – it is set in the heavens – to conquer the great island found by Kupe – the Land-of-Mists – the place from which you and Seumas were taken by us some decades ago. Of course I know your feelings about this.'

Seumas shook his head. 'There are wild tribes on those shores – a proud people.'

'In that case,' said Kieto, 'they must be subdued.'

Seumas smiled ruefully. 'I have given you two main reasons why you cannot win such a land – iron and horses – of which you have neither.'

'You don't understand the nature of the people you are planning to attack,' interrupted Dorcha. 'They make war against each other, but if a common enemy comes, the tribes will join together under one leader. *"I am against my cousin, but my cousin and I are against the stranger."*'

'We will find a way,' Kieto said with confidence. 'It is why I have called this meeting. To talk to you of Ru's voyage. Boy-girl has been communing with her ancestors. As you know, the spirits of our forebears can see into the future and they tell Boy-girl that in the course of his voyage Ru will touch the shores of an island where giants roam. On that island is a gateway to another world. In that Otherworld is a nation of Oceanians called the Maori, a magnificent warrior race, who have colonised an island as great as Land-of-Mists – a country they call Aotearoa, or Land of the Long White Cloud.

'We must go and find these Maori, discover the secret of their success in war. We must learn their methods, their strategies, their tactics, and use this knowledge to conquer the Land-of-Mists. I know Albainn is your land, Seumas, and yours Dorcha, but this I also know – if we do not conquer the fair-skinned tribes of your country now, there will come a time when they will overrun *us*. We must do this thing, or our descendants will regret our faint-heartedness, and curse us for not taking our courage in our hands and striking first.'

Seumas understood all this, but nevertheless he was deeply troubled, as any man is whose loyalties are split.

2

Since King Tangiia and King Karika had founded their island domain, others had come in their canoes to swell the numbers of their subjects.

Tangiia chose, in the Tahitian-Raiatean way, to emphasise his divine origins. He was thus a very remote figure to the people, appearing mostly at night since commoners were obliged to sit with bowed heads when he passed.

It was lucky for them that he had not married his sister, instead of his beautiful cousin princess Kula, for then the commoners would have had to prostrate themselves.

Tangiia's servants carried him almost everywhere: his mana was so great that where he laid his foot became his property. Thus in order to disrupt daily lives as little as possible, and to allow the land to remain in the hands of commoners, Tangiia was only carried abroad during the night hours, when most of his subjects were asleep.

Karika, however, remained very much a man of the people. This was the Samoan custom. Samoan kings did not trace their line back to the gods, or if they did it was not made public knowledge. Karika was strong on dignity, could be stern and challenging, but did not stand on pomp.

From the Rarotongan commoner's point of view it might seem there was a king to despise and a king to love here, but each form of kingship brought with it certain rewards.

With King Tangiia's divine heritage came colourful ceremonies, music and dancing and a strong sense of religious fervour. He and his priests wore cloaks and helmets of brilliantly coloured feathers, while the Tangiia himself was resplendent in the scarlet sash which proclaimed his right of kingship. His royal canoe was a marvel of regal ornamentation and craftsmanship, heralded always by trumpeters, drummers and flautists of superior musical skills. His house, standing on the slopes of a mountain, was an architectural wonder. The people were immensely proud of such a haughty aristocrat.

Karika, on the other hand, remained very much a warrior king. He organised games and sports, was keen on bird hunting and fishing for bonito and albacore. He was not averse to removing his tapa bark shirt and helping in the fields. Karika introduced hunting with a hawk – Rarotonga's koputu fishing hawk – which was caught by lowering oneself down a cliff face, staring the bird unflinchingly in the eyes, then snatching it from its nest. If the hunter took his eyes from the raptor for a second, or gave way to the bird's piteous cries, the hawk dropped as a dead weight in free fall, opening its wings just before hitting the ground far below the edge of the cliffs. Karika was adept at capturing the koputu.

The people loved such a king as this too, and felt they were getting the best of both worlds.

Such an island then, with its two great kings and its unsurpassed landscape beauty, was bound to attract settlers from far and wide throughout all Oceania.

They came from Samoa, from Tonga, from the Tahitian group, from the Hivan Islands, and from many others. So many Tahitians arrived within the first year that two of Tahiti's oldest mountains also magically transported themselves, since they missed the company of their human friends, and became Rarotonga's Ikurangi and Te Atu Kura peaks. The basins where they once stood in Tahiti remain as a testament to their departure.

On the day Kieto's expedition was about to depart, the great adventurer Hiro arrived at the island on his weather-worn pahi.

Dorcha and Seumas went hurrying down to the beach, to see the seafaring hero, who almost rivalled Kupe in his wanderings, pass through the gap in the reef. Hiro had been to the far corners of the ocean, even to Hawaii. He had tales to tell which chilled his listeners to the pith.

Hiro was an important friend and visitor and King Tangiia broke his rule and appeared in daylight on the beach, carried high on his litter. Still only in his late thirties he was a fine figure of a man in his feather cloak and helmet, but necessarily pale and serious in aspect. His lovely wife Queen Kula, resplendent in her own right, accompanied him.

Along with Tangiia came his retinue: counsellors, priests, a masseur, guards, a storyteller, the jester, a wise man, his treasurer and his valet. Tangiia stood on his litter with wide arms, welcoming Hiro to the shores of Raro- tonga, while a chosen warrior – one of Karika's personal bodyguards – made a show of pretending to attack the visitor with a spear, running forward, jab- bing at the air, rolling his eyes up to show the whites, lolling his tongue, slapping his thigh, and distorting his features with furious grimaces and angry sneers.

Hiro reached the high-tide mark and was greeted by Karika, who rubbed noses with the adventurer, bidding him welcome.

The feasting and dancing began. Dogs, chickens and pigs were slaughtered, breadfruit pits were opened, pandanus leaves were laid down. Musicians fetched their instruments and played lively tunes, filling the island air with song. In the high green valleys of the bladed mountains, the birds rose and fell in clusters, wondering what the noise was about.

Kieto and Seumas managed to get Hiro on his own, by the fire later that night, and discussed their own plans with him.

'Have you come across an island where giants are said to walk about and command attention?' asked Kieto.

Hiro, broad-chested and tall, square-faced and hawk-nosed, with long flowing black hair and deep brown eyes, looked thoughtful.

'I have never been to such a place, but I have heard tell of it on my travels.'

Seumas said, 'Could we persuade you to come with us, lead our expedition?'

Hiro smiled, shaking his head. 'My path lies in the opposite direction. I hear that the island you speak of, which is called Rapanui, the navel of the world, lies just above Fee Tietie on the windflower from this island – but far off, so far away it must be in the corner of Oceania. I must sail Nuihiti no Pare on the windflower, or the gods will be displeased with me.'

'Why do the gods tell you to go in that direction?' asked Kieto. 'What is beyond Samoa?'

'I have to seek out an art form, called *writing*, which is like speech only silent.'

This was gobbledegook so far as Seumas was concerned.

'How can it be like talking, yet be silent? It doesn't make sense. Are you sure the gods are not having a joke with you? Which gods do you mean? If it's Maui, then you had better think again, Hiro, for you know what a trick- ster he is – that demi-god would lead you into Hine-te-nui-po's mouth.'

Hiro smiled and said, 'I cannot reveal which of the gods direct my path, but it is no trick. There is such a thing as *writing*, for I have heard the word on the wind, when the Great Wind-God Maomao blows from Nuihiti. I must seek out this mystery and bring it back to my people.'

Hiro would be drawn no further than that and Seumas had to be satisfied with feeling that Hiro's journey would be a wasted one and that this *writing* would turn out to be silly pictures of some kind that did not talk at all.

The following morning, the pahi carrying Kieto's expedition set forth on the high seas. The expedition consisted of Kieto, Seumas, Dorcha, Rinto, Pungarehu (the killer of the Poukai bird), Polahiki, Boy-girl, Po'oi and the Farseeing-virgin, Kikamana. There was also a hired crew and the owner of the pahi on board.

Rinto was the son of the famous Manopa, right-hand man of Tangiia when that king had been struggling against the tyranny of his half-brother, Tutapu. Manopa had once saved the life of Seumas, even though the two were not basket-sharers in any sense and actively disliked each other. Manopa had died with the debt unpaid. Seumas therefore looked for an opportunity to save the life of Manopa's son, in order to discharge his obligation.

Kikamana was now an old woman, but still one of the most powerful priestesses in Oceania. Her knowledge of the occult was unsurpassed and her magic exceptional. Dorcha had learned much of her skill from Kikamana.

Polahiki was there on sufferance. A dirty, scarred and flea-bitten scrounger who stank of body odour and bad breath, this old Hivan fisherman invaded the space of others with all the sensitivity of a swamp hog. Polahiki had pestered Kieto night and day until at last the young navigator agreed to take the fisherman along with him. Polahiki said he was bored on Rarotonga and wanted to be out on the high seas once again. However, immediately the voyage began he started to complain that he was feeling sea-sick and home-sick and wanted the canoe to turn round and take him back. He only shut up when Seumas threatened to throw him overboard.

Po'oi was the son of Blind Kaho the navigator and Feeler-of-the-sea. The son was almost as adept as the father had been and Kieto had included him in the expedition for his great skill of knowing where the craft was in the ocean simply by testing the temperature of the water with his hand.

These, then, were the people chosen by Kieto to seek the legendary Maori nation, whose skill at war was unequalled, and whose mythical homeland could only be reached by a fairy gateway on an island somewhere far away, under the roof of voyaging.

Kieto followed a kaveinga to his birth place, the island of Raiatea, asking questions from time to time of the other navigators on board – Po'oi and Dorcha. Dorcha owned the only form of chart known to Oceanians, the shell-stick map, which she had fashioned from strips of criss-crossed bamboo studded with small cowries. The chart had been constructed on the first voyage between Raiatea and Rarotonga, and depicted the major navigational points islands, setting and rising stars, reefs and rips – used on that original journey.

Halfway to Raiatea they sighted a magnificent flotilla of around one hundred and fifty pahi canoes coming towards them, heading in the opposite direction, with around eighty souls on board each of them. Seumas feared it might be an invasion fleet, on its way to conquer Rarotonga. He had never seen so many vessels in one group.

Polahiki said, 'If that's a war flotilla, I'm telling you now, I'm on *their* side.'

Po'oi replied scornfully, 'We know you'd betray each and every one of us, if it meant saving your own skin.'

'I'd betray my own mother,' agreed the incorrigible Polahiki. 'In fact, I did.'

'Well,' said Dorcha. 'If it is a war party they'll swarm over us straight away. We don't stand a chance of fighting or outrunning them. What are those colourful pennants they're flying? And they all have tall yellow sails. They don't look like war banners to me – they seem too stately for that. Best make friends with them.'

Kieto agreed with this plan and as the magnificent fleet approached he stood on the front of the pahi.

'Who are you?' called Keito. 'Where are you bound?'

A man stood on a high platform of the leading pahi, dressed in yellow and red leaves and wearing red body-markings.

He was a lofty, lean figure with a very handsome face. Droplets of water from the salt spray glinted in the sunlight like multi-coloured jewels on his muscular body. His hair was fashioned like two raven's wings, sweeping up from the sides of his head. Around his neck he wore a garland of hibiscus blooms and there were frangipani flowers decorating his ears.

He grinned broadly on hearing Keito's question, as if he could not believe his ears, and shook his head in amazement. Instead of answering, he thrust forward one of his legs: an almost black limb which was literally covered in thick tattoos. The other leg was devoid of markings.

'So what?' said Seumas, mystified. 'So he's got a few tattoos!'

'Only on *one* leg,' breathed Boy-girl, suddenly coming to life. 'You know who that is?' Her voice was full of deep reverence, as if she had just encountered a god. 'Do you know to whom you are addressing your mundane remarks? We are indeed favoured of the gods. This is beyond everything.' As she spoke her voice rose to an excited high-pitched squeal, which grated on Seumas's nerves.

'So what's his name?' asked the Pict, wondering why he was so annoyed at Boy-girl's reaction. 'Tell us.'

'I don't know his name.'

They all stared in the direction of the white bow wave which preceded the yellow-sailed pahi.

Dorcha said, 'But you said you knew him?'

Boy-girl quivered visibly from head to toe.

'Know him? His name is not known to me, but his profession is. That man you see smiling at us is an exalted Painted Leg, one of the sacred ones. A *Painted Leg*. He's the leader of that group. Higher than a king – almost a demigod. You know what that means? It means that the fleet is the Arioi, sacrosanct to the Great God Oro.'

Now Seumas knew what Boy-girl meant, and was aware of the reasons for her great excitement. The Arioi was a unique society of dancers and singers, players and entertainers, who travelled Oceania building enormous stages on which to perform their various acts. There would be musicians and comedians amongst them, too, and other kinds of performers. There were seven grades of performer, the highest being the Avai parai, the Painted Leg, and the lowest the novitiates, the Poo-faarearea, known as *flappers*.

Arioi shows included such diverse acts as histrionic orations, spear fighting, satirical plays, sparkling dialogues, chants on ancient history, laudatory songs of heroes and heroines, and provocative hura dances. The Arioi had sprung up from the Tahitian culture, in the years between Tangiia leaving Raiatea and the present day.

The Arioi had never visited Rarotonga before, it being a relatively new and small island. Seumas had heard of the troupe, but had not seen it. Now he and his wife were heading away from Rarotonga, it seemed the wonderful show was going to visit his home.

'Damn!' he said, disappointed. 'The one time they come to Rarotonga and we miss them!'

Now that the mighty fleet of travelling players was aware of another boat in the vicinity, the Arioi began dancing and singing in a lively manner, giving Kieto's expedition an unexpected treat out on the great ocean. The occupants of the six vessels behind the leader had locked their canoes together on the calm waters and were performing a hura dance. As the several pahi floated sedately by Kieto and his group, the Arioi drummers thundered out a fast rhythm on their log drums while women swished their grass skirts and men leapt and strutted.

The male dancers hopped and jigged around the swaying females, making lewd gestures with their hands and hips. When the shy 'maidens' retreated, the men followed them like rutting creatures of the wild, becoming more and more frenzied in their movements, their eyes rolling, their hands and feet flying. The music raced like hot blood through excited bodies, firing the dancers to a pitch which seemed to Seumas and Dorcha to be almost insane.

Boy-girl's cockerel ran up and down, crowing at the top of its voice, while Dirk barked excitedly, chasing the fiery feathered creature around the deck.

As the pahi drew alongside the male dancers leapt and bound up to the females with jerking bodies. Dorcha's eyes opened wide as she noticed that many of the extravagantly decorated men had erect penises jutting through their leafy kilts.

'Goodness,' she said, suddenly feeling hot and bothered. 'Do you see …?'

It was true that the Oceanians were normally quite strait-laced when it came to exposing their genitals, going to great lengths to cover their private parts, yet on sacred occasions, such as when the Arioi danced, all their reserve was thrown to the winds and they became totally uninhibited.

In fact the dance in front of the expedition ended with one couple actually copulating to the encouragement of the other dancers, who showered them with flower petals.

'Yes, I see what you mean,' muttered Seumas primly, the priggish highland Pict coming out in him. 'Not very tasteful is it?'

'It's *wonderful*. It's a religious dance, you oaf,' said Boy-girl, who was obviously enjoying every minute. 'It's been blessed by the gods.'

'Well, we all know which gods they might be,' replied Seumas, his lips as tight as pahi sennit sheets. 'And we don't need to approve of them do we?'

The next two pahi had wrestlers on board, who were covered in coconut oil and struggled with one another, forming a tangle of bodies.

'And goodness knows *what's* going on under that lot,' cried Boy-girl, hot with excitement. 'For a few flower petals I'd swim over to them and join in.'

Next came the orators of ancient history and myth, chanting a song about Tawhaki's grandson, the great Rata:

'… one day the navigator king, Rata, began building a ship in which to make a voyage. As he went through the forest carrying his adze, with his men around him, he noticed a serpent struggling with a white bird.

' "Help me, O Rata!" cried the bird. "For I will perish under the coils of this terrible snake."

'Rata did not like to interfere with the natural order of the forest however, so he pretended not to hear and passed on.

'The next time Rata passed the spot the snake and the bird were still locked in an intense fight.

'The snake on seeing the sea-faring adventurer said, "This is a private battle, Rata – you should leave us alone." And Rata saw the justice in this remark, for the serpent was entitled to his prey, just as the birds were entitled to their insects.

'As he walked away, the bird cried, "If you aid me I shall help you finish your ship!" But Rata walked on, thinking that the bird was simply pulling lies out of the air in order to save itself from its fate.

'However, when he and his men reached the spot where they had previously felled the trees, there were none lying on the ground, but all were upright once again and growing tall.

'Angrily, Rata and his men felled more trees but this evening when they passed by the still battling snake and bird, Rata suddenly severed the snake in two, decapitating it, and the bird was able to escape the creature's coils.

'Thank you,' said the white bird, 'you will not regret your actions, O Rata, for I am Ruru, King of the Birds, and I and my kind will assist you in your efforts to build a canoe. The trees you felled are in a magic wood and you will need my help to overcome the local sorcery.'

'That night Ruru gathered together all the birds of the forest, who pecked and drilled at the felled trees, boring holes and stitching them together with sennit cord. Before morning a magnificent double-hulled canoe stood waiting for Rata and his men to carry it down to the sea. However, the sea was far away and the craft heavy, and finally it was the birds who with supreme effort managed to lift the pahi and fly it gently above the forest, to place it in the island's lagoon.

' "A pathway through the air for the ship," the birds had sung as they carried the pahi above the land. "A pathway of sweet-scented blossoms for the boat of Rata!"

'Rata set sail that evening, after thanking Ruru, but refusing to take a magician named Nganaoa with him.

'When the ship was out at sea a calabash floated alongside the craft which was taken aboard by one of the seamen.

' "Where are you going, O Rata, grandson of Tawhaki of the Thunder and Lightning?" said a voice from within the sealed calabash.

' "Where do you *wish* to go?" asked Rata.

' "To the Land of Moonlight, to seek my parents," replied the calabash.

' "What payment do you offer for your passage?" asked Rata.

' "I will look after your great sail."

' "There are mariners to do that work," replied Rata.

' "I will keep your hulls empty of seawater by bailing."

' "There are seamen for that job too. And the calabash is hollow, my friend. Why not sail to the Land of Moonlight in your own little craft."

' "Because I can't get out, without your help," replied the voice.

' "Then you are no use to me," replied Rata, "for a creature who can squeeze himself inside a calabash should surely be able to get out again without assistance."

' "Don't throw me overboard," cried the voice in panic. "I'll tell you what I will do – I'll protect you from three terrible monsters – the Gigantic Clam, the Ferocious Octopus and the Ship-swallowing Whale."

'Rata had heard of these awesome monsters and had entirely neglected to protect himself against them. He ordered that the calabash be opened. Out came Nganaoa, the magician.

'A few days later the craft was passing between two strange, fluted, white cliffs when they started to close on the vessel, hinged as they were below the surface.

'Rata cried, "It's the monstrous clam!"

'Nganaoa the magician immediately picked up a magic spear and with a spell on his lips threw the weapon down into the water. It struck the Gigantic Clam in a soft vulnerable area and the beast disappeared down to the depths of the ocean without closing around the great canoe.

'Several days later, a fantastic octopus, the size of which Rata had never seen before, came lashing over the surface of the sea, its tentacles flying and its mouth open and ready to devour the hapless mariners.

'Nganaoa flung a kotiate club, which passed through the flailing tentacles and struck the octopus a death blow on its bulbous temple.

'Next an enormous whale came rushing at them with its cavernous mouth wide open, ready to swallow the pahi and its crew whole. Nganaoa quickly seized two tall spears and jammed open the whale's jaws with the weapons, while chanting a sorcerer's song into the beast's face. The whale was defeated.

'"Well done!" cried Rata. "You have earned your passage, Nganaoa."

'But the magician did not need to seek further for his parents, for when he looked down the throat of the whale, he found them in its belly, trussed in sennit cords and waiting for their son to rescue them. Nganaoa made the whale vomit his parents by sticking a lighted stake down its throat. They fell on their son's neck, showering him with thanks.

'Rata, the great captain, navigator and king went on to discover many new islands, and to return to his homeland safe and happy with his successful voyages ...'

The song drifted away on the breeze as the last few yellow-sailed and colourful-bannered pahi of the Arioi passed by Kieto's solitary craft. Soon the enormous flotilla was out of sight over the horizon and the still ocean, with its running cold currents carrying the craft, seemed a silent lonely place. Kieto disappeared into the deck hut with Kikamana to commune with his ancestors. Boy-girl went to sit in the bows of the double-hulled, twin-sailed canoe and dream of being a member of the elite Arioi herself.

Others drifted away to various parts of the boat, there being room to be alone on such a large craft with only half-a-dozen or so passengers and a crew of not more than twelve.

Dorcha tied a lead around Dirk's neck and left him lying by the mast, before taking Seumas by the arm.

'Where are we going?' whispered Seumas, bemused by her leading him to the stern of the vessel. 'What's going on? Have you something to tell me?'

Hidden by a sail from the rest of the passengers and the crew, Dorcha fumbled with her skirt, removing it. She then lifted Seumas's garment and pressed her hot body against his, making him open his eyes wide in astonishment.

'What's going on?' he whispered in her burning ear.

'If you don't know that by now,' she said hoarsely, 'you're less of a man than I thought you were, Seumas Black. *Cha toigh learn neach ach thusa,*' she added, slipping into Gaelic, as she often did when she was embarrassed by having to initiate a love-making. 'Come on, man, you couldn't witness a dance like that and still be soft down there.'

He wasn't 'soft down there' as it soon became apparent, but he was shocked to find that his wife of many years, a woman of fifty, was lustful and musty-breathed. He would have been startled had she been only twenty. She pushed him on his back and climbed on top of him, lowering herself on him.

'Is this right?' he moaned, wondering at the rush of pleasure, the electri-city in his loins. 'It seems not to be proper to me.'

'Proper be damned,' she groaned. 'Just lie there and enjoy it – or not – I don't bloody care, so long as you stay stiff.'

So he did 'stay stiff' and he did enjoy it. In fact it was one of the most excit-ing love-makings he had ever experienced, even though he was grey-haired and fifty, and thought his time was past. And his wife, magnificent creature that she was, sat poker-backed moving rapidly up and down, her face and wild hair framed against the blood-red sky. When her orgasm came it seemed as if she were howling silently at the rising moon.

In the bows some sailor had begun welcoming the evening by beating the tai-moana, the Threnody-of-the-Ocean, a long drum carried by ocean-going canoes. The loving pair kept time with the beats, almost all the way, only overtaking the drummer at the very end of their session. Then they both lay there in each other's arms, glistening with sweat.

'By the gods, woman,' he whispered softly to her, as they drifted off into sleep, 'when I'm rich I'll *buy* the bloody Arioi and make them dance for us every night, so help me I will.'

And she laughed throatily into his ear.

3

Ao, the God of Clouds, was very important to seafarers in Oceania, for in the shapes and colours of the clouds the seamen recognised certain navigational signs. One particular cloud formation might indicate the presence of land beneath, another a dangerous reef below shallow water. Red clouds, grey clouds, white clouds, black clouds: all had significance when predicting future weather patterns. The reflection of sea colours, from lagoons and shal-lows, could be seen from several hundred miles away on the base of a cloud.

So, Ao knew of his standing amongst mariners, but he was not puffed up or arrogant. He could not afford to be, for he was subject to the whims of other gods, especially Maomao, the Great Wind-God, who blew Ao's children all over the sky.

Yet Ao had a certain power, being a close friend of one of the most powerful gods in the roof of voyaging.

Tawhaki, the God of Thunder and Lightning, who was greatly feared and respected both amongst the gods and amongst men, used Ao's clouds as hiding places.

One day Tawhaki asked Ao to take him down low, close to a vessel crossing the ocean from Rarotonga to Raiatea. Ao did as he was bid and Tawhaki was able to listen to the words of Kieto, who spoke of his intention to attack and subdue the peoples of the Land-of-Mists. Tawhaki knew the land of which Kieto spoke and he was not happy. Tawhaki was aware that there existed other gods, *different* gods, in the skies and earth of Land-of-Mists, and in the seas around Land-of-Mists. If Kieto went to war, then the Oceanian gods would have to do likewise.

'We shall have to battle these strange gods of that distant island,' Tawhaki told Ao, 'for the mortals take us where they go, and if Kieto goes to Land-of-Mists he will take the First Ancestor, Tiki, with him on the front of the canoes, and you and I, and all the other gods, will follow too. Those gods of that distant land will regard us as invaders and will attack us. We shall have to war with them in their skies, under their seas, beneath their landscape.'

Ao replied, 'But we are such *powerful* gods, Tawhaki. There is the Goddess Pele, of the Volcano, shooting fire and molten rock with her mouth. There is Milu, Ruler of the Underworld. There is Ruau-moko, God of Earthquakes. There is Maomao, Tangaroa, Papa, Rangi, and so many others. Let us not forget Io, the Supreme One, who dwells in the highest of our twelve upper worlds, a hundred times more puissant and as remote from us as gods are from ordinary men.'

'Their gods are powerful too, the peoples of that land, and I foresee a long and weary war between us. Perhaps we shall win, but then again, we might lose. I think I might have to destroy Prince Kieto and his little band.'

'But what do Io and the other gods think?' asked the timid Ao, afraid of upsetting his superiors. 'Do they agree with you in this?'

Tawhaki growled in anger, his voice rumbling across the roof of voyaging.

'Io says the affairs of men are not our business, provided we are treated with respect and receive our due sacrifices.'

'Then should we not obey the Supreme One?'

'Not if it means the death of us, for what would he be to us then, but another fallen god!'

Ao realised now that Tawhaki was in rebellion against the highest order of the gods and he was a little afraid.

'And who do you have with you?' he asked. 'Who strides across the land-scape, seascape and heavens beside the great Tawhaki, out of whose armpits comes the lightning, out of whose chest comes thunder? Who agrees with Tawhaki that Kieto must fail in his endeavours? Which of the gods is with you?'

'With *us*,' corrected Tawhaki. 'Why none, for they are all cowards where Io is concerned. Even Rongo and Tane refuse to brook the Father of the Gods. And Oro.'

'Not even the Atua? Even they are not with us? Tiki? Marikoriko? All the ancestor spirits? What about the demigod, Maui? Surely, little Maui is with us?'

'Maui would help men make war on his grandmother if he thought it would be exciting,' snarled Tawhaki. 'And the ancestor spirits fear no mortal combat – they revel in it.

'And before you ask,' added Tawhaki, 'the beast-gods are also with Kieto. Dakuwanga the Shark-God, Dengei the Serpent-God, Moko the Lizard-God – they all revel in bloodshed and wish to feed on the dead souls that combat brings.'

'Then we are utterly alone.'

'Yes.'

In truth, Tawhaki *was* concerned by the prospect of a war with the gods of Land-of-Mists, but this was not his reason for wanting to destroy the Ru-Kieto expedition. In point of fact he was feeling jealous and spiteful. The island which Tangaroa was giving to Prince Ru of Raiatea was the very island Tawhaki had intended giving to an Hawaiian nobleman. It irked the God of Thunder and Lightning that Tangaroa had beaten him to it. Tangaroa, however, was much more powerful than Tawhaki, and there would be no use in the Thunder-God trying to overrule the Great Sea-God, master of all the oceans.

Ao would not countenance the idea of destroying Ru, so Tawhaki pretended it was Kieto he was after.

'Together we can crush this upstart Rarotongan,' Tawhaki growled. 'We can smash him.'

Ao saw then what he had let himself in for and he was very concerned for his own safety.

'Sneakily, then,' he said. 'We must do it with cunning and guile, not openly, with force.'

'Agreed,' muttered Tawhaki, 'but if we fail to do it on the sly, then I shall blast their pahi from the water with thunderbolts and lightning.'

'Oh dear,' murmured Ao, the gentle God of Clouds, regretting already that he was a close friend of the brashest and noisiest of all the Oceanian gods. 'I hope you won't have to do that, for Io will surely come to hear of it.'

'A last resort,' promised Tawhaki, striding out of the clouds and marching purposefully across the broad expanse of sky. 'Only as a last resort.'

Ao hoped so, or they would both find themselves standing on heaven's equivalent of earth's leaping place of souls.

Ragnu, once the high priest of King Tutapu of Raiatea and Borabora, now the high priest of the dying King Haari, waited in his dark Raiatean temple courtyard which stood next to Tapu-tapu atia, the Investiture Stone 'Most Sacred, Most Feared'. In this marae of Ragnu's stood an ahu, stained black with the blood of innocents, upon which the high priest, a kahuna of great power, had sacrificed men and used their kabu to work his sorcery. Even now he commanded souls, held them in thrall, and used them for his devious schemes, which were mostly designed to increase the power of the priest over the islanders.

Ragnu's hunched shape moved like a spider through the stone-cold dimness of his temple bounds, muttering to the unfortunate captive souls, as they gathered in the corners of the ancient marae, their expressions of utter misery comforting to the priest.

'You serve me, you pathetic wretches, yet you are only of use for short-arm schemes. Once you leave my island, you scuttle down to Milu's Underworld and hide from me, out of reach of my magic. So, we cannot use you to destroy my Rarotongan enemies, can we, my wraiths, my wisps of mist? I have to trust instead one of my own kind, who are never to be wholly trusted.'

The dead souls, safe only from the ravenous Dakuwanga while they remained in Ragnu's thrall, wailed piteously.

'Yes, yes,' snarled the kahuna, 'I know you kabu are full of your own misfortunes, but what about *mine*? Almost twenty years ago Tangiia and his people – Kieto, Seumas and Dorcha included – made a fool out of me. They destroyed the finest king that ever sailed the ocean – my own Tutapu. Now they have come abroad again and must be ripe for my revenge. I will have it. I will have it. They must suffer pain and humiliation, just as I suffered. They must be brought down, humbled, stamped face-down into the red clay.'

The wooden temple gods stared broodingly from the chill shadows at the ranting priest as he paced the worn floors. Their thick noses, their hollow eyes, their brute-lipped mouths dripped with moisture and moss. They had seen death in multiples, witnessed the bones piled high on the ahu, beheld altars running with blood, watched organs eaten raw by novice priests craving power. The dark gods were steeped in death, it clung to them as a foul gas to a marsh, it permeated their porous forms. Death had weathered their shapes, eroded their spirits, turned them into coarse, jaded beings. They were sated, glutted with death. They had been corrupted and corroded by the atmosphere of death, which had rotted their timbers.

There was a noise outside the temple close and someone peered through the curtains of vines that draped over a doorway which led to the marae.

'Lord Ragnu?' a voice called, full of trepidation. 'Are you there, o priest?'

The ancient, shrivelled figure of Ragnu, with its wizened features and bright eyes, waited in the darkness, enjoying the visitor's fear, savouring the man's terror. There was a faint moan from the man. His legs seemed to buckle under his own weight and it was obvious he was about to turn and run. Ragnu came out of the shadows and confronted him.

'You are here, Titopika.'

The man addressed as Titopika jumped visibly, but then sighed in relief on seeing the priest.

'My lord – this place ...'

'It worries you?'

'There are spirits here, ghosts, clinging to the walls like spider's webs.'

Ragnu said, 'I am here to protect you.'

This remark did not appear to ease Titopika's apprehension. His eyes were switching back and forth in his skull and his hands shook. Ragnu decided to light a torch, in order to calm his man down a little, so he would concentrate on what was being said to him. There were the embers of a fire in a clay bowl in the centre of the marae. Ragnu took a brand and lit it from the charcoal, blowing on the redness to create a flame. Once the place was lit Titopika did indeed become calmer.

'You know why I have asked you here?' said Ragnu. Titopika gave a final shudder and said, 'You wish me to do something further for you?'

'You have made yourself a part of Prince Ru's expedition with his family?'

'Yes, I obeyed the command you sent.'

'There is a party of six or seven Rarotongans who will journey with him. They are at this moment on the high seas, on their way here. I have seen their crab-claw sails in my farseeing bowl. Amongst them is a man called Kieto. For some reason which I have failed to divine Kieto and his friends are accompanying Prince Ru on his search for a new island.'

'How is it you cannot find out?'

'I'm being blocked by another power – no doubt that damned high priest-ess Kikamana, with the help of the goblin Dorcha and that shred of whimsy, Boy-girl – which will not let me discover their reasons for going with Ru.'

'Oh. And what must I do?'

'You must ensure the destruction of this group. Do not enquire as to my motivation. It is enough for you that I wish them all dead. You must sabotage the whole expedition, if need be, but you must annihilate the Rarotongans.'

'Am I the person for this work?' quailed Titopika.

Ragnu studied the beautiful young man, seeing deeply handsome features and a finely wrought body.

'Yes, you are. Don't worry, I have a plan which will be acceptable to you. I understand you like women?'

'Doesn't every man?'

'Not in the quantities you do. But that is neither here nor there. If you do as I tell you, you will succeed.'

'And how is it to be accomplished?'

Ragnu said, 'I will tell you this before you leave. You are sure Ru has agreed to take you with him? What is your function on board his pahi?'

'I am to be the island's first resident priest, when he finds a new home for his family.'

'Good. Good.'

The young man was quiet for a while. He was considering the moral issue of what he was being asked to do. To destroy a group of Rarotongans was not of great serious concern to Titopika, but to sabotage the voyage of a prince blessed by the Great Sea-God Tangaroa was another thing altogether.

However, Titopika bore no love for Ru's family. They had refused to allow Ru's daughter, a puhi of great beauty, to marry Titopika's older brother. Titopika's family were almost commoners and that made the match unlikely, but the love was genuine and the result had been that Titopika's brother killed himself at the leaping place of souls.

So, Titopika had no qualms about destroying the Rarotongans and he bore a grudge against Ru's family which might one day have to be settled.

He was however afraid for himself for a number of reasons.

He was quite rightly and properly frightened of Tangaroa's wrath. And if he ruined the expedition completely he destroyed his own chances of becoming a high priest on a new Faraway Heaven. Finally, if he was on board the same craft he was being asked to wreck, why then it followed he was going down with it.

'What about me?' asked Titopika. 'How will I survive?'

'By special dispensation of our ancestors,' smiled Ragnu. 'The spirits of the dead will return you safely to this isle. I happen to know that Ru's expedition is not finding favour with certain gods and they wish him eliminated. Kieto is also under suspicion. Naturally as the agent of my scheme to destroy these two, you will be blessed by the gods and transported back to us here on Raiatea by the ghosts of our forefathers.'

'Are you certain of this?' whispered an elated Titopika. 'I will be kept from harm?'

Ragnu's eyes half closed as he smiled into the face of his spy and saboteur.

'You have my promise.'

PART TWO

'The valleys are thick with people'

1

The arrival of Kieto's pahi at Raiatea coincided with the death of King Haari.

A messenger called 'the bird' was sent running around the island to proclaim 'King Haari is dead!' from every hill and every valley. Near relatives had immediately visited the house of the deceased king with gifts of cloth. The young men of the island prepared for the event known as 'the slaying of the ghosts' where they fought a battle with malignant spirits who would do harm to the king's soul on its way to heaven. The ghost-fighting was a serious dance in which young warriors struggled with unseen forces and were hopefully victorious, defeating the bad spirits before the king was wafted through the gateway into the place where his ancestors dwelt.

Even as the Rarotongan canoe entered the lagoon through a gap in the reef, there were people on the beach wailing and tearing their hair, and lacerating themselves with shark's teeth. The mourners, commoners and nobles alike, had dressed themselves in filthy floor mats and had daubed their skins with the ash from their fires to humiliate themselves. The sincerity of their grief was unquestionable.

One man had oiled his hair and as the Rarotongan pahi glided over the still surface of the lagoon, disturbing the fishes in the lime-green shallows, he set fire to his head to demonstrate the honesty of his penitence. Friends quickly doused the flames with sea water, but not before the poor fellow had suffered terrible burns to his scalp, face and neck.

Others were having fits, thrashing in the sand, throwing themselves bodily at tree trunks and rocks, to knock themselves unconscious. Yet others beat themselves with clubs, branches and sennit cord whips. It was a terrible if impressive sight and one which both Dorcha and Seumas found disturbing.

'Why do they do that?' asked Seumas of Kieto, appalled at the injuries the people were inflicting on their own bodies. 'Surely they can show others that their grief is genuine without such mutilation?'

'They do it to stop even more terrible things happening to them and their families.'

'Explain.'

'Well, as you know, a king or chief is close to the gods – when a king dies the gods are very upset. The great ones and the king's powerful ancestor spirits start to ask questions like, "Is anyone responsible for this death? Is it a necessary death?" Thus the people are afraid they are going to be held responsible. Were they neglectful of their duties to deities? Was there something they could have done to keep their king alive? Did they pray enough, offer large enough sacrifices while he was ill, do enough to drive out the demons which eventually took his life? All these questions worry the people, so they try to prove to the priests and the gods that they are so distressed by the king's death that they could not possibly have been in any way to blame for it.'

Seumas shook his head slowly. 'And what if the gods do decide someone was responsible?'

'Some terrible catastrophe might occur – a volcano might erupt, a great wave come, or the earth might shake.'

Po'oi added. 'They are not *just* considering the gods, but also the king's spirit. It will be angry that the body has not been able to hold on to it. It's possible the king's sau will go insane and cause untold damage, if not placated in some way, if not calmed and pacified by the solemnity of mourning.'

Once again, Seumas felt like an outsider in this world which had adopted them. There were times when Seumas considered himself an Oceanian through and through; times when he believed he had been on the islands for so long that he had become part of them; times when he saw no difference between himself and someone like Kieto or Po'oi. This was not one of them. Now he felt like the alien he actually was, witnessing strange and unfathomable rites, as different from the people around him as a fish was from a dog.

'I think I understand,' he said to Po'oi and Kieto, so as not to hurt their feelings.

'Understand?' grumbled the smelly Polahiki, coming up alongside Seumas and leaning on his shoulder. 'You understand *nothing*. Even I do not understand. Look at those stupid fools, hurting themselves.' Polahiki picked his nose as he spoke and wiped the mucus from his finger on his soiled loin cloth. 'Do they think a god is going to send a bolt of lightning because one old fool's heart stops beating?'

Seumas winced and pushed Polahiki away from him.

'Why are you so different to them?' he asked the dirty fisherman. 'You think your fleas will protect you?'

Polahiki grinned, revealing a mouthful of black teeth.

'I don't believe in these things as deeply as do most people. There may be gods, or there may not be – who cares? They've never shown themselves to me. I've never visited them. We get on famously by ignoring each other. The gods don't bother Polahiki and Polahiki doesn't give an owl's hoot for the gods. That's the way it should be.'

'Perhaps you're not worth it?'

The fisherman spat on the deck and grinned again.

'Perhaps, but I think the secret is – I don't believe in them, so they don't exist for me. I'm safe from beings who don't exist. I live in a bubble of unbelief. A *dirty* bubble, but who cares, it's my private bubble.' He laughed again.

Despite his loathing of the man Seumas felt there was something profound in what the fisherman was saying. He couldn't altogether dispute it. What if it were true?

'It sounds too easy,' he said. 'Too easy a trick.'

Polahiki grimaced now and his expression went deadly serious. 'You think so? Try it.'

And Seumas knew the man was right. It was not easy to stop believing. You could tell yourself something wasn't true, didn't exist, but deep down you felt afraid that you were wrong, that there was a supernatural force, omniscient and omnipotent, ready to crush you like a ripe breadfruit. His doubt must have showed on his face, because Polahiki nodded.

'See?' said the fisherman. 'Not easy at all.'

Seumas turned his attention to the island itself now, as they cruised into the shallows. He took hold of Dorcha's hand, called to Dirk, and the three of them jumped from the deck of the canoe and waded ashore together. Once on the beach, they stood and stared at the scene around them. Raiatea had been their home for seven years after they had been abducted by Kupe and his crew, taken from the shores of Albainn and carried away against their will. It had been the making of them, as individuals.

The sand on the beach was warm beneath their bare feet. A soft breeze gently stroked their shoulders. It felt good. Coconut palms curved over them, laden with nuts in various stages of ripeness. There were the scents of bananas and ti-lilies in the air, and the rustling sound of fields of sugar cane leaves fell like waves upon their ears.

Orange drala blooms, their shape and colour attempting to fool hungry parrots into believing they were also birds of spectacular hue, and not flowers at all, hung with many beaks from dangling stems.

Overhead the birds, sooty rails, wheeled and cruised on the thermals. Small fish like silver darts sprayed into the air from the shallow water near them, raining back into the lagoon again, as they were chased by some large predator hidden beneath. The green-ridged mountain before them was wearing a hibiscus shrub behind its unmarried ear.

Seumas put his arm around Dorcha. He inhaled the perfume of wild ginger sap which she wore on her skin and deep in her dark hair. He felt her hug him close and she kissed his cheek. It was as if they had come home.

Suddenly the foliage parted and two men stood before the couple. There was a look of indignation on the features of the intruders. Dorcha recognised them before Seumas did.

'Rian? Ti-ti?' she said, guardedly. 'How are you both?'

It was Rian who spoke. He had always been the belligerent twin brother. He was the one with the temper.

'What is our wife doing with her arm around another man?' cried Rian. 'You adulterous woman!'

Dorcha gasped. She had been away from the island for two decades and had almost forgotten that she was actually still married to these twin brothers who were as one in the eyes of the commoner's law. Now she had been to bed with another man. It suddenly struck her that this was a serious matter. Adultery was punishable by death, if the injured party requested such a sentence.

'Rian,' she said, 'I can't believe you're still interested in me. Surely you and Ti-ti have taken another wife? It's been almost twenty years.'

'We have taken no new bride,' Ti-ti interrupted. 'We have been waiting for our lawful wife to return.'

There was a hollow laugh from the Pict, who had thus far kept his peace, but now felt the situation was becoming ludicrous.

'Oh sure,' cried Seumas, 'you've had the dinner on the table for twenty years, waiting for her to walk through the door.'

Rian stepped forward, anger in his eyes. 'You mock us? You are an adulterer too! I shall see to it the judge chooses a very painful death for you, goblin!'

The tone in his voice made Dirk snarl. The dog took a couple of paces forward. Rian went pale and Ti-ti actually turned and ran back into the rainforest, to hide.

'You keep that hound away from me,' whispered Rian, pulling a shark-toothed club from his waistband. 'I'll kill it.'

'Not if he kills you first,' snapped Seumas. 'And as for this other thing, this judgement, I know the law as well as you, Rian. You can bring us in front of a judge, but listen to this – I'll opt for a trial by single combat. I'll take it out of the hands of men and put it in the hands of the gods. Remember what happened the last time we fought? This time I'll split your skull open. I'll leave your brains on the coral dust. I'll cut out your liver and throw it to the dog here, so help me. Then I'll do the same to your brother. Bear that in mind before you run whining to the priests.'

Ti-ti, hidden somewhere in the forest, gave out a cry of fear as he heard these words.

'Rian,' he called. 'Leave him alone.'

Rian ignored Ti-ti, saying to Seumas instead, 'My brother is a coward – I'm not afraid of you, goblin.'

Dorcha intervened here. 'Rian,' she said, 'why do you want to hurt me?'

'Because you went to the man we all hated!'

'But if you have him executed, then I shall be executed too. We are adulterers together, he and I. Do you want me to die in the hands of the priests?'

'If it has to be ...'

'No,' screamed Ti-ti, from the bushes. 'Not her. You promised not her.'

Dorcha whispered to Seumas, 'The little one always loved me much more than the big one.'

Then to Rian, she said, 'You know if you have me killed, then your brother will never forgive you.'

Rian faltered now, glancing back into the forest.

'He will – in time he will.'

'I *won't*,' shrieked Ti-ti. 'I'll kill you myself if you hurt her. You promised it would only be *him*. I'll cut your throat while you sleep, brother. I'll poison your drinks. I'll rub deadly fungus into your meat.'

Boy-girl had now come up the beach, where the group was standing amongst the debris of the high-tide mark, where copra, dead leaves and driftwood formed a ragged line.

'What's going on?' she said. 'Seumas? Dorcha? What is this silly man brandishing a club for?'

Seumas said, 'He wants to kill two adulterers.'

Boy-girl raised one eyebrow. 'You two?' she said.

'Yes,' snarled Rian. 'And I won't brook interference from you, Boy-girl.'

The tall, elegant Boy-girl brushed away some locks of hair from her forehead, making her shell-decorations jingle. She stared down imperiously at Rian. Then she wet a finger and wiped it slowly down the flinching Rian's cheek, while he stood mesmerised by those dark eyes of hers.

Boy-girl said softly, 'My, my, Rian. Here you are, willing to call people adulterers, when you and I ... but that was so long ago, wasn't it? Still, you *were* married to Dorcha at that time. You know, that sounds awfully silly, accusing someone of doing something you've done yourself, doesn't it? We could *all* be in serious trouble, couldn't we?'

Dorcha looked sharply at Rian, then at Boy-girl, while a groan came from Ti-ti, still hidden in the forest.

'I – I ...' began Rian, looking confused.

'Yes, *you*, you naughty man. You and I, that is – remember – behind the breadfruit pits? And what about that virgin youth you used to desire, the sweet boy who used to tread the breadfruit? – yes you did – you told me so – did you ever manage to steal his chastity?'

'I – never ...'

'Oh, I'm sure you did, you big liar you.'

Rian looked broken. He dropped the club and turned dazedly to stumble away, into the rainforest. He was shaking his head as he left to join his brother, but his eyes showed how unsure he was of himself. It was almost as if an argument were raging inside his skull.

Seumas heaved a sigh of relief. Dirk began to relax. Dorcha was still staring fixedly at Boy-girl, her head on one side. Finally she spoke to Boy-girl.

'Did he really – you and Rian, I mean?'

'What *do* you mean?' smiled Boy-girl, her cockerel brushing against her ankles and darting its head at Dirk.

'Well,' said Dorcha, 'you could be hypnotising him – I know that trick of yours.'

Boy-girl let out a tinkling laugh, before walking away, saying over her shoulder, 'You'll never know, will you? Even if I tell you one thing, you'll still wonder whether it was the other. Don't lose sleep over it, Dorcha. Rian isn't worth it. You have your chosen man, now. Worry about *him*. I've still got plenty of time to get my sticky fingers on his sweetmeats too – and I will, if you're not careful.'

'Never,' snarled Seumas, giving a little shudder. 'Not me, Boy-girl. And take this damn chicken with you. It keeps bothering my hound.'

'You leave my cock out of this,' called Boy-girl in that infuriating way she had which made Seumas so uncomfortable. 'You're always trying to get your hands on it.'

'Why do you always do that?' shouted the exasperated Pict. 'I wish you wouldn't use that kind of double-talk. Listen, I don't like you that way. I've told you a million times.'

'Oh you,' laughed Boy-girl, from halfway down the beach. 'You don't think you would have any say in the matter, do you? You're just a shell to be played with, a flower to be plucked. No one takes *your* opinion seriously. When I want you, I'll just take you, Seumas.'

Seumas snarled again. 'She's been saying that ever since she met me, damn it,' he growled. 'I won't have it. Of course I've got something to say in the matter.'

Dorcha laughed and took his arm again. 'You really think so? You're still hard and strong, Seumas – a warrior through and through – but you're no match for Boy-girl. She could eat you alive. Don't even imagine you could do anything to prevent it. She has thousands of years of experience, in comparison to yours, when it comes to sexual matters.'

'Has she, by the gods!' muttered the ruffled Seumas, peeved by the fact that he was being laughed at. 'Has she?'

'Thousands of years. And what she can't get by any other means, she can certainly get by hypnotism and magic. You'd be like a little fluffy chicken in her hands. You'd be helpless. It's a good thing I'm here to protect you from that jaded libertine, isn't it? Or you'd end up being her slave.'

'Damned rubbish,' said the uncomfortable Seumas, walking off with Dirk at his heels. 'You talk so much nonsense, the pair of you. And I'll have that bloody rooster of hers in a stew one of these days – feed it to Dirk.'

'She's been promising to do the same to your dog,' said Dorcha, laughing. 'I'd watch out, the pair of you.'

*

The new king was crowned within the confines of Tapu-tapu-atia, with the ancestor spirits looking on, and the gods smiling benevolently. The old heroes and demi-gods were also in attendance, standing in the shadows, to watch the donning of the red girdle. The sacred red girdle, maru-ura, a section added for each king, told the story of Haari's reign and many others before him. The scarlet feathers were woven into cloth and formed a genealogy and history of the kings: their work, their accomplishments in war, their enemies and friends, their wives, their sons and daughters, their achievements in peace time.

Early that morning the people had come from their houses and lined the route to Tapu-tapu-atia, while great canoes from other islands entered through the holy channel, the first one bearing the God Oro, the commander of the spirit world warriors. Like the other ocean-going craft, this one carried gifts for the new king, of fruits, and livestock, honey and fish.

There were sacrifices too.

Towards the end of the colourful ceremony the new king walked into the lagoon, and two grey shapes came from outside the reef, to rub against him, one side, and the other. Even the sharks of the ocean were loyal to the successor of Haari, as they had been to the old king. People saw this happen, or believed they did, which Polahiki would say was the same thing.

Then the king dressed again with great solemnity, and was presented with his fan of frigate bird feathers, his royal spear, and his mace of office, a wondrously carved stick.

Later, the feasting began, and it was here that Seumas and Kieto managed to talk to Prince Ru. Ru was not one of the new king's basket-sharers, so they found him sitting at one of the smaller fires away from the rest of the nobles. The prince, in his thirty-fifth year, listened to what Kieto had to say. He explained why he was leaving Raiatea.

'The valleys are thick with people,' he said, 'and I have been shown a star by the gods. Under that star lies the island that will provide us with a new home.'

'Will you take us with you?' asked Kieto.

Ru seemed puzzled. 'But the star I seek, the island home, hangs over the seas around Rarotonga. My new island is somewhere near your own island. Why do you come all this way back to Raiatea, just to make the return journey to Rarotonga?'

Kieto glanced at Seumas, before replying. 'Our priests have looked at your voyage through the mists of time. They have seen, vaguely, how you are swept off course by events you will be unable to control. During your wanderings, similar to those experienced by our people under Prince Tangiia when we were seeking a new Faraway Heaven, you will touch an island called Rapanui. The island of the giants.'

They saw Ru's eyes narrow in the firelight.

'I have heard of this place, from fishermen and adventurers who were blown off course. No one has ever disembarked on that island and lived to tell of it. It is far away, thousands of miles from my destination.'

'Will you take us? What have you got to lose if you *don't* sail to Rapanui, but go directly to the island under your star? The problem will be ours, not yours. We could assist your crew with their work.'

Ru shook his head determinedly. 'My crew, as you must have heard, consists of twenty royal virgins – puhi chosen for their virtue, strength and beauty. This was a command from the gods, from Tangaroa himself, if I am to succeed in my mission. The maidens will be my mariners. Already my brothers and their wives are afraid of the long sea voyage. I have promised them that the Great Sea-God himself has given his word that we will reach our destination, provided we follow his instructions.'

'We can cook, can't we?' said Kieto. 'We can sew. We can make fires, twist fibres into sennit, make mats. There are a multitude of tasks to be carried out on board, which don't involve handling the great canoe.'

'If your party comes with me, it will be as passengers, but I am of the mind that if I don't take you on board perhaps we will not be diverted to this island called Rapanui?'

'I think you know that what has been seen by the kahuna will come to pass, whoever is on board your pahi.'

Ru nodded thoughtfully, before saying by way of dismissal, 'I shall give you my answer in the morning. The name of my canoe is Te Pau-ariki ...'

'*The Princely Flower*,' murmured Seumas, as the pair walked away from the fire. 'A very pretty name for a craft which has such a gruelling, difficult task ahead of it.'

'No doubt this too came as instruction from the gods,' replied Kieto. 'They are quite particular when they inform their adventurers of the details.'

'Do I detect a note of sarcasm?'

'I do not,' said Kieto, 'see why Ru should consider himself chosen of the gods, that's all.'

Seumas laughed. 'By damn – you're jealous!'

Kieto looked uncomfortable. 'I'm not, but I think our mission has far more importance. Why wasn't I given instructions from the gods! Why did I have to use priests to find out where I was going?'

'You forget – you *were* chosen – to conquer the land of my birth. If you have a few difficulties in doing that, I'm not going to call the gods unreasonable.'

Kieto grunted a little petulantly at this remark.

At that moment someone came along the edge of the forest path, walking towards the great fire in the darkness. 'Out of the way,' snarled the man, 'I am a tapu.'

The figure was dressed splendidly in a cloak of feathers, a beautiful helmet, and carried a staff which proclaimed him to be a high priest. As a high priest he was indeed taboo to the touch, if not to the sight. Seumas stared at the features of the priest in the flickering light of the many fires, and recognition filtered through to his memory.

'Why,' he said, 'if it isn't Ragnu, the man we whipped like a dog some twenty years ago!'

Ragnu stared into the face of Seumas, clearly not recognising him for a while. Then the old priest nodded and smiled grimly. 'The goblin! Well, well. I would have taken you for an Oceanian, if it hadn't been for one or two tattoos on your body. And this I suppose is Kieto, full grown and looking only a little less like the runt in a litter of rats?'

'Still insulting people, Ragnu?' remarked Kieto, unimpressed. 'Have you nothing better to do?'

'Yes, I have a king to attend, if you would now step aside. I would hate my mana to be the cause of some illness, or even death.'

'Well, isn't that the truth?' murmured Seumas, in a deeply sarcastic tone.

The two men did as they were asked however and watched the kahuna stalk off, into the night, between the many fires. Seumas noticed that as he passed each fire the people sitting around it fell silent for a few moments, until he had gone. It seemed he was still feared, probably still hated, yet he held the highest priesthood in the land.

'I've often wondered,' said Seumas, to Dorcha later, 'what that man wants out of life. He's next to the king, despite being defeated alongside Tutapu at the battle at Rarotonga, yet he still seems to crave something. He knows he can't be king himself, he hasn't the blood line, so what else is he after?'

'Eternal life,' replied Dorcha, instantly. 'It's what every man wants, once he has all the earthly power he can get. Ragnu is probably directing all his energies, all his magic, towards making himself immortal.'

Boy-girl, sitting on the far side of the fire, said, 'To do that he has to eliminate all his enemies – take vengeance on those whom he has sworn to destroy. That's a long, arduous task, and one fraught with dangers and difficulties. I might wish him all good luck in his enterprise – if we weren't among the number he has to punish before achieving such an end.'

Kieto said, 'We have to mind our backs while we're here – I suggest we sleep on the pahi and set a watch.'

'You're afraid of that old man?' sniffed Seumas.

'I'm afraid of the power he wields,' Kieto said. 'And you would be too, Seumas, if you were sensible.'

'I've never been sensible,' Seumas said. 'It's saved my life on many occasions.'

'I doubt it,' Polahiki growled. 'Anyway, I'm in no danger – I was on Ragnu's side in that battle. I only swapped sides when Tutapu started losing.'

Dorcha grinned and said, 'And me.'

'In that case,' Kieto said, 'you two can take the first watch, because you have nothing to fear.'

Polahiki's face fell and Dorcha laughed, saying to him, 'Don't worry, fisherman, I'll do it alone. I don't want to spend the early hours picking nits from my hair after sitting next to you. You can sleep on the shore.'

Polahiki stared at the main fire, where Ragnu sat next to the new king.

'No,' replied Polahiki, after a moment's hesitation, 'I think I'll sleep on the ship. Maybe Ragnu didn't like the idea of me changing sides in the middle of the battle. I'll stay among friends, I think.'

Seumas growled, 'Friends? You've got to be mocking us, fisherman. No one here likes you.'

Having seen his enemies again, Ragnu was full of anger. He still intended carrying out his main plan, of sabotaging the voyage of *The Princely Flower*, but there was a longing in him for the quick death of the goblin, Seumas. Now that they had come face to face again, Ragnu was filled with repugnance, that this creature from beyond Oceania should be living amongst them as if he too were a proper man like any other on the islands.

'His very presence on the soil of Faraway Heaven is an affront to the gods,' whispered Ragnu to himself. 'I must remove this vile creature from our society. I would be thanked by kings and commoners alike. He lives on us like a leech, flouts our conventions, and has his own strange code of honour. I will do it tonight, while he is within my reach.'

When the ceremony for the new king was over, Ragnu did not return to the marae at Most Sacred, Most Feared. Instead, while the nobles were getting drunk on kava he stole a pig from a pen outside one of their houses. He stifled its squeals, holding it tightly under his arm. He entered the hinterland jungle. In the darkness, with only the starlight to show him the way, Ragnu found a narrow winding path up through the green gorges, to a cave on the steep hillside.

A tapu had been placed on the cave many years ago, by Ragnu himself, who had hung wicker sharks over the entrance, warning any casual passerby, hunter or gatherer, that it was forbidden to enter this place on pain of a horrible death.

Once inside the cave, Ragnu lit a torch with a set of flints, then prepared his magic herbs and potions. First he drank several of the potions, to protect himself from the spirit world, taking care also to mark his own skin with certain symbols of which only priests of high rank had knowledge.

The walls of the cave were already hung with various objects – heads and hair of men and animals, strange idols made of clay and feathers, sharks' teeth, whalebones, dried skins of barracuda – which served to keep any visiting spirits from going berserk. Ghosts were highly strung beings, whose sanity was close to the edge, and in calling them one risked mindless destruction.

Down below, in the villages, the sacred drums were still beating, even though the new king had retired. The adulation of the people was not suppressed by lack of sleep. They would be sounding their praises, with shell trumpets, wooden flutes, and other instruments, throughout the next few days. Ragnu used the rhythm of the drums to chant a fangu, summoning ghosts from the well of darkness, calling on them to assist him.

First, he took some nail parings, dried skin and hair from a bamboo tube, where they had been for many years.

They had once belonged to Seumas, stolen from the floor of his hut when he was not at home. Ragnu had many such grisly collections, gathered in secret, once belonging to every important person on Raiatea and Borabora. These scrapings assisted him in his gruesome tasks of murder and spell-making. When you had some part of your enemy's body, you had your enemy's likes and dislikes, strengths and weaknesses, imprinted on his bodily parts, waiting to be revealed.

'Now we shall find out what will draw the Pict from the safety of his pahi,' murmured Ragnu.

He placed the body parts in a clay pan and heated them over a fire, weaving a spell at the same time. Taking a live owl from a cage he cut its throat and allowed its blood to squirt on to the parings. Next, he tossed various magic powders into the pan, and into the fire, releasing and searching through odours that had been imbedded in the hair and nails from long ago. The smells came one after the other, as Ragnu unlocked the secrets of Seumas's impregnated tissues. Finally, he found an aroma he believed would be irresistible to the Pict and captured the gas in several foot-long bamboo tubes.

He then took the pig and ritually slaughtered the animal, frying its heart in a bowl, offering the sacrifice to his own atua, asking his ancestor spirits to help him fashion a puata. Eventually, the smell of the blood and the fragrance of the herbs brought a powerful ghost into Ragnu's presence and this being promised him a puata. The ghost smelled foul – of rotting tissue and polluted earth – and once the promise had been extracted the priest wanted rid of the creature.

Ragnu thanked the spirit, profusely, sparing no compliments for dead souls are not immune to flattery and eat it like breadfruit. It took some time to persuade the atua to leave, for having confronted a mortal, it wanted to stay and talk. Eventually, however, the ghost went through the eye-socket of a human skull, hanging on the cave wall, and took its stench with it, back to its own personal hell.

'Now we have the power, we make the *thing*,' murmured Ragnu.

He was, by this time, shaking with exhaustion and fear. Oh yes, he told himself, he was frightened. He was afraid, but he was also very excited. What he was about to do was fashion a living monster out of clay and twigs, out of leaves and wicker: a dangerous creature, very strong, very big, but very stupid.

It would be able to talk, and though a beast walk on its hind legs, but it would need special guidance to its target, or it might rush off into the forest and prey on Raiateans for centuries to come.

Thus, Ragnu was agitated by what he was about to do: by the idea and the act of fashioning a supernatural creature.

Out in the forest Ragnu surrounded himself with ti'i. These wooden idols had a two-fold purpose: to protect the magician and to assist him with his magic.

A karakia was chanted into the blackness of the trees.

A whirlwind came, hurtling out of the darkness, carrying with it masses of twigs and leaves. It wrenched turf from the ground, moss and bark from logs, reedy stems and willowy saplings. First a cage of wicker was formed into a shape not unlike a boar standing on its hind legs, but much bigger than that beast – a *giant* boar. Onto the wickerwork was daubed a mixture of clay, twigs and leaves, until the towering shape was solid. Two curved branches stripped of their bark, white and smooth, formed the boar-man's tusks. A monstrous head with great ears and small eyes was seated on the torso. Rocks formed the boar's feet and dried grasses its shaggy hair. It was a boar, but a *mockery* of the real thing, a parody standing on two legs, over a head taller than the priest.

Yet it was a terrifying mud-wood statue: it drove fear into the priest's heart like a stake.

The final fangu came out as a hoarse whisper from the sorcerer's lips.

'O Rongo, breathe life into this creation,
Make it your own creature, a thing of the night,
Out of the ancient memory of the forest itself,
A thing conceived in a time before men,
A monster of an older earth –
O Rongo, breathe your breath into this clay.'

And Rongo the Great Plant-God did as he was requested and made flesh of vegetable and put air into leafy lungs.

For a moment nothing occurred and Ragnu almost decided that his spells had not worked properly.

Then the incredible happened.

The tall, muscled monster boar moved some steps towards the priest on its hind legs, a little ungainly at first, but becoming surefooted with each pace. Legs covered in coarse hair grew stronger and less clumsy with every second. A great belly, overhanging a tiny set of genitals, swayed with the motion. Only around the navel and nipples were there no bristles: the rest was dark bushy whiskers. The boar's cheeks hung in flaccid folds of loose flesh.

The priest saw its tiny eyes flicker. A large flattened snout dribbled mucus onto the mossy floor. The creature's slitted mouth opened. Rows of strong-looking teeth were revealed between the bases of the sweeping tusks.

Stinking hot breath struck Ragnu on the cheek.

'Yes,' muttered Ragnu, his heart racing beneath his ribcage. 'It is *alive.*'

'I-am-alive,' said a dull, torpid voice.

The puata seemed too sluggish of mind to attempt an attack on the priest, but Ragnu was taking no risks and remained well within the circle of ti'i.

Ragnu issued his instructions to the creature, which swayed under the starlight, occasionally blinking.

'Have you got that?' asked Ragnu, hopefully.

'What?' growled the boar in a listless tone. 'Got what?'

'You stupid oaf,' muttered the impatient Ragnu, who once again explained his plan, slowly and carefully, hoping that at least a little would be absorbed by the immensely obtuse creature with whom he was placing this task.

Finally, all was ready: monster and man took the path to the beach.

On board the hired pahi the Rarotongans slept, while the waves curled along the outer reef, falling with a rhythmic booming sound upon the drum of coral. The moonlight glittered on the rearing waters as they reached upwards, then fell crashing on their faces: gleamed on the milky foam that washed back over the channelled lips of the reef, back into the broad ocean.

Beyond the sleepy island, the heart of which still throbbed with its own sacred sounds, the wide waters of Oceania would have been quite still if it were not for the footsteps of invisible fairies running over its surface: a million of them, playing their fairy games around the early-houred watch. The dancing wavelets and small lights had beguiled the dozy Polahiki, who was now draped over the steering oar, as fast asleep as those whom he was supposed to guard.

Far in the distance, where the dark sea met the dark sky, little gods laughed at the schemes of devious men.

Seumas woke with a start and sniffed the air.

'Is it?' he muttered, sitting up and sniffing again. 'By the gods, I think it is!'

He stirred himself. Dorcha had kept the first watch and had handed over to the lousy Polahiki. She had then crept under the blanket with her husband. Seumas now shook her and she tried to open her eyes without success.

'What is it?' she murmured.

'Haggis!' said Seumas, excitedly. 'I can smell haggis cooking – really. Take a whiff.'

'Don't be foolish,' grumbled Dorcha in a sleepy voice. 'Leave me alone.'

Seumas saw that he wasn't going to get her to stir.

'Suit yourself,' he said. 'I'm going to get me some haggis – someone knows how to cook on this island.'

So saying he walked to the side and slipped into the warm waters of the lagoon. They were like a tepid bath, soothing away his tiredness. He swam slowly towards the beach, trying to ascertain which direction held the source of that wonderful aroma. When he reached the shallows, he stood and let the water drain from his body, before wading to the beach.

'Where is it coming from?' he muttered to himself. 'Hell, my stomach is ready for some of that.'

The aroma seemed to be issuing from the direction of the forest, so he followed a path in the starlight. At one point, he stopped and stared behind him, thinking he was being followed. When no one was forthcoming, he continued his search for the fire on which the haggis was being boiled.

The trees closed in around him, causing the path to disappear beneath his feet, but Seumas had been on this island for seven years, he knew the ways like he knew himself. There were no dangerous creatures – no snakes or savage beasts in the forest – so there was nothing for him to fear. Only the birds were disturbed by his thrashing along the path and they simply moved on their roosts to a shadier part of the tree.

'Where are you, where are you?' muttered Seumas.

Once more he heard the crack of a twig behind him, turned and stared, but again no persons revealed themselves. In his belt Seumas had his lei-o-mano and he felt he could handle any attempt at an attack, should it come.

He walked on.

Finally, he came to a clearing within which was an old disused hut, its palm leaf roof collapsed at one corner, its walls running with roaches. A dark doorway beckoned as the smell seemed to be coming from within the hut.

'A secret cook,' murmured the Pict, for the first time thinking rationally and suspecting something was wrong. 'Why would someone come right out here to boil a haggis? Where would they get a haggis in the first place? I must be going mad.'

He drew his lei-o-mano, wishing he had thought to carry a patu club, and went through the doorway.

Inside the hut, on the floor illuminated by starlight coming through the broken roof, were several tubes of bamboo.

'What the hell ...?' he began.

Just at that moment a tall huge beast came charging out of the dark corner of the hut, struck him and bowled him off his feet, sending him flying backwards through the doorway. His lei-o-mano went sailing from his hand to land somewhere in the bushes. The brute who had collided with him using its chest and shoulders now stood snorting and bellowing above his supine form, glaring down at him with wet-pebble eyes.

'Shit!' muttered Seumas, staring up at the monster.

The tusks of the beast gleamed in the starlight as the creature dribbled down their curves. Seumas saw the mouth open slightly and knew a blow was coming. He rolled aside just as a hoof smashed into the spot where his head had been.

Seumas was chilled by the strength of the stamp, which raised a great divot and penetrated the earth. This was no ordinary creature, no boar taught to walk on its hind legs. This was a product of the occult, a supernatural being dragged out of some hellish place not fit for the eyes of mortals, and thrust into the real world. The fear coursed through Seumas, who in his fright reverted to Gaelic.

'Tha e cho laidir agus a bhitheas e!' he cried, exclaiming at the beast's brawn.

The boar took a step back at these words, as if they had startled it.

'What-say-you-human?' it boomed, dully. 'What-words-make-you?'

'Arrrgghhh!' screamed Seumas, on hearing the brute talk, more terrified by this aspect of the situation than any other, 'You speak, you fiend!'

'I-kill-you,' intoned the boar. 'Now.'

'Ann an comhairle nan aingidh,' shouted Seumas, trying to push himself backwards into the forest with his feet.

'Go talk to some other poor man.'

The puata put his hooves over his ears on hearing the strange language again, as if the words hurt his head. 'Say-not,' he boomed. 'Speak-no-ugly-speakings.'

Seumas tried to get to his feet, desperately thinking of something else to say in Gaelic, since doing so clearly confused the creature. As he got to his feet however, the monster charged at him, its head lowered, its great tusks pointed at the Pict's chest. Seumas tried to scramble out of the way and was caught on the right shoulder, pierced by a tusk, then flung against a tree by the momentum of the brute's charge.

'I-kill-you,' boomed the puata.

'You've already said that,' gasped Seumas. 'Now do it, you thing of the mist. *De'n cheo.* I'm caught between tree and rock. *Tha bi eader a' chlach agus a' chraobb.'*

'Arrrrghhhh!' cried the beast, much as Seumas had done on hearing it speak. 'Say-not, say-not.'

It charged again, and would have trampled over the body of Seumas, had not a black shape come out of the darkness like a winged demon and buried its teeth into the throat of the puata, hanging there, snarling, rending the flesh.

Seumas recognised the demon instantly. It was Dirk III, sired by Dirk I, out of Dirk II. His hound had followed him into the lagoon, up from the beach, but had not approached before because it knew it had not been given permission for this walk in the night forest. Now though, the master was in danger, and it had come running to the attack.

'GAAAA!' cried the boar, its throat tearing open, spilling out twigs and dirt from within.

It tried to shake the dog loose, and pounded it with its forelegs, but once Dirk had his teeth into something they met and locked and there was no way the beast was going to get rid of its attacker by simply shaking and striking it. This the brute realised, even in its stupidity, and it ran at a tree intending to crush the dog against a hardwood trunk.

Seumas leapt to his feet now, grabbed a thick branch, and struck the puata across the back of its hind legs. It fell crashing to the forest floor with Dirk still gamely seeking a better hold on its throat. Seumas brought his club down hard on the creature's skull several times, smashing it open.

More dirt spilled out.

Seumas jumped on the puata's belly and, turning, struck it between the legs, splitting it to the navel.

Once the brute had started to crumble it was broken apart remarkably easily, as if one small crack in its facade had been enough to cause weaknesses to radiate throughout its whole frame. Dirk worried the top half of the beast, tearing and ripping chunks away with his teeth, while Seumas continued to smash the lower half apart with the branch. When Seumas paused to begin pounding the head, the beast's mouth opened for the last time and out of its torn throat came the feeble words, 'Hit-not.'

'Sorry, friend,' said Seumas, 'you've been used.'

He hammered with the branch-club and scattered the fragments of the head amongst the trees, and it was over. There was a wooden tusk here, a leafy ribcage there, something which might have been an eye lying in the dust. Seumas kicked at the dead leaves and twigs, strewing them still further.

'Damn beastie,' he muttered. 'Where the hell did you come from?'

Since there was no answer from the creature, Seumas decided it was not in his interests to remain in the forest.

The Pict gave his dog a hug and stroked him, telling him what a hero he was.

'Boy-girl's blasted chicken couldn't do that, now could it?'

Dirk wagged his tail in appreciation of the praise. Seumas then staggered away, along the forest path. His wounded shoulder was hurting him badly. He made it back down to the beach safely, with his faithful Dirk trotting by his side.

When he entered the waters of the lagoon, the salt both stung and did his injuries good. He was not seriously hurt, but his wounds did not heal as well these days as they had done when he had been a young man. Dirk swam beside him, head high, nose well out of the ripples, eyes bright with the satisfaction of having saved his master from almost certain death.

Back on the ship, Kieto was awake and standing watch. 'Where have you been?' asked Kieto.

'Fighting boars made of rubbish,' muttered Seumas. 'I'll explain later.'

'You want a compress on that wound.'

'In the morning,' said Seumas.

He crawled under the blanket next to Dorcha, slipped an arm around her waist, and was almost asleep, when he heard her murmur sleepily, 'Where have you been, lover?'

'Chasing haggis,' he replied.

2

Kumiki sighted Rarotonga on the horizon and almost wept with relief. Since he had left the shores of Nuku Hiva, to search for his father the demon called Seumas, he had been through much. The loneliness of being at sea without company had almost turned him mad. He had not only been having terrible dreams at night, but during the day too, while he was awake. They were acted out in front of him, on the platform of his double-hulled canoe, and he was afraid they were terrible portents of things to come. Yesterday, Maui and Ro themselves had appeared before him and acted out the story of when they had changed heads:

Maui had been summoned by the gods to discuss with him some mischief for which he had been responsible. Perhaps they intended to punish him? No one knows that part of the story, for it took place in heaven. What mortals do know is that the person who brought him the message to accompany her to heaven was Ro, who had been Maui's wife until she became disenchanted with his tricks and had gone to live in the netherworld.

'I shall come with you,' said Maui, 'but I must avoid a certain village on the way, for there are people there who plan to attack and hurt me.'

Ro led the way, but ignored Maui's pleas not to pass through the area where there were men who wanted to harm him, for she knew he was capable of avoiding such an attack and wanted to see how he would do it.

When they were outside the village where these men lived, Maui turned to Ro and said, 'Give me your head.'

'No,' replied Ro, 'for how can I find the way to where the gods dwell without a head?'

'You shall have mine,' said Maui.

And so, after more arguments, Maui finally persuaded Ro to exchange heads with him and the pair of them walked through the village. Just as they were emerging from the other side, a gang of men pounced on Ro and dragged her off, while Maui made his escape into the rainforest. There he waited for Ro. Indeed she appeared some time later.

The pair exchanged heads again and Maui asked, 'What happened?'

'It was just as you said,' replied Ro. 'They tied me to a stake to burn me, pulled away my garments, and were amazed and frightened to find that I was female.

'They said, "Has Maui become a woman? What magic is this? We are men of a tribe which does not harm women!" And so they let me go.'

Maui laughed again. 'I knew this was so – they would not hurt a female – now they will forget the tricks I played on them and leave me alone.'

This scene had been played through on the deck of the canoe the previous morning and Kumiki's brain was still reeling with the images which had been dancing before his eyes. It was as if it had all been real – Maui, Ro, the village, the ambush, the rainforest – and these people, these things, had actually stood on the front of Kumiki's deck.

Yet he knew he was feverish from lack of good fresh water, and the solitude had plucked and tweaked at his mind.

The reason he had needed to mix seawater too heavily with his fresh water, thus not only making it unpalatable, but dangerous to his sanity, was because of the last island he had stopped at.

The island had looked innocent enough, but in fact it proved to be the home of some terrible spirits. While collecting drinking coconuts Kumiki was chased by a spirit known as the putuperereko, a monster with huge testicles who devoured people when he could catch them.

Kumiki was a fast runner however, and managed to outdistance the putuperereko, but dropped all his coconuts in the chase. When he went back for them later, feeling it was safe, he came across a beautiful creature who attempted to seduce him.

Remembering in time that this was a strange island he was on, home of peculiar spirits, he recalled that there was a spirit called a tarogolo who seduced people of the opposite sex and when it had them in their power, killed them by cutting up their genitals. When he refused to lie with the creature, it screamed at him with foul words, and its face became distorted.

With a half-coconut shell held between his legs, to protect his valuable private parts, Kumiki had run back to the shoreline and boarded his canoe. The island was clearly enchanted by horrible creatures. Despite the fact that he had only three drinking coconuts on board, Kumiki set sail and left the region as fast as the wind would carry him.

Thus he had to mix his fresh drink with largish quantities of seawater, which might have brought on the hallucinations. To cure himself of these daytime dreams, Kumiki had invoked the Healer-God, Ro'o, whose chants had been taught to men to help them drive out the bad spirits which cause illness and death. Ro'o had now helped him by bringing him to his destination, Rarotonga.

Before he entered the lagoon, Kumiki prepared himself for war. He put on his feathered helmet, took up his kotiate club in one hand, and a spear in the other. He had no cloak to put on, but he squared his muscled shoulders and wore a ferocious expression, his tongue lolling out, his eyes swivelling up occasionally to show only the whites. He knew the three solid bars tattooed across his face made him look fierce. He was also aware that his Hivan hairstyle, the two horns jutting from an otherwise bald pate, frightened his enemies. He had his terrible battle cry ready in his throat.

Since he knew Oro, the Great War-God, would not come to the aid of a youth about to go into single combat, for Oro commanded armies not individuals, Kumiki asked his ancestors to invoke the Goddess of Volcanoes, Pele, to assist him by permitting him to spit fire. Kumiki did not think this too much to ask.

He tried spitting flames once or twice, with no success, though thought that perhaps Pele might be waiting to give him fire to cough up in the heat of the battle.

When Kumiki's canoe drifted around a corner of the island he was amazed to see a whole fleet of ships anchored in the lagoon. A hundred at least: perhaps two? They jostled each other in the rippling waters, their sails folded away somewhere, leaving their masts to fence each other in the wind. Kumiki wondered if some king were visiting, from Samoa, or Tonga, or perhaps even Tahiti? He tried to not let it influence him in any way. He was here to kill a man. That must be paramount in his mind.

When he reached the beach, it was crowded with people. Some were singing, some were dancing, others were telling jokes, doing somersaults, acting the buffoon. Kumiki was a little daunted by this, but was determined to carry his plan through. He swelled his chest like a hero should and took up a fighting stance on the hot sands.

'Where is the demon they call Seumas?' he cried. 'I shall slay him in single combat.'

To his annoyance, hardly anyone took notice of his words, still carrying on with their leaping and prancing, their chattering and running through the musical scales. One or two gave him an uninterested sidelong glance. The nearest man to him said, 'Oh, very good – not bad at all – but you'll need to sharpen up those accents.'

'Bring out the Seumas creature,' screamed Kumiki at the top of his voice. 'Let me see the fiend I am to kill!'

'That's *much* better,' said the other man. 'I can hear the Hivan warrior in that one. Needs just a *little* more venom. Just a teeny bit more fire. Who are you anyway? Want to join the ghost dancers, do you?'

Frustrated, Kumiki stamped his foot. 'I am Kumiki, son of Seumas the goblin, whom I am about to kill – if someone will take the trouble to find him for me.'

The man stroked his chin. 'Seumas, Seumas – oh, yes, I know, I've heard of him – the Pict. Oh, he's not here at the moment. You'll have to work up another act if you want to join the Arioi. Seumas has gone on a long ocean voyage in search of an island.'

Kumiki almost wept. 'A voyage?'

'So I hear from the locals. He's joined with Ru, the Raiatean prince. They'll be gone – oh, ever so long. Chances are they'll never come back again. You know what these adventurers are like. They'll brave the world, but they're as vulnerable as the next man. I shouldn't be surprised if he drowns or gets eaten by sea monsters.'

Kumiki sat down on the beach and hung his head. His enemy was not on the island. All that time, all that courage, wasted. Kumiki had made the journey of a lifetime, alone across vast tracts of dangerous ocean, and all for nothing. The demon was not here. He was off somewhere on one of his jaunts, raping women no doubt, pillaging innocent islands, tearing down graven images and flouting the gods. Seumas was with Prince Ru on a voyage to nowhere, out of reach of Kumiki's club and spear.

'It's not fair,' sobbed the youth. 'I have come so far – so far – and all for nothing.'

'Where have you come from?' asked the man, who appeared to be some sort of dancer. 'Tell me, boy?'

'From Nuku Hiva,' sighed Kumiki.

'Wow, that's impressive,' replied the man, squatting down near him 'Look, my name's Ramoro.' He didn't ask Kumiki *his* name for that would have been extremely impolite. Kumiki might be someone famous and you were expected to know famous people by their aura. Instead he simply waited for Kumiki to tell him.

Kumiki stared at the man's face and saw by his tattoos and the way he arranged the flowers in his hair that he preferred men to women when it came to love-making.

'I'm Kumiki,' he said at last. 'I'm on a mission to kill my father, Seumas.'

'Wow!' said the other delightedly, 'that's impressive too. I've never heard of anything like that. But you'll be disappointed. As I said, Seumas the Pict is not here. He and his wife have gone with Kieto to join Ru's voyage.'

'And no one knows where Ru is bound?'

'That's it. What are you going to do now?'

'After I get a drink of water?' said Kumiki, realising that his mouth was lined with a white crust. 'I don't know. Wait here for Seumas? Go home? I don't know.'

'Come on, boy, let's get you something to drink,' said Ramoro, taking his hand. 'And you needn't worry about me trying to seduce you. I've already got a lover.'

'I wasn't worried,' lied the Hivan youth.

After he had drunk a refreshing coconut full of water, sipping it carefully to prevent stomach pains, Kumiki stared about him at the activities on the beach. It seemed a sort of controlled chaos, with people practising all sorts of skills. And very interesting skills they were too. Kumiki liked the noise and colour of the scene. It filled him with excitement. Who were these people? They clearly did not belong to Rarotonga, for Ramoro had called the islanders 'locals'. Then Kumiki remembered the word Ramoro had used.

'The Arioi?' he asked. 'Did you say the Arioi?'

'Yes,' laughed Ramoro. 'I'm one of the dancers. My best friend is a singer – he has a divine voice. He's as beautiful as Kopu, the Morning Star, and I love him very much. We joined the Arioi together, two years ago.'

'The *Arioi*,' breathed Kumiki. 'I've never seen it before. When I was a boy,' he gabbled, 'very young, I wanted to run away to join the Arioi. It was the dream of all my friends, to take to the seas with you people.'

Ramoro laughed again. 'It's the dream of every young man or woman – those with any imagination. And who can blame them? This is a wonderful life, travelling from island to island, being praised for our performances, enjoying the best of everything, having no other responsibilities except to the company. I adore it. I wouldn't change places with anyone in Oceania.'

'Nor would I, if I were a member of the Arioi. I would like to be a Painted Leg. That's what I would like to be.'

'Oh, *that's* all?' said Ramoro, amused by the boyish enthusiasm and reverence in Kumiki's tone. 'Just a Painted Leg.'

Kumiki nodded and looked serious. 'Well, I know that's very ambitious. I know a Painted Leg is, well, the *first* rank amongst you Arioi. But *someone's* got to be there, haven't they? And I think I've got a lot of talent. I'm sure I have.'

Over the next few days Ramoro explained to Kumiki what he would have to do if he were to join the Arioi.

'You need to have a talent, of course – what can you do? Sing? Dance?'

'No, not really.'

'What about clowning? We have one man who dresses up like a baby and rolls around the floor making baby noises. What about doing something like that?'

Kumiki screwed his face up in disgust. 'That sounds demeaning and humiliating.'

'All right, it's not amongst the more highly regarded of our performances, I admit – but how about spear fighting, or wrestling?'

Kumiki nodded enthusiastically. 'I'm quite good at wrestling. I'm very strong.'

'Good. We'll try to get you in as a wrestler. Now what you have to do sometime in the next few days is attract a lot of attention to yourself, to show you're not afraid of audiences. The normal way is to dress yourself in brilliant yellow and red leaves, paint yourself all over with dyes, stick leaves and mud to yourself, and act as if you're absolutely crazy. When people look at you, spring in front of them and behave as if you're deranged.'

'Do I have to?' asked the unhappy Kumiki. 'Couldn't I just go and say I wanted to join?'

'You'd be laughed and jeered all the way back to Nuku Hiva. You've got to prove to everyone that you don't care what people think of you. You've got to prove you'll do *anything*, go to any lengths, to become a member of the Arioi.'

Kumiki sighed. 'Well, if I *have* to.'

He did as Ramoro said, he painted himself to look like a madman and decorated himself with leaves and twigs. There were leaves sprouting from his nose and ears, stuck to his chest with mud, sticking out of his waistband. There were twigs entangled with his hair. There was a broken branch poking like an erect penis from his skirt. A bunch of feathers trailed from a cord around his waist. Grass was stuck to his underarms like hair.

He jumped out on people, leapt into rings of talking elders, made noises like a chicken being strangled, rolled his eyes, burbled his lips, snorted like a pig. He hooted and shrieked, he danced like a maniac, he fell down and gibbered. One night he leapt into a huge basin of warm soup and pretended to swim, splashing startled onlookers and causing havoc.

In short, he looked and acted crazy.

Within a week he was asked to join the Arioi as a wrestler. He sold his canoe, joined the performances, and by the time the troupe was ready to sail away from Rarotonga, Kumiki had small circles tattooed on his ankles, denoting he was an Ohemara and in the sixth class – one up from a flapper.

He was as proud as Io.

PART THREE

God of all the sharks

1

The Princely Flower set sail from Raiatea, bound for Maraamu tairoto on the windflower.

Seumas did not discover for sure exactly what or who was behind the attack by the puata. If he had not been woken in the middle of the night, but had smelled haggis during the more sane daylight hours, he would have been extremely suspicious. The night hours and a sleepy head however lulled one into accepting things at face value.

Seumas had many old enemies, as well as friends on the island, and it could have been any one of them. Rian and Ti-ti might have paid a priest. Or it could have been Ragnu. He was in no doubt that he had been lured away from their pahi, to face the puata, but he could prove nothing.

'Best let it lie,' said Dorcha. 'We're leaving this place in any case. It's not our island any more.'

She and Seumas had been bothered by the presence of Rian and Ti-ti and were glad to be out of their sight. The two brothers had not openly attacked them again, but had often stood with smouldering eyes some way off, watching Dorcha. Seumas had wanted to bash their heads together and probably would have done if not prevented by Dorcha.

The Scot was aware she and Seumas had technically broken the law and the brothers could have caused a lot of trouble for them had the pair not been divided in their opinion over the matter. Ti-ti was the gentler of the two and did not want Dorcha to come to any harm, though the same gentle soul would have been delighted had Seumas been skinned alive and hung up in the noonday sun for the ants to eat.

'I'm certainly sure those two paid a priest to make that creature out of clay and twigs,' grumbled Seumas, 'then lured me away from the pahi with the smell of cooking haggis.'

He sighed as he recalled the aroma, thinking how good it would have been if the smell had led him to a pot over a fire, and a friendly Raiatean ready with a spoon.

Most of the rest of the party had gone abroad on the island, and on nearby Borabora, visiting relatives.

Polahiki was one exception, since his home was somewhere in the Hivan islands, but Kikamana had found her sister, and Boy-girl her parents. Po'oi had also visited his brothers and sisters, who were scattered over the island.

Pungarehu had cousins who wished to make a fuss of him, people who lived in the hills: he managed to reach them, stay a short while, then had to make the long trek back to the coast.

Rinto, son of Manopa, had hardly stepped off the chartered pahi onto Raiatea. The place had been his father's home, not his, and this was his first time on the island. Unidentifiable cousins, aunts, and various other relatives, all of whom were unrecognisable to Rinto, kept coming up to him and telling him he looked just like his father. Strangers to him. They rubbed noses with him, hugged him, called him Manopa's boy, made him feel extremely uncomfortable. Rinto was glad they were on their way. He didn't like people he didn't even know touching his body, making him squirm with embarrassment inside.

Prince Ru was in sole charge of the craft, a single pahi with only his extended family and a few other passengers on board, besides the contingent from Rarotonga. Although technically Ru was entitled to call himself king, once he had set sail, he told his crew and passengers he would remain a prince until he found the island he was seeking.

'There would be problems with mana on board and I will not *feel* I am a king until I have an island under my feet.'

Ru was a navigator prince of great renown, known throughout the Tahitian Islands as one of the best pathfinders in Oceania. For this voyage to find his family a new home he had obeyed the gods and crewed his vessel with twenty virgins, who now worked the sails, rived the ropes and bailed the water from the twin hulls. They were magnificent women, strong yet lithe and comely. With frangipani and hibiscus blooms behind their ears, they sang at their work as they steered the ship towards an invisible point on the horizon, following the swell beneath the craft.

Seumas couldn't take his eyes off them at first.

'If you stretch your neck any further, your head will fall off,' remarked Dorcha, drily. 'I'd be very careful, laddie.'

'Looking at what?' he feigned innocence. 'Oh, *them?* I was just interested in the way they do the work, that's all. Very efficient lasses, every one of them. Very efficient. Up with the sails, down with the sails ...'

'It's not their competence at sailing which attracts, you dirty old man. You just mind yourself.'

He laughed and shook his head, knowing that very little passed Dorcha by.

'They're forbidden taro, anyway,' said Seumas. 'Nono nuts, that's what they are. Apart from anything else, Ru would execute any man who touched one of those maidens, since it would bring him into direct conflict with the gods.' Seumas sighed, adding, 'It's part of their attraction – that they are unobtainable.'

'Would you like me to make *myself* unobtainable,' Dorcha said, arching an eyebrow. 'It's easily done, you know.'

He slipped a tattooed arm around her waist and grinned at her.

'You're desirable, whether you're out of bounds or not, lassie. I could eat you for breakfast, dinner and supper, so I could.'

'Mind it stays that way, *laddie*,' she said.

Another passenger, a handsome Raiatean man, witnessed this banter with an amused expression on his features. Dorcha knew his name was Titopika, but was ignorant of the reason for him being on the voyage.

He said he was a novice tohunga, a priest specialising in removing taboos from people and places – a purifier of tapu – and in touch with the spirits of the air, sea and earth, having knowledge of their language. A tohunga is necessary to any new Oceanian society, because he is qualified to perform funeral rites. Dorcha assumed this young man was going to the new island to set up his own temple. Promotion would be quicker at a new location. Raiatea itself had priests by the several dozens. Competition for top places was fierce and nepotism was rife.

'What are you laughing at?' asked Dorcha, already uncomfortable with the feeling of claustrophobia a voyage on a craft induces. 'Can't we talk in private?'

'I'm sorry,' said the man, not at all put out by her tone. 'It was rude of me.'

Seumas said, 'Take no notice of her – she gets touchy unless she's got a mountain range to stare at.'

'I'll remember that. Do forgive me. I meant no offence.' Dorcha relented under this barrage of profuse apologies and told the man it was all right.

He smiled and left them to their personal chores.

Tawhaki hid in a cloud Ao sent to him and after roaming the skies for some time finally came across Tui Tofua, God of all the sharks. Tui Tofua was not a relative or even a friend of Dakuwanga, who was the Shark-God who ate sau, the souls which were lost on their way to the Land of the Dead. Daku-wanga was a spirit-shark dwelling in the ether, while Tui Tofua was in human shape and commanded all the real sharks in the real ocean.

Tawhaki asked a favour of Tui Tofua, who hated human beings and saw them only as food for his sharks. He asked that Tui Tofua's sharks do a service for him. Tui Tofua asked what that service might be and when Tawhaki told him, the God of all the sharks agreed to assist the God of Thunder and Lightning.

A multitude of sharks gathered under *The Princely Flower* and no matter how hard the crew pulled on the steering oar, or set the sails with Maomao's wind behind them, the vessel persisted in following a different bearing to the one Ru had set. With sharks under the two hulls, jammed there, it was impossible to control the course of the pahi. The sharks took them off their chosen route and into unknown waters.

It took the combined efforts of Dorcha, Kikamana and Boy-girl, each chanting their own powerful fangu, to rid the pahi of the sharks. Gradually, as the chants worked their spells, the fish left. Finally, the craft was free again and the royal maiden on the steering oar asked Ru for a direction.

Even Seumas, who was no navigator, could see that the shapes of the waves were all wrong. They were in some part of the ocean where the sea birds were strange and the clouds had no real definition. The colour of the water was a dark blue, almost black, indicating great depths. There was no te lapa to give guidance under the surface and a strange calmness had beset them, accompanied by sweltering days and restless nights.

Tui Tofua would surely be punished for what he had done with *The Princely Flower*, when Tangaroa caught up with him. In the meantime the pahi was becalmed on sultry seas, a hot sun pressing itself down on the necks and backs of the seafarers. The crew had little to do but wait for the wind, for which Ru sent prayers daily, bound for the ears of Maomao.

Seumas rose one night in the stillness to fetch a drink from a gourd lying in a cooling tank forward. As he picked his way amongst sleeping bodies that tossed and turned in the hot inert air, he heard a quick rustling movement from the direction of one of the hulls. Seumas reached the halved water gourd and dipped the wooden ladle for a drink. A moment later the young man known as Titopika appeared to come away from the port hull.

He came up short against Seumas, visibly jumped, and then hurriedly tried to find a lost composure. Clearly Seumas had startled Titopika with his presence, but it was not surprising to find more than one person at the drinking water on such a night. Possibly Titopika had been half-asleep and unready.

'I – er – would like a drink, if you've finished with that ladle.'

'Sorry,' said Seumas, 'did I frighten you?'

'No,' replied the other in an unexpectedly irritable tone. 'I just didn't think to see anyone about at this hour.'

'So I *did* surprise you.'

Titopika looked huffy. 'If you insist. Now may I have a drink of water, or are you going to hold onto that ladle all night?'

Seumas handed over the ladle without another word, but there was something about the man's manner which interested him. It was as if Titopika had been caught doing something illegal. Had he been stealing rations? Not this early in the voyage surely? Yesterday they had caught several albacore using ouma fish as bait. The albacore were huge and there was more than enough to feed the whole vessel for many days, so even the strongest appetite could not be suffering at that precise moment.

Perhaps Titopika had smuggled kava on board? Or had a store of honey? It was all most intriguing.

When the young man had finished his drink of water and had gone away to his bed, Seumas went to the area of the vessel from which he thought he had seen

Titopika emerge. It had seemed to be on the very edge of the deck, just where it met the port hull. Seumas felt around, under the boards, seeking a hiding place, but found nothing. Refusing to give up on the puzzle he looked further afield.

In the hull itself, some of the crew were sleeping: royal virgins swathed in pareu, curled up together in the bottom like litters of newly born pups. Seumas stared at the dark shapes lying on pandanus mats in the shallow swilling water at the bottom of the hull, trying to keep cool. There seemed to be nothing untoward there: no obvious place to cache illicit food.

Suddenly he was aware of a set of brown eyes on his face. He stared into the features of one of the women, whom he appeared to have woken. She looked frightened. It seemed she might scream any moment. His skin prickled with apprehension.

'It's all right,' Seumas whispered. 'I'm not going to do anything – I was just looking – just looking for something,' he finished lamely, aware of how feeble it sounded. 'Nothing to get alarmed about.'

The woman continued to stare unblinkingly at him and eventually he crawled away. The incident remained in his mind as mildly disturbing, but there was nothing to substantiate his feelings that Titopika had been up to something unauthorised. When he saw the young man the next day, there was nothing with which to confront him, but it was significant that Titopika would not look him in the eye, and passed by him close to the pandanus mat sail without a glance.

Ru's pahi lazily approached an island which seemed to move as the mist drifted over it, revealing now a mountain, now a valley, now a forest. People on board had smelled sweet potatoes cooking and knew the island was inhabited. As Oceanians they loved sweet potatoes, sacred to Rongo, and had long since eaten all those on board. As Oceanians they would brave any strange island to replenish their depleted stores.

'Be careful,' Seumas warned Ru. 'Remember what happened to me when I chased the smell of cooking haggis.'

'That was different,' Kieto interrupted. 'Your haggis food is back in your own homeland, Land-of-Mists, while sweet potatoes are to be found over the whole of Oceania.'

Yet, as they approached the island in the early evening through a narrow gap in a dead coral reef, grey and depressing, both Dorcha and Boy-girl reported seeing things dancing on the water behind the pahi. It was as if they had gone blindly into a trap and their captors were rejoicing at having caught the prey. Dorcha said she wouldn't have been surprised to see the pincers of coral snap shut behind them.

'What did you see?' asked Ru of Dorcha.

'I can't be sure exactly,' replied Dorcha. 'Perhaps nothing at all? Maybe a mirage. I just caught movements out of the corner of my eye. They flashed silver, like fish, but they weren't fish, of that I'm certain. I got the impression of – of human-like forms.'

'Ponaturi,' stated Ru with conviction. 'Sea-fairies. This is an enchanted place.'

Ru explained that the Ponaturi lived in the divide between the visible and the invisible world. One caught them in the glimmering light of a dawn, or in the last stray wispy tails of a disappearing sun. 'You think you see them, perhaps you do – but you can't be sure.' They were bright shadows that flitted past the corner of the eye, as they soared through the glooms of twilight, of too tenuous a nature to be completely discernible – but tangible enough to attack humans.

Seumas asked, 'Are the Ponaturi like the Tipairu, the Peerless Ones?'

'No – the Tipairu are gentle creatures, who love their dancing. The Ponaturi are savage sea-fairies who live in hordes, more willing to fight than dance. Once they latch on to a vessel, they won't let it go until all the seafarers are dead. Their chant is:

"Scent, scent,
Odour, odour,
My food is man,
My drink is blood."'

Polahiki gave out a low moan of fear.

'The hero Rata slew them in great numbers,' continued Ru, 'using deadly karakia chants as well as physical force. We must keep our weapons handy – we may need them. Where's Kikamana, our priestess? Dorcha the Scot? And that young tohunga?'

Kikamana, Dorcha and Titopika came before Ru.

'I want you three to protect us from the Ponaturi when we have to leave here,' he said. 'Can you do it? We're not a large enough force to beat the Ponaturi on purely physical terms. They'll swarm all over us.'

Kikamana said, 'For the karakia to be effective we need human bones to beat together, preferably those of an ancient warrior hero. Otherwise the karakia will be slow to work. We are not carrying such a cargo.'

Boy-girl took Polahiki by the hair and pushed him forward.

'We could kill this otherwise worthless specimen and use *his* bones as drumsticks.'

'True,' argued Seumas, 'Polahiki has done nothing so far – it's his chance to be useful.'

'You leave me alone!' screeched the terrified fisherman. 'Who catches your fish for you?'

'I think we do that ourselves,' Boy-girl said. 'You eat anything you catch.'

Boy-girl's cockerel ran up to Polahiki and began pecking around his feet. The fisherman had become so agitated he was dislodging some of his lice and other tiny parasites which infested his body. They were falling to the deck, to be devoured by the colourful rooster pet of Boy-girl.

The Farseeing-virgin interrupted. 'I'm afraid this is serious. We do need the bones if we're to escape a battle with the Ponaturi. Rata's tohungas used the bones of Wahieroa.'

Seumas said, 'We could search this island for graves. I'm not above grave-robbing if my life's at stake. I doubt we'll find a hero in a place like this, but if we don't do something we'll be trapped in this lagoon while those sea-fairies wait for us on the other side of the reef. What do you say, Kieto?'

'I don't like the idea of robbing graves. Our ancestors, and perhaps even the gods, would not approve of such a thing. But if we scour the caves on that ugly-looking mountain, we might find some bones. I see no signs of civilisa-tion here – this is a primitive place. There are islands where they do not bury their dead, but pile the bones in some cave.'

'Isn't that the same as stealing from a grave?' said Dorcha. 'I can't see much difference.'

'The difference is that the bones will not have been subject to funeral rites,' replied Titopika. 'They will not be so powerful, their mana will have dwin-dled, but Kieto's right we're more likely to find bones in a cave than anywhere else.'

A three-person team was chosen to go ashore to search for the bones. These were Seumas, Dorcha and Kikamana. Ru was taking Pungarehu and Po'oi to look for sweet potatoes. All the others were to remain on board the pahi, which floated on a scummy tideless stretch of lagoon where the flies and other insects were persistently annoying. Rotten stumps of palm trees projected from the water under which lifeless coral was corroding and filling the lagoon with grey sludge.

Polahiki was attempting to fish, but the only thing he was catching in that dull, torpid water were moray eels with thick slimy skins.

'The goddess Pere has deserted this place,' he moaned. 'She has left it to stagnate.'

Those remaining on board prayed to Tiki to protect them from the onslaught of the Ponaturi fairies, while their captain and pathfinder was on the island. Ru had assured them the sea-fairies would not attack while the ship was anchored in the lagoon, but a little trust in Tiki did not harm. The First Ancestor's wooden face remained impassive as he imbibed the prayers, glad to be of some comfort to his many descendants.

When the party of six reached the beach, they followed a trail of coconut shells and fruit skins up the beach to a village just inside the rainforest pale. There they found a listless, apathetic tribe, who seemed to be living in a state divided between fear and boredom. They poured out their misfortunes to the visitors, complaining of everything and anything, and finished by telling Ru not to send anyone into the middle of the island because no one had ever managed to come back alive.

'All the best land is there,' moaned the chief. 'We could grow better crops, if it weren't for the fact that a monster lives on the mountain. It eats anyone who ventures into the hinterland.'

'A monster?' queried Ru. 'What kind?'

'What kind is your *fear*?' asked the chief, rhetorically. 'It is a taniwha whose name is Hotu-puku.'

'I have heard of this noxious monster. And the lagoon why is that dying?'

The chief replied, 'Tipua. The Ponaturi allow them to come and feed on the coral and weed. Without weed and coral there are no fish.'

Ru nodded. 'We need some human bones to escape the Ponaturi – can you let us have some?'

'We would if we had any ourselves. Most of our people are taken by the taniwha, but the Tipua also carry away the dead in the middle of the night, to feast on the rotting flesh. We have no graves, no corpses, no bones. Our ancestors haunt us nightly, keeping us awake and in fear, because their bodies have been treated so badly after death.'

Ru turned to Dorcha, Seumas and Kikamana.

'Well, do you still want to go into the high country?'

'We had no choice before,' said the Farseeing-virgin.

'And even less now, if we want to escape from this place.'

'Off you go then – and good luck.'

The three went out of the village on an overgrown path which led into the jungle of the foothills. Seumas was glad they had Kikamana with them, for though he considered himself a good warrior, and Dorcha also a fighter, the high priestess had powerful mana – much stronger than any they owned themselves – and this would be useful if they came up against a monster.

'What kind of monster did he say it was?' he asked Kikamana.

'It is the colour of your fear,' replied that kahuna. 'If you fear cockroaches, then be prepared for the mother of all cockroaches. With me, it is lizards.'

Dorcha shuddered. 'Snakes,' she said. 'I hate snakes.'

'Women,' said Seumas. 'It's women that terrify me.' Dorcha shot him a look, but Kikamana, who was unused to humour in serious situations, stared at Seumas in surprise.

'Really – you fear women?'

'Actually,' said Dorcha, 'he's only terrified of one woman and if he doesn't behave himself you'll soon see why.'

Kikamana was still bewildered, but decided to let the matter drop, since she didn't seem to be getting anywhere.

They made their way inland, up the gradually sloping ground, until they came to a steeper climb. Here the jungle thinned out to become rainforest, and after that more open country, with bushes and bamboo, rather than tall trees. All the while they sought caves to investigate. When they found them they went inside cautiously, discovering most of them empty. Just occasionally there were the bones of birds, or a ceiling covered in bats, but no human skeletons.

Finally they approached an enormous cave which stretched like a mouth under the brow of a cliff. There was something in the aspect of the cave which warned all three that this was probably the home of the taniwha Hotu-puku. In any case they were on their guard for a meeting with the monster. Seumas asked the other two if they had any plan.

Kikamana said, 'We could entice it from the cave then bring magic to bear on its size. A karakia might be effective in shrinking it, whatever it looks like to each one of us. However, as you both know, we have no ancient bones to ensure the effectiveness of the chant.'

Seumas shuddered. 'Put our faith in a fangu chant, without sacred bones? You must be crazy. I couldn't do that.'

'Well, what then?' asked Dorcha. 'Give us an alternative.'

Seumas looked around him. They were standing on the edge of thick jungle. There was a clear grassy slope ahead of them, leading up to the cave and the tall cliffs. To either side the land fell away as steep escarpments. If the monster came on foot, it would have to run down the narrow slope and follow them into the dark undergrowth beneath the dense canopy of the trees, where vines and branches hung thick as curtains.

Of course, it might have the ability to fly, depending on what each of them saw it as, but then they would be safe in the jungle, below the path of its flight.

'I suggest we make snares out of the vines,' he told the two women. 'Then when we have nooses around its neck ...'

'Or *necks*,' said Kikamana.

'... or necks,' added Seumas, giving Kikamana a sidelong glance. 'When it's securely roped we kill it with clubs and spears. We'll probably need the help of others.'

Kikamana said, 'It will only complicate matters if there are more people here – it means more variation to the shape of the monster. However, it sounds a reasonable plan. Dorcha and I shall protect ourselves with a karakia. What will you do?'

Seumas said, 'A good warrior doesn't need a magic chant – I'll face the monster without it.'

'Fine, then let's make the nooses.'

They set to work, tugging out the blades of cabbage-trees and twisting them into ropes, the vines being a little stiff to knot and use for snares. They were already armed. Kikamana had a carved rib-bone of a whale, which had been shaved into a sword. Seumas had a short wooden cleaver. Dorcha carried a long-handled club with a serrated hardwood edge on one side and shark's teeth down the other. All three held a spear each.

The ropes made from the ti fronds were hung amongst the vines, disguised as normal growth amongst the trees, their nooses hanging limply ready to be filled. The ends were fixed to tree trunks or stakes hammered into the ground with rocks. The knots were draped with blossoms and wild flowers to hide their presence and this was so well achieved that birds used the loops of the snares as perch swings from which to make their calls.

In the mid-afternoon they were ready to take on the taniwha and each of them prepared their nerves for the coming ordeal.

'I shall call the monster down,' said Kikamana. 'It is my privilege as a kahuna.'

'Help yourself,' said Seumas, with a gesture.

'Likewise,' Dorcha added.

Kikamana, that magnificent priestess, left them to walk up to the opaque orifice of the mountain which pushed earth and rock apart in a cracked grin. The two Albannachs watched her progress with hearts beating rapidly faster, camouflaged by the slats of sunlight that shafted the canopy. They had the unenviable task of pulling the nooses tight if the monster's head (or heads) did not automatically do so.

Kikamana was about halfway up the slope when a blast of bats came from the cave, millions of them, blackening the air for a few moments. Then the taniwha's foul breath came hissing from the mouth of the cave. She smelled its rank odour and felt the damp warmth of it on her cheek. Then suddenly, there it was, the taniwha Hotu-puku, its fierce great head filling the entrance to its den, its burning eyes like two suns glaring down at her. It was indeed the head of a giant lizard, as Kikamana had expected; having explored herself thoroughly during many years of meditation she knew her own fears intimately. She shook in apprehension.

'Moko!' she cried. 'Lord of the Lizards, protect me from one of your deviants!'

The God of the Lizards made no obvious reply, nor had she really expected one, not having prepared the way to his ears with sacrifices and prayers.

Kikamana was absolutely terrified by the scaly beast before her, as Hotu-puku emerged from the cave. She witnessed its spear-like crest and the dreadful forest of spines protruding from its head and back. Its head jerked back and forth in the manner of reptiles as its tail pounded the earth in the cave behind it. A flat belly slid with a rumbling sound along the ground, dragging loose rocks and broken limbs of trees along beneath it. Those loose scales which dropped from its sides as it scraped through the cave mouth fell like turtle shells to the ground to shatter on the stones. A long tongue flicked in and out of its horrible split jaws, lapping the shrubs around the terror-stricken priestess as she fought for the will to move.

'Kikamana,' shrieked Dorcha's voice behind her, 'run away from the snake – quickly, quickly.'

But still those baleful eyes held her as the hot musty breath engulfed her own and made it difficult for her to breathe or think, fogging her reason with the lack of fresh air. Hotu-puku's mouth opened, revealing a blood-red interior which disappeared into a black throat. A hissing roar issued from this region, blasting the kahuna's ears.

'Look out, look out, the taniwha is upon you!' yelled Dorcha. 'Run away Kikamana!'

Finally, as the ridged spiny giant began to run forward, its claws thumping the moss-covered earth, Kikamana found some youthful strength in her tired old body and turned on trembling limbs to run.

When she reached the safety of the trees, skipping neatly through the loops of the snares like a little girl, she found that Seumas had fled, leaving just the two women to deal with the monster.

On it came, its head appearing halfway up the tall trees at the pale of the forest, then its forelegs entered, and one was caught within the snares. Kikamana slashed at an anchor rope with her whale-bone sword, releasing a tethered young tree to which the noose was tied.

A double-noose tightened around Hotu-puku's throat, which drew even tighter as the monster thrashed in its coils. At the same time the one snared foreleg was raised off the ground by the sprung tree, causing the beast to unbalance, while the second foreleg frantically clawed at a nearby trunk tearing the bark from the bole in one complete strip. A tail lashed the hill behind Hotu-puku, the spines ripping the turf to pieces and raining soil and grit upon the broad leaves of the undergrowth, adding to the noise and confusion.

'Kill it, kill it,' shrieked a wide-eyed Dorcha, clearly almost stupefied by terror.

She did not remain transfixed however and ran forward to slash at the monster's throat with her tooth-edge club, ripping the loose skin open where it flapped as the taniwha tossed and jerked its head. A foam-flecked mouth sprayed the women as they fought to bring the creature to its knees, splattering and drenching them in disgusting fluids that plastered their hair to their skulls and blinded them with its acidic properties.

'Get its legs,' cried Kikamana. 'Chop at its ankles.'

'What legs?' shrieked the Scot. 'I can't see any. Snakes don't have legs.'

Kikamana drove her whale-bone sword up into the sagging skin of the underjaw, pinning the beast's mandible to the roof of its mouth.

Kikamana then took up her spear and forced it hard into Hotu-puku's belly, spilling hot, thick steaming juices onto the floor of the jungle. Then the brave priestess went for neck and upper torso, stabbing with her long spear, piercing lungs and heart. Each time she struck the creature let out a shrill wail which was both pathetic and horrifying in its tone.

In the meantime Dorcha, emboldened by their success, chopped at the taniwha's head with her club, trying to split its skull and causing great wounds to its eyes, as it convulsed and moaned under the onslaught of the two warrior women.

Its hideous head gradually sank to the earth, as the stranglehold of the double-noose around its neck tightened further, stemming all oxygen to its body. The spear went in repeatedly, the club struck at kidneys, liver, and other vital organs, until with a final forlorn sigh Hotu-puku delivered itself up unto death and was rolled sideways to hang there by the springiness of the tree to which its foreleg was attached.

The women let fall their weapons and hugged each other. Both were pouring sweat and showed signs of their ordeal in their lank hair and limp muscles. When they were able to, they let go of one another and went to a nearby pool to bathe away their grime, to help relax, and to wash the monster's phlegm and spittle from their skin and clothes. Their own blood besmirched their garments too, where they had scratched and cut themselves in the mêlée. They went back to survey their kill.

'What do you see?' asked Kikamana of the Scot.

'A snake,' answered Dorcha, shuddering. 'What do you see?'

'A giant lizard, bristling with poisonous spikes. A scaly monster of a thing. I wonder what Seumas saw that terrified him so much? He must have run all the way back to the village, judging by the speed at which he left.'

Dorcha shook her head. 'He'll be so ashamed, I know he will. Poor Seumas. He'll never live it down.'

'There's no shame attached to it. Either one of us might have turned and run too. I'm sure I would have done, in the beginning, except I was frozen to the spot. Had we enough sense, we would have done exactly the same. There's only a split second between so-called cowardice and bravery. His survival instinct is obviously stronger than mine, that's all. He should be proud of that fact.'

Dorcha said with a sigh, 'He won't see it that way – he'll curse himself for being afraid, he'll hate himself for leaving us to do what he will see as his work, he'll despise himself for running when women stood and fought. It'll be a long time before he stops loathing himself for this act.'

Returning to more practical matters, Kikamana said, 'I think we ought to disembowel the monster, to make sure of its death. We don't want it resurrecting itself once we leave it. Magical monsters have a habit of reviving and returning to avenge their own deaths.'

So the two women set to work once more. They began by sawing open the belly with the shark-toothed club, spilling out the liver and lights, scattering them amongst the forest ferns. They removed the heart and burned it on a fire and broke open the skull with rocks to drain it of brains. Finally they came to the stomach, opening it with knives of obsidian and sharp mussel shells. They cut through the layers of fat and through the folds of muscle, until they had opened the sac, to reveal a horrible and disgusting sight.

Whole bodies of men, women and children fell out, some severed in the middle, some without arms or legs. There were also piles of greenstone weapons, hardwood clubs and lei-o-mano. A great variety of body ornaments were clustered in heaps, from shell brooches to wooden amulets to necklaces of bones and teeth. There were garments and cloaks of every kind, including flax war-cloaks woven with dogs' tails and embroidered with parrots' feathers, so thick they were impervious to the strong juices of the beast's stomach. There were cloaks of white dogskin with fine borders and others of rich red kula feathers. Piles of old bones, steaming with enzymes, dropped to the ground.

All these the women gathered in a great mound, to collect later when they returned with more people.

It was a treasure trove, but more importantly, amongst the fresh victims were the ancient bones of distant ancestors, which Kikamana assembled in a cloak ready for use against the Ponaturi. There were legbones and armbones which could be used as drumsticks to beat on old skulls.

'That's enough then,' said Kikamana. 'We must make our way back to the village.'

They cut out the taniwha's tongue to carry with them as proof of its death.

On the path back to the village they met Seumas cowering behind a rock.

'What happened?' he cried, hugging Dorcha to his breast, clearly in a state of shock. 'I thought you were both dead.'

She was both pleased and touched that the first thing he thought to do was take hold of her, glad that she was safe, and did not immediately whine about his own cowardice.

'We destroyed the monster,' she said. 'It went exactly as you planned it. You should congratulate yourself for a brilliant scheme which worked. Otherwise I think we should all be dead,' she added generously.

'No,' he said, hanging his head, 'the credit all goes to you – to both of you. I turned and ran, coward that I am, but it was impossible for me to stand. I could not. What I saw was invincible – the thing which terrifies me most in the whole world. I still could not have fought it, even were it to happen again right here on this very turf. I would still turn and run, I'm ashamed to say. But there, it's done, and I must live with my shame.'

Kikamana said, 'I blame no man for being quick enough to preserve himself in the face of his worst nightmare. You must know that it is no shame for an Oceanian warrior to turn and run at any point in the battle? It is accepted that a good warrior is fleet of foot too. He is expected to be ferocious when he stands and fights, but is applauded if when he flees he outruns the enemy chasing him. That is our way.'

'But it isn't the Albannach way. A man who flees the field is a coward and deserves death. I have dishonoured my name.'

'You'll get over it,' said Dorcha, grimly. 'I want no man of mine pining for his honour so much it puts him into the grave. That's a weakling for you – not a man who runs – but a man who can't face up to his failures. Yes, you damn well failed, you running Pict, but you'll have to live with it. I'll only think the more of you, if you do. It's love's way.'

He hugged her neck with his arm, a tall man gripping a short woman, one strong in body, the other in spirit – but both strong in mind. He wanted to argue with her, tell her he should by rights go and hang himself from the nearest tree, that this was the only honourable way out for a real man, but he knew she was right, that it was harder to stand and fight with his own inadequacies.

'All right, woman, I won't mention it again, so long as you don't. If you bring it up in some argument in the future, I swear I'll kill one of us, you hear.'

'Agreed,' she said, and smiled. He was her man, strong in spirit too. Not as strong as her, but close. 'Now let's get down to the village and tell them we've killed the monster. We've got the bones we need too, to fight the sea-fairies. It's been a successful day.'

As they made their way along the path, the women asked him what he had seen, when the taniwha emerged from the cave.

'You'll *never* know,' he said to Kikamana, 'but I may tell Dorcha later, when I feel more myself.'

And they had to be satisfied with that, staring at the man's muscled back, as he strode ahead of them, eager to be done with this place where his weakness had overwhelmed him.

2

While *The Princely Flower* was at rest within the reef, Tawhaki plotted his next move against the expedition, calling on his old friend Tawhiri-Matea the Storm-God, the smiter of trees, the lasher of waves. Tawhiri-Matea had little respect for mortals and though he was aware that Io would be angry with him for assisting Tawhaki, the Storm-God was thirsty for human lives.

'You must wait for the canoe to leave the waters of the enchanted island,' said Tawhaki, 'then strike.'

'It shall be as you say, Thunder-God,' replied the brutal god of storms. 'I taste death on my teeth.'

While the party of six were on shore some of those left behind on the pahi were becoming impatient. Titopika spoke to Polahiki, saying that he feared something had happened to Ru, Kikamana, Seumas and the others, and that they should go and search for them, to see if they needed help.

Polahiki scratched his sores, picked at his scabs, and replied, 'You sure we should? We've been told to stay here.'

'That was not an order to be taken literally. After all, if something *has* happened to the shore party, we can't just sail away and leave them here, can we? They might still be alive, trapped in some cave, or locked up in cages. Who can tell what dangers there are on that island. I say we take some men and go over there to look for them.'

'All right,' said the fisherman, licking his salt-encrusted lips. 'I could do with a drink of cool fresh water. Let's go and speak with Kieto.'

Titopika shook his head. 'Leave Kieto out of this – he's not as flexible as we are. He's rigid enough to follow Ru's orders to the letter. We'll just take a canoe and go and look for them ourselves. What do you say?'

Polahiki was not stupid and soon realised that Titopika had his own reasons for wanting to do this thing, but on the other hand the fisherman had no love for anyone on board the pahi, he was desperately thirsty for some good clean water and he had a naturally belligerent and rebellious nature, which of course was why Titopika had chosen to persuade him.

'All right,' he said, 'but I'm not paddling all that way in a dugout. It's too much like hard work. You get one more man and I'll come with you.'

Titopika went off and found a cousin of Ru, a man of twenty years named Kiaru, who was jealous of the fame of his older relation. The thought of disobeying Ru's orders both scared and excited Kiaru, who wanted his own name to be as revered as that of his noble cousin. Titopika tempted the young man with visions of him as the saviour of the expedition.

'We should take the initiative then?' said Kiaru. 'After all, orders are for the guidance of wise men and for fools to follow to the letter.'

'We need to weigh up the circumstances of the situation and act accordingly,' confirmed Titopika. 'It seems to me that Ru and the other five have been gone far too long. If they're not in any danger, why aren't they on their way back to us? We would see their dugout on the lagoon.'

The young man Kiaru stared at the dull grey waters of the lagoon, empty of any craft.

'Let us go now,' he said to Titopika, 'while Kieto is at rest in the deck hut.'

The three men armed themselves, two in order to protect themselves should they meet with hostile forces, the third with more sinister intentions.

Titopika hoped to be able to find Prince Ru on his own once they were on the island. The six already there would be gathering stores – sweet potatoes and breadfruit mainly – and Titopika meant to sneak up on Ru. If and when he did, Titopika was going to kill the prince, quietly and efficiently. Ragnu had said this would not be possible on the pahi during a voyage, with so many people in so small a space, but out there on an island it was a very workable plan. The undergrowth in the rainforest was often thick enough to hide men from one another's sight, even though they were but a few paces apart.

Ragnu's long-term plan for the destruction of the expedition was proceeding gradually, according to that priest's intricate and devious scheme, but it was a slow process and this was a much quicker way of bringing the voyage to an end. With their navigator prince gone one of the several brothers of Ru would take over command. Ru's brothers had no love for the Rarotongans and could be persuaded to put them ashore somewhere, on a deserted island, where they would rot and die. Ragnu would be delighted by such an end for his enemies – and of course the pahi would be there to carry Titopika to the new island, where he could one day become a great kahuna like Ragnu.

The dugout slid away from the pahi before the warning could be given and they were halfway across the lagoon when the shout came from an enraged Kieto.

'Come back,' cried Kieto. 'What are you playing at?'

But the three men knew Kieto could not follow, since there were only two dugouts on the pahi, and both were now in use.

Kiaru looked anxiously back at the ocean-going canoe.

'Don't worry,' soothed Titopika, 'he'll thank you when you rescue your cousin and bring him back safe and well.'

Polahiki sniffed and lay back in the canoe as if he were on a leisurely boating trip to visit an aunt.

'Personally, I couldn't care less whether Kieto snaps a gut and goes spinning off in space.' He picked his nose and spat to emphasise his carelessness. 'Just keep paddling, boy, don't worry about nits like *him*.'

But Kiaru was still a little worried. 'Kieto has a great deal of mana. He sailed with the great Kupe to the Land-of-Mists when he was but seven years of age. He is not a man to be dismissed lightly.'

'Yes, his mana is strong, but we are doing the right thing,' said Titopika, thinking he would have to sacrifice this finicky youth once the main job had been done. The young man's disposition was too particular. 'Kieto is too much the seafarer to understand what dangers lurk on the land.'

Kiaru had to be satisfied with this explanation and paddled harder to reach the shore, while the other two discussed which way they would go once they reached the beach.

They landed on the dingy sands and took the path into the rainforest. Soon the three men met with a fork. They argued as to which way they should take and Titopika won. The party struck off left, away from the density of the jungle.

Despite the fact that they had taken the easier path it was humid and unpleasant under the rainforest canopy and storm flies stuck to the sweat on their skin. The dank smells of areas always in shadow assailed their nostrils and in one place there was a danger of quicksand, when Kiaru sank to his thighs and had to be extracted by the other two.

'Where are we going?' grumbled Polahiki. 'We don't seem to be getting anywhere.'

'Listen,' said Titopika, 'I hear running water!'

They carried on, following the narrow path, until they reached a stream just at the point where the foliage met the beach.

'We've come to an inlet,' Kiaru said. 'It cuts deeply into the island. We'll need a canoe to cross this.'

Titopika was now beginning to realise he had chosen the wrong track and that they should have taken the *right* path at the point where it forked.

'Let's drink and then turn back,' he said. 'We haven't come too far in the wrong direction.'

All three fell to their knees to slake their thirst on the crystal waters which tumbled down from the hilly interior. As they refreshed themselves they heard twittering noises, as if people were imitating birds, coming from the beach hidden behind the water-edge shrubs and plants. It was almost a musical sound, yet at the same time irritating. Titopika went down on his stomach and wormed his way through the shrubbery to see what kind of creature would make such peculiar chatter.

The sight which met his eyes was truly wondrous and made him gasp in astonishment.

Landing on the beach from the clouds were a dozen winged women, fairies from regions in the sky, all of them naked and beautiful, with pearl-coloured skins and silvery hair. They were uniformly two-thirds as tall as Titopika, a man of average height, and their limbs were slender and pretty. The hair which fell from their heads was long and straight, dropping to their ankles, and it shone like the waters of a lake caught in the bright sunlight. Their eyes were magenta and as cruel and deep as an ocean trench. Heart-shaped faces, with small sweet mouths, perfectly shaped noses and tiny abalone ears, captivated the watching Titopika, as the fairies clustered around the pool formed by the stream as it flowed onto the beach.

Even as he watched the entrancing creatures, Titopika sensed a ruthlessness about these beings, who he was sure would think nothing of taking a man's life. There was about them an air of strangeness beyond their mere physical forms, an alienness as far from a mortal as the moon was from the earth. It made him shiver with apprehension.

By this time the other two had crawled to where he was lying and they two were staring open-mouthed at the fairies whose figures no mortal eye should ever behold.

'Look – look what they're doing,' whispered the enthralled Kiaru.

As the three men stared the women removed their white wings and these they left above the high-tide mark, amongst the shards of broken shells tossed up by the ocean, before plunging joyously into the pool to wash themselves and play in the cool water. Their games were sexual yet at the same time innocent, and all three men felt red-hot knives of lust burning in their loins. These women were incredibly desirable and at that moment Titopika would have gladly passed over a kingdom for just one hour lying with the fairies on the warm sands of the bay.

'Quickly,' he whispered to the others, 'here's our chance to destroy Ru. If we can steal those wings the fairies will do anything to get them back. I shall take as my price for the return of the wings, the death of Prince Ru.'

'No!' said Kiaru, sharply. 'I did not come to harm Ru – I came to rescue him.'

'Fool,' hissed Titopika, 'do you want to be a king or a prince's doormat for the rest of your life? Don't you realise the power these fairies can give us? We can become legends – think about it! This is a chance that comes along once in a thousand years. We can be masters of the world!'

Kiaru wriggled with uncertainty in the sand. The idea of being so powerful that no one could touch him was stunning. He was afraid of what Ru might do to him, if he went against his brother, but as Titopika had inferred the three of them would wield so much puissance Ru would not be able to do anything. Kiaru would be in a position to crush all his enemies, stand tall and proud amongst his kin, and rule with bamboo rod.

The vision was all too tempting and he crawled forward to where he could reach for the wings, pulling them gently one by one into the shrubs and passing them back to Titopika and Polahiki.

The two older men worked with quickened breath, well aware of the horrible fate they would suffer were they detected in the act. Their lives would not be worth a pinch of sand. They gathered the soft white wings into three piles. When all were safely in their keeping, they took one bundle each and ran into the rainforest, to hide them under a bush. They covered the fairies' wings with fresh grasses, to camouflage them in case the now wingless women were to search the forest.

As the men returned to the beach, they heard a high piercing wail which threatened to split their eardrums.

'Oh – oh – oh,' cried Polahiki, his spirit shattering under the shrillness of that cry. 'They're coming for us!'

With that the fisherman ran off, back along the track down which they had come, eager to escape the wrath of the sky-fairies with wicked eyes that held promises of torture beyond that which any normal man can suffer, let alone a Hivan coward.

'What shall we do?' whispered Kiaru, who had gone as pale and grey as dead coral.

'You go back and protect the wings,' ordered Titopika. 'I'll speak with the fairies.'

Kiaru did as he was bid, trotting back to the hiding place, glad to let the tohunga deal with the delicate but vicious women against whom the men had committed a terrible sin. Such creatures would tear off a man's genitals with their slim pretty fingers, or suck out his eyes with their sweet lips, or blow into his mouth with their perfect noses until his chest exploded. The word *compassion* was not in their vocabulary.

With his heart pounding Titopika stepped out onto the beach to find the fairy women tugging on their breasts and wrenching at their long hair. Some were screeching in torment as they sought their lost property along the high-tide mark, while others clawed at the sand, digging holes at random, believing their precious wings might have been buried by envious crabs. Any live creatures which were unfortunate enough to be in their way, they crushed or stamped into the ground. The barbarism of their actions drove fear into Titopika and he almost turned and ran away like Polahiki, but managed to fight his panic into a small corner of his mind and there control it.

'Stop,' he cried to the fairies. 'I know where your wings are – they shall be returned to you.'

One creature with little pointed teeth came running up to him, screaming, 'Where? Where? Where?'

'They were taken by the birds,' lied the tohunga, 'and hidden in the bushes. I – I shall need payment for my services – payment in kind. If you agree, I'll lead you to the wings immediately.'

'Payment? What payment?' chorused the women. 'You wish to enjoy our bodies? You wish to make us love you?'

'No, no – that is, the thought is as delightful as you are all beautiful – but I have a more urgent need. There is a prince somewhere on this island, a noble from Raiatea. I want you to tear him to pieces and throw him to the sharks. If you do this, I'll tell you where your wings are hidden …'

At that moment a shadow passed over Titopika: that of a great bird. The tohunga looked up and so did the fairies. The man let out a gasp of astonishment as he recognised Kiaru, who had attached a pair of white-feathered wings to his back and was now flying over the lagoon.

'Kiaru!' shouted Titopika.

Kiaru was not only flying away from the island, but he carried the other sets of wings under his arms.

'Come back,' yelled Titopika. 'Where are you going?'

'I'm flying home,' came back the reply on the wind. 'I shall be famous …'

Titopika watched the young man sweep low over the waves. He did not seem to be able to get any height. Then he reached the outer reef. As he passed over the wide lip of coral, the ocean's waves crashed against it sending up spume and salt spray, which drenched him. Suddenly, his wings seemed to peel away from his body, and drifted downwards like falling leaves. Kiaru fell with them, hitting the surface with a splash. He could not hold on to the other sets of wings and they floated away from him on the surface of the sea.

On seeing Kiaru fall the fairies let out shrill cries and dived into the lagoon to swim out to fetch their precious wings.

While this was happening, Kiaru seemed to be striving in the rollers, thrashing and flailing with his arms. Titopika knew him to be a good swimmer and could not understand the reason for the youth's struggle. Did he have the cramps? Was a shark attacking him? Then Titopika noticed thick white stems, like headless flowers, growing around the young man. What was that? Surely not? But, yes, they were tiny arms, reaching up out of the water to grip Kiaru around the waist and head. The distant cousin of Prince Ru was then pulled down, to some awful fate below the waves, and never surfaced again.

'Ponaturi!' cried Titopika, shuddering. 'The sea-fairies have taken him.'

In the meantime the sky-fairies had reached their wings and were attaching them to their shoulders.

Titopika made off quickly, into the forest, aware that Kiaru was being torn to pieces somewhere on the ocean bed.

He ran all the way back to where the path forked: ran almost into the face of Ru.

'What are you doing here?' demanded Ru. 'I ordered all passengers to remain on the pahi.'

'It's your cousin, Kiaru,' gasped Titopika, pointing back along the path. 'He's been taken by fairies.' The tohunga then realised he had better not tell Ru the whole truth. 'Some sky-fairies came and took him away, up into the clouds. Others were after Polahiki and myself, but we split up and escaped. At least, I *think* the fisherman escaped.'

'My cousin, Kiaru?'

'Gone,' cried Titopika. 'I tried to save him but they wrenched him from my arms. They were savage creatures with terrible claws. I did my best, but I couldn't keep them from him. There were too many. Ask Polahiki.'

Prince Ru's expression was uncompromising. 'You disobeyed my order to remain on the craft. This is what happens when discipline breaks down. You shall be punished.'

Titopika's back straightened and his voice took on a harder note. 'No one punishes me – not even a prince. I did what I did for the common good. You were gone too long. We thought you had been attacked and were captured – or dead. Were we supposed to wait for ever? I think not. We are not children without initiative, or a will of our own.'

Ru conceded that the shore party had been longer than anticipated.

'Yet you should have obeyed my orders. I left Kieto in charge. Why did he not organise you?'

'Kieto was asleep. I did not wake him because it was unnecessary. I am quite capable of organising a rescue party without the help of a Raiatean.'

'Yet you lost my cousin.'

Titopika thought it prudent to hang his head for a moment, then he looked the prince in the eyes again.

'True, and if I could undo that part, I would, but this is a dangerous island. One can't prepare for every eventuality.

'Accidents will occur on voyages such as ours. Lives will be lost. We will be lucky indeed if Kiaru is the last person to forfeit his life to our great adventure.'

Ru nodded, thoughtfully. 'I shall be lenient,' he said, 'but if you disobey my orders again, I shall have you flogged and dragged behind the pahi in shark-infested waters. Is there anything of my cousin to recover?'

'Nothing – he was torn to pieces in the air and the remnants cast down into the sea.'

'Then let us be done with this island now.'

Titopika allowed Prince Ru to pass him, carrying sweet potatoes in a tapa cloth sack. Not for the first time did Titopika regret he was not an expert in the art of makutu, or 'killing by thought' which had been the gift of very few Oceanian priests in the long august history of the ocean islands.

Other members of the shore party went by, each carrying fruit, drinking coconuts or breadfruit. Finally, Seumas brought up the rear with another sack, this one bulging with sharper objects.

'Bones,' grunted the Pict, as he passed the tohunga. 'Bones of ancient warriors taken from the stomach of a monster.'

'A monster?' whispered Titopika.

'A taniwha, killed by Dorcha and Kikamana.'

'And you?'

Seumas scowled and said sourly. 'I had little to do with it.'

There's a story there, thought Titopika, allowing Seumas to pass and tagging on the end of the single file. And as for the mighty Prince Ru, second son of a second son. He shall be lenient, shall he? How gracious he is in his mercy. How free with his compassion. I would like to give him a second mouth, with which to dispense his generosity to us lowly minions, a mouth below that which he already owns. I would like to slit his throat and watch him bubble out his lofty proclamations through blisters of blood. Indeed, I am quickly arriving at the conclusion that it might come to that shortly.

At that moment, a face leered at the tohunga from within the rotten recesses of a hollow tree. There was a creature there. It had long knotted arms and legs with which it pressed the sides of the wooden chimney, to hold itself halfway up inside the twisted bole. Its complexion was green, its features hideously ugly, and the consistency of fungi.

An enormous phallus and pendulous scrotum swung between its spread legs. A tongue came out, as long as a man's arm, to rasp in the face of the startled tohunga. Then it licked, stripping off a piece of Titopika's facial skin with its sandstone-rough texture. Rheumy eyes stared triumphantly as Titopika whined, then stumbled, badly shaken by the experience.

'A lipsipsip,' croaked Titopika, wondering why the gods were not happy with him today.

'What?' asked Seumas, turning to face him. 'Did you say something.'

'Tree-dwarves. I saw a tree-dwarf.'

'Well, don't shout it out, or everyone will want one,' joked the Pict.

Titopika was in no mood for such jests and might have struck Seumas had not the lipsipsip let out a monstrous fart that echoed in his hollow trunk and once again startled the priest.

'This is an evil place,' muttered Titopika, heaving because of the stench, 'and I shall be glad to be out of it.'

When they reached the shoreline they found only one dugout. Polahiki had taken the other one to get back to the pahi. They managed to cram in this small canoe however, since no one was willing to remain behind to wait for a second trip. When they reached the pahi they found Polahiki there.

'Took your time,' said the fisherman, standing by the pandanus hut, eating mashed breadfruit out of a banana leaf with his fingers. 'I've been back ages.'

'You deserted me,' growled Titopika.

'You mean, when you led us into that den of fairies? Too right, I did,' snorted the fisherman. 'And you watch your tone – there are too many secrets on this canoe to start using accusing tones with people.'

'What secrets?' asked Ru, suspiciously.

'That's for me to know and you to find out.'

'Don't tempt me,' said the prince. 'I haven't burned the soles of someone's feet for a long time.'

Polahiki looked put out by this and went to another part of the pahi, to lie under the umbrella of a lo lop palm leaf. Titopika decided to let the whole thing drop. The fisherman was right. If he, Titopika, started taking Polahiki to task, revelations might follow, and things would be none too comfortable for the tohunga. Better to leave things as they were and continue with the long-term plan, which *was* making progress, if a little slowly.

Ru was now making an inventory of their stores. They had only one dog left which had recently been on heat and had been made pregnant by Dirk, who was called a 'libertine and profligate' in Gaelic by Dorcha as a result. It seemed sensible to keep this animal until they reached their destination island, in order to breed her puppies. There were three pigs, which would be used as sacrifices as well as for food. Also, there were over three dozen chickens, which provided eggs and some meat for the basket.

The vegetable larder had now been restocked with pandanus fruit, green bananas, yam, taro pudding and sweet potatoes. Ru had been given turtle eggs and turtle meat by the villagers, as a gift for the people who had slain the taniwha. From the old stores they still had plenty of hard poi, dried breadfruit, dried bananas, sugarcane, arrowroot flour, nyali nuts and coconuts in various stages. There was also plenty of dried skipjack and akule reef fish.

As for fresh fish, Polahiki and one or two others would provide. Unfortunately, they had no shark-callers on board, like the great Aputua who had sailed with Prince Tangiia, but the number of people on board was not great, and the odd hammerhead or grey shark was caught without the need of callers. Turtle kebabs would fill any menu that was short of fish or meat, and there was always jellyfish, cuttlefish and other surface sealife to gather in the trailing nets as they went.

'We must now make a sacrifice to the Great Sea-God Tangaroa,' ordered Ru, 'before we go out to battle the sea-fairies.'

Every member on board the pahi took part in the prayers, worship of the gods being a group activity. Afterwards, individuals went to various parts of the pahi to pray to their own ancestor spirits for victory and a safe voyage.

One or two called on the demi-gods, such as Maui, or his sister Hine-uri (the dark form of the moon), though not the two together for Maui's sister had been angry with her brother since the time Maui had changed her husband Irawaru into a dog, for eating the bait which Maui wanted for his fishing hook.

Ru ordered his virgin crew to raise the sails of the pahi, one on either mast. The pandanus mats filled with wind. Then Ru put on his cloak of feathers, and his feathered helmet, took up a patu club in one hand and a spear in the other.

Others armed themselves, all except Kikamana the kahuna, Titopika the tohunga, and Dorcha with her occult powers: these three held the bones found in the belly of the taniwha and would beat them together while chanting karakia. The three magicians had surrounded themselves with Ti'i to protect them from the sea-fairies while the battle raged around them and also to assist them in their spells.

Seumas had a wahaika club which he would wield double-handed, while Dirk guarded his back.

'Let go the anchor!' cried Ru.

This done the vessel lurched forward, skimming over the slick grey waters of the enchanted lagoon and out into the open sea.

Immediately the pahi had crossed over the reef the sea began to boil with silver-grey bodies as the Ponaturi rose up in their hordes to attack *The Princely Flower*.

PART FOUR

People of the darkness

1

By the time the Arioi fleet arrived in Tonga, having been to Fiji and Samoa, Kumiki was a Hua, an Arioi of the fourth class. On his shoulders he proudly displayed the tattooed figures which denoted his rank. His friend, Ramoro, was also a Hua, and thus Kumiki had caught him up and intended to pass him by and become at least an Otiore, a second-class Arioi. Since Ramoro was not an ambitious man, this feverish ride to the top was not a hindrance to their friendship.

'You have done wonders, my friend, especially for a Hivan,' said Ramoro. 'Especially for a man with dark-red hair and a pale skin.' He was not speaking out of bitterness, but was genuinely happy for his comrade.

The truth was the Arioi was essentially Tahitian and ninety-five per cent of its players were from the Tahitian island group. Men and women from other island groups were permitted to join, but they were regarded as slightly inferior to the Tahitians, whose culture was full of colour and light, wonderful ceremonies, and the splendour and opulence of a wealthy, divine kingship.

Only such islands as Tahiti or Hawaii, with their love of display and their reverence of dancing, acting and games, could have produced the Arioi. The Tongans were pirates and sea raiders, the Samoans were too starchy and conservative and the Fijians were too fond of fighting to find time to develop such a marvellous troupe. Other island groups were either too remote, or too small, or just too busy living ordinary lives.

Indeed, Kumiki's home, the Hivan islands, had a smaller, looser circle of travelling players than the Arioi, called the Hoki, a wandering set of musicians, poets and dancers. But whereas the Arioi were a revered semi-religious group said to be of divine origin, the Hoki were despised by their own warrior nation as being effete and effeminate.

Hawaii could have produced an Arioi Society, but those islands were far off and though seafarers had touched their shores, all that came back were stories of wonderful courts, glittering ceremonies, and wild wars. The Hawaiians loved gambling too. They were a bright people: creative. Their temples were full of wicker images, marvellously interwoven with thousands of tiny feathers, the hideous mouths of which were doubled-looped, like a figure eight on its side.

So, Kumiki's pride in rising so quickly amongst the ranks of the Tahitian players was evident in his whole demeanour. This did him no harm, for its artistes were expected to be fine strutting characters, different from ordinary people.

The fleet of three hundred ships approached Heketa on the tip of Tonga-tapu. They made sure their yellow sails were in evidence in order to ensure that the fierce Tongans, eaters of men, would not mistake them for an invasion fleet. The singing and dancing, which never really stopped even on a long voyage, increased in fervour and energy.

'I must be at my drums,' said Kumiki to Ramoro. 'You go to your dancing.'

Kumiki had found his niche. After trying almost everything from wrestling to poetry, he had discovered in himself a talent for drumming. He was becoming a superb percussion musician, whose flying sticks were studied in awe by the less able drummers of the Arioi. Whence this natural skill had derived Kumiki had no idea, but his household deity was now Lingadua, the God of Drummers, whose single arm equalled a thousand mortal limbs in its ability to produce frenetic rhythms.

Kumiki knew there was more to drumming than just producing superb rolls, sustained highly imaginative rhythms and inventing new patterns. One had to be a showman too. In this Kumiki excelled, dressing himself dramatically in black tapa cloth, and using athletic movements. His fitness was essential to his act, since he did somersaults, high leaps, and handsprings when leaping from drum to drum. He had an assistant now, a woman named Linloa, who tossed him drumsticks and changed his instruments at crucial times during his act, and indeed made suggestions for enhancing his performance.

Linloa was a Harotea, a third-class dancer in her own right, and she was in love with Kumiki.

As the fleet approached the beach the Tu'i Tonga, the lord of the islands, was waiting in his chair. His mana was great since he was ruler of one of the most feared fleets in the whole of Oceania. The Tongans believed themselves to be superior people, warriors first and last, and even though they owned no large trees (their land being coral reef islands and not heavily forested) they had managed to pillage the wood they needed from neighbouring Fiji to build the fiercest navy on the ocean. They were raiders, and sometimes mercenaries when Samoan or Fijian chiefs needed support, and other island groups fearfully kept watch for the Tongan canoes, hoping never to see them appear in their waters.

The Arioi landed on the beach and the dancers and flautists leapt ashore to entertain the king, while the others were left to unload the equipment and stores.

'You carry the big drum,' ordered Kumiki to Linloa, 'while I get the smaller ones ashore.' Linloa did as she was bid, but when she jumped down into the surf carrying the large drum, a Tongan man rushed forward and tried to take it from her.

'We do not allow women to do the hard work,' he admonished Kumiki. 'Women are delicate creatures to be cherished and protected.'

'Release that drum,' ordered Kumiki, 'it is a valuable instrument. I am not a Tongan, I am a Hivan. This woman is not a Tongan, she is a Tahitian. You will therefore allow us to be the judge of whether she should carry the drum or not.'

The man scowled darkly. 'You may not be Tongans, Redhair, but you are on our soil. You are expected to respect our customs while you are here, or there may be trouble.'

'I respect your customs,' replied Kumiki, leaping down into the surf and striding onto the beach. 'I would not dream of asking one of your women to help me with my drums. This lady is trained in drum-carrying. She is an expert. In her hands what would be a heavy load for a man, is light and easy, for she has the knack of carrying drums. In fact, you could say she is the top drum-carrier in all of Oceania.'

The man's eyes narrowed. He was tall and lean, with supple movements. In his hand he carried a patu club.

'You are making fun of me, Hivan. Be careful. I do not take insults lightly.'

'I should think not. Insults are heavy things to carry. Much heavier than drums. I always ask Linloa to bear my insults. They're far too weighty for me.'

The man's eyes opened wide in anger and he drew back his paddle club to strike Kumiki. However, a shout came from behind him and he stayed his hand. One of the island's nobles had intervened.

'Tuloa, these people are our guests!' cried the noble. The warrior lowered the raised weapon, but stared hard at Kumiki. There was the strong suggestion in that stare which carried a message of a future meeting. Kumiki shrugged and shook his head slowly. Tuloa walked away.

'Funny ideas these people have,' muttered Kumiki to Ramoro and Linloa later, as they sat around a fire in the darkness. 'Where do they get these peculiar notions about women from? Hivan females are almost as strong as the men.'

Ramoro said, 'It is just their way. Who's to argue with them? They are a ferocious people.'

'So are we Hivans,' replied Kumiki, proudly, 'but our women work in the fields, carry water from the streams and do all kinds of heavy tasks. Why should they not? I think the arrogance of these Tongans is hard to bear. Have you ever been treated with such lofty disdain before in your life?'

Linloa poked the fire with a twig. She had eaten on reef fish and coconut and was feeling pleasant. Later Kumiki would make love with her. She felt no resentment towards him for treating her as a servant, but she could also see the Tongan point of view. Why should they not refuse to let their women do heavy manual labour? Every woman here was a princess.

'I don't think they mean any harm,' she said. 'It's just their way – they're a proud people. I – I think the women look very pretty, don't you, Kumiki? They don't have rough hands from digging and their complexions are softer, since they seem to stay out of the sun more.'

'Well, crazy ideas or not, that Tuloa had better keep out of my way, or I'll show him who is the great warrior,' promised Kumiki.

'You Hivans,' remarked the impressed Ramoro. 'You're just as strong-headed as the Tongans.'

The next day the whole troupe was engaged in building the mighty stage, as long as seventy men lying toe to head, on which most of their performances would take place.

Some of the Tongans assisted in building the stage. Both Kumiki and Linloa were engaged in carrying planks, strapping together posts, and fitting joints. While they worked storytellers entertained them, with tales of Pele the Fire-thrusting Goddess of Volcanoes, Maui and his tricks, Tawhaki, Rata, and other gods and demi-gods.

Kumiki and Linloa heard the story of Hutu, the man whose love had died, who went into the Underworld to fetch her back again:

'You know of the Underworld', began the storyteller, 'for it exists under our feet. You will recall the time Maui pulled up one of his house posts and looked down the hole. Maui was amazed to see his ancestors below, carrying on their daily tasks in the life beyond this one.

'So it was then, that Hutu, a young nobleman, but not of very high birth, was playing darts near the house of a puhi, a high-born virgin, whose tapu was so strong there was not a man in the land noble enough to be her husband. The puhi's name was Pare, and she dwelt alone in a beautiful house set aside for her use only and protected by three sets of palisades.

'Pare wanted for nothing material. There were plaited flax mats on the floors of her dwelling, made white by boiling. Its rooms were scented with the fragrance of kopuru moss and karetu grass, and perfume from kawakawa and tarata. Her clothes were wonderful cloaks with black borders and long black thrums, some made from the hair of dogs' tails plaited into the thick strong selvage.

'However, she was a puhi, and it seemed would never marry, and for this reason she was dreadfully unhappy. She saw only high-ranking servants, who gave her food, and the birds of the garden. In this garden she wandered during the day, weeping for the unknown lover she could never meet.

'Now one of the darts thrown by the youth Hutu, who was a handsome and intelligent young man, passed through the gate of Pare's house. He went to the fence and called to whoever was in the garden to return his dart. Pare looked through a crack in the fence and saw the beautiful young man and fell instantly in love with him. She tossed him back his dart and then cried, "I have formed an affection for you. Come into my house."

'Hutu, however, was afraid, for he knew this house belonged to a puhi and he knew the punishment for attempting to consort with a virgin of so high a rank.

'"I cannot," he said "I am a stranger here and must obey the customs of your people."

'So he went away, troubled in heart and mind, and later the tribal elders came for him to execute him, for Pare had died in the night of sorrow, and they blamed Hutu for her death.

'When they took him to see the body Hutu was struck by her amazing beauty, and when he remembered her voice he too was overcome by sorrow.

'"Leave her body here," he said, "for I shall make the journey into the Underworld and retrieve her spirit."

'So saying he chanted a karakia taught him by a tohunga and when he rose he walked down into Te Reinga, the Land of the Dead, where Hine-nui-te-po sits as guardian. On reaching her, Hutu told her his story and the goddess took pity on him and pointed to the path used by the spirits of dogs when they journeyed to the Underworld. Hutu then gave her a mere of greenstone, a jewel which pleased her, and she then allowed him to use the path for the souls of men. She prepared him a basket of Ngaro, in case he became hungry in the Underworld, but Hutu was eager only for the soul of Pare and did not eat.

'When Hutu reached the Land of the Dead he asked for Pare and was shown to a village. Pare was still upset with Hutu though and even now he had come to fetch her from the Underworld, she would not come out to see him. So Hutu organised some games amongst his ancestors, who delighted in the sports they had left behind them in the real world. While Hutu was throwing darts, he let one fly purposely through the doorway of Pare's house where it stuck to the wall. She laughed on seeing his dart again and came out to meet him. They hugged and rubbed noses and professed their love for one another.

'Soon it was time for Hutu and Pare to return to the real world, but the path back to life was so complicated and tangled that it was impossible to retrace one's journey. Hutu however had an idea. He asked his ancestors to bend down the tallest palm tree near the village and tie it with ropes. When they had done this he took Pare on his shoulders, climbed into the bushy head of the coconut palm and ordered the severing of the rope. Hutu and Pare were catapulted towards the roof of the Underworld, where Hutu gripped the turf and roots of this world and finally hauled himself and his new bride into the light.

'When Hutu returned with Pare the people said he was a great man, of considerable mana, and allowed the couple to live together as husband and wife.

'And that is the story of Hutu and Pare.'

*

The platform was completed in a day and that evening the performances began. Tongans from all over the islands came in their canoes to witness the dancing, the wrestling, the tumbling, and to listen to the poets, the musicians, the songs. Once again Kumiki astounded the audience with his phenomenal skill on the drums, leaping from small drum to large drum, from log drum to skin drum, pounding out natural and artificial rhythms. Even the Tu'i Tonga was impressed and asked to meet this young man with the pale skin and dark red hair. Kumiki went before the Tu'i Tonga, careful to keep his head lower than the king's, staying at a safe distance from the king's mana.

'You are my special guest here,' said the Tu'i Tonga. 'You may have what you wish – food, female company, any present you choose for yourself, it shall be yours.'

'Thank you, my lord,' said Kumiki, his heart full.

Of course there were several other 'special guests' of the Tu'i Tonga, who had pleased the king with their performances, but none so gratified as Kumiki. That night he slept with a local girl who giggled and kept him awake, while unknown to him Linloa spent a miserable night lying alone.

Tuloa the Tongan who had formed an enmity for Kumiki cursed his luck, for he could no longer kill Kumiki with a group of his friends as he had planned earlier, without falling foul of his king. A special guest was protected by the king's decree and if anything untoward happened to Kumiki while he was in Tonga, those responsible would answer to the king's personal guard.

'If I ever see him again,' snarled the thwarted Tuloa, 'I swear I shall cut out his liver.'

His ancestors sympathised deeply, but what could they do?

The sea-fairies came in silvery-skinned hordes, attempting to swamp *The Princely Flower* with their vile bodies, but the crew and passengers beat them back with clubs, and chopped off their gripping fingers with sharp shells, while Boy-girl, Kikamana, Dorcha and Titopika sat one on each corner of the pahi and clashed the bones together and chanted karakia.

During the battle three of *The Princely Flower's* passengers were dragged overboard. They died screaming in the mass of fairy bodies, torn apart before the eyes of the rest of the mortals. The Ponaturi were merciless once they had you in their strong hands. They stripped the flesh from your bones quicker than barracuda and left the sea stained red with clouds of blood. They pulled arms from sockets, legs from joints, opened the abdomen with their sharp talons, devoured the pieces even as they fought for more human bodies to rip and tear. One creature was chewing on the flap of a dead man's cheek when Seumas severed its head from its body with his kotiate club.

As the fairy's head floated away on a pool of ambergris its jaws continued to masticate mechanically, out of habit.

The canoe ploughed through the water, helped by Maomao's wind, and gradually the Ponaturi began to fall back. The deck was littered with their finger-claws, their crushed skulls floated on the waves of the sea. Their sundered limbs and fingers wriggled like silver fish, attempting to re-join their bodies.

One or two fairies kept their grip on the craft. They gnashed their teeth, and thrashed their clawed limbs, but to no avail; *The Princely Flower* was soon surging forward over the surface of the ocean, out into sweeter waters. A few more hacks from clubs and adzes and the last Ponaturi slipped away.

'Well done, my comrades,' cried Ru. 'We have escaped the clutches of those horrible creatures. Now we must set sail for Rarotongan waters again.'

Even as he spoke the wind picked up in strength, but it was not a wind of Maomao's making, it was a false wind created by Tawhiri-Matea. The Storm-God had brought with him two of his brothers, Apu Hau, God of the Fierce Squall, and Apu Mantangi, God of the Howling Rain. They began to lash the pahi canoe furiously, creating a chaos of white and dark. Forest-high waves rose around the canoe, which was suddenly very small in the midst of the fury generated by the three gods.

The twenty virgins, strong and able, worked at the rigging and the sails. Seumas and the other passengers crowded into the deck hut, keeping out of the way of the busy maidens. Ru stood by the mast, directing his crew, sometimes managing the steering oar himself, at other times lending a hand with a slack or wayward sheet. The women worked tirelessly, their purity assisting their stamina, magnificent in their efforts.

Divested of their garments, which tended to get tangled in ropes and other equipment, the rain whipped at the skins of the naked maidens, ran in rivulets down their backs and breasts, streamed from their brows, soaked their long hair which plastered itself to their shapely forms. If the situation had not been so precarious, Seumas might have been lost in sexual fantasies, as he watched these beautiful nude females plying their sailing skills. Instead he was appalled by the severity of the storm, and was simply glad they were mariners whose mastery of their trade was keeping the pahi from plunging into the ocean depths.

Lightning flashed – Uira darting from the armpits of a watching Tawhaki – illuminating the turbulent darkness. Lithe bodies gleamed in the brilliance. Then the thunder crashed, punching the belly of the sky, robbing Rangi of wind for a moment. Colours patterned the leaping waters, running like live creatures over the dark hills of the sea. Hollows appeared in front of the pahi as the ocean sucked in its stomach.

Try as they might though, the storm brothers could not sink the pahi with its proficient crew, and gradually they tired. First Apu Hau, God of the Fierce Squall, began to flag, he being the one who expended the most energy in the shortest time. He left to go and sleep. Then Apu Mantangi, God of the Howling Rain, ceased his screaming. Finally, the leveller of forests, the lasher of waves, Tawhiri-Matea, could no longer find the strength to stir the ocean, and he too sought a haven of rest. Tawhaki had to be satisfied with the thought that *The Princely Flower* had been flung even further into unknown waters, and that Captain Ru would be well and truly lost.

The first thing Ru did was thank his crew for their expert seamanship. Then he offered prayers of thanks to Tiki, for his part in seeing them through the storm. Finally the whole pahi offered prayers to Tangaroa, who had not swallowed them despite the opportunity, but was still their patron.

Ru did his best to find the right stars that night, but the kaveinga were unknown to him. He sought any local te lapa beneath the waves without success. The shape of the waves, the direction of the swell, meant nothing to him. They had gone well off the edge of Dorcha's bamboo and shell chart, so this was of no use to them. Even the fixed stars, the fanakenga, were in strange positions and of little assistance to him in his navigating. The constellations were little help – Ru found Ara Toru, the Path of Three, and Te Rua Tangata, the Double Man, but they were on the edge of the sky and not in a familiar position.

The morning brought a little more success. Po'oi had inherited his father's skill, that of the Feelers-of-the-sea, and found the waters warmer than deep ocean would suggest. There was a cloud in the distance: the kind of cloud which hangs over a mountain peak. In the briny there was driftwood and in the skies some red-footed boobies. Land was nearby.

'Even though this atoll is in the wrong part of the ocean,' said Ru as they approached the ring of low islands, 'we may settle here if things are as we wish them.'

There were eight long islands in the circle. Around the whole atoll was a ring of coral, making for a massive lagoon in the centre, but each island also had its own reef and its own lagoon facing the ocean. Between the islands there were either tidal sweeps of deep water or a ridge of coral just below some shallow water which could be used as a pathway.

In the middle of the atoll's lagoon was a greater island, making the ninth in the whole group. Thus there were eight elongated islands coming from a central round body. Ru, or some other member of the party, might have guessed what this place was from the mere shape of the landscape.

'This seems like a good place,' said Ru, smelling the fragrance of sandalwood on the breeze. 'A low set of islands, but with some large trees.'

They rode the breakers over the reef, to enter the outer lagoon of the largest outer island, and all seemed well enough. However, as they approached the beach they saw what they first thought were millions of crabs. On closer inspection, these turned out not to be crustaceans, but spiders. The nearer they drew to the strand, the thicker seemed the number of spiders. Every conceivable type of arachnid seemed to live on that shore, from tiny creatures with minuscule spinnerets, to massive weighty lumps with large unsegmented bodies.

'Ugghh.' Dorcha shuddered. 'I can't stand them.'

'Look at them,' said Boy-girl, equally uncomfortable. 'All different kinds. There are some with yellow-and-black legs – big ones – I hate those. And the red bulbous ones. And some with long hair. My cockerel, Lei-o-mano, can have a feast. Millions of them. What is this place?'

Kikamana said, 'This must be the earthly home of Nareau, the Spider-God. See, they're all over the trunks of the trees and there are nests of them in the palm leaves. Look at those webs – thousands of them – hanging between the fronds.'

'I am not stepping ashore here,' said Dorcha in a determined voice. 'I refuse to go amongst those – those creatures.'

Ru ordered the sounding of the tai-moana, the ship's long drum, to scare the spiders from the beach. Indeed, this worked, for when the drum was sounded the spiders scuttled away, into the hinterland, leaving the sands clear. Dorcha still refused to leave the canoe, but Seumas went with the landing party, accompanied by Dirk, who had been kept tied while the vessel had been at anchor off the island of the taniwha. The dog was restless and needed a good run. Dirk was not frightened of spiders, of course, and delighted in chasing some of the bigger ones up the trunks of trees, leaving him to bark at them.

Seumas was secretly pleased that both Kikamana and Dorcha were too frightened to step ashore amongst the spiders. It gave him a chance to prove himself again, retrieve a little of his lost honour and dignity, left behind on the island of the taniwha. He said nothing to the two women, but held his head high, kept his face grave, and stepped ashore without a falter.

The two women and Boy-girl, along with half the crew and passengers, male and female, waded the shallows of the lagoon searching for shellfish while the shore party went on its way. There were no spiders to bother them in the water. There were deadly stone fish, whose poisonous spines could kill within a minute or two, toothed moray eels as thick as a man's thigh and smoky sting rays that hid in the grey coral dust. These they would brave – but not spiders. They gathered the bounty of the ocean: cones, spires, conches, cowries, turbans, combs, razors and other molluscs, risking death in unknown shallows.

Ru stayed with the canoe, to await the shore party's report when they returned. The leader of the shore party was Pungarehu, the man who had killed the Poukai bird on the voyage with Tangiia. He stayed close to Seumas, being an old friend. They fought their way forward with difficulty, through the sometimes thick nets of webs that were spread between trees.

As they neared the centre of the island the spiders became bigger and uglier, until they were the size of small pigs. The arachnids stared with their four pairs of compound eyes, their several jaws working like mechanical devices.

Some would stand their ground, while others rushed away into the under-growth, timid creatures on spindly legs.

They lit torches with a flint, partly because it was dark under the canopy, and partly to keep away the spiders.

They entered a large clearing with soft green light falling on the surface of a still pool.

'Look out,' cried Pungarehu, shouting a warning to Seumas. 'On your left flank!'

Seumas turned to see a giant black spider charging at him like a wild boar, bearing down on him with terrifying speed on its eight bamboo-like legs. Seumas saw the jaws working and salivating, and knew he might lose a limb if he was not quick. The rest of the party including Dirk scattered, running for the trees, unsure of whether or not they would meet equally horrifying spiders inside the woods and rocks.

The Pict stepped to one side and swung his club, bringing the weapon down with great force onto the spider's back. The creature buckled in the middle, as if made of tree bark, and spilled its innards on the mossy floor. Out of its stomach poured thousands of tiny white spiders, which swarmed over Seumas, biting him with the severity of wasp stings. They seemed to be going for his earholes and nostrils, trying to enter his body by his several orifices.

'Ow, ow!' the Pict yelled, slapping at them.

Pungarehu came rushing back out of the trees, carrying a torch of dry grass. He ran it quickly over Seumas's body, not lingering long enough to burn him, but ensuring that the spiders either frizzled or ran. Some became tangled in the Pict's long hair and Pungarehu removed these like someone picking lice from their friend's head. They bit his fingers, making him yell too. Dirk did not come out of hiding until all the white spiders had disappeared.

'A lot of help you were,' yelled Seumas at the dog. 'Get on with you.'

Dirk cowered and slunk ahead, aware that his cowardice was unworthy of him.

They caught up with the rest of the party, who had by now lit more brands. It was the most effective way of removing the cobwebs from their path and keeping the spiders at bay. Compound eyes shone from the darkness of the trees. Millions of them. The spiders watched but kept their distance, secure in the knowledge that this island was their home, a sanctuary of Nareau the Spider-God, the weaver of sticky silken ropes on which he hung mortals like pendulum weights. When Seumas looked up through the canopy, he saw thousands more of the tinier spiders, using threads like kites to carry themselves along on the breeze. They seemed to be heading towards the anchored canoe.

'I hope those women don't take over the ship and run,' he muttered to Pungarehu. 'I wouldn't want to be stranded on *this* place for very long.'

Finally the group reached a central clearing in the island where they were surprised to see a long hut raised on stilts, as long as a hundred men laid toe to head, and very wide. It was made of the trunks of trees plugged along the gaps with mud. There were no windows and no visible doors. The roof was thatched more sturdily than usual. It looked for all the world as if this were a solid structure, with no entrances.

'What do you think it is?' asked Seumas. 'A store house of some kind?'

'That's what it looks like,' remarked one of the crew, a tall woman carrying a spear. 'But I've never seen a store house that size before. Either this place has a large population hidden away somewhere ...'

'Or it's a land of giants,' muttered Pungarehu, looking around him nervously.

They went forward to inspect the hut and found some tightly fitting trap doors underneath. There were no handles however, with which to open these doors, as one might expect. Moreover, there were steps leading down from them, as if this was a place to enter and leave, rather than allow dried food-stuffs to spill out into sacks or some other kind of container.

Carvings adorned the exterior of the long house, of moons, stars, comets and meteors. There was the figure of Hine-nui-to-po, Lady of Darkness, on one end of the hut and Hine-uri, the goddess of the dark phase of the moon, on the other end. Black dye covered the whole building, even underneath. The space beneath the hut was hidden by dark flaps of cloth pinned to the edges of the floor.

'This is very puzzling,' remarked Pungarehu.

Darkness had begun to sweep in swiftly, as it does in tropical regions, where the sun drops down behind the wall of the ocean like a hawk stooping for its prey. Soon the torches were needed for something other than keeping spiders at bay. No sooner had the light disappeared, than the trap doors began to open beneath the hut. The shore party retreated to the trees, quickly snuffed their brands because they would surely be seen, and there they waited to see what or who would emerge from this long house in the middle of spider country.

The people who came out – if they could be called real people – were pallid and wan creatures. They drifted over the ground rather than walked, like evening ghosts. They carried no lamps or brands, yet they seemed able to see their way without difficulty in starlight. Once outside, it was as if they had just woken from a long sleep. They stretched and yawned, then stared at the sky as if watching the dawn come up, while they slaked their thirst from gourds which hung from lines on trees.

Pungarehu, Seumas and the others watched hidden in the trees, curious as to the nature of these strange people.

The children came out of the long house and almost immediately began playing games, in the way that children do, probably having been eager to be out for some time now. They played hunt the shoe, blind man's bluff, played with spinning tops and various other games which seem universal amongst the young. The older female children juggled expertly with kukui nuts, while others stood around and chanted rhymes until a nut was dropped.

No rough games were begun, however, such as the ball games played on Rarotonga and Raiatea, in which women and men sometimes broke limbs in the scramble to get the ball over the goal line, especially since there was no limit on the number of players.

Curiously, no fires were lit and the wan people seemed to keep to the shadows of the hut. There was no moon but there was the starlight, though even this seemed too bright for the islanders. They shaded their eyes when they crossed open ground, as one might do in intense tropical sunlight. Some of the shore party began to wonder whether they were witnessing the activities of creatures from the spirit world. Yet the local people seemed simply blanched rather than insubstantial: their movements were not the motions of ethereal creatures.

Although there were no open flames, umu were used, and the smell of roast pork, baked chicken and edible rat came wafting over to the group in the trees, making their stomachs churn in anticipation of a feast. Eventually Pungarehu decided they should make their presence known to the islanders, before they were discovered accidentally. The group stepped out of the trees.

'Hello,' cried Pungarehu. 'We are visitors here – can we share your food?'

The result of this call was electrifying. All movement amongst the wan people stopped immediately. If someone had dropped dead on the spot the response would probably not have been different. Then the children took to their heels, running towards the hut. Some of the adults too, made off. The braver ones stood their ground while Pungarehu and Seumas approached, leaving the rest of the party on the tree line.

They went first to an old man, who stood quaking by an umu.

'Sir,' said Pungarehu politely, 'forgive the intrusion. We are not hostile. We are seafarers lost on the wide ocean and have come across your island by sheer chance. Is it possible to sit and talk with you?'

Once the old man had been assured he would not be harmed, he seemed to settle down a little. He called to others, younger men and women, who now approached the pair cautiously. Although Pungarehu and Seumas carried arms, there were no weapons of war in evidence amongst the wan people, and Seumas wondered if they were an entirely peaceful people. Perhaps they did not even hunt, but took their meat entirely from domestic livestock?

The first question the old man asked was a strange one. 'Are you day-people?' he said.

'Day-people?' questioned Pungarehu. 'What do you mean by that?'

'Do you go abroad during the light hours?'

'Of course we do,' said Pungarehu. 'Doesn't everyone?' The old man and some of the others shook their heads. 'We do not. We are the people of the darkness. Our bodies dissolve in strong light.'

Seumas doubted the truth of this last statement, though he was quite sure the old man believed it to be the truth. The Pict felt that perhaps these people had got into the habit of staying out of the sunlight for some reason and now *believed* the light would harm them. Back in the old country of Albainn there had been an eremite who entered a cave in the mountains. He lived on worms and fungi, and bits and pieces brought to him by outsiders. After a few months he convinced himself that he could not go out of the cave again, telling visitors that his body would fall to pieces in the open air.

This was surely much the same situation. Perhaps these people had been driven into their hut as a means of protection and had grown dependent on the darkness? That seemed more likely than the bizarre idea that they would disappear if struck by the sun's rays.

'Would you like to eat with us?' asked one of the young men. 'Tell us news of the outside world. Because of what we are we cannot travel like you day-people. We would be honoured to have you share at our baskets.'

Pungarehu accepted on behalf of the whole shore party.

They were led to the area beneath the stilted hut. A flap was rolled up to allow them entrance. When they were all underneath, the black flap was dropped again leaving them in complete darkness. Seumas was suddenly suspicious of their situation. A panic began to rise in his throat. Nothing but blackness all around: no sense of who lay where. The whole shore party could be slaughtered here, where they could not see. There was no room to man-oeuvre. Claustrophobia overwhelmed him. He drew his dagger and took up a fighting stance, wondering from which direction in the blackness the attack might come.

'Pungarehu! Are you still here? Hello! What's happening? Are we being attacked? To me, Pungarehu! To me, man. Here, here. Hello?'

2

Seumas felt a hand descend on his shoulder. 'What?' he cried, jumping.

'It's all right,' came back the voice of Pungarehu. 'It's me. Once your eyes get used to the darkness, it'll be fine. I don't think these people trust us. They don't like the light – and having lived in the darkness for so long, they can see quite plainly in it.'

Seumas was not happy. 'The feeling's mutual. I don't trust them, either.

And I don't like being surrounded by people I don't trust in a dark, confined place.'

'They have no weapons,' reminded Pungarehu. 'If they try anything, we can give as good as we get. Just settle down and try to get some rest.'

Pungarehu was the leader of the shore party, so Seumas did as he was told. After a while his eyes did indeed get a little more used to the darkness and he saw shapes moving around, carrying platters of food. He stayed on the alert, expecting an attack at any moment. He had his club and would use it if he had to. Pungarehu was not so concerned and was tucking into fruit and vegetables.

'Keep your wits about you, man,' whispered Seumas, wondering if the right leader for the shore party had been chosen. 'This is not a good time to relax.'

But Pungarehu had his eyes on one of the local women and he waved Seumas away impatiently.

'Stop worrying,' he said. 'I've got one hand on my club.' Seumas snarled, 'Which club is that, man? The one between your legs?'

Pungarehu ignored this remark.

Seumas was given a plate of banana porridge, but he scraped it away surreptitiously, fearing poison. All the while, he was aware of being watched intently. Perhaps these people might be without weapons, but they could fall on him in numbers and beat him to death with their fists, or strangle him in the dark. To Seumas the situation was highly volatile.

While he was eating something struck him as extremely odd and he asked one of his hosts warily, 'Why are there no spiders in here? Elsewhere, the island's covered in them.'

'You must not have seen the carvings of Nareau which surround our village area. The Spider-God keeps his creatures from our house. We are not afraid of spiders, but they get into everything – into the soup and sticky fruit – so it's best they remain outside the village.'

'I quite agree. I wish we'd done the same thing,' said Seumas, but the man failed to hear the irony in his tone.

When the meat came round, Seumas's appetite got the better of him. He asked, 'Is that pork or dog? I don't eat dog meat.'

'Pork,' came the reply. 'Here, smell.'

Having smelled he decided to trust to the God Rongo that it was not poisoned.

It was indeed succulent pork, roasted crisp and even, and pungent with the odour of singed bristles.

The women, as in most Oceanian societies, did not eat with the men, but sat in their own group. They were not allowed pork or dog meat, only fish and shellfish. It was a taboo which Dorcha did not mind respecting, since she had never much cared for meat anyway. Occasionally she had deliberately eaten with the men, to show them that they were not special, but since she was a strange person from the Land-of-Mists she had been allowed to get away with it. When she and Seumas were alone together, she ate with him as a matter of course.

Seumas found the pork running with the hot fatty juices of the roasted pig. It was delicious. The first taste, for a long time, was delectable. Pork fat dribbled down his chin, onto his chest. He discovered the joint was stuffed with wild herbs and wild bananas. There was fermented poi on the side. Baked yams to follow. Fresh spring water was available to wash it all down. He ate until he was near bursting. Then he rolled over and unfortunately fell asleep, having had an exhausting day getting to the night-people's village.

He woke much later to find a figure wielding a weapon standing over him. Seumas reached quickly for his own club and was about to swing it up at the crotch of the man who threatened him, when he saw it was Pungarehu. He gave a shout of annoyance at having nearly crippled his friend.

'What is it? Why are you standing over me like that? You crazy fool, I almost killed you.'

Pungarehu sounded distracted.

'They've run back to their long house. I think they have weapons there. We should get back to the ship.'

Pungarehu threw back the flap and sunlight flooded in, hurting Seumas's eyes.

'It's morning,' said Seumas. 'They can't follow us in the light, can they? I don't understand it? Why didn't they kill us while we were asleep if they wanted to?'

'We didn't sleep,' said Pungarehu, indicating some of the shore party. 'They turned nasty just before the dawn, but we couldn't wake those of you who ate the pork. It must have been something in the herb stuffing. Some of us avoided eating that, since it was the obvious place to put a poison or a drug, in something with a strong overpowering taste.'

Seumas felt guilty. 'What happened next?'

'We stood over you,' said a young Raiatean. 'We stood around you, guarding you with our weapons. They shouted and waved their fists at us for a while. Then the dawn came and they had to go up into their long hut.'

Seumas was still bewildered. 'But why did they turn nasty all of a sudden? I mean, they could have attacked us when we first came into the darkness. I still don't understand.'

The young man glanced towards a spot on the ground. It was where Pungarehu had been sitting beside one of the local women when Seumas fell asleep. There appeared to be two depressions in the sand, quite close together. Looking up at Pungarehu now, he knew that the leader of the shore party had been indiscreet, had made love to one of the night people.

'Pungarehu, what have you done?' said Seumas.

Pungarehu looked angry. 'None of your business.'

'Of course it's my business. You've put the shore party in jeopardy. You knew these people did not trust us, were watching us like night hawks, yet you took one of their women? That's madness. They'll slaughter us now. Couldn't you curb your lust for one night?' growled Seumas, furiously.

The killer of the Poukai Bird looked shame-faced. 'I – I couldn't help myself. She is so beautiful. My arm was touching hers – soft, delicate skin against mine – I could smell her hair – it was driving me crazy, Seumas. We – we began by exploring each other secretly with our hands and it led to more – and soon she came to sit on – on my lap, and she had nothing on under her loin cloth ...' Pungarehu groaned.

'I don't want to hear any more,' growled Seumas.

The night-people had had to go into their lightless long house, but once the darkness came they would no doubt fall on the intruders and attempt to slaughter them. The shore party started back, battling their way through spiders once more and eventually reached the lagoon. Seumas found to his relief that they had not panicked and sailed away, but had dutifully waited for the shore party to return with their news.

Pungarehu made his report to Ru while Seumas sought out Dorcha, who was gathering shellfish and anemones in the lagoon. He found her lifting a rock with a hooked stick. A moray eel shot out from under it, snaking through the shallows to look for a new hiding place. Under the rock was a murex shell with occupant, which Dorcha popped into her basket.

'Oh, you're back,' she said, giving him a peck on the cheek. 'And what was my fine brave Pictish warrior doing out all night? Did you find people? Were there any women? I can smell pork fat on your breath. You've been feasting on piggies. Did you get drunk too? Was there any kava?'

'Not drunk, no. There was no booze. People, yes.'

She stared at him. 'Beautiful women?'

'To some they may have *seemed* beautiful, but to me, who has beauty at his fingertips in the form of a lovely Scots lass, why they were turtles by comparison.'

'Bletherer!'

'It's true. They couldn't hold a candle to you, my love. Besides, they were a sort of ghostly hue. Not my type at all. I like my beauty substantial.'

'And the other men and women? Did they think these people unattractive?'

'I can't vouch for all of them. I know Pungarehu slept with one of them. We're going to have to leave here as soon as we can because of it.'

'Pungarehu? The fool.'

'Yes, you'd think he had more sense, wouldn't you?'

'Men's brains are in their loins,' snorted Dorcha. 'I don't think I'm really surprised at all. Are you sure you didn't bed one too? You look guilty.'

'I'm looking guilty because I was asleep while all this was happening. If I'd stayed awake I might have prevented it.'

She touched his cheek. 'I believe you, Pictish man. You're more sensible than most of them. Didn't used to be, but then you're older now. Wiser. And more handsome.'

'Now who's blethering?'

Dorcha bent to pick up a money cowrie. 'What are they like, these local women?'

'Strange as snow in summer. The men too. They hate the light. I think they believe daylight would melt them. It was only the coming of the dawn that saved us from attack.'

Seumas explained what had happened to them. Dorcha shuddered at the bit about the huge spider and acknowledged that she could not have stood her ground in the face of such a horror. Seumas knew better, however, since she had been attacked by the thing she feared the most – a giant snake – and had remained to support the Farseeing-virgin Kikamana. When he told her about the night-people, she was intrigued.

'You mean they *never* go out into the light?'

'Never,' confirmed Seumas. 'They think they would dissolve in the sun.'

'Hmmm, I'm inclined to believe what you said before, that they've been avoiding it for so long they've forgotten why. If one or the other of them disappears occasionally, when they go out into the light, it's probably because they're blinded and get lost in the forest. Probably get eaten by *spiders*. Ugghhhh. Anyway, you're all back safe and sound.'

'Safe and sound,' confirmed Seumas. 'You were right about the feasting though – we were fed like kings. I don't suppose they've had visitors in a long time. They were most hospitable at first – until one of their virgins was breached.'

When Ru heard about the strange night-people he wanted to sail immediately. Pungarehu admitted he had violated the spider islanders' trust, but begged to be allowed one more visit to the long house, alone. It was obvious to most of the passengers and crew of the pahi by now that Pungarehu had found a soul mate amongst the weird people of the island. He made no secret of it.

Ru said he would wait until midnight only, then he would set sail, even if Pungarehu was not on board.

Seumas, Kieto and Boy-girl, basket-sharers, sat talking about it in the early evening. They still remained on the pahi because of the spiders. It was true that familiarity bred contempt, for Boy-girl was no longer afraid to go ashore. But the spiders got into everything, including human orifices, and it was unpleasant to sit around in a place where eight-legged nuisances were crawling all over you.

There was still the occasional attack by bigger spiders, whose bites were no doubt quite virulent, all spiders being poisonous by nature. Some of the littler arachnids floated out on threads, but a quick once over with a swat and the canoe was clear.

So, the three friends remained on board the pahi, and now sat around a low fire talking. They had their weapons in their hands, as did all the other people on board, expecting an attack from the strange night people. Seumas had strung his bow and had a quiver of arrows.

Pungarehu had gone to abduct his pale woman. Seumas had wisely decided not to accompany him, but he felt guilty about it. Pungarehu had said it was best he went alone. He had left a secret message with his paramour, telling her to meet him in the forest, once darkness fell. Pungarehu would meet her and they would run together towards the waiting pahi.

Seumas wondered at the wisdom of Ru, allowing this kidnapping to happen, but admitted privately to Dorcha that he still did not know these Oceanians whom he now called friends.

'What's it going to come to?' asked Boy-girl, in her throaty tones. 'I mean, it's all right if he just wants *sex*, but what if he's fallen in love with the creature?'

Seumas was never very comfortable talking about sexual matters with Boy-girl, who professed she wanted to experience the Pict's body more than anything else in the world.

Kieto replied, 'Yes, I know what you mean.'

'I think he should just stick it to her and then wave bye-bye,' sniffed Boy-girl, twirling one of her many dangling ribbons around her forefinger. 'What do you think, Seumas?'

Seumas felt uncomfortable with the question.

'Me? Oh, I don't know. Ask somebody else.'

'No, come on – do you think he should just—'

'Look, Boy-girl,' said Seumas hotly, 'you know how I feel about these matters. I don't believe in sex for its own sake. I think it has to have a spiritual side to it. You have to be in love with someone to make it work properly.'

'You didn't think that when you first came to us.' Boy-girl sniffed again. 'You went through about twenty of our Raiatean maidens, just like that! I was absolutely amazed at your virility and capacity for sexual variety. You had no shame. I mean, twenty, in as many days. I think you set a record. Even we Oceanians, advanced as we are in sexual matters, thought that was a bit extreme. Were you in love with *all* of them?'

'That was different,' snapped Seumas, glowering. 'I was – I was very young in those days – irresponsible. And I was trying to teach Dorcha a lesson. After all, the first thing she did when she got to Raiatea was marry those stupid brothers.'

Kieto took up the teasing too, now that Boy-girl had Seumas on the run. 'Oh, so you didn't actually *enjoy* those women? You did it just to spite Dorcha. It must have been tough for you, making love when you didn't want to. Did you have problems with your potency?'

Seumas's manhood was now at stake. 'I don't say I didn't *want* to. I'm just saying it's much more pleasurable doing it with someone you're in love with.'

Boy-girl was grinning now. She smoothed out the skirt which covered her long lean legs. 'Better leave him alone now, Kieto, or we'll be getting challenged to single combat before the night's out. You know what he's like when it comes to sex. He's thoroughly inhibited.'

'I am not,' cried Seumas.

But the matter was dropped by mutual consent and they got to talking about their expedition to reach the Maori in the Otherworld beyond the Rapanui cave.

'We must be getting close to the island of the giants now,' Kieto said. 'Ru never expected to come this way, but as it was foretold to us, we have been pulled and pushed over the ocean by sharks, storms and all manner of strange winds and currents, until we are truly in unknown waters. Soon we shall step foot on Rapanui and our search for the cave begins. Are you both ready?'

'I'm ready,' Seumas replied.

'So am I,' replied Boy-girl.

The three friends clasped hands.

Seumas sometimes wondered if he should start to feel he was getting too old for this kind of adventure. His hair had begun now to turn silvery-white. He oiled it, making the excuse to Dorcha that he liked to smell fragrant for her, to darken it. Most of the skin on his shoulders was tattooed now, with sweeping lines of dark blue and black, which made the grey of his hair stand out more. His chest too, was covered with zig-zag lines, like the patterns on mats, and the nipples were the centre of great whorls which covered his hard pectoral muscles. There were other lines which led to his thighs, where the serious tattooing began again, covering most of his thickly muscled legs. The crisp white bodily hair stood out in contrast to the candle-nut powder imbedded in his skin.

Yet, when he really thought about it, the great Kupe was an old man of seventy before he gave up long sea voyages. King Tangiia's father, once ruler of Raiatea and Borabora, was an old man before he stopped testing himself on the ocean. Why, so long as the air was clean, the sea was warm and the skies were bright blue, why not seek adventure? It wasn't as if Seumas was trying to be young again. He didn't mind being old. But he would mind being put out to grass, like a veteran donkey.

At around midnight there was a shout from the beach. Seumas and everyone else leapt to their feet, weapons in hand. Soon Pungarehu came paddling furiously towards them in a dugout canoe, a delicate pale figure in the boat with him. The pair were being pursued by about a hundred ghostly warriors, with slings in their hands.

The night people first let fly from the beach, showering the water around the dugout with rocks and stones. Then they rushed to canoes, hidden in the foliage by the shore, to pursue Pungarehu on water.

Ru had already ordered his virgins to raise the sails and the pahi strained at anchor ropes, ready to leap forwards like a flying fish being chased by a shark.

The air was full of yells and threats, as Pungarehu finally reached the pahi and almost threw his abducted bride on board, where she was grasped by Ru. A stone struck Seumas on the shoulder, painfully. He saw that it had come from a spectre with a slingshot, standing up in the bows of a pursuing canoe. He fitted an arrow to his bow and fired at the man, hitting him in the foot, seeing with satisfaction that he fell back amongst those paddling his craft, thus disrupting their progress.

'Let's get out of here!' cried Ru. 'Let go the anchors!' The order was obeyed and the pahi shot forwards, over the reef, and away from the island of spiders. Behind them they left shouting, screaming warriors, who wanted blood. The islanders were to be disappointed.

Once they were out at sea, one of the two huts on the pahi's deck was converted. This hut had no windows. During the day it was to be occupied by Pungarehu's new wife, Wiama, who would lay under a thick blanket of pandanus leaves inside its walls.

For the first day or so the scabby Polahiki hung around the edges of the hut, hoping to be shut in with Wiama, not because he wanted her sexually, or because he was curious about what she did locked up in there all day long. He wanted to be shut in because no one could open the door during the day and he would not have to do any chores. Pungarehu chased him away saying that if he caught him hanging around the hut again, he would personally throw him overboard, where the fisherman could get all the rest and quiet he needed – for a whole eternity.

Wiama came out at night, a waif whose skin was almost luminous. Seumas could see the framework of her bones. On a full moon she stayed in the shadows. She claimed that Hine-keha's face was too brilliant for her, and blinded her. Wiama had made the ultimate sacrifice for love. She risked death on a daily basis, simply to be with her new husband, Pungarehu. She was fascinating to the rest of the people on board. You could see a taper through her hand. Her eyes were so pale they were almost white. Her skin was a network of blue veins and arteries, crazing her porcelain skin. Everyone saw her as some kind of fragile spirit who would one day simply shatter like a bird's egg before their eyes.

PART FIVE

Island of Giants

1

While resting at the spider islands, Ru had found and shaved a new mast to replace one damaged in the storm. There was a good wind behind them in the form of the goddess Hine-tu-whenua, whose benevolence was ever bountiful. The ship was heading in the direction of Fee tietie on the wind-flower, but since Ru did not know where they were on the vast face of the ocean, it was impossible to tell whether they would reach a destination. Pola-hiki was as usual despondent and negative, telling everyone they were going to their doom.

'The fish in these waters are strange. I think we're going to sail for ever and not find land.'

And indeed, it seemed that way. They appeared to be in a particularly empty quarter of the great ocean. Each day they searched the sky for cloud formations which would indicate land beneath them and found nothing but puffs of white and endless blue. At night the roof of voyaging kept its secrets close to its breast. Gradually they ate through their stores, until food was dangerously low. Water too, was becoming a problem, though there was some rain during the nights.

Ru stood at the mast, day in, day out, staring at the distant horizon. Occasionally Kuku Lau would try to fool him with a false image, an island shimmering in the heat waves, but Ru was a navigator with much experience and did not allow his wishful thinking to overwhelm his senses. Occasionally too, they would be given hope in the form of a white flush of surf in the distance, only to find rips or flocks of seabirds.

One evening Ru held a meeting with Kieto, Seumas, Dorcha, Kikamana and Boy-girl. He asked for their opinion on the situation.

Kikamana said, 'There are signs in Tiki's face that all is not well on board. Nor can I reach Tangaroa in my dreams. The Great Sea-God has abandoned us.'

Ru said, 'This he would not do unless he was displeased with us for some reason. Do you think it is Wiama? Perhaps Pungarehu should never have taken her from that island? Maybe her presence on board is making Tanga-roa angry.'

Kikamana shook her head. 'No, things started going wrong before she came on board. It is something more deep-rooted and less obvious than that. We have broken some command.'

'Well, I can't think what that is,' said Ru, irritably.

Seumas suggested they keep a watch between them, and they agreed, but since none of them knew what to look for it was a very unrewarding business.

Things became even worse. The wind died down: Hine-tu-whenua deserted them. One of Ru's relations disappeared one morning, hooked up into the clouds by Amai-te-rangi, the fisher of people. Ua sent no more rain for many days and they began to seriously thirst. There was a herb they could put in the seawater to make it palatable, but one could only drink a certain amount of salty water before retching it up. Dakuwanga was seen swimming in the mist between the earth and sky, waiting to devour any sau which came his way. The kabu of the man lost to Amai-te-rangi was witnessed floating like a balepa over the roof of voyaging one night, giving everyone the chills.

'We are surely going to die soon,' said Polahiki. 'I have never been on a voyage where the gods hated me so much.'

One night Ru dreamed he visited Limu, the Guardian of the Dead, in his vast wooden palace beneath the ocean. Ru passed through the Land of the Dead without incident, as one does in a dream, seeing neither the terrible Nangananga, nor the Ruler of the Underworld, Milu. When he reached the palace of carved and polished woods, he found it surrounded by guardian lizards feeding on flies, which seemed strange to Ru since they were below the waves and one does not find insects like flies under the water. The lizards allowed him to enter the huge halls of the palace and Ru went straight to the heart, where he was told the god Limu was waiting to give him audience.

Inside, the palace was magnificent, with hundreds of huge pillars of wood supporting a high roof, and beautiful wooden floors and ceilings, covered in carvings of men, fish, birds and other forms of the natural world.

There were balconies reaching up into the misty heights of square towers, tier on tier of them, all filled with curious spirits of the dead, waiting for an audience with Limu. They peered down in resentment on the intruding Ru, who seemed to be jumping ahead of them in the order of things. None spoke to him however, nor tried to bar his progress through the sweeping wooden arches, for the lizards kept watch on their behaviour, and fiercely ejected any soul that caused upset.

Finally Ru came to a darkened room with a wooden throne ten times the height of a man. The throne was decorated with skulls and bones, and masks of men with long tongues, and lizards, and other representations of the dead. On this seat sat the Guardian of the Dead, who told Ru he had been petitioned by Tiki, the First Ancestor, and his wife Marikoriko, First Woman, to give Ru due warning of the consequences of his circumstances.

'If you do not sort out your troubles soon,' said Limu, 'you will end up here.'

'Is there no alternative?' asked Ru. 'I do not think we are going to discover the source of our problem. We have tried and nothing comes to light. I hate to think I have led my people to their deaths.'

'I could arrange for you to land on the Islands of Eternal Souls,' Limu said. 'On Lotophagoi there is singing and dancing – happiness – for ever.'

Ru said, 'It would seem that this would be no different from death.'

'It is death of a kind,' agreed Limu. 'All that is left to you is to make a discovery on your ship.'

Ru then left the palace and travelled up towards the stars, where the Oceanian Star-God Rehua sat in the tenth heaven at a place called Te Putahi Nui O Rehua, The Great Crossroads of Rehua. It was from here that Kaitangata, the beloved son of Rehua, fell one evening. The blood from his fall washed over the sky and now forms the colourful sunrises and sunsets.

Ru was not allowed to enter the tenth heaven, where only one more heaven would have separated him from the Supreme Being, Io, in the twelfth and topmost heaven. No mortal has ever been that close to the highest deity and Ru was to be no exception. He had to shout to Rehua from below, to ask him if he could help.

Rehua replied, 'I can only tell you this – it is in the dark hours when you break your word to Tangaroa.'

'I, break my word? How is this?'

'I can tell you no more,' said Rehua, sparkling with a thousand stars, dazzling Ru with blazes of brilliant light, scintillating in his aura of cold fire. 'The rest you must discover for yourself.'

While Rehua was speaking, Mareikura, heavenly angels and attendants of Io, were passing by Ru and brushing him with their ethereal forms. These creatures were the Supreme Being's special envoys, carrying messages between the highest deity and the other gods of Oceania. Where they touched Ru's skin they left a smudge of precious glittering stardust.

Ru left the Crossroads to the Stars, and returned to his own body, sleeping on *The Princely Flower*. He was convinced now that Wiama was their problem, for Rehua had stipulated that the disobedience occurred during the dark hours, which was the only time Wiama was abroad. Ru waited until night, then demanded she be brought before him.

'You must be the perpetrator of our difficulties,' Ru said, 'for you are the only one who does not sleep through the night, but has the freedom to do as you choose while others are not so alert.'

'This is not quite true,' whispered Wiama in his ear, taking up her defence. 'There are others who do not sleep.'

'Who are they?' demanded Ru, quietly. 'Tell me their names!'

'Better I should show you,' Wiama said, softly.

She rose and crossed the deck to the starboard hut, the one used by her during the day. There she took hold of a large piece of tapa cloth and under

Ru's gaze, whipped it away. Underneath were two naked bodies, struggling together in the throes of love. One was Titopika, the tohunga, the other was one of the crew of twenty virgins, plainly no longer a maid.

Ru let out a loud cry. No wonder his voyage had slipped from Tangaroa's favour. The Great Sea-God had demanded but one condition for his assistance, that virgins only were used as mariners to sail the craft. Here was one of his crew, her maidenhead taken by a priest who should himself be chaste. This was in flagrant violation of his orders and those of the Great Sea-God, Tangaroa, whose very breath was law on the ocean.

Ru ran to his bed on the deck and snatched up a weapon, a club made of nokonoko. He rushed back to the fornicating pair, intending to dash out their brains. Others had been roused from their beds and had gathered around the guilty couple, staring down at them as they slipped from each other and tried to cover their nakedness. As Ru raised the club over the woman's head, Seumas reached out and gripped it, holding it fast.

'You dare to touch a prince?' cried the stricken Ru, the source of whose mana was great nobility.

'I don't touch your head,' said Seumas, 'nor even your arm – only your club. I can't allow you to murder this woman. It's not her fault. It's *his*. He seduced the maiden. I remember now, seeing him sneak back and forth across the deck at night. I thought it was for drinking water, but he was obviously visiting this woman. He has used his magic to make her his slave.'

Ru managed to control his anguished spirit for long enough to be able to speak with Seumas and a hastily formed council, while the Titopika and the woman dressed.

Ru said to the council, 'Seumas has said the woman was seduced, but not against her will, or she would have reported Titopika's actions.'

'She is a young woman, without experience in these matters,' Kieto agreed. 'Yes, she has done wrong, by disobeying your orders, Prince Ru, but her wrong is *nothing* beside his. Titopika has done this thing, perhaps with the intention of sabotaging the expedition? I have no doubt it was deliberate.'

'You think it was done on purpose?' Ru cried, incensed. 'Why would a young priest do such a thing?'

By this time Titopika had been brought before him and spoke in his own defence.

'I am only a novice priest. I am Ragnu's agent. He told me what to do. I was afraid of him.'

Kikamana said, 'Once you were on the voyage, what did you need to fear? Ragnu's arm is not that long.'

'So you believe,' snorted Titopika. 'I think otherwise. I have seen the punishments he hands out to those who fail to do his bidding. I have seen men's souls in torment, their bodies signifying nothing, yet they scream for mercy.

Ragnu is a very powerful priest, a kahuna with magic which can reach a thousand miles—'

'If he's that powerful,' snorted Seumas, 'why bother with creatures like you – why not just sink us with his magic?'

'I am not a man with great mana, like Ru, and I'm not protected by the gods.'

This was true. A kahuna, no matter how powerful, would not openly be able to sabotage an expedition led by such a man as Ru, whose actions had been guided by the gods. Such destruction would have to be done furtively, out of sight of any deity, so that it might seem an accident, or weakness of human nature. The gods were very disparaging about the frailty of mortal will and would not look too closely at any reason for failure which seemed to spring from mankind's deficiencies.

'Get out of my sight,' said Ru to Titopika. 'I shall consider how to deal with you later.'

Once Titopika had taken himself to another part of the canoe, where he would be guarded by some of Ru's relatives, Ru put his mind to the problem of rectifying their situation.

'We must make a sacrifice to Tangaroa,' he said. 'I would like it to be Titopika, but his soul is stained with dishonour and as such he is not a worthy sacrifice. Instead, it will have to be either another person on board, or at the very least a deserving animal. We wish no harm to come to any member of this expedition and we have no domestic livestock left.'

Seumas suddenly realised all eyes were on him and Dorcha, and he leapt to his feet as it dawned on him where Ru's hints were leading.

'No,' he said, 'I absolutely forbid it!'

Kieto said, 'We know how you feel, Seumas, but if we don't do something we shall all die anyway.'

'Think of another way,' cried Seumas, putting an arm around the neck of his dog, Dirk. 'Dorcha, help me.'

Dorcha said, 'Give us until dawn, Ru. If we can't think of anything else, then you'll have to go ahead. At least give my husband until the sun rises.'

'Until morning,' agreed Ru. 'If Seumas has no other answer, then we shall sacrifice his dog. In the meantime, I have to replace the crew member, or we shall still be in violation of Tangaroa's command.'

'You're not going to execute her?'

'No – I'm going to marry her to Titopika. They deserve each other. But more importantly, do we have any more strong, healthy maidens on board? I need an able female virgin to man my ship, or we shall founder in these doldrums for ever. Do we have such a woman amongst us – one who is not a child – who can replace the wayward maid?'

There was silence amongst the council for a moment, then one voice spoke up.

'Yes, we do.'

It was Kikamana, the priestess, personal kahuna to King Tangiia of Rarotonga.

'You?' murmured the prince. 'Of *course*.'

He did not ask if he could trust her. If Kikamana said she was still a virgin, then it was so. One did not question a kahuna of her status. Though in her fading years, her spirit was as pure and unblemished as that of a newly born infant. Kikamana, old in age, but young in her virtue: chaste as a high mountain spring. Her body unviolated, her soul and integrity flawless, she was the perfect replacement for the fallen maiden.

'So be it,' stated Prince Ru.

Titopika was married to the young woman the next day. She clung to him possessively, while he himself exhibited nothing but an air of boredom. Seumas wanted to reach out and bash their heads together, believing them to be as stupid as each other.

A close watch was kept on Titopika after this. Ru had warned that any further attempts to impede the expedition would result in the death of the spy. Most thought it a miracle that Ru had not slit his throat and thrown him overboard already.

In the night Seumas had come up with what he believed to be a solution to his problem. Dirk was his dog, raised by him, trained by him. He would not allow his dog to be killed. There would be no ritual sacrifice.

Seumas told Dorcha what he was about to do and her eyes widened in astonishment.

'You're either mad or stupid. You can't love a dog *that* much. Give him up.'

'No,' replied Seumas, determinedly, 'I will not. It has nothing to do with being fond of an animal,' he added, grimly. 'Dirk is my responsibility. If you take on the responsibility for a life, you do everything possible to see that life is preserved. Nothing to do with sentiment at all. I feel nothing of that sort for the dog – he's a good hunter, quick and obedient, and he would die for me – but I am without the kind of silly emotions you're talking about.'

Dorcha raised an eyebrow. 'Are you indeed? I know you, Seumas, you're my man. When you were in love with me and couldn't have me, you were sentiment from your toes to your eyeballs. I used to see you mooning around the beach, staring at my hut. It turned me off my dinner.'

'A dog is not a woman,' he stated, flatly. 'And in any case, I didn't moon around after you. You must have imagined things – that's your vanity working there, lassie. I did nothing of the sort. I was simply—'

'Responsible for my welfare?' she interrupted.

'In a way, yes. It was because of me you'd been taken from Albainn, so of course I felt I had to protect you.'

'What a bletherer,' she said. 'Look, man, you can't risk your life for a scruffy *cú*,' she used the Gaelic word for dog, in order to get through to him, 'so come to your senses.'

'My mind's set,' he replied. 'I won't have it changed by a woman.'

'Oh, no, a woman couldn't influence you, could she – but a bloody dog can. Preserve us!'

That day there was a clear sky like a blue bowl over the curving ocean. There was a swell on the seascape, but the waves were small – 'licking waves' Dorcha called them – and a brisk following wind filled the pandanus mat sails sending the great pahi shooting like a small vaa fishing canoe over the surface. Fairy terns from some nearby island, which Ru sought in vain to locate, skimmed through the air above them.

In a clay bowl on the deck a small fire was going and some cooking was in progress. A mother and her small daughter, relatives of Ru, were baking taro. From the hulls came the ever present sound of the bailers as the crew removed the water which constantly seeped through the stitched planks caulked with vegetable and shark oils.

Despite the calm weather the women were working hard, getting the most out of the sails, using the steering oar to its best advantage. The salt spray glistened on their teak skins, which had grown darker since they had begun the long voyage. A new Oceanian infant was as fair-skinned as any baby Dorcha and Seumas could produce. It was the constant exposure to sun and the elements which turned an Oceanian's naturally pale skin a darker hue. Many noble women never went into the sunlight and retained an ivory complexion for their whole lives.

The twenty virgins, Kikamana now amongst their number, were becoming weathered and brown, but were still no less attractive for all that. They were a beautiful people altogether, thought Seumas, the men and the women, with their muscular lithe bodies and long black hair, with their handsome features and dark eyes. Very handsome. No wonder they were so vain.

'Well?' said Ru. 'Have you come to a decision?'

Boy-girl and Kieto stared from behind Ru at their basket-sharer, Seumas, also waiting for his answer.

'I suggest,' said Seumas, evenly, 'rather than slaughtering my dog, in which I have invested many years of patient training, that we sacrifice a great white shark.'

Ru frowned and shook his head, as if there were water in his ears from swimming.

'A great white shark?'

'Yes.'

'But,' said Ru, 'we don't have a great white shark, we only have a dog.'

'Then we must catch one,' replied Seumas. 'We must drag some bait behind the pahi and catch a great white.' Boy-girl, as puzzled as Ru, intervened here.

'But we have no meat to use as bait – you know that, Seumas. A fish will not do. It needs to be a chunk of bloody meat.'

'There is meat walking around on the deck right now,' Seumas pointed out.

Polahiki shook his head and said, 'If you're talking about rats, we ate the last one two days ago. There are no more rats on board. I've looked in all the hollow bamboos and amongst the vegetables – everywhere that they hide. I admit they are devious creatures, good at squeezing into small places, but we've definitely eaten the last one. I had some myself.'

'You had it *all* yourself,' grumbled one of the women passengers. 'I saw you eat it half raw.'

Seumas said calmly, 'I meant two-legged meat.'

Kieto took a sharp intake of breath. Others had stopped their tasks to listen now. Ru frowned again.

'I think I know what you mean, Seumas. Titopika! We should use the new husband as bait?'

Titopika heard this and came striding over the deck.

'Goblin! You have always hated me, haven't you? This is your revenge, is it? Because I am Ragnu's creature? Have pity, man, on someone who has been ill employed.'

'I did not mean to use you.'

After Seumas had made this remark all eyes swung naturally to where the dirty fisherman, Polahiki, sat peeling his scabs and scratching his lice bites.

'Me?' cried Polahiki, leaping to his feet. 'Oh yes, pick on a poor defenceless fisherman, who's only trying to do his best. That's typical. Naturally because I'm a Hivan I'm fair game, to be pushed around, bullied and persecuted, just to satisfy some cruel—'

'Oh shut up,' Seumas said, wearily, 'I meant *me* – *I* will be the bait. Make some cuts on my legs so that I trail blood, put me out on a line, and when the great white comes, make sure you harpoon him before he gets my feet. That's all.'

There was stunned silence around the Albannach as passengers and crew digested this extraordinary suggestion. One or two glanced at Dorcha, to gauge her reaction, but realised she already knew what Seumas was going to say. Boy-girl gave Seumas a tragic look.

'Oh, *no*,' she said. 'Not for a *dog*. Here, let's use Titopika after all? He's the cause of all our troubles anyway. Let's use him as the bait.'

Titopika said nothing, his lips tightening, but his new bride clung to him and started to weep. Seumas called Titopika to him. The fake priest roughly pushed away his distressed bride and walked up to face Seumas.

Seumas said, 'Are you really a full tohunga?'

'No – I was hoping to be – but Ragnu has destroyed all that for me.'

'But you know how to slow-bleed a man?'

Titopika and a number of others around him looked puzzled.

'Yes.'

Seumas handed him a sharp-bladed shellknife.

'Then you can cut my ankles for me, man, so that I leak, but not gush blood. Can you do that?'

Titopika smiled, nodded, and took the knife.

'No!' cried Boy-girl. 'He'll cripple you.'

Titopika looked scorn upon the unhappy Boy-girl.

'I shall do as I was asked and no more. Do you take me for an idiot? If I cut him any more than necessary, you can feed me to the great white and have done with it.'

Boy-girl looked at Dorcha, who said, 'I trust him – in this anyway. If my husband is such a fool to go through with this, he needs to be sure he won't bleed to death before noon. Cut him, Titopika.'

Ru, once he saw that Seumas meant what he said, had his crew make ready a harness of sennit, with a trailing rope. Then some bamboo logs were lashed together to make a small raft on which Seumas would lie, his legs dragging behind him in the water. Dirk looked on, bemused by all this activity around his master, wondering whether or not to attack the man with the knife, who was making thin incisions on his master's ankles. Seumas, in the harness, was lowered off the back of the pahi on the small raft, which rode the water like one of those boards which Hawaiian's used to ride the booming surf.

Kikamana beat together the bones she had used to drive off the Ponaturi, and chanted a karakia, while Boy-girl threw some magic stones into the sea to attract their quarry:

'O, great shark of the seas,
Great white hunter of lesser hunters,
Here is the bait for you to devour,
Blood draining like a sunset drains from the sky,
Clouding the waters, bringing frenzy to your senses,
Come and take him – if you can!'

The karakia over, Kikamana picked up a thick bamboo harpoon with a whalebone barb on the end and stood with the others, waiting for the great white to come to take the bait.

'Let us hope Magantu, the monster who can swallow a pahi whole, does not take the scent of the blood,' whispered Po'oi, the son of old Kaho. 'If Magantu comes, then we shall all be bait and snapped up pretty quickly.'

'Stop trying to put cheer into our hearts,' moaned Rinto. 'We're happy enough as it is.'

Seumas skimmed the waves behind the canoe, a thin red trail of smoke in the water behind him. The wash occasionally went over his head, making him splutter and snort. It was difficult to discern his feelings from his face, on which he deliberately kept the wooden expression of a suffering Pict.

Seumas's greying hair flowed behind him like the kelp tresses of the female who dwelt in the monstrous seas far below the islands, in that foggy, misty and dark ocean – the frozen sea of pia, with its mountainous waves – where she lived with a deceitful creature called the sea-elephant, who dived to great depths and was hidden from hunters by her long mane.

After some time, when no great white appeared, Dorcha had Titopika cut her own ankles and took some sponges, soaking them in her blood then throwing them overboard. Others began to do the same. Seumas began to look chilled and miserable, unable to keep his expression bleak any longer. More blood-soaked sponges were thrown into the sea. There was a danger of tiger sharks coming to take the bait, instead of a great white, but this was not spoken of, for tiger sharks were not worthy sacrifices to the Great Sea-God, Tangaroa. Only a great white would do.

The day dragged on and Seumas appeared to be growing weaker, through exposure and loss of blood.

Suddenly Po'oi, having climbed the mast to get a good sighting, yelled excitedly, 'Here he comes! The great white shark of the seas!'

A dark fin was seen cutting through the water, approaching Seumas at right angles.

'Pull him in!' shrieked Dorcha, grabbing the taut line.

'Not yet,' murmured Boy-girl, gently taking her hand from the line. 'We might lose the fish if you take him in too early – just a little while longer.'

The tail of the shark flicked above the surface and Dorcha could see the black fringe. She was astonished at the length of the beast. It was a monster. It could surely swallow Seumas *and* the surf raft whole in one bite. The dorsal fin sliced through the waves with amazing speed, as the great white began to circumnavigate the pahi, its circles growing tighter with each revolution. Soon it was cruising just two body lengths away from Seumas, whose face was once again impassive.

Ru said, 'Pull him in – gradually.'

'No, no, *quickly*,' said Dorcha, her heart in her throat.

Those on the line took no notice of her, but did as they were told by Ru, taking in the raft and Seumas by slow degrees, with the great white decreasing his circles all the time, being drawn in closer to the waiting harpoons and nooses.

'The rope's fraying,' cried Dorcha. 'It's snapping!'

'Slowly, slowly,' murmured Ru, ignoring her. 'Easy, easy.'

To Dorcha it seemed to take a year before the gentle bump of the raft on the back of the pahi was heard. Seumas remained where he was, waiting for the moment when the great white turned in the water as he must to take his prey, his mouth being on the underside of his monstrous head. In that moment the softer underbelly of the shark was exposed. Seumas was snatched literally from the crescent mouth with its saw-tooth jaws. Then the harpoons flashed in, seven of them burying their barbed points in the shark's belly.

There was much yelling and calling from the harpooners, amongst whom was Ru himself.

'Hold him, hold him!'

'Watch it – his skin's like sandstone!'

'The mouth, the mouth – keep away from the mouth.'

The great fish thrashed once against the side of the canoe and immediately four of the harpoons broke or came out. The owners of the other three held on grimly, waiting for the tail to thrash again. When the tail showed, a noose was swiftly thrown around it by Polahiki, the expert, the man who had killed more sharks than any other aboard. Once that was tightened another went on, and another. They had him now and let go the harpoon lines, so that the great white was dragged along behind the pahi, half as long as the ship itself, a burden on the sails.

'Oh laddie,' said Dorcha, her eyes afire and her expression a mixture of anger and relief. 'You are the most bone-headed Pict I have ever had the misfortune to – to marry.'

Seumas grinned sheepishly at his fretful wife, while Dirk wagged his tail and nuzzled his neck, as if the dog knew his master had saved his life at the risk of his own.

Dorcha wiped Seumas down, drying his body, then set about putting ointment on his cuts. Tenderly he did the same with hers, kissing her now and then on the soles of her feet, licking the salt from between her toes to make her mad, blissful in the knowledge that she loved him fiercely.

Occasionally he whispered in her ear as they were ministering to each other, things which must be secret between a husband and wife of middle age, gradually bringing a smile to her face, sometimes allowing her to punch his arm when he became too outrageous in his suggestions. To Seumas it was worth the risking of his life, to find himself so close to her again, as when they were young and freshly in love.

2

Tangaroa was aware that some god or gods, either to spite him or the humans on board the pahi, was doing their best to ensure *The Princely Flower* did not reach its destination. It was a puzzle that Tangaroa could not solve at this time, since the perpetrator kept himself or herself hidden. And well they should, for Io himself had proclaimed the voyage to be worthy.

The Great Sea-God had not searched too hard for this interfering god, since he himself of late had been misdirecting the canoe. It was not spite on Tangaroa's part, but punishment for those on board not adhering to his strict orders. Now things had improved and he had been propitiated.

Tangaroa watched the great white shark being dragged on board the pahi, taking up half the ocean-going canoe's length. The shark was ritually slaughtered, offerings were made to the Great Sea-God. Tangaroa was gratified and appeased. Now that the situation on board had been rectified, with regard to his instructions, he saw no reason to delay the pahi any longer. First, however, the ship would need to call in to an island, to replenish its supplies.

The nearest landfall was an island called Rapanui.

After the sacrifice and the feasting on the great white, most of those on board fell into a deep sleep. Wiama almost came out of her hut, thinking that it was nightfall, but was warned by her lover Pungarehu not to open the door. Pungarehu had heard her stirring behind the walls of the hut and though he was waiting impatiently to see her he was terrified she would leave the hut too early and destroy herself.

When indeed it was dark, the waif left her hut. She fell into her lover's arms. The pair of them went to the front of the canoe to sit and watch the darkness flowing over them from the direction of Apa toa on the windflower.

'I have missed you, my love,' said Pungarehu. 'The day is long without you, even though I sleep to pass the time.'

'You *must* sleep then,' she said, 'for you would get no rest otherwise. You must regulate your hours to mine, for you do not dissolve in the darkness, as I do in the light.'

Pungarehu saw the logic of this, though he was growing increasingly upset with their need to part during the day.

'I could come into your hut with you.'

She smiled and touched his cheek with a hand as translucent as a bubble shell that floats on the ocean waves. 'Then we should both get no sleep at all.'

'Please, let me stay with you in your hut tomorrow?'

Wiama sighed and considered this request. The truth was, she liked Pungarehu to be on the outside of the hut, so that he could protect her from accidents, or possibly even deliberate attempts to harm her. While he was out there he could stop anyone going near to the deck hut. There might be those who might forget that she was in there and absently open the door in search for stores. There might be those who were jealous of Pungarehu for some reason and who sought to harm him by destroying her. It was best he remained on the outside, while she was on the inside, in order to control access.

'It's best ...'

'Please?' he murmured into her ear, delicate as a nautilus, with such deep longing that she could not resist him.

'All right,' she said. 'Just for one day.'

'Tomorrow?' he cried.

'Tomorrow.'

Back on Raiatea, in the temple at Tapu-tapu atia, Ragnu was pacing the floor in fury. He had used his far-seeing devices and was aware that his agent on board *The Princely Flower* had failed him. At first he had wanted to destroy the young man, but once he had calmed his fury was no longer directed towards Titopika, whose efforts at destroying the pahi had not in Ragnu's estimation been worthy of a high priest's spy.

The irony of the situation was not lost on Ragnu either. His machinations had actually contributed to the successful outcome of Kieto's expedition. The Rarotongans were about to land on Rapanui and would undoubtedly discover the passage to the Otherworld which they sought. This was due in part to Titopika's seduction of one of the crew and Tangaroa's subsequent misdirecting of *The Princely Flower*.

A white-bellied sea eagle had been despatched, with a calabash in its claws, to seek out the vessel and to deliver the container to Titopika. There were symbols scratched on the calabash, which Titopika would recognise as the product of Ragnu's hand. These symbols would also lead the young man to believe that there was poison in the calabash, to be administered to the enemies of the kahuna of Raiatea.

There was something far more deadly inside the container, however, but less reliable.

Ragnu's difficulty had been in the numbers of his enemies. It was unlikely that Titopika would be able to poison everyone on board the pahi. Even a delayed-action poison might not be imbibed by all the passengers and crew. Then there was the problem of Titopika himself. Ragnu did not wish *anyone* to survive the voyage, including his agent, who would have a hold on the kahuna for the rest of his life. The new king would not be pleased to learn his cousin Ru had been murdered by his own high priest and supposed guardian of the noble families.

It was possible of course, that the bird would not make it, that some accident or incident would befall the raptor. He could do nothing now but wait for the outcome and hope that his booby trap managed to destroy the whole contingent aboard *The Princely Flower*.

In the meantime, Ragnu prepared himself for a new sacrifice to his ancestor-spirits, who were waiting to be appeased by the death of Seumas, Kieto and the other original members of the Tangiia expedition to Rarotonga.

'A young boy, I think,' murmured the priest. 'I'm sure my great-grandfathers would appreciate some roast long pig.'

Tomorrow he would lead the other priests of the island in a gathering to honour the Great Creator-God, Rongo, god of all things growing. These gatherings were now the only times Ragnu had the opportunity of meeting other ordinary people, for his mana was so great now that it almost equalled that of a king. If his shadow should fall on a commoner, that man might die. Power had its bad side, in that he was a lonely old man, too lofty for the masses and too sinister for the nobles. They were all aware of his great mastery of the occult and were afraid of him, commoner and nobleman alike.

He was a friendless old man, bitter and cold, with nothing to take pleasure in except the deaths of his enemies.

When morning came there was deep mist over the sea. Hau Maringi, God of Mists and Fog, had decided it was a day in which to cast his cloak over the ocean. *The Princely Flower* entered this bank of sea fog, sliding over a still sea, and cruised on into its heart. The crew paddled in the absence of wind, to take their craft through the vaporous barrier, and out on the other side, while Ru stood at the mast.

'Listen!' he cried, after a time. 'Hold the paddles.'

The women rowers did as they were asked. Seumas strained his ears. He was rewarded with the faint sound of waves dashing themselves on rocks. There was land somewhere around, but the fog disguised the direction.

'Which way?' he asked Ru.

Ru, whose navigator's ears were more tuned to such sounds than a warrior from Albainn, pointed.

'That way,' he announced. 'Paddlers, follow the direction of my finger.'

The women did as they were bid. Seumas and Dorcha, and the rest of the passengers from Rarotonga – Po'oi, Rinto, Boy-girl, Kikamana, Kieto and Polahiki – all crowded onto the front of the craft. Pungarehu was inside the second deck hut with his new wife, Wiama, enjoying a honeymoon. He and Wiama heard all the scuffling outside and called to ask what was the matter.

'An island,' cried Polahiki, excitedly. 'We're approaching an island.'

Suddenly, the mists cleared, and there indeed was the source of the breakers: a high volcanic island. The scene was dramatic. Before them lay a heavily wooded land, rising from a small sandy bay directly in front of them, to the rim of an enormous crater. In some places the heads of giants appeared above the trees. They had either red or white bodies, but all had red topknots on their heads. These figures with their distinctive features, their long heads and long noses, dominated the landscape. The red giants had long ears, the white giants short ears. Several of these creatures were moving, as if along paths through the forest.

'Do you see that?' breathed Seumas. 'A land of giants.'

'Rapanui!' confirmed Dorcha. 'I shall add it to my shell chart tonight, relative to the stars in the roof of voyaging. We have found the place we were looking for.'

On hearing this, Ru interrupted angrily, 'But this is not *our* destination. You said we would be taken here and I hoped you were wrong. Are you sure you did not use your magic to take us off course and to this godforsaken place?'

Kikamana, whose magic it would have been if anyone's, replied, 'If we could have used magic to guide a canoe here we would have had no need of you, Prince Ru. We would have come to this place ourselves directly from Rarotonga. We are here because it was foretold that *The Princely Flower* would touch these shores. It is part of your destiny, part of our destiny, and unavoidable.'

Ru seemed to be satisfied with this answer.

As the canoe entered the bay and cruised slowly towards the sandy cove a man burst from the treeline. He was tall and thin with an aquiline nose and long ears, not like an Oceanian but with the appearance of the giants, and he was running as if pursued by someone. Every few moments he darted a look over his shoulder in a terrified manner, sometimes stumbling when he did so, as if he expected those chasing him to emerge from the forest.

'Do you think a giant is after him?' whispered Polahiki. 'He looks as if demons are on his trail.'

Indeed, at the next moment a group of warriors, heavily tattooed with claw marks, stripes and bars, came hurtling out of the forest. They were dressed in dried grass skirts, with long grass leggings, and carried spears with huge obsidian points. Their appearance was ferocious and terrifying. Their frenzied manner, wild hair and grass garments, and their sinister body markings, were all obviously designed to make them appear diabolic in the eyes of the uninitiated. Skulls hung from belts of what looked like human hair. Necklaces of dried body parts decorated throats. Bones dangled from locks of hair.

Seumas for one had no doubt this was a barbarous death cult. He had known them before, both in Oceania and in the land of his birth. He knew their ways: dark and savage ceremonies taking place in the dead of night, victims speechless with terror, fear ruling the communities in which such cults operated.

One of the warriors pointed to the fleeing man and they set off in pursuit of him, over the rocky ground towards the beach.

The fugitive looked up and suddenly saw the pahi, gave a frantic wave, and set off towards the canoe. His hunters followed, yelling and screaming at him. They seemed determined he should not escape. Ru realised that his ship was being placed in a dangerous situation and ordered crew and passengers to arm themselves, which they did with alacrity.

Soon the man with the long ears was close enough to be heard, and he yelled out in absolute terror, 'Birdmen!'

'Birdmen?' said Seumas. 'What does he mean?'

The chasing warriors were near to their quarry now, as he splashed through the shallows, only a short distance from the pahi. They let loose their spears, throwing the short-shafted weapons at the back of their target. The first four missed their mark, but the fifth struck the desperate man squarely in the back, its large stone head probably smashing through his spine, the point coming out of his abdomen.

The sixth spear seemed to be lifted by a strange gust of wind, which carried it over the heads of those on the deck of *The Princely Flower*, to bury its point in the wall of the second deck hut.

Blood gushed from the wound, as the fugitive managed to stagger another few paces, before he slid down into the water. The waves rippled over his head and the water around him became scarlet and smoky. The grass-covered warriors on the beach, the 'Birdmen' as the dying victim had called them, gave out screeches of triumph, like raptors who have caught their prey. Then they were off, running up to the woods again, yelling insults over their shoulders at those on the deck of the canoe. 'What do you think of that?' said Po'oi in an awed voice. 'We witnessed a manhunt in our first few moments. This is not a happy island. He knew they were going to show him no mercy. I'm sure if we had harboured him, they would have attacked us too. They looked a very fierce clan.'

'I think you're right,' said Seumas, grimly. 'They looked like marauders. When he said "Birdmen" I think he meant birds of prey. Did you see those claw tattoos? They were no ordinary symbols – they were the mark of the pirate.'

Polahiki turned his back on the island and said, 'Perhaps we should leave here now?'

After he had turned he noticed the spear sticking out of the wall of the second deck hut. He was amazed at the size of the spearhead, which was more like a long knife. Rushing over to it, he grasped the haft. A shout came from within the hut, a command *not* to remove the spear, but Polahiki was already in the process of pulling it out. There followed a scream which chilled the blood of every person on board. Then came the sound of weeping and the beating of fists on the deck.

Next, to the amazement and horror of all, the door to the hut flew open and Pungarehu appeared. His hands were cupped and full of golden dust, like fine beach sand, which blew away on the stiff offshore breeze. Tears were streaming down his face. He uttered one word which said everything.

'Wiama!'

Polahiki backed away from the ravaged face of Pungarehu, the stranger's spear still in his hand.

'It wasn't my fault,' cried the fisherman. 'Don't come near me – I'll kill you.

I didn't know. You called too late. Don't look at me like that. Somebody hold him!'

Dorcha walked into the hut and stared at the walls. There was a hole left by the removed spear. Through this hole came a thin but brilliant piercing ray of sunlight. The Scot imagined it must have struck Wiama in the chest, as she lay with her lover on the deck, for there were two depressions in the straw. One of these two imprints was glittering with golden dust. The shaft of light illuminated a spot one third down this indentation. The waif had been mortally wounded by a javelin of sunlight, as solid to her frail body as the point of a real spear.

Outside, they were trying to comfort the distressed Pungarehu, who cursed Polahiki with every sobbing breath, until finally it was Seumas who intervened.

'Stop your oaths, man, do you not realise? It was the wind which carried that spear into the wall of the hut. No ordinary wind, for they are heavy weapons, not meant for throwing but for jabbing at close quarters. If Polahiki had not removed the spear I'm sure it would have been blown out by the wind.'

'The wind?' said Pungarehu, fighting against his tears still. 'What has the wind to do with it?'

'There is a god of the wind, is there not?' explained Seumas. 'His name is Maomao? I seem to remember a priest telling you that Maomao was angry with you and had promised to make you sorry. Yes? Yes, you remember. You are the killer of the Poukai bird, the giant bird under the protection of Maomao – I was with you man – I helped you kill the creature. This is the Great Wind-God's punishment for slaying the Poukai. You killed the giant bird with a stone axe, broke its wings first, then its jaws and skull. Remember?'

Pungarehu stared at his friend's face and knew this to be true. His wife, the beautiful and delicate Wiama, was the innocent victim of a long-standing dispute between a god and a man. Now the debt had been repaid, the man was no longer under threat – but the price had been unbearably high.

3

A meeting was held between the Rarotongans and the Raiateans. It was decided that Kieto and his Rarotongans would go out into the island, to search for the entrance to the kingdom of the Maori tribes. Ru and the Raiateans would stay with the canoe, replenish supplies, and defend their position against any attack from either the Birdmen or warriors from any other clan on the island, the giants included.

'Once we have supplies on board, we may anchor a good way offshore,' explained Ru. 'We must be in a position to sail away out of reach of any war fleet. But we will not leave you for good. Come to this beach and light five small fires in a straight row, the length of a man's arm between them, and if we're out on the ocean we shall come for you.'

'How long will you wait?' asked Kieto.

'One month at the longest. If you do not return within that time, we shall assume you are all dead.'

Kieto nodded. 'That's fair.'

'May your ancestors smile on your expedition,' said Ru, to the Rarotongans.

They nodded gravely and each sent up a prayer to Tiki, the First Ancestor, even Dorcha and Seumas. Besides the two Albannachs and Kieto there were Kikamana, Polahiki, Boy-girl and Rinto, son of Manopa. Po'oi and Pungarehu were to remain behind with the vessel. The former because he was unwell with some digestive complaint and the latter because he was still grieving over the loss of his bride and not in his right senses.

Heavily armed, the group set off into the interior of the island, hoping to find a person or tribe friendly enough to help them with the location of the magical cave.

When they reached the forest and entered it they felt a little more secure. At least the trees masked their movements. Out on open ground they were vulnerable to attack from the Birdmen, who both Seumas and Kieto felt would return with more warriors. Ru was no fool though and would not risk *The Princely Flower* in any foolish gesture of honour. The prince would weigh up the consequences and act accordingly. He was the right kind of hero to have in such circumstances: neither rash nor given to stupidity or temper. The ship, at least, was safe.

Polahiki, as usual, dragged his feet and complained the whole time about the amount of walking he was having to do, but Kieto would not wait for any stragglers and the fisherman was having to keep up with the rest of the party.

It was only a short while before they came upon one of the giants, this one obviously without movement, for it was lying flat on its back, its massive top-knot missing. They studied its strange long ears and enigmatic expression. The giant had been *painted* red, and its eyes were white coral with red pupils.

Kieto went forward and touched the creature, which appeared either dead or dormant.

He withdrew his hand quickly, then tentatively touched the still form again.

'What is it?' asked Seumas.

'Stone,' said Kieto. 'It's made of stone.'

He chipped at its face with his club.

'Yes, solid stone.'

'Did it turn to rock when it died, do you think?' asked Rinto.

'Look at the size of it,' muttered Kieto. Even just the head was three times his height. 'I hope we don't meet one of the living ones.'

Polahiki said, hopefully, 'Maybe those we saw were being moved by humans? We couldn't see their legs for the trees, if you remember.'

'I saw one turn and look behind it, and bend and stoop to pick something up – could men make it do that?'

'No, I suppose not,' replied an unhappy Polahiki.

The group continued along a path, which eventually led to a village of distinctive houses. Kieto told his group to stay hidden until they had observed the natives for a while. This they did and were soon rewarded as they watched people moving around the village. Their appearance was not like that of the victim of the Birdmen, but Oceanian, but they were not dressed for battle, nor did their tattoos give the same impression of hostility as those of the Birdman cult.

Finally, Kieto judged it right to call softly from the shadow of the forest to one of the villagers, a young girl fetching water from a surface pool. She was a sad-looking spindly creature who hummed to herself softly. The water container was a third the size of herself.

'Child!' he called. 'Come here.'

The girl looked up, gave a startled yell, and ran back into the village, shouting, 'Long ears! Long ears!'

Almost immediately warriors came running from the houses, brandishing spears and clubs, yelling their heads off.

Kieto said, 'Steady, don't fight unless we have to.'

When the shouting warriors of the village were a few yards away, the leader suddenly stopped and stared. Others gradually came to a halt behind him. One young man, whose battle fear had made him blind to all about him except the need to kill, continued his screaming charge but was deliberately tripped by one of the more experienced men of his village, sending him sprawling in the dust.

'What was the girl saying?' asked the front man. 'These are short ears like us – but new to the island, yes?'

This question was directed at Kieto, who nodded his head.

'We have landed here in order to replenish our supplies, but so far have seen nothing but a horrible murder.'

The leader of the party stuck his spear head first into the ground and the other villagers copied him.

'You have come at a bad time,' said the man. 'There is a war on, between the Long Ears and the Short Ears. In ordinary times visitors are welcome, to fill their water gourds and gather drinking coconuts, fruit and vegetables for their voyage, though we see few such sea-farers on the Navel of the World.

'Now, though, the smell of blood is in the air night and day. There are many bad men around, who will kill anyone, whoever they might be.'

'War tends to do that to people,' agreed Kieto.

Seumas said, 'These bad men – would they be called *Birdmen?*'

The village leader nodded. 'You have seen some of the Short-Eared warriors of this clan? They are as dangerous as the Long Ears ...'

'What about the giants?' asked Kikamana. 'Are the living ones made of stone too?'

'Living? Dead?' said the man. 'These are strange times. Some move, but are they living? Some are motionless, but are they dead? Who can tell, but the sorcerers.'

'Why are they painted different colours?' Kikamana queried.

'The red stone giants are on the side of the Long Ears, the white ones with the short ears are on our side. Sorcerers on both sides work to control the giants. Some give them the power of movement, while others seek out new spells in order to turn them back into solid stone again. The giants fight each other, try to crush enemy villages, cause much damage. No one seems to be winning except Hine-nui-tepo.'

'In war she is always the winner,' Kieto said.

'Come into our village,' said the leader, 'and take of refreshments. If we can help you, we will. I hope we can show we are not entirely devoid of hospitality, even though our island is torn apart in these dark times.'

The group of seven were led into the village where there was a temple with its marae. There were also several ahu around, some stained black with blood, others clean. Kieto asked why there were so many altars and was told that some were platforms where giants had stood, when they were dead stone.

Seumas, like others with him, retained a firm grip on his weapons, in case they were being lured into a position which they would have to fight their way out of. It would not be the first time warriors pretended to be friendly in order to slaughter their guests.

'We have recently killed a Long Ear,' said the leader of the warriors, who appeared to be an ariki of some kind. 'We still have some of the meat left – liver and thigh mostly.'

'Don't you have any pork?' asked Kieto. 'We are not used to eating human flesh.'

'Pork?' said the chief. 'What is that?'

And, looking around them, the Rarotongans realised there were no hogs to be seen, only chickens. It appeared that these people did not have pigs, nor dogs.

Seumas was glad he had left Dirk behind on the pahi, or the locals might have killed him for fear he was a demon. So, if they wanted red meat, they would have to eat people. The thought turned the stomach of the Pict.

'Just fruit for me,' said Seumas, quickly, still not over his first experience of long pig on a Hivan island. 'I've promised Rongo I would remain his faithful servant for three months, since a coconut struck me on the shoulder and not on the head.'

There were a few raised eyebrows at this hastily contrived excuse not to eat the liver of a human.

Seumas added quickly, 'It could have killed me, if it had hit my head – I owe my life to Rongo. He obviously steered the coconut away from a death blow.'

Kieto shook his head sadly.

Dorcha did not protest because she knew that as a woman she would not be offered meat. She and Kikamana would have to eat apart from the men, as was the tradition. It would be interesting to see what the natives would do with Boy-girl, who was a woman in appearance, but still possessed a man's genitals.

Boy-girl took one look at the half-cooked flesh of a roasted human being carried to the mats on wooden platters and promptly sat herself down with the women.

'These two,' said the chief, pointing first at Dorcha and then at Seumas, 'there's something curious about them. They have unusual eyes. And their hair is different. They have strange faces.'

'They are not Oceanians by birth,' Kieto replied, 'but they are now our basket-sharers.'

'I see,' said the chief.

He sat down on a mat and gestured for the Rarotongans to do the same. Food was being brought by women and placed in front of the men. Then a basket of fruit and fish was taken to the women. Polahiki dived in without any ceremony and began chewing some of the liver and thigh meat, while Seumas kept to breadfruit paste and taro, along with some dried fish. The rest of the Rarotongans, not cannibals by tradition, picked a little at the meat, then settled down comfortably with the rest of the fare. The villagers did not mind that their meat was being spurned by most of the newcomers, since it meant more for them.

'So,' said the chief, 'you are from a distant island?'

'Rarotonga.'

'And who is chief there?'

'We have two kings who rule jointly and peacefully, King Karika who came from Samoa and our own King Tangiia who came from Raiatea. We have only settled the island in the last several years. Rarotonga is a long way from this island, which we believe is called Rapanui?'

'This is correct,' said the chief, human fat dribbling down his chin. 'Rapanui is the name of our island, and the king who first found it was called Hotu

Matua, who taught us how to make these beautiful houses. Hotu Matua is our most revered ancestor and he will deliver us from these Long Ears.'

'When did the Long Ears first come?'

The chief shrugged. 'Perhaps they were here when Hotu Matua landed?'

He did not seem inclined to speak any further on the subject and Kieto wisely dropped it.

However, the chief went on to say, 'Yes, Rapanui we call our home, but it should be called Blood Island at the present time. There have been too many deaths – massacres of whole villages – and we do not know where it will end. You would do well to leave quickly. Things here have degenerated into a dark swirling chaos. Men are not in their right minds.'

'Thank you for your advice, but we are looking for a cave, the gateway to another world. I was told it would be on this island. Do you know of such a place?'

The chief looked about him nervously and shook his head.

'On this island there are many, many caves.'

Kieto was disappointed with this reply and the chief saw that he had been the source of unhappiness to one of his guests.

'I think I know of a man who could tell you the answer to your problem,' the chief said, by way of reparation. 'He is a great sorcerer – but he is a Long Ear.'

'Tell me his name?' asked Kieto.

'His name is Tapu Tao.'

'And where does he live?'

'In the mountains.'

At that moment there was a crashing sound from the jungle path and on looking up, Kieto and his group saw the head and shoulders of a red stone giant parting the crest of the trees.

'Look out!' cried Kieto, leaping to his feet.

The earth shook with a 'thump, thump, thump' as the giant continued its progress towards the village. Its topknot, which was of red sandstone and had not needed painting, perched on its head like a strange-looking hat. Its expression seemed more monstrous for being blank and lifeless, than if it had shown fury or lust. The coral eyes with their red pupils were penetrating. Heavy arms swung pendulum-like from the giant's shoulders. Its head made grinding noises, rock rubbing against rock, as it turned this way and that.

Kieto and the others were unsure what to do and looked to the villagers for some sort of guidance. Should they run? Should they attempt to hide? The natives however showed little enough fear, but appeared to have urgent tasks to perform. They were alert and primed for something. Splitting into two groups which went to different sides of the village they gave the impression of being annoyed rather than scared.

The giant came on, its gait ungainly but seemingly determined, into the village. Its right foot crushed a house to matchwood under fifty tons of solid rock. Its left foot squashed a chicken run, killing some of the livestock and sending the rest fleeing and squawking. Here the giant stopped and paused for a moment, turning its great head with its topknot balanced on its crown, the squealing, grating sound making the Rarotongans cover their ears. It was an appalling noise that set the teeth on edge. The massive stone man then started to move again, into the heart of the village.

As he did so, ropes suddenly sprang up criss-crossing the village, strung between the tops of tall trees with strong thick buttresses. The lines caught on the topknot of the colossus and strained as the giant continued his progress. The monster seemed unaware of the net of ropes, or did not care, and continued to walk forward while the lines stretched. One or two of the thickly woven ropes snapped like cord, whipping away and lashing the treetops on either side of the village. Gradually, however, the red topknot began to slide backwards, held by those lines which remained. The tops of the two great trees to which the lines were attached bent like bows under the strain.

Finally, as the huge stone man took another step forward, his topknot was dragged off, several tons of it falling to the ground, the thump of the impact causing the baked earth to shudder so hard it threw people off their feet.

The losing of its topknot was obviously a magical trigger which robbed the giant of its power of movement. The legs of the colossus slammed together like stone gates, closing and welding into one single pillar. Its head locked in the forward position. Its arms crashed to its sides. Chips of stone flew in all directions. Dust billowed from the armpits. Its nipples, standing proud, quivered.

The giant's momentum so suddenly checked caused the monolithic creature to fall forwards like a massive felled tree.

'Look out!' cried Kikamana.

The group scattered, heading away from the direction of the fall and into the trees. The local people dropped to the ground where they stood. They were wise in the ways of falling giants. The newcomers were not so knowledgeable.

This impact was tremendous.

The visitors, some still caught in the act of running, were catapulted into the air.

Trees were shaken from their roots by the hammer blow. Houses, outbuildings and stalls leapt and rattled their hardwood joints. Around the village the whole forest had gone remarkably quiet, with not a bird sound to break the silence. The stone giant had been defeated by some prior knowledge of its vulnerability. It lay face down in the dust, next to its topknot, obviously unable to stir.

The villagers then jumped to their feet and ran to the fallen idol. There was a joyous shout and they began to beat the inert statue with stone axes, hammers and other implements, as if it were capable of feeling their blows. They spat and urinated on its head. Children ran up and down the spine and old women attacked the creature's feet, throwing mud cakes onto the soles so that they stuck there. Cockerels were encouraged to climb on the topknot, to crow.

It was bedlam.

Kieto motioned for his party to move on, since they were having trouble getting any sense out of the villagers.

The group entered the forest once more, heading inland towards the mountains.

Kieto decided they should avoid any other villages, since even hospitality would slow them up. Everywhere they went they came across the signs of war. There were areas of burnt scrubland and deserted houses. Every so often they met with fences, corrals where domestic livestock had been penned, which had been torn down. Occasionally they stumbled on a corpse, a pile of fresh bones, or skulls in a heap. Dead animals and birds littered clearings in the forest.

'War is such a waste,' said Seumas. 'And here we are preparing for a new one.'

He meant the war Kieto was planning to take to the Albainn, which Kieto insisted was inevitable.

'That's not a war we can avoid – anyway, I prefer to call it a conquest. It is in our destiny to conquer the whole of Land-of-Mists. I keep telling you this, but you don't believe me, Seumas. Why is that *The Princely Flower* was driven on to the shores of this unhappy island, when Prince Ru wanted to search the seas around Rarotonga? Destiny, my friend.'

Seumas looked at Dorcha, who shook her head in sympathy with his point of view. But there was nothing they could do about it. It did seem an inevitable course; now that Albainn had been discovered the Oceanians had to conquer it.

At one point they were on the rim of an extinct volcano crater and looking down could see a light swathe of green reeds in the collected water below. They passed an unfinished stone giant, half-hewn from the rock, as tall as twelve men standing on one another's shoulders. Not far from this was a rock covered in strange symbols, pictures of a kind they had not seen before, as if they were intended to be informative signs.

'This is a strange place,' said Boy-girl with a shudder. 'It arouses the curiosity in my womanly instincts, but at the same time my manly intuition tells me to run back to the pahi and get away from here as fast as I can.'

They reached the foot of the mountains by the early evening and made camp in a low valley. Behind them were the rainforests, down to the shores.

In front of them were fantastic bladed green mountains, like shards of flint or frozen sea waves, thrown up by volcanic action into mysterious shapes. Here they refreshed themselves with rainwater which had gathered in natural rock bowls. When night fell, and the spirits of the landscape were abroad, they fell in with their learned fears of the supernatural, and where their knowledge of the island was limited they invented, allowed their imaginations creative licence. It was not difficult to find something to be afraid of, on an island which was steeped in dark wars and mysticism.

Also, they were physically cold, for this was an island nearer to the frozen seas than their own: a near sub-tropical climate with a different flora to Rarotonga. The temperature dropped when Ra took his golden face down below the skyline. Cool winds swept down from those sharp heights above them.

'We should have brought blankets,' said Dorcha, shivering. 'Why can't we have a fire?'

'Because it's dangerous,' Kieto replied. 'A fire can be seen for many miles. Even though we're in a valley it might reflect on any tall rocks around us.'

So Dorcha, who had been raised until her womanhood in a land which froze solid for four months of the year at least, had to suffer the indignities of a cooler climate than Rarotonga.

Seumas mentioned this fact to her.

'In Albainn I had a cat-skin shawl to keep me warm during the day and a wolf-skin blanket at night. Anyway, I've been living under a hot sun for most of my life now – my blood is thinner. That other life was a thousand years ago.'

'It does seem a long time ago – so far in the past it's become a faded memory.'

'Well, if Kieto has his way, we'll be going back again soon, though I'm not sure I want to.'

They woke the next morning, chilled and eager to walk again to get warm. However, they soon found their muscles were still stiff from the walking they had done the previous day. The trouble was, they were not accustomed to hiking over long distances: they were seafarers, not land travellers. Even when at home on Rarotonga, they had little need to walk far. So the trek began to tell on their tempers, fraying them at the edges, and they began to snap and snipe at one another.

Around noon they came across an elderly male with a bundle of sticks on his back twice his own height. The elder and his burden were going in the same direction up the mountain path, but he was moving so much slower than Kieto and his party. They saw that though he was bent, he was actually quite tall and lean. His ear lobes were long and hung low. Catching up with the old man, they confronted him, Kieto throwing questions in his face.

'Where are you going?'

The old man glared, not in the least confounded.

'To my village, weevil brain. Now if you'll step aside? This stack is heavy.'

'Can you not see we are short eared?' said Kieto. 'Are you not afraid we will kill you?'

'Well, if you're going to do it, do it *now*, because I'm old and tired and don't want to carry this load a step further if I've only got a short while to live. After all, I collect the wood to make a fire to cook myself a meal in order to keep myself alive. If I'm to die very shortly, then my labour is all for nothing and I might as well rest until the end comes.'

Kieto smiled at this speech.

'We're not going to kill you.'

'Then get out of the way, hog's turd, so that I can be about my business.'

'Look,' interrupted an exasperated Polahiki, 'we're newcomers to the island, having only arrived just yesterday and we want to find a man named Tapu Tao. We were told he's a Long Ear. Where can we find him?'

'I don't know.'

'You don't know him?'

'I didn't say that, you flea-bitten fool, I said I don't know where you can find him. Everyone knows Tapu Tao, but no one knows where to find him. He's a hermit. He lives up in the mountains.'

Seumas said, 'I thought we were in the mountains?'

'No – higher up. Up there!'

The old man's bony finger pointed dramatically to the peaks of the sharp, bladed mountains, where the hawks and high birds circled. Up there amongst the damp misty regions alpine flowers clung gingerly to precipitous ledges and overhanging crags. There an Oceanian rat would have difficulty in finding a wide enough path. Polahiki groaned. Seumas's heart sank. It seemed impossible. The ways were too steep, the escarpments too sharp. Perhaps the Pict could do it alone, but Kieto would never allow that, in case something happened to him.

This was turning into a nightmare journey.

'This is crazy,' said Boy-girl. 'I can't climb up there – I'd die.'

'That goes for the rest of us,' muttered Dorcha, 'except maybe my husband, who used to collect fulmar birds for their oil from such places, but that was when he was young.'

'We're never going to find this cave,' moaned Rinto.

'What cave?' asked the old man, apparently entertained by the idea that he had been the cause of so much consternation amongst these Short Ears.

He had divested himself of his huge bundle now and was staring from one face to another with a half-smile on his face.

'We are seeking the cave to an Otherworld, where the Maori dwell,' said Kikamana.

'Oh, *that* cave,' replied the old man, reaching down for his bundle again.

Seumas grabbed the stack himself, to help load it on the old man's back, and found it extraordinarily heavy. In fact he could not lift it on his own. Rinto lent a hand.

When the burden was in place again, resting like a house on the old man's spine, Seumas said, 'When you said *that* cave, it sounded as if you knew it yourself.'

'I do,' replied the old man, walking on with painfully slow steps. 'All of our elders know where it is.'

'Could you share your knowledge with us?' asked Boy-girl. 'Or do we have to be Long-Eared elders?'

'Yes and no.'

'Yes and no what?'

'Yes, I could share it with you and no, you don't have to be an elder of my people.'

Boy-girl looked significantly at Kieto.

They waited, but nothing more was forthcoming. Finally Kieto said, 'Will you tell us?'

The old man paused in his stride.

'I might do, but I have to get this bundle to the top of this path. It's heavy.'

'*Very* heavy,' muttered Seumas.

'Why don't we carry it up there for you,' suggested Kikamana, 'and you can explain to us where to find the cave as we walk?'

The bundle of sticks hit the floor with a thump as the old man let go of the carrying strap.

'What a good idea,' he said, smiling.

So they split the bundle into four and Seumas, Polahiki, Rinto and Kieto took a stack each, leaving the women to walk one either side of the old man. He seemed to enjoy their company more than that of the men, who trailed on behind, the bundles being heavy enough even though a quarter of what had rested on the old man's back. Boy-girl walked on ahead, like a tatterdemalion leading a parade, waving away the clouds of insects that infested the rockside grasses.

The women spoke low and earnestly to the old man, who took great delight in the touches he received on his arms every so often, and occasionally patted a shoulder in return. When they reached the top of the winding path, where they found a cave with an old woman sitting hunched over a tiny fire of dried bird's dung, they had all the information they needed. The old woman wanted to know what in the name of Ara Tiotio was going on and they left their informant to face a barrage of abuse for being so long with the wood.

The group descended the mountain again, happy to have found the location of the entrance to the Otherworld.

According to the old man the cave was actually only accessible from the sea and the party had to get down to the shore. 'There are high cliffs,' the old man had told them, 'so you can't get to it from above, but the water is actually quite shallow – too shallow for your ocean-going canoe. You'll have to find some outriggerless canoes and paddle into the cave.'

In fact, the cave entrance was on the other side of the island to where the pahi was anchored. Kieto had decided they would borrow some canoes from the locals and hopefully return them at a later date. There were seven of them altogether, so they would need at least two canoes.

As they descended from the mountain they could see the island below them littered with stone giants, both white and red, some standing on ahu, others clumping around the landscape. The moving ones had their topknots in place, the motionless ones had their topknots missing. Here and there too, was the smoke from burning villages. Great areas of forest had been shorn. Deserted villages, some in ruins, were like patches on the ground. It was an eerie scene. This was Rapanui, land of stone carvers, going through a bad time in its history.

PART SIX

The Armies of the Dead

1

The group travelled over hills and through valleys, using the tree's high plants for cover, until they came to a grassy clearing which they had to cross to reach the fringe of forest which ran along the shoreline. They had just started over this open patch of ground, when a long-eared red giant appeared out of the trees to their left. It had obviously seen them and began striding towards them.

'Look out!' cried Polahiki. 'Kieto, do we stand or run? Which way shall we go?'

The obvious course of action was to take flight – men could not fight stone giants with puny wooden clubs and spears – but for the moment Kieto was indecisive.

'Quick man,' said Seumas. 'Make a decision!'

Although the stone giant was awkward in movement, the sheer length of its strides brought him almost upon the group. Then suddenly, it stopped, and turned its grating head towards the forest. It seemed to be listening for something.

'What's the matter with it?' asked Dorcha.

Her question was answered by the trees parting again and another giant emerging, this time a white giant with short ears.

The two monoliths stood and stared at each other with baleful eyes. Their split peg legs had no feet on the bottoms, which meant they walked as if on stilts. Although they tried to stand on one spot, they in fact had to totter this way and that to keep their balance. No sound came from their big-lipped mouths, which remained sealed. Only in the way their heads swivelled did the Rarotongans, tiny by comparison, feel there was any hostility expressed.

Then as if by some given signal, the colossi moved towards one another, clearly ready to do battle. The humans were about to witness single combat between two massive stone giants: a spectacle they wished to observe from a place of safety. They felt vulnerable and exposed out in the clearing.

'Quickly,' cried Kieto, firm at last. 'To that rock overhang over there – let's get out of their way.'

The mortals ran across the grassy area to the shallow cave pointed out by Kieto and crowded underneath. The red giant's head swivelled on its shoulders, making that horrible grating sound again, and observed their progress. While he was doing so the white giant struck him a terrible blow on the shoulder.

Chips of stone whined through the air as part of the red giant's collar shattered. Bits of gravel came zinging from the fist of the white giant too. The flying fragments hit the cliff around the rock overhang in a hail of stone splinters. Had the group of humans been exposed, they would have been cut to pieces by the blast. As it was, they clustered behind their rock shield, hoping the giants would destroy one another.

The red giant now turned on his opponent, charging with his damaged shoulder. They met like two mountains clashing together, making the ground shudder with the impact of their collision. The white giant developed a fissure down the left side of his body: the humans heard the ear-splitting sound of the stone cracking. It was like a cry of agony.

The force of the blow had not only damaged the white giant, but his opponent too. In the meantime the shattered white monolith had been in the act of swinging his free fist at the topknot of his antagonist, only to make contact with the arm of the red giant blocking his blow. Instead of hitting the topknot, he struck the red giant's wrist, snapping off the ruddy statue's hand and sending it spinning and crashing into the forest, felling several trees.

Miraculously, the topknots of both giants remained in place, as if attached to their heads by more than gravity.

'The red one is winning,' groaned Polahiki. 'Look at that crack down the white giant – he's falling apart.'

'But the red giant has lost a hand now,' said Seumas, hopefully. 'Maybe he'll turn and run?'

But neither monster stone image seemed ready to yield. Both of them appeared stubbornly ready to fight until they crumbled to sand. They might have been made of hate instead of stone, the way they swung their arms at one another's topknots. It was a strange combat, silent of battle cries, but noisy with the clash and crack of stone on stone.

A red nose went whizzing past the rock overhang, to ricochet with a humming sound off a boulder. This loss of his olfactory organ seemed to spur the red giant to more drastic action for he suddenly head-butted his opponent just below the ear, endangering the safety of his own topknot, but managing to destabilise the balance of the white giant. The white giant's earlobe fell to the earth and buried itself in the moss. A hunk of rusty chin followed the descent of this lump of anatomy as the white giant's elbow came up under a red jaw.

'Have you ever seen anything like it?' whispered Rinto, the youngest member of the group.

'No,' said Dorcha, 'and I don't want to ever again. I wish the white giant would finish off that red devil, so that we could be on our way ...'

Her words turned out to be the death knell of the white giant, for at that moment his peg leg accidentally found a hole in the turf and he went flying backwards to land in a sitting position. He struggled to get off his backside, but his noseless assailant picked up an enormous boulder, as big as a house, between his right hand and his left wrist stump. He threw this chunk of moraine full force at the white giant's face. The force of the blow rattled his head. At last the topknot toppled to the earth and rolled away down a slope. The white giant immediately became immobile and rigid as a pinnacle.

'Now we've had it,' moaned the pessimistic Polahiki. 'That red oaf will come for us next. He'll make fish meal of us within a few moments.'

However, the cardinal giant seemed more intent on turning his blanched foe into gravel before taking care of any other matter. He began pounding the head and torso of the white giant, steadily, almost rhythmically, with his broken arm. His stone victim began to shatter and break, chunks falling off easily now that he could no longer ride with the blows. The ochre giant was not satisfied even with this and seemed intent on reducing his conquered adversary to powder. Blow on blow rained down on the unfortunate and helpless Short Ear, while in the meantime the humans managed to sneak away around the base of the cliff, into the long grasses on the far side of the clearing.

Seumas, the last in the line, looked back to see the red giant holding the white giant's sundered head in his good hand, about to pitch it into a long slope which led to a bog. The deed was done and the head rolled like a pale massive cheese down the gradient. The red giant's ochre face was as expressionless as ever, but the Pict got the feeling that the victor of the contest was experiencing a moment of triumph as he watched his enemy's pate sink slowly in the morass.

'By the gods,' Seumas muttered, 'those creatures might not have any hearts, but they have a taste for winning.'

The Pict was right. Just as Seumas turned to follow Rinto, the last but one in the line, the giant saw him. An ochre hand reached down for a missile. Before the grasses closed around Seumas a triangular stone nose zinged past his ear. It buried itself deep in the nape of Rinto's neck. Rinto fell to the ground without a murmur, dead before he struck earth. Seumas was in turn astonished at the speed at which it had happened, then shocked to the core by the tragedy.

He quickly examined his friend, but it was clear there was no life in him. Seumas could do nothing. Stepping over the body of Manopa's son, he caught up with the others, knowing if they waited they would become further victims of the red giant's callous enmity. When the group was far enough away from the scene, Seumas called softly to Kieto.

'We've lost one man.'

Kieto, at the head of the line, turned and stared.

'Rinto?' he said. 'We'll wait until he catches up.'

'No, you don't understand,' murmured Seumas, as the others were looking at the path behind him. 'He's dead. Killed by a stone. The red giant threw his own nose. It struck Rinto at the base of the skull. He's lying back there.'

'We have to fetch his body,' Kikamana said. 'We have to give him a burial ceremony.'

Kieto stared at Seumas, a look of comprehension entering his eyes, and he shook his head.

'No, Seumas is right. The giant's back there and anyway, we can't carry Rinto into the Otherworld and home again. He's lost to us. We have to go on without him.'

'You can't,' snapped Kikamana. 'His father was a hero. Rinto deserves to join his family. Without a ceremony his sau will be at the mercy of Dakuwanga.'

Kieto replied, 'You think he will get past Nangananga? Better his soul is swallowed by the Shark-God than be left to rot inside the womb of that foul goddess.'

'What's the difference?' sniffed Polahiki. 'One end or the other.'

It was true, Rinto was a bachelor and had not the protection given to priests and virgins. He had no excuse for being single. Kikamana might give him a fake wife, a doll, to carry with him down the purple path to Milu's land, but these artefacts seldom fooled the monstrous goddess who waited beyond the entrance to the Underworld. Rinto would be stuffed up inside Nangananga's womb with all the other bachelors, a hell within a hell, for the rest of eternity.

Behind them came the sounds of the giant crashing around in the forest, looking for their trail. Kikamana shook her head sadly and realised that more of them would die if they went looking for Rinto. It was true he would be a burden on them, heavy to carry, and jeopardise their mission. They had to go on and Rinto's sau would need to see to itself.

'On then,' ordered Kieto.

The group continued down towards the shoreline. Once there they followed the coast until they came across a village similar to the one they had first encountered. There were marauders at work there though, pillaging and burning houses. These were tall men, whose ear lobes had been stretched by some method and hung down long and loose.

Down on the beach some of the invaders, who had obviously arrived in their own narrow canoes, were busy smashing holes in the bottoms of their enemies' boats. Their own vessels were grouped on the sand at some distance from the village. Kieto and his party took the opportunity to seize two of the Long Ears' canoes and paddle them out into the sea. They were spotted when one of the wreckers looked up and gave a shout.

Four canoes set out in pursuit. The lead canoe was fast and covered distance quickly. The other three were strung out behind this speedy crew.

'Here we go!' muttered Seumas, gripping hold of his whalebone club and placing it in his lap. 'If they catch up to us, you carry on paddling, Dorcha.'

'Who are you handing out orders to, laddie?' she muttered. 'I'll do what I think best.'

Seumas sighed, knowing his spirited wife would do exactly what she believed to be necessary, without thought for her own protection. It was what he would do himself of course, but then he was a man and she a woman. Since she had left Albainn however, the difference between them meant little to her. It was really only at meals or in bed that their genders were obvious and even then Seumas sometimes became confused.

In Seumas and Dorcha's canoe was Polahiki. The other three, Kikamana, Boy-girl and Kieto, were in the lead canoe. The three in front had weapons to hand and looked ready to defend themselves at a moment's notice.

Polahiki, who only needed the flimsiest of excuses to stop paddling, which was hard work, dropped his oar and felt around in the bottom of the canoe. He found what he was looking for and gave a shout of triumph. It was a canoe breaker, carried on all Oceanian war craft: a lump of volcanic rock lashed to the end of a sennit rope. Polahiki was a fisherman, skilled in the art of flinging heavy nets, having to be accurate enough to hit shoals of fish as they flashed by a boat. He began swinging the canoe breaker round his head in every increasing circles.

The lead canoe of the Long Ears drew closer and closer. Spears began to plop into the water around Seumas. Stones from sling shots sang around his head. He could not turn and throw back because it was an awkward movement returning spear throws from a front canoe: he might overturn his own boat. Besides, Polahiki was in the way, still whirling the canoe breaker around his head.

'Hurry up,' he snapped, irritably. 'What are you waiting for, man?'

'Patience, patience,' muttered Polahiki, his dirty arms swinging the plumbline around in widening steady circles. 'I need to be sure ...'

A spear thudded into the rim of the canoe.

'For the love of the gods,' moaned Seumas. 'Throw the damn thing.'

At that moment Polahiki let go the line. The weight of the volcanic stone carried it sailing through the air. It smashed into the bows of the lead Long Ear canoe, just on the waterline: a perfect shot. The damaged canoe was flooded immediately, seawater gushing through the gaping hole in the front. Warriors yelled excitedly, diving overboard. One of them, a strong swimmer, tried chasing after his assailant. Polahiki showed him a filthy backside, knowing the man could never catch up.

The second war canoe did not pause to pick up the men in the water, as expected. They left that to the third and fourth boats. Since they were quite close to their quarry now, rescue attempts could be left to stragglers. This was a tactic quite unanticipated by the Hivan fisherman and he sat down and began paddling furiously.

'They're still coming,' he cried.

The second Long Ear's canoe also began to gain on Seumas and his party, having five men at the paddles. Kieto looked back, saw what was happening, and made a brilliant naval decision. There was only a canoe length between his vessel and Seumas's. However, the distance between the lead Long Ear canoe and his two remaining companion craft was widening.

Kieto ordered Kikamana and Boy-girl to turn the canoe round and they began heading back towards the oncoming Long Ears. Seumas was at first puzzled, then realised what was happening. It was now two canoes against one. Seumas shouted orders to Polahiki and Dorcha and they too swung their canoe back to face the Long Ears. The Long Ears glanced behind them and began to understand the quandary they were in. They had no support.

'We don't want to fight you,' cried Kieto, as the two Rarotongan crews approached the enemy canoe. 'Turn back and we'll let you go.'

There was a snarl from the leader of the Long Ear's canoe and he leapt from his vessel's bows towards the nearest of his enemy: the Pict.

Seumas, despite his age, was blindingly fast. He dropped his paddle, snatched up the whalebone wahaika club resting across his knees and struck the leaping man all in one smooth movement. The body hit the side of the boat, rocked it dangerously, then slid into the water.

There followed a short period of inactivity. Everyone was trying to assess the situation and decide what to do next. The man in the water was bleeding but not unconscious. With one injured shoulder, he struggled to reach his own canoe again.

One of the Long Ears then stood up and shouted. His arm came up as he pointed. Hammerheads were homing in on the bloody swimmer. The predators were incredibly swift, flashing grey and white through the water. In less than a moment they were on their prey. The Long Ears tried to drag their man out of the water, but a hammerhead shark had gripped him by the legs and was shaking him as a dog shakes a rag. No sound came from his throat, but the victim's eyes were wide with pain and fear. Seumas guessed the Long Ear's voice was locked tight by the terror which must have been surging through his brain.

The hammerheads won the tug of war. There was nothing anyone could do. Hammerheads are infamously tenacious and persistent. The victim was dragged under the canoe, out of the grip of his comrades, and the water around became a furious flurry of lashing fish forms with log-like heads, swilling blood and pieces of floating meat.

Seumas signalled to Kieto and the two Rarotongan canoes slipped away, out towards the big waves, leaving the Long Ears to garner what they could of their comrade. The sun was going down behind the horizon, Ra had finished his task for the day, and the light was fading rapidly. Phosphorescent light danced on the waters in the gloaming. The paddlers reflected on the day's events, each lost in images of red and white giants, the untimely death of a comrade and hammerhead sharks tearing human flesh.

Fortunately Hine-keha was at her brightest. The two canoes slipped under the brow of the sea-facing cliffs, passing cave on cave, and eventually found the one they were looking for with striations around the mouth. Seumas was carrying a fire-making stick, Polahiki the block, and Kikamana and Dorcha the brands. Soon they had torches in their hands and entered the cave, paddling slowly and warily, their flitting shadows acting out different lives on the walls of the tunnel to the Otherworld.

The water in the cave seemed to go deep into the heart of the island, before they could beach the canoes. It was here the tunnel widened to a cavern. They dragged the two canoes up on to the grey sand and began walking, surrounded by stalactites and stalagmites. Above them there was a black, moving ceiling, as they disturbed millions of roosting bats. It was an eerie and claustrophobic journey for the Oceanians, though the two Albannachs felt curiously at home: they had experienced such places in the land of their birth.

The cavern grew ever wider and wider, until they seemed to be walking in a wide landscape, but still the sky and horizons remained rock, from which emanated a soft grey-green light. There were thousands upon thousands of moths in the air and on the ground. Why these creatures were in such abundance was a mystery, but they appeared to be multiplying all the time.

'We don't need the brands any more,' said Kieto, indicating the strange light. 'Best put them out.'

They snuffed the torches and left them where they would be found on the return journey. They had another problem now, however, which they had not anticipated. With each step they took they were vaguely aware of a growing hunger, which they could not satisfy. There was water in pools, but no food, and the party began to experience ravenous cravings for nourishment. They also had to keep stopping for sleep, becoming tired again after only a hundred paces or so once they woke up. It was a confusing and upsetting episode.

'What's happening?' asked Kieto of Kikamana. 'It's not that long since we last ate. Why do I feel starved? Why do we have to stop and drink every few paces? Why do we need so much rest? I don't understand it.'

Kikamana looked about her at the undulating rocky landscape and shook her head.

'I think – I think something is happening to time in here. It goes by much more quickly. It's as if a day is passing with every two or three hundred steps we take. If we continue, we'll starve to death. Look at Polahiki. He's lost weight since we entered the cave. And me. We all have.'

'If we turn back,' asked Polahiki, 'will we reverse what's happening to us?'

Seumas growled, 'We're not going back, Polahiki. Get that out of your head. We've come this far and I for one am curious about what lies at the end of our journey.'

'Me too,' said Dorcha. 'I want to meet the Maori.'

'What if I go back on my own,' said the belligerent fisherman. 'What then?'

'Off you go then,' said Kieto, with a wave of his hand. 'But if you take a canoe, we'll hunt you down and kill you ourselves. But don't let us stop you.'

Polahiki gave his leader a sour look and said no more on the matter.

The party continued for a while, growing steadily weaker with malnutrition, until suddenly Polahiki began grabbing handfuls of moths, scraping them off the floor, and stuffing them in his mouth. The others, famished, followed suit. The six of them now scooped moths from the ground, grabbed them from the air, and crammed them into their mouths. No words were spoken, they simply knew they had to eat something. Sometimes, with a handfuls of moths from the floor came red clay and this was eaten along with the lepidopterous insects, helping to fill the huge cavity in their stomachs.

Seumas had to take mouthfuls of water to wash down the dusty, dry creatures, some still wriggling as they descended his oesophagus. Their wings stuck to his teeth and the roof of his mouth, their antennae tickled his throat. He felt it was a disgusting thing to be doing, but he was so hungry he could not help himself. It was either this or eat one another.

After a while they all sat down, a little pale around the corners of the mouth, and Kieto spoke to them.

'Let's hope we get to the end of this journey soon – I don't think I could do that again.'

'You'll do it,' said Kikamana, 'if you have to.'

When they had rested, for they were extremely tired, they continued their journey.

They came to a shallow river flowing over a rocky bed. It struck Seumas that the stone walls of the cavern had moved back. This was probably the largest part of the whole cave system, the centre of their journey. They were now at the heart of the monstrous cavern, with its echoes, its moths and bats, its spikes of lime. The river, however, appeared to be some sort of boundary line, because as they began wading over to the other side, the party began to see visions, hear sounds, which must have originated in the preternatural world.

'Do you see them?' whispered Seumas to Dorcha. Dorcha nodded. 'Kikamana, what are they?'

There were translucent men and women, all very tall and straight, marching a foot above the surface of the river.

They moved in ranks and files, fifty wide, thousands long, relentlessly towards the six Rarotongans. The figures were humming some kind of marching tune and carried torches in their hands, but the flames did not illuminate the cavern, they burned with an uncanny light whose rays went no further than the face of the carrier. At their head was a leader, who moaned incessantly in hollow, emotionless tones, 'Kill them, kill them, kill them.'

'The armies of the dead,' replied Kikamana, softly. 'Quickly take off your clothes. Lie down in the water.'

No one thought to argue with the priestess, who knew about the culture of the Dead. They tore off their skirts and lay down on the pebbles and rocks in the water, letting it trickle over their backs, keeping their noses just above the surface, and waited apprehensively for the spectres to pass by.

Over their bodies marched the armies of the dead, the ghostly feet not far above their heads. Seumas found the whole experience ghastly. He shook, both with fear and the chilling waters of the river. Grisly men and women with dark sunken eyes, sallow skins and vacuous voices tramped above him, creating in him a feeling of grey sickness and horror. They seemed endless too, these great battalions of spectres, while Seumas just longed for the last line to pass over, and be gone.

Suddenly, Polahiki stood up and tried to run, screeching at the top of his voice.

'I can't stand it. I can't stand it.'

He managed to reach the rocky shore, but appeared to fall there, and be held by an unseen force. The troops now ceased humming their dreadful monotonous tune and followed their leader in chanting, 'Kill him, kill him, kill him ...'

The line of marchers weaved towards the spot where Polahiki was lying, wretched and quivering with terror. They stretched out grisly hands, on the end of grisly arms, as if to welcome him into their ranks. They pursed their grisly lips, ready to kiss his cheeks, while blowing foul gases down their grisly nostrils. Their sunken eyes glowed with an acquisitive light. He was theirs. It seemed they were going to lift him up like a child of the departed, carry him off, take him to their asylum. Polahiki was gibbering with fright, making the horrible whimpering noises that Dirk made in his sleep.

Then one of the marchers cried out in louder tones that overrode the chanting, 'Leave him. He is mine. Touch him not. He is mine.' This was repeated a dozen times over.

On hearing this call the armies of the dead turned back into their straight line again, gliding over the surface of the river, leaving Polahiki still sobbing and gasping on the bank. For reasons yet unknown to Seumas, the Hivan fisherman was safe. Yet it had seemed that he had been doomed until that single voice had cried above the chanting, 'Leave him. He is mine ...'

Finally, the last battalion of the army of the dead passed over the group and they were able to rise and dress.

Polahiki joined them again, considerably shaken, but probably no less so than the others. They all took some time to recover from the experience, which had bitten into their minds and souls with cold teeth. They began walking again, Seumas and Kieto taking the front position. Dorcha deliberately remained at the back, so that she could speak with the priestess.

'Why was he saved?' asked Dorcha of Kikamana.

'Polahiki? He will probably tell you that.'

The fisherman nodded. 'My father,' he said. 'My father was in the ranks of the dead. It was he who told them to leave me alone.' Polahiki's eyes appeared to mist over a little. 'When I left my home isle, my father was still alive. He must have since died.'

'I'm sorry,' Dorcha said, though she could not bring herself to touch the fisherman, whose unwashed body and dirty habits revolted her. 'You must be grieving.'

'No,' said Polahiki, candidly. 'I never liked him much. He used to beat me as a child. In fact, I hated him. I'm glad he's dead. I hope it was very painful. I hope he trod on a stonefish and died in agony. It would be too much if he just died quietly in his sleep.'

Dorcha was shocked by this speech.

'Then why did he save you?'

'Well, I never did anything to *him*. He probably thinks I had a wonderful childhood. He probably thinks I revere him for drumming his knowledge into me. He probably thinks he was a good teacher, strict and firm. In fact he was a cruel monster. I remember the bamboo cane swishing down on my bare back and legs, while he beat some piece of useless wisdom into me. It didn't occur to him that I would forget what he was telling me and remember only the pain. He thought it was the only way to learn things, since that's the method *his* father used.'

'Your grandfather.'

'Yes – he was an old bastard too. I hated his guts as well.'

There didn't seem to be much Dorcha could say to this and she joined her husband up front. They were coming to a narrow place now, where the light had undergone yet another change. Here the rock walls of the cavern were much closer together and had dark shadows at their bases. The group could hear movements amongst the shadows, but could see nothing.

'What is it?' asked Seumas of Kikamana. 'Monsters?'

'Demons,' replied the priestess, firmly. 'We will need a karakia.' She took some bones from her waistband and began to beat them together, chanting a fangu as she walked. The others followed after her, keeping well to the middle of the cavern.

Suddenly, out of the shadows came showers of stones and rocks, striking the Rarotongans.

'Don't run,' cried Kikamana, breaking her chanting for a moment. 'Walk.'

The others did as they were told, but the missiles were extremely painful. At the same time the hidden demons began hooting and jeering at them, challenging them to do battle, calling them cowards, saying they were poor specimens of human beings. Seumas gripped his club. Dorcha grabbed his wrist.

'No,' she said, as the stones rained on them. 'Follow Kikamana's lead.'

As if running this gauntlet were not enough they came to an even narrower passage, where the walls were slamming together in an irregular fashion. It meant they would have to run a short stretch at the risk of being crushed to breadfruit pulp. Such a daunting prospect once again had Polahiki complaining, as rocks struck him on the back and head, opening the festering sores which seemed to be so much a part of his life.

'Now this?' cried Seumas, more irritated than afraid. 'Do we make a dash, or what?'

Once again the knowledge of the kahuna, Kikamana, was necessary to their survival.

PART SEVEN

Land of the Long White Cloud

1

Kikamana ordered every member of the party to find some large stones, as big as they were able to carry. The demons in the shadows seemed to have run out of ammunition now and were watching the humans with bright eyes. There was no more hooting and shouting, just curiosity. The demons wanted to see what would happen when a mortal was caught between the slamming cliffs.

'They spurt,' said one.

'Squish and spurt,' muttered another. 'You see.'

'They crack too,' murmured a third. 'They squish, spurt and crack – like a ripe fruit with a kernel.'

Polahiki threw a wicked glance in the direction of these creatures, but said nothing.

Kikamana said, 'Select hard rock, if you can – not sandstone, or limestone, or anything too soft.'

This they did. There was nothing as tough and brittle as flint in the enormous cavern, but there were chunks of gneiss. These they gathered at the entrance to the clashing cliffs. When they had accumulated as many as they could find, Kikamana told them what they must do.

'When the cliffs draw back, we must throw as many of these rocks as possible inside, so that when the walls slam together the next time, hopefully they will jam them wide enough apart to create a tunnel.'

So, they waited for the cliffs to smash together, then when they drew back there was frantic activity to roll and throw boulders into the gap. They had about three-quarters of their load within the space, when the cliffs slammed together again. Some of the rocks were crushed, smaller ones on the edge, but essentially a gap was created. When the cliffs drew back again, the group filed through at a rapid pace.

Boy-girl, Polahiki, Kieto and Dorcha made it through before the next coming-together of the cavern's savagely mating walls. Seumas and Kikamana were caught towards the end of the passage. The cliffs managed to smash more rocks this time, narrowing the gap considerably. If Seumas had stretched his arms out either side, he would have touched the walls. However, they would surely get to the end before the *next* blow.

Seumas was about to step out to safety when the cliffs unexpectedly shut again. This time he was actually grazed on one side of his body and had but a finger's-length to spare on the other. Kikamana was not far behind him. The walls drew back. Seumas leapt out.

Again, it was only a moment after they had drawn back, that the cliffs smashed together again, as if determined to trap at least *one* victim. Kikamana was in there, as the walls met with a thunderous sound, causing the floor to vibrate. Boy-girl screamed. Every member of the party imagined the priestess was blood-and-bone paste on the faces of the two cliffs.

The walls drew back again, and miraculously Kikamana came on through, stumbling out to freedom.

'You're alive?' cried Boy-girl. 'You must be the greatest kahuna of all time!'

'Not so great,' said Kikamana, getting back her breath. 'There are hollows on the cliff faces. I just happened to be opposite one. Very lucky.'

'Not lucky,' said Kieto. 'You are beloved of the gods, Kikamana. If it had been one of us, we would have been crushed.'

The slamming cliffs appeared to be their final obstacle in the great cavern, which now began to narrow again to the size of a normal cave. A breeze was felt. There was an opening, somewhere ahead, into another world. Every member of the party gathered their mental strengths, ready to face this fresh challenge. They all had their own ideas on what the new world would be like.

The light of the sun was in their eyes and they followed it.

Seumas was the third to step out into the Otherworld. The light dazzled him for a while, but when he was able to look around him he saw a landscape of undulating grasslands beyond an area of bubbling hot springs and tall hissing geysers. This did not appear to be small-island terrain, but more on the scale of his homeland Albainn, and its attached neighbour, Engaland. This was a big country, with a vast blue sky above, and elongated clouds that stretched like lazy giant sheep over the heavens.

Seumas heard a sound next to him and turned to see an enthralled Kieto.

'Aotearoa,' breathed Kieto in wonder. 'Land of the Long White Cloud.'

'Land of the Maori,' Seumas said.

'Yes, land of the great Maori warrior race, whose fame has reached our world through the dreams and the visions of kahunas. We must be cautious here, for we are out of our own place and things will be different – customs, manners, perhaps even gods? Who knows, we may be the first of our people to come here?'

Kikamana looked about her in awe. 'I have often dreamed of this land, during trances and fevers, when my mind was able to reach out beyond our own world. It is larger and more beautiful than I imagined. See, in the distance, the blue ridges of mountains. And here, beyond this hill, the spouting hot waters shooting up into the air like quick-growing trees. This is a land of contrasts, the very hot and the very cold.'

'Cold?' said Polahiki.

Kikamana said, 'I have seen a coldness beyond belief, in its high places – there it becomes so cold the rain falls as white powder and the water hardens to stone.'

'This is surely not true?' argued Polahiki. 'Hard water? And rain like dust?'

'It is true,' Dorcha confirmed. 'These things are called snow and ice. We have them in our land, the birthplace of Seumas and myself. Snow and ice, made from rain and still water. Snow settles on the land and turns everything pure white, muffles it in a cold powdery coat. Lakes and ponds ice over and turn hard as stone. They make for wicked winters, when everything freezes, and mind and body go numb.'

The other members of the party shook their heads, as if it was all too much for them. They stared around them at the magnificent rolling landscape, leading as Kikamana had said, to the distant ranges of mountains. On the grassy hill where they stood they were able to see the hot springs surrounded by simmering pools of lava. Hissing, yellow-edged holes sent out a pungent gas which stung their eyes and nostrils. Steam drifted over the landscape in rising veils, making the scenery quite mystical to Rarotongan eyes.

Despite the warning of cold weather, Polahiki was much impressed with this new land. All his life he had lived on boats or small islands and now here was a land, perhaps an island, perhaps not, which stretched as far as the eye could see. It was an ocean of grass and trees. Surely this was a place where one could settle in comfort, fishing in a calm lake instead of a vast sea, where there was so much land one might build a house and never have to see another human being again?

There was something of the eremite in Polahiki.

Around the hot springs were ferns as tall as many coconut palms, decorated with butterflies and birds. There were rainforests in the distance, dark green and moody. There were valley pockets thick with rotting vegetation and nets of vines, and littered with fallen and leaning trees. It was a richly layered land, full of life, with a cooler climate than they were used to, but with more shades of green to its covering. The travellers had no doubt of the wealth of the country in which they found themselves: it was evident in its every aspect.

Kieto scanned the horizon and eventually found the sight for which he was looking.

'Smoke,' he said, pointing. 'We must head in that direction.'

The party set off, with Kieto at their head.

Polahiki asked of Boy-girl, 'How do we know these people, these Maori, won't be hostile?'

'I expect they will be,' replied Boy-girl, cheerfully. 'Kieto will be disappointed if they're not. After all, that's what we've come here for, to meet a warrior nation.'

The answer did nothing for Polahiki's worries, except to reinforce them.

Pathfinding a broad landscape was a little like navigating on the ocean, except there were more markers. Kieto dropped down into a valley and followed a braided river the width of which astonished him. Everything was so much larger here in the Land of the Long White Cloud. The river led him in the general direction of the smoke he had seen and he guessed the makers of that smoke would not be too far from a source of fresh water.

As evening fell on the broad land, they began to approach the place where they had seen the smoke. Now they could see the lights of the fires. Kieto had decided on a bold entrance, since they did not have a great deal of time and they had to make contact with the Maori soon. Ru would only wait for a month off the coast of Rapanui.

It was true that Kikamana was with the exploratory party, and she was a member of Ru's crew, but no doubt Ru would find himself another virgin to take her place from amongst the Short Ears if he found it necessary to do so.

Kieto and the group came to a bend in the mighty river. At that moment there was a yell from a Maori sentry. A hundred warriors leapt to their feet and came charging down a slope in a tight formation which looked like a solid unit.

'Don't touch your weapons,' warned Kieto. 'Stand your ground.'

Seumas was itching to draw his club, but he did as he was ordered and hoped they would not be subject to the worst.

When the Maori saw that there were only six intruders, three of them women, they broke formation. The front ranks of the Maori stamped forward, step by step, with lolling tongues, distorted mouths and rolled-up eyes to show the whites. At the same time they sang a harsh song which sent shivers of fear through the newcomers. This was a terrifying spectacle and Polahiki turned to run, would have done so, had not Boy-girl grabbed him by the arm and held him there.

By the dying light of the sun the visitors could see that the Maori had tattooed their faces, a custom which was repugnant to Kieto's people. It was true Hivans had tattoos on their faces, back in their old world, but not people from the Tahitian group of islands. Hivan tattoos tended to be straight bars and lines, whereas these Maori faces bore fantastic designs which followed the contours of their cheeks and mouths, around the eyes, on the brow. There were curlicues and whorls on the chin and down the nose the spine of a fish with spreading bones, and circles within circles, maze leading into maze on either side.

One man now came forward, brandishing a spear, his face twisted into a demonic expression. His legs in a wide stance, he stamped the ground, chanting oaths. With the spear he jabbed the air before him, continually.

Kieto cried, 'Brave warriors of the Maori, we come in peace. We are from a distant island. Give us your hospitality.'

The words had their effect. The warrior in front became less aggressive in his pose. He stared hard at the group. Finally he slapped his thigh and called.

'You are ship-wrecked here?'

'We are Rarotongans,' said Kieto. 'We have come to find the Maori tribes!'

'We are the Maori,' replied the warrior. 'Come with us.'

They were surrounded by the warriors and led towards the campfires. Seumas realised, as they approached the fires, that there were many more warriors than they had first imagined. There were several hundred men around the fires. This was no village either, but the camp of a force on the move.

The group was the object of curious interest as they were led through the camp by those who had captured them. Finally they were brought before a standing man who was flanked by two carved wooden posts stuck into the ground. The carving was of such superior quality that Seumas almost reached out and touched the posts. These he knew were staff-gods, probably ancestors-gods, and it would not have been wise to defile them with a stranger's hand. Nevertheless, he was impressed by the sheer craft of the artist, who must surely have been a genius.

'I am Chief Tuwhakapau,' said the tall stately figure between the posts. 'Where are you going?'

Seumas knew immediately why the chief did not ask who they were or where they were *from*. It might be that they were famous Oceanians and therefore to ask who they were would reveal ignorance in the chief. If they were notable men he would be expected to know who they were on sight. So, good manners dictated that he should not ask them their names, nor their homeland, but their destination only, since of this he could not be expected to have foreknowledge.

'We are Rarotongans,' said Kieto, 'but from an Otherworld, out of the cave by the hot springs.' He named each of the party in turn. 'We come to learn of warfare from the masters of war, the great Maori race, O king.'

The chief stared at this motley group and suddenly grinned. His warriors laughed to see him smiling. Kieto and the others joined in the mirth. Then the man spoke again.

'You must not call me king, for the Maori do not have kings, we have only chiefs. We are not puffed-up Tahitians, with so much mana that we cannot walk among our own people. We are fighters—'

'That's why we have come to see you,' said Seumas, interrupting.

Heads turned to look at this new speaker. The Maori chief stepped forward and looked into Seumas's eyes, studied his hair, then stepped back again. He nodded.

'A Captain Cooker,' he said. 'You come from King George?'

Seumas did not know what to say to this, since it meant nothing to him.

'A Captain Cooker?' he asked at last, when the silence became unbearable. 'What is that?'

'You are a man from the tall ships,' said the Maori. 'You come with guns?'

Seumas looked helplessly at Kikamana. She was the one with the knowledge of this land. She was the one who should know what *guns* and *tall ships* were.

Kikamana said, 'I am a priestess. You must know we are from the Otherworld. We do not have such things as King Georgers and Captain Cookers there. You must forgive us for our ignorance. This man comes from Land-of-Mists, and his wife here, the same. Their land is without a sun.'

'Just the same,' nodded the Maori. 'Just the same as Captain Cook.'

'I do not know this Captain Cook,' said Seumas, evenly, 'and I have no king called George. My king is called Tangiia.'

The chief looked startled at this.

'You know the ancestor heroes?'

'Where we come from, Tangiia is no ancestor, but is alive and well.'

'Then,' said the chief, clearly impressed, 'you are from Hawaiki, the Old Homeland, where we all began!'

'What is he talking about?' Seumas asked Kieto, quietly.

'Hawaiki, the cradle of our people. Some say Raiatea was once Hawaiki, but no one really knows. It is the beginning and the end. A sacred land whence the earliest of our fathers and mothers emerged.'

'Hawaiki,' murmured the chief, this time a little more suspiciously. 'If you are from Hawaiki, then you must either be gods or ancestors.'

'Neither,' replied Kieto, 'but from *another* Hawaiki. Just as a palm overhanging a lake has an image in the water, a reflection of itself, so we come from a world which is the image of this world. Yet the lake ripples with the wind and so the two palms, the one on the bank and the one on the water, are not *exactly* the same, but have some differences. So it is with the two worlds, which are remote from each other, and similar in appearance. Without one, the other would not exist however, and each has its own importance in its own time.'

'What my leader here says is true,' Seumas confirmed. 'We can talk of reflections, or shadows, or the great ocean and the roof of voyaging. There are many examples.'

The chief nodded thoughtfully.

At this point Seumas felt he should not put himself forward any more and excused himself and stepped into the background, leaving Kieto and Kikamana to speak to the chief. Afterwards, when they were around a camp fire, not far from the Maori and under guard, they spoke amongst themselves.

'These people do not trust us yet,' explained Kieto, 'so they put a watch on us. But I believe they will let us take part in the battle. It's the only way we will get to fully understand their strategy and tactics. In the meantime, we must study their ways, try to understand them.'

Dorcha said, 'First I would like to understand what this place is and what it means to us. Seumas and I are completely confused with all this talk of King George and Captain Cook. Do you know who they are, Kikamana?'

The priestess shook her head. 'No, I have never heard of them, but what you must understand is that this world roughly mirrors our own. In this world there is probably a Kikamana somewhere, and maybe a Dorcha and Seumas. Or was. Or will be. This is not only a different place, but a different time. Perhaps in this world the Picts are the civilised race? – maybe the Picts rule Oceania? Perhaps George is king of the Picts and Captain Cook a Pictish hero? Who knows.'

'George doesn't sound like a Pict name,' grumbled Seumas. 'It doesn't sound like any sort of name at all.'

'That's not my point,' Kikamana said. 'My point is that you can take the same elements that make up the real world, put them in a pot and shake them up, then pour them out and find *this* world. Do you see what I mean?'

'No,' replied Seumas, 'and my head's spinning. Can we just leave it at that?'

They spent a cold night, shivering under their thin individual blankets. The following morning Chief Tuwhakapau appointed an elderly warrior as their companion. His name was Tangata. He was tall and very thin, his muscle tone beginning to flag, but he had an honest face. He explained what was happening.

'Maybe we kill you, maybe we don't,' smiled Tangata through broken and missing teeth. 'Chief Tuwhakapau is not sure whether or not it would be a good thing to kill the Captain Cookers just yet. Killing Captain Cookers might be tapu. He has consulted the tribe's two tohungas and one says kill you, the other says not to kill you. They argue a lot. In the meantime my advice is you must get our chief to love you, so even if it isn't tapu to kill you all, he lets you live because you're nice people.'

Tangata smiled again. His ancient leathery face, covered in blue-black tattoos the exact lines of which had disappeared into the creases caused by old age and the weather, had a kind of warm grotesque quality to it. With his thin grey hair, his wispy white beard, and his almost black eyes, he might have been someone's great-grandfather. He had the matter-of-fact, no-nonsense style of speech of the chief, and perhaps all Maori, and he left you in no doubt where you stood. An old, respected warrior, he would treat you right if you were genuine, but kill you instantly should you prove treacherous.

'What happens today?' asked Kieto. 'Do we break camp?'

'Yes, we go to the village of our enemies, where we make war with them.'

Boy-girl said, 'Why do you make war?'

The old Maori shook his head slowly. 'War is our destiny. Only in war can man find glory and honour. Perhaps you would not understand, being a stranger, but respect from other warriors is most important to us. And when we die, the great warrior goes to a shining paradise, where he will hear his praises sung by those he left behind to mourn his passing.'

'In other words,' said Boy-girl, in an aside to Kikamana, 'they don't need a reason.'

The Maori broke camp and the warriors went on the march. The six Raroton-gans and their guide took up the rear. For them it was quite some feat, to travel overland at a near trot. It was a fatiguing journey. They went through bush and over grassland, into rainforest, uphill paths, along gorges, and finally in the middle of the afternoon Tangata pointed to their destination, a fortified hill village.

'The enemy pa,' said Tangata. 'They have seen us coming and sound their drums.'

To both the native Oceanians and to the Albannachs the pa was an astonishing sight, a piece of engineering beyond the experience of any of them.

The whole hillside had been flattened at the top and fell in tiers on all sides. A ring-ditch circled the outer defences, with a rampart and palisade immediately behind the trench. Along the outer palisade of sharpened stakes were fighting stages with ladders leading up to them. Behind the outer defences, on a higher level, was a second rampart and palisade, within which were thatched buildings, houses and store rooms. Placed at intervals along both the outer and inner stockades were posts of carved figures – ancestor gods – who along with the warriors of the tribe would help protect the village against invaders.

The defending warriors on the fighting stages looked down upon the approaching aggressors and seemed utterly superior. To Seumas, Kieto and the others their position appeared to be unassailable. To these visitors an impossible task lay ahead of the raiding party: overwhelming a foe in a position of such strength would take an army of thousands.

'It can't be done,' said Seumas. 'We chose the wrong side this time.'

The invaders ranged themselves on the plain below the fortified hill village and began a haka.

Warriors in serried ranks, Tangata among them, began to leap in unison first one way and then the other, at the same time letting out a deep resonating cry which curdled the blood. Their spears and clubs rose and fell in a perfect imitation of a breaker curling along a beach, so that they appeared not as many individual men, but as a single beast with a single mind. It was as if a monster were performing out there on that warm sunlit plain, a dark frill with white trimmings rippling along its front and flowing in waves back through its broad flat body.

Terrible screams came from the monster now, as the invading warriors alternated their deep bass notes with high blood-chilling shrieks. Fury foamed from every pore as they roused themselves to a fervour of battle-lust, their passion for killing evident in every brandish of a weapon, in every athletic leap of the body, in the rolling of eyes and the jerking of heads.

'Perhaps thousands of warriors will not be needed after all?' murmured Kieto, now thoroughly impressed. 'Perhaps these warriors will just flow over the fences like a giant octopus, sucking the life out of what lies underneath?'

On the ramparts of the village the defending warriors had gathered. Many of them were on the fighting stages, ready to cast rocks and spears down on the attacking forces. Others stood inside the palisades or behind the pa gate, over the lintel of which stood the tekoteko, an artistically sculpted statue of a demon possessing great magical powers of defence.

Once the haka was over, Tangata came running back to his six charges, to watch over them. If any treachery was to be done, it would be now, while the backs of the invaders were exposed to an attack from the plain. Tangata did not seem disappointed that he was unable to take part in the battle. He told them he had seen many wars, many such attacks, and having survived until a ripe age he intended to spend the rest of his years being a little more cautious in his fighting.

'What's happening now?' asked Kieto. 'Will there be a full frontal attack?'

Tangata was dubious about this. 'What we tried to do was shame them into coming out and fighting us on the plain, but unless they're touched by the sun they won't do that. The village is too high to throw hot stones on the roofs of their houses, so we can't do that either. I think the young men will attempt to gain honour with a few rushes at the palisade, then we'll settle down into a nice long siege.'

The old man's words were no sooner out of his mouth when a group of young warriors, eager to gain respect and glory, ran to the palisade and launched their spears at the enemy. This action flushed a rash of spears from behind the ramparts of the fortified village. Most of the javelins missed their mark, but one or two struck flesh. A warrior on a fighting stage fell to his death. Three young men were either wounded or killed amongst the attackers.

One young attacking braveheart tried to rush and climb the palisade, club in his teeth, only to be crushed by a hail of rocks from the defenders, delighted to have a clear and available target for their missiles.

Following this foolhardy move the attackers sat down at a distance from the pa while one of their number strutted up and down, challenging the enemy to send out a warrior to do single combat with him. He shouted insults, boasted about his own prowess and skill at fighting, called those behind the wooden stakes 'babies' and 'little fish'.

His call was answered with alacrity by a member of the village and a hand-to-hand fight ensued between the two. The attacking forces gained the first victory and a great cheer went up amongst them. The next man from the pa was also despatched, but with less ease. Finally, on the third acceptance, the attacker's champion went down under a fierce blow and a groan went up from his companions. From the fort came the first cheer and the victor was allowed to return to his comrades behind the palisade to receive congratulations.

All this was pure sport to wile away the time.

Thereafter, the siege settled in and the attackers camped around the village, spending their time in eating and drinking and taunting the occupants. The hope was they could goad the warriors inside the village to come out and battle with the waiting besiegers, but so far the men of the village proved wisely invulnerable to this assault on their manhood. After all, Kieto pointed out, what was the point in spending a great deal of time and effort in building defences for a village, if you were going to abandon it for a handful of insults?

Kieto was extremely impressed with the pa. He saw in it great possibilities.

'It could be used as a fort, an encampment, when we set out to conquer the Land-of-Mists,' he said to Seumas. 'Have you seen anything like it before?'

'I have heard of such things amongst the Angles.'

'Then we will adopt this fortification too, and put it to our own use.'

The idea of a siege, starving or thirsting one's enemy into submission, was very new to the Rarotongan experience. Rarotongan battles were fought out in the open, with warriors dressed in their fine and colourful war garments.

The Rarotongans had, it was true, certain forms of organised warfare. There was the fatatia method where armies met face-to-face. Or the more sneaky aro nee where only they met the enemy on a narrow front and the larger flanks remained hidden behind trees or rocks, ready to pounce. And there was the aro ro where the army advanced in lines and when the first line had been battered or beaten, the second line moved up to take its place.

A more manly tactic was the paitoa, where the army was ordered to stand as firm as a stone wall, while the enemy hurled themselves against them.

In uura tama faarere no man was allowed to leave the battlefield alive before they had conquered the opposing force.

One method which might turn an enemy army around, if it had weak leaders, was the ropa tahi. In this the whole attacking army made it known they were concentrating mainly on killing chiefs and warriors of high rank. This tactic was enough to frighten the bravest warrior king, faced with a horde of fanatical hot-blooded young men intent on killing him alone, regardless of who might get in the way.

Kieto got to speak with Tangata.

'When we first approached your camp,' he said, 'your warriors came out in a tight formation – what do you call that?'

'This we call the *turtle*,' replied the old man, grinning. 'We will use it again – against *them*.'

He pointed to the forces behind the pa, which numbered around nine hundred men. The attacking force was in the region of fifteen hundred warriors. It was almost two against one, if it ever came to an open fight.

Tangata was quite happy to sit down and talk about the fighting methods of the Maori. He had seen much and was full of knowledge on the subject. Kieto took it all in, asking many questions, receiving information on strategy and tactics of famous battles. Tangata was a fund of fighting experience, which he was quite happy to share with his questioner, since it made him the centre of attention.

'What about sea battles,' asked Kieto. 'Are the Maori good at fighting on the water?'

'Not as good as on the land,' admitted Tangata with a show of honesty. 'The people of Hawaii are much better, I have heard. A ship called here not long ago telling us of a great sea battle there, between two kings.'

'Tell us about it,' said Kieto.

There had been news of a war between two cousins on the Hawaiian Islands. Kamehameha and Kiwalao, whose decisive sea battle off a beach known as Mokuohai had resulted in a victory for Kamehameha. The Hawaiian God of War, Kukailimoku – a fearsome deity with lustrous eyes and blood-red head – had ensured the felling of Kiwalao with a stone from a sling and one of Kamehameha's warriors had dispatched the chief by slitting his throat with a lei-o-mano. Thus the Hawaiian islands of Kauai, Oahu, Molokai, Lanai, Maui and Hawaii now came under the domination of one man.

As Seumas listened to the story unfold, once again he marvelled at the Oceanian memory. Each detail of the battle was recounted by Tangata and Seumas had no doubt it would be entirely accurate. This was a war which Tangata had not personally seen, but which had taken place thousands of miles away, at the farthest reaches of the Ocean. Yet the old man had committed to memory all that had been told to him by the visiting sailors from that land, whose own memories were as reliable as day following night. In turn, Kieto would have all these particulars locked in *his* memory.

The Oceanian's ability to retain minutia was phenomenal, making him one of the greatest navigators of all time, one of the finest oral story-tellers the world has ever known and unmatched by any other race at recounting personal and national history.

2

Ragnu had learned through his occult powers that the son of Seumas the Pict was now travelling with the Arioi and was indeed one of its number. This discovery was a revelation to the priest, who now saw further possibilities of wreaking revenge on the Rarotongans. To kill the son of Seumas would be to ensure that the goblin's line ended with his death. What more could a bitter man ask for than the total destruction of a family?

'Now I have you,' muttered the priest. 'I have you and I have your soul.'

The idea of killing one of the Arioi, a member who had risen quite high in its ranks, despite being a Hivan, fitted in with the priest's wider plans. He had long since become jealous of the rising power of the Arioi. Its Painted Legs were now regarded almost as equal to kings in rank. In fact, one of its Painted Legs *was* a king who had placed his duties and obligations behind him to join what Ragnu considered to be riff-raff.

Ragnu discussed his plans with his other priests, underlings who would follow their lord to the depths of the ocean if he so desired.

'To kill this creature, a Hivan youth called Kumiki, I must first be able to penetrate the ranks of the Arioi.'

'How will you do that, lord?' asked one of his priests. 'The Arioi might be a troupe of travelling singers and poets, but there are warriors amongst them – wrestlers, spearmen, others – who are quite capable of protecting their comrades. One hundred and fifty ships – that's a fighting force if necessary.'

'True,' said Ragnu. 'A hundred and fifty ships. In any other guise it would be an invasion fleet, would it not? But we have a navy to equal it. The last king feared invasion from the Hivans and so built a flotilla of ships which would meet such a need. What if I were to be given command of the Raiatean war ships and was sent out to attack the Arioi?'

The younger priests looked at their kahuna with mystified expressions on their faces.

'But who would give such an order?' said one at last. 'The Arioi are welcomed everywhere they go. They are a peaceful group. That's why they show their yellow sails, so that no island nation will attack them, thinking them to be aggressors. Who would order such an attack?'

'Our own king,' said Ragnu, enjoying unravelling his scheme for his followers. 'If he believes the Arioi to be something else – an attacking force from the Hivan Islands.'

There were nods amongst the other priests now. They had learned over the years not to underestimate their lord's intellect and magic. His sorcery was equalled by none. His knowledge of the secret ways was legendary amongst them. He could make beasts of the night, turn men into frogs, change the shape of the weather, destroy the indestructible.

'You must have worked out a plan,' said one of his students, 'for poisoning the king's mind against the Arioi.'

'Not *poison*,' Ragnu explained, his eyes glinting, 'but misrepresentation. The king will perceive a threat and I shall step forward and offer my services, to remove that threat. When the mistake is known, I shall be horrified, but who will blame me, since my own king has ordered me to attack?'

One of the priests opened his mouth to speak, but Ragnu continued by saying, 'I know what you're about to ask – how will I make the king perceive a menace where there is none? – but that must remain my secret for the time being. If I told you all, you would be as clever as I am, and that cannot be.'

This made the other priests laugh and even brought a smile to the face of the would-be questioner.

One young man, a newcomer to their midst, had one last question to ask.

'Will you be satisfied, my lord, with just *killing* the son of Seumas? I would have thought torture ...'

'Yes, yes,' snapped Ragnu, waspishly, 'of course you would have thought torture more appropriate. Killing a man quickly does not salve the desire for revenge, does it? But when a man dies slowly and in great agony, this is as good as having him to oneself and killing him by painful degrees.'

Ragnu went to a shelf on the temple wall and took down an object wrapped in cloth. He laid it on the floor and unwrapped the item carefully, to reveal a horrible weapon called an airo fai. It was an implement invented by the devious high priests of Tahiti, kept hidden until a crucial point in any battle, then brought out and used to terrify the enemy. Used like a dagger, the sharpened bone with its flexible backward-sweeping curved spikes, went *in* smoothly and easily. It was when the instrument was wrenched *out*, with the backbone barbs opening like jointed spines, that the terrible damage was done.

Many of the young priests present gasped at the sight of the ugly weapon and one or two went pale as images entered their heads, of the weapon being used.

Ragnu smiled at their squeamishness and said, 'The serrated back-bone of a sting ray, fashioned thus into this long dagger, will inflict such terrible wounds on a man – rip his insides out, tearing the flesh ragged – that he will die in the most dreadful circumstances. He will suffer such pain as would cause a god to howl. He will drag himself from enemy to friend, begging to be clubbed out of his misery.'

The priests stared in awe at the weapon, knowing Ragnu's words to be true.

Ragnu picked up the dagger and began to walk amongst his men, as if musing on an interesting subject.

'Of course, one cannot use such a weapon without testing its capabilities, and fortunately it has come to my attention that there is a spy amongst us – someone sent by King Tangiia of Rarotonga to report on my affairs. That person will be a suitable testing ground for my Tahitian gift, will he not? Don't you agree? Do I hear murmurs of assent?'

He heard nothing, for the whole group had gone deathly still. Several priests had begun trembling, though this was not proof of guilt, for any man with even the faintest threat on his head might be forgiven for shaking in such circumstances.

Faces had drained of colour. Even those who were secure in the knowledge of their innocence realised they would have to witness a gory execution and were not looking forward to the prospect.

Up and down their ranks strolled the crooked figure of Ragnu, highest of high priests, his hand clutching the weapon the Tahitians called the airo fai. Sweat rolled from their brows as they stared straight ahead, unwilling and afraid to look their lord in the eye. The tension in the room grew with every second, until its silent scream could be heard by every ear, its tautness in every breath taken by the waiting men.

Finally, one youthful priest could stand the suspense no longer, jumped to his feet with a cry, and tried to flee the room in which the stress was unbearable.

Ragnu was quick as a spider across the floor. He reached the youth, spun him round with a swift hand, and buried the airo fai in the young man's stomach. The youth gave out a terrible scream. Ragnu twisted the weapon half a turn in the wound, then tore it out, pulling with it on its many hooks of bone part of the priest's stomach and intestines. The grey, bloodied innards dangled like a gory umbilical cord from a hole no bigger than a man's eye socket, while the victim fell to his knees and tried to push them back inside again, screaming incessantly as he did so.

Ragnu made his priests sit where they were and witness the victim's slow death as he convulsed and shrieked – the air reeking of blood, gore and human excrement – taking as long as the great fire in the middle of the temple to finally die.

When the ashes of the fire were cold, and the young traitor had finally breathed his last, Ragnu allowed the others to go, knowing the scene would have impressed them beyond any words he could have uttered. Of course the youth had not been a traitor – there were no such creatures amongst the ranks of Ragnu's priests – but it did no harm to occasionally make an example of one of them, just in case.

3

Finally, the goading of the attackers drew the young manhood of the defending force outside the walls of the pa. The Rarotongans, still under guard, watched from a nearby hill as the two armies clashed with great ferocity on both sides. Kieto was eager to be down there in the melee, but the Maori chief forbade it. The Rarotongans were still under suspicion.

The quality of the fighting was superior to anything Kieto had ever seen before. It was clear to him that the training and philosophy of the Maori youth resulted in a warrior who was of the highest excellence when it came to warfare. Even Dorcha, the person least impressed with violence, acknowledged the fact that she had never seen such accomplished fighters as the Maori.

As with most open-plain warfare amongst Oceanians, the battle swayed back and forth, despite the disparity in numbers. When a bad omen appeared in the sky – a cloud shaped like a lizard – the attackers took flight and ran towards their distant home, even though their numbers were vastly superior. It was not cowardice to run, it was proper battle form. A few moments later the fleeing army decided there was nothing to fear from the gods, since no further bad portents appeared, and they turned on their pursuers, whose valour had now dissipated. Suddenly hunters became hunted, running in the opposite direction!

In the end, as the day died so did many of the defending force, and the remainder retreated into the pa. The following morning negotiations took place, with envoys like birds flying between pa and invaders' encampment, and finally some agreement was reached between Chief Tuwhakapau and the chief of the pa. Seumas, Dorcha and the others never did find out what the original argument had been, but it seemed to follow Tangata's explanation: warfare for its own sake, in order that men might gain respect, glory and fame amongst their kind.

It transpired the defending force had recently been wasted by an epidemic of some kind (brought to them, said Tangata, by Captain Cookers) and an earlier war with a tribe in the next valley along. The pa was therefore a lot more weakly defended than it had first appeared and the families inside were fearful of being overrun by blood-crazed warriors who might burn and loot, kill and maim, in the heat of the moment, possibly to regret their impulsiveness later.

The reason the youths came out to do battle with the attackers was so that honour could be satisfied and the fire could be taken out of the invading force who had worked themselves up to a fever pitch for the battle. Once these two goals had been accomplished, the chief of the pa could take the unusual step of surrendering his village to the enemy, rather than face a long siege or the threat of fire.

Now that the war was at an end, on both sides there were ceremonies to purify the warriors. At the start of the war the priests had consecrated the fighters and that tapu had to be erased before the terms of any settlement could be negotiated. The drums of peace sounded within and without the walls of the pa.

Once these formal rites were over the defeated chief came out with a bundle of sticks and some leaves. These were the materials for his own roasting, should the invading chief think it necessary to kill and cook him. It was an old Samoan custom, no doubt picked up by the Maori chief from some mariner, to take the sting out of the occasion. The materials for the fire were symbolic only, a gesture, not to be taken seriously.

Chief Tuwhakapau was magnanimous in victory however and exchanged bonds of friendship with the defeated chief.

'You were great in your generalship,' said the pa chief. 'You deserved to win.'

'No, no, my strategy was of little account,' the victor demurred. 'The weather was good to us, the wind was in the right direction for the flight of our spears and we probably surprised you with the suddenness of our attack.'

It was good form for the victor to make excuses for the failures of the defeated army, to give them back a little of their honour. It was all right to boast before the battle, but afterwards the winners were expected to be modest. They had, after all, seized the day, and had nothing more to prove.

Once terms had been agreed, the pa chief went back to his village to prepare for the entrance of the victorious chief, his nobles and priests. Instead of opening the gate to let him in, a section of the stockade was lowered, for Chief Tuwhakapau was now a special guest and the right courtesies had to be shown to him. The pa chief needed to show he was going through a certain amount of trouble to receive his guest.

Kieto asked the old man Tangata whether they would be allowed to accompany the nobles to see the inside of the pa.

'I shall ask the Chief Tuwhakapau,' said Tangata. 'No doubt you are considered lucky for him since he has won the battle and you have shown no treachery. Had he lost, you might be roasting on a fire now, but since he won ...'

The chief said he would be pleased for visitors from sacred Hawaiki to form part of his retinue.

The group of six found themselves the objects of much curiosity from the inhabitants of the pa. It was a strange time, for there was mourning in progress, for the dead warriors on both sides, yet there was festivity in the air, because the war was over and honour had been satisfied. Kieto and his band had to be cautious in what they said and to whom they spoke, so that no tapu was violated in any way.

Dorcha was amazed at the quality of the carvings on the houses of the Maori.

'Look at the designs on the walls too,' she said, after viewing the wooden figures which made the house posts, 'and the patterns on the ceiling!'

The interior of the meeting house was indeed very beautiful, no less than the exterior. When she and Seumas walked around the village they found other houses, not quite as artistically wrought as the meeting house, but with carvings and patterns of high quality. A storehouse was among the most attractively carved buildings and it sported a carved figure on the point of the pitched roof which had something similar to the topknots of the giants on Rapanui perched on its head.

Seumas, however, was more interested in the fortifications than the artistry of the carvings.

He walked along the palisade in the early morning while the sun glinted on the dew-covered sharpened stakes and wondered about his own people in Albainn. Dorcha walked beside him, occasionally looking up into his worried features. She knew he was battling with his emotions and she knew too that she was important enough to him for her advice to mean something.

'What are we to do?' he asked Dorcha. 'When it comes to the point where we must choose whether or not to join the expedition to Albainn, what are we to do?'

'What does your head tell you to do? Forget your heart.'

'We both know that even if we hated our birthplace, it would still give us pain to see it conquered. What you must do is put your feelings aside and think about the best course of action.'

'Am I to be concerned about being called a traitor, reviled by my clan?'

'You should not let it influence your decision, if you have a greater good in mind.'

He nodded thoughtfully.

Dorcha knew that Seumas had grown in mental and spiritual stature since he had been amongst the Oceanians. When he had arrived on Raiatea he had been a headstrong Pict, full of the vanities of manhood, whose fear of peer opinion dictated his actions. In those far-off days, he had to act like the man he was expected to be. Now his wisdom had matured, he had grown away from that bull-headed Pict and had a much more thoughtful and sensitive nature which he was not ashamed to display, knowing it made him no less a warrior for it. He made decisions himself and no longer automatically fell in with general opinion.

'It must be,' he said at last, staring over the fence at the grassy plains beyond, where the shining river wound its broad flat back, out of the distant mountains, 'that I at least will go with Kieto when he attempts his conquest of our homeland. You shall come too, if you wish, of course – but I will not persuade you to do that for which I have little stomach myself.

'I will not take part in any fighting nor assist either side in any way, but I must be on hand to smooth the path to peace. Whatever happens Kieto will go with his Oceanians to the Land-of-Mists and my refusal to join him will make little difference to the outcome. If I am there, however, I shall be available as a go-between, knowing both sides as I do. Someone who understands both Oceanian and Albannach *must* be there, to explain any misconceptions, so that unnecessary bloodshed can be avoided.

'Think what a Scot or a Pict would make of a man running away on the battlefield! By his own code he would be entitled to consider that man lower than dirt and to be shown no mercy. Think what an Oceanian would make of men who ambushed him! By his code he would be entitled to believe those men cowards and worse than beasts in their behaviour. Someone must be there to explain that under the rules of their own kind, both are legitimate actions and not to be taken as an insult.'

Dorcha put an arm around the waist of her man. 'You have more wisdom in you now, Seumas, than I would ever have believed you capable of in the old days. You know that if the Oceanians lose, or if you get captured, the clans will burn out your eyes, cut off your testicles – and then, when they think you are numb with pain, they'll quarter you with horses.'

Seumas sighed. 'I know it. They won't understand my position. It's impossible to expect them to make the leap that has taken me half a lifetime to achieve. I will be an abject traitor in their eyes – less than pigshit. Their hate for me will be very deep. They'll feed my remains to the crows.'

'But you have to go.'

He nodded, his eyes on hers.

'I have to go.'

'And I shall go with you.'

'You don't have to. I know how it'll distress you. When it's all over, I'll come back to Rarotonga. I wouldn't live very long in those winters, not now, now that I know a different weather. I want to end my years in the sun.'

She shook her head. 'And what if you *don't* come back because you can't, I mean? I want to be there with you, when you die – if you die. It's right I should be there.'

'It might be the death of you, too.'

'So be it.'

He turned and studied the landscape around him, admiring the shape of it, noting the contrasts. Here, in the Land of the Long White Cloud there were many scenes. There were the hot springs, the geysers, the forests, the volcanoes, the grasslands, the braided rivers, the hills and mountains, the plains – and Tangata had told them of an island below this one, where there were glaciers whose snouts reached the sea, and high mountains covered with snow, and areas of perpetual rain. It was an interesting landscape, a coat with many different cuts.

'I could settle for this land, except that it's not in our world,' he said.

'We must go back.'

'Yes, we must.'

He stared at her for a moment and her features were caught in the light of the early sun. He touched her greying hair then looked away from her, quickly. She caught the gesture and mistook it.

'I know, I'm not as young as I once was.'

'It's not that,' he said, turning back, his eyes shining. He looked close to tears. 'I was thinking – I was thinking how I wronged you once, and how much I love you now ...'

She said, 'We were never to speak of that again.'

'No, not me. You said you would not speak of it. Dorcha, I killed your husband – killed him in a fight over a sword. You hated me for it long enough, even when I'd learned to love you, but then you put your hate aside.'

'I learned to love you too, Seumas.'

'And you are prepared to come with me, to the place where I took your husband from you. You're willing to return to the land where we hated each other. You know what your clan will say to you, don't you? They'll call you a whore, a slut, for bedding your husband's murderer ... oh, I know it wasn't like that, it was a fair fight, but all that won't make any difference to them. Those Scots, they'll despise you for sleeping with a Pict, an animal, a man who covers his skin with pictures, a savage, one of the Black unwanted memories, bring back the bitterness, call up the hate we once felt for each other?'

She smiled and took his hand. 'Do you think I'm still beautiful, Seumas the Black?'

He looked serious. '*A kotuku is seen but once,*' he replied, using an Oceanian saying. 'You're the finest woman – Dorcha, I love your body so much it chokes me to look at you. I can't believe how lucky I am to have such a woman at my side.'

'Good enough, Seumas. Yes, I may think on my old life, on the man I once had when we were young, but that was a different woman then. I was with him three years. You and I have been together for over twenty ...'

'It's not the time.'

'No, it isn't, but it is the *feeling*. We're going there together,' she said, 'and when we've been there, we'll come back home again – to *our* home.'

He seemed happy with that and they said no more on the subject. They would both accompany Kieto. They had seen the boy grow into a man. They loved him. He had been their guide in Oceania, to the ways of its people, as well as its secret paths, its hidden places. He would need them on his campaign, his crusade to take the gods and culture, the ways of Oceania, to the people of Albainn and Engaland.

4

The Arioi fleet had been at sea for a month. They had climbed the waves of the ocean, descended into its valleys, and now they were – almost to a person – glad to see the shores of Nuku Hiva, one of several Hivan islands they would visit.

The Hivans themselves, a tall, handsome people, were not supposed to be generally enamoured of the Arioi. They called themselves a warrior race who believed actors and singers to be rather effeminate creatures. However, there were many among them who secretly enjoyed a good show, who publicly scorned the travelling players but secretly admired them. Certainly there was a kind of suppressed excitement amongst them.

Thus, as with any island group visited by the famous Tahitian Arioi, the beaches were crowded with people. There were indeed warriors amongst them, men such as Kumiki had once been, with twisted horns of hair on their otherwise shaven heads and tattooed on their faces with forbidding solid bars. Dedicated to cannibalism more than any other Oceanians, Hivans were rightly feared by their neighbours. Workers in stone, their marae and ahu stood outside temples of hewn rock. They were a formidable race with solid foundations.

They stood and stared quietly, while around them women and young people chattered with excitement as the yellow sails of the Arioi fleet drew closer and the singing could be heard.

'We are the Arioi, full of colour and light.
'We come to entertain you with our dancing and song.
'Witness our acrobats, hear our musicians, listen to our singers!
'We have poets and storytellers, we have enchanters!
'The Arioi are come! The Arioi are come!'

The chants reached the shore and filled the waiting Hivans with great glee. Children ran back into the villages to rouse invalid grandparents, haul them down to the beaches to watch this wondrous sight. Grandsons carried grandmothers and grandfathers on their shoulders. People cleared a pathway for those so old that they were laden with a tapu, in order that they should not be touched, even accidentally. Fat dogs, some only hours away from the pot, caught the excitement and yapped and barked. Pigs squealed, running around their pens, wondering what all the fuss was about. Cockerels crowed. Clamour was the order of the day.

On board the pahi the entertainers were in full swing, letting rip with their voices in song, leaping and dancing across pahi, playing their various instruments.

On one of the front pahi were gathered the drummers, pounding out their various exciting rhythms, while at the mast stood their leader, for the moment not playing, reserving his greater talents for the entertainment of chiefs. He was a tall, proud man, a Painted Leg, the first drummer ever to reach this exalted position. His right leg, tattooed black, was thrust forward for all on the beaches to see, and when the watching Hivans stared into his face they saw three solid bars tattooed across his cheeks and nose.

A Hivan! The words went hissing down the beach with the speed of surf on a curling breaker. The Painted Leg was a Hivan, a man from their own islands! A surge of immense pride went through the crowd. Chief Api Api was sent word. One of his own people had become a Painted Leg!

No matter that travelling players were regarded with some disdain by Hivan warriors – that was when they were Tahitians, a rather foppish people in any case – here was one of their own kind now a king of song and dance, of singers and dancers. Here was a Hivan supreme amongst all the artistes of Oceania. In the whole world the Arioi were the best, the most talented and lauded of entertainers, close to the gods, and of their number the best of the Arioi was one of their own kind. It was incredible.

Chief Api Api listened in amazement, hurried down to the beaches with a guard and retinue of priests, stood waiting as the Painted Leg – who in any case seemed to be a drummer, which happily unlike dancing or poetry was a fairly masculine vocation when all was said and done – stepped into the surf and strode onto the shore, to stare about him in a haughty manner.

The crowd moved in, not close enough to touch the Painted Leg, for he was surely a tapu, but to stare into his eyes, to see if they knew him at all. One woman, whose mouth had dropped open in wonder, suddenly found her voice and informed the people of Nuku Hiva of the name of this great man.

'Kumiki!' she cried. 'It is my Kumiki!'

The Painted Leg's face lost its disdainful expression for a few moments as his eyes anxiously searched the crowd for the owner of this voice. However, before his eyes could lock onto those of the person who had identified him, the people parted, and Chief Api Api stood before him. Kumiki's face assumed its former cavalier aspect and he greeted the chief.

'My Lord,' he said, 'I am happy to return to my home island as a Painted Leg, an Avae Parai,' he thrust his decorated limb forward for all to see, 'honoured among the distant islands. I am your own Kumiki, a humble bastard prince of Nuku Hiva. I return in triumph to greet my Chief, Api Api, and bring him gifts of mother-of-pearl, sharks' teeth, greenstone carvings, wooden ornaments, weapons and other treasures …'

A bundle was brought forward and unrolled at the chief's feet to reveal these items, and more, under the solemn but barely contained gaze of the chief.

'Kumiki,' said Api Api, after clearing his throat, 'I accept the gifts you bring and add my own praises to those already heaped upon your young head. You have brought great honour to me and my family, to these islands of the Hiva nation, and we are proud you are one of our sons. Come, you will share my basket with me, and tell me all about your conquests.'

Kumiki, followed by his faithful friends, the Otiore dancer Linloa and Ramoro, an Harotea, went with Api Api. Linloa was sent by the Chief to eat with his daughters. Since she was an Arioi, where women were regarded the equal of men, she was actually allowed to eat pork and dog meat with the men, but she made no complaint which might have spoilt the day for Kumiki.

Both Ramoro and Kumiki were allowed to share from the chief's own basket. A very great honour indeed. Ramoro was not entirely at ease, a Tahitian who preferred men to women amongst the savage Hivan people (who knew of what they were capable?), but Kumiki was relaxed and glowing with immense pride. He had left this island a boy in search of a father and had returned a great man.

Chief Api Api had no idea who Kumiki was at first. Now he had been surreptitiously informed by his priests that this was the son of a captured enemy chief's wife. She too had been a Hivan, but from another island, not Nuku Hiva. The boy had unfortunately been sired by a goblin when the Raiateans had briefly touched the island and killed many people in his father's time. Then, when the youth had reached his manhood, he had set out to find this goblin father and kill him, for raping his mother and causing so much grief amongst the Hivan people. There was more to the story than that, as the chief well knew, but he kept his secrets to himself.

'Have you completed your mission yet?' asked Api Api of Kumiki, as they gnawed on dog meat. 'Did you find the lustful demon who forced himself between your mother's plump thighs?'

Kumiki frowned. He was a sensitive man and he did not like the picture of his mother conjured up by Chief Api Api's words. It seemed to him that things could have been put a little more delicately. There were certain adjectives used here which trivialised his mother's terrifying, humiliating and degrading experience and might have been dispensed with given the circumstances. However, even though he was now a Painted Leg, and felt himself to be vastly superior to the grubby chief of a Nuku Hivan tribe, he could hardly call to task a man who commanded several thousand fierce warriors.

'I am afraid I have not yet had the pleasure of slitting the goblin's throat,' replied Kumiki. 'It seems the foreigner called Seumas is on a voyage with the great navigator Ru, on his way to find a new island. When he returns from his seafaring, I shall seek him out and dispatch him.'

Chief Api Api seemed a little amused.

'I have never heard of a man hunting down his own father before. One usually reveres one's father.'

'This is surely a father like no other,' interrupted Ramoro. 'This Seumas is a creature from hell.'

'And what does that make your friend here?' said the chief, sipping kava juice and allowing himself to become very slightly drunk. 'A son of the creature from hell?'

Ramoro said, 'A man cannot choose his own father. The seed of the goblin has been overwhelmed by the long line of Hivan forefathers held by the mother of Kumiki. This demon's seed was but a trigger, to activate the birth of Kumiki, whose talents as a drummer have shown him to be worthy of his ancestors, to be a culmination of their collective selves. He has gathered within him all the skills of his grandfathers, going back to Tiki, and the demon's seed has been smothered, lost, in the flood of pure Oceanian which forms our friend.'

Api Api nodded. 'I agree. There is little enough of the goblin in Kumiki – yet, it is still a strange exercise, to chase one's own father with murder in mind. Shall you eat him, when you finally cut out his heart?'

Kumiki, to whom the question had been addressed, stared thoughtfully into the distance.

'If his flesh is not tainted, not nocuous in any respect, then I shall roast him like a lizard on a stick and eat every vital part of him – brains, liver, heart and lungs. The rest I shall throw to the sharks.'

'Sounds suitable,' said the chief, nodding his approval. 'I would do the same.'

Later, after they had left the chief to sleep off the effects of the kava, Kumiki and Ramoro went to supervise the building of the great stage. It was important that a Painted Leg should be there, while the gods were being invoked for a good performance. Oro, the God of War and Peace, was their patron, and as the platform was being erected sacrifices of lizards, a pig and a dog were made in his honour. While the sacrifices took place a story teller informed the thousands of Hivans watching the building of the stage how dancing first came to Oceania, through Koro, son of Tini Rau, Lord of the Fishes:

'One day when the world was young and the sea so blue it hurt a man's eyes to stare at it, Tini Rau, Lord of the Fishes' who lived on the Sacred Isle, but sometimes stayed on Mangaia, went for a walk wearing a necklace made of pandanus seeds. At this time Tini Rau was indeed staying on Mangaia, near Rarotonga, enjoying a pleasant break from his normal duties. His son Koro caught the fragrance of the seeds, which perfumed the air all around Tini Rau, and decided to follow his father.

'Koro watched as his father shinned up the trunk of a palm tree and knocked down some coconuts. These he husked on a sharpened stake, then broke open the kernel and scraped out the sweet meat of the coconut, wrapping it in a pandanus leaf.

'Tini Rau then carried the parcel of coconut meat to a place on the shoreline, where the rocks met the sea, tumbling down into its depths and forming a kind of rough ramp. Tini Rau stood ankle-deep at the head of this ramp and commenced to scatter the coconut like ground bait on the surface of the sea.

'First came all the shoals of tiny silver fish, millions of them, with brightly coloured cousins. Soon the water was swarming with yellows, blues, stripes, and all the colours of the ocean as the small fry came in to feed on the food being fed them by the Lord of the Fishes. Then came the larger reef fish – parrot fish, trigger fish, angel fish, red snapper and a thousand other kinds of largish fish. These were followed by big fish like sharks, dolphin, porpoise, whales. Then octopi, squid, sting rays, manta rays. Soon, to Koro's amazement, the whole sea was frothing with fish of every shape and size.

'Koro's awe at the number of fish was short lived, for an even more wonderful thing happened as the Sacred Isle itself came over the horizon and slipped over the reef of Mangaia.

'At this point all the fish in the lagoon came up the rocky ramp on to the Sacred Isle, some having assumed full human shape, and others remaining partly in the water but having taken on the form of mermaids. Once they were all on land, or in shallows, the Sacred Isle began to float away like a boat, while the figures on it danced and sang, creating a beautiful sight.

'Koro, nor indeed any other man but Tini Rau, had seen dancing before and it was a sight which took his breath away with excitement. Never before had he seen movement which was so exquisite. Once the Sacred Isle was out of sight, however, Koro's exhilaration dissipated and he was left forlorn.

'The following evening Koro climbed a palm and gathered some coconuts, spreading the meat on the waters of the Mangaia's lagoon and chanting the fangu he had heard his father sing.

'Fishes came from far and wide, and eventually, also the Sacred Isle, gliding over the top of the reef. There were the fishmen dancing on its beaches, in its shallows, and Tini Rau, smiling, waving an admonishing finger at his son.

'Tini Rau welcomed Koro on to the Sacred Isle, where the dancing went on for many nights and days, at the end of which Koro decided that this activity had to be given to all men and women, whoever they were, and having obtained permission from his father made sure all ordinary mortals knew how to dance.

'This is how paradise came to earth, when Koro taught mankind the wonderful art of dancing!'

Once the stage was built, Kumiki was able to leave the place and find a spot in the forest to rest. Linloa, his faithful friend and assistant went with him, making a bed for him out of dried grasses and standing watch while he slept. Kumiki slept the sleep of the weary until he was woken in the early evening by the sound of argument close by.

He opened his eyes to find Linloa restraining a local female and ordering her away from the place.

'How dare you tell me where to go!' cried the young woman. 'This is my island. I go where I please. And I wish to speak with the Painted Leg they call Kumiki.'

Kumiki sat up and rubbed his eyes, before asking, 'And why do you wish to speak with me.'

The girl turned a shining face on him, her teeth gleaming like mother-of-pearl as she smiled.

'It is I,' she cried. 'Your own beloved Miro!'

Kumiki leapt to his feet in excitement. This was the woman for whom he had done everything: joined the Arioi, climbed its ranks, become one of the fabulous and rare Avae Parai. This was the woman he had left behind, but swore to return to in triumph one day and sweep her off her feet, away from covetous relatives.

'Miro!' he cried. 'It is all right, Linloa – this is my long-lost love, my own beautiful Miro.'

Linloa's face fell as she regarded the plump and shining Hivan woman beside her and the little Tahitian girl who had ministered to Kumiki since he had joined the Arioi quietly left the glade.

Kumiki, left with his excited Miro, was moved to kiss the woman of whom he had dreamed since he left Nuku Hiva. Her lips tasted like ripe fruit. His hands roved over her soft firm body, touching her round breasts, her fat thighs, exploring the secrets of her hidden garden. Suddenly, she giggled.

Kumiki was annoyed. 'What is it?'

'Nothing,' she murmured, playing with a necklace of seeds, and looking at his Painted Leg, the symbol of his greatness, 'but we mustn't you know, not *really*.'

His irritation grew and he was astonished. He had been away for many, many months, and now he was being told 'he mustn't'? It was ludicrous. He desired her and once they had made love he intended to ask, nay *demand* her hand from her father, who would not dare refuse a Painted Leg, beloved of the people, king of entertainers, friend of Chief Api Api.

'What are you talking about?' he asked. 'Speak, my beloved. Your father cannot refuse us now.'

'Why,' she said, slyly. 'I might let you do something to me, on this moss, but you must promise never to tell.'

'For what reason?'

'Because I'm *married*, of course,' she growled playfully, as if to a child. 'My husband would kill me.'

Kumiki was stunned. He took a step back from her and stared. Had he heard right? Married? It was not possible. She had promised to wait for him. There was a pact. They had sworn an oath to each other under the gaze of Hine-keha. How could she possibly be wed to some other man?

'Married?' he repeated, stupidly.

'Yes, but you can have me now, here, on the ground. I want to feel you inside me. Look, my legs are trembling with excitement ...' She took his penis in her hand and began pulling him forwards by it, guiding it towards her vagina. 'Quickly, before someone comes – put your seed in my belly!'

Kumiki gave out a great cry of emotional pain, pulled his tapa skirt over his genitals, and pushed her away from him.

'Get away from me. Married? How could you be married? You said you'd wait for me. We both promised we'd wait for each other.'

She pouted. 'Yes, but you were gone so long. I thought you might have met someone else.' She said, 'You can't expect a person to wait for years you know.'

But that was just what he *had* expected. Now this, to return to his home isle in triumph, to be feted by kings, only to find that the girl he had left behind had waited how long?

'When did you get married?' he asked, dully.

She told him. It was only a few months after he had left her standing on the beach. He sighed, realising he could not blame her. It was he who had sailed off over the horizon. She would have been happy had he stayed and forgotten his so-called father. Now all his dreams had been felled like trees, all in one day, one hour, one moment. And it was his own fault. He could not blame her for that.

'Leave me,' he said, wearily. 'Go back to your husband.'

She looked annoyed at this. 'Aren't you going to make love to me? I want to tell all the other women I've been with a Painted Leg. They'll be so jealous.'

'Go back to your husband,' he repeated.

Her face screwed up into a vicious expression.

'You can't do this to me,' she snapped, 'I'm precious.'

With that she flounced out of the glade and was gone.

Kumiki sat down on the moss. His spiritual pain was beginning to subside a little. It was true he would never get over this terrible blow, but he had seen his beloved Miro in a different light today. Her demands had been for selfish reasons, for petty reasons, so that she could brag to the other women at the water place, not because she regretted her rash actions and still felt an over-whelming love for him. He considered himself lucky to have escaped so lightly. Had he married her instead of going off to search for his father, she would now be cheating on him.

There was a rustle of leaves and he looked up sharply, wondering whether the ghosts of one of his ancestors was spying on him in his grief. However, Linloa stood there.

'She's gone?' said Linloa.

Kumiki nodded. 'It seems she is already married.' Something like a look of relief passed over the features of Linloa and her tone suddenly became almost light-hearted. 'Well, never mind, there are more women in the world. You are desired by a great many.'

'They are impressed by my drumming, by my Painted Leg,' he said mournfully, 'but who would love me for myself? Miro knew me before I became famous.'

'So did I,' said Linloa, looking at him steadily in the green light of the glade. 'I knew you when you were a flapper – I saw you the day you painted yourself with yellow clay and acted like a mad creature, to become one of us.'

He nodded, still staring away from her. 'Yes, it's true, I have good friends in you and Ramoro. You did not jeer at me like the other Tahitians. You did not make fun of my red-coloured hair. You were good friends to me.'

'We still are – and I, perhaps, am more than a friend.'

This was delivered in a hushed whisper and Kumiki looked up to gaze into the features of Linloa. What was she saying? What was she trying to tell him?

'Linloa?' he said.

'I love you!' the words came out in a rush. 'I love you, and you hardly know I exist. You prefer girls who wave from the beach, to me. You do not find me beautiful. You prefer women who would go with any man, if he was an Arioi.'

'Linloa? I didn't know. I mean, I thought we were friends.'

'Friends, yes,' she said, sadly. 'That's all we ever will be I suppose, since you do not find me attractive.'

He felt chagrin. 'I never really thought about it. I mean, we rehearse together, we do so much – you're just always there. I'm very, very fond of you.'

'I'm grateful for that.'

He studied her now. He had always seen her as a very pretty woman. She was small and waif-like, with slender hips and narrow shoulders. Her hair hung down to her waist in rivers of black. She was as light as a feather to look at and he knew he could pick her up with one arm. Compared with him she was one of the Peerless Ones, a forest fairy.

'In fact, I think you're quite beautiful,' he admitted. 'It's just that, well, I haven't thought of you in that way before. It never occurred to me ...'

'Does it occur to you now?'

As she spoke she released her waistband and let her skirt fall to the forest floor. She was caught in a shaft of golden sunlight from Ra's lips, which pierced the canopy above. Her slim, delicate form glowed palely against the background of green misty light from the ferns and broad-leafed plants. She trembled a little, vulnerable in her nudity, allowing his eyes to roam over her diminutive figure. Indeed she was one of the Peerless Ones in human shape. He wanted to gather her up in his arms, safeguard her fragility with his male strength. Her presence awakened in him all the protectiveness of the male of the species.

Within moments they were making love and he was whispering promises in her ear, telling her he had loved her all along without even knowing it, saying she was the most beautiful creature in the world and that he wanted to spend the rest of his life with her by his side.

When it was all over and they lay on the damp moss in each other's arms, he told her, 'I want to look after you.'

'I know,' said she, 'that is my strength.'

'Your what?'

'It was my intention that you should feel this way – that's why I did it.'

'Did what?'

'Spoke as I did, stood as I did, made myself look small and weak, so that you would feel strong.'

Kumiki had the distinct feeling he had been manipulated, but he actually didn't care. He knew he had found his life's love in this glade and none of those things would ever matter again. Linloa was his for ever, and she loved him passionately, he realised that. What did it matter that she had deliberately set out to make him want her? All was now well.

'I love you,' he said.

'I love you too,' she murmured. 'And we must be careful how we break this news to Ramoro. I don't want him to feel betrayed by both of us. I don't want him to feel we have conspired behind his back. It has been the three of us together until now. We must be gentle in the way we tell him, not rush out and say isn't it wonderful, let's all rejoice. I shall tell him we have gradually developed feelings for one another which have just made themselves evident, that we haven't been sneaking off, making love behind his back, hoping he would go away so we could be alone. Let me deal with it, in my way.'

Kumiki was impressed by her thoughtfulness. It was not that Ramoro would be jealous of him, Kumiki, because of his good fortune, but that Ramoro might think he had been the odd one out, while the other two enjoyed an intimate relationship. It was important that Ramoro should know he was being informed from the very start of the relationship, that nothing had gone on previously, that their joy was to be shared with him from the outset – indeed, that their joy was his joy too.

'Yes, you're right. I shall leave it to you.'

Once the stage was ready the show began and people came flooding in from the hills and valleys to see the marvellous Arioi. There was an emphasis on re-enacted battle scenes and heroic recounting of legendary exploits for the benefit of the Hivan population, who being made up of martial clans liked blood and gore more than they enjoyed singing and dancing.

This gave Kumiki full opportunity to use his drums in a martial role, adding drama to the actors' efforts during the mock fights and producing a slow funereal beat when the war was over and the dead were being counted. Kumiki could use each note to its best effect and his performance as always was excellent. He had a high profile during such exhibitions, which satisfied this particular audience's desire to see the Painted Leg who was one of their number, one they could claim for their own.

As usual, Linloa was energetic in her efforts to assist Kumiki during his performance. She was selfless and tireless, even though she had her own acts to perform. It was at one point in the evening, when the sweat was streaming from Kumiki's back as he leapt from drum to drum, thundering out a magnificent roll, when one of the audience leapt to his feet.

'Die, you wife-stealer!' cried the Hivan warrior who had a javelin in his hand. 'Adulterer!'

No sooner than these bitter words were out of the man's mouth than he launched his spear at Kumiki. The Painted Leg was trapped behind his instruments, unable to leap out of the way of the missile. Linloa saw in an instant that he would die if she did not do something. She threw a small drum she was carrying, like a disc through the air, and it struck the spear in mid-flight, causing it to be knocked from its course. It glanced from the corner of the stage and stuck in the trunk of a nearby palm tree, where it quivered.

When the warrior saw that he had failed to kill the drummer he gave a cry and leapt up onto the stage wielding a club. This he swung at Kumiki's head. This time however Kumiki was able to duck from the waist. The stone club whistled over his right shoulder. Kumiki then came up from under his drums and struck his adversary across the side of his head with a drumstick as thick as a man's wrist. The Hivan warrior dropped to the stage as if his legs had been boned. There he lay, still.

There was pandemonium amongst the Hivan audience. Warriors jumped to their feet, threatening to storm the stage. They had no idea why one of their number had attacked the Arioi drummer, but they didn't like the fact that he had been clubbed senseless. Only the intervention of Chief Api Api's personal body guard prevented any further violence from taking place.

The chief came to the stage and questioned Kumiki. 'Have you seen this man before?' he asked.

'Not to my knowledge,' replied the Painted Leg.

'Then why was he trying to kill you?'

Kumiki shrugged and Ramoro said, 'Never before has a Painted Leg been attacked during his performance. It is disgraceful. I thought the Hivan peoples were civilised.'

Api Api said angrily, 'We are civilised. Something must have been done to goad this man into his attack. Some insult, or long-standing dispute. Are you sure you do not know him?'

'I tell you ...' cried Kumiki, angrily, but suddenly out of the corner of his eye he caught sight of Miro, standing amongst the women, glaring at him. Her eyes fell occasionally to the inert body of the man on the stage. 'Wait a minute,' Kumiki murmured to the chief, 'who is this man's wife?'

Api Api, who could not be expected to know every warrior's family personally, shrugged his shoulders and looked for assistance from his priests.

'This is Akamiku,' said the high priest. 'He is married to a woman called Miro.'

'I thought so,' said Kumiki, angrily. 'This is the husband of the woman I was once to marry. She failed to wait for me to return to these islands, however, and when I refused her favours – because she is married – she swore to get even with me. I expect she taunted her husband with untrue tales of our liaison so that he would attack me.'

'Lies!' shrieked Miro, from out of the crowd.

'In that case,' Kumiki said, calmly, 'we shall have to wait for this Akamiku to revive so that we can ask him.'

'You raped me!' screamed Miro. 'I told you I was married, but you took no notice.'

'It is you who is the liar,' replied Kumiki.

There was silence now, as the crowd observed both partners in this argument. An accusation had been made and refuted. Even under normal circumstances there was a difficult judgement to be made, one which lacked proof on both sides. A woman claimed she had been assaulted by a man. The man denied the assault. Without witnesses, unconnected with either party, there was no way of proving innocence or guilt with any degree of certainty. What usually happened in these circumstances was that a high priest, chief or king made a decision based on his own feelings, given the known circumstances of the case.

The high priest spoke to Chief Api Api.

'There must be a trial,' he said. 'You must preside.' Ramoro stepped forward on hearing this.

'There will be no trial,' said the Arioi. 'The accused man is a Painted Leg. His status is at least as high as that of a king, perhaps almost as lofty as that of a god. Never has an Avae Parai had to defend himself against the petty accusations of an ordinary person. If that were necessary Painted Legs would be spending all their time defending themselves, because there are many who envy their talents and are jealous. No, it cannot happen. An Avae Parai is above the law.'

There were murmurs of agreement from the whole troupe of Arioi and even from amongst the Hivan crowds. What Ramoro had said was true. No one would dare accuse a king without proof and a Painted Leg was at least as elevated as a king.

Chief Api Api raised his eyebrows in the direction of his high priest, requesting guidance in the matter.

'Under normal circumstances, I would agree with what you say,' said the high priest to Ramoro, 'but here we have a case of a woman who was betrothed to a Painted Leg, before he became exalted amongst us. This is not just a member of the population trying to become famous by attacking a god. This is between two people who are known to one another, who have had intimate relationships in the past.'

'Nevertheless,' replied Ramoro, 'there is no proof of any misconduct. If the woman wishes to provide proof, that might be a different matter.'

'Do you have any proof?' asked the high priest of Miro.

Miro looked sulky. 'My body is my proof. My damaged reputation is my proof. My feelings ...'

'These are not proofs,' said Ramoro. 'They are simply words.'

Chief Api Api shook his head sadly.

'This is a very difficult problem.'

Suddenly, Kumiki himself spoke up.

'The accusation of rapist is particularly abhorrent to me, since this is how I came into the world. My life's ambition is to eventually find the violator of my mother and make him pay for his crime against her body and soul. Yet here I am, accused of the same offence! I know I am totally innocent in this affair and that is why I'm willing to stand trial but not a trial presided over by mortals – one which is conducted at a higher level – one which is decided by our ancestors.

'We shall leave it up to spirits. There is a game we play here on Nuku Hiva, called spear-stick. If I remember correctly from my youth, we push five sticks into the earth, in a line. The contestant has five throws at the sticks and has to knock down as many of the five targets as he can. The opponent may attempt to thwart the thrower, by running across the target area as the throw is being made, but of course this is dangerous for the runner, who may be speared by accident.

'I suggest we each choose a champion, this woman and I, and leave it to them. If the gods favour her champion, then I will bow to my punishment. If my champion wins, then she must withdraw her accusation and publicly apologise.'

The high priest nodded at these words and said, 'I think this is a wise and fair way of deciding the truth. However, accusing someone of a crime as terrible as this has its consequences. Only a chief can decide the punishment for the Painted Leg, if it transpires he is guilty, but if the woman loses; she forfeits her life, for false accusation.'

'Good,' said Api Api, 'now choose your champions.'

'I choose Chief Api Api!' cried Miro, quickly.

A murmur went through the crowd as swiftly as a shoal of fish sweeps through a lagoon. The chief was the best spearman on the island. His fame as a marksman was renowned throughout all the Hivan islands. In fact, he had never been beaten at spear-stick. Not only that, his psychological advantage over any opponent was strong. Who would not feel intimidated, throwing against the chief of Nuku Hiva?

Perhaps a man might be a little surer with a spear than Chief Api Api, but it was like a son throwing against a father: there were other factors to consider. There was respect for superiority of position, reverence for status, fear of a powerful but angry loser. These were difficult obstacles to brush aside. They manifested themselves in hesitancy, trembling arm and wavering eye. As with all such sports, success depended as much upon what was in the head as the skill in the hand.

Chief Api Api nodded his assent.

The high priest called across the heads of the crowd. 'And who does the Painted Leg choose?'

'I choose Telufo the Tongan,' said Kumiki, 'one of our troupe.'

There was a gasp from the thousands of people watching this drama unfold as an elderly man, grizzled and grey, thin as a stick insect, stepped forward on the stage and nodded.

'A Tongan?' cried Chief Api Api, wondering whether he was being insulted here. 'What is this?'

'My chief,' said the high priest, 'I have heard of these people. The Tongans play a similar sport to our spear-stick. They place a short post in the ground and throw the spear so that it drops down onto the post. I have heard they are very adept at this variation of spear throwing.'

'But this Telufo is an old man.'

'Old, but still skilful, lord,' said Telufo.

'Do not presume to make a fool of me, Painted Leg,' said Chief Api Api. 'I want a good contest.'

'The ancestors will decide,' replied Kumiki. 'This is not a contest between two men of unequal rank and age, for your throwing arms will be guided by unseen hands – those of the divine ghosts of our forefathers. There will be no shame in losing, for this is a judgement on me and on Miro, not a test of your individual mastery at spear-stick.'

'So be it,' said the chief, removing his clothing and standing in a simple loin cloth. 'Bring the targets and the spears. Let the judgement commence. One set of five throws each no more – and the one with the most sticks lying flat on the ground is the winner. Agreed?'

'Agreed,' said Telufo.

A large space was cleared and two thick marker posts were driven into the earth. Between these posts, using them as a line of sight, five sticks were thrust vertically into the ground. Straws were drawn and Chief Api Api won, electing to throw first. Telufo went down to the right of the line of sticks, to run across the target area if he so chose, in order to disorientate his opponent.

The chief threw his first spear without any interference from Telufo. It struck the first stick in the line, furthest away from the Tongan. There was a great cheer from the crowd, while the Arioi shuffled and looked apprehensive. Chief Api Api was clearly a good spear thrower and had not been given an honorary title simply because he was a ruler.

The second spear was thrown, then the third, and each time a stick went down. The crowd was silent now, some of them glancing at Kumiki. Linloa had taken his arm and was waiting as calmly as the Painted Leg himself for the outcome of the contest. There was a worried look in her eyes, but she did not transmit this to those around her, possibly for fear of influencing Telufo, for whom the pressure to win was already strong.

The fourth spear was thrown, with the same success as the three previous throws.

Chief Api Api was handed the last spear. Still Telufo had not moved from the spot. He watched with the glinting eyes of an elderly man as Chief Api Api, now completely absorbed in his own skill and success, drew back his arm. It was clear that the chief had been lulled into a state of preoccupation. During the first two throws he had anticipated some sort of intervention from Telufo, but the old man had not moved, and now the chief had forgotten his existence as he stood quietly on the side-lines, as still as rock, just another one of the forest shadows that fell over the scene.

A split second before the spear was launched a shade detached itself from its fixed position and flitted across Chief Api Api's line of vision. The spear flew from the chief's hand, but the unexpected distraction was enough to spoil his aim ever so slightly. The javelin went through the air and passed through space between Telufo's arm and his skinny chest, grazed the last standing stick, and skidded along the ground into the forest beyond. The final target remained standing, albeit slightly skewed. Api Api had failed in his final throw.

However, Chief Api Api had laid flat four out of the five sticks: a great achievement. There were not many spear throwers in Oceania who could match this score.

The chief grunted in disappointment, but once he had got over that initial rush of annoyance for not felling all five and making a legend of himself, he stepped back in satisfaction.

'Your turn, old man,' he said. 'Good luck.'

With that the chief strolled out and stood in front of the replaced targets, a smile upon his face. Miro, standing to the left of the row of sticks, looked very smug. Her champion had proved himself with a brilliant display of spear throwing. Now the old man had to do something even more brilliant, which was very unlikely, and since Api Api's habit was to expose himself to danger by standing directly in the line of fire, ready to dodge the spears as skilfully as Rarotongans who were adept at evading spears thrown at them in quick succession, it seemed that Telufo stood little chance of matching the score, let alone beating it.

Telufo might well have been intimidated by Api-Api's presence in front of the targets. If he struck the chief with a spear and injured or killed him, he would be executed and roasted by the Hivan population. Somehow he had to knock over the sticks without harming the chief in the process.

A spear was handed to Telufo. He weighed it in his gnarled hand. It seemed he at least knew how to hold it.

'A very nice spear,' he said. 'My congratulations to the man who shaped it. A good balance.'

He inspected the stone head of the spear.

'Well-crafted point too. Excellent workmanship.'

While the crowd was thus captivated by his soft speech, they were hardly expecting his next action. With a sudden swift movement, which took everyone by surprise, Telufo launched the javelin at the first target. King Api Api hardly had time to spin away from the target. The spear missed the first stick by a hair, burying itself in an earth bank beyond, leaving the target quivering like a sapling in the wind.

'Missed,' said the chief, recovering from his shock. 'Now you have to hit all the remaining four.'

'I expect so,' said Telufo.

The chief's priest cried, 'You *expect* so? We know so. Painted Leg,' he turned to Kumiki, 'prepare yourself for your punishment.'

Kumiki however, was talking to Ramoro, and he hardly acknowledged the high priest. There was a flick of the hand, no more. It was as if the Avae Parai did not *care* about the outcome of the match. Linloa stood at his side looking a little more anxious, but there were no signs of hysteria, as well there might be, given the task ahead of the old man.

'A little off target, I think,' murmured Telufo. 'A shade from the left.'

This time Chief Api Api was ready for the throw, as he danced nimbly in front of the target, always prepared to get out of the way but hiding the stick while the thrower took aim.

The spear flew. The chief was agile in avoiding it. Again, the javelin missed its mark by a fraction.

'That's it!' cried Miro.

Her husband had now recovered and was holding a cold compress to his wounded head.

'Kill the Painted Leg,' he growled. 'It was agreed.' Chief Api Api shook a finger at the man. 'I sentence transgressors, not you.'

'Excuse me,' interrupted Telufo, 'but the contest is not over yet.'

He took up a third spear and threw it. Then a fourth. Both missed their targets by the merest dog's whisker. It was true they formed a neat line of their own, the four spears, each at the same angle and precisely in line. However, that was not the object of the game. The aim was to knock down as many sticks as possible with five spears. So far all five sticks were still standing.

'Enough,' said the chief wearily. 'It is time for me to pass judgement on the Painted Leg.'

Telufo smiled politely and bowed a little.

'But, if you please, lord, I still have one spear left.'

It was true that the game was not over until all five spears had been thrown.

'Then throw it and get it over with!' snapped Api Api, not at all pleased that he had to pass on punishment to one favoured of the gods. 'Quickly.'

'Perhaps you would like to protect the target?' said the old man, cordially. 'But since there is only one of you and five targets, perhaps your priests would stand in your stead? One priest could cover one target each.'

'Is the old fool mad?' cried the high priest.

Api Api sighed. 'Do as he says. Let's get this over.'

Five unwilling priests were pushed towards the line of sticks. One could see why they were apprehensive. With so many of them out there, they might bump into each other as they tried to get out of the way of Telufo's last spear.

Miro poured scorn on the spear thrower, saying he was a senile old turtle, who could not hit a tree while standing on the root.

Kumiki simply watched through narrowed eyes, his expression entirely enigmatic.

Telufo waited until the five priests had covered a target each. Then he tested the wind with a few blades of grass to determine its direction and strength. Finally he wet the fingers of his right hand, drew back, and launched the spear at a marker post some three lengths to the right of the line of sticks, well away from the target area.

Miro let out a squeal of laughter.

Her glee was premature.

The spear struck the right marker post, which deflected it at an acute angle. It passed *across* the normal line of flight and struck the first target stick. The spear continued its flat, almost level trajectory, to take the other four sticks out of the ground. With a single spear Telufo had removed all five sticks and was thus the winner of the contest.

The watchers, several thousand of them, were stunned by what they had seen. Surely this was magic? Or more likely assistance from the spirit world? There were gasps of wonder and everyone began talking at once. Chief Api Api stared in astonishment, unable to believe what he had seen.

'Is this possible?' he asked.

Telufo bowed and said, 'With the help of our ancestors.'

'No!' screamed Miro. 'It's a trick.'

The high priest took her by the arm.

'The rules required that the sticks are removed by a throw of the spear, that is all. Clearly, from what we have seen, you are falsely accusing a Painted Leg of raping you. Do you confess to these untruths? The chief may be lenient with you, if you admit your guilt.'

Miro fell sobbing to her knees.

'It's true,' she wept, 'I accused him falsely.'

'Such accusations denigrate those of women who have justifiable complaints against men,' said the priest, severely. 'Your sisters will not thank you for this.'

'Take her away and kill her,' murmured Chief Api Api. 'Bring me her heart.'

Miro shrieked in terror as the priests grabbed her arms and began dragging her towards an ahu.

'Wait!' cried Kumiki. 'I beg for leniency. The woman was wrong in falsely accusing me, but I do not want her life on my hands.'

'Why not?' asked Api Api, genuinely surprised. 'It is a worthless life in any case.'

'Still, I would rather she lived. I loved her once and it is only my consuming need for vengeance which separated us. Let her live and I will do an extra performance.'

Chief Api Api looked at Miro, sobbing in the grip of two young priests, and then shrugged.

'So be it, the woman shall live. And you, Lord of the Drums, will entrance us once again with your flying sticks! But tell me, the old man, Telufo – he was once a great spearman?'

Kumiki glanced at Telufo, who was grinning.

'Once? He still is. It is part of his act for the Arioi. He does that trick with the five sticks every performance. Had not our show been interrupted, you would have seen it anyway. It is his speciality.'

Api Api raised his eyebrows. 'And it always works?'

'Well, perhaps not every time,' admitted Telufo, still smiling. 'I remember once, several years ago ...'

PART EIGHT

Kurangai-tuku, the ogress

1

The party of Rarotongans remained with the Maori for many days, enjoying the coolness of their climate while Kieto learned all he could about the art of warfare and the building of defences like the pa. There seemed to be three groups of pa: pa with terraces only, promontory or ridge pa with short transverse ditches, and finally, ring-ditch pa. Each was best for a certain type of terrain. Kieto spent his time examining the engineering, asking questions about the methods, and generally gathering knowledge from the Maori of the most effective way of building.

In the meantime, the other Rarotongans began to wander further and further out into the wildernesses of the Land of the Long White Cloud. They were uneasy, concerned that they had been gone too long from their own world, that Ru might have given up on them and put to sea again, thinking them all lost. Kieto, however, would not quit Aotearoa until he had all the knowledge he needed safely stowed away in his mind. He told the others that if Ru was gone they would need to build their own craft to sail back to Rarotonga, though how that was to be achieved in such a hostile environment as Rapanui he did not explain.

Boy-girl, who had entranced the Maori with her singing and consequently was followed everywhere by a band of suitors who were totally unaware of the dubious nature of her gender, expressed a desire to accompany Seumas on a hunt. Normally she scorned such activities, finding them 'tragically boring' but the attentions of her beaus were driving her distracted and she said she would do anything to get out of the pa for a few days and into the tranquillity of the countryside.

'Come on then,' said Seumas, grabbing a spear. 'Let's go and kill some birds.'

'*You* kill the birds,' said Boy-girl. 'I'll just watch.' However, before they had left the pa a young chief, seeing the two preparing for an expedition, came to them. 'You will bring her back again?' he said to Seumas. 'I forbid you to take her away.'

He was of course talking about Boy-girl.

Seumas raised his eyebrows. 'Of course, I intend bringing her back again.'

The young man stared passionately at Boy-girl.

'She will stay with me for all time,' he said, nodding his head slowly. 'If anyone tries to take her from me, I shall kill them. If any harm comes to her on this expedition of yours, I shall kill you, Captain Cooker. If she refuses my advances when you return, I shall kill her. So be it.'

With this little speech the warrior strode away.

Seumas heaved a sigh. 'Now what? You've got half the young warriors in love with you, and this one wants to cage you like a bird. You deserve all you get, Boy-girl, but you're putting us all in jeopardy.'

Boy-girl said in all seriousness. 'There's going to be trouble – we'd best deal with it later.'

They left the fort and went out into a region between lakes Rotorua and Taupo, bordered by the Waikato river, a district which the earthquake god ruled and kept in perpetual restlessness and bubbling activity. It was a place which seemed full of magic, yet so far in this Land of the Long White Cloud the Rarotongans had experienced no magic whatsoever. Seumas was beginning to think that there was no such thing here, in this Otherworld, and had begun to relax about such things.

The Pict began impaling some of the large edible birds which ran around the bushes, using a long thin flexible spear which had been fashioned for the purpose.

'Are you sure you don't want a try at this?' he asked Boy-girl. 'It's not difficult.'

'No thank you,' she said, playing with the ribbons which dangled from her long black curls. Seumas had made her remove all the seashells from her locks, because of the noise they made. Boy-girl said she felt naked without them. 'I'm not sure I should have come on this expedition. I'm just as bored here as I was back in the pa.'

'Nonsense,' said Seumas. 'Enjoy the countryside. The views are beautiful. This is a land made for the gods! The volcanoes make it interesting, there are wonderful mountains, and the lakes are like pieces of fallen blue sky.'

Boy-girl sighed. 'Yes, you're right, it is a wide and pretty land, but still I'm bored.'

'We'll go back soon,' promised Seumas. 'Just let me spear one or two more birds. You can help me preserve them in their own fat in calabashes, once we get back to the pa.'

'I'll look forward to that,' grimaced Boy-girl.

Seumas stalked a bird which landed on a large bush. He crept up to the bush and was about to spear the creature when it was suddenly speared from the far side. Curious, he crept around the bush to find himself staring at an enormous woman, who continued to spear birds while he watched. She had no weapon in her hands, but was shooting out her lips, impaling the prey on their pointed tips, then retracting them so she could remove the quarry with her hands.

Seumas was astonished and gave out a little cry.

The ogress turned and saw him, her eyes opening wide.

Fearful that she would spear him with her lips, Seumas began to run. The ogress dropped her birds and chased after him, catching him easily because she had wings on her upper arms which assisted her flight and though massive and bulky, she appeared very light on her feet. Seumas struggled in her grip, calling for Boy-girl's assistance, but failed to break free.

Boy-girl came running around the bushes on her long slender legs and came skidding to a halt when she saw the ogress, whose features were incredibly ugly.

'In the names of the gods!' she cried. 'What's this?'

'Two of them?' growled the ogress. 'Who comes to hunt in the territory of Kurangai-tuku? Do you not know these are private hunting grounds?'

Boy-girl must have realised she could do nothing against this enormous woman, so she turned and ran, hiding in the bushes nearby, watching to see what would happen to Seumas.

Seumas said, 'We had no idea this was a private place. We're newcomers to this world.'

'You will come back to my cave with me,' said Kurangai-tuku, 'where I shall decide your fate.'

Seumas struggled in the arms of this ugly ogress, but she was so large his feet were well off the ground and he could get no grip on her fatty flesh. She took him underneath her right arm, pinning his own arms to the side of his body. He yelled and kicked to no avail. When he would not stop striving to escape, she slapped him around the head, a stinging blow which half stunned him and made his ears ring.

Kurangai-tuku then went back for her string of dead birds, shooting out her lips into bushes as she went, probably in the hope of spearing Boy-girl who was now hidden.

Seumas was taken to a nearby hillside where there was a cave. Kurangai-tuku found some woven grasses and bound him tightly, putting him in a dark corner full of spiders and insects which crawled over his face and into his nose and mouth. There were other creatures in the cave: domestic birds, tame lizards and other creatures. Still a bit stupefied from her blow, Seumas made no more protests, but simply watched for the chance to escape.

Kurangai-tuku plucked and scraped the birds she had killed, and those Seumas had speared, and began eating them raw. She was a disgusting eater, spitting out the bones into a pile by the exit to the cave. When she had eaten enough for herself, she gave out a loud belch which echoed through the cave, and then came and tried to push raw bird meat into Seumas's mouth.

'No, no,' he spluttered, 'I'm not hungry.'

'If you don't eat, you'll die,' said Kurangai-tuku.

'I've eaten today already,' said Seumas. 'I don't need any more yet. Later, and you'll have to cook it for me. We humans don't eat uncooked meat.'

Kurangai-tuku, who stated she was always hungry, said she did not understand this, but left him alone.

'Once,' she told him, 'we had a big bird running through the bush, one of which was enough to satisfy me for a meal. It was called a moa. But the Maori people have killed them all.'

'I expect you killed your fair share,' said Seumas, for which remark he received another hefty slap around the head.

Later in the day, Kurangai-tuku had run out of birds to eat and left Seumas in the cave to go and hunt.

While she was gone the other creatures in the cave, Kurangai-tuku's pets, came to investigate her most recent treasure, nuzzling up to Seumas and inspecting every part of his body. He yelled at the creatures, and thrashed his bound body as much as he could, but they still came back.

Seumas was hoping that Boy-girl had followed him to the cave, but she made no appearance, and after a while he realised it was because Kurangai-tuku was hunting in the region all around the cave entrance. He realised he would have to persuade the ogress to go further afield and waited until she returned from her hunt.

'That's a poor show of birds,' he said, nodding at the string of prey she had brought back. 'Can't you do better than that?'

'Of course I can,' snapped the ogress, 'but I have to go a long way from here to get fatter birds.'

'Well, I noticed some really plump pigeons,' remarked Seumas, 'in that range of hills behind where you found me. Not the hills *immediately* behind, but two ranges back from there. Fat wood-pigeons they were. They looked delicious.'

Kurangai-tuku narrowed her eyes in her ugly face and stared at the Pict.

'You are a funny kind of Maori. You have strange hair and there's no tattoos on your face. I don't know whether or not to believe you. If you're lying to me I'll break every bone in your body, then eat you slowly. I'll eat you alive, bit by bit, so you last me several days. Are you lying?'

'No, it's the truth. You've never seen such a flock of pigeons in your life. They're so fat they can hardly fly.'

Kurangai-tuku nodded thoughtfully. 'I shall go and spear some of these pigeons with my lips.'

She left the cave and through the exit Seumas could see her striding across the countryside, using a karakia to assist her.

'Stretch out, stride along,' she was crying. 'Stretch out, stride along.'

These words seemed to lengthen her step, so that she was covering the plain in fewer than a dozen paces, and stepping from peak to peak when she came to the first range of hills, creating a great wind by her movements over the land.

When she was out of sight Seumas called for Boy-girl, hoping she was within earshot.

'She's gone!' he yelled.

However, instead of Boy-girl, someone else entered the cave. By his appearance it was a young man, a Maori, and he stared about him feverishly.

'Is she gone?' said the young man.

'Who are you?' asked Seumas, trying to sit up.

'My name is Hau-tupatu,' said the youth. 'I was once a captive of Kurangai-tuku like you, but I used a karakia my grandmother taught me and escaped into a rock.'

'Why have you risked coming back?' asked Seumas.

'To get this.' The youth crossed to a corner of the cave and picked up a beautiful cloak of red feathers made from the underwings of kaka birds. 'I have always coveted this cloak – and now it's mine.'

At that moment a ruru owl let out a hoot of alarm, no doubt calling for Kurangai-tuku. Hau-tupatu felled the bird with a blow from his club. But then another, a tiny grey bird called a riroriro, flew out of the cave exit. It flew off over the hills, no doubt to warn the ogress that she was being robbed.

'Let me free, quickly,' said Seumas. 'Before she returns.'

'I have no time for that,' said Hau-tupatu.

With that he ran out of the cave leaving Seumas still bound and helpless. It was only a short time later that Kurangai-tuku came bounding home, demanding to know what had happened.

'I heard the riroriro calling me,' she said. 'I thought you had escaped, but I see you are still tied.'

Then she let out a terrible cry and rushed to the corner of the cave where her cloak of red feathers had been. She found her cloak of thick dogs' fur and an ornamented cloak of glossy flax, but no feathered cloak. A loud wail escaped her.

'Where is it?' she shrieked. 'Who has stolen my beautiful cloak?'

She spun round and stared out of the cave exit, to see the youth Hau-tupatu running over the plain. Flapping from his shoulders was the scarlet cloak. With her wings on her upper arms beating fast she ran after the thief. Seumas, frustrated and helpless, simply had to lie there and witness this drama, wondering if he was ever going to get free.

'Boy-girl,' he yelled. 'Where the devil are you?'

To his relief Boy-girl appeared from outside. She looked anxiously over her shoulder and then entered the cave. Once her eyes became used to the darkness, she saw Seumas, covered in lizards and spiders.

'Ugghh,' she said, fastidiously.

'Never mind *ugghh*,' cried Seumas. 'Get me loose. That woman will be back again soon. She's a monster. Quickly, loosen the rope.'

Boy-girl came to him and began fiddling with the knots, finding them too tight to undo.

'I need something to cut them with,' she said, looking around. 'Or burn them through.'

Finally, she found a piece of sharpened flint that Kurangai-tuku used to scrape the feathers from the birds she ate, and with this managed to saw through Seumas's bonds. Once he was free they rushed from the cave together and climbed the hill. They followed the ridge of hills and eventually, before the evening swept across the landscape, they reached the pa.

'Where have you been?' asked Dorcha. 'I've been worried about the pair of you.'

'This is one of those places,' said Seumas, wearily. 'I thought we had left magic behind us, in our old world, but this place has it too. We ran into an ogress, a creature called Kurangai-tuku, who used her lips like a spear. She caught me and kept me tied amongst her pets. Boy-girl finally managed to let me loose when a youth who called himself Hau-tupatu came to the cave and stole the woman's red feather cloak.'

'Hau-tupatu has been through here, wearing that cloak,' confirmed Dorcha, 'just a short while ago.'

Boy-girl was alarmed at this. 'We'd better tell the Maori – so they can defend the pa against Kurangai-tuku.'

Dorcha shook her head. 'According to Hau-tupatu, the ogress is dead. He used the theft of the cloak to lure her into a boiling spring called Te Whaka-rewarewa. She died horribly in the scalding waters.'

Seumas shook his head. 'That's the last time I go hunting with Boy-girl – she's bad luck.'

'Me?' cried Boy-girl. 'I've never been so frightened in all my life.'

That evening, while Seumas was washing himself in a stream outside the pa, he heard the plaintive cry of a small grey bird drifting over the landscape.

'*Riro riro riro riro,*' came the mournful sound.

When darkness fell, the cries of the bird ceased, and the land moved into a deep silence.

At last Kieto got what he wanted, a full-blooded battle with the Maori.

A messenger came to Chief Tuwhakapau and the chief of the defeated pa to say there was a great gathering of clans from upper Aotearoa near lake Taupo, where the lower Aotearoa clans were massing for an attack. Kieto requested to join Chief Tuwhakapau's warriors and this was granted. Seumas and the others elected to remain out of the fight, not wishing to risk their lives unnecessarily.

They marched with Kieto and the other warriors, those who had defended the pa now being allies of those who had attacked the pa, towards Lake Taupo. There, near the hot springs, they found hundreds of other tribes encamped, all preparing for a massive battle the following day.

Seumas was astonished at the number of men. They were like a dark sea over the plain. There were thousands on thousands of them, all excited and primed ready for a fight. That night their campfires covered the landscape like stars. There was much praying to the gods, men communed with their ancestors, spear points were sharpened, club edges were honed. One or two of the chiefs had thunder sticks left them by Captain Cookers and these were cleaned and polished. These thunder sticks were marvellous magical weapons which apparently could kill at a great distance, if the user had good eyes.

Kieto was allowed to inspect a thunder stick but pronounced it unfathomable.

'It's just like a hollow bamboo stick made of cold stone,' he told Seumas. 'A very *hard* cold stone. It shoots a pebble – who knows how? – which hits the warrior and kills him, as a piece of flint launched from a sling will kill a man.'

'That sounds like an iron weapon to me,' Seumas replied, when the material was described to him, 'not stone.'

'Do the Angles, Picts and Scots have thunder sticks?' asked Kieto.

'No,' replied Seumas, truthfully. 'They do not.'

The following day Seumas and the other Rarotongans stood on a hill and watched the battle. It was a glorious affair with great sweeping tides of warriors gathered to rush down upon one another in a massive display of death and destruction. The dancing and singing beforehand was impressive enough and filled the valleys and mountains with sound. Once again Seumas was awed by the haka, which chilled him almost as much as the sound of the bagpipes scared the Oceanians.

Then, when the two sides ran at each other, and clashed, there was a mighty crash which echoed over the land. Spears filled the air like swarms of elongated birds. Clubs cracked on heads. Swords hacked at limbs. Daggers plunged into torsos.

Now and again there was the crack of thunder and a puff of smoke as one of the chiefs used his magic weapon. Somewhere amongst the thousands of warriors presumably a man fell with a pebble lodged in his head or body. Seumas was not impressed with the weapon, thinking he could have killed half-a-dozen men in the time it took to prepare the thunder stick for another crack. Still, it was feared more for the way in which it did its business, rather than for the amount of havoc it wreaked.

Upper island clan turtles were formed, bristling with spears, and these tried to force their way through the centre, but were driven back by hastily constructed spear-shaped columns of the enemy, who attacked the turtles on a narrow front, driving like a wedge into the packed mass of warriors.

Next, the upper clans tried sweeping phalanxes of warriors, running down a slope and clashing with the enemy like wave on wave from a limitless ocean. This tactic almost worked as the lower clans fought to keep any ground they had gained, trying desperately not to give way. However, they were made of strong stuff, these tribes from below Lake Taupo, and they withstood the onslaughts like a cliff of solid rock.

The lower clans' ranks refused to be broken and this began to tell on the upper clans, wearying them.

There was the smell of gore and blood in the warm air, mixed with the scent of vegetable oil. The warriors had smeared themselves all over before the battle, to make themselves slippery and difficult to grip. They shone in the sunlight with great beauty, their muscles gleaming, their tattoos standing out starkly against their brown bodies.

The whole plain reeked of the odour of sweat too: fear sweat and sweat from physical effort.

Thousands of feet drummed on the earth as the battle swayed back and forth, causing trees on ridges to shimmer and shake.

The tide of men hacking, jabbing, stabbing, cutting, swayed back and forth over the noonday. Finally, the tactics of the lower clans were successful. A panic began to set in. One side started running, those of the martial clans whom Kieto had joined, and Seumas and the others found themselves having to flee also. The battle had been lost to the tribes of lower Aotearoa. Those who had taken flight were pursued with some alacrity and glee, chopped down as they fled. The land was littered with oiled bodies, gleaming in the pleasant sunlight, and Seumas asked himself more than once, 'What for?'

Kieto happily survived this major battle with the Maori, breathless and sweating, high as a hawk on adrenaline. Shreds of flesh dripped from his whalebone club. Hanks of hair hung from his lei-o-mano. He was happy. He had been a hero amongst heroes and had discovered a love of battle within himself.

'War *is* glorious,' he said. 'No doubt about it.'

'But did you learn anything?' asked Seumas. 'Surely you were too much in the thick of it to see what was going on around you, generally.'

Kieto put a hand on the Pict's shoulder.

'I leave the tactics to you. You must explain them to me, as you saw them. You were watching it – what happened?'

'You were outflanked,' said Seumas. 'They sent a force – fleet of foot – around your right flank and these warriors drove your ragged edge into the middle of your line, causing great confusion there as they crowded with the centre.'

'See,' cried Kieto triumphantly, washing himself in a stream, 'I knew I could rely on you, Seumas.'

'Did you?' said Seumas. 'And you enjoyed yourself?'

'Immensely,' replied Kieto, his shining face dripping with water. 'But I'm sorry we lost. If I had been the general I would have strengthened the right, because their left had the best warriors they could muster. It was all too simple, wasn't it? We gained some experience there.'

'Yes,' agreed Seumas, 'I suppose we did. But we've got something else to think about now, you know. A young Maori chief has fallen in love with Boy-girl. He swears he'll have us all killed if we try to take her away with us, when we leave. I'm sure he means it, just as I'm sure he has the power to command enough warriors to do the job.

'We're going to have to think of some way out of this.'

2

Finally, it was time to leave the Maori and the Land of the Long White Cloud. They had been away from Rapanui for three months now and surely Ru had set sail? If Kieto was worried he did not show it. He seemed to believe he was beloved of the gods and that nothing would stand in his way of eventually taking an invasion fleet to Land-of-Mists. And if he were to do this, then of course he had to live to return to Rarotonga.

'How are we going to get Boy-girl away?' asked Seumas of Kieto. 'The young chief is just as enamoured of her as he ever was.'

'Boy-girl says she'll get him drunk on kava, then we'll have to make a run for it,' Kieto replied.

On their last evening Polahiki schooled Boy-girl in the manner of the dance of the tropic bird, which is a speciality of the Hivan islands. The tropic bird is one of the most beautiful creatures in Oceania: an angel in earthly form. Pure white with a long slender red tail the tropic bird's courtship dance is a heavenly display. Dressed in a white tapa cloth, with red feathers in her hair, Boy-girl gave the Maori one of the most moving performances they had ever seen in their lives and the silence which greeted the end of her dance was profound. The audience was so affected they could utter no sound.

The young chief who was in love with her prepared to lead her away to his hut afterwards, and Boy-girl turned and said her loud goodbyes to her old friends, saying she would be happy to remain amongst the Maori, a great warrior race.

Cheers greeted this speech.

Polahiki then asked to remain amongst the Maori as well, rather than go back to his own world, since he loved the wide open spaces. He planned to go off by himself into the wilderness, find a lake well stocked with fish, and live there out of sight and sound of the rest of humanity. There were sweet potatoes in abundance in the Land of the Long White Cloud and if there was one vegetable which found its way to Polahiki's heart through his stomach it was the sweet potato.

'What a pity the young chief did not fall in love with Polahiki,' said Seumas in an aside to Dorcha. 'Then we wouldn't have to worry.'

'I can't imagine anyone, short of that ogress you killed, *ever* desiring Polahiki's body for any purpose,' said Dorcha. 'Though no doubt he would have made a meal for the unfussy Kurangai-tuku, however unpalatable he looks to us.'

To Polahiki himself Dorcha said the rest of the Ru party would be quite grateful for his unselfish act of remaining behind, since they would not have to smell Polahiki's unwashed body when the wind was in the wrong quarter, nor have to watch him cracking his lice between chipped dirty fingernails, nor have to avoid brushing against him for fear of being soiled.

'Rarotongans young and old will benefit from this generous act,' she told him, as he scowled into her face, 'and will be eternally thankful.'

On the other hand, the party returning to their own world would not be short of numbers. Tangata, the old Maori, was dreadfully curious about this similar Oceania on the other side of the cave, and wished to see it for himself.

'You may never be able to return here,' warned the Farseeing-virgin Kika-mana. 'Do you leave any family?'

'No one,' replied Tangata. 'I am an old warrior without sons or daughters and my barren wife is dead. We were not blessed with children, so I am alone. Of course, I have brothers and sisters, and cousins, but they are not close to me in my old age. I want to do this one last thing – see this world from which you come – before I die.'

'So long as you know what you're letting yourself in for,' said the priestess. 'We do not wish to be responsible for your unhappiness.'

The next morning the party was ready to set out to return to the cave which led to Rapanui on the opposite world. At dawn Seumas crept to the hut of the young chief and called for Boy-girl. He received no answer. Thinking she had probably drunk kava along with her lover, he looked inside the hut with its elaborately carved door posts, into the gloom.

Boy-girl was there, looking distressed. She put a finger to her lips and pointed down, at something attached to her right leg. Seumas was horrified to see she was manacled, with an iron chain running to a central post. The manacle must have been left by the Captain Cookers, when they visited the Land of the Long White Cloud.

The young chieftain was asleep on the mat beside her, snoring noisily, dried kava juice rimming his lips.

'Where's the key?' mouthed Seumas. 'The *key?*'

Tears brimmed Boy-girl's eyes. 'Son of a pig has swallowed it,' she said in a normal voice, and gave the sleeping youth a savage kick in the stomach.

The boy jerked upright and was promptly sick on the floor. Seumas stepped forward and struck him a blow on the temple with his club, rendering him unconscious again. They searched his vomit with a stick, but found no key.

'*I think* he swallowed it,' said Boy-girl. 'It looked like it.'

'Wonderful,' murmured Seumas, gagging at the smell of the vomit. 'You *think.*'

'Well don't just stand there,' growled Boy-girl. 'Get me free!'

Seumas went out and got Kieto. Between them they dug away at the central post and then both men heaved on the chain. Finally the post gave way. The young chieftain groaned. Boy-girl gave him another kick and then dragged the post behind her, leaving the hut. They left the village with Seumas and Boy-girl carrying the heavy wooden post between them.

Tangata said, 'We must burn the post, or it will slow us too much.'

'No,' Seumas replied, 'we must get the iron off Boy-girl, or she'll be dragging the chain. Tangata, can you get one of those thunder sticks? Can you make one work?'

The old man grinned. 'I see what you mean.'

Tangata went back into the village, entering a hut. He came out again carrying one of the iron tubes. When he reached the others, he said to Boy-girl, 'I have loaded this thunder stick. Put your leg on the rock and turn your head away.'

Boy-girl, trembling in fright, did as she was told.

Tangata lit a piece of cord, then blew it out so that it glowed. He then placed the end of the thunder stick against the iron stud which pinned the two pieces of hinged manacle together. When he was satisfied with the position, he blew on the smouldering string to make it glow red again, which he then put to a small hole two thirds of the way down the whole weapon.

A terrible explosion made everyone's ears ring. Boy-girl screamed in pain and terror. Seumas started to run, a natural survival instinct taking over, then checked himself. He stared shame-facedly at Dorcha, who was white with fright. She had frozen on the spot, the other survival mechanism.

'It's done,' said Tangata, the only member of the party to be unaffected by the violence of the stick. 'Are you hurt?'

Boy-girl rubbed her ankle. There were powder burns all around it, leaving a pale band where the manacle used to be. It looked a little like a tattoo gone badly wrong.

'My leg stings,' she said. 'But I don't think it's broken, it's just bruised.'

'Can you walk?' asked Kieto.

She stood up and tested the ankle, finding she could. There was a slight limp, but nothing which would slow them down.

'Are we taking the thunder stick?' asked Kieto of Tangata.

'No we're not,' cried Seumas, gathering courage to pick it up. The tube was warm, where the thunderbolt had travelled through its length. He flung it far away from them, grabbed Dorcha's arm and said, 'Let's get out of here. The whole village will be awake now. We'll have to run.'

He was right, there was now a general call to arms. The young chieftain had come round and was yelling for his warriors to join him. A race began to reach the cave which led to Rapanui and the other world.

The sky was streaked with long wisps of cloud, against a deep red background. They ran over the broad landscape, each sorry for their own reasons to leave this beautiful yet mystical land. As they neared the cave entrance, the Maori came up over the hill. Spears began to fill the air, to thud into the earth behind the fleeing party. The Rarotongans entered the cave, just as the Maori found their range.

One spear hissed past Seumas's ear and he, being the last of the party, turned at the entrance to the cave and waved his patu club at the oncoming warriors.

'Good organisation,' he called, 'but this is a rabbit hunt – you've got to catch your prey before there's a fight!'

They were now close enough for Seumas to see the fierce tattooed features of the Maori. The warriors protruded their tongues and rolled their eyes putting on their war faces. The young chieftain who loved Boy-girl was hurtling down the last hill, right out in front of his warriors. Seumas took his slingshot from his belt, fitted a stone to the saddle, then whirled the weapon around his head.

The stone struck the Maori chief on the foot, sending him squealing, tumbling head over heels. He landed in a piece of boggy ground with a *splat*, his face going straight down into mud the colour of old porridge. Frogs leaped and jumped out of the way in fright, no doubt fearing the attack was directed at them. A wading bird rushed across the marsh, screaming blue murder, wondering what had fallen from the sky.

Slowly the chief rose, mud dripping from his features, the wading bird still screaming as it went over the next hill.

It was such a comical scene, Seumas could not but help laughing at the unfortunate man's somersaults. This had the effect of making the chief's own warriors laugh also. Finally the chief himself, having recovered his feet and wiped himself off, saw the funny side of things too. The Maori are big-hearted enough, confident enough, to laugh at themselves when they are involved in a ridiculous situation. Finally, all the pursuers were in a state of mirth, slapping their thighs and clutching their ribs. A laugh was as good as a victory.

Seumas gave them one last salute, before entering the cave and following his companions.

He received a cheer as his reward.

As he moved in the dimness of the cave's interior, he reflected on the Maori, on their greatness. They were a fascinating people with a true feeling for the artist, both in their wooden carvings, the quality of which the Rarotongans had never laid eyes on before this visit, and their buildings. In the science of war too, they were more advanced than the Rarotongans, with their magnificent pa and their tactics and strategies unknown to warriors of the small islands.

'It's a pity,' said Kieto, later, 'that we can't visit the Hawaii of this world too. It sounds as if we could learn much about naval warfare from them. That sea battle Tangata talks about sounds remarkable ...'

The party eventually reached the cave and passed through it, encountering the clashing rocks and the armies of the dead, but well able to deal with them. This time too they had taken enough provisions, so they did not have to eat clouds of dry moths. Finally, after a long and gruelling journey, they reached their canoes. They emerged from the mouth of the cave on to Rapanui and paddled to a landing point just below the volcano which the short-eared villagers had called Rano Kau. On meeting fresh air again they found the island in turmoil. Open warfare had erupted. The whole place was seething with violence.

Seumas and Kieto stood on the rim of the crater and stared down the length of the island.

There were ranks of red stone giants ranged against white stone giants, battling it out in great numbers. The air was full of the sound of stone on stone as the monsters clashed; topknots flying, rock bodies crashing to the earth with an impact that shook the landscape, dust billowing. Some giants had fallen into specially dug traps – deep pits – and were being buried alive up to their shoulders in the ground.

On the human front, even more horrific scenes could be witnessed. Down one end of the island the Short Ears had dug a huge trench, right across the Poiko Peninsula, just beyond the Rano Raraku crater. Within this ditch they had piled brushwood and logs, which had been set alight, so that a river of fire crossed the landscape from beach to beach. Into this horrible flaming trap the Short Ears were driving the whole Long-Eared population like domestic livestock, burning them alive. The screams of the Long Ears could be heard from the crater lake of Rano Kau, at the other end of the island.

'This is ugly,' said Seumas. 'This is open warfare for you. Do you want this, Kieto?'

Kieto stared at the dreadful scene. 'If it is necessary for victory,' he replied, 'then so be it.'

Yet Seumas, whose stomach heaved at the sight, knew Kieto was also affected by the suffering. It seemed that the young would-be general's ambition, predestined perhaps and thus unavoidable, outweighed his compassion. Kieto had so long been in the grip of his dream of conquest, a sight like this, however harrowing, was not enough to wrench him free.

Kieto was one of those men in history who look on colonisation as necessary to the progression of his people. The Oceanians were by nature migrants: as their nations grew they spread outwards, seeking new lands, where necessary wresting them from their present owners. Colonisation was in their blood. If the land they found was uninhabited, so much the better, but if sparsely inhabited by another race then that race must stand aside for the overwhelming numbers of settlers.

Kieto was also hungry for recognition of his intrinsic and learned talents as a general. To be a great man amongst the Oceanians was to be either a great navigator or a great warrior. Here was a chance to be a warrior on a scale never before envisioned or possible. Here was an opportunity to conquer a land the size of the country which the Maori had found and colonised. What dreamer of fame and glory could pass over such a chance to become the most famous general in the history of the world?

Not Kieto.

'We must discover if Ru has been prepared to wait for so long,' said Kieto, turning from the massacre. 'We'll need to take the path around this side of the island to avoid both the giants and the battle between the humans.'

'To avoid the slaughter, you mean?' said Seumas.

'If those are the words you wish to choose.'

The party, including the elderly Maori, Tangata, circumnavigated the island until they came to the beach where they had been put ashore by Ru. Sure enough, anchored off the coast they could see *The Princely Flower*. Kieto ordered the lighting of five small fires in a row and shortly afterwards *The Princely Flower* came gliding over the water. Dirk was there, standing on the bows of the craft, with the cock Lei-o-mano perched on his back. It seemed the two had consoled each other while their owners were gadding about in an Otherworld.

Soon everyone was aboard and Ru set course for Tooa o to ra on the windflower.

Once the pahi was on its way, with a misty spray drifting over the bows and drenching the score of maidens which made up the crew (among which Kikamana was of course numbered), Seumas and Dorcha began to relax.

Dorcha took out her bamboo-shell chart and added the dimension which included Rapanui, while Seumas went back to his old hobby of studying the efficiency with which the naked complement of mariners, glistening with fine-spray moisture, went about their seamanship. He simply sat dreamily watching the women, with his arm around the neck of Dirk, who was demonstratively pleased to see his master back on board.

There was a softness to the air, out on the briny, and overhead a pastel blue was restful on the eyes. Out on the great ocean the waves were large graceful beasts, rolling as a mighty herd across the seascape. Dorcha felt a surge of contentment go through her as she worked with the slivers of bamboo and small money cowries, completing her chart of voyages of Oceania. She felt closer now to Seumas than she had ever done before in her life.

There was a Seumas she hated, a figure in the past, but he was now gone, faded away. They had done so much together, upon this second great voyage in the middle of their lives. Their earlier seafarings had been done alone, with he a wild storm in front and she following like a furious wind behind him. Now they were intermingled, almost as one, and had made this voyage together. Now their pioneering spirit had merged and she was feeling great satisfaction in loving and being loved by her constant companion, the Pict.

Once her task of completing the chart was done she joined Ru at the mast.

'Thank you for staying for us,' she said. 'It must have been a long wait.'

Ru looked at her and raised his eyebrows.

'Not so long,' he said. 'You were only gone a few days.'

'But we were in Aotearoa for well over a month!' she exclaimed.

Ru shook his handsome head. 'A few days, that's all. Admittedly events on the island boiled over into bloodshed and chaos while you were gone, which made our wait *seem* that much longer, but in fact the days were only seven altogether.'

'In that case, time must have passed more quickly in the place where we were. At least four of our days for every one of yours.' She considered this more carefully, before adding, 'So that's why we grew so hungry on our journey through the middle of the earth. It makes sense now.'

'You amaze me with your words,' said Ru. 'I have not yet spoken to Kieto, but I must learn from him what wonders you beheld in the land of the Maori. I see you left the dirty fisherman behind. Was he killed?'

'No, he elected to remain there.'

'Their loss, our gain,' grunted Prince Ru. 'And you returned with one of their number?'

'Yes, his name is Tangata, an old Maori warrior. Isn't he magnificent?'

Ru studied the grey-haired gentleman in question as that man rested with his back against one of the deck huts. He seemed bright and alert, watching all that went on around him, studying the sea with a keen yet cautious eye.

'He tattoos his face, in the way of the Hivans, yet the tattoos are not of the same pattern. They are much finer and more artistically wrought. Is he a mariner?'

'I think not,' replied Dorcha. 'So far as I know he hasn't been to sea before in his life. He comes from an inland place, where there are great lakes, but his tribe was not a sea-going people. His was a martial clan, whose warriors lived for fighting. We saw them in battle. The glory of war seemed to be their sole reason for keeping fit and healthy.'

Ru shrugged. 'Each to his own. I prefer to pit my wits and strength against the ocean. The elements are tough enough adversaries for me. Speaking of which there have been strange goings-on amongst the gods while you were away. We had a dozen electrical storms in the first three days alone, which seemed to be trying to force us away from our anchorage and leave you behind.'

'Are you sure?'

'No,' replied Ru, 'but it appeared that way, for in the outer ocean there was a good wind – we could see it in the flights of the birds – and it was a clear sky. Only around the island was there thunder and lightning, dry storms without rain. If we had left Rapanui I'm sure we would have found excellent and safe sailing.'

'Tawhaki and his creation Uira? What could we have done to upset the God of Thunder?'

'Whatever it was, I think it is settled, for the electrical storms disappeared after those first five days.'

It was true that in his frustration to rid the world of Kieto's party, Tawhaki had overstretched himself. Tangaroa wanted to know why there was so much thunder and lightning necessary around Rapanui, when Ua and Maomao were not present to herald in the noise and lights which normally accompanied a howling rainstorm. Ao, the God of Clouds and Tawhaki's unwilling co-conspirator, finally broke away from the God of Thunder and confessed to Tangaroa that there was a plot to thwart Kieto and his party. Tangaroa complained to Io, who lives on the remote twelfth plane, away from the squabbles of the lower gods, and Io duly sent messengers to Tawhaki, chastising him and warning him not to interfere in the affairs of men.

The God of Thunder was much displeased with both Ao and Tangaroa, but had no choice but to cease stamping around the heavens and releasing lightning from his armpits. He went away to the far corner of Oceania to bother the Hawaiians for a while, to vent his annoyance on their ships and to stir an old friend of his to action, Pele, Goddess of Volcanoes. The navigator prince Ru would not be bothered by thunder and lightning again, not on his present voyage into the unknown waters of Oceania.

That night Ru sighted a fatigued bird on the horizon. When it drew closer to the pahi he saw that it was a white-bellied sea eagle and it was carrying something in its claws. As it flew over *The Princely Flower*, the sea eagle released its cargo. A calabash landed amongst some ropes and failed to break open. Titopika was the first to pick up this object, since it landed almost in his lap. He recognised some symbols carved on the seed pod. In triumph he followed the instructions of these symbols, twisting on the glued stopper to the calabash.

The stopper came out like a volcano plug with all the pressure of the Goddess Pele behind it, shooting up into the sky and killing the sea eagle which had transported it.

True to his nature, Ragnu wanted no living witnesses to his deeds, even should that observer be a bird. A kahuna with the powers of Kikamana might force that bird to speak, to reveal the name of the sorcerer who sent it. So the creature was betrayed by its own master and death was its reward for a duty performed with diligence and efficiency.

Out of the now opened calabash came an ear-splitting rushing sound as if all the demons of hell had been released.

3

Ragnu had at first intended to fill the calabash with poisonous gas, so that everyone on board the pahi would be killed. However, Ru himself was especially loved of the gods and there were all Ru's family and relations to consider. Ragnu decided in the end that while he felt no real concern over cold-bloodedly murdering a whole canoe full of people, whether they were princes or paupers, it might bring him unwelcome attention from the gods.

Thus he had filled the calabash with storm winds.

It was one thing to kill people with a deadly gas, quite another to present them with a situation like a storm. If Ru's vessel went under because of poor seamanship during bad weather, or because it was driven onto reefs or rocks, that could be attributed to the capricious nature of the ocean. A storm was a test to be passed or failed, depending on the captain.

When Titopika removed the stopper to the calabash, a hurricane was released. This mighty wind immediately filled the sails and drove the pahi far from its course. Waves grew monstrously high and lashed the decks of the oceangoing canoe. There was a white fury in the air, which smothered the ship. Those on board found it difficult to breathe, since the air was so full of stinging spray they swallowed sea water with every gulp of oxygen. Two men and a woman were washed overboard, never to be seen again. Pungarehu, still grieving over the loss of Wiama the night-girl, was one of those lost.

Dakuwanga swam in the midst of the storm, having just missed swallowing the sau of one of Ru's relatives as it made its way through the confused air to the entrance to Milu's kingdom. It was happily passed into the hands of

Limu. Pungarehu's soul also fortunately escaped the jaws of the shark-god and he and the woman made it safely to the purple road, and down into the underworld. There he met his beautiful Wiama, to whom he was married in spirit if not in fact: she proclaimed herself his wife in order for him to safely pass the terrible Nangananga.

As the furious hurricane tossed the pahi around like a toy, throwing it this way and that in its petulance, Titopika himself was killed. One of the masts snapped and struck him a skull-cracking blow on the head. His brains spilled out like milk from a split coconut and were washed overboard. His body slipped into the sea, later to become food for the sharks and barracuda, and the little nibbling carrion. His sau went up into the ether, buffeted by Tawhiri-atea, the Storm-God.

Dakuwanga, having been thwarted of three of his potential prey, was especially alert. His sharp cold eyes spotted the sau of Titopika, struggling through the blinding storm, and descended upon it just as it was about to tread the purple road. Milu was waiting, ready to answer the usual question asked of him ('Why, on the point of death, am I aware of the meaning of life?') and to testify as to the unfairness of it.

Titopika's soul was not destined to become an atua however, for Dakuwanga's ravenous jaws closed around it just an instant before it touched the purple road. Titopika, silently screaming his last scream, was swallowed by the Shark-God. There would be no life beyond life for the tohunga. He was now on his way to becoming incorporeal excrement, to be scattered on the winds, over the seas, and never to know awareness again.

Milu shook his head sadly and returned to the Land of the Dead, for he could foresee no other souls descending.

Titopika left behind him a grieving wife, the princess who fell for his dashing looks, his élan. The poor woman had gone from bride to widow in a few short weeks. She went to a sympathetic Dorcha to learn her fate. She told the Scot she was pregnant. Dorcha used her occult powers and discovered that the woman's son would one day become a great chief on an island yet unnamed. He would raise his mother high in status and the pair of them would rule with great wisdom.

When the storm abated, *The Princely Flower* found itself in a part of the ocean where the air was sultry and the wind sluggish. Those on board knew the signs well. They recognised the putrid nature of the waters around them, the lifeless weed and floating coral. There were rotten palm logs floating away on a desultory tide. Strange ugly fish fed off their own decayed dead.

'We stop at no island in these waters,' said Ru. 'I want no more of monsters, or deadly fairies, or giants. We will ignore any enticements. Dorcha, Po'oi, help me find my way amongst these new stars up there in the roof of voyaging ...'

For once the dark magic of strange islands was not allowed to delay them and after only a few days they had found their way out of the doldrums. They entered a sea, still unknown to them, which was sparkling and clear. Fresh breezes, surely from Hine-tu-whenua, took the craft in a skimming motion over the back of her sister Hine-tengaru-moana.

Many of the stores they had gathered on Rapanui had however been washed overboard in the storm and it was imperative that they stop at an island to replenish them. Indeed, a likely-looking cloud was seen at noon, under which there would be an island. By evening the next day they had reached the outer fringe of the island and passed over the reef. Once in the lagoon Ru dropped anchor and studied the palm-covered beaches with satisfaction. Here there would be food in plenty.

'I can see coconuts and breadfruit,' said Ru, 'and we may find yams and bananas, if we're lucky.'

A party was formed to explore the hinterland made up of Seumas, Dorcha, Ru and Tangata the Maori. Dirk was to be permitted to accompany his master, since he had been pining for him while Seumas was in the Land of the Long White Cloud.

'See you behave yourself, mind,' said Seumas sharply to his hound. 'No running into the bush, looking for smells. There'll be enough for you without you charging off.'

Dirk wagged his tail and looked suitably responsible.

Dorcha sighed. 'You talk to that dog as if you think it'll understand you.'

'It knows what I'm about, Dorcha, even if it doesn't understand the words. I'm the one who trained it after all. It knows by the tone of my voice what I'm about. You women never did understand the bond between man and dog. I think you females are jealous of the closeness between a Pict and his hound.'

'Are we now?' teased Dorcha. 'This closeness? Is it the same kind of closeness that a shepherd feels for his sheep I wonder? I know how the cold nights can improve such a relationship, up in the damp hills of Albainn. I've heard of stories …'

The prim Seumas was as shocked by her insinuation as he was meant to be.

'You know I don't mean it that way,' he said, prudishly. 'I mean in a spiritual sense.'

'Oh, chaste is it? Well, make sure this pure relationship you have with your mongrel includes discipline. I don't want to have to spend my time on that island chasing a stupid dog.'

They were able to wade ashore from the pahi, through the shallow waters, leaving Kieto in charge of the vessel. Ru's family and relations gathered coconuts on the shoreline, breadfruit from the fringe of the rainforest and shellfish from the lagoon. Others made rods, baited their hooks, and angled for reef fish all along the coral lip.

The party of four proceeded into the rainforest with caution. Too many times they had blundered on to a seemingly uninhabited island, only to find it crawling with monsters, or infested with hostile tribes. This time they were going to be ready for anything unusual or threatening.

The group were surprised, however, for the deeper they went into the rain-forest, the more pleasant became their surroundings. There were beautiful tall trees, their buttress roots as high as a man. Thin waterfalls jetted from high rocks, down on to mossy platforms, into fern gullies many shades of green.

Butterflies filled the dazzling air of sunlit glades. Dragonflies and damsel-flies hovered over moist banks. Lizards dropped from leafy boughs, to scamper through the undergrowth. There were all kinds of exquisite birds, with colourful plumage and elegant songs. Even Tangata the Maori was impressed, saying that Aotearoa had a wonderful variety of birds, but not as rich and plentiful as this small island.

Finally they came to an area where there was a huge pool, in the shadow of a volcanic rock overhang.

'Look how it sparkles in the sunlight,' breathed Dorcha. 'It invites me to bathe.'

Seumas looked around him. 'Not yet – you don't know what's in there.'

'What could be in such a pretty lake?'

Ru said, 'Seumas is right, Dorcha. We have to be careful. The pool might be attractive for a reason.'

Tangata, who was carrying a tall spear, bent down to look into the crystal waters. They promised to be thirst-quenchingly sweet. He was about to dip a hand into the pool to taste the water when he saw his reflection on the sur-face. With a startled shout he drew back and then jumped to his feet.

'What is it?' cried Ru. 'A creature?'

'No, not that,' replied Tangata, 'it is my own self – I have changed into a boy.'

He dropped his spear and ran his hands over his face, feeling his features. Then he looked down at himself, to find the same wrinkled limbs, gnarled hands and pot belly he had woken with that very morning. He was still a senior warrior.

'I don't understand it,' he murmured, going down on his knees again. 'There is an eight-year-old me in the lake, yet here on land I am still old Tangata.'

While Seumas gripped the nape hair on Dirk to hold him back, the others genuflected. They stared down into the pool and let out similar expressions of shock and surprise.

Dorcha said softly with nostalgia evident in her voice, 'A little girl – oh, I'm a little girl again.'

'A young boy,' muttered Ru. 'I recognise myself – it is definitely me.'

'Let me see,' said Seumas, unable to bear it any longer.

Still holding on to Dirk, he bent down and stared into the clear waters. The reflection was that of a male child, too young even to have tattoos. A junior Seumas. He smiled at himself and the boy smiled back. It was a miracle. Something wrenched at Seumas's heart – a feeling of lost childhood found again – and he sighed deeply.

Was this possible? Could they look back to the past, see themselves as they were, mourn for the innocence of infancy? It was a sweet-sour exercise, gazing at something which was locked in the past, unobtainable, yet so beautiful in its guiltlessness. A lump formed in his throat and a kind of yearning was like a pain in his chest, as he stared at himself as he had been, oh, at least a thousand years ago.

Seumas glanced across and saw an immature and artless Dorcha, a pretty little girl with matted black locks and black eyes, looking back up at him. He reached for the image with a small cry, as another kind of pain explored his breast. This was the child Dorcha might have borne, had they been able to have children. *His* child. These two, in the water, were their lost children, their unborn progeny, wistfully staring up at their parents.

Before his hand broke the surface it was gripped by Tangata, who despite being an old man was immensely strong.

'No,' said the old man. 'This is a magic pool.'

Seumas drew back, realising the Maori was right. Perhaps these images were bait to lure them into the pool? A hand might be clutched from under the surface and the owner dragged to his doom. There were goblins who lived at the bottom of stagnant ponds, who enticed victims into the water, then cut them up into pieces and hung the bodily parts from hooks. True, this water did not look torpid, but perhaps this was deceiving, maybe the impression of sweetness and clarity was false?

'Why …?' began Seumas, but at that moment Dirk wrenched free. The pool had been maddeningly inviting for the hound, who wanted nothing more than a swim in its cool-looking waters.

'Look out!' cried Dorcha, but before they could stop him Dirk had plunged in.

He swam around in a circle, his nose just above the surface, then climbed out onto the bank to shake himself. To the astonishment of the humans, Dirk had shrunk to about a fifth of his normal size. There was a youthfulness about him too, which became more evident with every moment, until finally, as he stood there wagging his little tail, they realised he had regressed.

'He's a damn puppy again!' exclaimed Seumas.

They gathered about the transformed dog in wonder, feeling his limbs, body and head.

Ru said, 'It's true – he is a puppy.'

Tangata stood and stared at the pool.

'I know what this place is,' he murmured. 'It's the Pool of Life.'

'I know it too,' confirmed Ru. 'You have the legend of these waters in your world also?'

Tangata nodded.

Seumas and Dorcha were at a loss.

'What does it mean?' asked Dorcha.

Tangata explained. 'When mankind was first put on the earth by the gods, they argued amongst themselves as to whether mortals should be allowed to live for ever.

'One god believed that a mortal's life should resemble a flaming torch, so that it could be relit many times, before finally burning down to the stub. Thus if a man was killed in battle, or died of some disease, he could be lit again. All men and women would live for ever.

'Another god suggested that a mortal might be fashioned in the way of snakes, and simply shed their skins when they grew too old, and thus replenish their beauty.

'A third god went ahead on his own and created a Pool of Life. He suggested that there should be one of these on every island in the world, where mortals could submerge themselves when they reached old age and come out a young child again.

'The fourth god, however, was full of bitterness and envy for everything which did not further his own importance. He maintained that to give mankind any sort of immortality would be a waste of time. "Let men and women just die when they are killed or fall fatally ill, and never return."

'Just at the moment this god spoke there was a heavy rainfall and the gods wanted to get under shelter, so they all cried out, "All right, let it be so." And thus, because of a shower we mortals are doomed to die an everlasting death.'

'But,' Ru added, 'this one pool, created by the third god, still remains here on earth. And this is it. We have found it. It has been lost to mankind until now. Many claim to have found it, in various places, but they always lost it again.'

'Maui was very angry with the gods,' said Tangata, 'for robbing mankind of eternal life. He tried to reverse their decision by stealing eternal life from Hine-nui-te-po, but as you know, she trapped him when he tried to pass through her body.'

Seumas stared at the puppy which was frolicking on the grass bank of the pool.

'So, this is it,' he said, 'the Pool of Life? We can all relive our lives again, do it over. I remember how it was when I was young – I was happy then.'

'Were you?' asked Dorcha.

Her voice had a strange tone to it and he turned and stared into her eyes. Some of the nostalgic fervour went out of him then. He began to recall, truly now, how he was a poor starved waif, risking his life on the cliffs to collect fulmar eggs. In those days his arms were hardly strong enough to hold him to the cliff in high winds. Several times he had almost fallen to his death. Even when he had the eggs, most of them would be stolen from him by brutish men, or women with the eyes and claws of eagles. Yes, in those days he ran around in rags, avoiding beatings only by staying out of sight and sound of his father.

Had he been happy then?

'Well, I was a free spirit. I had only myself to account to – and anyway, it would be different here.'

'I wasn't a free spirit, I was a drudge,' said Dorcha, firmly. 'I worked like a slave for my father, then when I married I worked like a slave for my husband. And my emotions were in a turmoil. I don't want to go back to that again, to a time when I was so miserable I couldn't think straight.'

'But it wouldn't be like that here, in Oceania,' insisted Seumas. 'We could grow up here amongst these people, *really* become one of them.'

'We shall never be Oceanians completely,' she argued. 'We will always be outsiders. You have a vision of how you would like things to be, not how they will be. Go on, swim in the pool. I have no right to take this chance away from you. If you want your youth back, then you have the opportunity now to find it once more. Take it. Be a boy again.'

Seumas stared again at the shining pool.

'It would be stupid not to take advantage of such an opportunity. It's the dream of every man, to return to the time when he was young and strong. If I don't do it, how long have I got left, before my body betrays me? – before my joints seize and my back aches? – before my eyes fill with yellow sap? – before things inside me begin to fail? How long before I actually die? Ten years? Twenty at the most. Yet now I have the chance to become young again, to become a boy.'

'Take it,' insisted Dorcha, 'but I shall remain as I am, shall become your mother – your grandmother – and in a few years I'll watch you choose a new wife.'

'You could do it too,' Seumas cried. 'We could grow up again together – live again as husband and wife.' He turned to the other two men, who had been whispering amongst themselves. 'We could all become children again. Think of what we could do with another life! With all the knowledge that we have gained so far and yet more to follow.'

'You don't know that,' Ru said, quietly. 'You don't know that you'll even be able to remember anything of the life you've led so far. Look at the dog.'

Seumas gazed at Dirk, now a floppy wide-eyed puppy chasing a breeze-blown leaf along the bank of the pool.

'Dirk,' he said, sharply. 'Heel, boy.'

The puppy took absolutely no notice and continued with its play.

'Dirk!' snapped Seumas, in his most authoritative tone. 'Come! Come! Heel, boy. Now.'

Nothing. Dirk did not even look up. He was totally absorbed in chasing the leaf. There was no automatic response to a command. The hound had been subjected to years of rigorous training and obedience was normally instinctive. Clearly the dog had lost all of the training instilled in him and was now an undisciplined creature.

'You're right,' said Seumas, quietly. 'The dog doesn't remember.'

'It's as if he's been born again,' said Tangata. 'A new life, with a new mind.'

Seumas turned his attention to Tangata.

'You, Maori man, surely you're going to go into the pool? You're an old man. What sort of life have you got left?'

Tangata smiled, his tattoos disappearing into the wrinkles on his lean face.

'I am an old man, yes, but I have led a good life. I'm a warrior. I have many victories to my name. It is a respected name. There are songs about me, Maori songs in which my praises as a warrior and a man are sung. I am assured of a place in a warrior's heaven.

'Perhaps, the second time around I will not do so well? Maybe I will fail? Who knows. Luck and the gods play important parts in our lives. Next time I might not be so lucky, not so favoured? I am happy to die a respected man, envied by the young warriors because of my achievements. Also I am weary of life now. I'm ready to go.'

Seumas was almost affronted by the Maori's decision. 'Even you? What about Ru?'

Prince Ru shook his head. 'Nor me. I have current responsibilities to fulfil. My people expect me to find them a new island.'

'And if you were not a navigator on a voyage?'

Ru sighed and looked longingly at the pool. 'It is tempting, but I think I would follow the example of Dorcha and Tangata.'

'I see.'

Seumas shrugged. 'Well, I'm not going to do it alone, not without Dorcha. Ru, what do we tell the others, back at the pahi? Shouldn't they be given the chance for a new life?'

'There are almost sixty people on that canoe, but I'm going to make the decision for all of them. We will say nothing to them about the Pool of Life. What they don't know, they can't grieve for later. What if some of them do take the plunge and regret it instantly? What if some *don't* take it and later wish they had? No, better we don't tell them.'

'How will we explain Dirk?'

'We met an old woman who transformed the dog into a puppy. She was a sorceress and we killed her. Once the provisions are on board we'll speed away from the island, in case there are more of her kind.'

Dorcha nodded. 'I think we're doing the right thing – I hope so.'

'I'm not so sure,' Seumas said. 'But you're the leader of this expedition, Ru. I accept your judgement.'

The group of four retraced their path, back to the beach, Seumas carrying Dirk. The other passengers and crew were amazed when they saw Dirk and some showed anxiety over the idea that there might be more witches on the island. The only one who seemed delighted by Dirk's new young state was Boy-girl's pet cockerel, Lei-o-mano, who had suffered much from being chased around the deck by a mature Dirk.

Now the tables were reversed and it was Dirk who had to run from the wicked claws and pecking beak of the rooster. Lei-o-mano wasted no time in getting his own back on the hapless puppy. It was as if the rooster knew that in a few months' time things would be back to normal again and the hunter would become the prey once more. The cock was making the most of it.

Stores were gathered in quickly, packed into the deck huts, and soon the pahi was gliding over the reef towards open sea. Not so long afterwards, the island was a mere speck on the horizon, as the wind filled the crab-claw sails and drove the pahi onwards.

Seumas stood at the mast beside Ru, staring back at the dark mote, wondering if he would ever get rid of that deep but unignorable yearning inside him.

PART NINE

Ararau Enua O Ru Ki Te Moana

1

Hine-tu-whenua carried *The Princely Flower* once more into a known and friendly sea. The surface was choppy, but there was a consistent swell which bore the double-hulled craft towards Rarotongan waters. Ru took this to be a sign that Tangaroa had taken charge of the craft and was leading it towards its destination, and the prince allowed the ocean to have its way.

Ru, like Dorcha with her bamboo-and-shell chart, had a record of the whole journey in a long length of knotted string, the device navigators used to prompt memory. It was not so much his own memory that needed the aid, but those navigators who would follow in his wake. Once the knowledge of the voyage became third or fourth hand, the captain of any pahi might need some sort of prompt to assist his knowledge.

The helmswoman was instructed to simply go where the currents took her, and not to force a direction.

Rongo-mai, God of Comets and Whales, sent a school of whales to guide the pahi. Kuku Lau, Goddess of Mirages, sent wavering forms to entice the ship onwards. The images Tiki and Marikoriko which sat on the deck seemed at peace with themselves.

At last all the omens were good and there was hope in the air.

One thing marred the anticipation of all on board: Tangata the Maori had begun to fade away. The further the vessel drew away from Rapanui, the more evanescent became the old warrior, until there came a time when he looked like a ghost. His body was almost transparent and those who stared at him could see the waves beyond him. When he walked in front of the mast, or rigging, these too were visible through his form. Also, his voice became thin and wasted, until one had to press one's ear to his mouth to hear what was being said.

'I think we're losing him,' said Boy-girl. 'I'm not sure what's happening, but one morning we'll wake up and he'll no longer be here.'

The Oceanians prayed to the god Ro'o to heal Tangata of his sickness, but still the old man grew dimmer and less tangible.

Then just before he disappeared altogether, his body began to darken in places. Patches like maps appeared on him, growing perceptibly stronger with each passing day. There came a point when Seumas remarked that he felt as if he were seeing double. There was a blurred secondary image, another outline, which seemed part of Tangata, yet somehow detached from him. It was as if an ill-fitting soul were trying to escape the mortal part of the old Maori and was struggling to detach itself.

Finally, the crew and passengers of *The Princely Flower* woke one morning, to find one of the figures, that part which had been fading, completely gone. The other shape, the form they had believed to be the soul, was growing stronger and more tangible. Now that the lithe, lean figure of Tangata had gone, they could actually recognise this materialising being. It was Polahiki, the Hivan fisherman, reappearing in his old world!

'What's happened?' cried Polahiki. 'Where's my cave?'

'You tell us,' said the astonished Kieto. 'We left you in the Land of the Long White Cloud, and now you manifest yourself out of the declining remains of Tangata the Maori. What have you done with the old man, that you should surface from his ghost to stand before us on the deck?'

Polahiki moaned and tore at the roots of his hair.

'I've come back,' he wailed. 'I was happy in my cave on the hillside of that Otherworld, and now I've come back.'

'But where is Tangata?' repeated Kieto.

'Why,' groaned Polahiki, 'he must be where I was living, in the cave that used to belong to Kurangai-tuku the ogress. It was a beautiful cave, right away from smelly humanity, and now I've lost it to that damned Maori.'

Seumas laughed on hearing this. 'I'm not sure Tangata wants to be in Kurangai-tuku's cave either.'

Kikamana said, 'It seems the winds of time and space will not allow a person to stay in the world in which they were not born and raised. Tangata and Polahiki have changed places again.'

'And to think we were rid of you,' said Dorcha to the fisherman. 'Now you're back and you smell worse than ever – I think we should order a bath.'

'Never,' snarled Polahiki, backing off. 'I'll kill the man or woman who touches me with water.'

But they managed to overpower him and get a line on him. They dragged his filthy body in the wake of the pahi, keeping a watch for sharks. He screamed the whole while, as the surf rushed over him, sometimes submerging him. Ru was merciless however and would not allow the line to be hauled in until he was sure Polahiki was in some measure clean. There on the deck they bathed him in sweet-smelling oils and perfumes, until he smelt as pleasant as a frangipani blossom.

They knew his nits would hatch again, and that he would be covered in fleas once more, but at least the worst of the dirt was gone from his body. Those who slept down Polahiki's end of the pahi remarked that the fresh air they had been enjoying until now remained to some degree clear of pollution.

The day after the washing of Polahiki a star was sighted in the roof of voyaging.

'There it is!' cried Ru, with great satisfaction in his voice. 'Under that star lies my island.'

Three days later a green glow was sighted on a cloud base. *The Princely Flower* was heading in the direction of Tooa o te ra on the windflower. Rarotonga was directly off the port side of the craft, in the direction of Apa toa, though many miles away. By noon they had sighted a hook-shaped island and by evening they were gliding through a huge and magnificent triangular lagoon.

'How have we Rarotongans missed this island, in our voyages across the ocean?' questioned Kikamana, in astonishment. 'It's almost on our beach.'

'Not more than twenty days sailing,' confirmed Ru, 'but I think the gods have kept it hidden until now, for me and my people to settle its land.'

Ru and his maidens carried Tiki ashore on their shoulders and built a fire on the beach as a sign that they had arrived at their new home. The great pahi was dragged up onto the sands where it was unloaded of all the tubers, seeds and shoots carried from Raiatea, these to be planted. There were pahua clam shells in plenty, in the lagoon, which quickly became a delicacy amongst the newcomers. The only dog still alive on board the pahi was Seumas's puppy, Dirk, so there were none to breed for livestock. Wild pigs had been found on the island of the Pool of Life and these would be domesticated.

Boy-girl's pet rooster was let loose amongst the few remaining hens, to become the father, grandfather and great-grandfather of all the new chicks on the island. He strutted and crowed as if he was actually aware of his unique status on this new Faraway Heaven, flashing his red and green feathers, shaking his sunset wattle with great dignity.

Sacrifices were made to the gods, especially Tangaroa, who had led them to the promised land. Ru officially named the island 'Ararau Enua O Ru Ki Te Moana' – *Ru in search of land over the sea* – but since this rather pompous title was too much of a mouthful for most of his people, it had a second name 'Aitutaki', meaning *to keep the fire burning*, because that was the maidens' function with the symbolic blaze while Ru climbed to the highest point on the island and surveyed his kingdom.

When Ru returned to the beach there was trouble, followed by tragedy. He had come down from the high place to say he had divided up the island into twenty sections, one section for each of the virgins who had crewed *The Princely Flower* from Raiatea to Aitutaki. This created dissension amongst Ru's four younger brothers, who immediately announced they would not stay and dragged *The Princely Flower* down the beach to launch it again, so they could set off on their own to find another island.

In their haste to get away before they could be stopped by Ru one brother fell under the rolling logs and was killed.

The bitter brothers and their wives and families were not prevented from leaving the island and they set sail for other climes. Ru, now king of Aitutaki, never did explain his reasons for not including his closest relatives in the distribution of land. Ru was and always had been an enigmatic man, not given to making excuses or explaining his actions.

The Rarotongans decided to leave King Ru to establish his kingdom. They built an outrigged sailing canoe, a vaa motu, of sufficient size to carry them back to Rarotonga. There was Kikamana, Kieto, Po'oi, Boy-girl, Polahiki, Seumas and Dorcha, and the now maturing Dirk. These had safely completed what was to become one of the most celebrated of the legendary voyages. Pungarehu, the slayer of the Poukai Bird, and Rinto, had been the only ones to lose their lives amongst the Rarotongans.

Fully provisioned for a short journey, they set sail on a morning when the sky was red with promise. Dorcha and Po'oi were the navigators. The outrigged canoe, less than half the length of a pahi, skipped over the rich wide lagoon of Aitutaki and out into the open sea. They left the new island behind them, with its initial teething problems.

Kikamana still owned one twentieth of the land on Aitutaki, which she had offered to give to Ru's brothers. King Ru had forbidden the transfer, telling Kikamana that she must remain the owner, which led her to believe that some god or other had sent a message to Ru while he was on his solitary vigil and insisted that the twenty royal maidens be the ones to own all the land. So she left her section to be managed by an overseer and said she would return in the future to take possession herself.

'Well, we're on our way home again,' said Dorcha to Seumas.

Dorcha always referred to Rarotonga as 'home' whereas Seumas had difficulty in throwing off the feeling that home was actually Albainn and Rarotonga was a foreign land.

'I suppose so,' he conceded. 'Still, we've had ourselves an adventure, haven't we? I doubt there's a Pict alive who's seen what I've seen in my lifetime. It's been a full and rich life and I'm glad I've lived it.'

'You sound as if you're going somewhere,' Dorcha said. 'You're not feeling ill, are you?'

'No, no. It was that chance to return to boyhood which got me thinking again. I mean, I'm sure we made the right choice, by remaining as we are, but it still made me mull over my life and set me to wondering about whether I would change it. The only thing I would change, at this moment, is that thing ...' he could hardly bring himself to talk about the fight which had resulted in the death of her man. The whole episode was still quite painful to him, not because of anything he personally felt over the incident, but because he had hurt her. 'You know, the death of your first husband.'

'We would not be married now, if it wasn't for that,' she said, pragmatically.

'I know, and that troubles me. I killed your husband and this resulted eventually in our marriage. I benefited out of a bad deed, which isn't right.'

'Look,' she laid a hand on his shoulder, 'you can't change the past no matter how much you think about it. Things happened we both regret, but now is now. You can't look back. We still have the twilight of our lives to look forward to and I'm not going to have that time spent in turning over events which can only cause us grief. Forget the past. I have.'

'Are you sure?'

'Of course I'm sure.'

In the middle of the afternoon Kieto sighted a fleet of pahi on the horizon. As they drew nearer the Rarotongans saw that it was the Arioi. On this occasion, when there was no hurry to get back to Rarotonga, Kieto felt they could board one of the Arioi vessels and talk to the troupe. The seafarers had missed the Arioi the first time around and everyone on board agreed that it would be exciting to see some of the acts.

The yellow sails drew nearer. When the first vessel was close enough, Kieto called and asked if they could come aboard. The answer was yes. Polahiki dropped the sail of the outrigger, a line was taken, and the smaller vessel was towed behind the lead Arioi pahi. Those on board the outrigger were soon on the deck of the pahi, full of interest and excitement.

On board a choir was singing, practising scales. There were tumblers running through their acrobatics. On the other pahi, around and behind the lead ship, performers were running through their acts. A canoe drew up alongside on which a drummer was leaping from instrument to instrument, rehearsing his show. Kieto was most impressed with what he saw.

'Who's that?' he asked the captain of their pahi. 'The drummer?'

'A Painted Leg,' answered the captain, with reverence in his voice. 'His name is Kumiki and he's from Nuku Hiva.'

'Brilliant,' Po'oi said, admiringly.

'That's why he's a Painted Leg,' replied the captain, laughing. Then he asked, 'Where are you people from?'

'We live on Rarotonga,' replied Kikamana. 'We've been on a long voyage – to an island called Rapanui.'

'I've never heard of this island. Would they enjoy seeing the Arioi?'

'They might, when they've settled all their differences. There's a civil war on there at the moment. You would do well to stay away until that's over. In any case, the island is in the far corner of the ocean, many months away.'

The captain grunted. 'I wouldn't want us to get mixed up in a war,' he said. Then he changed the subject. 'We went to Rarotonga some time ago. Did you see us there?'

Kieto replied, 'No, we left just as you arrived, and we've been voyaging ever since. Not that craft you're towing for us, but in a pahi much the same as this one. We went with Prince Ru of Raiatea to search for a new island.'

'And did you find it?' asked the captain.

'Oh yes, it's called Aitutaki and it's about twenty days sailing from Raro-tonga, Apa toerau on the windflower.'

'Ummm, we'll let them get settled then pay them a visit in a few years' time. So, you all went with Prince Ru ...'

'Now King Ru.'

'Of course – but you all went with him?'

The captain was obviously fishing for names, but as it was impolite to ask directly he did not do so.

'Yes, there is myself, Kieto – Kikamana the priestess; Po'oi whose father was Kaho a blind navigator and feeler-of-the-sea; Polahiki a fisherman from the Hivan islands; Boy-girl, a hypnotist and ventriloquist, and finally Dorcha and Seumas, of whom you must have heard: they are people from the Land-of-Mists, the great country discovered by Kupe and myself.'

The captain stared at the couple about whom Kieto was speaking.

'Ah, that is the man called Seumas?'

'I knew you would have heard of him. That dog he's patiently training, des-pite all the noise going on around him, is the one he calls Dirk. We're not allowed to eat it,' laughed Kieto. 'He feeds it meat and uses it to hunt lizards and birds. Seumas is a strange man in many ways. You should get him to play his dead pig for the Arioi. A new act! He makes it wail in the most horrible way.'

The captain was affronted by this suggestion. 'Why would I want him to play in our troupe? We are a company of entertainers. We're not in the busi-ness of frightening old women and children to death.'

Kieto smiled and shrugged. 'Seumas says the music of the bagpipes – that's what he calls his instrument – he says it grows on you. An acquired taste. You might find your audiences clamouring for more, after a few years.'

'After a few years,' snorted the captain. 'You think we're going to allow him to screech and wail for a few years, chasing away our customers, in the hope that one day they'll become tone deaf and find his music acceptable? Not in my lifetime.'

Kieto laughed and later told Seumas about the conversation, which Seumas did not find in the least bit funny.

The Rarotongans were gathered around one of the masts, sitting in a circle, discussing all they had heard and seen that day. It had been an interesting experi-ence, but not a full one. Obviously on board one pahi amongst three hundred, they could only watch one or two acts close up and a few others at a distance, but most of the pahi were too far away for the group to see or hear what was going on. Kieto had asked the captain his destination and found it to be Raiatea.

'We have no need to hurry back to Rarotonga, now our mission has been successfully completed,' said Kieto. 'Who would like to go to Raiatea once more? We could see the Arioi in full splendour, watch their performance over a number of days, then find a larger vessel than our outrigged canoe, and travel back to Rarotonga in style some time later?'

The vote was almost unanimous. Only Polahiki said no, grumbling about missing out on his fishing.

Kieto told Polahiki he could take the outrigger.

'We're sure to find a vessel going to Rarotonga from Raiatea – if you want to leave us, do so.'

Polahiki left shortly afterwards, the slovenly fisherman bidding everyone good riddance. The feeling was mutual. He was not the best of companions.

'It's a short voyage,' said Dorcha, 'but I don't envy Polahiki – stuck in that canoe alone with a dirty fisherman for several days.'

The others laughed at her joke.

Later that evening, when the group were preparing to go to bed, someone came on board from a neighbouring pahi. In the light of the torches, Kieto recognised the man as the drummer he had seen and admired during that day. The Painted Leg came with the captain and glared at the group, his eyes going from face to face, and finally resting on the features of Seumas.

'You are the goblin they call Seumas?' said the Painted Leg.

Up until that moment, Kieto had been awestruck by the fact that they were being honoured by the presence of a Painted Leg. He had been about to express his profound admiration for the man's talent at drumming. Now, however, a feeling of irritation swept through him at the Painted Leg's words.

'We do not refer to Seumas as "the goblin",' said Kieto. 'He is a respected Rarotongan, a warrior who has earned his place in our society.'

'You might not call him the goblin,' snapped the Painted Leg, 'but I do. In fact I call him worse. I call him a murdering rapist. Tomorrow, goblin, we will fight to the death, here on this deck. You and I. Prepare your mind for your last night on this ocean. You will not see another.'

Seumas climbed slowly to his feet and stared at the Painted Leg. He was now in his middle years and, though fit, knew that a match with a man half his age was a dangerous exercise. He had wily old tricks, certain skills which are only learned over a number of years, but he might not be a match for this super fit drummer, who spent his whole life leaping and dancing. Not if the drummer were as good at single combat as he was at pounding his instruments. Yet the Painted Leg was in years merely a boy, despite his grand title, and perhaps unseasoned in war.

'You call me names, Painted Leg, but I don't know what you're talking about. Kumiki from Nuku Hiva? Have I insulted you in some way, while we have been neighbours today?'

'You insulted my mother,' said Kumiki in a choked voice. 'You insulted her by raping her and leaving her for dead. She died in childbirth, giving me life. I am your son, for what it's worth, you ugly monster. I'm your *son*.'

Kumiki spat the word as if it were so loathsome and foul it tasted like bile in his mouth.

Seumas was genuinely bewildered and shook his head. 'I have never raped a woman in my life,' he said. 'You have the wrong man.'

Dorcha stood up and put her arm around her man.

'Listen to him, Painted Leg. He is trying to prevent you from making a terrible mistake. Seumas is my husband. If you kill him, you will have to kill me too. I know this man, and I know him to be honourable. He would not take a woman against her will. I am his wife. I know this.'

'I have the *right* man. Be here and armed tomorrow morning, goblin. If you are not I shall strike you dead where you stand. And anyone else who stands with you. You may all be armed, but I shall have *him*,' he pointed to Seumas. 'I shall avenge my mother and myself in the light of the dawn.'

With that, the Painted Leg left them, striding back to the dugout canoe where a paddler was waiting to take him to his own pahi.

Seumas stood there bemused. What was the Painted Leg talking about? It was a mystery to him.

'Have we ever been to Nuku Hiva?' he asked Kieto. 'When were we in Nuku Hiva?'

Kieto nodded, replying, 'We stopped there for a short while on our voyage with King Tangiia. It was where you, Po and Manopa, and some others were trapped up on a plateau. Don't you remember? You escaped by tricking the local people with a climb up to the peak of one of the mountains. Later, Manopa rescued you by coming back in a canoe with Wakana.'

'Oh, *that* island,' recalled Seumas. 'Where they forced me to eat long pig?'

He remembered now, having to chew on the flesh of a cooked man, the husband chief of the woman he was later forced to make love to in front of his Hivan captors. She too was a captive, from another island, and both had submitted to the act knowing they had no choice, but gaining little emotional pleasure from it. Yes, Seumas had raped a woman on Nuku Hiva, but at the point of a spear, and she too had been forced into the performance by a hostile and lustful tribe.

It was not as if he had attacked a local woman and taken her against her will. He had told no one of this shameful incident and those with him had held their peace too, having been forced to do the same. None of them wanted the details to be spread abroad. Now most of those men were dead – Manopa, Po, the young priest who had stolen the God of Hope from Raiatea – dead and gone. Certainly in the present company, Seumas was the only one who knew the truth of the incident.

'But that was so long ago,' murmured Seumas, more to himself than any other. 'It's not something I want to remember.'

Dorcha frowned and stared hard into Seumas's eyes. 'You did rape a woman?'

'Against my will, as well as hers. I was forced to do it. There was a club raised over my head – a dagger at my throat – I had no choice in the matter.'

Dorcha said, 'No choice? But you mean you were ready for it – capable of making love to a woman?'

'I know what you're thinking,' replied Seumas, angrily. 'But there was danger in the air. We were anticipating a struggle, a fight to the death, because there was no way I was going to submit to execution without a battle. The anticipation of deadly conflict does things to a man ...'

Seumas went to his bed and lay on his back, staring up at the stars. It was as much a shock to learn he had a son as it was to know he might have to fight that son to the death. When he and Dorcha discovered, through time, that they were unable to have children, Seumas accepted the fact philosophically. He was not one to brood on such things. And now he had a son, a young man who had materialised out of thin air! And that son was a Painted Leg, a man supreme amongst his kind. Kumiki's achievements were something of which to be immensely proud. His son, an Avae Parai! He *did* feel proud.

They must have lied to the boy, his guardians on his home island. They had told him his father raped his mother out of pure lust. And because Seumas had been too ashamed to speak of the incident, there were few who knew the truth. Certainly this was the first time Kieto, Boy-girl and Kikamana had heard of it and they would be wondering why Seurnas had kept it so secret. It made Seumas's story appear suspicious. Perhaps they too were wondering if Kumiki was speaking the truth? There was a man, a survivor of the group that went ashore with Manopa, Seumas and Po onto the island of Nuku Hiva, but he was back on Rarotonga, and could not speak for Seumas here.

Dorcha came to him and put her arms around him.

'I believe you,' she said, 'in case you're wondering if the whole world is against you.'

'I was thinking that, yes,' admitted Seumas. 'Did you see the way Kieto was looking at me?'

'It was just a shock, that was all. Certainly it was a shock for me. Forgive me for my outburst?'

He kissed her tenderly. 'It was a shock to us all. How can I fight him, Dorcha? I don't want him to kill me, and I don't want to kill him? What do I do?'

'Refuse to fight.'

'You saw him. You saw his anger. He's been living his life for the moment when he could confront me. He's been feeding off his hate since he was a child. He won't take that for an answer. He'll simply cut me down where I stand.'

'Then you'll have to defend yourself.'

'I can't do that either.'

'Oh, Seumas, man.'

Seumas felt empty inside. Neither of the alternatives were acceptable. To stand and be killed, or to fight his own son to the death. It was an impossible choice.

'But he's a fine-looking boy, Dorcha, isn't he?' Seumas said, another feeling altogether surging through him. 'I can't help but feel proud of him.'

Dorcha sat up and looked at Seumas in amazement.

'You can feel fatherly love for the son who hates you on the eve of a battle to the death with him? You are crazy, Pict. That youth might have risen through the ranks of entertainers, but he has no maturity. Any sensible young man would have listened to your side of the story and weighed it against the tales he had heard from poisonous mouths. Instead, he charges in like a headstrong Albannach bull, not for a moment considering you might be innocent of the accusation.'

'True, but I can see myself in him. Was I not like that at his age, woman? You remember? A wild impetuous youth, hot-blooded and full of righteous vigour.'

She sighed. 'I suppose you were, but don't sound so proud of yourself. I thought you very stupid in those days, Seumas from the Blackwater, and I'm glad you grew out of it. If you hadn't, we wouldn't be lying here together now.'

Kikamana came to where they lay and asked to speak with Seumas.

'Are you going to fight this young man? If you win, they'll kill us all you know. He's a Painted Leg. They wouldn't be able to allow you to kill one of their greatest performers without some form of retribution.'

'What would you have me do?' asked Seumas. 'The truth is I raped his mother, though not willingly. What shall I do, offer to kill myself?'

'We can slip away now, in our own canoe. The captain of this pahi doesn't want the fight. He'll allow us to slide away during the night.'

Seumas had already thought about this.

'No,' he said. 'He'll continue to hunt me down, with all that hate festering in his heart. If he doesn't find me, it'll eat away his manhood and all the good aspects of his character. Bitterness and hate can turn the most talented person into a dry husk, worthless to the world. Let it stand.'

'But you can't kill him!'

'No, I can't – but I have to let him fight me, get it out of his system. Perhaps I can wound him seriously enough to stop the fight? Perhaps if he wounds me, it will not be fatal, but will be enough to cleanse him of his hate and anger? We shall see. Running away will not help me, or him. This confrontation has to take place sometime. Better now than later, when I'm a weak old man and he's twisted inside with fury and enmity towards me.'

'He's already twisted inside,' muttered Kikamana, 'but I accept your decision. I'll tell Kieto, Boy-girl and Pooi. I'm sure they'll be behind you.'

'They – they don't think I'm lying?'

Kikamana looked surprised. 'Of course not, why should they?'

'I don't know,' said Seumas, miserably. 'I just thought they might believe the youth over me. You saw that hair. He *is* my son, no doubt about that. And I've never been open about this incident. I just thought – I thought—'

Kikamana interrupted, firmly. 'These are your friends, Seumas. They know you to be an honourable man. They trust and love you. Have no doubts on that.'

'Thank you,' mumbled Seumas, feeling uplifted. 'Thank you, Kikamana.'

Seumas and Dorcha tried to get some rest after that, but they were woken in the dawn hours by chanting from the pahi which kept pace with their own. There were prayers to Oro, God of War and Peace, patron of the Arioi, going up into the roof of voyaging from the mouth of Seumas's son.

Seumas wondered whether he ought to pray to some god too, but he had never been completely comfortable with the Oceanian gods. They were not his deities. He wondered if he should pray to his own god of war, whose name was buried deep in the back of his brain, but his own Pictish gods were back in Albannach and had no power here on an alien ocean.

Instead, he prepared himself mentally for an impossible task: a battle in which there were to be no winners.

2

Kumiki came on board as he had promised, bringing with him a woman. She carried his weapons: a lei-o-mano and a patu club made of nokonoko. The woman looked upset and Seumas guessed this was either his son's wife, or his betrothed. In the light of the day, Kumiki looked younger than ever. Seumas guessed the boy was not more than twenty years of age. This, coupled with the fact that he was Hivan and not Tahitian, made it even more amazing that he had managed to become a Painted Leg. He had to be a uniquely brilliant drummer.

However, this did give Seumas some hope. A boy so young, one who had concentrated on becoming a top entertainer, was not likely to have had much experience at war. In fact he looked green and unseasoned. It might be that Seumas could disarm the youth and gain a submission. On the other hand Seumas knew he himself was not as lithe and supple as he had once been, and would need all his learned battle skills to stay alive.

'Good morning son,' said Seumas, selecting a club for himself. 'Are you ready to kill your father?'

This opening greeting clearly disconcerted the youth.

'I shall do what must be done,' he snapped back.

Seumas's club was made of whalebone. Unlike Kumiki he had deliberately chosen one which did not have tearing or cutting edges of shark's teeth or razor shells. He wanted to stun the boy, knock him senseless, and then call the fight a draw.

'Then be very careful,' said Seumas, as a space on the deck was cleared for them. 'I have powerful mana – my head is full of mana. My skill at single combat is renowned throughout all Oceania. I have killed many men, both in battle, and at contest. There are those who go in fear and trembling when they hear my name. The great magician, Ragnu of Raiatea, has long sought my death, but has been unable to bring it about.'

This bragging was an essential part of the psychological attack on one's opponent, before the actual fighting began, and it was significant that Kumiki neither took part in it, nor seemed affected by Seumas's taunting.

All he said in reply was, 'Normally, as a Painted Leg I am tapu, but the priest removed the tapu last night, in a special ceremony, so we fight merely as two men.'

'Nothing *mere* about me, son. I have beaten giants in my time. I have slaughtered Ponaturi with this very kotiate club. I have been chosen as an ariki by my tribe. Beware of me, boy, for I will take your head from your shoulders. If you manage by some freak of nature to kill me, my kabu will haunt you for the rest of your days, bringing terror into your life.'

Dorcha, standing on the side-lines with Boy-girl, Kikamana, Kieto and Po'oi, raised her eyes to heaven at these words.

However, his taunting was beginning to have an effect on the young woman who had carried Kumiki's weapons and she gave a little cry, burying her face in her hands.

'You are upsetting my wife Linloa,' hissed Kumiki. 'Stop talking and let us fight.'

'Your wife?' cried Seumas. 'Then she is my daughter-in-law! How do you do, daughter? My son has chosen well, you are a credit to him. Son, she is beautiful – plump and beautiful. If I had not a fine wife myself, I should envy you. That's her over there, by the way, your step-mother.'

Without meaning to, Kumiki turned and saw Dorcha staring at him with her black eyes. He swung back angrily, annoyed at having been tricked into looking behind him. Linloa however, was staring at Seumas in an agitated manner. Seumas smiled at her, hoping to put her at her ease, but instead it seemed he frightened her with his goblin's face and red-grey hair.

'Fight, damn you,' snarled Kumiki.

The two men went into crouching positions, one with a leg almost black with tattoos and bars across his face, and the other with no facial tattoos, but with strange elaborate designs down his tanned chest, shoulders and back. The Hivan tattoos made the youth's face look fierce, while the Pictish whorls and spirals broke up the shape of the older warrior, made it difficult for his enemy to see him with any clarity.

The Hivan youth's inexperience soon became obvious, as Seumas tried various moves. The blows were blocked, but not quickly enough, and Seumas knew that if he had swung more swiftly, as he was able, the parry would have come too late. Several times during that first encounter, he could have felled his son and cracked open his skull. The boy knew it too, for there was comprehension in his eyes.

'An old dog, eh?' he murmured to Kumiki. 'You need to be a little more athletic.'

At these words the boy changed his tactics completely, and began a series of astonishing acrobatic moves which startled Seumas and sent him into retreat. Now it was he who had difficulty in blocking the blows, but luckily he did anticipate each strike with accuracy. It was clear that the boy was extremely fit, knew how to weave, leap and somersault, and that Seumas would have to watch his back as well as his front.

'Clever, very clever,' he said to Kumiki. 'This old body has forgotten such tricks.'

The pair of them then went to it seriously, closing and engaging with ferocity, Seumas desperately trying to knock the youth down without killing him. The air was full of the sounds of clashing clubs. Neither man had drawn his lei-o-mano. Finally, Seumas managed to hook his club under Kumiki's wrist, and the youth's weapon went flying through the air like a black bird on the wing.

There was a gasp from the crowd and a startled cry like that of a bird from the girl Linloa.

Seumas could have felled the youth there and then, but he hesitated, looking for a clean swipe to the back of the head. While he paused in indecision Kumiki leapt forward, grasped his arm and wrenched it back, causing him to drop his own weapon. As he stooped to retrieve it, Kumiki drew his lei-o-mano and sliced Seumas across the upper arm, cutting into the flesh and severing a sinew. The Pict winced in pain.

Still, the kotiate club was soon in his hand and despite his wound he continued to defend himself, until Kumiki managed to force him back with his slashing dagger to the point where the youth could pick up his own club. With this larger weapon in his right hand he rushed at Seumas, causing the Pict to stumble on a pile of ropes. Seumas fell backwards, his own club raised in self-defence. This was knocked from his hands and went spinning over the deck.

There was another cry from the spectators as the boy stood over the man, the patu club ready to split open the older man's skull. It was poised to deliver a killing blow, but it failed to descend. Seumas looked into his son's eyes and saw the anguish of indecision there too. The youth was fighting with something inside himself, some emotion which was staying his hand, preventing him from destroying his hated foe.

'Ahhhh!' moaned the boy, clearly trying to overcome his reticence.

To no avail.

He finally shouted in frustration, dropped the club, and rushed to his bride to bury his face in her breasts.

'I can't do it,' he sobbed. 'He's my father.'

It was so. One's ancestors were to be revered, not destroyed. A father was a father, however worthless. The gods would not approve of patricide, no matter what the cause.

The ropes were untangled from his feet and Seumas was helped up by the Rarotongans. Once he had regained his dignity, he went to his son.

'You fought better than I imagined you would,' he said. 'But you were mistaken in your beliefs, my son. The gods would not let you kill me because I am innocent. I never loved your mother, it's true. I never really knew her. Like her I was a captive of a hostile tribe and we were both forced to the act in front of jeering warriors. I had no choice.'

Kumiki turned and stared at his father bleakly.

'However,' continued Seumas, after catching Dorcha's eye and remembering an early morning conversation. 'I do think that your mother was a proud and stately woman, distinguished in her courage, and had we but met under different circumstances, I might easily have loved her. She was the wife of a great chief, the daughter of another great chief, ariki through and through. A noble woman who like me had fallen into the hands of conquerors. We respected one another, your mother and I, even as we performed for the scoffing warriors. You could say the union, which eventually resulted in our son Kumiki, was as dignified as it had to be in the circumstances.'

The youth continued to stare at him, but there was no longer any terrible hate in his eyes, only confusion.

Kumiki took his trembling young wife by the hand and led her across the deck, to the dugout canoe. With her on board the small craft, he paddled away from the pahi to his own, where his friends and fellow performers were watching, hanging from the rigging, clinging to the mast. They had witnessed the whole fight from beginning to end and there was an air of respect about them as their Painted Leg's canoe approached.

When he stepped back onto the deck, they greeted Kumiki by cheering him as a victor, telling him his act in not killing his father was noble and worthy of a Painted Leg. And indeed it was a laudable act which had helped the young man rise above the less finer feelings in him. It had come out from within him, despite the driving deadly hatred, and surfaced at precisely the right time. Surely this was the spirits of his ancestors at work, guiding him to right and proper judgement? This was the work of more than just one man.

For his part, Seumas was happy that it was all over. He had not had to kill his son and the relief came through his pores in the form of sweat. Yet he felt cold. He sat on the deck with a cloak thrown round his shoulders, shivering and perspiring just as if he were suffering from a fever. Dorcha sat with him, her presence a great comfort to him. Boy-girl and the others remained a little way off, ready to assist if necessary.

'I didn't have to kill him, that's the important thing,' said Seumas.

'The important thing,' Dorcha corrected him, 'is that he's your son. You must do what you can now to get to know him. Now that he's aware of the truth, he may let you be his father, in the way that's best for both of you.'

'Perhaps he doesn't believe the truth?'

'Even if he still doubts you now, he'll come round in the future. He *wants* to believe in you. You're his father. Until now he's looked on you as an ogre, but I'll bet he's surprised that you're not such a monster after all. He'll want to get to know you too – you're his family.'

Seumas sighed. 'I hope you're right.'

'I'm right,' said Dorcha, in that infuriating tone she used which was full of confidence. This time he hoped she *was* right.

Over the next few days, as the fleet sped towards Raiatea, Seumas caught his son watching him from the other pahi. When he knew he was being observed, Kumiki pretended to be doing something with his drums, or helping the crew with the canoe, but Seumas knew that his son was inquisitive, and that curiosity was gradually softening the boy. Dorcha was right, as she usually was about these things, and Seumas simply had to wait.

A week after the fight Kumiki came on board again. He was treated like royalty. The captain of the pahi brought out a stool for the Painted Leg to sit on, while they both talked in undertones about the weather and any navigational problems the fleet was experiencing. Seumas kept one eye on his son, who did not look his way once, though the Pict had a feeling that the youth was aware of his presence.

'He's here to talk to you,' whispered Dorcha. 'I've heard from the crew that his wife has been urging him to make friends with you. She's got a good head on her shoulders, that one. Look at him. He's being too deliberate about not noticing you. Make an excuse to speak to the captain while he's there.'

'What?' said Seumas, panicking a little inside. 'What would I have to speak to the captain about?'

'Invent something,' hissed Dorcha. 'Use your head.'

It was not easy. Seumas was scared. What if Dorcha were wrong and his son simply ignored him, or worse, insulted him? What if that hatred had not dried and Kumiki was still seething inside, looking for an excuse to fight again? Seumas was worried that his son was still in a destructive mood, hoping for an opportunity to crush his father to a pulp.

Seumas eventually went to the captain and waited for the two men to stop speaking, before saying, 'I noticed the drinking water was brackish this morning – are we having to mix it with seawater?'

'We're a little low on fresh water,' replied the captain, surprised at this interruption. 'Does it bother you? There are drinking coconuts, if you wish.'

'No, no,' said Seumas, anxious not to be considered a whingeing passenger.

'I'm quite used to brackish water from my long voyages with Tangiia and Ru. I was just curious that's all, because it looks like rain. We can fill the gourds if we get a downpour. I just wanted to be ready.'

The captain raised his eyebrows at this extraordinary interruption, but the talk had its effect on Kumiki.

'You sailed with Ru?' cried the youth, enthusiastically. 'I hear he set out for an unknown island, but was swept away to the far reaches of the ocean.'

'Yes, I sailed with Prince Ru,' replied Seumas. 'He has now made his home on the unknown island, Aitutaki, and is a king. It was a long and dangerous voyage though. We did indeed get taken off our course and made a landing on the island of Rapanui, place of the red and white giants. On another island we met the People of the Night, who fade away when confronted by the light. We saw the armies of the dead, the Maori warrior nation, monsters, fairies …'

The youth's mouth was open in wonder, then he seemed to draw back a little and became slightly haughty.

'I have seen great wonders too, on my solitary voyages.'

'I'm sure you have,' said Seumas, 'and I would be pleased to hear about them. Why not come and share a basket with me and my friends?'

Kumiki stood up and nodded gravely.

'I should like to meet these people who sailed with Ru.'

Seumas tried not to smile and motioned for his son to go ahead of him, to where Kieto and the others were sitting.

'I must warn you,' said Seumas, 'that we eat with women, when we're travelling.'

Kumiki looked surprised. 'Eat with the women?'

'Yes.'

The young man did not pause in his stride however as he considered this unconventional behaviour.

'Well,' he said at last, 'I expect this is a custom you have brought from your own land.'

'I expect it is,' agreed Seumas.

He had reached the small group now and stood over Dorcha, a little too imperiously for Seumas's liking. 'Yes, this is Dorcha, who is also from my homeland.'

Kumiki suddenly flashed Dorcha a most charming smile and sat down beside her.

'What do we have to eat?' he asked her, boyishly. 'You must tell me all about this place where you were born. Is it hot? Are the mosquitoes bothersome? Who is your father and mother? Do you have pigs and dogs there?'

The questions poured from his mouth and from that moment Seumas knew things were going to be fine between them.

PART TEN

Moikeha and the winds

1

So eager was Kumiki to get to know his father that he sent for his wife Linloa and the pair of them stayed on board the pahi carrying the Rarotongans for three days. However, at the end of those three days he suddenly remembered he was a Painted Leg and should be practising. He sent for several drums to be fetched from his own pahi. With these he gave the Rarotongans a semi-private performance, witnessed only by others because the night air carried the sound.

Seumas was amazed at his son's skill and pronounced himself to be very proud. He could not stop speaking of the youth to Dorcha, who continually nodded and smiled. Then Boy-girl caught Seumas's eye and had a quick word in his ear. The Pict's sanguine mood was mellowed a little by Boy-girl's advice. He nodded gravely at Boy-girl, going back to Dorcha's side.

'I keep forgetting,' he said later to Dorcha, 'that he's not your son too. I wish he were. He should be. Boy-girl told me I enthuse too much. I'm sorry.'

Dorcha smiled wistfully. 'It doesn't matter. You're excited by Kumiki at the moment – by the fact he exists. He's new to you. I understand that. Don't worry about me.'

'But I do,' he said. 'Your happiness is of the utmost importance to me.'

She put an arm around his shoulders. 'I'm glad of that. I hope I can regard him as my son too, and Linloa as our daughter. I like her. She has a sensible head.'

'A sensible head,' snorted Seumas. 'What's so wonderful about that?'

'Where there are men like you and your son, who have never managed to grow up completely, you need sensible women.'

'Huh!' Seumas grunted weakly, never knowing quite how to deal with this side of Dorcha.

After the performance, when the praises died down a little, Seumas and Dorcha had a long talk with Linloa, a beautiful young lady with fine manners and a shy disposition. Seumas could tell she loved her husband with a great passion. Her eyes never left his face when he was speaking. Seumas was not sure this was a good thing, for young men are apt to become a little conceited by such adoration, and begin to treat their wives uncivilly. However, Kumiki seemed hardly aware of his wife's devotion and occasionally plucked her arm to let her know he knew she was there and that all was well between them.

Over the past few nights, with the help of Dorcha and Boy-girl, Kikamana had been seeking to find a source of bad dreams. Now, while the group were engaged in conversation Kikamana had been communing with the spirits of her ancestors. They had passed on to her some alarming news.

'Someone's out to destroy us,' she said. 'There's a dark cloud coming from Raiatea. The cloud carries a poison meant to destroy us all. We must be vigilant.'

The buoyant mood of the Rarotongans was suddenly dampened as they stared over the sea ahead of them. Seumas knew of only one man who wanted them all dead.

There would be no peace for them until that man had been removed from the face of the earth.

'Ragnu,' said Seumas, quietly. 'It must be him.'

Ragnu had also been communing with his ancestors, asking them to act as his go-betweens. He had obtained from the ghosts of his forefathers the assistance he required in order to gain the attention of the gods. Hau Maringi, God of Mists and Fog, carried a thick blanket of damp vapour to the Arioi fleet and enveloped it. The miasma clung to the pandanus mat sails, dank and dismal, not letting Ra's rays reach them.

Over the course of a few days the sails began to rot for want of dry air. A black mould formed on the mats, eating away at the bright yellow colour, until the original ochre was no longer visible. When the captains of the pahi ordered replacement sails to be fitted, these too had formed the same black mould while the pandanus mats had been folded and stored in the deck huts. There was no other choice but to continue the journey with the sails as they were, hoping that they would not rot into tatters and force the fleet to use oars.

'I don't like the look of this,' said Kikamana. 'We must arm ourselves.'

'Against whom?' asked Kieto.

'Against an unknown enemy,' replied Boy-girl. 'I understand what our kahuna is saying. That fog is not natural. Hau Maringi is helping our enemy.'

The captain of the pahi was reluctant to inform the rest of the fleet about Kikamana's fears, concerned that he might look foolish, but Kumiki persuaded him that it was better to err on the side of caution, than to be caught out.

When individuals throughout the flotilla had armed themselves and were staring into the impenetrable mists, a heavy swell came to rock the pahi fleet violently. Although it was not a storm, for there was no wind, the motion of the ships caused great distress. Many were seasick, hanging over the gunwales and vomiting into the ocean. All singing and dancing stopped and those who were not unwell were comforting and assisting those who were incapacitated.

For the first time in its history, the fleet was silent, its crews and passengers simply wanting to be on dry land again.

Then suddenly, as they approached Raiatea, the mists cleared and the day was bright.

'A great flotilla of ships is coming,' Ragnu told the new king of Raiatea. 'A fleet with black sails.'

'Black sails?' questioned the young king, who was not at all experienced in international matters. 'What does that mean?'

'You will remember,' said Ragnu, 'when King Tutapu pursued Prince Tangiia over the oceans, his ships were rigged with black sails. It was a symbol of war. Henceforth, we understand those flotillas who carry black sails to be war fleets, out to sack and pillage, to plunder innocent islands. This island of Raiatea and its sister Borabora are rich islands, my lord, and as such are likely to fall prey to such marauders.'

'Show me this great fleet, with its ominous sails.'

The king was carried down to the beaches by his attendants and he saw the black fleet for himself. It was a silent and dreadful flotilla, raiders who seemed bent on ravaging Raiatea and Borabora. There were no friendly drums beating, no Tai Moana. Nor was there any singing and chanting, as there would have been if these pahi had been on a long journey and were glad to see friendly land again. The king had no doubt this was a war fleet, probably sent from Tonga. The Tongans were some of the fiercest pirates on the seas, though they had never sailed this far in search of quarry before.

'What shall we do?' he enquired of Ragnu. 'We must defend ourselves.'

'Give me the Raiatean navy, lord, and I shall sail out to meet these impudent marauders on their own terms.'

Over the years of the last king a fleet of warships had been built for defence purposes. These were not sail-rigged ships, but pahi tamai: double-hulled paddled war canoes. They carried up to three hundred warriors. They were solidly built of strong hardwood frames: narrow craft with only an arm's length between stout twin hulls which stood high out of the water, so that those on board overlooked any much lower sailing vessel built for speed on the open sea.

The structure of these canoes consisted of transverse cross pieces and longitudinal girders. On the bows was an elevated platform where the warriors were gathered ready to do battle. The paddlers of these craft stood up to do their work inside the deep basins of the hulls. The king's banners flew from the prows, from which carved posts protruded vertically.

The king listened to Ragnu, but seemed indecisive.

'The only alternative,' said Ragnu, 'is for you to lead the Raiateans in battle.'

This new king was no great warrior, having gained his position through his bloodline rather than his courage. He was a good intelligent ruler, who kept peace amongst his peoples, but he was no admiral. Ragnu's suggestion had its desired effect.

'I give you command of the navy,' said the king. 'Go out and defeat this invasion fleet.'

These were the words Ragnu wished to hear.

That night, when Ragnu performed occult ceremonies for the favours of his ancestors, he learned of the presence of the Rarotongans on board the Arioi fleet. This was a wonderful bonus. He could now kill both Seumas and his son, the other Rarotongans, and destroy the Arioi all in one. Ragnu could hardly contain his elation.

Everything was going according to his schemes.

At dawn the Arioi fleet was within reach of the war canoes and with two hundred vessels, some sixty thousand warriors barbed with weapons, Ragnu set out to meet the oncoming ships. In case the Arioi had recovered from their seasickness and began singing, Ragnu had every drummer on every war craft pounding their instruments, to drown any sound which might reach Raiatea from the oncoming fleet.

The old sorcerer, streaked through with hatred and bitterness, stood on the bows of the leading war canoe looking like a monitor lizard about to catch its prey.

Kikamana, on seeing the war canoes launched from the beaches of Raiatea, knew that something was seriously wrong. It was true that the canoes were sometimes used ceremoniously, sent out to meet important visitors to the island, but she could see armed spearmen on the platforms, warriors with clubs in their hands, men wielding basalt canoe-breakers. Her instinct told her these men appeared agitated, as if they had worked themselves up to a pitch of frenzy, and she knew they were primed for battle. Her dreams, over the last few nights, had been foreboding. This flotilla of war canoes was the manifestation of her nightmares.

'Send up an alarm!' she cried to Kieto. 'We're about to be attacked!'

'Are you sure?' asked Kieto. 'Perhaps we're just being met?'

'Do as I say,' she snapped, 'or the Arioi will all be slaughtered by that fiend Ragnu.'

Kieto wasted no more time. He called to the captain that they were being attacked and to raise a signal to all the other vessels in the fleet. At the same time he woke Seumas and told him to arm himself.

'What's happening?' asked the Pict.

'Ragnu,' said Kieto. 'A war fleet.'

Seumas leapt to his feet, grabbing his whalebone club. Others were doing the same. His son Kumiki was already armed and ready for battle. The youth looked quite fierce with his battle face on, the horns of hair standing from his head. They glanced at each other, father and son, and gained spiritual strength from each other's presence.

Soon, most of the Arioi were ready for the onslaught, but Seumas knew they were not fighters. These people were entertainers – musicians, dancers, orators – not warriors. Of course there were those among them who knew how to fight, but they were untrained and uncoordinated. They might fight as individuals, but the attackers were a cohesive force which would probably sweep through the Arioi and set the decks of their pahi awash with fire, blood and gore.

'Take heart, my friends,' cried Kieto. 'Stand together!'

The intention of those on board the battle canoes, now that they were closing, was plainly obvious. They were indeed prepared for conflict. Ragnu could be seen on the lead canoe, his thinning black hair floating on the breeze. His face was a mask of savage triumph as he bore down upon his enemies.

Maomao, the Great Wind-God, was angry with the Raiatean priest. There was a legend attached to Maomao, of which he was justly proud. In the early days of Hawaiian history there had been a mariner, a hero, by the name of Moikeha. Moikeha sailed to Raiatea, on the way back stopping at Kauai Island, where King Puna was running a sailing contest. The prize was the hand of Princess Ho'o Ipo, King Puna's daughter. The finishing post was the island of Kaula, one hundred miles distant. Chiefs and princes in sleek fast craft had gathered to take part in the contest, eager to gain a puhi for a beautiful bride.

Maomao disguised himself as an old man and requested passage with Moikeha, who in truth did not want the extra weight on board but out of politeness could not refuse the elderly gentleman. He took Maomao on board promising to transport him to Kaula, even if it meant losing the race.

Once under way, the princes and chiefs surged ahead of Moikeha's canoe. However, Moikeha's passenger had with him a calabash, full of winds, which he released and filled the sail of the small craft. Moikeha's vessel overtook those of his rival princes and chiefs, and reached Kaula first, winning a trophy of a carved ornament with which the Hawaiian hero returned to Kauai and claimed his bride. Ho'o Ipo bore him seven children and Moikeha ruled the island wisely until his death.

Now this story was well known throughout Oceania, but this upstart priest had copied the Great Wind-God's trick of releasing winds trapped in a calabash. This infuriated Maomao, who did not like to be imitated by mortals and was concerned that this repeated use of the calabash might outshine his own, or in some way become confused with it. Maomao therefore decided to punish the priest who had usurped his inventiveness.

Maomao blew the lead war canoe, containing the arrogant priest, far ahead of the rest of the navy, so that it met the force of three hundred sailing canoes – alone.

*

Suddenly, Ragnu's craft was swept ahead by a freak gust of wind, which whipped the paddles from the hands of his rowers and blew his accompanying warriors from the platform into the water. The fighting men were left behind, struggling in the waves, to be picked up by the rest of the war flotilla.

Ragnu's craft ploughed through the water and glided past the first Arioi canoe. Seumas stood waiting on the bows of the pahi. At great risk to himself the Pict leapt on board the war vessel and confronted Ragnu on the platform.

Ragnu was resplendent in his battle dress. A feathered helmet adorned his head. A huge cloak of kula feathers swept from his shoulders. In spite of the fact that he was a thin and wasted old man, he looked bulky and strong. The priest's eyes glittered with triumph at being presented with the one enemy he wished to have destroyed.

'Kill him!' cried Ragnu to the paddlers, deep in their hulls.

The paddlers, however, were unable to climb up to the platform swiftly enough to save the priest.

'Now,' said Seumas, gripping his whalebone club. 'Now we meet hand-to-hand, priest.'

Ragnu, clutching a spear, whined, 'You would not kill an old man? I'm a priest. Your soul will blacken and shrivel if you harm me, goblin.'

'So be it,' replied Seumas. 'You have been too devious for your own good, priest – this is your last glimpse of the world.'

Ragnu snarled and threw the spear, skimming Seumas's shoulder in its flight.

The priest's next action horrified all those who wished Seumas success in single combat. Ragnu had drawn a weapon from the folds of his cloak. It was an airo fai, the Tahitian dagger made of a stingray's backbone. The wicked hooks of bone, sharp curved spikes, lay sleek and flat against the blade like innocent feathers on a bird's back. But Seumas knew that if he was stabbed by this weapon he would have his innards ripped from him when the dagger was retrieved and the hooks splayed open.

'What's the matter?' said Ragnu softly. 'Don't you like what you see, coward?'

Seumas said, 'Let's get to it, priest.'

Ragnu laughed and lunged with the dagger, careless of Seumas's club. Seumas's fight with his son had left him with a shoulder wound that slowed him down. His club hit Ragnu on the shoulder, ineffectively. With his left arm Seumas tried to parry the priest's thrust, but only managed to knock it higher. The airo fai struck him on the chest, between two rib bones, and the point jammed there, unable to penetrate further.

Ragnu wrenched the weapon back savagely, tearing a small hole in the muscle on the Pict's chest.

Seumas groaned and staggered back, the pain excruciating. Blood poured from the wound, running down to soak his tapa skirt. Ragnu moved in, stabbing, stabbing, trying to find a target on the abdomen of the Pict. Seumas's flailing left arm managed to divert the blows, but he was being beaten back, towards the edge of the canoe. If he faltered once, or tripped, the airo fai would be inside him, wreaking wounds that would not heal.

The Rarotongans on board the Arioi pahi looked on in dismay as they saw Seumas was off-balance. Their pahi could not lock with the Raiatean war canoe, however, the latter being more manoeuvrable having rowers instead of sails. None the less, Kumiki could not stand to see his father in such dire circumstances. The drummer took up a spear, ran the length of the deck, launching the missile at the distant Ragnu.

By some miracle of the wind the javelin was carried the distance, but looked like falling short of its main target. At that moment however, Ragnu saw his chance for plunging his dagger into the weakened Seumas and stepped forward for the final thrust. Kumiki's spear struck and pinned the priest's foot to the deck of the pahi.

Ragnu screamed in pain, diverted for a moment.

Seumas gathered his strength and brought his club up in a sweeping movement, hoping to knock the airo fai from the priest's grip. Instead he hit Ragnu's wrist, driving the dagger up under the kahuna's chin. The terrible weapon was forced through the floor and roof of Ragnu's mouth and into his brain. The priest's eyes bulged. A reflex action caused his arm to jerk downwards, wrenching the dagger out.

With a shock Seumas saw the bulging eyes disappear as if sucked into his skull. It was a moment before the Pict realised the dagger's tiny bone hooks had caught on some muscles and had pulled the eyeballs down into the priest's mouth.

The dagger fell to the deck.

Shreds of eye muscle, mouth tissue and the dying man's tongue hung from the ugly weapon.

Ragnu coughed once and grey flecks of brain matter splattered the front of his chest.

Seumas stepped forward and with one swift blow knocked the priest sideways, tearing his foot from the spear. The Pict took up the body, held it aloft, then tossed it into the sea. It floated there, face down for a few moments, before hammerheads came swarming in to devour the bloody corpse, ripping it apart.

Dakuwanga was waiting for the ripe plum of all sau to pass into his multi-toothed mouth. Ragnu, ever devious, had a surprise for the Shark God. In life using his occult powers, the kahuna had swallowed the soul of a dog in anticipation of just such a predicament. This he now tore away from his own soul and tossed it to Dakuwanga, thus distracting the great spiritual predatory fish. The Shark God gobbled up the dog's sau while Ragnu laughed and made his escape.

'I am even trickier than Maui,' he praised himself. 'Even the gods cannot match my cleverness.'

Just as he was about to put his foot on the purple road, however, there was a whoop of delight from the clouds. Ragnu just had time to look up in horror to see a huge basket descending upon him. Amai-te-rangi, the angler god, scooped him up and carried him high into the clouds. The fisher god, eater of men and souls, had like Dakuwanga been appraised of the coming battle by certain ancestors of mortals, and was on the scene ready to snatch any morsels of food which fell from Dakuwanga's lips. Yet here was a complete sau, missed by the Shark God, and Amai-te-rangi devoured it gratefully, not forgetting to belch afterwards, in appreciation of a good meal.

Ragnu was to spend an eternity travelling through the gut of the giant angler.

Seumas turned to the paddlers in the war canoe and said, 'Take me back to your fleet, quickly. They are attacking the Arioi by mistake. Our yellow sails have turned black with mould, no doubt the work of that excuse for a man the sharks are eating – we have no intention of invading Raiatea.'

'It's Seumas,' cried one man. 'I know him. It's the goblin who went to Raro-tonga with Prince Tangiia – he's an honourable man. Do as he says. Stop the war canoes before they reach the fleet and massacre the Arioi!'

'We have our orders from Ragnu,' complained another.

Seumas said, 'I give you my word, this flotilla is that of the Arioi. Ragnu is dead and the responsibility is now yours. What will you tell your king, if you slaughter a troupe of performers and players – artistes who have no training in war? Ragnu will not be there to take the blame. You will.'

There was a hurried exchange of words between the paddlers in which the second speaker was heavily outvoted, then the canoe set off to cut a line between the Raiatean navy and the Arioi flotilla. With great effort the rowers managed to put themselves between the two armadas. A great deal of yelling and shouting followed, until finally the Raiatean warriors understood that this was all a mistake, that the Arioi had come.

Anxiety and dread, which is in the mind of every man before a battle, suddenly turned to relief and joy. The Arioi were here! There was to be no death and destruction, only festivities. The war canoes accompanied the Arioi to the lagoon, where the king waited in some apprehension and puzzlement. At last the Arioi found their voice and began singing. Others began dancing. Musicians took up their instruments. Tumblers did acrobatics on the decks.

Poets recited at the tops of their voices, trying to throw their words over the wavelets of the lagoon, to the people on the beach.

There was happiness and laughter in the air.

Kumiki found his father and spoke to him.

'If ever I doubted your honour and courage, I beg your forgiveness now, Father,' said the youth. 'I have greatly wronged you in the past.'

'Out of ignorance, not malice,' replied Seumas, magnanimously. 'You believed what you were told.'

'I should have consulted others.'

'What's done, is done. Let it be.'

Once on shore Kikamana explained to an uneasy monarch that there had been a plot to destroy the Arioi. The king was told that Ragnu, out of jealousy, had tricked the noble ruler into a situation which was now under control.

'Bring me this erring priest,' cried the king. 'I shall have his head.'

'Seumas took it for you,' replied Kikamana. 'It was necessary to kill the priest in order to stop the battle.'

'In that case Seumas the Pict is my honoured guest,' said the king gravely, 'for he has saved me much sorrow. I am embarrassed to be in his debt. Ask him what favour he requires as payment of this obligation on my part.'

Seumas, when asked, said he would like a gift: the cured hide of a pig. And also permission to play his pipes with the Arioi. The king had heard of this terrible screaming hog which the Pict claimed was a musical instrument and being rather timid in nature took some time in granting the request. Even so he made himself absent from the performance, making excuses for a journey to Borabora for a few days' rest, having had enough shocks for one month. He had been assured by his priests that the evil sound of the pipes could not reach him at that distance.

Seumas made his bagpipes, drilling hardwood for the chanter and using bamboo for the drones.

Three days later the Pict stood on the huge stage alongside his son and played the bagpipes: a dirge that brought tears to the eyes of Dorcha it was so beautiful, then a martial pibroch, and finally a lilting melody out of the hills. The tunes reminded her of the craggy mountains of her homeland, of the heather-covered hills, of the ptarmigan and hare, of the eagle and stag, of the wildcat, of the fir and the oak.

She could smell the sweetness of the frangipani, but she wanted to smell the pine. The gaudy colours of the hibiscus were in her eyes, but she wanted the delicacy of alpine flowers. The sound of parrots rent the air, but she wanted the howl and bark of the wolf and fox. Nostalgia took her heart in its fingers and caressed it, bringing forth a flood of feelings, some good, some not so pleasant.

For others around her it was difficult to find beauty in the sound. Some were clearly nervous and their eyes darted to those of their friends, seeking comfort. Others wore pained expressions, but kept their silence out of politeness. Others still looked longingly at their boats, clearly wondering if they could get up and go fishing without seeming ill mannered.

At the end of the recital Seumas bowed low to his audience and there was a kind of ragged cheer. Boy-girl maintained later that it was one of relief, that the performance was over. Dorcha however was convinced there were some amongst the Raiateans who appreciated the music of her homeland.

Kumiki got up from his position at his drums, took the hand of his father, and held it high, to show that at least one musician amongst them regarded the sounds as being that of euphony, however strange.

And who would doubt the judgement of a genius, a Painted Leg, a god amongst those who knew melody when they heard it?

After the bagpipes came the hura dancing and once more Seumas was embarrassed and shocked by the public display of sex.

'You would think they could learn to control themselves, wouldn't you,' he said to Dorcha.

'That's the whole point, I think,' she said. 'They become so immersed in the dance that they forget there's anyone watching. They forget about the world and go into a kind of trance.'

'Trance? They're as shameless as hares in spring. A trance is where you stare into space and do nothing. They're certainly not doing nothing. It's – uncomfortable.'

'For you,' she laughed, 'but not for everyone.'

'Humph,' he grunted. 'Well some of us have to retain a sense of decency.'

'You liked watching naked virgins run the sail up a mast.'

'That's different – that's sort of – natural.'

'And this isn't, you prude? I suppose you want to have the hura banned?'

He squirmed uncomfortably as the hura women in grass skirts began swivelling their hips faster and faster, keeping up the hot pace of the drums. The swishing of the skirts, the beauty in the faces of the women, the breasts bouncing underneath the garlands of flowers, all added to his discomfort. The rhythms became intense and he kept having to pull himself back from the edge of drowning in music and movement.

'I wouldn't dream of interfering,' said Seumas, 'any more than I would think of joining them. But one of these days someone's going to land on these islands and be very shocked and offended. Someone like that Captain Cook we heard about from the Maori. A man like him would put a stop to all this, you mark my words.'

2

When the performances were over and the Rarotongans were preparing to return to their home island, Hiro arrived back from his travels in distant lands. They had last seen him on his weather-beaten pahi in Rarotonga, before setting out for Rapanui, and he looked as strong and fit as ever. He was also very cheerful, greeting them with a wave and a smile on his salt-encrusted tanned face.

'Where's the king?' asked Hiro. 'I expected a lot of fuss as usual.'

'On Borabora,' replied Kieto.

'Good, I hate all that pomp and circumstance.'

Seumas said, 'Did you find it?'

'Did I find what?' asked Hiro, grinning. 'Oh, you mean the *writing*. Yes, I found it.'

They crowded around the adventurer, staring at him, looking for some kind of bundle: Boy-girl, Dorcha, Po'oi, Kikamana, Kieto, and of course, Seumas.

'Well, where is it?' asked Seumas, looking Hiro up and down. 'Is it on the pahi?'

'No, it's here with me now.'

'Show it to us then.'

Hiro laughed and picked up a stick. With this he drew strange symbols in the sand. They looked like tattoos gone wrong. Seumas could sense that despite his jovial mood, Hiro was excited. He wondered why.

'Is that it? That's the *writing*,' said Seumas, bemused and disappointed. 'Tattoo signs?'

'They're not tattoos,' replied Hiro. 'Wait a minute – I'll show you.'

He called to a friend who was coiling ropes on their pahi. The woman came wading through the clear waters of the lagoon and joined the group.

'This is Wheena,' said Hiro. 'Now, Wheena, we have to give a demonstration.'

Wheena, a large and jolly-looking woman, nodded and went away to a distance down the beach. Hiro in the meantime found a piece of coconut shell and a chunk of charcoal from a fire. Then he stood in front of Seumas.

'Give me some words,' he said, 'any old words. Something perhaps that only you know. Not too many for the moment. This shell is not that large.'

Seumas thought for a moment, under the scrutiny of the others, then said, 'I have found my only child, a son.'

Hiro scratched away at a concave piece of coconut shell and then when it was covered in marks handed it to Seumas.

'Take this to Wheena,' he said. 'I'll stay here.'

Seumas took the shell gingerly and walked down the beach with his retinue trailing after him.

Boy-girl said, 'I thought writing was silent words. That's what Hiro told us it was before he left.'

'There's no such thing as silent words,' snorted Kieto. 'How can there be? Words are sounds.'

'Wait and see,' said Kikamana. 'It may be magic.'

'Yes,' Dorcha agreed. 'Keep your minds free.'

They reached Wheena and Seumas handed her the chunk of shell. She turned it upside down and then studied it for a moment. Then she smiled at Seumas.

'Congratulations,' she said. 'I'm pleased for you.'

A prickle of fear went down the Pict's spine.

'Why would you be pleased for me?'

'Because it says here that you have found your only child, a son.'

Chilled, Seumas took a step back from the woman and regarded her through half-closed eyes. Surely she had heard the words on the wind? Or perhaps some creature, a bird or a rat, had carried the message to her on its lips? This was magic, pure and simple, and beyond the reach of ordinary men. Of course, a signal could have been used, but for such an elaborate message, delivered word for word at the other end, and moreover a set of words which had only just left Seumas's mouth a few moments previously. How could they have worked out a signal for something he had not known he was going to say himself?

'What is this?' whispered Kieto. 'Is it magic, Kikamana?'

'I don't know,' replied the priestess, truthfully. 'It doesn't feel like magic.'

By this time, Hiro had walked up to them, still smiling. 'You want to try it again?' he said. 'This time I'll go off and one of you can send the words through Wheena.'

The pair of them did the trick over and over again, until gradually, Seumas allowed himself to be convinced that it was not magic.

'So you make the shape of the words with the charcoal?' he said.

'Just so,' replied Hiro. 'If I draw a pig, you know pig by the shape. Well, you can give words shapes too. That's what writing is. Spoken words drawn in shapes. When you see what the words mean, understand them, it's called *reading*.'

Kieto was the most impressed of the group.

'We can use this *writing* in battle,' he said. 'If I have a general who is out of earshot, I can send a message to him without worrying that the messenger will get the words muddled, or forget what to say in the heat of the battle. I can *write* my message and my general can *read* it.'

'I'm not sure it's the best use of writing I've heard,' admitted Hiro, 'since I'm not fond of war myself, but I agree, it's possible to use it for this purpose.'

Later, the Arioi had to set off to sea again, anxious to be out under the roof of voyaging. Seumas experienced a painful parting from his newly discovered son and daughter, who were of course remaining with the Arioi.

'I shall come and see you, Father,' said Kumiki, gravely, 'when next I can.'

'Do so,' said Seumas, 'and expect to see me at any time. One day, when I am through with voyaging and war, and you are ready to settle down to a farmer's life, we can live on the same island together, as a family should.'

Kumiki grinned. 'I will give you some grandchildren then – Linloa will anyway. At the moment we are not permitted children. The rules of the Arioi state that we must remain childless, or leave the group. But when we settle down, we shall have masses of them.'

Linloa laughed. 'Will we?' she cried.

The couple were about to board their pahi when Seumas took Kumiki aside one last time and spoke to him quietly.

'Listen, son, you – you don't do that dance – that *hura* thing – with Linloa, do you?'

Puzzled, Kumiki said, 'I'm a drummer, not a dancer, Father.'

'So you don't do it?' said Seumas, relieved.

'No – I play the drums.'

'Good, I would hate to think that my grandchildren were conceived in public view.'

The youth shook his head and smiled at his father's priggishness, then boarded his canoe.

Seumas's heart was full as he stood with Dorcha, his arm around his wife, and waved his son and daughter goodbye.

However, it was Hiro who dominated his mind, when there was leisure to ponder on the gravities and vagaries of life. This idea of *writing* was surprising, yet hardly as important as a wondrous new weapon, or the invention of a new kind of sailing vessel, or even a good fishing hook.

'I think Hiro makes too much of this *writing*,' he said to Dorcha, testing his own feelings by challenging the usefulness of the concept. 'It seems simple enough to me.'

'Then why were you so astounded in the first place?' she asked. 'Why have we never heard of such a thing before.'

'Oh, I've not heard of a lot of things, but that doesn't make them astonishing.'

Dorcha took his face in her hands and looked into his eyes.

'Listen to me, Seumas,' she said. 'You know I love you, so I always speak the truth to you. This *writing* which you pretend to scorn is probably the most important thing you'll ever discover in your life. It gives the user great power, even Kikamana said so. A man who can write is a man who can talk to others over oceans, without leaving his home. Think of that! It's miraculous. Words you speak now, write now, can be given to your unborn great-grandchildren, after you're dead. Writing crosses time and space, leaps oceans and centuries.'

Seumas was an egg-gatherer, a warrior, a lover, a bagpipe player, a man with many talents. He was still fit and able and could match any man in sport. He could probably outrun Hiro in a race, climb a mountain with more speed, hit a target more accurately with a spear. Yet he knew deep within himself that Hiro was a greater man than he, though he was big enough not to let this observation disturb him. If Hiro was a greater man, then Seumas could learn from him, without loss of pride.

'I will ask Hiro to teach me this *writing*,' he said, patting the head of Dirk, now grown to full size again, 'before we leave for Rarotonga. If Kieto and Boy-girl are beginning to understand it, I can learn it too. At least, I'll try. You should do it too, Dorcha, you're better at these things than me.'

Dorcha put an arm around his waist and hugged him. 'My man,' she said, proudly.

He laughed. 'My woman,' he said.

Together they walked along the sands to where Kieto was talking earnestly with Hiro, drawing things in the dust with a small twig, learning the great secrets of the universe.

LAND-OF-MISTS

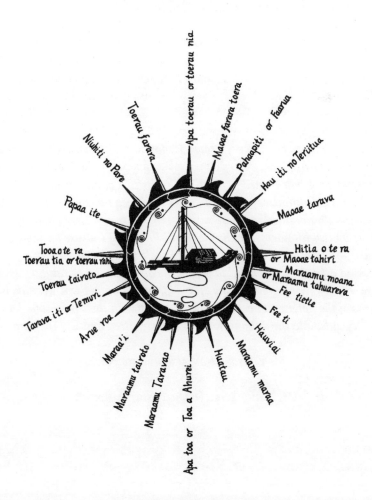

Apa toerau or toerau nia
Maoae farara toera
Pahaapiti or Faarua
Hau iti no Teriitua
Toerau farara
Maoae tarava
Niuhiti no Pare
Hitia o te ra or Maoae tahiri
Papaa ite
Maraamu moana or Maraamu tahuareva
Tooao te ra
Toerau tia or toerau rahi
Fee tietle
Toerau tairoto
Fee ti
Tarava iti or Temuri
Hauviai
Arue roa
Maraamu maraa
Maraa'i
Huatau
Maraamu tairoto
Maraamu Taravao
Apa toa or Toa a Ahurei

This, the third novel in the Navigator Kings trilogy, is for the children of the two sets of adults to whom the first two books were dedicated. Coincidentally, and rather aptly, these young men are like the Oceanian hero Craig of this final novel in the series, all half-Celtic. They are:

Peter Fedden
Craig Fedden
Richard Fedden

and

Craig Chidlow

This book is also dedicated to those on the far side of the world in Oceania: the dancers, drummers, poets and others who keep the ancient traditions of Polynesia alive and well in these culture-eroding times. They are represented here by two islanders. Firstly, the then Minister of Culture for the Cook Islands. Secondly, an oral storyteller, the Speaker-for-the-Seventh-Canoe, who was kind enough to meet and talk with me on his island of Aitutaki. Others were equally giving of their time and help, even though I was weaving fragments of the Polynesian people's history, along with their myths, fables and legends, into the dubious form of a westernised fantasy. They are:

Mr Kauraka Kauraka: anthropologist

Mr Tunui Tereu (Papa Tunui): historian

PART ONE

In the land of firewalkers

1

The Fijian war chief Nagata and his warriors were paddling up the Sigatoka River. They travelled cautiously, for the Sigatoka was the ancestral home of two particularly unpleasant gods: Dakuwanga the Shark-God and Dengei the Serpent-God. While both these deities were concerned mainly with the dead, they would quite happily destroy the living, if sufficiently annoyed to rouse themselves from their resting places.

'Use your paddles smoothly,' warned Nagata, 'in case we waken those who sleep lightly.'

The chief and his warriors were on their way to their warclub tree. Warriors all over Oceania were arming themselves and making ready for a long voyage. The great Rarotongan ariki, the noble Kieto, was massing Oceanians for a long voyage to a place called Land-of-Mists. There would be fleets from distant Hawaii, from Rapanui, Samoa, Tahiti, Aitutaki, Tonga and many, many others throughout the blue watery world of Oceania.

Along the murky river swirling with brown mud went the canoe, battling upstream against the sweeping flow of the Sigatoka, avoiding dead floating trees taken from the valley's edges. On all sides were stone-walled hill forts, for the Fijians were mighty warriors and their various clans were forever battling against one another.

Suddenly as the canoe rounded a bend it snagged a fishing line. The line went taut and halted the canoe. The hands of the fisherman on the bank were obviously very strong.

Nagata was annoyed and indignant. The paddlers had just got a good rhythm going and it was upsetting to have that brought abruptly to a dead stop. The war chief was particularly incensed as on this part of the river the current was so strong it was difficult for his warriors to build up any speed.

'Whose line is this?' cried Nagata, angrily, as the thick sennit continued to hamper the canoe's progress. He reached over and wrenched a massive pearl-shell hook from the bows. 'Whose hook and lure are these? Come out and be recognized. I shall brain the person to whom this fishing tackle belongs with my gata waka club.'

The leaves of an hibiscus tree on the bank parted in response to this shout. Two large hands appeared, one holding the line, the other forming a shaking fist. Nagata was suddenly appalled to see that no body was attached to these hands.

He knew immediately to whom the severed bodily extremities belonged.

Tui Delai Gau, God of the Mountain, was a giant who lived in a tree. He sent his hands fishing whenever he was hungry. He could also send his head up into the air, to spy on trespassers.

'I'm sorry,' said Nagata to the hands. 'I – I did not know I was speaking to you, my lord …'

There was, of course, no reply, for hands cannot speak. However, a head appeared over the rainforest, some distance inland, and a loud moan escaped its lips. The hands began walking down the bank on their fingers in response to this cry. They entered the water. Then they began swimming towards the canoe with funny fish-like movements. The thumbs stayed above the water, as if guiding the hands in the right direction.

One of the paddlers shouted in fear, 'I have a wife and child – it was not my fault!'

He dived over the edge of the canoe and began swimming towards the opposite bank. One by one the other men dived over the side of the canoe and did likewise, leaving Nagata to deal with Tui Delai Gau's hands on his own. The god's hands gripped the end of the canoe and pulled downwards quickly. Nagata, at the other end, was shot high into the air. His precious club went flying and he himself landed on his head and shoulders in the mud of the shallows ahead of his swimming comrades.

When they reached Nagata, they rescued him, pulling him out of the clay bottom.

In the meantime Tui Delai Gau's hands were destroying the canoe, ripping it apart. They tore the gunwales from the hull, the sennit stitching ripping like cloth. They wrenched the prow from the bows. Finally they broke the back of the canoe, sending the debris floating back down the river towards the sea.

When the hands had finished their work, they swam back to their fishing spot and pulled in the line. The awed men watched as the hook was baited with something that looked suspiciously like a man's liver and was then cast in the deep middle part of the River Sigatoka. They nodded in admiration as the bird's-feather lure was played on the current, so that it skipped and danced like a live thing on the river's ripples.

Within a few moments Tui Delai Gau had caught himself a handsome fish.

'What are we going to do now?' asked one of the men of their chief. 'We have no boat to reach the weapon-tree.'

'We must walk,' grunted Nagata. 'How else will we be able to arm ourselves with war clubs?'

So they crept through the rainforest, but this was a dangerous business in Fiji. Since they were visiting the warclub tree, they were not heavily armed. They needed to arrive empty-handed to carry the weapons home. And not

only were there old clans of Fijians established in territories along the Sigatoka, but recently some Tongan clans had arrived.

These were fierce people who had been banished from their own islands
for being troublemakers. The Tongans had quickly established hill forts and
ring-ditch forts of their own. Once a clan was embedded in a fortification of
this kind, it was almost impossible to root out and destroy. From this strong
base they would raid less fortified villages and prey on passing travellers.

Within each village was the dreaded Killing Stone at which the clan would
slaughter their prisoners as offerings to the gods, and afterwards cook and
eat them.

At this moment the Fijian group was passing through the land of the Waiwai clan who owned just one of the hundred ring-ditch forts along the
Sigatoka. They were a terrible people. Their village was surrounded not by
just one moat, but three, plus a loopholed stone wall. Once you were taken
prisoner and carried beyond that wall, those ditches, you were lost for ever.

'Keep close to me. Make no noise,' whispered Nagata, promising himself
that next time they selected a warclub tree, it would be much closer to home.

The trouble was, one needed a young nokonoko tree for such a purpose,
and the nokonoko grew in only a few locations.

Finally they were through the land of the Waiwai and they could see their
sacred tree, up on the bank of the river. It was protected by magic charms –
wicker sharks, dangling from its branches – and no other tribe would dare
steal from a tree which was protected by the magic of a priest. Their skins
would blister, their eyes would pop out completely from their heads and their
tongues would swell and grow pustules.

A warclub tree is certainly a wonderful sight.

When a clan selects such a tree, it does so with a view to growing its weapons over the long term. Each branch, each bough, is trained in a particular
killing shape from the time when the tree is supple enough to be bent and
twisted easily. Sennit cord, stones and logs of wood are used to make the
shapes around which the branches are bound. In time the nokonoko wood
becomes harder and tougher than rock. From a distance one could recognize
all the different varieties of club: the i wau, of which there were eighty different types, and the i ula, the lighter, more personal throwing clubs. These
merely needed to be detached from the tree to become a weapon to wield.

Indeed a warclub tree, bristling with such weapons, looks like a festival
tree hung with gifts for warriors.

'Quickly, cut some weapons from the tree,' said Nagata. 'We must not
linger.'

He was not only worried about the other clans, there was still Tui Delai
Gau to worry about. The god might send his head up high above the forest
again, to see where they were. Sometimes these lesser gods brooded on

things and decided at a later time that a little mayhem, destruction and murder would not go amiss. The minor gods were less secure than the greater gods, and insults festered in them.

'Quickly, quickly!'

The clubs were cut down with small flint axes, gathered in bundles, strapped to the backs of the warriors. Finally, everyone had as much as they could carry. Nagata led his men back through the rainforest along the valley towards the sea. His was a coastal clan, a people who felt themselves quite superior to those hot musty peoples living in the sweltering villages of the hinterland.

Nagata's people had fresh sea breezes to cleanse their huts, light-bright sunshine to lift their spirits, clean sand for their floors, pretty decorative shells on their hut walls, laughter, gaiety, the soft sound of the surf on the reef and the cry of the seabirds over the ocean. The tribes of the hinterland had mud, thick dank jungle and still, stale air. They were definitely inferior peoples to those who lived on the coast.

But dark places breed dark thoughts, and dark thoughts make savages of men. Thus the interior tribes were fearsome, bellicose creatures who would rather crush a skull with a battle club than remember the birthday of a loved one.

When Nagata and his men were creeping through a tunnel formed by strangling fig trees and she oaks in the land of the Waiwai, they suddenly saw a pair of hands before them. In one of the hands was a sokilaki barbed fighting spear. In the other, a sobesila mountain club.

'Tui Delai Gau!' cried one of Nagata's men.

But he was wrong. The hands were human and belonged to a warrior of the Waiwai. In the darkness of the rainforest, behind him, were twenty other warriors. They had heard the commotion on the river earlier and had found Nagata's men's footprints in the soft sand at the river's edge. Now they had caught the trespassers sneaking back.

'Thieves! Plunderers! Pirates!' yelled the first Waiwai warrior, with a snarl.

Nagata felled him with a quick strike to the throat.

A brawl ensued, with several blows falling on heads and shoulders, and many spears being exchanged. There was much fierce yelling and scuffling, but in fact the area was too hemmed in by trees to allow the fight to develop into anything more than a restricted skirmish. Finally, Nagata's men managed to fight their way through the Waiwai, with the loss of only one warrior and two wounded. The Waiwai were satisfied. They had their feast for that night. Nagata's men were not pursued.

When Nagata finally reached the mouth of the Sigatoka River, he fell on his knees and kissed the sand. Mangoes and breadfruit were picked from the trees. Fresh coconut water was extracted from the shells. The people rejoiced at the safe return of their chieftain, mourned the loss of the one warrior, whose widow was instantly compensated. A necklace of shark's teeth was given her by a deputation of great woolly-headed Fijian warriors with glum round faces.

Sacrifices were made to Tui Delai Gau and hung on a lantern tree. There were many-coloured fruit doves, orange-breasted honey-eaters, black ducks and white-collared kingfishers. A cloak made of the skins of ocean geckoes and green tree skinks was draped over one of the branches. Mats with strong geometrical patterns woven by women were laid around the base of the tree covering the root area.

That night there was feasting and dancing in the village of the Naga. Drums beat healthy rhythms, scented leaves sent up heady fragrances from the fires, kava was drunk into the small hours. Warriors walked on white-hot stones to prove their manhood, for this was the land of the fire-walkers. They were seemingly careless of the heat, a trick of the mind learned over the centuries.

They had their weapons of war, with which they would follow the mighty leader of their expedition, Kieto, to the Land-of-Mists. There these weapons would be put to good use, slaying a people with red hair and white skins known as the Celts.

Later that night, when the village was asleep, tipua came to the lantern tree and stole the cooked birds and the beautiful lizard-skin cloak with its shiny green scales and small tight stitching. Giggling they went back into the forest with their treasures, knowing that the tribesmen would wake in the morning and believe the Mountain God had been appeased.

Goblins are like that: they care for no man's honour.

2

Mist drifted low over the heather, falling down the sides of deep gullies, over the lintels of rockhangs of the glen. The man who tramped resolutely through this mist, scattering these vapours with his walk, was in the fifth decade of his life. He strode on thick red legs, his feet bound with rags to keep them from the cold, along a ridge towards a needle of rock. He was a Celt, a Scot from the kingdom of Dalriada, sworn enemy of Angles, Britons, Jutes and, above all, Picts.

The Celt's hair was dark and as shaggy as the mane on a mountain steer. His neck was thick and bullish. The width and muscle of his shoulders were a testament to his great physical strength. In his right hand he held a roughly forged, wide-bladed sword with a rusting trailing edge. In his left fist was a wooden targe with the bark still gripping it.

The granite monolith which appeared to be his destination pierced the late winter sky like a black twisted tree. This rock was riven with dark magic, which was why the old crone sat at its base, the smoke from her fire curling around its tortured shape. The Celt hailed her as he reached the snowline and stamped along its edge to where the shrivelled hag was hunched.

'Old witch,' he growled, 'what have you for me?'

'Ah, Douglass Barelegs. Do ye bring me gifts? Even a woman with powers needs her wee surprises.'

He threw her a lump of something wrapped in a dirty rag. Whatever it was, it sweated grease in thick patches. She took it with a claw-like hand and sniffed it noisily, making appreciative sounds afterwards.

'Is it a dead man's heart ye bring me, laddie?'

'Whatever it is,' he replied, 'you'll eat it, so why bother with its identity. Have you news for me, woman? Someone told me you had something to tell.'

'Was it a corbie told ye so, eh, laddie?' she cackled, stirring her little fire with a stick then placing the bag of offal on a hot stone beside it. 'D'ye listen to sich creatures?'

'Don't play games with me, old hag,' he said, sweeping his sword-arm backwards as if about to take her head from her shoulders with the honed edge of the blade, 'or I'll chop your neck off at the roots.'

She screwed up her features. 'No need to get testy on me,' she snarled. 'I can keep things to myself if I wish it.'

He gripped the oakwood handle of the sword, its two halves bound with sweat-stained cord around the hilt-spike, ready to deliver the blow. She looked along the iron blade, the light dancing erratically over the hammered surface where it was pitted and flawed, and knew she was a second away from death. Her sneer turned to a look of pathetic terror.

'Don't …' she said. 'He's coming.'

The Celt stayed his hand, letting his arm fall down by his side. His face registered a look of mixed hope and disbelief.

'He? You mean Seumas-the-Black is finally on his way back to his homeland?'

'Aye,' she laughed, 'but whether he'll reach here is a matter for the gods.'

The Celt chose not to indulge in the same doubts as the crone. He preferred to imagine Seumas stepping from a boat while he himself waited to take his head from his shoulders. Douglass wondered whether his mother would be with the Pict. He did not dare ask the witch for this information, in case her answer was not the one he wanted.

The hag drew her ragged shawl around her thin shoulders and peered at him through the smoke of the fire.

'The man who killed yer fether has a son,' she croaked.

His head came up quickly. 'What? He and my mother, the Dark One?'

She smiled, enjoying the fact that he was shocked by this news. 'Nay, laddie – his spawn from another base union. The young whelp is a mongrel. I see his name written in the smoke. Craig, it is. The Man of the Crag. He comes too.' The witch stared into the middle distance. 'It is of great import- ance that ye kill him quickly, for he is a Man of Two Worlds. The prophecy says that sich a man will open the tower and destroy my kind for ever ...'

'Damn you and yer prophecies, you old crone – who cares whether your kind is gone?'

'Ye will, Douglass Barelegs, when there's nay magic for ye to draw on and work yer schemes, yer sedition, yer betrayals. Ye dream of power, ye have great ambitions locked in yer breast, Douglass, but ye cannae get onything wi'out the likes o' me. Ye have to kill this Craig the moment ye set eyes on the man, or we'll bayth perish. We'll bayth vanish in the mist.'

The face of Douglass twisted into a mask of hatred and he raved into the wind. 'I'll kill the two of them! I'll kill them all! At last my fether's death will be avenged. I'll kill fether and son – and that wipperjinny of a mother too if she's with them. I was ten years old when she ran away with that murtherin' bastard – took off with some sea raiders from the outer islands I'm told. Gone to Yell, Fetlar or Unst, to soil his blanket with their greasy union.

'That wipperjinny ran off with her dead husband's murthurer, to fill his bed with her slattern's body. If I had not been with my grandfether on a raid, I would have killed her then. Now the bitch will die with him. My only regret, my only shame, is that they've lived so long. A whole life together. My fether had none. He was struck down in his prime by a cowardly cur ...'

The old witch stirred the fire again, looking at him through the veil of black smoke with narrowed eyes.

'It was said that yer fether taught ye how to beat yer mither wi' a heavy stick in them far-gone days. Maybe a tween the two of ye she couldna stay? She drudged for ye and ye rewarded her wi' nothing but hurts and bruises. I think I micht have run away ma'sel in sich circumstances.'

The sword arm came up again.

'Watch your tongue, you old bitch, or I'll cut it out and hang it from a bush.'

The witch wisely kept her counsel after that while the greybearded man raged about how he was going to stomp faces into the ground, break bones, sever heads. While he was talking he put the end of his sword in the fire, leav- ing it there like a poker heating itself. From down below in the glen came the blast of a horn, which echoed around the mountainsides. Douglass stopped ranting and stared down into the trees. His clan was being attacked, but it was useless to hurry down there, for it would finish before he arrived. Raids tended to be swift, merciless and all over in a short while.

Douglass picked up his sword again. The end of it was now glowing red. Without any warning he placed the hot part against the bare skin of the crone's withered arm. The spot sizzled, sending up a rank smell of burning flesh. The witch screamed in agony, jerking her arm back. She sucked the spot where the shrivelled flesh had been burned with her toothless mouth, moaning in the back of her throat as she did so.

'That's just a taste of what you'll get if I find you've lied to me, you bag of bones. Next time it'll be your eyes.'

With that he strode back along the ridge, leaving her whining against the face of the stone tor. He could not hear what she was saying but he knew it would be bad. She would be asking the demon of the stone to suck his brains through his eyesockets while he was asleep. Douglass was not afraid of threats of this kind from the witch. She was good at seeing the unseeable, but not so good at persuading the forces of evil to destroy her enemies.

'May yer heart rot in yer ribcage, Dark Douglass,' she shrieked after him. 'May yer testicles shrivel like kernels in auld nutshells! May yer ...'

And so they went on, while he found his path down the mountainside, to the pine-scented glen below.

3

Azure skies, blue seas, white sands. It did not seem right having a funeral on such a bright day, in such a colourful place. There were multi-hued shells on Rarotonga's beach as he walked: sea combs, green turbans, scarlet tops, textile cones. Dorcha had loved the sea shells. Back in Albainn the whelk and mussel shells had been terribly dull by comparison. Dark shells out of dark seas: almost black seas on some grey stormy days.

Seumas suddenly remembered he had companions: his son, Craig, and the ageing Boy-girl.

'I was thinking how much your adopted mother loved the colour of these Oceanic isles,' said Seumas to Craig. 'She was a dark woman with a dark soul, but she liked the world around her to be colourful.'

Boy-girl, with grey swept-back hair, still walking tall and stately, with impeccable elegance, protested.

'A dark *soul*? Surely not, Seumas. She was the best of people – loving and kind.'

'I don't mean dark in that sense. I mean she was *mysterious*. I never really got to know her, deep down. There was some place she used to go inside, where I could not follow. It used to make me very jealous. I wanted *all* of her. I wanted to follow her into every little corner of herself, but I got used to being denied.'

Craig said, 'She loved you, Father. You had more love from her than any man can expect. If my own wife Linloa loves me half as much, I shall be satisfied.'

Seumas sighed. He did not want to sound ungrateful. It was true, he had felt loved. But Dorcha had been such a prize for him he could never quite believe she had been his. And perhaps every man wanted more? Perhaps the best of women always withheld some part of themselves? It ensured they were not owned by the men they loved. No one should give everything, or their partners will have nothing to strive for, nothing left to desire. We all want what we cannot have.

'Stung by a box jellyfish,' he snorted. 'You would have thought she might have fallen from a cliff in a tragic accident, or be taken by a shark while bathing. But to die of a box jellyfish sting! It does not seem right.'

'If she'd been taken by a shark, and mutilated, you'd have hated it, Seumas,' said Boy-girl. 'You'd have spent the rest of your life hunting sharks and killing them, you know you would. As it is, it's not very practical or very dignified to go on the rampage slaughtering jellyfish. And her body was whole. She looked so beautiful this morning, on her bed of flowers.'

'Boy-girl is right, Father,' said Craig.

The young man who walked beside Seumas had one leg completely tattooed. This was a badge of the highest office in the Arioi – a Painted Leg – the top rank. The young man had been one of the finest drummers Oceania had ever known. In those days he had been called Kumiki, but had taken on a Celt name to honour his father. His wife Linloa still called him Kumiki in private, to show that his mother's side of the family should not be forgotten and her ancestors were respected.

His mother was dead, however, and his father still alive, so it seemed right and proper to propitiate the living, especially since Craig had spent the first eighteen years of his life hating his father and threatening to kill him.

So half-Celt, half-Hivan, Craig was part of two worlds – the world in which he lived and the world which Kieto was going to conquer. His father, he knew, was torn in two by this expedition to the Land-of-Mists. Seumas loved his adopted people, but blood runs thick and he hated the idea that he was about to become a traitor and help lead an invasion against his ancestors, the Picts of Albainn.

Seumas was now an old man, over sixty years of age with creased muscles and hollow cheeks. He had gone back to wearing his hair in a long braid, but now it was white instead of red. It was Craig who had the red hair, but his skin tones reflected those of an Oceanian. Craig-Kumiki was truly the offspring of a union between mist and sunshine.

'What did she want that damned cross on her grave for?' grumbled Seumas, going off on another tack. 'Those silly ideas of hers.'

'Well, there I must agree with you, Father,' Craig said. 'She had some strange notions about the gods – said they were not much longer for this world – whatever that meant. She seemed to think that only Io, the Great One, had any significance whatsoever, and that he was known by many peoples under many names.'

Boy-girl said, 'We must respect her wishes though. She asked for a simple wooden cross and white flowers on her grave. That's what she wanted and that's what we had to give her. I like the idea, actually. It has taste.'

'Taste,' grumbled Seumas. 'You're always on about taste – heel, Dirk.'

The last two words were directed at a dog which had come bounding along the beach to meet them.

'Taste,' said Boy-girl, her nose in the air, 'is one of the most important things in life.'

Seumas made a non-committal noise which was meant to be a protest. He had argued too long and too often on this subject with Boy-girl, and he almost never felt he had won. Boy-girl was much too clever for him. Much too witty. Much too quick with words. Boy-girl had a dagger for a tongue, which could cut a man down to half his size in less than a moment.

Seumas turned to Craig and said in his original tongue, *'Tha mi seann duine.'*

'What, Father?' faltered Craig.

Seumas shook his head and sighed. 'Have you learned no Gaelic, since I first tried to teach you? I said, *I am an old man.* It's an easy sentence. Did you get nothing from it?'

'Nothing,' Craig replied, sadly. 'I'm afraid your lessons have been a waste, Father. I'm as ignorant now as I ever was, where your old tongue is concerned.'

The old man shook his head again in sadness at this news.

The group turned at the end of the bay. The dog was gambolling around them, dashing into the water here, into the rainforest there, generally making a nuisance of himself. He was one in a long line of Dirks which stretched by into Seumas's past as a string of hounds. Seumas had never felt whole without a dog, though he knew the islanders made fun of him for it. They ate their dogs, raised purely on a diet of fruit, while he turned his meat-eating pets into hunting hounds.

As they rounded the point, they came across great activity. Industrious carpenters and priests were in the process of building thirty great tipairua canoes. Mighty trees had been felled for the twin hulls of each canoe, across which their platforms would be built. On these platforms would stand two masts, to bear twin crab-claw sails. And two huts, to store the food for the voyage to the Land-of-Mists. These were invasion craft, built to travel thousands of miles to go to war.

Kieto was supervising the building of the canoes, with his older brother, Totua. They were drawing pictures in the sand with a stick, using the marks of writing brought back by the great Hiro from his travels in the direction of Tooa o te ra on the windflower. The priests were studying the marks intently. None were used to this new form of communication and great concentration was required.

On seeing the Pict approach, Kieto said something to his brother Totua, and then left his side.

'Seumas?' said Kieto, looking up as the three approached the group of priests. 'How are you feeling today?'

'Much like any man who has lost the better part of himself,' replied Seumas.

Kieto put a hand on his shoulder in sympathy. Now that Kieto was a highly eminent ariki, second only on the island to its two kings Tangiia and Karika, he carried great mana. But Seumas was also considered to be a distinguished warrior and he too bore much mana. So the two were able to be familiar with one another, without fear of harm.

'Yes, she was a wonderful woman.'

Standing close to Kieto were twins, a boy and girl, about eighteen years of age. These were the ariki's children, Hupa the girl, and Kapu the boy. Both were carrying bows and quivers of arrows, made for them by Seumas. Both were wearing necklaces of shark's teeth as a symbol of the high rank of their father and thus of themselves as his heirs.

'We are sorry our aunt has gone,' said Hupa, who was more of a warrior than a maiden. 'We miss her.'

It was rumoured that Hupa was the head of a secret society, formed of women warriors. They called themselves the Whakatane, which literally means 'turn into a man', but in essence meant to act like a man, to do manly things. It was said that Hupa's name within the society was Wairaka. In legend Wairaka was a chief's daughter who saved a troubled voyager canoe while the men were distracted by the beauty of a foreign landscape. She was the first Whakatane and Seumas had heard that Hupa and her followers made sacrifices to Wairaka in a sacred place.

'Thank you, Hupa, I'm sure she misses you too.'

Seumas was himself a little distracted at that moment. He was thinking about the coming invasion of Land-of-Mists. It was with some despair that Seumas realized there was nothing which could stop it now.

'Your plans seem to be progressing,' he said to Kieto in a disapproving tone. 'When is the fleet to sail?'

'Before Hine-keha shows her full face.'

'Within the month. And we sail first to Raiatea?'

Kieto nodded, warily, knowing that Seumas was torn in his loyalties.

'I must make sacrifices to my atua, at Tapu-tapu atia, Most Sacred, Most Feared. Raiatea is my birthplace and where my ancestors reside. Then we shall sail to Tongatapu, where the fleets from other islands will gather prior to sailing to the land Kupe first discovered, the Land-of-Mists.'

'Kupe did not discover it first,' growled the elderly Seumas. 'There are people living there.'

'You know what I mean,' replied Kieto.

'You will not win this war, Kieto.'

Kieto sighed. 'Do not go over this again, Seumas. It is inevitable. It is unstoppable. There will be voyager canoes from Hawaii, from Rangiroa, Manahiki, the Hiva Islands, Samoa, Tonga, Tuvalu, Tokelau, Rapanui – even from Fiji. The Oceanians gather in great numbers. Never before has a flotilla of this size been assembled against a common enemy.'

'Enemy? They have done nothing to you.'

'But given time, they will. We shall invade them, before they invade us. It's as simple as that.'

Overhead there were some dark birds wheeling through the skies. These were saddlebacks, brown with orange wattles, and were considered a good omen to the priests and carpenters who were building the canoes. In legend a pair of saddlebacks had guided seafarers from Hawaiki to a safe haven. These two became the pets of a tohunga named Ngatoro-i-rangi. It was believed that they could foretell the coming weather.

In point of fact, saddlebacks were sacred birds.

Seumas noticed the birds and a rash and unworthy idea came to him which he grasped without thinking.

'May I borrow your bow and arrow, Kapu?' he said, reaching for the weapon.

The boy-twin handed the weapon to his 'uncle'.

Seumas fitted the arrow to the cord and drew back on the bow. Aiming into the air he released the missile. It flew straight and true, striking a saddleback through the breast. The unfortunate bird fell to the beach. Dirk, like the good hunting dog he was, ran and picked up the bird in his gentle jaws, carrying it back to his master.

The priests around Kieto let out a cry of shock and some put their faces into their hands. Even Boy-girl was appalled by what Seumas had done. Kieto stared at his friend in disbelief and then shook his head sadly.

'I know what you have tried to do, Seumas, but it will not work. The bad luck will fall on your head, not on ours. This is no way to stop the fleet sailing.'

Seumas stared into the ariki's eyes. Then he let the bow fall to the sands and walked away. Craig followed him. Now thirty years of age, Craig was a mature man, one who had travelled almost as widely as his father, but even he was shocked by what Seumas had done.

'That was not good, Father,' said Craig, catching him up. 'You must have known that such an act would not be enough to stop Kieto. *Nothing* can stop him now. Even if he were to announce tomorrow that he was not leading the invasion, another would spring up and take his place.'

Seumas shook his head grimly. 'I know – I didn't think. There is still inside me a little of the impetuosity of my days as a Pict, running through the heather of Albainn. Then we did things first and thought about them afterwards. I killed your adopted mother's first husband that way. Struck him down without a second thought, so that I could steal the sword he carried.'

He sighed. 'Dorcha was able to curb my rash acts, when she was around. I would always stop and think, would Dorcha approve? Now she's gone and see how quickly I slip back into my old ways. Well, the deed is done, the bird is dead.'

Dirk came trotting up, still carrying the saddleback carefully in his mouth. Craig took it from him and tossed it away into the rainforest.

'Stay, boy,' said Seumas, as Dirk looked confused and about ready to dash into the undergrowth to retrieve the bird. 'Leave it, Dirk.'

'Father, you must dine with Linloa and me tonight. She is cooking fish and sweet potatoes. I mentioned I might be bringing you back to our hut and she was pleased.'

Seumas knew this was untrue. Linloa was very good, but she had fed and watered Seumas over the past month, while Dorcha had been ill with the jellyfish poison. Seumas knew she would have had enough of her father-in-law for the time being, for he had not been a good guest while his wife had lain dying. Restless, complaining, and becoming irritated with his infant grandchildren, Seumas had not made Linloa's hut a happy place.

'No, I prefer to be on my own tonight, if you don't mind, son. It's good of you to ask, but there are things to think about. I'd better make some sort of sacrifice to the gods, to try to appease them for killing that innocent bird.'

He stared into the sunset. 'Why did Dorcha have to go and die now?' he said bitterly.

'We all have to die, Father.'

'Yes, but box jellyfish do not normally kill adults, not even elderly ones. Your mother died on purpose, I'm sure of that – she went because she wanted to go. She could have held on, recovered, but she left me anyway.'

Craig did not disagree with his father.

'Perhaps – perhaps she had experienced the best of her life and felt she had to go? You know she often said to me, "Craig, if I die tomorrow I will have had a good life, one with more happiness than a woman has a right to expect." It is a great compliment to you, Seumas, that she felt that way.'

Craig did not know how to deal with his father when he was in this kind of mood. Seumas was still an alien to him in many ways. The Pict had once told his son that his head was still full of strange white winters. Craig was not able to understand this, not able to comprehend what he had never known. There was a desperate need in Craig to really understand his father, to know him deeply, but all Craig's efforts at this ended in failure. He realized after a while that he would never be able to get inside Seumas. His father was a great mystery to him and this fact made the young man very unhappy.

'She did it on purpose, to upset me,' Seumas growled. 'She always wanted her revenge. She never really forgave me for killing her first husband, you know.'

'She loved you to distraction, you silly old man,' cried Boy-girl, who had come up behind them quietly. 'I've never heard such nonsense. Dorcha punish you after all this time? – oh yes – she was prepared to die in pain to do it, was she? Go home and drink some kava, Seumas. If you're not careful I shall be consoling you so much, you'll be inviting me to share your bed, and then you'll have something to complain about.'

'You'll never get into my bed, you old witch,' growled Seumas. 'You keep away from me.'

'I'd rather sleep with Dirk, these days,' she sniffed, smiling. 'He snarls less than you do.'

The goddesses and gods of Oceania held a gathering somewhere within the Twelve Worlds on earth, under the sea, or in the heavens. Only Io did not attend. This was because the Old One never left his dwelling in the Twelfth World. His pleasure or displeasure could be felt in the lower levels, when it was necessary for him to make his mood known, so there was no need for him to leave his place of residence. In respect of this gathering, the subject of which he knew in advance, his messengers let it be known that he would not give an opinion and that his state was too lofty to join any campaign.

It was noted by the other gods that some of Io's celestial Mareikura, his personal messengers and attendants in the Twelfth World, were hovering quietly within sight and sound.

When Oceania itself was in turmoil, the gods were also in a state of agitation. There was no separate earth, for mankind, gods or ancestor spirits: all dwelt in the same place and felt the same effects of any upheaval. They were either for the invasion, or against it. No god or atua could be impartial, except perhaps Io, who had the right to reserve judgment until such time as he felt it necessary to give it.

'We all know what is happening amongst the men and women of Oceania,' said Tawhaki, the God of Thunder, whose armpits gave birth to Uira, the Goddess of Lightning. 'There is to be a war, but such a war as Oceania has never known before. Our peoples – those who live on the islands of our blue waters – are going on a long voyage to a strange land. There to do battle with an alien people who worship gods not of our ilk. What I ask is, do we let them go alone?'

Papa, Goddess of the Earth, nodded sagely. 'You are saying we should go with them?'

'He is saying,' said Tane, God of the Forests and Lord of the Fairies, 'that the enemy will have an unfair advantage. They will have their gods to assist them, while our people will be without supernatural guidance.'

Hine, that powerful goddess with many forms and faces, including death, was surprisingly not in favour of going to war, even to assist Oceanians against an unknown foe.

'You know I have many shapes and colours,' she told the other gods, 'from the Indigo Lady to Lady of the Early Gentle Floating Shadows. I can be useful to you in war, in several ways, and will go if there is general agreement that we should, but I fear this conflict will end in disaster for us all.'

Ira, Mother of the Stars, spoke quietly in favour of supporting the Oceanians in their endeavours.

'We may find these new people need new gods and goddesses, and here we are to fulfil that need.'

Next, Rangi, the Great Sky-God, spoke, evoking a response from Tangaroa, the Great Sea-God.

'What say you, Prince of the Ocean? Do we travel with the fleet and battle against these strange gods of these alien people – the gods of the Celts and the Angles? Do we fight in those dark skies above the Land-of-Mists? Do we battle with them in their dark ocean? Shall Tane go to war in the gloomy forests where only one kind of tree seems to grow? Will Rongo trample their ugly vegetation underfoot?'

Tangaroa deliberated long and hard before answering. 'As to whether we go or stay, I do not think we have a choice. I feel an attraction for this island which is impossible to resist. You feel it too, all of you, or we would not be here today. But are we all capable of fighting? You, Rangi, are not the warring kind. Nor Papa. Myself, Tawhaki, Whatu, Maomao, Pele – we have weapons of thunderbolts, hail, wind and fire. Others, such as Oro, are ready armed for war. But many of you will be struggling without weapons, with just your own strength, your own will.'

'No matter,' said Ra, interrupting, 'it is clear we must all go. If Rangi must fight it will be with their Sky-God and the struggle will be equal, in so much as Rangi and the Other will both have the same weapons. It must be on these terms, that each will fight his matching equal. Tawhaki will fight their God of Thunder, I shall fight their Sun-God.'

'And all of us must go?' asked Nareau, the God of Spiders. 'Even those of us regarded as lesser gods? Moko, the God of Lizards? Dakuwanga, the Shark God?'

'All,' said Ra, 'with only one exception – the Old One, Io, will remain to watch over our domains. If you have no counterpart with whom to fight in single combat, then you will serve those of us who have. You may act as weapon-bearers, you may stoke the forges of the weapon-makers, whatever is necessary. So, are we in agreement – the gods of Oceania will go to war?'

'We will,' came back the consenting chorus.

Ra replied, 'Then let us gather with the fleet at Tongatapu and follow them into the Unknown Region.'

Craig left his father and wandered back to the hut he shared with his wife and three children. Despite his savage appearance – the three bars tattooed across the bridge of his nose and over his cheeks – he was no more ready than his father to go to war. Consequently he was in a contemplative mood. The Hivan warrior in him urged him to take his well-built frame and expend his energy on the battle-field, winning honours and glory. The father and husband in him however, which was rapidly becoming the more dominant part, told him to stay at home.

Entering his hut, he rubbed noses with the small, round-limbed Linloa, whose cooking was only second to her good nature. Craig loved his wife in that comfortable way which some successful men manage to acquire. Celeb-rities such as himself, the greatest drummer the world had known, could have had many affairs, several wives.

Craig was one of those men who had known dazzling achievements at a time in his life when they could have caused great conceit, but he managed to remain level-headed and faithful to one woman, because that was his nature. So long as his marriage and his home life was stable, Craig was cap-able of the most outstanding accomplishments. Take that rock base away from him and he became insecure and uncertain.

'And how is the greatest Beauty that Rarotonga has ever known?' he said, kissing Linloa's lips on entering.

She placed a fresh ei on his head, made of frangipani and flame tree blossoms.

'Ever? I think the Princess Kula might have something to say about that – or perhaps some of those virgins, the crew of Ru's *Princely Flower*? Beauty? I think not.'

'In my eyes you are unequalled,' he said, smiling.

'Now that's different. In the eyes of a short-sighted man. Yes, I can accept that.'

'I'm not short-sighted!'

'You must be if you think I'm beautiful.'

She turned away from him but he could see that she was happy.

'I'm – I'm *pleasant* to look at, I'll grant you that, husband. If that satisfies you, then I'm a contented woman.' Then she turned back to look at him, her face intent, and added fiercely, 'But if you ask who on Rarotonga has the most *love* in her heart for her man, why then you may compliment me, husband.'

He laughed and kissed her gently, 'You are a funny mixture of passion and homeliness, Linloa. I suppose I must be the luckiest of men – I *know* I am. Where are my children? I must see them before they fall asleep.'

'I'm afraid you're too late,' she answered, now stirring the sauce for the fish, 'they exhausted themselves running around the boatbuilders today. They're already asleep on their mats. You can give them a goodnight kiss if you like.'

He went to the back of the hut, where the delicious smells of his wife's cooking were hovering in the air and driving the house spirits crazy, to find three little curled bundles on a mat of woven pandanus leaves.

The youngest and the eldest looked so sweet and magical, with their brows clear and their skin so bright. The middle child, the gods watch over her, was unfortunately extremely ugly. This did not matter to Craig of course, and Linloa, like any mother, would refute it hotly. She saw only beauty in *all* her children. But it was a fact, the middle child was as ugly as a baby hog and perhaps would suffer a little for it, though she had a quiet, placid nature and was a sunny child in all other aspects.

There was a god who was responsible for and watched over such children as the middle-child. The god's name was Punga, who first gave the world bugs and beetles, and reptiles of a repulsive nature, and grotesque fish like the stone fish, the sting ray, the sunfish, the blowfish. Punga was the God of Ugly Creatures, and as such, his creations were special to him. The homely, the hideous, even the ghastly, were cherished by him. This middle-child was one of Punga's charges. Punga loved dearly all the world's ugly creatures and protected them against unjustified mockery and vindictive bullying. Punga would not let the infant suffer too much under the taunts of others.

'Sleep well, my little ones,' whispered Craig. 'May your dreams bring you spiritual riches.'

After the meal was eaten, Linloa enquired guardedly after Seumas.

'I invited him back for the meal,' said Craig, 'but he wouldn't come.'

'Why not?'

'He thought he had imposed enough. He thinks he's becoming a cranky old man.'

'He is,' said Linloa, 'but we love him just the same. Still, I'm glad he did not come with you. We have not been together alone for many days now. It is pleasant just to sit here with you in Ra's dying rays and listen to your voice.'

Craig sat with his back against the wall of the hut and watched the sun swoop down below the horizon, like a hawk stooping on a rat. He too was glad his father had not joined them, though he felt guilty for being selfish. There would not be many evenings left to spend with his wife, before he went away to war. Craig needed such evenings to remember, to sustain him, for the voyage itself would be hard and lonely.

And at the end of that journey, why nothing but a bloody war with an unknown enemy!

Yes indeed, he would need such memories to keep him from the darkness, in the time ahead.

Punga, the God of Ugly Creatures, felt a great tenderness towards the mortal Craig. It was not often that mortals prayed directly to the gods themselves. They usually went through intermediaries – through their atua ancestors – but Craig seemed especially indebted to Punga because of his protection of Craig's child. Thus the god was wont to protect the father of the child also, because of that man's strict devotion.

Punga was also going to this war in the Land-of-Mists and while he was there he resolved to watch out for his charge, the young Craig, to keep him as safe as was godly possible. The beautiful-ugly child needed such a father and Punga would try to make sure he returned to her unharmed.

There was a bond between man and god which both cherished.

PART TWO

Lioumere's iron teeth

1

The fleet set sail at the end of Breadfruit season, when the winds were favourable and the currents set true. There was a brisk sea and the tipairua canoes were running dogs carrying logs of foam in their mouths. The crew were kept busy taking in and letting out sail, seeking the maximum thrust from the wind. As always the bailers were occupied with their half-coconuts and severed gourds, shovelling out the excess sea water. Lines were run out behind, in the hope of coming across a shoal of bonito or barracuda. All the signs were favourable for a good voyage to Raiatea, once the home of Chief Kieto.

Seumas, who was travelling in the second canoe, behind the chief's, was shocked to learn his captain was Polahiki, the Hivan fisherman who wove his way in and out of the Pict's life like a rusty old needle drawing a filthy thread.

'How did you get here?' he asked Polahiki. 'The last time I saw you was off Aitutaki, when we returned with Prince Ru from Rapanui.'

'Came in on the evening tide three days ago,' said Polahiki, picking a scab and wiping the deposit on the tiller oar. 'Kieto was short of captains for his thirty tipairua, so he asked me. I am a good navigator, you know.'

It was true; Polahiki might have been the dirtiest sailor on the high seas, but he knew the ocean and he was familiar with voyager canoes.

'You better get us to where we're going, or I'll strangle you with my bare hands,' growled Seumas. 'And stay downwind of me.'

Polahiki sniffed. 'I'm captain of this craft – I go where I please. If you want to get off, be my guest. I see your manners haven't improved any. You're still a bad-tempered goblin. The only difference is, you're an *old* goblin now, which is worse.'

Seumas saw that he was going to have to put up with Polahiki, at least until they reached Raiatea. Over the first few days he kept out of the captain's way, but curiosity got the better of him in the end. There were still some holes in Polahiki's history which had never satisfactorily been explained to Seumas. The fisherman had been left behind with the Maori, when Kieto, Seumas and Dorcha, with Boy-girl and Kikamana, had fled from the Land of the Long White Cloud.

One evening, after Polahiki had taken some readings of the kaveinga, the natural star paths, Seumas spoke with him on the matter of his missing days in the land of the beautiful pohutukawa tree, with its magnificent scarlet blossoms.

'What happened to you, after we left with the old Maori man – where did you go?'

'I went to live in the cave once owned by Kurangai-tuku, the ogress who held you prisoner.'

'This much I know,' said Seumas, sitting on the edge of the platform in the bows, so that the cool hissing spray bathed his feet. There was starlight on the water ahead, picking out the green wavelets in the darkness. Kieto's canoe was up in front and a little to the starboard of Polahiki's craft. 'But you mentioned that you were involved in some fighting.'

'Not exactly fighting,' Polahiki replied. 'You would not believe what happened to me. I was the sole survivor of a massacre ...'

'You usually are,' grunted Seumas, knowing Polahiki's ability to survive was his main skill. 'But go on.'

'Perhaps after I tell you my story, you will consider me worthy enough to share the food in your basket? Well, I was sitting outside my cave one day, when I was approached by a young chieftain of one of the Maori clans that lived locally. He told me to fetch my war club and join him in an expedition to a distant pa, where a sorcerer named Paka had taken a young maiden by force. Her name was Rona.

'When we were close to the place where Paka had the girl, an evil spirit told the young chieftain a lie, saying Rona had now been taken to Puke-tapu, near Manukau. So we went to this new place, but when we came near I realized how dangerous it was. There were skeletons of warriors scattered over the countryside, and rotting corpses, and freshly dead men. We soon found out how and why these men had been killed.

'There were two sorcerers living in the pa at Puke-tapu, by the names of Puarata and Tautohito. On the walls of the pa they had erected this massive wooden head, in the skull of which gathered hundreds of powerful atua. When a force such as ours approached the pa, the head would shout in so loud a voice that it stopped the heart of any man who heard it.'

'If it shouted at your army, why are you here?' asked Seumas. 'Why aren't you lying dead with the Maori?'

Polahiki adjusted the tiller just a fraction, according to his sense of the direction of the swell, and then continued his story.

'I was coming to that. Obviously I didn't die, because I'm here – though even death is not always an end to things, as I'll explain to you in a minute. Anyway, as we approached the pa this terrible wooden head, taller than five men, began to bellow in the most frightening tones. Its thick wooden lips below the nose that ran from brow to mouth, did not move, but wisps of something like mist came flying from them.'

'Atua,' muttered Seumas. 'Powerful spirits.'

'Precisely. Looking around me I saw that my companions had stopped in their tracks, their eyes bulging, their hearts pounding. Greenstone weapons fell to the earth, some point-first, sticking there. I could see the rib cages around me and it was as if the warriors had dwarves inside their chests, punching in fury to get out. Then by ones and twos their hearts burst and they fell dead on the ground.'

'Still ...' Seumas said, but Polahiki held up his free hand for silence.

'I survived. Yes, for my ears were so full of wax I could hardly hear the great head shouting.' He grinned with a mouthful of rotten teeth. 'Sometimes it pays to be a dirty old fisherman who never washes his lugholes. I felt the shaking of things around me – the tree roots and the meadows beneath my feet – but as for the voice itself, it was like distant thunder, or the sound of a waterfall deep in a forest.

'I can tell you, I ran from that place, intending to go all the way back to my cave. On the way there I met another force, with a great Maori chief called Hakawau at its head. I told him what had happened. He said we had been tricked, that the maiden Rona was still with the tohunga Paka at Rangitoto. He forced me to join them and once again I went into battle with the Maori.

'This time, however, Hakawau was victorious, since he had brought with him his own potent atua. Hakawau had great mana and easily defeated Paka and rescued the girl. We then went on to fight Puarata and Tautohito at Puke-tapu. Before we got there Hakawau told his men to give me a good bath because he said he could not stand the stink. The bastards washed out my ears and made me vulnerable to the raving of the head.'

'But you survived yet *again?*' asked Seumas.

'Naturally. I am one of life's great survivors, for this time Hakawau's atua swept away the evil spirits from their nest inside the terrible wooden head. All the head could do was wail pitifully – sort of a thin whining sound made by the wind that blew across its mouth – and Hakawau's men stormed the pa. Hakawau went into the house of the two sorcerers, but did not kill them there and then. He refused their gifts of meat and kava, and when he left he struck the threshold of their house with the heel of his hand.

'When I went into the house a little while later, everyone inside was dead.'

Seumas nodded. 'That's some story, if it's true.'

'If it's true?' cried Polahiki, his hand jerking the tiller. 'Of course it's true – ask anyone.'

'Well, there's no one to ask, is there?' said the sixty-year-old Pict. 'We're a little short of Maori witnesses in this part of the world.'

'It is true, every word. What's more, my troubles weren't over. When I finally got back to my cave, I found it occupied. There was a man named Te Atarahi living there, if *living* is the right word to use.'

'You mentioned something about that before.'

'Yes, I did, didn't I? Well, if you saw this fellow Te Atarahi you wouldn't complain about how bad *I* smell. He stank so much the stench offended even me. His head was quite normal, except there was no hair on it, but the rest of him was just bones with skin dripping from them. He was a corpse, I tell you, but with a normal head – which looked huge on a skeleton.

'He was perched in front of my cave like a hunched bird on a stone, drinking the dew from the flax blooms. When I went near him he flapped his bony arms in a threatening manner and I was alarmed enough to run off.

'I went down to the village and told them what I'd seen and they told me the man's name. They said they'd buried him a year previously, dead as a post. Now here he was, come back from the dead, to steal my cave from me.

'Some of the villagers came back with me and we managed to chase the creature off into the wilderness. I threw stones at him that time but he kept coming back again, to haunt me. I noticed after a time that flesh began to gather on his bones like bird lime on a bare branch and one day when he came back he seemed quite normal. "Where did you live?" I asked him. "Did you have a house?" He told me that his house had been on the edge of the village. "Well, go back there and live in it," I told him angrily. "Stop pestering me for my cave."

'And he did, and that was the last I ever saw of him.'

Seumas shook his head, wonderingly. Some strange things had happened to him in his time, in the land of the Maori as well as on enchanted islands, and he knew that all things were possible. Polahiki had come out of the Land of the Long White Cloud reluctantly, so there was no reason for him to lie.

The Pict had to admit that Polahiki's adventures were interesting, but he did not want the man for a basket-sharer, and said so quite brusquely.

'Suit yourself,' sniffed the captain. 'You and that son of yours think you're better than other people ...'

Seumas did not want to listen to this and moved aft to sleep.

He was woken roughly in the early morning. Craig was standing over him. Behind Craig was Hupa, the girl-twin of Kieto. Her brother was with their father, but she had elected to travel on the second canoe. There were occasions when she and her brother quarrelled violently and both thought it best they were not cooped up together on the same canoe.

Seumas sat up and rubbed his eyes. He was dripping with salt-spray, but that was not unusual. Most sailors spent half the voyage wet and cold, which was why they had to be so hardy. They developed a layer of fat which protected them from the rigours of their journeys.

'What is it?' he asked. 'Why am I woken?'

He was an old man now, not required for watch duties.

Then he realized why. Around the craft Seumas could make out mountainous waves building in the darkness: waves with huge white crests. They were in a vast trough, but none of the other vessels in the fleet could be seen.

White spray blinded him, whipping into his face from the dipping bows. It stung his eyes and cheeks. He sat up, coughing and spluttering, wondering how he had stayed asleep until now.

'We're having a visit from the god Apu Hau,' said Craig. 'Polahiki needs all hands, Father.'

'I can see that,' Seumas replied.

He climbed to his feet just as the canoe hit the wall of a wave and tipped at a steep angle. Craig, who already had a hand-hold, gripped his arm. Stores wrapped in pandanus leaves bound with sennit cord went sliding off the edge of the deck into the water. A dugout canoe, used to reach shore in shallow harbours, strained at its lashings but thankfully remained tied. A man on the port side went overboard, quickly lost in the spindrift flying off the hull.

'A line,' cried Craig, immediately leaping overboard with one end of a rope.

Seumas quickly snatched at the other end and tied it to the mast. He saw his son disappear into the black maw of the ocean, swallowed instantly by the heaving darkness. Then his head appeared a few moments later, awash with foam, like a coconut husk being swept backwards as the canoe surged into a new wave that seemed to lift itself from as far down as the sea bed.

'Back there,' shouted a mariner, pointing to a form which had bobbed out of the water. 'Two lengths to your left!'

Craig, who now had the line tied around his middle, struck out for the drowning sailor. Reaching him he kicked sideways, to get behind the man. Wisely he did not want to be pulled down to a watery grave with a panicking man. Finally, he had him in a head lock as Seumas and the others began to haul in.

While this rescue was in progress one of the masts suddenly let out a tremendous *crack* and snapped in two. Its sail flew away like a flapping ghost, out over high ranges of waves with flecked and twisted tops. The broken spar crashed to the deck, narrowly missing Polahiki and the man with him, as the pair of them struggled at the steering oar. Ropes whipped through the air, lashing at men's bodies. One sailor screamed as the flail cut into his bare back.

Now the voyager canoe was in a funnel of water, with two great waves on either side, running down a valley with its one good sail. There was respite from the furious gusts down in this trough, but it was a dangerous business. If one or both of those waves folded over it would swamp the tipairua and possibly take it down so far that it would not rise again.

The night above was swirling madness, and even the stars appeared to be spinning, as the wind sucked up the ocean and whipped it to froth. Polahiki was clearly trying to follow the kaveinga called Kau Panonga Roroa – the Long Group – but was continually being swept off his course. The extent of leeway drift was lost in the tipairua's wake and the captain would have few of the more reliable natural navigational aids to assist him in his direction. Only the bright, stable Sacred Timber constellation flashed in and out of view, but this was of little help when the other stars churned in the night's whirlpool.

Polahiki yelled to his helpers, asking them to watch the ocean depths for signs of any te lapa, those underwater streaks of light which are visible at night.

No such reports came back to his ears. One more navigational aid was absent.

The tipairua broke out of the end of the wide tube of water just as Seumas and the other mariners hauled the struggling pair back on to the platform. But rescuer and rescued man were exhausted by their ordeal and simply lay there like fish dragged from the depths and left to gasp out their last. Seumas too was weary from the hauling. He was no longer a young man who could go from one task to another without stopping for breath.

'We nearly lost you there, Craig,' he said, stroking his son's wet hair. 'But it was a brave thing to do.'

'I didn't think,' wheezed Craig. 'I went without thinking too much.'

'It's the only way,' said a mariner. 'If you stop to think, you don't do it, and a man drowns.'

'It might have been two,' muttered Seumas, 'but never mind that ...'

The storm raged for a long time, until finally it faded away with the coming of the dawn. The tipairua slid out into calmer seas in an area of the ocean unfamiliar to Polahiki or any of the other navigators on board. Apu Hau had carried the canoe into strange waters and the Farseeing-virgin Kikamana, ancient and wizened, believed it might be for a purpose.

'The gods are with us on this voyage,' she told Seumas, 'so why would Apu Hau or any of the storm gods try to wreck our canoe? It must be that we have been carried here for some reason to our advantage.'

'More likely that fool Polahiki failed to avoid the storm like the other captains,' grumbled Seumas.

'I'm sorry, Father,' replied Craig. 'You're wrong this time. Polahiki stood no chance of avoiding it. I was standing on deck when a squall swept into the fleet from starboard – it carried us out of line and scattered the other canoes. There was nothing Polahiki could do.'

The captain was at that moment sleeping off his night's ordeal, having spent all of it at the steering oar himself. Seumas had to concede that the fisherman, as old and cranky as himself, was a good sailor. Apu Hau was God of the Fierce Squall. No doubt his son was right.

Atanua, Goddess of the Dawn, rose now that the sky had been cleared of darkness by Atea the God of Space. She wore her rosy garments and her face was flushed with pink beauty. Some akiaki, fairy terns, were seen flying in the direction of Niuhiti no pare on the windflower. This was the direction in which the damaged craft, like a wounded butterfly on a breeze-swept pool, was being carried.

'Let us go with the wind,' said Kikamana, 'and see where we fetch up.'

'So long as we don't fetch up in Manu's Armpit,' grunted Seumas, referring to a constellation of stars.

The Oceanians, his son included, stared at him in such a puzzled way he suddenly realized that once again he had forgotten how different were their separate cultures. He had meant of course that they might find themselves dead and up amongst the stars. However, Oceanians would not expect their spirits to go higher than the trees after death – where the atua was known to cluster – and most would anticipate going under the waves rather than up into the sky.

'Never mind,' he sighed. 'Forget I said it.'

They were in a windless calm, the air sweltering and thick. Men and women swooned in the midday heat, giddy with the oppressive atmosphere. Sluggish waters drooled from the mouths of rips, past which the canoe moved at a maddeningly slow pace, as if drifting through a dream. In the distance an island came into view, a hogback ridge running across its dark form, the main peak a plateau, like a cloven hoof against the skyline. At the back of a beach scattered with white driftwood resembling the bones of monsters was a thick jungle of cabbage trees.

'Dead-pig island,' said Craig. 'I passed this once in my travels, when searching for my father.'

'You know its name?' asked Hupa, standing with him by the deck hut inside which most of the crew and passengers were finding shade to sleep. 'You've been on it?'

'No, it frightened me so much I didn't stop – I gave it the nickname. It looks like a pig lying on its back, don't you think? A slaughtered pig.'

'Is this where Apu Hau wants us to go? I can't think what would be here for us, can you?'

Craig at first inclined to the same opinion. He wiped away the irritating bodies of insects which had stuck to the sweat on his face. Looking at the island he could see a high column of cloud resting on its shoulders. To his father clouds were a source of darkness, but to an Oceanian clouds were associated with light. Ao, God of Clouds, was not a dark deity. The fact that the island had a tall white cloud as a headdress indicated that the place was not entirely forbidding.

'We must search this island,' he said. 'Will you come with me? I'll need someone at my back.'

Hupa took up her bow and quiver of arrows.

'I am ready for any adventure,' she said. 'Shall I wake my companions?'

She meant the three other maidens who were constantly in her company.

They too were armed like warriors, much to the disapproval of the men on board. Craig believed they were part of her secret society, the Whakatane.

'I think it best if we go alone. If too many of us stumble around in a drugged state, on an island with unknown qualities, we're liable to lose someone. You and I seem to be the only clear-headed ones at the moment. I think we should go alone and see what we can find first.'

'I agree,' she replied, eagerly.

Hupa was a small, slim but athletic-looking maiden, whose lithe movements had attracted many a suitor. She had however discouraged any lover from entering her life. Her face had a fresh, round, open appearance, set with a small nose and clear brown eyes. Her hair was cut unusually short for a woman, though her pretty – some said boyish – features made up for what some men regarded as a strong defect. However, their prejudices might have had something to do with the fact that when competing with these men, that which she lacked in physical strength she made up for in sheer determination and skill.

Craig found her company pleasant, as he would any young person eager for experience in the world. She displayed no real traits of bad temper, except with herself when she failed in some physical feat, like not hitting the target with her arrows, or being beaten in a running race by a youth. Then she would chastise herself verbally in front of an audience, careless of those who heard her call herself a 'stupid vahine'.

Once they had moored the craft with a lump of coral for an anchor the pair took the dugout canoe and paddled towards the shore. Craig kept a wary lookout for signs of the Ponaturi, those savage sea fairies who would tear someone to pieces as quickly as would barracuda in the water. He remembered being told of his father's experience with those creatures, in just such a place as this.

'Why are you looking like that?' asked Hupa.

'No reason,' said Craig, not wishing to frighten her.

'You're wondering if there are sea fairies here, aren't you?' she muttered. 'I considered that too. But I think they would have been on us by now, if they were around.'

Craig allowed himself a smile. He was underestimating this female warrior. She knew exactly what the world was all about and needed no protection from him.

After passing over a lagoon where the dead coral lay broken and grey like old bones on the shallow bottom, they reached the beach behind which stood the army of cabbage trees. These proved to be very dense, so the pair walked along the weed-covered sands until they found an opening. Just before going through the gap in the ti, Hupa gave a shout and called Craig's attention to a footprint in the sand.

'Look at this!' she cried, excitedly. 'It's huge!'

Craig stared down at the massive spoor of what was surely a monster of some kind. The print was deep, which meant the creature was heavy as well as large. On first glance it might have been the footprint of a large man or woman, possibly a giant. The bridge between the pad and heel was narrow, revealing a high instep. But it was the toes that showed this creature was not entirely human. They were long and thin, more like fingers than toes, and there were only four of them. There was no 'big' toe. The gaps between were wide which made the footprint spread like a banana tree leaf.

'I had a feeling something nasty like this lived here,' muttered Craig. 'This is not an ordinary island.'

'How do you know the creature is malicious?' asked Hupa. 'It might be friendly. Could be one of Apu Hau's children – perhaps that's why he led us here?'

'I'd like that to be true.'

The couple then went through the gap in the ti. A short way into the trees they came to a wooden wall. This took the form of a palisade fashioned from massive tree trunks with sharpened tops. It was the tallest fence either of them had ever seen. It reached to the top of the rainforest canopy. In one or two places there were narrow tunnels in the sand going under the palisade. It was as if Oceanian rats as big as men had burrowed underneath the enormous posts.

Walking this way and that, the pair failed to find any gates or door, so eventually they scrambled down one of the tunnels, to come up in a village on the other side.

It seemed deserted at first, except that there were fresh smells around: the aroma of cooking, coconut oil, fermenting breadfruit mash. And the animal dung was fresh and ripe, with hundreds of flies buzzing around it. Here and there half-eaten fruit lay, the juices still oozing from the flesh.

Yet the huts and houses in the village were all in a state of disrepair. There were holes in the roofs. Thatch walls were hanging loose from posts. Totems had fallen to the ground and were lying face-down in the mud. Pigs were roaming loose amongst the chickens. Dogs had fouled the pathways and lay scratching in run-down vegetable gardens.

'Someone doesn't care how they live,' said Hupa. 'Look at the state the village is in.'

Almost the moment she spoke, a figure poked a shy head around a doorway. Some whispers passed between hidden bodies. Finally many villagers began to emerge. Unlike their houses the people looked to be in good condition. Their hair was glossy, their bodies plump and clean, their eyes bright with health. Only their melancholy looks gave any indication that things were not well on this small island.

'Greetings,' said Craig. 'I am Son-of-Seumas, a Hivan by birth. My red hair and blue eyes are natural and come from my father's people, so you need not worry about them. This is Hupa Ariki, daughter of the great chieftain, Kieto.'

'Hail, strangers,' said a fat man who appeared to be the chief, for he was wearing a headdress. 'Welcome to the larder of Lioumere-the-Ogress.'

Hupa looked askance at the man. 'Larder? That is a joke, I hope.'

The chief grinned and made a sign to his warriors, who immediately surrounded Hupa and Craig.

Craig reached to his waistband for his club. Hupa managed to string an arrow. But the villagers were on them before they could use their weapons. The luckless pair were soon disarmed and forced to kneel before the fat chief. This personage grinned at them in a friendly way and then shook his head.

'It is very sad. You have such nice names. You introduced yourselves so politely. Now we have to offer you as sacrifices to Lioumere. I am sorry our hospitality cannot offer anything better than this, but we have no alternative.'

The chief spread his hands and gave them another friendly smile.

Craig glared at the fat man and shook his head. 'The gods will punish you and your people if any harm comes to us. We are part of the great fleet which has been sent to conquer the Land-of-Mists. Out beyond your coral reef lie thirty tipairua canoes, each carrying a hundred warriors. These will be joined by hundreds more, from all over Oceania. You shall be hanged by your thumbs from a beam and your skin flayed from your bones if you touch one hair on this maiden's head. She is the daughter of the ariki leading our vast flotilla!'

'And this warrior, Craig, has great mana. All those who touch him will die in agony,' cried Hupa.

'Alas,' sighed the chief, 'none of this matters, for you see this island is ruled by the ogress, not by us. There are four more villages like this scattered around the island. Each month she takes one person from one village, moving around the other villages in rotation. So you see, we will gain ten months respite while we have you two to offer as sacrifices. Should any more of your people come, they too will become meat for our patroness, the large and very ugly Lioumere.'

Hupa paled, saying, 'You mean she eats people?'

'It is her preferred source of food. She will have fish when we can catch it for her – whole whale-sharks disappear down her gullet in a week – and sometimes dogs or pigs. But she maintains that human bones are nourishing. She will not do without them.'

'Bones?' repeated Hupa

'She loves them.'

'Why not let her starve to death?' snapped Craig. 'Why feed her at all?'

'We have these defences, it is true,' replied the chief in a patient tone, indicating the palisade, 'but they are only strong enough to keep her out while she is in a reasonable frame of mind. However, if she were starving, frenzied, driven mad with hunger, even this palisade would not prevent her from entering. She would smash her way in with great boulders from her mountain, or use a stalactite from her cavern to batter down the walls.

'Then it would be a slaughter, like a wild dog in a chicken coop, like a hawk among a nest of rats. Our bodies would be scattered over the rainforest floor.

'At least in this way we are able to survive as a tribe, albeit we have to let two or three people go during the course of a year. There are some three hundred of us in this village – it does not seem too high a price to pay to be left alone.'

'Except for the families of those you sacrifice,' Hupa said. 'What of them?'

The chief shook his head. 'They do not exist. A young woman is given, an old man, a child. Once they have gone they were never born. No one ever speaks of them again. It is as if they were never here. A man may lose his bride on his wedding night, or a mother her youthful son on his reaching his manhood. They never existed. We continue. We live on. We may not flourish in great numbers, but we still generate.'

'You seem such a strong and fit people. Why not go out and attack her? Finish her. Rid the island of this monster who treats your tribe as livestock.'

The chief shook his head. 'We are too afraid. It was tried once or twice. She threw boulders into our midst. She smashed our skulls with her stone stalactite club. We were slaughtered. Lioumere feasted on the bodies and that kept her wrath in check long enough for our treachery to fade from her thoughts. She does not have a long memory. Her brain is very weak. In fact you could say she is a moron.'

'So, you are cowards,' cried Hupa. 'Strong, fit and able warriors like you!'

'It is because of Lioumere that we are so healthy and sound of limb and body. Those who are given first are the ill and ailing, the crippled, the mad. All our sick people, anyone who is not perfect, is a prime sacrifice. Of course, occasionally we have to sacrifice a healthy person, but for the most part there is usually someone who is not well.'

'Nice people,' muttered Craig to Hupa. 'Throw the sick and helpless to the slaughterer.'

'Put them in the bamboo hut,' said the chief. 'Lioumere will be here in the morning.'

2

Hupa and Craig spent an uncomfortable night in what was clearly a prison hut. The door was made of hardwood set in stone-hard mud walls as thick as the length of a man's arm. There were strong bamboo bars at the small narrow window. The floor too had been pounded until it was as solid as rock. They tried in various ways to escape, but even the roof proved to be made of stout bamboo poles. Guards sat outside the hut all night long and kept peering in at them.

'Look at this,' said Craig, when the dawn came and they could see their surroundings more clearly. 'I don't think many of these people went to their deaths willingly.'

There were pictures scratched into the mud walls, of weeping men and women, of children, of graves and burial mounds.

All morning they were retained in their prison. Water and food was brought to them. No one spoke to them or looked them in the eye. It was as if they were pigs ready for the slaughter. Craig put on a show of being unafraid, but he found it unnecessary, for the plucky girl was quite pragmatic herself. She did not cry out once, nor weep, nor reveal the terror which she undoubtedly felt. Instead she spent her time scowling at the guards and calling them names.

Round about noon the door was opened and two men came in and grasped Craig by the arms.

'No!' yelled Hupa, kicking at one of them. 'Leave him alone.'

But they ignored her. The door was barred against her, after they had hauled Craig outside. They dragged the struggling man near to one of the holes under the wall, which the people used as entrances and exits to the village. There they waited while drummers pounded out rhythms on their hollow-log drums, and flautists played strange tunes on their flutes. Craig felt it was ironic that he should be led to the slaughter to the sound of drums, since they were his instrument. He nodded to one of the drummers who obviously felt he was quite good at his art.

'I could drum you into the ground, my friend,' he said in a dry tone.

The drummer blinked and raised his eyebrows at the man pounding away on the log next to him.

'No, I really could,' said Craig. 'You see this?' He put his tattooed leg forward through the front slit in his tapa bark kilt. 'I'm a Painted Leg. I was once the pride of the Arioi. My instrument was the drum. You have never heard the drums played as I played them. I would like to be modest but I am no liar.'

The chief on hearing this stopped pretending that Craig was not there. He came scurrying across the village with an eager look on his face.

When he reached Craig, still being held tightly by the two guards, he said, 'You were with the Arioi?'

'I was their leader, a king, almost a god.'

'I have heard of the Arioi. It is said they had many canoes with yellow sails. Are there not poets and singers, dancers who do the exotic hura dance? Do they not have storytellers and wrestlers? Do they not put on plays of great renown on stages which are longer than a village is wide?'

'All this is true,' said Craig.

'Prove it,' the chief said. 'Show us how you play the drums.'

One of the men already drumming began to protest, saying that he was playing the rhythm which would bring Lioumere to the village for her meal. The chief waved this protest away impatiently, ordering that Craig should be released.

'You pick up the same rhythm,' he ordered Craig. 'If you're so good that won't be difficult. Perhaps we may allow you to live after all.'

Craig went and stood behind the drums. He was not sure how all these delaying tactics were going to help him in the long run. It seemed logical, however, that if he impressed these people, he might work himself into a position where he had an opportunity to escape. The problem was he knew he could not leave Hupa behind, for by the time he returned with help, she would probably be ogre meat. If he left it would have to be with her at his side.

He picked up the sunbleached, worn drumsticks.

'Behold,' he cried, 'the drumming of a Painted Leg.'

Then his practised hands became a blur to the watchers as he hammered on the hollow logs with sticks the thickness of a man's wrist. The sound of his immaculate and intricate drum rolls, his brilliant interpretation on a rhythmic theme, went out over the rainforest, into the hollows of the distant mountain. He saw the villagers' eyes open wide with disbelief at the speed with which he played. They had never heard anything like it before in their lives. They were mesmerized.

Craig played for quite a time and had almost forgotten about the predicament he was in, when suddenly there was a very loud scream from outside the walls. He stopped drumming and felt the blood drain from his face. The sound had been horrible. Its maker was clearly not human. Then it came again as an ear-piercing shriek, that had the parrots in the trees squawking and screeching themselves.

Villagers put their hands over their ears as the cry penetrated their skulls. Then a monstrous hairy hand and part of an arm appeared, up through one of the holes under the wooden wall. Long fingers with broken, dirty nails began to feel around, as if expecting to find something within reach. Coarser tufted bristles on the knuckles of the fingers stirred the dust as the fingers scrabbled in the dirt, feeling, feeling.

The chief cried, 'Fetch the girl – we must keep this one for his drumming. Fetch the girl!'

But Craig now had weapons in his hands, the two drumsticks, almost as thick as logs. He leapt in front of the warriors and began beating them back with his clubs, keeping them away from the door of the prison hut. Not only was he a drummer, but a great athlete, who could leap and somersault from drum to drum. From outside the village walls, the sound of the shrieking started to become hysterical.

Foul stinking breath came through the cracks between the barricade's posts. Then green spittle oozed through, where Lioumere's saliva dribbled onto the outside of the wall. It too had the nasty odour of rotting meat.

Another high-pitched shriek followed, which might have come from the lips of one insane.

Clearly the ogress was not happy at being kept waiting. The hand on the end of the scrawny, muscled arm began snatching at thin air. Villagers already out of reach scrambled back in panic, away from the clawing hand.

'Get him,' yelled the chief. 'It must be him then. She's becoming impatient. Quickly, quickly – give her the food.'

Once more Craig had become a *thing* rather than a person.

Still his truncheons thudded on the heads and shoulders of warriors who tried to reach him. Finally, one young man got through and tried to wrench the drumsticks from his hands. Craig let one of the sticks go and grasped the youth by the throat, flinging him away with all the force he could muster.

The young man, who was not more than nineteen years of age, lost his footing and went rolling in the dust. Unfortunately for him the momentum of his fall took him within reach of Lioumere's hand. The hairs on the fingers were brushed by his body and, like a rat's whiskers, they told the owner that something was there to be grasped.

Lioumere's fingers scuttled this way and that, found her victim and clutched wildly at him. She caught him by his long hair at first, making him shout in pain. Then she had his legs. She began to pull him towards the hole, making chortling sounds on the other side of the wall.

'NO!' screamed the youth in panic.

The whole yard now halted in its efforts to get hold of Craig and turned to stare in horror at the boy.

His arms reached out for something to grasp, something to prevent himself behind dragged down the hole.

'My son!' cried the chief. 'Save my son.'

The boy managed to grip a wooden post used to tether pigs. He wrapped his strong limbs around this anchor, whimpering in terror as Lioumere got a better hold on him. Finding that her prey would not move she gave a quick wrench. The boy's eyes bugged as his arms were torn from the post. He cried out once more to his father, his arms wide in supplication. Then he was drawn through the hole by his legs and was gone.

'My son,' shrieked a woman, who must have been the chief's wife. 'She's got my son!'

There was a slobbering chuckle from behind the wall, then the sound of undergrowth being trampled.

Lioumere was satisfied with her catch and was on her way back to her cave.

The woman fell on the floor in a heap, sobbing hysterically, beating the ground with her fists. The chief began pulling out his own hair in bunches, leaving bloody marks on his scalp. Other villagers were wailing and crying. One of their favourites had become Lioumere's supper. Soon his bones would be splinters and powder in her jaws and his flesh washed down with several gallons of swamp water.

The chief came over to Craig. 'You have murdered my son,' he hissed in hatred. 'You fiend. I wish we had never laid eyes on you.'

'Better him than me,' said Craig. 'It is all your fault in any case, for putting up with this situation for so long. If it were up to me, I should have killed that ogress long ago, cut off her head and thrown it to the sharks.'

'That's easy for you to say,' yelled the head man in his grief. 'You're not the one who has to go out and do it.'

Craig saw his chance of escape now.

'If you give me back my club and restore my companion's weapon, we will kill this monster for you. Perhaps we may even be in time to save your son?'

At this, the whole village went quiet. Even the missing youth's mother stopped sobbing. They stared first at Craig and then at the chief.

'It's been tried before,' replied the chief. 'She has bitten off the heads of those who went after her. Her teeth are like splinters of rock and harder than flint or greenstone. Magical teeth. Why do you think you will succeed where others have failed?'

'We can only try. Tell me, has she any weakness – any weakness at all?'

'Only her instep. She has a tender instep. They say when she was born she was ripped from her mother's womb by her father, who used his teeth.'

Craig decided this would have to be enough. He secured Hupa's release and told her what he intended to do.

'I shall go after this ogress and attempt to kill her – but you need not come with me. You can return to the tipairua if you wish and wait for me there. I have no right to ask you to come with me.'

Hupa, who had got her bow and quiver of arrows back, shook her head fiercely.

'I go with you.'

Craig sighed. 'If anything happens to you your father will burn me at the stake.'

'If anything happens to me, it will surely happen to you as well. We'll both be ogress's dung. There'll be no need to concern yourself after that. The two of us will be fertilizing the wild hibiscus trees.'

Craig smiled ruefully. 'You have such a delicate way of putting things, Hupa, being a maiden.'

She laughed in her hearty sportswoman's way and slapped him on the shoulder.

The chief said to them both before they left, 'How do I know you won't just run away, back to your canoe?'

'You don't,' replied Hupa, 'you have to have something which is hard to find in yourself.'

'What's that?'

'Trust. After what you have done to us we would be within our rights to leave your son to die. However, we are honourable people. We have made a promise and we'll honour it.'

The chief could do no more than accept this, which he did with uncertain feelings.

That night they left the compound, going up into the rainforest by the light of Hine-keha's face. Quite rightly, the chief was worried that they might run away, back to their canoe, for there was no one to stop them now. But both had given their word and they were anxious to try and save the youth if they could, despite what the tribe had intended for them. Their fate was to have been the same as his and he would not have cried for them when their bones were powder.

They followed the fresh footprints away from the walls of the village, up into the foothills to the mountain. The spoor followed a stream which eventually led to the sad-looking mouth of a cave up on a grassy rise, below a rock shelf. Here they watched and waited for the sun to rise.

When the Hine-nui-te-po had fled the scene in her cloak of black feathers, Ra the Sun God appeared behind them and crept up into the hills.

Once the sun was up there was movement in the cave. Craig and Hupa watched carefully as a horrible figure stumbled out into the day, stretched and yawned. Despite the fact that they were anticipating a strange creature, they were both shocked by what they beheld.

'What a monster,' whispered Hupa.

It was a naked female ogre but of monstrous proportions. Her head was half as large as her torso, which in itself was as long as the height of three ordinary women standing on one another's shoulders. No neck was visible below this huge ugly head, the hair of which hung lank and grey to the creature's waist, as coarse-looking as frayed rope ends. Two lidless eyes stared out from a face with no prominent nose, only twin cavernous nostrils with wrinkled edges. The same rough grey head-hair came out of these caverns, and out of thick brown ears resembling enormous figs. It was as if they were sprouting hoary bracken.

Craig murmured, 'She could bite off the head of a wild boar with that mouth.'

Her massive scallop-shaped breasts, her navel and the area between and around her legs also grew coarse grizzled hair. Her thighs were thick and muscled, as were her forearms. Her feet were long and prehensile, with cracked and broken nails. There were lumps and boils on her body, calluses and corns on her elbows and feet.

The pair watched as she picked up a log of hardwood and began crunching it in her jaws. Within a very short time the log was a pile of kindling. This Lioumere put to one side, presumably to use as firestarters at a later time.

She obviously liked chewing things, for the next thing she popped into her mouth was a fist-sized piece of rock. This she noisily ground to gravel, which she spat out on occasion, showering the leaves of the forest trees. Her mouth worked methodically, reducing some of the gravel to powder, which she blew down her nostrils like smoke.

After another yawn and stretch, she cleared her throat and hawked and spat a wad of powder-sludge mixed with mucus into the rainforest.

The phlegm landed high above the spot where Hupa was hiding, and it hung there elongating itself, bending a sapling with the weight of a gobbet of thick swamp slime.

'Charming!' muttered Hupa, getting out of the way in anticipation of the fall.

Those fig-shaped ears were not for decorative purposes only though, for the huge head came up at this single word and the ogress stared into the forest. Lioumere's mouth dropped wide open and the watching pair got another shock. The orifice, which stretched almost from ear to ear, was full of comparatively small jagged red teeth as even and sharp as a shark's, stacked in ever-decreasing crescent rows from the front of her palate to the back of her throat. There must have been over a thousand teeth in that ugly opening.

In the next moment the figure was running at great speed towards the clump of foliage behind which the ogling pair sat to view their enemy.

'Quickly!' cried Craig, fear freezing his heart. 'Run! Run!'

Hupa needed no second telling. She was on her feet and racing back down the slopes to the thicker rainforest below. Craig was right behind her. He did not look back. All he could hear were those terrible feet crashing in the undergrowth behind him. There was a fast-flowing torrent at the bottom of the slope. Hupa turned on the bank and fitted an arrow to her bow, firing almost in one movement. Craig turned as the arrow struck the instep of the ogress in the act of lifting her foot.

Lioumere screamed in agony and dropped like a felled giant kahikatea tree with a mighty thump which reverberated through the forest.

She sat up and plucked the arrow from her foot, still screaming at the top of her voice.

Without waiting any longer the two Rarotongans leapt into the fast-flowing water and allowed themselves to be swept swiftly away downstream towards the sea.

Once they had dragged themselves out of the torrent, they assessed their chances of killing Lioumere.

'It's not going to be simple,' said Craig. 'She's obviously been attacked in the normal manner before and knows how to respond quickly. We have to think of a plan to put her off her guard.'

'That's your side of things,' Hupa said, quickly. 'I'm more of a straightforward person. I'm not much good at thinking sideways. You have the right hair on your head for that sort of brainwork.'

'What's that supposed to mean?' asked Craig, indignantly.

'Well, you have red hair,' replied the artless Hupa. 'It must be a strange soil which grows such hair, with strange thoughts buried in it. I'm just a normal person.'

'Oh,' he growled, much as his father would, 'so I'm the offspring of some sort of weird goblin, am I?'

'Exactly,' answered Hupa. 'That's exactly it.'

He could detect no maliciousness or insult in her tone and concluded she was simply speaking her mind. Hupa was a guileless young woman who spoke without inferences of any kind. She said as she found. Instead of fuelling his anger it made him want to laugh. It was the kind of thing an ingenuous Oceanian might say to Seumas. He found he was pleased to be compared with his father by this innocent maiden.

'Well,' he said, after some thought, 'it just so happens I do have a plan in mind. It's a very dangerous one and a little too reliant on the ogress herself, but it may work. I can think of no other ...'

He outlined his scheme to Hupa, whose brown eyes went big and round as the explanation came forth.

'It'll never work,' she said, flatly. 'She'll crush you under her heel the moment you approach her. And anyway, how do you know she understands human language?'

'I don't, but language is something other than just sounds – there are gestures too, which aid communication. I used to watch my father and adopted mother speaking in that tongue they called *Gaelic*. I found I knew what they were talking about, even though I did not understand the words, simply by the way they used their hands and positioned their bodies.'

'And you've seen the tree?'

'Yes, my father described it to me after his visit to the Land of the Long White Cloud. It produces a gum which the Maori chew to heighten their senses and enhance their appetite. We must collect enough to make a mouthful for Lioumere as well as myself.'

In the end Hupa agreed to the plan, though she still had grave reservations. The pair then hunted through the rainforest, collecting gum from the trees which Craig identified, until they had a huge wad of it. Craig took a piece of the gum and put it in his mouth, chewing it tentatively. Hupa did the same. She nodded thoughtfully after a while.

'The Maori are right, it does substantially increase one's feeling of well-being, as well as sharpening the taste buds.'

They spat out the chewing gum, almost simultaneously.

'Good,' said Craig. 'Let's hope they are right about the rest of it.'

So, with the gum in a hastily fashioned wicker knapsack, he went back up the slopes towards the cavern of Lioumere, with Hupa following some way behind.

Craig found the ogress sitting cross-legged outside her cave tending a fire. Lying beside her, trussed to a peeled greenwood spit, was a terrified-looking, blubbering youth. Craig was relieved to see that the boy was still alive. However, if he were not quick the young man would soon be roasted, as Lioumere was at that moment fitting two forked branches into the earth on either side of the fire, across which she presumably intended to lay the spit.

'Good day to you,' cried Craig, emerging from the undergrowth. 'How are you, Lioumere?'

The ogress's head shot up at these words and she stared in astonishment as Craig approached the fire she was poking.

The youth too was looking amazed as Craig sat down by the flames, smiled and rubbed his hands.

'Nice cooking fire you have here, eh? No earth-ovens for the great Lioumere. An open fire, with roasting hot flames! Very good. I'll bet you're looking forward to your meal.'

Craig nodded pleasantly at the trembling youth, who could not take his eyes off him.

Lioumere made a whining noise in the back of her throat and her eyes narrowed. Craig knew that she was a hair away from reaching across the fire and snapping his neck. He could see a bruise on her instep, no doubt caused by Hupa's arrow. This was going to be a very delicate operation.

'I bring you gifts, Lioumere,' he said, in a soft and friendly tone. 'Here, look, in this basket on my back.'

Craig undid the crude wicker basket they had quickly woven that morning. She looked on, curiously now. He reached inside and lifted out the wad of gum. Breaking a piece from it like dough, he put it in his mouth. Then he began chewing with a play-acted enjoyment, rubbing his stomach at the same time.

'Good,' he murmured. 'Good appetite.'

Lioumere continued to stare into his features. Craig spat a gob of juice on the ground. He nodded.

'Very, very good,' he murmured in a contented way.

He held out the remainder of the wad. Craig was counting on the guess that Lioumere could not resist anything to do with food and drink. She loved her stomach, would pander to her greed even if it meant it was her last act. She was a self-indulgent glutton.

She looked at the chewing gum for a moment, sniffed the air above it with those ugly pits she used for a nose. Then she snatched the wad from his palm, painfully scoring his skin with her sharp nails as she did so. The wound was nasty but Craig kept a smile on his face as Lioumere held up the piece of gum, studying it carefully, breathing its aroma.

Finally, to his utter relief, she popped it in her mouth. The pair of them squatted on opposite sides of the fire, chewing away stolidly for a few minutes. Gradually the muscles on Lioumere's face relaxed, the lines became less evident. Her eyes took on a slightly softer look as she masticated on the gum with her many rows of russet teeth. Finally, she revealed a benign side to her nature as the drug took effect.

'Good, eh?' said Craig. He pointed to the youth, still strapped to the peeled log. 'Make him taste better. Yes? Give you stronger appetite for cooked flesh!'

'Ahhhh,' moaned the boy, hanging his head. 'You are a traitor to your kind.'

'Not necessarily,' replied Craig, but still smiling at Lioumere when he said it. 'Watch this.'

He then made a great show of swallowing the gum and belching hard. He rolled his eyes in appreciation and patted his abdomen. 'Mmmmmm,' Craig murmured. 'So good.'

With pattering heart he watched as Lioumere kept chewing her gum, but then, just when he thought he might get to his feet and make a run for it again, she swallowed.

Craig sat there, watching hard, praying the poison would work quickly. The gum had its own toxins, which would not harm a man so long as he just chewed on it. However, once swallowed, the stomach juices attacked the gum, which subsequently released a poison deadly enough to kill a human being. His own piece of gum was lodged under his tongue on one side of his mouth.

The Maori warriors were aware of the lethal properties of the gum, but they chewed it anyway, possibly to affirm their manhood and courage. Or perhaps they enjoyed the effects so much they were willing to take the risk? Whatever, the gum was virulent, fatal to a man, once in his gut.

Lioumere stared at Craig for a long time, her eyes revealing nothing. Then suddenly they opened wide and she lurched to her feet with a loud yell. Staggering forward she stepped directly into the fire, scattering sparking logs and embers.

'Hupa, quickly!' cried Craig, as the ogress lunged for him. 'Help me!'

He spat out his own wad of gum and jumped backwards out of her reach.

Clearly Lioumere's sight was affected, for she took great swipes at the air around and above Craig's head. The Rarotongan picked up a large stone with both hands and hurled it at Lioumere's head. It struck her temple and glanced off without felling her. Hupa came running up then and loosed an arrow into the ogress's face. The missile struck an eye, which made the monster scream, before plucking it out.

'She's going,' Hupa cried, stringing another arrow. 'Look, she knows she's in trouble.'

Lioumere was not interested in attack now, she was concerned about survival. She started to run down the slope, escaping on those thick legs of hers. Her movements were giddy and weaving, like that of a drunken creature. Down the incline, away from the cave she reeled. Into the rainforest, her body crashing through lower branches and undergrowth, careless of any injuries she might receive. It was clear she knew she was in trouble and wanted somewhere hidden to work off the sickness which had come upon her so suddenly.

'Quickly, follow her,' cried Hupa.

The pair ran down after the ogress, leaving the youth protesting, asking to be set free. The boy obviously wanted to get away while Lioumere was gone, thinking that once she recovered he would still be her prey. Craig and Hupa's priorities were different though. They felt it was essential to kill her while she was being attacked by the poison.

The youth need not have worried, nor indeed the pursuers of the ogress.

When they had traversed the winding trampled path to its end, following crushed bushes and broken trees, she was lying dead on her face. The poisons had at last reached her vital organs. Her monstrous head was half buried in the soft moss. One arm was hanging limply over a rotten log. The other was flung forwards, grasping a protruding rock. Already an army of ants was marching across her back, indignant to find their pathway blocked by this hairy mound of flesh.

'Are you sure she's dead?' whispered Hupa. 'Shall we crush her skull with rocks?'

'No,' murmured Craig.

The son of Seumas was now feeling some remorse for having destroyed this wonder of supernature. It was true that Lioumere had preyed on the people of the island, cooked and eaten them for goodness knew how many years, but that was because she was an ogress. That was how her kind survived. In her ignorant state people were considered pigs, chickens or dogs. Human beings were livestock and quite properly slaughtered for the purpose of ensuring one had food in the larder.

'Help me turn her over,' said Craig. 'Then I must make a pair of pincers out of some hardwood sticks and coconut fibre.'

When both tasks had been carried out, Craig then began to extract the Lioumere's teeth. He found some pitcher plants and began to fill them with the teeth. It was his guess they were hard stone of some kind, though they felt heavier than any rock he had come across. When he had finished there were ten pitchers of teeth. He strung them together in two fives on a piece of vine and slung the whole lot around his shoulders. The load was immensely heavy.

'I'll go back and let the boy go,' Hupa said. 'Your club is back there under the hill. I suggest you cut off her head and carry it back to the village. Otherwise we won't be believed and it'll take an age to get away.'

'Right,' answered Craig, not relishing the idea of hacking off Lioumere's head, even though his paddle club was rimmed with shark's teeth and was probably as sharp as any axe. 'Come and find me once you've released the youth.'

He did as she suggested, however, once he had his paddle club in his hands, and chopped the ugly head from the shoulders of the fallen monster. Hupa then returned and the pair of them dragged the head through the rainforest by its coarse grey hair. When they passed a forest pool a singing log called out in an eerie whistling voice, asking if it was the head of Lioumere. The pair replied that it was. The log, which was probably a taniwha in disguise, then demanded they throw it in the pool.

'It belongs here, hidden in the forest,' sang the log. 'You must leave it here, not deposit it in a village of fools and cowards, so that they might make a trophy of it.'

Craig saw what the log meant. It was not right that the tribe should use the skull to brag of their prowess, when they had done nothing but submit to Lioumere's rule for many years, allowing their children to be taken away and eaten. That chief would put it on a pole and puff about his bravery.

'How will we prove she is dead?' asked Hupa of the singing log, 'if we relinquish her to you?'

'You have her teeth,' whistled the log. 'How would you get her teeth without her head?'

'That's true,' said Craig. 'Throw the head into the pool – it's getting too burdensome anyway.'

The couple dragged the head to the pool's edge, then let it roll into the waters. It went down like a stone to the bottom, where they could see it looking up through the lidless eyes, the toothless mouth half open. The hair floated like fronds, forming a cushion of follicles around the log.

Soon the fishes began to nibble at the lips and ears. Within a few days there would be nothing but a gigantic skull greening on the bottom of the pond. The grey hair would remain and no doubt grow to fill the shady hollow.

'Those are magic teeth,' called the log after them, as they went on their way. 'Use them wisely.'

3

Having restored the youth to his father and mother, Craig and Hupa took their leave of the village. The locals would come nowhere near them anyway, even to look at Lioumere's teeth. They believed the couple must have so much tapu they were highly dangerous to normal people. Even as the pair were leaving, the villagers were fencing off the places where they had sat, so that no one might come to harm by touching those spots. Once the tapu had worn off, then the fences would be removed.

Hupa and Craig paddled back to the tipairua, anchored just outside the reef. When they arrived an anxious-looking Seumas was pacing the deck. Others were awake now and seemed refreshed after their sleep. Hine-tu-whenua was blowing a fine brisk breeze, away from the island and in the direction of Raiatea. Tai-moana, the voyaging canoe's drum known as Threnody-of-the-seas, was being sounded. Tiki, in his pride of place before the mast, looked woodenly solemn and intent of purpose.

As soon as they were on board and the dugout secured, Polahiki ordered the sails to be raised.

They were on their way again.

'Where have you been?' demanded Seumas. 'We've been worried since yesterday about you both.'

'No you haven't,' replied Hupa with her usual candour. 'You were all drugged with sleep when we left. It was only after we completed the task for which Apu Hau must have brought us here that you woke and started biting your nails.'

A wry smile appeared on Seumas's hoary face.

'Trust you to pierce my pomp,' he said to her. 'You're right. It's not long since we woke. But finding you missing, both of you, we began to panic.

585

Polahiki was convinced the sea-fairies had got you and had dismembered you both. So, tell me about your adventures! What is this about the God of the Fierce Squall and his purpose?'

They sat on the deck in the shade of the pandanus-leaf hut eating taro and telling Seumas the story of Lioumere. While the story was in progress Seumas kept stealing a glance at the pods of teeth on the vine which Craig had unslung from around his neck. When they had finished Seumas asked, 'Can I see these magic teeth?'

Craig opened one of the pitcher plant pods and revealed the heavy russet teeth. Seumas picked one out and held it up, studying it in the light. His expression changed so alarmingly that Craig asked his father if anything was the matter.

'What? Oh, no, no. Everything is fine. Are these really magic? What could one do with them?'

Hupa said, 'If they harbour magic, then one could do almost anything. It is obvious though that they have something to do with the coming war. We must keep them well preserved, ready for the time when we need to use them.'

'For what?' snapped Seumas.

'Father?' said Craig, surprised. 'Why are you angry at Hupa?'

Seumas seemed to bring himself under control with great difficulty.

'Ah, I'm sorry. I'm getting to be a testy old man. I didn't mean anything by it. Could you – could you let me have one of those bags of teeth?'

'For what purpose, Father?'

'I – er – for an experiment. I'll return them to you later. I would be very grateful.'

Craig looked at Hupa who shrugged and nodded.

'No need to return them, Father – you may keep them.'

Thanking them both, Seumas took the bag of teeth and secured them to his waistband.

Craig and Hupa now went off to get some sleep. They were exhausted after their labours on the island. Around them the mariners were busy at work. Shark-callers were beating the water behind the canoe, using their chants to attract the sharks into the nooses they trailed in the water. Some were casting coloured stones into the wake in a further effort to get the creatures into their clutches. Everyone was looking forward to shark steaks for supper that evening.

Seumas went to a quiet spot to study Lioumere's teeth. He knew exactly what they were made of – *iron*. The Oceanians at last had some iron in their clutches, but they did not know it. Arrowheads could be made from Lioumere's teeth, which would penetrate the shields of the Celts. A thousand arrows with metal points would help to even the imbalance between the metal swords and spears of the Celts and the wooden and stone weapons of the Oceanians.

Seumas was not interested in creating balances between the two potential warring factions. He needed the teeth for another purpose, a selfish purpose. He required them for their magical properties only. If he told his son the teeth were made of iron, then Craig might demand their return, for they were precious metal. Seumas hoped the magic in the teeth was strong enough to do what he required of it.

'What have you there?' asked a voice behind him. 'They look like chips of redwood.'

Seumas clutched the pod of teeth closely to his chest.

'Nothing, Polahiki,' he blustered. 'They're mine.'

Polahiki looked surprised. 'I didn't say they weren't,' muttered the fisher-captain. 'I was simply making conversation, but never mind. I have my navigation to attend to.'

'Yes, go away and adore your fleas.'

'Huh!' muttered Polahiki. 'No need to get nasty.'

Seumas realized he was being unreasonable but could not help himself. He knew there were those on board who were saying he had become haggard since his wife's death. His face had grown leaner and had adopted a haunted expression. They probably knew the grief was working at his soul, gnawing on his spirit, reducing him to a wretch of a man. When he had last looked at himself in a basin of water, he himself had been shocked by what he saw – shadowy gaunt cheeks, grey pallor, grizzled chin. There were deep furrows in his bony brow and red rims around the hollow eyes. It was the face of a man condemned. He looked like a wasted man, a man of sticks and straw.

'But I have the magic now,' he told himself, in that quiet voice that men going mad are wont to use. 'I can do what must be done ...'

Prince Daggan stared from the main window of his house built high on the slopes behind the beach at Raiatea. It was a magnificent house, better even than the house of his father, the king. Made of hardwood, with a roof of woven leaves, the floor space was ten times that of a normal dwelling. There was lat-ticework in the walls to allow the cool breezes which blew up from the ocean to penetrate the room. The window itself, hanging from thongs, could be closed against storms. Now it was propped open with a short pole, to permit viewing.

And a fine viewing platform it was too, positioned up there above the bay. Prince Daggan watched as the fleet from Rarotonga sailed into the lagoon. He could see his rival, Kieto, standing at the mast of the leading tipairua. It grieved Daggan that a man who had begun life as a commoner, should now be considered worthy enough to lead a whole nation into battle. It should not be so. Was royal blood worth nothing in these times?

'It should be *me*,' muttered Prince Daggan. 'I should be the war chief, not that crass labourer.'

But Daggan had not even been considered for the position. People had only ever spoken of Kieto, simply because as a boy of seven Kieto had sailed with Kupe to the Land-of-Mists.

So what? Daggan had thought. The whole expedition had been an accident. To follow an octopus and discover an unknown island! And certainly Kieto's presence on board that craft had been a matter of pure chance. It could not have been Daggan, of course, who had not been alive at the time, but did that give the new ariki Kieto a precedence over those of higher rank?

'I am a prince – born a *prince* – while this man began life as a fisherman's son. It is not right he should lead us. I should lead. And perhaps listen to advice from such people as him – but not necessarily take it. I have been trained in the arts of war, as befits a king's son. My grandfather was King Tutapu, a mighty warrior who was brought down only by the trickery of his so-called wily brother Tangiia.'

'Your grandfather was one of the most feared kings in the history of Rarotonga,' said Daggan's wife Siko, sitting on a mat in the corner of the room. 'You should be proud you have his blood.'

She was preparing some breadfruit mash with taro and roasted rat meat.

'Of course I am proud,' replied Daggan, unable to turn away from the window as the fawning populace of Raiatea were paddling out into the lagoon in their thousands to greet a long-lost son of their soil. 'Look, there goes my father – damn him. It's a sickening sight when a king gets dressed in his dog-skin coat and feathered helmet to greet the whelp of a lowly fisherman and his bitch wife. Is he not afraid his tapu will strike the commoner dead? Is he not afraid his mana will overwhelm the tutua, the low-born Kieto?'

'I heard your father say that Kieto was a natural noble, rather than one born or bred.'

'A *natural* noble,' spat Daggan. 'What is that? Do the gods confer nobility on toads? Do they fill the worms with grandeur? Better than *this* I would think.'

Daggan's wife, tall and sleek and smelling of fresh coconut oil, came and placed a long-fingered hand on his bare shoulder. Her sharp nails rested lightly against his skin. There were times when those nails inflicted pain on him – a pain which he enjoyed – but at that moment there was enough ache in his heart to sustain his masochistic tendencies.

'We must think of a way to rid ourselves of this Kieto, so that you, my husband, will be able to step forward and offer your valuable services as leader of the invasion fleet. Already I have plans in progress to make this possible. We need but a little more time.'

Before marrying her half-brother, Siko had been a sorceress of some renown.

She still practised the black arts, without the knowledge of her father-in-law, to whom she had made a promise to give up her former ways. Now her husband was in need of her skills and she was happy to come to his assistance.

'Can you do that?' asked the prince, turning and looking eager. 'Is it possible?'

'Of course it is possible,' she replied, 'but we need to be very careful. Should any hint of a plot reach your father's ears, both of us will be banished. He dotes on that Kieto too much, while his own dear son ... but never mind. We will make that good. I just need a little time to fashion a scheme.'

'Well, be quick,' cried the prince, a little too aggressively for her taste. 'Be quick.'

She let the sharpness of her husband's words pass her by. She was used to his impatience. Instead she revealed what she had already found out.

'We may have an ally soon, in our endeavours,' she said, standing in the speckled shadowy-lights of the latticework. 'I have consulted my atua and they send me favourable messages concerning the goblin.'

The prince's head came up swiftly. 'Seumas? What of him?'

'He has need of me and my magic, while bringing a little magic of his own.'

'This doesn't involve the screaming of his dead pig?' said the prince, turning pale. 'Not the bladder and bamboo pipes with which he professes to produce music? I couldn't stand that. The last time I heard them I almost wet myself ...'

'No, nothing like that. He wants me to weave a spell for him. Raise someone from the dead. I shall soon have him in the palm of my hand. We can use him for our own purposes, my husband.'

Daggan moved closer to his wife. She was beginning to excite him with her words.

'How do you know all this?' he asked, huskily.

She laughed. 'Am I not the queen of sorcerers? How should I not know? Spiders come to me in the night and whisper hallowed secrets. Bats fly in at my window with messages from afar. Goblins, fairies and dwarves stop me in the forest and pour their poisonous schemes in my ears.'

His eyes opened wide at these words and he began to tremble a little.

'Stop,' he said. 'I don't want to hear these things. They trouble me. But if we can do it, sister! If we can do it, my lovely wife! To rid ourselves of this Kieto? Why, that would be worth almost anything.'

His hands were running over her breasts now, dropping down to feel the hidden crevice between her legs. There were beads of sweat in the corners of his eyes. His breath had a strong musty smell to it

She undid her tapa bark skirt and let it fall to the floor.

'Make love to me, brother-husband,' she said, her nostrils flaring. 'I must have you, *now*.'

They clutched each other and fell on the floor. There was a short struggle, she reaching and trying to untangle his clothes much like a fisherman will grapple with a fish caught in his nets. Finally she had freed the fish and it slipped quickly into her grotto. Too soon though, it left that narrow cleft for open waters again. She would have preferred that it visited for a longer period, but she knew her own husband's strengths and weaknesses.

'So when shall we make our move?' asked Daggan as they dressed themselves again. 'Can I leave things to you?'

'Of course,' replied the unsatisfied Siko, wondering if that tall male servant was still pulping the breadfruit just inside the forest pale. 'I shall go now and make preparations this instant. You rest your weary body, my husband, for you have served me well today.'

'Yes, I have, haven't I?'

PART THREE

The Indigo lady

1

When he arrived in Raiatea, Kieto was still one tipairua missing: the one with his daughter and Seumas on board. Kieto was beginning to wonder whether he had been right in appointing Polahiki as the vessel's captain. The Hivan fisherman was probably not up to handling a great voyager, despite the fact that he was an excellent navigator.

Two other tipairua had gone missing in the storm which Apu Hau had forced upon them, but these two quickly caught up and re-joined the main fleet after the storm had blown itself out. Where was Polahiki's craft? Had it gone down with all passengers and mariners? It would be a tragedy if it had, but Kieto was not yet willing to accept such a terrible scenario.

He told his son Kapu, 'I cannot go to Most Sacred, Most Feared. I will speak to King Rangari and tell him the ceremony must wait until I am satisfied the craft is not lost.'

'Yes, Father,' said Kapu, who was as anxious as Kieto about the missing tipairua. His twin sister was on board and while they fought a great deal, he still loved her as a brother should and wanted her to be safe.

Seven days later a sail was sighted on the horizon. To Kieto's relief it was Polahiki's craft which came scudding over the reef into the lagoon. There was much joy on the island at the news. People streamed down to the beaches in their hundreds, forsaking their chores for a glimpse of Seumas-the-Pict and his famous son Craig, whom they knew as Kumiki the Painted Leg – next to Lingadua, the greatest drummer who ever existed.

They were not disappointed. Craig had always liked the adulation of his followers. Seumas was less enthusiastic about the praise which poured forth, as garlands of frangipani were hung around his neck and a ring of blossoms placed on his head. Nevertheless he accepted it with a smile and good grace, sending a priest-messenger to thank King Rangari for taking the trouble to leave his house to greet him and the others with a wave.

The great king did not of course go too close, for his tapu was so strong his shadow might have destroyed those on whom it fell. There were those who professed they could feel the presence of his mana too, from a great way off. Instead the king remained partly up the hill, where he could be seen by all, but could not inflict unintentional harm. He was surrounded by his priests, who, being his half-brothers and cousins, were virtually immune, though even they did not go so far as to actually touch his person.

His son and heir was by his side too, but left him to come down to the beach to extend the king's welcome to Kumiki-the-Drummer and Seumas-the-Pict.

'Greetings, Seumas,' cried the nobleman, 'you remember me, Prince Daggan?'

'Yes indeed,' murmured Seumas. 'How are you?'

'I am well,' smiled Daggan. 'I was sorry to hear about your wife Dorcha. I remember she was a special favourite of my grandfather Tutapu. We all grieved at the news.'

'Thank you,' replied Seumas.

'May I then invite you to a private gathering, Seumas? Just myself and my wife. We would like to share in your sorrow – not openly of course – just the three of us sharing a basket. You have been the basket-sharer of a prince before, so my rank should not hold any special fears for you. We might talk of old times, of mistakes made, of glories not yet forgotten.'

'I seem to remember your family and mine were on opposite sides of the conflict,' said Seumas, soberly.

'All history now,' smiled Daggan. 'Today we are all friends – let there be no more strife amongst Raiateans or Rarotongans.'

'Then I should be honoured,' murmured Seumas, remembering now that Daggan's wife Siko was a sorceress of some note.

'It is the time of Hine-uri, so bring a torch in order that you might see your way up the mountain path. That is my house up there on the slopes. We shall expect you this evening.'

'Hine-uri,' nodded Seumas. 'The Indigo Lady. The lady of the occult. They say the dark arts are practised during her rule of the moon.'

'Do they? I suppose they do. Well, then? Tonight.'

With that the prince turned on his heel and made his way back up to where his father sat on a high wooden chair, waving a scarlet feather at the tutua below.

Seumas returned to where Kieto and Polahiki were talking with Craig.

'You did the best you could,' Kieto was saying to Polahiki. 'If Apu Hau wanted to take you to that island, there was not a great deal you could do about it. And these teeth you took from the ogress, Craig – you have them with you? Let me see them.'

The teeth were fetched, all except the one set which was now in Seumas's possession.

Kieto studied them, weighing the pods in his hands.

'They're very heavy. I have never felt stones as heavy as these before. What sort of magic do you think they are good for?'

Craig shrugged. 'I am no tohunga or kahuna. We had best ask someone like Kikamana, the Farseeing-virgin, that sort of question.'

'Kikamana is still resting after the voyage. She's quite frail these days.

'When she emerges from the temple I will ask her,' said Kieto. 'In the meantime you had better leave these in my keeping. They may be valuable. On this island we have enemies as well as friends, eh, Seumas?'

This remark was clearly intended to draw out from Seumas the reason why he had been engaged in conversation so long with Prince Daggan, a sworn foe of Kieto, but the elderly Pict merely shrugged.

'We have had our enemies here in the past, it is true, but I think we should put those days behind us.'

Kieto stared at his old friend for a long time, but then, it seemed, overcame his fears.

'You're probably right, Seumas,' said Kieto. 'Let's forget local enemies and look to the common foe – the Celts and Angles. Perhaps we could go over some stratagems while sharing a basket this evening at my campfire? You should be there too, Craig – and one or two others I shall inform.'

Seumas uttered a sharp 'No' without meaning it to sound so abrupt.

'What?' asked Kieto, looking affronted.

'I mean, I'm sorry, Kieto – like Kikamana I am very tired after the voyage. I need to rest and clear my head of salt-spray and too much sun. Please forgive me when I say I am *unable* to attend – but you go ahead, with your chiefs.'

Kieto's brow cleared instantly of its dark look and he put a placatory hand on his friend's shoulder.

'No, *I'm* sorry, Seumas. You have been the energetic warrior for so long now I keep forgetting that you are past being a young man. A *fit* man, I hope, but needing more rest these days. It is I who should beg your forgiveness. I am thoughtless of the needs of others in my single-minded endeavours for a successful expedition, and my manners are not what they should be.'

They parted then on good terms, Seumas going to the hut of an old friend to get out of the blazing sun. He felt guilty that he had not told Kieto the truth, but he knew the younger man would not understand. Seumas did not want to be persuaded out of his present course of action, and so intended that it should remain clandestine, as befitted its dark nature.

When he took off his waistband, a short time later, there were two leather pouches hanging from it. One contained the teeth of Lioumere. The other, his wife's ashes.

That evening, after dark, Seumas took a lighted brand and made his way up a winding path to the house he could see lit by lamps above on the slopes. There was a delicate darkness that had settled softly on the island. Overhead a puff of cloud hid the stars directly above the island, but around the edges of this limited vaporous veil the sparkling chips of light clustered. Had there been no cloud it would have been bright enough to see the path simply by their light alone.

It was one of those nights on which any man at peace with himself might have expected to encounter wonderful fairies, or tree dwarves or even mountain goblins. But Seumas's mind was not on such ethereal creatures. He was thinking of Dorcha. A tipairu, lipsipsip or tipua could have leapt out in front of him and shouted 'Boo!' and Seumas would have brushed it aside in annoyance and continued on his way.

When he reached the house he looked back down the path, to see the sea glinting below, the white surf thundering along the reef visible in the starlight.

'Who's there?' called a female voice, causing a flutter in his heart for a second. 'Make yourself known!'

'Seumas-the-Pict,' he answered. 'Known in my own country as Seumas-the-Black, of the Blackwater clan.'

A moment later the beautiful Siko appeared in the doorway, holding a lantern in her hand. It was peculiar because she had sounded just like Dorcha, though of course he could see it was not his beloved wife. A strange coincidence, but he put it down to the fact that he had been dreaming and praying so hard it would not have been surprising had she materialized before him.

'Is that your full name?' Siko asked, curiously. 'Seumas-the-Black. I never knew it before.'

'Oh,' said Seumas, a little distractedly. 'Yes, yes it is. Why do you ask?'

'Names are sources of power to a witch. You should not be so free with your name, Seumas. Come in.'

He stepped into the magnificent house, saying, 'Those who may wish to do me harm may have it so far as I'm concerned.'

'Oh,' she said, the light from the lamp giving her face deep shadows, 'that sounds like the voice of despair.'

'I am not the same man since my wife died. She was everything to me. Now I am not only old and a dried husk of what I once was, but I am lonely. Very, very lonely. There does not seem to be much to live for now, except my son and his wife, and my grandchildren. My son is with me but I doubt I shall see the others again. I have a strong feeling I shall not return from this war. My bones will lie in Pictland, in Albainn, before the winter hammers that land to hardness.'

'Is that why you carry your wife's ashes on your belt? So that you can be in the Land-of-Mists together? You want your resting places to be one? Doesn't her other husband lie there too? Won't you be taking her back to him as well?'

Seumas's hand went to the pouch which contained the fired remains of Dorcha.

'How did you know?' he asked, quietly. 'How did you know what was in the pouch? And about Dorcha's other man?'

She smiled. 'The one you killed for his weapon? I am a sorceress after all.

Come through and see my husband. He awaits with the feast we have had cooked for you. Pork, dog, rat and fowl, as well as parrot fish and manta ray wings. Taro, arrowroot, banana ...'

'I don't eat dog meat,' he said, following her. 'I never have.'

Prince Daggan rose as Seumas entered, in the way that even nobility rises when a distinguished elderly man enters the room. Once again Seumas was reminded that he was now in the evening of his lifetime. He was given due deference, but he was not important any more. Discussions went on around him rather than through or with him. His words were listened to politely but a marked tolerance showed on the faces of those who harkened. Regard to his age and affection for him as a person ruled over interest in what he had to say.

'Good evening, Prince Daggan.'

'Good evening. I understand we must congratulate your son on defeating an ogress? That was some exploit.'

'He had help – the young Hupa Ariki was with him.'

'She is but a maiden. I doubt she influenced the outcome of the battle too much.'

'No, no, I understand from my son that she took an equal part in the giant's slaying. Young women these days are very skilful with weapons. Hupa in fact is unmatched in the use of the bow and arrow.'

'Really,' smiled Siko. 'We do not altogether approve of such things on Raiatea, but perhaps it is different on a new Faraway Heaven such as Raro-tonga? You probably need female warriors to supplement your numbers? Anyway, enough chatter, please eat – I shall leave you alone.'

Seumas remembered that in the main, women on Raiatea did not eat with the men, especially when there was pork on the table.

'Can your wife not share our basket this evening, Prince Daggan?' asked Seumas. 'I especially wanted to ask her something – something about her profession.'

The prince nodded gravely and motioned for his wife to sit with them on the mat, with the feast spread out within the triangular shape they made.

They began to eat the food set before them, though Seumas only picked lightly at this and that, still distracted by his reason for being in this house. Delicacies laid out on pandanus and banana leaves, soaked in coconut sauce, or garnished with wild honeycombs, or marinated in mango juice, were all there to be had, but none of them excited his taste buds in the least. Finally he blurted out his reason for being there.

'Siko, madam, in your capacity as a magician are you familiar with the art of *kapuku*?'

'That of reviving the dead? Of course.'

'Could you raise someone for me? Given the right conditions of course. I have payment.' He touched the other pouch on his belt.

Siko waved aside the mention of the payment.

'I must know some things about the dead person. How long have they been interred? Is the body still whole? What is the reason for the raising …'

'Love,' said Seumas, quickly. 'The reason is love.'

'And the answers to the other questions?'

'The death has been recent, within two months. There is no body. Only ashes.'

'Ah,' murmured Daggan. 'You speak of your wife, Seumas. It is she who hangs on your belt you wish to revive?' He turned to Siko. 'Can you work with ashes, my dear? Is it possible to bring back the person whole after fire has wasted the body?'

Siko shook her head, sadly. 'Nothing can bring back the whole person, but we can call the sau, bring it back in its human form, though that form will not be substantial. Her presence will be there, but you may not touch her, Seumas. She will be here as mist, though you will be able to see her as she once was, speak with her, listen to her words. Is that enough?'

Seumas felt his jaw go rigid and he was silent for a long time. Finally he answered, 'It will have to be.'

The atmosphere in the room had become quite sultry by this time. The burning lamps were giving off some kind of thick, cloying perfume. Seumas began to wonder what kind of oil was being used in those lamps, but he was too single-minded about his needs to complain about his discomfort.

Siko said, 'You realize what you ask? We would be breaking the king's law here. If we were discovered raising the dead, we would probably be put to death ourselves. People have a great fear of breathing life back into those who have gone.'

'I know.'

'And we shall have to appeal to Kahoali, the God of Sorcerers.'

Seumas said, 'Is that so terrible?'

'It can be. We need to make suitable offerings in order to obtain his assistance. One of the essential ingredients is the eyeballs of a freshly murdered man floating in a cup of kava. Does that trouble you?'

Seumas looked at Prince Daggan, who turned his head to avoid their eyes meeting.

'Where would we get such things?' asked Seumas, turning back to Siko again.

Siko gave him a tight smile. 'We already have them.'

He knew what she meant and he realized with a sinking feeling that he was slipping deeper and deeper into the horrors of dark magic. In the past Seumas had always felt men and women should be free to follow their own gods, whoever those gods might be. But there were some deities who required offerings no honourable or law-keeping man could or should consider.

If they had not actually done it themselves he knew that Siko and Daggan had ordered the murder of a man in order to obtain his eyes. Through her dark arts Siko had foreseen the coming of Seumas and his request for her aid. The preparations for that aid had already been carried out.

Seumas found himself mumbling, as he unhooked Lioumere's teeth from his belt.

'These are from the jaws of an ogress called Lioumere. They are said to be magic. You may take them in payment for your services.'

Siko smiled, accepting the pouch of iron teeth.

'This is only part payment,' Daggan reminded his wife. 'Seumas needs to provide us with a service too.'

'I'll do anything,' replied Seumas, sinking even further into the morass of crime, 'if you will give me back my Dorcha, even if it be for only a night.'

The atmosphere in the room was stifling now. Seumas wanted to gag and throw up his meal on the floor. He forced it back down his throat with difficulty. His skull ached and a fierce pain throbbed behind his eyes. He felt as if he were drowning in some pool of viscous fluid. His movements were sluggish and heavy as he buried his face in his hands.

Siko said softly, 'You will warn us when the Rarotongan Kieto is on his way to Tapu-tapu atia, to pray to his ancestors for a successful voyage and campaign. You will do so from Fisherman's Rock, down on the beach. If it is day you will signal to us here with a wave of a piece of indigo cloth. If it is night you will use a lamp to send an occulting signal ...'

'Why? Why must you have this information?' croaked Seumas, knowing in his heart that they meant to do some harm to his friend. Kieto would be at his most vulnerable when he went to Most Sacred, Most Feared, for he had to commune with his atua alone, unarmed and most probably in the darkness. 'You will not assassinate him?'

'That is not for you to know. Do you want to see your wife here, this evening? Do you want to have her with you? She will be your slave. You will be able to summon her whenever you wish it. Do you want that?'

'Yes, yes, anything,' groaned Seumas. 'It doesn't matter. I only want to see her one last time. The last thing she heard from me was angry words. I had no time to say I loved her. No time to say I was sorry. No time to say goodbye. How could I know that such a wound would kill her? I was angry with her for swimming in the lagoon when there was a swarm of box jellyfish about. She died with my shouts in her ears.'

Daggan, now that he had what he wanted, reassured his guest concerning his fears. He told Seumas not to worry, that it would not be necessary to harm Kieto. That all they wanted to do was ensure that he did not take the fleet to Land-of-Mists.

'Other atua will replace those he intends to speak with,' said Daggan, 'and these others will persuade him that the gods do not wish him to lead our warriors into battle. No real physical harm will come to him.'

Seumas allowed himself to be consoled, knowing deep down that he was a fool for doing so.

'Give me the dust,' said Siko. 'Hand me your wife.'

Siko took the ashes of Dorcha from Seumas and told the Pict to follow her. Leaving Prince Daggan behind she went off into the night without a lamp. Seumas stumbled after her, wondering how she could see in the dark when he had to cling on to her garment in order to keep to the path. Eventually, after weaving their way up a narrow trail, they reached a remote place in the high hinterland where there was a large cave. A musty smell came from the interior.

Inside the ceiling rustled with bats and long fat cave worms crawled over the dung-covered floor.

'We must begin the ceremony in a state of iniquity,' she told him. 'Lust and carnal desire are part of Kahoali's requirements. You must take me here on the floor, amongst the worms. I must have your seed inside me before we begin the rituals. Take me savagely and with loathing.'

She let her skirt fall to the ground and then lay on top of it with her legs open.

'Forgive me, Dorcha,' groaned Seumas, as he went down on her body. 'It's for you ...'

While they were fornicating, Seumas forced his mind to the time when he and Dorcha had first witnessed the release of the coral-egg bundles in the Rarotongan lagoon. The female corals prepared their eggs in advance of the release, while the male corals developed the sperm. Some corals were both male and female, needing only themselves. A few days after the fourth full moon in the year the corals released their bundles of sperm and eggs simultaneously all over the reef, so that fertilization could take place.

Seumas and Dorcha had seen this event several times now and never ceased to be amazed at the spectacle. Pinks, blues, oranges, reds: a huge variety of coloured bundles released by the polyps floated to the surface of the water to mate mindlessly in the gentle ripples of the lagoon. A delicate coming-together of the sexes: the tranquil sea their copulating agent.

Not like this violent struggle between two bodies in the bat shit on the floor of a witch's cave.

'I've finished,' he said with relief, thinking his orgasm would never come. 'It's over.'

She rose and unlike him chose to remain naked.

Further in the cave she lit a lamp which let out a foul-smelling stench. There were ti'i all around the cavern, standing on ledges. Ugly effigies with leering mouths and lolling tongues. Siko, with her hair wild and stained skin, began to intone karakia, while setting up various objects to do with her spell. Cave spiders and rats came out of their holes to witness this ritual occult magic, their small eyes gleaming in the light of the single lamp. Seumas felt uncomfortable.

'Do I have to wait in here? Can I go outside?'

'As you wish,' murmured Siko, hardly paying him attention.

Seumas left the cave and sat amongst the trees within hearing distance. He was wondering what would happen if Siko was pregnant from his ravishment of her body. It was a thought he did not allow to develop, the consequences of it being too awful to contemplate. He picked some wild flowers in the light of the stars while he waited: a bouquet to hand to his beloved when they met once again.

While he sat and waited Seumas fell into a doze, from which he was awoken by the sound of grating high-pitched voices coming from within the cave. It seemed that Siko was arguing with someone inside that inner blackness. Neither of them was the voice of Dorcha. He imagined that Siko was now conversing with atua, or even the God of Sorcerers himself. He was glad he was outside. It was not something he wished to witness. There were enough nightmares in his head without adding to them.

Later, there was silence. Seumas rose, wondering whether he ought to go in now that the noises had ceased. He did not relish the thought of witnessing some ugly exhibition, however, so still remained hovering on the threshold. A few moments later Siko came hurrying out of the cave. She looked ghastly, as if she had come into contact with all the demons of the underworld and had only just escaped unscathed.

'It is done,' she murmured, then hurried off down the path into the rain-forest, without another word.

Seumas remained at the cave entrance in trepidation, not daring to enter. All at once a terrible fear had gripped him. An apparition was beginning to form out of the inner darknesses of the cave. He knew by the unnatural cold wind which blew from within that this would not be *his* Dorcha, but a Dorcha now reluctantly released by the keepers of the dead. This was her mindless soul coming to him, not her real temporal character, the person he had loved while she had been on earth.

He shivered violently in the unhealthy atmosphere.

Dorcha then came out to see him. There was a smile on her face, but it was not one which warmed his heart. It was the fixed smile of the dead. He recognized only the fragrance she had carried on her body when she was alive. This and only this told him he was in the presence of Dorcha. She spoke to him in a soft wasted voice, her body drifting apart in places and then re-forming like smoke from an unseen fire.

'Seumas, you have asked for me and I came.'

Seumas swallowed hard, wondering what he had done, remembering what he had promised in order to have it done.

'Is that you, my darling?' he whispered, hoarsely. 'Is that really you?'

'It is I, Seumas, my love, my life.'

He reached out to touch her, their relationship having always been strongly tactile, then remembered she was but a shade from another world.

'Did they force you to come, or did you come willingly?' he asked. 'I would not have you do something you did not desire, Dorcha. Will you chastise me now for my actions? I betrayed Kieto in order to get you to return. I wanted to say I was sorry – sorry for being so furious with you. But you went and died in my arms before I could recant.'

'I do not remember you being angry and I care nothing for Kieto,' she replied, coldly, her eyes melting and resetting in a disturbing way. 'I care nothing for the living, except for you of course. I only care that you love me enough to want me here, even though this world is a frightening place to me, full of the energy of the quick.

'I come from a place where there is a slow movement into a dark void called eternity, where time does not exist, where flowers and other objects bearing worldly contours are regarded as the shapes from which insanity is formed.'

He let the posy fall from his grasp to the forest floor.

'I – I thought you would disapprove of my actions.'

'How can I disapprove of things I do not understand? When I was alive I must have comprehended these things, but now they are so foreign to my way of discerning they mean nothing to me. It is good to hear your voice, Seumas. I might have forgotten you too, but you are an essential part of my spirit, the essence which is *me*. In life we became one, so part of me is still alive in you and part of you died with me.'

He sobbed, his voice full of anguish. 'I knew it was so, Dorcha. I knew that was how it must be. We were one person, you and I. I want us to be whole again. I want us to know ourselves as we were. I am not myself any more. I am this shadow of a man, not fit for anything except carrying an obsessive dream.'

'It is not possible, Seumas. We cannot be as we were. But we can accept how we are now.'

He nodded, the misery in him more than he could bear. He had thought he would be overjoyed at seeing her again, hearing her voice, but it was as if he had raised the worst part of that darkness which had always resided within his spirit. This was not good. He did not feel well again. He felt as if he had swallowed grave earth and the clay was creeping through his veins with the cold and ugly purpose of destroying his spirit.

'Shall we talk?' he said, in despair. 'Shall we talk of old times? I shall remind you of our life together. You will see how happy we were once ...' and without waiting for her answer he began the story of their love as if it were a litany, letting it come from his lips in a monotone.

Even before the dawn came she had begun to disappear, the terrible boredom of his presence, his tale of two people in love, overwhelming the forces which had demanded she be there. She evaporated gradually, while Seumas was still caught in the agony of his narrative, trotting out the words which now meant nothing at all to one of the subjects of the tale. The tedium, the dullness of his account was driving her mad and she had to leave or turn into one of those insane spirits that haunted the woods and hills of Rarotonga never knowing the peace of death.

'Don't go,' he cried, the tears streaming down his cheeks. 'The price to call you forth was treachery. I have not yet had the value of that tarnished coin ...'

'Goodbye,' she whispered from the mist which now drifted over the grasses revealed by the dawn. 'Goodbye, my grand Pict – we will be together soon.'

He was left alone on the hillside with nothing but the sound of the wind – and a lingering fragrance.

2

Seumas followed the path down the slopes. His mind was whirling with thoughts. He had promised to betray his friend, Kieto, and payment for that promise had been delivered. Dorcha had appeared and might have stayed with him, had he wanted it. The dead are different from the living, however, as Seumas had found to his cost. The Dorcha who had returned was not the Dorcha who had left. They were too strange to one another and could not remain in each other's company.

'Where have you been?'

Seumas looked up quickly, the guilt flooding through him.

'Nowhere. What's it to you?'

It was Boy-girl who had asked the question. Her long hair decorated with sea-shells and ribbons was wet through. She had obviously been for an early swim in the lagoon. She looked thoroughly taken aback by his abruptness and bad manners, and raised her eyebrows in that arch way she used on occasion.

'Sorry I spoke to you at all,' she said. 'You'd better let everyone know you're in a bad mood, or we'll all get our heads bitten off.'

'I – I'm sorry, Boy-girl,' said Seumas. 'I was thinking of something else. I'm tired.'

'You look tired. Have you been for a dawn walk?'

'Yes, that's it. I went up into the mountain. I can think more clearly up there. I had bad dreams and wanted to wipe them from my head. You know.'

She nodded, now mollified by his tone.

'I do know, yes. I have bad dreams all the time. It comes with age I suppose. No – that's not true, I used to have nightmares as a child. We're coming full circle, that's what it is, Seumas. We're slipping back to childhood.'

'Oh, if that were true,' he said, wistfully. 'I would love to be a boy again.'

Seumas left Boy-girl and went back to his hut. Dirk was with Craig and so there was no one to greet him. The place seemed very empty. Feeling both exhausted and miserable he lay on his mat and fell fast asleep.

Much later he was awoken by a sound and sensed a foreign presence in the room. Sitting up quickly, he saw two silhouettes in the light of the doorway.

'Who is it?' he murmured.

'Rian and Ti-ti,' came the answer.

Instantly Seumas was on his feet, a club in his hand. These were two brothers who had been married at one time to Dorcha. Rian had been trying to kill him ever since she had left them. Both brothers had accused him of enticing her away, despite the fact that Dorcha herself had told them she had a mind of her own and could make her own choices in the matter.

'It's all right,' said Rian, stepping forward and making a placatory gesture. 'We're not here to harm you.'

'Why are you here then?' he asked, reasonably.

It was Ti-ti who answered this. 'We – we wanted to hear how she died.'

'Dorcha? You think I killed her I suppose?'

'No,' replied Ti-ti, 'for we know you loved her as much as we did. We were here and you were there. We could not even come to her funeral. We thought you might tell us how it went and whether she ever spoke of us, when you both went to live in Rarotonga.'

Outside the hut the sun was going down quickly, leaving a red flush in the sky. It seemed he had slept through the whole day. He motioned for the two men to sit down on a mat. He noticed now that they were both grey-haired and Rian was quite thin, his muscle tone having gone. Once upon a time he had hated these two, but now they looked like harmless old men. They nodded at him as he gave them something to drink in a half-coconut shell.

'You want to know how she died?' he said. 'She was in pain at first, but then her body began to go numb. A jellyfish sting. Can you believe that? Our Dorcha taken by something as silly as a jellyfish sting? She spoke of you before she died, of course. She told me to tell you both she had been happy with you, while you were all together.'

Ti-ti let fall some tears at this news and even the tough Rian's eyes looked misty.

'She said that?'

'Yes,' lied Seumas, who had made the whole thing up, 'I was going to come and see you, but the voyage has made me weary. I'm not the man I once was.'

'None of us are,' said Rian, standing. 'We thank you for your time, Seumas. Death brings men together. We'll leave you now. The funeral was a good one?'

'As grand as they come. She went out in fine style. The flutes were playing, the drums were pounding. There were a thousand blossoms for her shroud and palms for her path. People wailed and pulled at their hair. Others cut themselves with sharp shells. One man gave me a carved canoe, sacred and cherished, to serve as her coffin when she was cremated. She was greatly loved and admired.'

'You had her body burned?' said Ti-ti.

'She wanted me to bring her ashes here, to scatter them on the island she loved.'

'It was done?' asked Rian.

'Just as she wished, up there on the slopes.'

Satisfied, the two brothers now left, going out into the darkness of the evening. Seumas went out to one of the fires and brought back a brand to light his lamp. This he placed on the window ledge of his hut, so that its light shone within and without. He remembered miserably that he had a task to do. He had not told Prince Daggan and Siko, but he had already known that this night was the time when Kieto would be going to the temple.

Some time later, as Seumas sat outside the door of his hut, Kieto came past.

'You are going to commune with your atua?' asked Seumas, dully. 'Is that where you're going?'

Kieto looked down at his old friend. 'Why, of course it is. You know that, Seumas. I shall come and talk with you afterwards. We have one or two things to discuss. Perhaps you could ask Boy-girl and Craig to join us?'

Seumas said that he would. Kieto went on his way, towards that part of the island where Most Sacred, Most Feared was situated, deep in the rainforest, under the shadow of a rock hang. There were the island gods, images planted in the ever-damp moss around the terrible Investiture Stone.

Seumas's spirit was in agony as he watched Kieto go into the rainforest. The Pict stared up at the house on the hill, knowing he was being watched for a sign. If he was going to keep his promise to the sorceress, it would have to be now. But how could he do that? How could he betray his friend? Why had he agreed to such treachery? His selfishness, his obsession with his dead wife, had led him along an ignoble path.

Standing now, he paced up and down in front of his hut, wondering what he should do. Now that it came to the point, he could not betray Kieto. That much was impossible. The right thing to do was to go up to Prince Daggan's house and tell him and Siko that he could not carry out his side of the bargain. They would probably murder him, but he deserved as much.

He looked up again at the house. The lamps had been extinguished rather abruptly. That was puzzling. Had the pair gone out somewhere? Surely they would be watching for the signal from Seumas, desperate as they were to know when Kieto would be at Tapu-tapu atia. It was almost as if they had already received the sign they wanted from him.

Suddenly, Seumas looked at his own lamp. It was situated on the ledge in the window, at about chest height. He had been walking up and down in front of it. *An occulting light.* Seumas realized in horror that he had inadvertently given the signal by pacing backwards and forwards blocking and unblocking its beams from the sight of those above. To the couple on the hill it would have been an occulting light.

Seumas began running towards a clutch of visitors' huts that were some distance apart from where Seumas dwelt.

'Craig, Craig, come quickly! Kieto's in trouble. I think he's about to be abducted.'

Craig appeared almost at once. Hupa and Kapu came from another hut. Soon there was a party of them running towards the path which led to Most Sacred, Most Feared. Seumas was trying to explain on the run.

'It's my fault,' he told Craig, 'I betrayed him to Prince Daggan and his wife Siko.'

'That witch?' muttered Craig, with Dirk at his heels. 'What are you talking about, Father? Keep silent until we have dealt with the matter.'

Seumas, anxious to confess his guilt, nevertheless bit his tongue.

When the party was halfway there, a deep-throated and bloodcurdling howl went up somewhere in the rainforest. The tone sent shivers down Seumas's spine. It sounded like a large wolf, which was impossible in an Oceanian land. There were no wolves. Therefore it must have been a dog, but Seumas had never heard one of the local dogs howl like that. It sounded as if the creature was out on a hunt, out to kill.

Dirk's hackles went up and an ugly growl formed in his throat.

'What is it?' cried Hupa. 'What made that sound?'

Kapu, her brother, turned pale and stopped running. 'I'll get help,' he said, turning back to the village along the path.

When the others reached the clearing of Tapu-tapu atia they saw Kieto standing with his back against the tall Investiture Stone. He was holding his left arm. Facing him, with its back to the group, was a fearsome creature out of a nightmare. Its naked body was that of a muscled, hairy man. Its head was that of a huge dog. The monster was making ready to rush Kieto.

Seumas quickly grabbed the snarling Dirk by the fur on the back of his neck, to keep him from hurling himself to almost certain death.

'Father!' shrieked Hupa. 'Don't move!'

She quickly fitted an arrow to her bow. Just as the fiend was making its run she fired. The arrow struck the beast in the nape of the neck. The shock of the wound stopped it in its tracks but failed to bring the brute to its knees. Instead, it turned, with fury on its face, to regard the intruders. The eyes in the great head burned with anger, the slavering jaws opened to reveal blood-ied fangs.

'Get my daughter away from there!' cried Kieto. 'This Kopuwai will kill you all.'

Craig seemed not to have heard this order. He moved forward with the agile grace of a drummer turned warrior. Planted in the ground halfway between him and the beast was the stone image of Paikea, God of Sea-Monsters. Craig wrenched this totem from the ground. It was shaped much like a large war club with a spike at the bottom and a rounded head with a face on the top. Craig began swinging the weapon back and forth as if daring the Kopuwai to attack him.

A second arrow loosed from Hupa's bow struck the man-animal in the chest and it was distracted from Craig's gaze. It let out one of those mind-splitting howls. Then it rushed forward, intent on getting to Hupa. Craig braced himself, planting his feet at shoulder-width apart. He swung the stone club at the creature's rib cage as it tried to run past him.

The club smashed into the side of the Kopuwai's breast and the watchers heard the crunch of bone.

This caused the Kopuwai to turn its attention back on Craig. It reached out with strong arms to grab him, its savage jaws snapping with a ferocious and ugly sound. Standing over a head taller than Seumas's son, it almost got a grip on his shoulders. But Craig was already swinging for the second blow. This time the club came down on the monster's skull, crushing it like a breadfruit. Human hands came up to protect the canine head against further injury. The creature howled in fear and agony. Its tongue lolled from its mouth.

A third blow from the stone club was delivered to the creature's left shoulder.

Still the beast did not die, but ran off into the rainforest, its feet crashing through the undergrowth.

Seumas let go of Dirk's ruff and ran to Kieto, to find him holding a stump where his left hand should be.

'Severed at the wrist,' growled Kieto, obviously in pain. 'Take me to a fire.'

Craig replaced Paikea where he had found him, the stone god being some-what blood-stained. Paikea was the son of Papa, Goddess of the Earth, and Craig would make reparations to her later. In the meantime there were other things that were of more importance.

They hurried Kieto through the rainforest back to the village. There the wound was cauterized with a blazing torch. Kieto's face registered his agony. Once the flame had been applied he passed out and was carried to his hut. Craig went to speak with Seumas, now standing quietly by.

'Well, Father, what was this about a betrayal?'

'They said no physical hurt would come to him,' Seumas whispered hoarsely. 'They promised he would be unharmed.'

'You are talking about Prince Daggan and Siko? What did they say to you? Why are you involved, Father?'

Seumas hung his head. 'I wanted to see Dorcha one last time. I *had* to see her – you *must* understand that. I wanted to say goodbye, to explain things ...'

'Father, we all want to do that. But unfortunately our loved ones do not die when everything is perfect. There are always some things left unsaid, things left undone. Death is not something to be wrapped up neatly like breadfruit in pandanus leaves, the sennit knot tied, the ends of the cord clipped.'

'I had to see her.'

'You keep saying that, but we all feel that way. We all want that last conversation. We all want to be forgiven for our transgressions. We all want to reaffirm our love. But death doesn't usually wait for such occasions. Sometimes, yes, we are lucky and manage to shed our guilt, but more often than not all the loose ends are left untied, all the wounds open.'

Seumas hung his head, finding his son wiser than himself, which given their respective ages he felt should not be.

'I'm sorry. In return for the sorceress Siko letting me have one last time with your mother's ghost, I promised to give Daggan a signal when Kieto went to the Investiture Stone. I was promised no harm would come to him. I thought they meant to kidnap him until after the fleet sailed with Daggan at its head. I will go to the king and speak against his son.'

'You will do nothing of the kind, Father. They'll certainly execute you too, if they find the pair guilty. Treason is regarded as just as heinous a crime as attempted murder. We are virtually at war. At such times punishment is always meted out with more severity than in times of peace. Even your friendship with Kieto might not save you.

'It's best you remain silent over this. I hope no one overheard you when we were running to Kieto's assistance. If asked why you thought something was wrong, you had better say you heard an earlier howl, which none of us did.'

'I don't care what happens to me,' said Seumas. 'I deserve all I get.'

'You might not care at the moment. Your wife has just died and you feel empty and wasted. You probably don't care whether you live or die. But *I* care. You are my father. I have just lost the only mother I have ever known. I do not wish to lose a father in the same year. Stop being a selfish old man. Think of others. You have your grandchildren to consider, as well as me. You

were never a pathetic man before. Stop feeling so sorry for yourself, Father –
pull yourself together.'

'That's easy for you to say.'

'No it isn't – it's very difficult. I hate being disrespectful to my father. But if
I let you alone you'll follow this path of self-destruction. What else did you
give to Siko in payment for producing Dorcha's phantom?'

'Lioumere's teeth.'

'Well, she'll probably use the magic they can produce to cause some polit-
ical strife on the island. At least we won't be here to witness it. Is that all?'

'Yes, I suppose so,' said Seumas, finding it a new experience to be chastised
by his son. 'By the way, the ogress's teeth are made of iron. I have told you
about iron. We can use the rest of them to make arrowheads.'

'Iron? That rock you call *metal*?'

'It isn't rock, it's something you get from rock, by melting it down. The
essence of rock, the soul of stone. It will pierce the strongest shield, the thick-
est hide. There's enough teeth to make a thousand arrowheads.'

Craig put an arm around his father's shoulders and gave him a tight smile.

'We'll give them all to Hupa – that woman is a marvel with the bow and
arrow. Did you see that shot she made? In half-darkness too. Smack on
target.'

Seumas nodded. 'She's a good archer. I don't think I've seen better. But
there will be enough to fill her quiver and those of many others. It won't help
us a great deal against swords, but it's a start I suppose.'

'Come, Father, you're determined to be the pessimist, aren't you? Let's go
and eat with Boy-girl. She always brings you out of yourself. You usually end
up arguing with her over some point or another, but at least it takes you away
from morbid thoughts. Drink a *little* kava, but not too much, or you'll get
maudlin ...'

Oh you gods, thought Seumas as he followed his steady and confident son,
is this old age, when the young treat you like a child? Let me get to the Land-
of-Mists and into battle, where there's swords and horses. I'll show this laddie
who's the father and who's the son then. He'll know then who has knowledge
of real battle and who does not.

PART FOUR

King of the fair-haired Fairies

1

Later Seumas was called to Kieto's sick bed, where that man lay recovering from the loss of his left hand. After the cauterization the wound had been smeared with a balm and bound with healing leaves. Kieto kept slipping in and out of a fever at this point, but he was anxious to know the answers to a few questions.

Seumas was asked by Kieto why he had known the ariki had been in trouble. The Pict told him that he had been visited in a dream by Dorcha. Though Seumas did not say so outright, he implied that Dorcha had warned him that Kieto was being attacked. Kieto accepted this explanation, dreams being one of the main ways spirits of the dead communicated with the living. Hupa was not altogether satisfied though and asked why Seumas had called out that Kieto was being abducted.

'The warning was rather vague,' said Seumas. 'I understood it to mean he was being carried off.'

Kieto would hear no more criticism of his friend Seumas.

'What does it matter how he knew?' said the ariki. 'He saved my life. Seumas is a true friend and always has been, ever since I was a small boy. I love him as I would love my father or my brother. He is a man among men, a great warrior, and mana is gathered in him like stars are clustered in the roof of voyaging.'

Seumas suffered this embarrassing praise in silence, fortunately taken by others for modesty, under the hawk eyes of his son. The two did not mention the matter to each other again. There were other people who knew his secret of course – the prince and his sorceress wife – but they had good reason to keep silent. Craig paid them a short hostile visit.

'When the gods made the first people,' Craig told the prince and his wife quietly, 'they ran out of human blood and had in some instances to use the blood of animals ...'

'I am familiar with the story,' said the prince, coldly.

'Then you know that in certain cases people take on the traits of particular animals. A person with traces of rat's blood in them will most likely turn out to be a thief. Someone with the blood of a parrot will be a loud-talking brag-gart. Those bearing the blood of ants will be busy, energetic people ...'

'Get to the point,' snarled the prince. 'You wish to tell me I have the blood of some foul beast in my veins?'

'No,' said Craig, looking him straight in the eyes, 'I'm here to tell you about me. I have the blood of the shark in me. I kill coldly and without mercy. Once I have targeted my prey, nothing short of death will stop me from tearing him to pieces. Do you understand me?'

Despite the protection of his rank and arrogance, a visible quiver of fear went through Prince Daggan on looking into the fathomless blue eyes of this young man.

'I am tapu,' he told Craig, haughtily. 'I am a prince.'

'And I,' replied Craig, 'am a hammerhead.'

Craig left the prince smouldering with rage at being spoken to as if he were a tutua by a half-Hivan, low-born son of a goblin.

'I'll roast his eyes,' snarled the prince to his wife as he crashed around the house in a blind rage destroying objects whether he loved them or not. 'I'll have his liver on a spit.'

Siko, who was never one to worry about lost causes or those which held no profit, brushed his anger aside.

'You waste your fury and energy on nothing,' she said. 'He is the one who is suffering, or why would he come up here to front a prince in that way? He is the one who desires revenge. We failed in our objective, that worries me more than some boy whose soul is seething with shame for his father's actions. Forget him and his father. Had he come here because of some malicious intent, I would have said yes, have him put to death. But he is suffering – let him continue to suffer.'

Prince Daggan calmed down immediately. 'How well you put things, my dear,' he said. 'How inadequate I am.'

Yes, she thought, but said nothing.

In the village below there were problems with the Kopuwai. The creature had not died and was still on the loose. It had gone back to a secret cave in the rainforest and returned with a pack of vicious two-headed dogs, which it set on the village. The dogs slaughtered chickens and livestock until the Rarotongans managed to kill most of them. The remaining two or three were driven back into the rainforest.

A band of warriors under the leadership of Kikamana then found the cave where Kopuwai lived. They tried to smoke him out by lighting fires at the entrance to the cave. When he failed to appear they went inside and found he had crawled into a narrow passage in the ceiling of the cave to escape the smoke and had become stuck and suffocated to death.

They took his body, severed the dog's head from it, and gave the two parts a ritual burial at either ends of the island.

'I feel sorry for the creature,' said Hupa. 'He and his fiendish hounds were created by some warped sorcerer. It was no fault of the Kopuwai that he was a monster. It might have been kinder to have captured him and set him free on some uninhabited isle where he could do no harm.'

'Then some poor unsuspecting castaway might end up on the island and be eaten for breakfast,' replied her brother Kapu. 'In any case, he was so ferocious it would take an army to get him into a cage alive. I wouldn't want to be one of those who tried it.'

Hupa shrugged. 'I just felt sorry for him,' she repeated.

Attention was then taken up by the arrival of the Hawaiian fleet under one of the sons of Nana-Ula, King of Hawaii. On board, much to the delight of ex-Arioi members like Craig, was the famous Oceanian bard and astrologer, Kama-Hau-Lele. This old man had recited epic poems on the voyages and exploits of ancestor heroes, during Nana-Ula's passage from his original homeland in Tahiti to the island of Hawaii.

'Kama-Hau-Lele is one of our greatest people,' Craig told his father. 'And I am going to meet him.'

Seumas said sourly, 'Your people.'

'And yours,' replied Craig. 'You have been here longer than you were ever in your birthland. You are an Oceanian now, Father, whether you like it or not. Your Picts would not recognize you as one of themselves now.'

The Hawaiian war fleet was one of the most magnificent sights Craig had ever seen. Though the canoes were necessarily voyagers they had flying war pennants of yellow, red and black streaming from the prows. High, curving staves came out of the prows, elaborately carved, with Tikis standing on their tops facing the occupants of the canoes, rather than the open sea to the front. Warrior platforms had been built fore and aft and were now full of chiefs in splendid yellow and red cloaks and capes falling from their shoulders. On their heads they wore tall glossy helmets, which gleamed in the bright sunlight, their colours reflected in the shimmering lagoon waters.

Hupa, standing with Craig, professed to have lost her breath in the wonder of the sight. Seumas and Boy-girl were quietly admiring the scene. Kieto was now up and on his feet, almost his old self, and was off somewhere else, greeting the son of Nana-Ula.

'I hear the Hawaiians fight in a crescent-shaped formation, like that of a quarter moon,' said Hupa. 'Their warriors are greatly feared for they seem invincible in battle.'

Craig, who no longer wore his hair in the Hivan style of two horns jutting from his head, felt bland and dull beside these men and women who imitated the birds in their appearance. He had seen such splendour before, amongst the Tahitians, but not to this degree. The Hawaiians seemed to him to be a higher form of life, a magnificent people, each one of them a prince.

The Hawaiians began to come ashore accompanied by the music of drums and flutes and other woodwind instruments. One of the drummers glanced at Craig as he passed, seemingly noticing his three bar tattoos. The man then looked back with a puzzled expression, to inspect Craig's legs. His eyes opened wide when he saw the painted one. Finally he looked up at Craig's hair, as his companions began to wonder what was the matter with him, since they were trying to keep time to his drum.

'Red hair!' cried the Hawaiian, excitedly. 'Painted Leg!'

All the musicians stopped and the chiefs and lesser individuals marching up from the shallows on to the shore with much pomp and circumstance stared disapprovingly at this little knot of young Hawaiians failing in their duty.

Now one of the flautists took up the shout. 'It is the famed Kumiki, the drummer of the Arioi! He is here! He is here!'

They rushed forward excitedly to crowd around the embarrassed Craig. They showered him with questions, telling him they had heard of his marvellous drumming, and wished he would give them a performance. Hawaiian chiefs then came and stood with the group, catching some of the excitement, realizing who it was that had caused the fuss. Finally the crowd parted for an old man with a crooked stave, who came up slowly and stood before Craig.

'I am Kama-Hau-Lele,' he said, staring into Craig's flushed features. 'You are the Painted Leg, Kumiki?'

Craig looked into the kindly face of the old man, covered with wisdom lines.

'Yes,' whispered Craig, finding himself confronted by one of his heroes. 'I am Kumiki.'

'Will you play for us, young man? Tonight, at the feasting? I have been told your performances are unequalled in the skill of their rendering.'

'And I, yours,' said Craig, growing bolder. 'Perhaps you would favour us with one of your stories, if I take to the drums this evening?'

The old man smiled. 'It will be fair exchange.'

The young man who had first noticed Craig was busy collecting shells from the hands of his friends and, after the crowd had broken up, Craig asked him what it was about.

'Why, I won my wager,' said the Hawaiian drummer. 'I whispered to the others that you would play for us – they bet against it. We Hawaiians love to gamble, on anything, anything at all,' he laughed. 'You seem puzzled.'

'We do not know this sport,' said Craig. 'Father, have you heard of "gambling"?'

'Oh, I've heard of it all right,' said the crusty Seumas. 'It's a fool's game. You can lose all you have in a single evening. I once knew a man who lost his wife and children to another, simply because he thought his beetle could win a race against a frog over twenty paces. Another man bet a companion that he could gather fifty eggs in one morning, from tall sheer cliffs in a high wind. He failed and lost the croft which had taken him six months to build.'

Craig grinned. 'That egg man was you, wasn't it, Father?'

'It could have been,' said Seumas, 'and if it was, you can be sure I'll never gamble on anything again.'

The Hawaiian youth laughed at these exchanges, saying, 'I love to gamble. Nothing would stop me. If I had a kingdom I would gamble it for another.'

'Then there's no help for you, young man,' Seumas said. 'You are lost to the world.'

'What about archery,' Hupa said. 'Do you wager on the outcome of archery?' The boy noticed her bow and quiver of arrows.

'It is one of the major events on which we gamble.'

'Would you like to gamble on me hitting something now?' she asked, stringing an arrow.

Craig put his hand on her arm. 'Not now. Later, when you have some competition, Hupa.'

'A young maiden?' said the youth. 'I'd bet against you anytime – our archers are brilliant.'

Hupa nodded, putting away her arrow.

Craig said, 'All right, you get your best archer and then we'll have a little competition.'

'Excellent!' cried the youth.

That night at the feasting, Craig played his drums for the Hawaiians, who listened enraptured. Seumas could not help but feel immensely proud of his son. One or two Hivans present claimed him as their own, as did the Rarotongans. When a hero emerges from the crowd he is divided up amongst his fellows.

Afterwards, true to his word, Kama-Hau-Lele told the story of how the demi-god Maui and his father pushed the sky further up so that people below it had more room.

'Rangi the Sky-God and Papa the Earth-Goddess had already been forced apart by Tane's children, the trees,' intoned the old man, 'but at that time trees were themselves bent double by the weight of the sky and people had to crawl around on their hands and knees, trying to get their work done – their fishing and hunting, their growing of crops, their building of low squat houses – while in this crouched position.

'Even the sun was upset with the situation, since it could not travel very far over this low region, which meant men spent most of their time in darkness.

'Finally, Maui decided he had had enough of working under a low sky made of blue rock against which everyone cracked their heads and knocked their noses on sharp and blunt projections. He asked for his father, who was a minor god called Irawhaki, and suggested that the two of them lift the sky up higher. His father agreed that it was a poor state of affairs when men could not do their work for fear of breaking their skulls.

'The pair of them put their shoulders under the sky and gradually forced it higher and higher. When they had it almost head-high they started to push with their hands, but even when it was above their heads it was still not high enough. Maui's father, being a god, made himself and his youngest son grow tall while still pushing up against the sky. Eventually the blue rock was way above the heads of people, above the tops of the trees, and even higher than the tallest mountain.

'Maui's father then told his son he had worked enough and went back to his favourite Underground world, which was not the world of the dead, but some other place where a different kind of people lived. The same world in fact which Maui discovered when he lifted a house post and looked down through the hole to see people moving about below the earth.

'Still the sky did not look quite right to Maui, who was more artistically inclined than was Irawhaki. The trickster hero did not like the rough bits, sticking out all over the place, and he climbed up onto the sky and with a stone hammer knocked off all the knobs and sharp projections. Then he smoothed out the bumps. Finally the sky was as you see it today, a beautiful flat blue dome of rock.'

Craig was spellbound by the deep, resonant timbre of the orator, and nodded enthusiastically when the story was finished.

'I like that,' Seumas said, 'father and son doing things together. But one thing I've never understood. Why is everyone so keen on him, this Maui.'

'It's because he's one of five brothers,' replied Craig, 'and is in fact the youngest. Our culture is full of stories of younger brothers, their ranking in the family being very low, using their ingenuity and cunning to raise their status.'

The following morning there was an archery competition. Since people had been talking about it at the feast the night before the whole affair had expanded. Many youths and some maidens – Craig suspected they were all from Hupa's secret society, the Whakatane – gathered to test their skills against one another.

Before the contest started the Hawaiian and Raiatean youths were scoffing at the young women, asking them why they were pretending to be good at manly sports. Their taunts died on their lips, however, when the maidens began to put arrows in the targets. Finally it came down to a match between one of the Whakatane and a Hawaiian youth. By this time many of the gamblers in the crowd were quietly backing the maiden.

They lost their bets, but only by a very narrow margin. It was clear to the men that the women were just as good as they were with the bow and arrow and that only good fortune had allowed one of their number to triumph in the end. A second contest might have easily had a female winner. The men went away quietly and soberly, a little wiser than before the competition had begun.

'Well done, Hupa,' said Craig. 'Pity about that last arrow.'

Hupa had been knocked out of the competition earlier than her skills really deserved, but she expressed satisfaction that the men had not run away with the contest.

'I think we women showed them that they had better keep their mouths shut the next time they see one of us with a weapon in our hands.'

'I believe you've given them more than enough to think about – the Hawaiians lost a lot of their wagers in the beginning, when they were betting on their boys.'

Hupa nudged him and gave him a little satisfied smile.

'Good,' she said.

The combined fleets of Rarotonga, Raiatea and Hawaii set sail for Tongatapu, where they would rendezvous with the Samoan, Hivan, Tongan, Fijian, Tahitian and many, many other fleets to form one mighty armada for the invasion of Land-of-Mists. Coloured banners flowed in the breezes, crab-claw sails filled their chests with wind, steering oars cut the surf.

On board the tipairua and other craft, navigators conferred with navigators, comparing shell charts and talking of points of the windflower. Captains called to captains, wishing each other the fortune of the gods, especially Tangoroa, the Great Sea-God, on whose back they would be scudding. Crew called to crew and warriors to warriors. A great excitement was in the air as Ra crossed the blue roof of voyaging and smiled down upon the brave Oceanians about to dare the unknown. Sacrifices were made to Ira, Mother of the Stars, under whose guidance the vessels would remain for the next several months.

Kahuna and tohunga were busy with rituals amongst the voyagers and in the temples on the island. Ancestors were being petitioned, asked to act as mediators between the people and the gods. Fires were burning offerings and ahu were smothered with fruit and meat, awaiting unseen hands to bear them away. Religion and magic were humming through the trees, whistling through the rigging of the canoes, crackling through the hair of the seafarers.

They received a tumultuous send-off as Raiateans, and even people who had canoed all the way from Borabora, massed on the beaches to wave them away. Drums pounded on sea and shore. Blossoms were tossed into the ocean to float on the waves. Tiki in his many images set his face to Te muri on the windflower.

Once out on the ocean the fleets did not attempt to keep in constant touch with one another. There was no sense in clustering so many craft together over such a long distance. In certain circumstances – a squall or a fierce wind – it might even be dangerous. They might be driven into one another. In any case, some were faster and went ahead, others preferred a different use of the wind, a slightly different course. After the first few days they fragmented, spread over the face of the sea, yet most in sight of at least one other craft.

The crews and passengers fell into their usual routine of dividing the day up into three parts, so that one watch was always awake, always on the alert. On Polahiki's craft that unwashed but reliable sailor allowed the main fleet to sail close to the wind, while he took a course which he knew would lead him into faster currents that would eventually assist his voyager in overtaking the other canoes.

Inevitably he eventually found himself alone. Sighting a green glow on a distant cloudbase, he knew there was an island with a reflecting lagoon beneath. They were beginning to run short of supplies on board, having lost a batch of coconuts to a freak wave. He decided to stop at this unknown island and stock up on whatever the place had to offer.

It was dawn as Hine-tu-whenua gently assisted the canoe into a rather pretty and tranquil lagoon with colourful corals, which seemed to be teeming with fish, crabs, eels and shellfish. There was no smoke coming from the island, no signs of it being inhabited. It seemed they had stumbled accidentally on a Faraway Heaven. Seumas, Hupa, Craig and the Boy-girl were standing on deck as the tipairua cruised into the turquoise inner waters and bumped gently against the coral sands of the shallows.

'Right,' cried Polahiki, 'water and coconuts, and anything else we can find. Let's get to it. Come on, move yourselves. I want to be away from here before darkness falls. I don't trust these lonely islands stuck out in the middle of nowhere.'

'What a forceful captain we seem to have chosen for ourselves,' murmured Boy-girl. 'Well, I for one am going to see what lies beyond the shoreline trees.'

'Is that wise?' asked Seumas. 'You know we've got into trouble that way before. What if this island is a magical island? Perhaps there's a fierce taniwha just waiting to devour some poor wayward sailor ...'

'I haven't seen a taniwha yet,' said the excited Hupa. 'Perhaps we should go to look for one?'

'I'm too old for that sort of thing,' replied Seumas. 'It's true, however, that all the magical islands I've visited so far have not been attractive at first sight. They're usually hot and sultry, with dead coral lagoons and ugly mangroves that come right up the waterline. This island looks as if it's just been modelled in the hands of some happy god.'

'Well, I'm not too old,' Boy-girl said, 'not quite yet. I think this place is absolutely charming. There are not even any flies or unpleasant insects in the air. And listen to the birds singing! What about you, young Craig? Will you come with us? Let's go and explore the hinterland, just for a short way.'

'I'd better go to make sure you don't get into any trouble,' Craig answered.

Hupa did not like this reply and told him so. She said she was quite capable of taking care of herself. Craig apologized, saying he knew how competent she was, '... But you need more than youthful courage, Hupa – you need experience too. I have been to many strange islands in my time. So has Boy-girl. You've only just left Rarotonga.'

So the three of them went inshore, leaving Seumas to supervise the gathering of the stores with Polahiki.

2

Once the three explorers had got past the initial tree line, they came upon hilly grasslands beyond. It was an amazing place. Craig told Hupa that it was somewhat similar to the landscape Seumas had described to him when speaking of Land-of-Mists. One or two trees studded the scene, but for the most part it was like a green swell out on the ocean, dipping and rising in a smooth feminine way, with valleys which dropped into clefts through which streams tumbled and rushed, banks of wild flowers on either side.

The three companions strolled across a meadow dripping with small plants whose tiny blooms caused their stalks to curve over gracefully in miniature arches. Insects like small bright stones hummed and buzzed above the plants. Birds dropped down into the tangled grasses, to rise again with something in their beaks: a piece of dried hay; a fluffy windblown seed; a fragment of food. Pockets of herbs here and there exuded wonderful fragrances.

'How delightful,' said Boy-girl. 'Have you ever seen anything more entrancing?'

A lethargy began to creep through Hupa. She watched as the others sighed and stretched out on the grass. Craig was settled a bit further away. Boy-girl allowed her elegant length to decorate a hillock nearby. The three of them rested there in the warm sunshine, each pair of eyes gradually closing as the balmy breezes caressed their lashes. Finally, they all dropped off to sleep within a short time of each other.

When Hupa awoke there was a cool breeze blowing up the hillside which chilled her. Boy-girl was snoring softly, still in the same spot where she had fallen asleep. Craig was nowhere to be seen, an impression in the grass where his body had lain.

Hupa sat up and stared all around. The scene had not changed except for the shadows of the clouds which now swept across it. What a stupid thing it had been to fall off to sleep in a place of which they knew nothing! The three of them could have been slaughtered while they dozed, by some tribe of people, or perhaps a taniwha. And where was Craig now? Surely he would not have gone off without waking her and Boy-girl.

'Boy-girl, wake up!' cried Hupa. 'Craig's gone.'

Boy-girl stirred, sat up and rubbed her eyes, the ornaments in her hair and on her clothes rattling.

'What? What is it? Did I drop off for a moment?'

'We've all been deeply asleep for ages,' answered Hupa, striding about. 'And now Craig's missing. He wouldn't have gone off and just left us, would he?'

Boy-girl suddenly came to her senses. 'No, he would not.' She felt her head. 'Some of my shells are gone,' she said, 'and one or two ribbons. Who would have stolen them? Who *could* have, without waking me. Look, there are tiny handprints on my tapa skirt. Can you see anything? Any tracks?'

'I'm just looking,' replied Hupa, peering at the ground. Then she came across a tiny track where the grass had been flattened. Near to this were footprints, made by some person. They had to be Craig's imprints. Here and there was a crushed flower, a squashed fungus. Whoever or whatever had taken Craig, it seemed he had gone by persuasion rather than force, since the prints were indicative of a casual stroll.

And why would they take just one of the three, leaving the other two? It did not make sense. Had Craig been walking in his sleep? Why hadn't he shouted an alarm?

'I'm going to follow these tracks,' said Hupa. 'You go back to the beach and tell Polahiki what has happened.'

'Shouldn't we both go back to the canoe?' asked the elderly Boy-girl. 'I mean, it might be dangerous for you.'

'I'm well armed,' replied Hupa. 'Would you argue with me if I was Craig and it had been *me* who had been abducted.'

'No,' said Boy-girl, truthfully, 'but you are the daughter of our war chief. I – I feel somehow responsible for you. I'm not sure it's right for me to let you go.'

'There's no right or wrong about it,' snapped Hupa. 'I'm going and that's flat. You either come with me or you go back and get some help. One or the other.'

'Since you put it like that, then I haven't got a great deal of choice, have I? Be careful, Hupa. As Craig said, you have the ability, but not yet the experience. Take things very slowly, weigh up situations ...'

'Yes, yes,' replied Hupa, now walking down the other side of the meadow. 'Tell the others.'

The impetuous young maiden was soon striding out, following a plain trail across the meadow. Through brook and vale she went, past woodland copse and over downy slopes. Now the clouds were racing her on the roof of voyaging above, like canoes anxious to get back to haven before the night fell. Their boating shadows rippled over the hills ahead, disappearing into the mountains beyond. The island was larger than Hupa had first imagined, having a high range of crescent peaks.

To keep her spirits up Hupa began to quote poetry, often turning it into tune with her high clear singing voice. She felt it was pointless to remain quiet. Whoever had stolen her companion away knew she was there in any case. On and on she went, following the clear track until she suddenly realized she was not alone, that there were creatures around her, walking along and keeping pace with her.

She glanced about her in surprise to see fair-haired women and men no larger than children half her height. They were not looking at her, but simply strolling along beside her and behind her. Dressed in a gauze material which billowed gently in the wind and revealed their perfectly beautiful naked forms beneath, they seemed quite undisturbed by the fact that she had discovered them. In their hair and about their bodies they had the swollen blooms of multi-hued flowers, dozens of them. The perfume from these was overwhelming. On their arms and legs were strange shimmering tattoos, but none on their torsos or their faces.

Hupa knew at once she was in the presence of fairies.

She stopped and asked one of them, a male, 'Are you the Peerless Ones, the Tipairu of the hills and forests?'

'No,' the fairy replied, his voice sounding like the rustling of crisp dry leaves. 'We are a different race of fairies – the Turehu of Rarohenga.'

'Rarohenga?' she said, alarmed. 'I have heard from our storytellers that Rarohenga is a land below the earth.'

'This is true,' replied a female fairy, her long, light, tawny hair lifting in the breeze, 'but here in this land we may come up for one month of the year.'

'Can you tell me where my companion is?' she asked the fairy, fearfully. 'He is a man with red hair.'

'Yes,' said another fairy as they crowded around her, touching her legs and waist with their tiny delicate fingers, 'the beautiful man whose hair is the colour of the evening sun is with the King of the Fairies, Uetonga. There are plans to marry him to Princess Niwareka. There is to be dancing. It will make the flowers burst forth on the hillside. There is to be music. It will make the blossoms spring to the branches of the trees.'

'Who is Princess Niwareka?'

'Why, she is the daughter of the king, of course,' came back the answer, accompanied by tinkling laughter. 'She is a fairy of incomparable beauty, whose lovely form makes the trees sigh with contentment. She is much prettier than *you*. Niwareka is virtue itself. She is purity itself. Niwareka is as chaste as spindrift on the waters of the ocean. Not like some we could mention, if we felt like being rude to strangers.'

The fairy looked pointedly at Hupa and its companions tittered nastily.

Hupa was taken aback by this reply, but only for a moment. She realized that the fairies believed her to be Craig's lover and expected her to be jealous. They were expounding the virtues of their princess because they believed Hupa wished to win Craig back from this creature.

'I'll have you know I'm a virgin too,' said Hupa, assertively, 'and I have no desire to have a lover at the moment. In any case, the man you have in captivity is already married and is the father of children. Would you steal a man away from the wife he loves for your own selfish requirements?'

'Yes,' replied the fairy, simply. 'We are selfish creatures, don't you know?'

The Turehu led Hupa to a village surrounded by a natural briar hedge covered in finger-long thorns. One of the fairies trilled a strange language. A spiked gate swung open and the small creatures bustled Hupa through it. Inside the rolling hedge of thorns there were small huts with carved portals and one large meeting house in the centre of the village.

Around the meeting house were clustered a thousand more fairies, with one rather petulant-looking, slightly corpulent male sitting on a throne carved out of a living pohutukawa tree in full bloom. He was cushioned on red blossoms that seemed to curl lovingly around his compact form.

Hupa guessed this must be King Uetonga. As she looked into his eyes, she could see they were purple with tawny flecks. They were not the eyes of a human. They looked as if they belonged in some exotic animal, some fabulous creature from another world. His bountiful sandy hair billowed long and soft around his small body, making his head appear twice as large as that of anyone else. Like the other fairies he was wearing some sort of wispy material which was wafted by the slightest of breezes.

'Who is this who comes here?' cried the king. 'Another person from the outside? Have you brought me presents? A fine cloak? A leather carving?'

'I have come for my friend,' said Hupa, boldly. 'The other member of our tribe who you hold here.'

'The man I enthralled? He must stay. He is to marry my daughter. If you have no gifts for the King of Fairies, for the Lord of the Turehu, then you must go quickly, before we trick the eyes from your head, or the toes from your feet.'

But Hupa was determined not to leave without Craig, who would be lost forever if she did not get him out from under the fairies' spell quite soon. Once the small creatures returned to Rarohenga, below the earth, Craig would never be able to find his way back, even if he wanted to leave them. And they were very good at making mortals believe they *wanted* to stay.

She strolled away from the main knot of fairies and stood at the back when

Craig came forth, his eyes vacant-looking and a silly smile on his face. By his side was a fairy with tawny hair so long it trailed after her in the dust. Her face was as pretty as a white shell. She had a sweet smile on her lovely features and kept looking up at the stupefied Craig, as if he were the most handsome creature in the whole of Oceania.

'You see!' cried the king, for Hupa's benefit, 'he does not want to leave. He loves my daughter, the fairy princess. And she dotes on him – adores him. You have lost him.'

Hupa ignored this and remained in the village until nightfall. The fairies did not seem to go to bed at all, but danced the night away, and looked just as refreshed in the morning. Their music kept Hupa awake most of the night, though she managed to get some rest. Fairies came up to her in the morning, their faces flushed with the excitement of the dances, to place garlands of flowers around her neck.

Craig looked worn out, but still there was more dancing as the dawn turned to a full light.

'I want to take this man away with me,' she said, confronting the fairy king once again. 'What must I do to make you let him go?'

The king looked her directly in the eyes and her mind began to spin in giddy circles.

'Can you play a flute so sweetly that we will be beguiled by your talent and be forced to let him go?' asked the king.

'No,' admitted Hupa, 'I have no musical skills.'

'Can you recite poetry so beautiful it robs one of breath to hear it?'

'No, I have written no poems or songs.'

'Can you sing in a voice that will charm the scarlet pohutukawa blossoms from the trees?'

'I cannot play, I cannot recite, I cannot sing.'

'Then what can you do?'

In a flash she fitted an arrow to her bow and aimed it directly at the king.

'I can split your tiny heart in two from a hundred paces,' she said, 'with one eye closed.'

There was a gasp from the fairies, who stopped dancing immediately. They stared in horror at this mortal maiden who was threatening their king with her weapon. Princess Niwareka let out a high-pitched cry.

The king gave Hupa a faint smile.

'What, would you kill a fairy king with flint and wood? Don't you know it is stone and tree from which we fairies spring?'

'This haft has an arrowhead made of iron, from the teeth of Lioumere the ogress! These are magic arrows. They never miss their target. Look into my eyes if you doubt the truth of this statement, for I'm sure a fairy king can separate truth from lies from the mouth of a mortal.'

The fairies gasped in shock yet again.

'Iron?' said the fairy king, weakly. 'What is *iron?*'

Hupa repeated what she had been told by Seumas.

'Iron is metal. Metal is the essence, the very soul of stone. It will bring kings low. It will level armies. Iron will pierce the toughest wooden or hide shield, the strongest turtleshell breastplate. And – more important to one such as yourself, a fairy king – this iron is magical!'

Hupa turned and loosed her arrow at a palm. It struck the soft trunk like a neck of flesh and pierced it through. The sharp iron arrowhead split the slim trunk in two halves, which fell away from each other on each side. It was as if someone had cleft a piece of kindling with an axe. And this deed had been performed by a slim young maiden!

The fairy king stood up, now impressed by this maiden and the use of her weapon.

'You have more of these arrows with the magical iron points?'

Hupa spoke slowly, quietly and precisely, for fairies' ears are sensitive and fairy language is more formal than that normally used by ordinary people.

'I have three such arrows and this magnificent bow, which was made for me by the Pict, Seumas-from-the-Blackwater. He is a mountain goblin from a strange place, called Land-of-Mists. The man you have captive, Craig with the red hair, is the son of Seumas-the-Black. I ask you to release him or I will surely kill you, King Uetonga.'

There was another gasp from the watching fairies, obviously appalled that this human was threatening their king, even though they knew him to be immortal. They moved back, expecting Uetonga to shrivel her with a look. Instead the wise royal creature cocked his head to one side and smiled.

'You are in love with this man, or you would not dare menace a fairy king in his own land.'

Hupa blushed to the roots of her hair.

'I thought so,' said Uetonga. 'My daughter was told never to take a man who was beloved by his own kind, but to be sure he was free and loose, like a log drifting on the ocean.' He turned to Niwareka. 'What, daughter? Did you think to steal another maiden's lover? I am of the feeling he must go back.'

Princess Niwareka stepped forward, her pale face turning pink with passion.

'NO!' she cried.

'Quiet, daughter,' replied the king.

Uetonga stood up and stepped down from his throne to stand in front of Hupa. The top of his billowing hair, like a dandelion in seed, only came up to Hupa's waist. Yet she could sense a tremendous power in this little being. There was the feeling that if he wished he could leave her charred to a crisp with a mere click of his fingers.

Yet the Turehu were known to be honest fairies, who struck bargains more often than they stole. The king took another of the arrows from the quiver at Hupa's waist and examined the point carefully.

'It's very sharp,' he said, 'smooth and heavy.'

'There is nothing like it in all Oceania.'

'Show me to how to shoot your bow.'

Hupa instructed the king, who seemed to pick up the technique remarkable quickly. Soon a second arrow thudded into a palm tree, which then split in twain as before. The king kept hold of the bow after he had shot the arrow. He reached across and took the third arrow with the iron tip from Hupa's quiver. He fitted the arrow to the cord and aimed it at Hupa's heart. She lifted her chin and stood without a tremble. The fairies waited with bated breath for the release of the arrow, but finally the king eased the tension on the bow.

'Take your bow and arrows,' he said, handing them to her. 'Now let us hear from the redhair. I think I might release him, if I have a mind to.'

With that he snapped his fingers and Craig shook his head as if coming out of a trance. Princess Niwareka screamed shrilly enough to burst the eardrums of a hog. She clung to Craig, who was now looking bewildered.

'I found him,' she shrieked, hurting Hupa's ears. 'I found him asleep on the cold hillside. I beguiled him with sweet honey dew delivered from my very own lips. I kissed him awake, I kissed him entranced, I made sweet love to him. I *want* him. I *want* him. He's mine. You can't let him go. I *want* him, I tell you! I will keep him.'

She stamped her foot and several patches of flowers nearby withered and died. She spat fury at the ring of fairies closing around her and a tree shrivelled down to its roots. She blew hot air down her sweet little nose and a stream dried up, leaving its fish to gasp and choke in the air.

'What's happening?' Craig asked, looking as if he thought he were still caught in a nightmare. 'Where am I?'

'You were on your way to Rarohenga, courtesy of King Uetonga, grandson of Ruau-Moko, God of Earthquakes,' replied Hupa. 'You have been captured by fairies, but the gracious and generous king is about to set you free.'

'Perhaps,' replied Uetonga, his expression entirely enigmatic. 'Perhaps.'

'And who is this?' asked Craig, trying to shake off the wailing princess, who nonetheless clung to him like a ramora sticks to a shark. 'What have I done to her?'

'Nothing,' smiled Hupa. 'She wants you to love her.'

The normally pretty princess's face was now screwed up into something quite ugly. Craig stared at her in pity. One or two fairies wrenched the princess from him, prising her little fingers open to get her to let go. She bit the hands of several of her companions with her tiny white teeth, leaving a perfect crescent of marks on their skin. She scratched at their faces. They seemed used to her tantrums and laughed.

'Niwareka needs a constant supply of young mortal males to woo,' said the king. 'There are twelve unhappy bridegrooms already in Rarohenga, discards of my fickle daughter. They are all deeply in love with her. They pine for her company, they sigh and weep, but she pays them no attention. Once she has had a pretty human for a short time, she grows tired of him. This may be your fate too, young man, unless you impress me.'

'If I can't have *him*,' said Niwareka, her tear-stained face coming up out of her hands for a moment, 'I want some presents. Give me some beautiful whalebone carvings: some scrimshaws fashioned by a seafaring man. Give me some precious shells: a wentletrap, a glory-of-the-seas, a sun shell. Give me some scarlet feathers from the kula bird. I want tapa bark cloth with nice brown patterns. I want pretty pearls from the ocean bed. I want – I want – I want ...'

'You shall be quiet, daughter, and show some graciousness in your defeat.'

The king spoke sternly to Niwareka, but Hupa could tell he was distressed by her behaviour. Uetonga obviously loved his daughter to distraction. There was some indication in the king's tone that it was by no means certain that Craig would go free at the end of it all.

Hupa desperately searched her mind for some way of showing King Uetonga that Craig was unique. Her eyes fell upon his painted leg. Of course, the *drums*, what else? Fairies loved exciting rhythms almost as much as dancing.

'Perhaps your daughter would like the young man to play the drum for her – he has been favoured by Lingadua, One-armed God of the Drums,' said Hupa. 'Craig, show us how you create your rhythms. Give us a display of your talent.'

Uetonga seemed very interested and nodded. 'Yes, young man – if you please me, you will buy your freedom.'

A small drum was brought, the largest the fairies owned, a sharkskin over the end of a hollowed log.

Hupa said, 'Play, Craig.'

Craig did not bother with sticks, but used the tips of his fingers and the palms of his hands to create a wonderful rhythm which had the fairies hopping and skipping. They jigged up and down, whirled each other around, did triple somersaults through the air. King Uetonga looked on, a slow smile gathering about the corners of his mouth and eyes. Clearly here was a man who had magic in his hands, beloved of the god Lingadua.

When Craig had finished the fairies crowded round him, catching their breath.

'May we go now?' asked Hupa, quietly.

'Leave us,' said the king, nodding. 'Be on your way.'

Niwareka let out another of her shrieks. This one split a third trunk in two halves, as perfectly as one of Hupa's arrows.

'Will she be all right?' asked Hupa, anxiously. 'She sounds as if she's unhappy.'

'My daughter,' said the magenta-eyed king, 'will never be all right.' He then turned to Craig again. 'Before you go young man, you may wish for some gift from us, to compensate for your distress. We have troubled you without your permission, so now you may ask something of us. Anything, name it – it shall be yours.'

At this point Hupa realized Craig could ask for riches – scarlet feathers, money cowries, livestock, many canoes – or fame – to be raised high in rank, to have some ambition for status fulfilled. He could have asked for long life, for everlasting health, for undying love. *Anything*, the fairy king had said.

Craig glanced first at Hupa, then stared at Uetonga, as if hesitating, as if what he was about to request was impossible, too much, even for a fairy king.

'I wish to understand my father,' said Craig, quietly.

The fairy king replied, 'It is done.'

Hupa took Craig's hand and led him from the fairy place, through the gateway of thorns, away from the village where the lovely Niwareka was stretched full length on the green turf, her sobbing face buried in the grasses. Craig seemed to come reluctantly.

'Hadn't we better make sure she's all right?' he said.

Hupa pulled him away with her. 'You're still besotted with her, Craig. It's not real love. It's fairy magic. Now think of your wife and children. Do you want to spend eternity in some underworld, pining along with all the other bridegrooms who've been discarded by that spoiled little bitch?'

'That's not the sort of language I'm used to expecting from you,' said Craig, stiffly.

'You'll hear worse if you don't hurry away with me,' replied Hupa, firmly. 'Stop dragging your heels.'

When they reached the brow of a hill they saw a group of people from the canoe coming towards them. There were Boy-girl, Seumas and the Farseeing-virgin, Kikamana, with several armed mariners. When Hupa reached them she said to two of the sailors, 'Get hold of this one. Don't let him go.'

Craig protested but Seumas could see she was deadly serious.

'Do as she says,' he confirmed.

On the way back to the canoe, during which Craig put up a half-hearted struggle, Hupa told Seumas, Boy-girl and Kikamana the story of Craig's capture by Uetonga's daughter. Kikamana was enthralled. She said she had never seen fairies in that number. One or two flitting through the shafts of sunbeams and shadows in a forest, playing touch-and-run in the half-light, but never a whole host of fairies.

'You are very privileged, young woman,' said the ancient Kikamana.

'It doesn't feel like it,' said the more pragmatic Hupa. 'I feel as if I've been into the jaws of sharks and have managed to escape unscathed by sheer good fortune.'

When they had Craig on board again, the canoe set sail. He stood at the mast, staring wistfully at the island as it slowly grew smaller in their wake. No one knew what was going on in his mind, but many could guess. He had fallen, or been made to fall, violently in love with one of the most beautiful creatures in the world, and was now being forced to leave her.

Seumas told his son to snap out of it.

'You're lucky you had a sensible girl like Hupa along with you.'

'I suppose so,' sighed Craig, 'but it's so hard.'

'Self-pity is something I can't stand to see,' Seumas said to Hupa. 'It sickens me to my stomach.'

'Do you mean pining over a woman you can't have?' she replied in an innocent voice. 'In the way that you languish over Dorcha?'

Seumas looked up with narrowed eyes, having been caught entirely off his guard.

'It's not the same,' he said.

'Oh, but I think it is,' replied Hupa, smiling tenderly at the old man. 'And you know it is too.'

He bent his head to his task, declining to reply.

Before she left him, Seumas asked her, 'Are the arrows really magical?'

'Of course,' said Hupa. 'At first I believed my aim had improved, but when I found I could not miss, even with my eyes closed and visualizing the target – I knew then it was not my skill, but the arrows.'

'It would be better to keep this to yourself.'

Hupa nodded. 'I agree – the fewer people know this, the better. There are forces out there which work against us. We would not want these to fall into the wrong hands.'

Seumas nodded, turning away, the guilt flooding through him.

PART FIVE

The sea raiders

1

Maomao, God of the Winds, was busy using all his resources to get the individual fleets to arrive at Tongatapu more or less at the same time. Tangoroa, the Great Sea-God, was also fully employed in such tasks. Oro, the God of War, and others followed behind the active Maomao and Tangoroa, he reshaping and cleaning his weapons of war and the others occupied with similar tasks. Other gods, like Ara Tiotio, God of the Whirlwind and Tornado, were necessarily doing nothing at all, simply keeping themselves quiet and peaceful.

Many of the smaller and less important gods had come along with the Great and Powerful, to be part of the glorious battle with a foreign foe. Amai-te-rangi, the god who angled for humans from the sky, was there with his fishing line and wicker basket. So too was Ulupoka, the god known as The Head, though his body was elsewhere. And Paikea, the God of Sea Monsters, with his following of giant octopuses, squid and gargantuan creatures for which man had no set name.

There were also potent local gods, such as Kukailimoku, the Hawaiians' God of War, without whom they would not consider going into battle.

All these followed in the wake of the two gods who managed the safety and direction of the Oceanian fleets, as they ploughed their way through benign seas to their meeting place. The gods were aware that down below, on the decks, there was martial singing and orations in progress.

Since Hiro had returned with the art of writing, there were men and women recording the events of the voyage by using charcoal to mark rush matting. The gods had nothing against *writing* as an art form, though not many of them understood it or saw the need for it, since they had given mankind 'memory' which should have been sufficient tool for recording purposes.

The same with poetry and song.

It was the Goddess Papa who remarked that Oceanians would soon lose their skill at remembering, if they continued to write everything down on a rush mat tube.

Kieto's voyage was not an easy one. He was still recovering from the shock of losing his hand. But there were enough able captains amongst his navigators to allow him plenty of rest. When he arrived at Tongatapu there were fleets from more than a hundred islands throughout Oceania, averaging ten canoes for every island, each canoe carrying eighty or more warriors. Eighty thousand warriors! It was a glorious sight.

Every so often the sound of conch horns drifted over the quiet evening waters, telling of some new arrival.

'I suppose you thought this day would never come, Seumas,' he said to the Pict. 'Well, here it is.'

'I *hoped* it would not,' replied Seumas.

That evening Seumas took his son aside.

'Craig,' he said, 'it's time I told you something.'

The two sat down by the mast, where a lamp was lit and threw its yellow light over their shoulders. Craig remained silent, knowing his father had something of a serious nature to impart.

'You are aware,' said Seumas, 'that I killed a man, the husband of Dorcha, back in my own land of Albainn. A Scot from the Kingdom of Dalriada, in those days ruled by Aidan-the-False. The Scots have their own region, you see, and the Picts have their Pictland. The two have always been at war, since the Scots came from over the sea to settle in Albainn. There were some people called "the Britons" around, but they have been of little account since the Scots arrived.

'Anyway, this Scot had an iron sword which I coveted. A sword with a *name*, which is always considered special in my homeland. I shall not tell you what the weapon was called, because that's unimportant now. What is important is that I was a savage man in those days and when I wanted something I would go out and fight for it until it was either mine or I was defeated. This was the way amongst the clans and I doubt it's changed very much.

'I don't know whether Dorcha was especially attached to her man, or whether her clan blood ran thicker than water, but she never really forgave me for that bad act. Perhaps it was just the act itself and not those involved which saddened her? I don't know. I could never fathom her soul to its depths, though I tried often enough.

'Don't get me wrong – it wasn't murder – I fought Douglass fair. He was a Scot, not from my people the Picts, and we might have indulged in single combat anyway, just because of our differences in race and clan. There were a dozen reasons to battle without the prize of the sword. Men of our stamp did not need excuses to cut each other down.

'All that is by the by, but in later years Dorcha confessed to me that she had a son, a boy of around ten years at the time we were whisked away by the Oceanians. Dorcha had not had much to do with the recent raising of that lad, even though he was hers, since her husband took him from her at six years of age and gave him to his own parents to raise thereafter, the grandfather of the boy being a man given to brutality and wanting to train the child in violent ways.

'He was also taught to despise the weaknesses of women, especially his mother's. Whenever the boy saw his mother after that he would abuse her, to prove to his grandfather how much he had learned in the art of spurning females. Dorcha suffered mental and physical mistreatment from her own.

'There was not much wrong with all this to the thinking of some people, even perhaps Dorcha, since a man had to be strong to survive at all. One had to make sure a boy could survive hard winters out of doors, fight off wolves, kill intruders before they killed him. It would ensure the boy's future. A baby was breast-fed, weaned by the mother, but the infant was taken by the father and fed with the necessary skills of survival in a land where life outside the clan was cheap.

'In many clans of course the women were treated with respect and deference, but not in all.'

Seumas paused for thought, as if he had forgotten where he was going. Craig remained silent, waiting patiently for the point of the story. Seumas never wasted breath on simple tales, even the history of his past life.

'The trouble is,' continued the Pict, 'that boy will have grown to a man by now – grown *beyond* a man. He's about fifty winters, if he's still alive. He'll be looking for me. His whole life he'll have been looking for signs of Seumas from the Blackwater, in order to put matters to rights. The man who killed his father must be killed. Clan against clan, family against family, man against man. A blood feud.

'When you find yourself in the land of the Albanachs you must seek out Douglass son of Douglass and make your peace with him ...'

Here Craig at last interrupted. 'You can do it yourself, Father – I shall help.'

'Certainly, if I am able, I shall do it,' replied Seumas, 'but I am an old man. We may go into battle and lose and perhaps I may fall. Perhaps *you* may fall. What I say is, if for any reason I cannot go out and seek this man, you must do it for me. One can't leave such a bloodstain on the land without trying to rectify things. It's been a long time, perhaps Douglass son of Douglass has forgotten me – but I doubt it. I think he'll still have me in mind.'

'I'll do my best, though I'm sure you'll be able to do it yourself.'

'Just one more thing – he may call your adopted mother a *wipperjinny*. If you are there with me I command you as my son to stop me from striking him dead, as I'm most certain to do. If you are there alone, then you must swallow the insult put upon her and explain that she was never unfaithful in her head, only doing with her body what a woman with her own needs must do to live a normal life.'

'A wipperjinny?'

'A promiscuous woman.'

For the last part of this conversation, Boy-girl had been present, since there were no secrets, since there was nothing sacred, so far as she was concerned. The fact that this was between father and son meant nothing more to her than that she must be silent for much of the time. But not *all* the time.

She said, 'Seumas, if he is such a man now as you were when you came to us, he will not understand about a woman's needs. If I remember correctly, in the order of things precious, women came after cattle and dogs. Am I correct?'

'This is not to do with you, Boy-girl,' said Seumas, stiffly. 'This is between father and son.'

'Huh!' snorted Boy-girl derisively. 'What's so special about that? The fact is, you pompous old puffer fish, you're thinking of trying to impart civilized thoughts to a savage. It won't work. This Douglass will roar with laughter if Craig mentions his mother's sexual "needs". You know that, I know that, so why try to tell Craig differently?'

Seumas looked thunder at Boy-girl for a moment, then nodded his head slowly.

'Boy-girl's right, I suppose. You will simply have to suffer any insults.'

Seumas then went off to another part of the canoe. Boy-girl followed him, presumably to make her peace with the old man. Craig was left to consider his father's words.

There came a time when the whole fleet was assembled. Kieto then called all the navigators – many of them kings – to a meeting. There he laid out the route for them, to the Land-of-Mists. His memory maps, learned at the age of seven, were perfect. He was not of the new warriors, who relied on the art of writing, though he saw the immense worth of such a thing, and his recall had not suffered accordingly.

He began by telling the navigator kings the fundamental direction as discovered by Kupe when he chased the renegade octopus to the colder parts of the world.

'Sail to the left of the setting sun,' he said. 'This is the time of year when Kupe and myself crossed the dark, cold ocean from Tongatapu to the Land-of-Mists.'

Prince Daggan, leading the Raiatean fleet, stood up to speak. 'Through our atua we have learned that the gods approve of our great expedition,' said the prince, 'but how can they themselves know what lies in store for us? You have told us of ink-black seas, of hard cold waves, of fierce freezing currents likely to wrench a canoe off its course. What I wish to know is, are you fit enough to lead us through these deadly waters?'

Kieto said, 'I assume, Prince Daggan, you refer to my recent injury. It has healed well and good, thanks to the High Priestess Kikamana's ministrations. You need have no fear that I shall fail you at the helm. I have worked all my life towards this goal – nothing could make me pass leadership on to you or anyone else at this point.

'But,' he added, 'you may take your own fleet and return to your Faraway Heaven, if this does not meet with your approval.'

Daggan scowled. 'I shall stay,' he said, sitting down.

This interruption over, Kieto then proceeded to describe the navigational aids that the captains of each craft should look for, in case they became separated from the main fleet. There were, beside the rising and setting stars, certain wave shapes and strange swells; new types of driftwood, seaweeds and birds; the sound of the sea in different regions, and many other smaller points of navigation.

When he had finished, Kieto told his fleet commanders to get some good rest.

'We sail in the morning.'

The next day's dawn was the colour of a chicken's wattle.

Group by group the crab-claw sails were raised and the mighty fleet began to sweep out into the ocean, on the heading of Arue roa on the windflower. Kieto had told all the captains that when they reached the Land-of-Mists they were to travel down the port coast to the bottom of the great island. There, where they had plucked Seumas from the waters, they would make their first landing. Kieto's reason for this was that Seumas knew nothing about the region of the Angles, which covered the top two thirds of Land-of-Mists. He did, however, know intimately his own landscape at the bottom-most tip of the island.

Nothing untoward occurred until the fleet reached the dark, cold waters of which Kieto foretold. Once in those hard, black waves which menaced the fleet on all sides, the leading canoes were attacked by a giant squid. Three tipairua were lost before frantic sailors managed to hack off two of the squid's tentacles and it submerged. Some said the squid was a friend of the octopus which the great Kupe had killed in these waters, but others reminded them that giant squids had no allies.

Next a school of monstrous whales plagued the fleet, swimming and diving in and about the craft, churning the water to a milky white froth which washed over the decks and swept away many warriors, carrying them to a strange, cold death below unfamiliar waves.

The horror with which the mariners regarded this unfamiliar ocean was universal. They could see no further than the surface, below which the darkness of a deepest night prevailed. Darkness and cold were the two aspects of the natural world which Oceanians feared and abhorred, and both were present in this miserable ocean in abundance. The impenetrable nature of the waters gave vent to the wildest imaginative terrors.

There were gargantuan monsters of immense size and ferocity down there, it was said, which waited for victims to enter the water before ripping them to shreds and crunching their bones in jaws full of jagged teeth.

Some of the fish that were caught, though not of giant size, gave a certain credence to these ideas. Lines which went deep came up with ugly monstrosities: fish with huge mouths, lumpy bodies and warty eyes. So repulsive were they the fisherfolk threw them back, line and all, without touching them.

One great eel, cold and slimy and thick as a man's thigh, was as long as one of the canoes. It had small cold eyes with which it regarded its captors and caused them to believe some god of this ocean was using the eel as a *familiar* to view them at close quarters. They hacked the eel to pieces and threw the bits back into the sea.

Although the fleet managed to avoid serious storms, there were squalls which took canoes away in a white blizzard of scattered foam. Fierce cold winds sprang from nowhere, counter to Maomao's efforts to help the fleet on its path, to rip and tear at the mat sails, and sweep away people without their hands on a lifeline. Black rocks suddenly reared up out of high seas, dripping and running with green-white water. It was as if the ocean were alive with monstrous tors which surfaced like whales in the path of the voyagers.

Sometimes gloomy stretches of still inky water dipped and swayed before the lead canoes, harbouring sinister menace which no sailor could name.

It was on one of these oily expanses that Seumas fell sick with a chill.

'It's because I haven't been in this climate for so long,' he said to Hupa and Craig, as they sat by him, piling blankets on his thin shivering form. 'It's a shock.'

'How do you think it is for us?' said Craig, wryly. 'I've never experienced anything like it.'

'And this is summer ...' replied Seumas, with an attempt at humour.

One morning a weak pale sun the colour of coral sand appeared in the sky. This brought with it a thick mist which swirled around the fleet, making them cling even more tightly together. They were locked together on still waters forming a massive raft, waiting for the mist to clear, when suddenly three long ships appeared off to starboard.

'Look!' cried Polahiki. 'War canoes!'

Craig, sitting by Seumas, looked up to see the three vessels, which had no outriggers, no double-hulls and a single square sail. Yet they were large, deckless craft, capable of carrying fifty or more men. They were long and sleek, with high curving prows. Weapons of war flashed in the weak sunlight as the intruders approached the raft of Oceanian canoes.

'Those canoes look like giant lizards,' gasped Craig. 'Father, look at them!'

Seumas went up on one elbow to view the oncoming craft.

The Oceanians who were watching this silent progress could see pale men manning the sleek vessels: men with dark, tawny and red hair. Burly, stone-faced men who looked like sea-washed versions of Seumas. They were wrapped in animal skins bound with leather thongs and there were thick,

shiny bracelets on their forearms and upper arms. It appeared to the Oceanians that they had no necks, for their heads sat firm on their shoulders.

Suddenly the three newcomers, having assessed the situation and found
themselves wanting in numbers, turned away together as if they were one craft
joined by invisible spars. They disappeared into the mists again, as swiftly as
they had become visible, one lone man shaking a heavy fist at the Oceanians.

'Who were they?' gasped Hupa, coming to Seumas's side. 'They looked
like demons riding taniwha.'

Craig asked, 'Yes, who were they, Father?'

'Sea raiders, from the outer islands.'

'Will they inform the Celts we are coming?' asked Craig.

'Doubtful,' replied Seumas, going back down to a state of rest. 'They pillage
the coastal villages themselves, so they're as much the enemy as we are.'

Hupa asked, 'Where did you say they come from?'

'There are small islands to the far south – the Rocks of Orca – which breed
men like those you have just seen. They are hard men, made of nothing but
muscle and tendon, with very little brain. They strip even the poorest village
of its meagre stores and skins. They are merciless creatures. Have no doings
with the likes of sea raiders. They would chew you up and spit you out like a
piece of gristle.'

This information was duly passed on to Kieto, who regarded it with some
suspicion. Seumas was known to exaggerate, especially when it came to stories
of his homeland. Dorcha had confirmed that much. There was something of the
tale-teller in Seumas: he could not allow the opportunity for a fine story to go
by without some embroidery. Kieto thought that perhaps the sea raiders were
to be avoided, but not if it meant any serious inconvenience to his mission.

Craig, on the other hand, had been very impressed by the savage looks of
those seafarers. The man who had shaken his fist had had hair the colour of
sunbleached driftwood. It had hung down below his shoulders in greasy tangles. On the top of his head had been a hat shaped like half a coconut, except
that it had been shiny and smooth-looking. Slung across his chest had been
a sword, similar to the narwhal spikes which some Oceanians made into
weapons, but flat-bladed.

'He would be a difficult man to beat in single combat,' Craig told himself,
staring into the thick curtains of mist before him. 'It would not be easy to
take him.'

However, though Seumas was sick in body, he seemed to recover in spirit.
He was all for chasing the sea raiders to the ends of the earth once the Land-
of-Mists had been won or lost.

'We could take a breakaway fleet,' he said to Craig. 'You and I, son, out on
our own. By the gods, it would be like the old days ...' His eyes shone with
enthusiasm. 'Just six or seven canoes. We could attack them quickly, while

they were in harbour, for those longships are fast under sail. We could board them in the night and have a fine old scrap.'

'I think it would be more than a *scrap*, Father. They look formidable fighting men.'

'They are, son, they are,' cried Seumas. 'Where would the glory be if they were not? But we could beat them, I know we could. They're arrogant bastards, but they're clumsy in battle, wielding heavy axes and swords. Us Oceanians, we're light on our feet. We could be in and away before they knew what was happening to them.'

Us Oceanians? His father was one of them again. But his Pictish ancestors did not go without mention.

'... also I was once an Albannach. We Picts are worth three times one of those sea raiders.'

Seumas picked up a patu club and began hacking away at invisible enemies, while the mariners ceased working at the shrouds and stood to watch and cheer, some of them yelling encouragements to Seumas during his mock battle. Craig had to admit his father's old litheness was still evident. Age had not dimmed his battle spirit. Seumas had fought with monsters and had walked away laughing. He was a hero of the old school.

Seumas quickly tired, his breath becoming short, but he smiled at his son. 'Like that,' he said. 'And with you at my side.'

'Yes, Father,' grinned Craig. 'We would stand like rocks, you and I.'

'Dorcha too, if she were alive. She could be a warrior when it suited her. Oh, yes, she used to bleat a lot about war being terrible, but when it came to protecting her own kind, why she could use a weapon I can tell you. Pity she's dead.

'But there's life in this body yet. Deeds to be done, Craig. I've been a bit morose of late. That's not good. I'm happier now. I have things I want to do.'

'Rid the sea of raiders.'

'Yes, by god,' roared Seumas, delightedly, holding his son behind the neck and bellowing into the wind. 'That, and other deeds!'

Seumas never recovered from the effects of the chill. His son and his friends took turns to sit up with him at night, during the dark hours, when the fear of death overwhelms any person close to its edge. There were times when he was terrified, there were times when he was accepting of it. More than once he felt ready to go. Some believed it was because he was faced with seeing his birthplace destroyed by an invader. Craig did not subscribe to this view. Craig believed it was merely coincidence, that his father was old and unwell, that his body, not his mind, was failing him.

'The black spectre comes to make me pay for my wrongs,' whispered Seumas to Kikamana, the Farseeing-virgin, as she watched over him alone one night. 'I have to atone.'

'If you feel remorse, then you are atoning,' she replied. 'Your wrongs are nothing beside the crimes of many men.'

'I should like my hands to have been clean, but I'm not that kind of man. If not the misdeeds I have done, then others equally as bad. I wish I had been a better made man.'

'There are many who will mourn you, be sad to see you go.'

'Then I am dying?' he said, his eyes misting over with sadness and fear. 'I am going.'

Kikamana was not one to lie. 'I shall be arriving at journey's end myself very soon,' she said. 'It will be good to stop travelling and rest.'

He grasped at this view of death like a drowning man clutches at thin air.

'Yes, yes, that's it. The end of a long journey. Not a thing to get upset about. Like stepping from a boat after a long sea voyage, eh? Not such a terrible end – more something we've been striving for, hoping to reach, all our lives?'

'That's how I see it.'

For a moment his face looked serene, then it hardened into a cynical expression.

'If you believe that, you'll believe anything. It's a bloody shame, that's what it is. Who wants to get off the boat while it's still out in the ocean?'

Seumas slipped lower and lower, until one morning grey cliffs appeared out of the mist on the starboard side. Boy-girl and Craig were with him, by his side, as was his hound Dirk. Seumas lifted a weak arm and pointed.

'Albainn,' he whispered in a voice like rustling leaves.

'Is this it, Father?' asked Craig. 'Is this your birthland?'

'This is where I was born,' confirmed Seumas. 'I climbed those cliffs, boy and man, to wring the necks of those fulmar birds you see wheeling about them. I killed them for the oil in their stomachs. Now the damn birds outlive me, for I am dying, son – slipping away fast. Listen to those bastards laughing at me. They're getting their own back. They don't see an old man dying – they see justice happening before their eyes – the Pict who killed their mates and fledglings is choking for want of air. I can hear them call to one another. They remember I used to rob their nests of their kind. Birds don't forget.'

'They're not the same birds, Father,' replied Craig, as if it were important. 'Those birds are long dead.'

'Then I've gone past my time,' sighed Seumas, his voice like the wind riffling the dry leaves of the pandanus hut. 'I should go. Yet I still cling fiercely to the world of the living. There's still a fire burning within me, which does not want to go out.' His eyes shone with an unusually bright light, as if there really were a flame behind them. 'I wanted to know more, my son, learn much more. But I had a bad start at learning. A good start at killing, but a bad start at gathering knowledge. You have a better one ...'

'Quiet, Father – you'll tax yourself.'

'Tax myself? I'm on my way out. How strange to think that in a few moments I will no longer be in this body. No longer able to draw breath, move these lips, make these sounds which mean so much to us. One moment there is life, the next nothing but an empty shell, a discarded coconut husk.'

Craig was holding his father's hand now, gripping it hard, as if he could anchor Seumas to the living world, stop him from drifting off into oblivion.

'The darkness is coming in, boy. Where are the cliffs? I can hear the fulmars' cries but faintly in the dimness of my fading brain. Craig, Craig, are you there, son? Don't leave me now.'

Dirk whined – a mournful note.

Seumas's fingers clawed at Craig's cloak, gripping it, pulling his son's face down close to his own. Craig could hardly feel the shallow breath on his cheek. He knew it was true, his father was dying. There was no sight in the eyes. They could see things now that no living man should see. Craig wrapped his arms around the tattooed Pict, holding him close as the lungs sighed for the final time.

In that moment, while crossing the pale of death, Seumas begged for a promise.

'Look after my people, son.'

'Yes, Father – I promise.'

Then the old man was gone – gone to join his Dorcha in the regions beyond life – where they could know each other again.

Dirk nuzzled the body, now cooling rapidly in the chill air. The dog was making strange noises in the back of its throat.

Boy-girl was weeping, her tears falling on Craig's shoulders as she reached over to touch the face of the corpse with the tips of her fingers.

'He never said goodbye to me,' she said. 'Couldn't he see me?'

'He was blind at the end – didn't you hear him?' replied Craig, wondering at her words. 'He told us so.'

'I couldn't understand a word he was saying,' sobbed Boy-girl. 'Not in that strange tongue of his.'

It was at that moment that Craig realized his father's deathbed speech had been in Gaelic. It was a shock. Craig had never learned the language from Seumas, though the old man had tried to teach him on a number of occasions.

Craig gently laid the body back down. It was as light as a straw. It was as if it had been the spirit of the man which had weighed heavy on the earth: the lifeforce which carried muscle, bone and blood. It was true, there was nothing of Seumas left but a husk. Hupa came and put her arm around Craig and he wept into her slim shoulder. She hugged him and held his head and rocked with him, imbibing much of his grief, letting it mingle with her own lesser grief, so that he could become whole again.

When Kieto learned of Seumas's death he ordered the fleet out to sea again. First he ordered that the Pict's heart be removed from the chest of the corpse and placed in a container of preservative fluid. Then he conducted the funeral of his lifelong friend and mentor, saying that Seumas was a man of two worlds and had belonged in both. The body was swaddled tightly in pandanus leaves and bound with sennit. The package was then strapped to a spar ready for a journey to some shore.

'We shall miss him greatly,' Kieto said. 'His close friends – Kikamana, Boy-girl and myself – and yes, to a certain extent, Polahiki – we shall all be the poorer for his passing.'

He paused for a moment's silent before adding one last comment.

'I-am-bereft.'

With those last three words Seumas's body was consigned to the dark ocean and the dry-eyed Kieto went into his deck hut.

Craig stared as the mummified body was taken away by the currents, wondering at his father's last request.

Look after my people!

Craig had said he would, but now that he thought about it, was unhappily confused.

Who were his father's people?

Which did he mean?

The Celts?

Or the Oceanians?

2

It was night and the watchfires of the Celts could be seen from the decks of the tipairua.

Seumas's death had left Craig with a terrible responsibility, since now their major guide and mediator had gone. It meant that Craig was the one to whom Kieto would turn for information: knowledge Craig had come by in a curious and convoluted way. Boy-girl had since told Kieto that Craig understood the language of the Picts and Scots, had learned it secretly from Seumas.

Yet Craig had not learned it, not in that way.

It seemed his visit to the fairies had been for a purpose, for now he remembered King Uetonga's gift to him on parting.

I wish to understand my father, Craig had said.

It is done, the king had replied.

Craig had of course meant that he wanted to understand his father's feelings, his thoughts, the roots of his culture, but the king had taken the words literally. He had given Craig the gift of understanding his father's *language*. Gaelic was now as much a part of Craig as it had been part of Seumas and Dorcha, who had kept the strange tongue alive in their heads between them during the years of their exile.

Other knowledge, too, was embedded in Craig's brain, and needed but direct questions to prise it out. Often he did not himself understand what he was talking about. It was as if he were a vessel full of exotic fruits, of which he knew all the names, but none of which were familiar to him.

Boy-girl came to see Craig as he stood by the mast. Dirk was at her side. She had taken on the care of the dog now that Seumas was gone. It was something she wanted to do. When Seumas had been alive, she had derided the Pict for his love of his hounds, but now he was no longer there she wanted some part of him to remain with her. Dirk filled that role.

'We land at dawn,' said Boy-girl.

'I know,' replied Craig. 'Are you ready?'

'For this? Never. It's been Kieto's dream, not mine. What would I want with a conquered land, a conquered people? It's some notion Kieto has of warding off a future invasion. Strike first.'

'And what if we lose?'

'Then we go home like curs, with our tails between our legs, and wait for the Angles or the Celts to come to us.'

'It's a big risk. They wouldn't have come to Oceania in *our* lifetime.'

Boy-girl nodded. 'I know, but Kieto's right – we must protect the future.'

When the slow dawn came rolling in, grey and monstrous, some time later, they made a landfall. A beach head was quickly established, then the warriors poured onto the shore, out of the cold waves that crashed on lonely grey sands covered in weed, dead birds and tangled driftwood. They made their way up craggy slopes to the land above the shore. There in the drifting fog and mists they began felling trees with flint and shell axes, to build fortified pa according to the instructions issued by Kieto.

With engineers supervising, the Oceanians worked furiously to give themselves some sort of protection before they were discovered. Soon there were palisades of sharpened stakes and deep ditches encircling the individual encampments. Samoans, Fijians, Raiateans, Hawaiians, all had their particular methods of getting the tasks done, and they did it with zeal.

One of the reasons for the speed of the operation was that the mist was gradually clearing. Sentries had been placed in a wide semicircle, to warn of any approach by the enemy. By noon there were reports coming back to Kieto to indicate that the natives were now aware they had foreigners on their soil.

Yet still the shock of the Oceanian arrival had not been felt seriously enough, for the Celts did not organize themselves on any large scale. What was happening was that clan members, out hunting together, would come and stare in amazement at the activity of close to a hundred thousand dark-skinned men stealing their trees to make forts, before going off again to pass on the news to chieftains and overlords. It was not until that night that the chieftains themselves began to come to the idea that they ought to discuss this invasion of their land between them.

Such was not an easy thing, for the clans were constantly at war with one another and the maintenance of blood feuds was more important than the threat of any casual visitors. Those who lived in hill cave communities hated those who lived in wee crofts in the lush glens below. Those who owned the mountain passes despised those who herded cattle around the shores of the lochs. Pict hated Scot, Scot hated Pict, both hated the Britons, all three hated those tribes of Angles who lived in Albainn and even more those Angles up in Engaland.

In short, none of them trusted one another. If anything, they wondered how they could turn to their own advantage the arrival of these brown-skins in order to kill a few more Kenzies or Leods or Phears. Some of the larger Scottish clans around their centre of Dunadd in the kingdom of Dalriada were even considering herding the lesser clans towards the newcomers, to see what occurred between them. Their chief, Ceann Mor, 'The Bighead', hardly mentioned the newcomers. The Pictland clans – the Cirech, Fiobh, Moireabh, Fótla, Cé, Fortriu and Cat – warned each other to stay away in case it was a Scottish ploy to get them all in one place and wipe them out. Their present war chief, Cormac the Venomous, who had recently murdered his rival, Eochaid Redhands, chose to ignore the situation, saying it was Scotch witchery, sorcery of a Celtic kind.

In consequence, the Oceanians found themselves with a week's grace, to build their pa and settle into the Albannach earth like hard little nuggets. The tipairua were kept moored off-shore at first, but wild winds and heavy seas drove them into bays unsuitable for a long stay. Finally, Kieto sent them off northwards along the coast to find a natural harbour somewhere, hopefully on a small island away from the mainland, leaving his army without any means of escape.

'We have to make good now,' he said, grimly. 'We must vanquish or we perish.'

After a week the clans were wise enough to see that they would be overrun by a foreign army if they did not quickly get themselves together. Already companies of Kieto's men were making forays into the wild hinterland, chasing local wildmen back into their bogs. Their first encounters with the Scots and Picts gave both sides a healthy respect for each other.

Kieto organized a system of messengers, to run between pa with written instructions and orders. Obviously the fleetest runners were used for this purpose. Parties of warriors were sent out to find sources of food. There seemed to be no coconuts, breadfruit or sweet potatoes. The landscape seemed devoid of edible crops of any kind, except for root vegetables as hard as stone and tasteless into the bargain.

As for meat, wild pig was found. Birds were there in plenty, often plump and sweet-tasting. Fish in the streams were abundant and very appetizing. There were dogs too though these were not suitable for eating, since they were mangy, savage creatures, all stringy muscle. The wild dogs attacked the Oceanians savagely when approached. They were worse than Dirk, who was well known throughout Oceania for his ferocious nature, and so the creatures were given a wide berth.

Hupa and Kapu were amongst the hunting party to first come upon a herd of cattle.

'What are they?' cried Kapu. 'They look like walking huts.'

There were about a dozen of the creatures, idly grazing on grass. The cowherd had run off on seeing armed tattooed brown warriors in strange dress come out of the forest. His cows with their long shaggy coats and large horns remained where they were, unperturbed. To the Oceanians they looked formidable creatures, with their huge curved horns and muscled bulk. One of the steers lifted its head and stared at Kapu.

'It's going to charge!' cried the young man, backing towards the forest. 'Kill it quickly, Hupa.'

But the creature merely ambled forward to a greener area of grass and began ripping and chewing again, seemingly unconcerned by the presence of the warriors.

Hupa walked forward slowly and found that the cattle edged away from her rather than charged. They did not run in fear either, though they appeared slightly timid. Finally she persuaded her group to prod the beasts with their spears, driving them back to the pa. There she presented this 'find' to Kieto, who was most impressed with the animals.

'We shall spit-roast one of them tonight,' he said.

And indeed, this they did, to find the meat wholesome and absolutely delicious.

'No wonder Seumas didn't want us to invade this land,' said Polahiki, burping loudly. 'With big horned pigs like these roaming around, just waiting to be cooked.'

'The hide will go to my daughter Hupa,' said Kieto, 'for finding the beasts – it will make a fine cloak.'

'I was there too,' grumbled her twin brother, Kapu, 'don't I get a cloak?'

Hupa said, 'The skin is large enough for two cloaks at least – we'll share it between us.'

'No,' replied the petulant Kapu. 'I don't want part of yours, I want my own. Why am I always being treated like an infant? Why do you and your Whaka-tane get all the credit, when others do as much?'

Kieto glared at his son. 'You will share the skin, or you will get nothing. Your sister is very generous. I hear you ran away when you saw these creatures.'

Kapu scowled and denied that he had 'run'. He told his father he was nat-urally cautious and had moved towards the tree line, for protection in case they were charged.

'We did not know at the time whether they were dangerous or not – I think my caution does credit to me.'

The war chief softened in his attitude.

'Perhaps you are right, but you will still do as I say – you will take half of the hide – the other half going to your sister. I will hear no more dissent.'

With that the matter was closed, but a festering jealousy was growing in Kapu which others recognized might one day be his downfall. Already he was beginning to hate his sister. In recent days he was much in the company of Prince Daggan and his sorceress wife, Siko. They seemed to have a lot to talk about, considering Daggan was an enemy of the boy's family.

Traditional Oceanian sources of food were not so forthcoming as the meat. There was very little fruit to be found, except for berries on bushes. Seumas had told them of tiny nuts and small hard, bitter fruit, called 'apples', both of which grew on trees like mangoes. These were not in evidence, it being the wrong season for such bounty. There were wild flowers every-where, and the purple and white stuff about which Seumas had waxed lyrical on many an occasion – a plant called 'heather'.

Kikamana was the person with the knowledge of fauna and flora, she being the person most interested in such things when Seumas and Dorcha were alive. From pictures drawn by those two Celts, she now recognized many of the different plants and not a few of the strange creatures of the landscape. There were deer, equally as good for eating as the cows but much fleeter of foot. There were woolly sheep and goats.

There was one fast little animal that made a good meal – provided a hunter could catch one – which Craig knew to be called a 'hare'. However, one had to be an excellent shot with a bow, like Hupa, or be clever at setting snares for the creatures. They ran like the wind in a wide curving arc and hid in little double-ended tunnels on the mountainside. The wild dogs chased them and the eagles fell on them, but their numbers seemed to be such that the loss of a whole col-ony did not appear to affect their ubiquitous presence on the landscape.

What with the stores they had brought with them and what they could forage from the landscape, the Oceanians were not likely to starve. Also, once they began taking prisoners, there would be meat for those Oceanians who still practised cannibalism. The Hivans and the Fijians said they could not wait to get their sharpened teeth into some nice white meat for a change.

The climate, however, was not to the Oceanians' liking. Although the season was supposed to be what Seumas called 'spring', it was still very cold on the skin of the sun-loving Oceanians. Winds swept up from the regions beyond the dark seas, the source of the world's coldness, and cut right through the warm-blooded warriors from the islands. Nights were brisk affairs to be passed under thick blankets, cuddled up to some loved one if at all possible. Mornings were always draped in mist and sometimes the warriors woke to find themselves chilled to the marrow by a covering of hoar frost on the ground.

'Where does Ra go to in this awful place?' asked Polahiki of Kikamana. 'Is he ashamed to show his face?'

'You forget, this is not Ra's domain, but that of another sun god,' replied the Farseeing-virgin. 'Even now our gods are gathering on the fringes of this land, ready to enter and do battle with strange deities for whom we have no names.'

'Craig knows some of the names,' replied Polahiki, shivering, and looking about him at the dreary aspect of a misty evening closing in. 'He told me some of them. One of the most important is a goddess called Brighid, who taught the Celts smithcraft and metalwork – that is how to use that iron stuff which Seumas regarded so highly. And Taranis, a thunder god, who no doubt will fight with Tawhaki when the time comes. Manannan mac lir, the Great Sea-God of this place, who will battle with Tangoroa for supremacy of the ocean ...'

'I am unable even to find a place for such gods in my mind,' said Kikamana. 'Their names are so utterly alien to me.'

'I know what you mean,' replied Polahiki, as the twilight wore unendingly on. 'Here in this land even the dusk takes for ever to disappear into its own gloomy hut.'

'Speaking of huts, yesterday Craig and I went out together. We were looking for streams with fish, but came upon a rocky place deep in a valley where there was a small dwelling made completely of unhewn stone slabs. I could not approach the place, for there were dark spirits there, glaring out at me. A *dolmen* Craig called it in the language of his father.'

'How did Craig know what to call it?'

'He has this gift of knowing, given to him by King Uetonga of the fairies.'

'Is this dolmen a dwelling place for the dead?'

Kikamana said she did not know for sure, but that it felt such a place.

Thus the Oceanians, with the help of Craig, grappled with their new environment and struggled with the strange atmospheres of Land-of-Mists, which disturbed some more than others.

There were certainly fairies and monsters here and other supernatural beings, which for the moment were holding their powerful forces in check. The Oceanians were as strange to the indigenous spirits of the place, whether fair or foul, as they themselves were to the newcomers.

There was a kind of magical stalemate while assessments were carried out.

The Celts finally managed to put traditional grievances aside and formed what they called an army, but was better described by Craig as a horde. One sunless morning thousands of them came charging down out of the hills, yelling and screaming, their wild hair streaming in the damp morning air. The Picts were recognizable by their tattooed bodies, but the Scots had also painted themselves with various dyes.

They were all completely naked except for a weapon belt around their waists.

The sight of naked hairy bodies and freely-swinging genitals shocked and unnerved the prudish Oceanians behind their defences.

'It's to do with going into battle unencumbered,' Craig explained to them. 'Weapons catch on clothes, and cloth can be driven into wounds by blades and make them fester ...'

But this explanation went over the heads of the Oceanian warriors, as some of the Celts stopped dead not far from the palisades and used their left hands to waggle their genitals in an obscene and insulting gesture at the enemy, while making strange gaseous noises with their tongues. Some of them actually turned to bend over and fart with bare arses at the shocked newcomers. Others pissed on the ground in front of them with a look of disdain on their features. Then the naked Celts threw themselves at the high fences, while the stunned Oceanian spearmen had to gather their wits before they could hurl their missiles down on them from platforms above.

Oceanians beat out battle rhythms on their drums, but the enemy responded with fearsome music.

'The screaming of dying pigs,' wailed some of those Oceanians who had never heard Seumas play his pipes. 'They have evil spirits trapped in those bags!'

Craig quickly sent messengers between the pa to inform the warriors as to the exact nature of the bagpipes and to tell them to put wax in their ears if they could not stand the sound.

Since there were no siege weapons the attack was not a great success, except for the opportunity for the two sides to get a good look at one another. It was an especially frustrating day for the Celts, who desperately wanted to get at the enemy and give them a good thrashing. The Oceanians on the other hand were impressed by those few Celts who were on horseback. To ride an animal like that obviously took great skill and man and creature would have been a formidable set of opponents on an open battlefield.

As it was the Celt horsemen could do nothing but ride up and down in front of the pa, waving their iron swords. There were grisly round objects suspiciously like human heads dangling from the manes of their mounts. Their horses, strong-looking muscled creatures with thick legs, wore masks of wicker and bark, which made them appear devilish creatures.

Kieto realized now why Seumas had warned them about the horses, for the mad-eyed, snorting, hoofed beasts with their clashing teeth were like something out of a nightmare.

When the Celts saw that they were throwing themselves against virtually impregnable defences, they tried to burn those defences down. Kieto, having lived with the Maori who invented the fortified pa, had foreseen this and seawater was available to douse the flames. At the end of the day the Celts went home, taking their dead and wounded with them. The Oceanians too had lost men, but the casualties were light on both sides.

'What now?' Craig asked Kieto. 'Do we follow them?'

Kieto considered this. It was a good tactic to creep in the path of retreating warriors and fall upon them in the dark, just when they thought they were safe. They would be busy building fires and making camp. Many of them could be slaughtered this way. But somehow, after seeing the Celts in battle, Kieto got the idea that the natives would regard this as a rather dishonourable way to conduct a battle.

'No, we'll see what tomorrow brings. Let's replenish our water supplies tonight and prepare ourselves for another day of fighting ...'

The following day's fighting produced more or less the same results, so that evening a deputation of Celts – some six or seven of them dressed in coarse clothing – came unarmed up to the gates of one of the pa and indicated with sign language that they would like to talk. Kieto was actually in another pa, but the fortifications were all linked by fenced passages. He arrived with Craig as the visitors were being sat down in front of a fire.

The leader of the Celts was a big bole-chested man with thick shoulders and one eye. He had a hound with him that was almost as ugly as its master. The cur lay with its belly to the earth, regarding everything around it through suspicious, narrowed eyes. It clearly did not like the smell of this place or the people in it and would, for less than the rib of a rat, deliver a few flesh wounds amongst these unwholesome strangers.

One-eye spat into the flames as he glared at the two Oceanians with his single orb. The phlegm sizzled on one of the logs as Craig opened negotiations.

'Greetings, chieftains,' said Craig in Gaelic, 'you have nothing to fear while you come to us unarmed.'

'Fear ye?' growled One-eye. 'I fear my dog more than I fear you.'

'A wise choice,' said Craig, looking at the ferocious beast. 'It is a fearsome creature.'

One of the other Celts, a thin man with whitish hair, smiled at this remark. This man cleared his throat now, ready to speak, and Craig gave him his attention.

'Ye speak our language,' said White-hair. 'How is this?'

'I am half Pict,' explained Craig, 'though this is the first time I have seen the land of my forefathers. My father was Seumas-from-the-Blackwater ...'

This speech was interrupted by a cry of anguish from one of the visitors, a thick-set man with black hair. The Celt leapt to his feet, snatched a club from one of the Oceanians guarding him, and rushed forward to strike Craig. One-eye grabbed his ankle as he passed and wrenched his legs from under him. The warrior, not a young man, went crashing on his face in the fire. The smell of singed hair filled Craig's nostrils. His attacker was back on his feet in an instant, still brandishing the weapon, but was felled from behind by One-eye with a log from the woodpile at the side of the fire.

'Get him out of here,' said the chieftain to two of his men, as the warrior lay unmoving. 'Lug the fool away.'

When the unconscious man was removed from the pa, White-hair continued to question Craig.

'Ye are the son of Seumas. I do not know this man. Is he amongst us?'

'Clearly your friend knew him, but no, he is not here. He died on the voyage to this land. And before you start thinking "traitor", it was not Seumas who led the Oceanians here. They found their own way many years ago and took Seumas captive along with a woman called Dorcha.'

Something registered on the old man's face.

'Ah, now I think I understand – Dorcha is the mother of Douglass Barelegs, son of Douglass ...'

'Stop this gabble,' interrupted One-eye, impatiently, 'and let's get down to what we came here for.' He turned to Kieto, recognizing him as the leader of the invaders. 'We cannot fight while you hide behind skirts of bark. Come out into the field and we shall see who is strongest. Are ye cowards to cringe and cower behind these wooden walls?'

With Craig acting as interpreter, Kieto learned what was being said and made reply.

'No, we're not cowards, we're sensible men. You know the lay of the land, we do not. You know the nature of your weather, we do not. We must use every advantage open to us, or you'll overrun us.'

'Overrun you? We are a tenth your number.'

'For the moment,' replied Kieto, 'but I am not so stupid as to think your numbers will not increase by the day, as word goes out to more of your tribes.

Even as we speak they must be flocking towards this place, eager for a good battle with outsiders.'

One-eye exchanged looks with White-hair and Craig realized that Kieto's guesses were accurate.

'My name is Cormac,' said One-eye. 'They call me Cormac the Venomous. What is yours?'

'Kieto.'

'Listen then, Key-toe – give us one good battle, the morn's morn. I'll be on the field with double the numbers I have today, but that's still a fifth of what you can put out. One good battle, eh? To get each other's measure.'

Kieto considered this proposal for a long time, then he nodded slowly. 'One good battle in the open – then we fight as best we know how. You will see that Oceanians are superior warriors and capitulate thereafter. But no horses.'

'No horses?' cried the chieftain, his bushy eyebrows arching.

'There must be a trade. You do not get something for nothing. We are giving up our pa, you must give up your horses. If you promise the beasts will be kept off the field, then we will meet you and do battle.'

Cormac nodded thoughtfully, reaching down to stroke his hound while he considered the matter. Kieto stared at the dog. Its hackles rose and it growled in the back of its throat as its head came up.

'I know you,' said Kieto to the cur. 'I have seen your kind before.'

The dog snarled, but its master held it by the ruff.

'I agree,' said Cormac, finally.

'Good.'

'Ye will see you waste your time attacking Celts, who will bite off your heads and chew your skulls to mush.'

After the Celts had gone, Craig followed his leader into a hut and sat with him.

'Is this a good thing, Kieto? I thought the idea was to wear them down first, by letting them exhaust themselves on the pa? But to go out there while they are fresh?'

'We must prove our worth on the open field, or we'll never get them to capitulate. You heard the veiled reference to hiding behind women. If they believe we are timid creatures afraid to come out of our villages, they'll simply keep on fighting until they exterminate us, no matter how many battles they lose. If, however, we put it in their minds that we are bold invaders, proud warriors who love the art of war – then we shall see a different frame of mind.'

Craig went to his bed thinking about the man they called Douglass son of Douglass, realizing this was one of those who his father wished him to befriend. It did not look a likely proposition at this point in time. To make his peace with such a man he would first have to knock him down, then tie him to a stake to render him harmless. Otherwise the Celt would open up Craig's skull at the first opportunity.

Craig sighed. It was not going to be easy.

The following day the two armies met on the open plain between the mountains and the shore. The moaning tones of conch shells drifting over the Albannach hills mingled with the sound of metal horns. Celtic drum beats melded with the rhythm of Oceanian sticks on hollow logs. There was a feeling in the air, the anticipation of battle, as warriors ululated, calling to one another from hill to hill, ground to ground.

This feeling increased amongst the naked Celts, many of them with combat erections, until they were delirious with battle-joy, rushing forwards without waiting for commands, thoroughly disorganized but eager to bite flesh with iron. The Oceanians were rigid. They had their set pieces and they awaited the command for the day.

Craig looked out on the battle lines of his own people, before the roaring Celts reached them. There were the gay feathered helmets, the magnificent cloaks of dogskin decorated with parrot feathers, the banners and standards of the chiefs flowing in the wind, the polished ironwood clubs glinting in the sunlight, the decorated white, brown and black kilts of tapa bark with their geometric designs. The wonderful tattooed shoulders of the warriors. How colourful they were! How brilliant to the eye! What a stirring picturesque vision they made.

The Celts themselves were drab in comparison, despite the blue and red dyes and the tattoos on the bodies of the Picts. Their naked bodies were quite offensive to Craig's eyes, their black iron swords looked rough and sinister, their sweat-stained, cracked leather weapon-harnesses quite ugly. The only real colour about them was the variety of hair types, that billowed red, brown, blond and black in the ripe wind from the coast.

They were like their own landscape, their own seascape and their own skies: rugged grey rocks below with mournful grey skies above. Yes, there was green and purple in there somewhere, with the occasional patch of blue, but swamped by grey.

Yet these too were his people, on his father's side!

The Oceanians were light on their feet, graceful, full of the flame of youth, closer to the sun and the stars, richer in skin tones, delicate, more spiritual in aspect!

The Celts were heavy on their feet, bulky in stature, strong-boned, ruddy-complexioned, big thundering fellows with big forearms and big thighs, full of savage courage that hurled them into battle with no thought of defeat or the safety of their lives and limbs.

Kieto, on seeing the wave of unruly, wilful Celts tumble in a torrent down the sides of the hills and wash out onto the plain, gave the order for paitoa: to stand like a rock and allow the enemy to hurl themselves at them. The messengers fanned out from Kieto carrying their prepared slates with the order scratched on them, using the 'writing' which Hiro had brought back to the peoples of Oceania from his travels.

The runners reached Samoans, Fijians, Hawaiians, Rarotongans, Raiateans, Hivans, and many other Oceanian islanders who then knew to stand unwavering, with weapons at the ready, while the wild Celts came charging forwards. They had received tapu from the priests and were full of the lust for battle. Victory would give them much mana, fill their heads with the potency of manhood and magic. Their faces were blackened with charcoal to make them appear that much more ferocious to the enemy. They were eager, hopping from one foot to another, as the drums pounded out blood-rushing rhythms.

Craig remained frustrated behind the lines, witnessing the action, his skills as an interpreter too valuable for Kieto to lose at such an early stage.

The land on the two sides of the plain consisted of brown peat bogs, with weather-scoured deep ditches. In order to avoid these, the Celts pouring across the plain were channelled naturally towards the centre of their front. Craig saw a thick wedge of naked Celts drive into the middle of the Oceanians, their iron swords wreaking havoc. The line of Oceanians gave at that point and almost let the Celts through, just managing to hold with a second line of reinforcements holding firm.

But the Celts' undisciplined attack worked against them as they pushed and shoved against each other in a massive tight knot of bodies, arms and legs, trying to get at the enemy. The Hawaiians, fighting in their traditional crescent-shaped front, closed their flanks round the foe, so the Celts were effectively caught in a passage lined by two walls of their brown-skinned enemies, whose battle clubs, some of them almost as tall as a man, cracked skulls and took off heads at the neck.

This meant there were some Celts caught in the middle of the mass of their comrades, Celts who were unable to use weapons on the foe for fear of striking friend. Spears and arrows rained down on these unfortunates hemmed in by their own confederates. They naturally tried to force their way out of the middle, thus propelling those on the outside of the column into the clubs of the Oceanians, eager to pay back in kind.

The eagerness of the Oceanians worked against them, however, as they drove the enemy back to firmer ground. Once outside the bottleneck the Celts were able to spread sideways and form a more cohesive and orderly battle line. However, this meant that the front had thinned and a group of impetuous Hivans broke through the line, which then closed behind them.

These Hivan warriors, some fifty men, found themselves battling behind the Celtic front line. With more space available both iron sword and ironwood club were wielded with more swing and thus more force.

Although it was metal against wood, the metal was not of the highest quality and the wood was one of the hardest on the earth, thus sword broke against club almost as often as club was hacked in half. In the main, both weapons held up well. The fighting in this small pocket of the field was heavy and furious, the warriors on each side seeing a chance to distinguish themselves on an isolated stage in front of their war chiefs.

The tattooed Hivans rolled their eyes, lolled their tongues and growled at their foes, clubbing this way and that, felling Celts with crashing blows of their great iron-wood weapons.

The painted Picts did likewise with their swords, hacking away at the enemy, hooting when one went down under the wide curving slashes of their swords.

Craig, seeing the Hivans were in trouble, as more and more Celts fell back from the front line to settle their frustrated wrath on this isolated group of Oceanians, motioned to a group of elite warriors, originally Samoan before they had co-settled the island of Rarotonga under their king Karika. With this small force of disciplined fighting men Craig attacked the Celt line with a wedge-shaped formation. With much cracking of skulls and chopping of legs they managed to push through and reach the now depleted group of Hivans.

'Fall back,' cried Craig into the ears of the nearest Hivans, 'drop back through the channel.'

His own men had formed an avenue between the Celt warriors on both sides. The Hivans slipped down this protected passage to re-join the main force. Once the Hivans were back in the Oceanian ranks the channel closed at the front, went wedge-shaped again and the Rarotongans themselves dropped back, with the loss of only a few of their number.

However, this movement had aroused the ire of those Celts who thought they had a bunch of the enemy amongst them which they could chop down at leisure. They attacked Craig's retreat with great venom and strength. Craig found himself looking into faces twisted with battle-anger, just a nose in front of his own. Hot breath was on his cheek as the knot of men struggled with each other. Sharp light-blue eyes stared into his own, startling in their intensity. Broad faces with blond stubble grimaced. He could smell the rank sweat under their armpits as they raised their swords and tried to strike in the solid knot of warriors that heaved and grunted, trying to get in a good blow amongst the tangle of arms and legs.

Then Craig fell, was in danger of being trampled by the thick-legged Celts. A foot crashed down on his chest, robbing him of wind. A heel struck him in the thigh, dangerously close to his testicles. Any moment he expected a sword to come down and divorce his head from his shoulders. Then he felt hands on his ankles and he was dragged unceremoniously out of the melee, back into his own lines. When he rolled over and looked up, he saw the face of Boy-girl smiling down at him.

'You naughty boy,' she said, wagging a finger. 'No heroics now – you've been told to save your tongue. Do as you're bid next time.'

'Thanks, Boy-girl,' he said, getting his breath. 'Here, help me to my feet. I'm winded.'

She did so and the pair dropped back a little, behind some stocky Fijians whose distinctive woolly-haired heads made them look a good deal taller to the enemy than they actually were, thus adding to their stature and ferociousness. Once more the fighting was at close-quarters, with muscled, pale-skinned men locked limb and trunk with dark-skinned warriors. There was much grunting and heaving amongst men who smelt differently from each other, looked strange to each other's eyes, and found the idea of touching a little distasteful. Dark men were slightly revolted by the fish-belly skin of the pale men. The freckled warriors were vaguely uneasy at grappling with shadows. The two groups found themselves fighting to get away from each other, rather than attempting to overrun and conquer those in their path.

The filed teeth of the Fijians and Hivans gave their wide faces a shark-like appearance. This aspect filled more than one Celt with terror when he looked into a mouth full of sharpened incisors. More than once a beleaguered Fijian or Hivan, whose weapon arm was trapped in the crush, simply sank his pointed teeth into the Celt warrior nearest to him.

'Nae biting! Nae biting!' screamed a young Pict, the first to be subject to this unfair tactic, soon to be spoken of as monstrously infamous by the Celts around their post-battle camp fires. Fear and dread swept through Scot and Pict. The Oceanians heard the gabble and guessed it was protest, but paid no heed. Great chunks of shoulder went missing, or an ear, or in some cases a few fingers. The Celts howled their dismay at such barbarism, renewing with vigour their attempts to hack themselves some space away from this ugly method of fighting.

Then one Scot, a brawler from the west coast, nutted a Fijian in the face, surprising that man. A howl of horror went up from the Fijian, who dropped his weapon to clutch his precious broken nose. Blood poured from his nostrils, soaking his triumphant attacker who saw that the Oceanian was not used to this kind of treatment and happily turned and nutted a second man.

Soon, many of the Celts who found themselves in this close-combat, hand-to-hand situation, used their broad foreheads to crack the noses of the Oceanians whose faces were closest.

'Use the nut, use the nut,' cried the Celts, realizing they too had a bare-body weapon to which the enemy were unused. 'Crack a few heeds, man!'

The Oceanians, who were not used to fists being used as weapons, let alone great-domed heads, began to back away as the Celts cracked skulls with their brows. The Oceanians could not understand how the Celts did not hurt *themselves* with this method of fighting and began to kick out at the bare testicles they could see waving obscenely in front of them. The Celts were on to this, however, being quite good at such foot-to-balls village fighting themselves, and gave as good as they got during this deplorable brawl in the thick of the battle.

Suddenly, to the astonishment of the pale-skinned Celts, Kieto gave the signal for the Oceanians to retire quickly, back to the pa. The runners went out with their slates, then at a sign from Kieto the whole Oceanian army turned almost as one man and swiftly ran to safety, leaving the Celts bewildered and upset, swinging at air. Scots and Picts alike were incensed at this cowardly action, just when the fight was warming up. They had never witnessed anything like it in their lives and screamed taunts after the fleeing brown-skinned warriors, calling them old women, children and mice, and yelling at them to stand and fight like real men.

Hupa covered the retreat with a line of her bow-women, ladies of the Whakatane, whose deadly accurate fire prevented the faster runners amongst the Celts from catching stragglers. She and her archers picked off the more adventurous of the enemy, whose blood lust was greater than their common sense. Some of them were so high on battle passion they did not stop running even with an arrow through the head or heart.

While Oceanians congratulated one another on the speed of their feet, the Celts gathered themselves and ran pell-mell at the fortifications, only to receive the same treatment which had been meted out over the last two days of fighting. They turned in frustration and began walking back to the hills, complaining loudly about 'yellow-bellied brown-skins' who ran from the field just when the fight was becoming interesting.

They were about halfway back when the Oceanians poured out of the pa, assumed fatatia, or long, straight combat lines, and began sweeping across the plain towards backs of the enemy.

Many of the Celts turned to meet them again, but were in disarray, their ranks shot with men who still believed they were on their way back to their camp to rest. They found themselves awkwardly placed at the bottom of the foothills, struggling to get up the same slopes they had rolled down so easily earlier in the day. Craig saw the pain of irritation and annoyance on their faces as they grappled with these peculiar tactics of fighting, then not-fighting, then fighting again. He could imagine they would be asking themselves what kind of creatures they were at war with, who, just when the outcome of the battle was about to be decided, turned and ran then came back when it was all supposed to be over and done with for the day.

Hand-to-hand fighting resumed, with both sides scoring minor victories.

Then Kieto gave the order for Ropa tahi.

Concentrate on killing the chieftains!

Although the Celts were naked, their chiefs displayed their wealth with shiny bronze amulets and torcs, decorated with spirals and centripetals. These were recognizable as the light caught their ornaments and signalled the rank of their wearers as surely as if they were helmets and cloaks. Oceanian warriors turned on these chieftains, ignoring fights with all others, and the slaughter of the Celt clan leaders began in earnest.

When those chieftains who were not at the forefront of the fighting saw what was happening, they began to panic. It was one thing to be part of a battle, but quite another to be selected out of the mass and have some thirty thousand savage warriors after your skin alone. One or two of the less courageous – or rather more sensible – of the chiefs turned and fled from the scene of the conflict.

Their clan members, on seeing their leaders flee, also decided to relinquish ground to the invaders.

Why should they stand firm when their supposedly most able warriors had shown them their heels?

Craig watched grimly as the whole army of Celts was in flight, racing back to the hills, while the Oceanians stood silently watching, gathering mana unto themselves. The day was won for the Oceanians, though Kieto was not quite so foolish as to think that there was an end to it. He knew this would only whet the appetite of the Celts, who would be back again with their numbers replenished.

3

That night Craig was sent up into the hills with a small escort to inform the Celts they could come down and collect their dead and severely wounded. He crossed the battle plain with Hupa and a dozen of her archers. When they sighted the fires of the enemy camps, Craig called out in Gaelic that he was entering under the sign of truce, to impart information. They were taken by escort to the Celtic war chief, Cormac, in his tent of animal skins high on the ridge.

Cormac regarded Craig sourly with his one eye.

'Why have ye come here, half-breed?' he asked with folded arms. 'To ask us not to use horses? Never again. Cowards are easily caught by men on horseback, for that's what ye are, damn ye. Ye run even when the battle's going your way.'

'I have come to ask for no favours, nor give any,' replied Craig. 'I come to tell you that you can collect your dead and wounded without fear of attack.'

'How is that?' snarled the one-eyed Cormac. 'Surely ye don't think we'll trust you after today? You'll probably fall on us like scavengers on sick deer and bite us like wee 'uns fighting at play with they sharp teeth. Probably when we've our backs turned, ye snivelling gilleans.'

'Why should you not trust us? We broke no agreements. We did nothing wrong.'

'Ye *ran*, damn ye!'

'This is not considered cowardly by our people, it is thought right and proper. A warrior must have fleet legs as well as strong arms. A warrior is judged on his skill in outrunning the enemy, as well as whether he can kill that enemy. You must understand our ways are not the same as yours – what is considered cowardly by you is considered bold and skilful by us ...'

'NEVER!' roared Cormac. 'He who runs is a coward, wherever ye hail from. He who attacks an enemy from the rear while he's walking back to his home is a treacherous cur. The brown-skins are both cowards and treacherous curs. I say it to your face, ye twixt-and-tweener.'

Craig was determined to ignore insults like 'half-breed' and 'twixt-and-tweener', references to his mixed blood.

'If you say that,' he replied in a firm, even voice, 'you're a liar and a man without honour.'

Cormac started forward, his one eye blazing, but he was checked by two of his fellow chieftains.

'Careful, Cormac – don't give them grounds for this man's accusations,' said one of his allies.

Cormac had his sword half out of its sheath and he snapped it back in again reluctantly.

'And what about that there today! We lost the chieftains of seven clans in that last ruckus. What a way to fight. D'ye hate us chieftains, laddie? Is that what it is? Do ye want to slaughter us all because we're born to lead?'

'It's one of the ways we fight – to single out the chiefs and attack them alone – ignoring all others. It puts confusion in the enemy. It makes them wonder who is next – maybe those with red hair, or black beards?' Craig folded his arms and stared at Cormac, adding softly, 'Why, were you scared?'

'Scared?' roared Cormac. 'Scared? I was shitting myself. I could feel my arsehole pinching with fear – what would you do if ten, maybe twenty thousand men were after *your* guts alone? You'd bloody shite yerself, laddie, and no mistake.'

Craig grinned, seeing his father in these hairy men of war, who stank of grease and animal fat.

'Yes, I would – I'd do that all right – and it smells just the same coming from us – same colour too – and it's just as humiliating to do it in front of comrades.'

Several of the Celtic chiefs present roared with laughter and Cormac could not help but join in.

'You're a strange one,' said the Celt war chief, 'but not as strange as the rest of them devils. Well, we'll collect our dead and wounded, but watch out tomorrow. The morn's morn we'll cut ye down like corn ...'

As he was leaving, Cormac called after Craig.

'Listen, laddie, I like ye. You're the only one of them brown-skins I trust. Maybe it's because you're half-Celt, or maybe it's because your fether was a Pict, or maybe it's just because I think ye an honest man. Tell that chief o' yours that any dealings will be through you, an' naybody else.'

Craig felt elated. If he was to do his father's bidding, of attempting to reconcile the two peoples, then both sides had to trust in him. Kieto knew and trusted him. Now Cormac had said he did too. There were those who thought him a fence-sitter, neither one nor the other, and mistrusted him for that reason alone, but it was the two chiefs who were important. 'Thank you,' replied Craig. 'I'll tell him.'

The following day the fighting was renewed. This time the Scots and Picts used their horses, though since these were highland clans and none too rich, there were not enough horsemen to make any difference to the outcome of the battles. Oceanians then thought it fair to use their fortifications more, throwing rocks down on the Celts who struggled to get over the ditches and dykes, raining arrows on the massed warriors who tried to storm the pa and climb the wooden palisades. Each new battle brought both sides nearer to the conclusion that they were not going to get beyond a stalemate.

Some of the lowland Scots and borderers arrived on the scene and threw a certain amount of panic into the Oceanians.

The lowlanders were better equipped, better armed, than the highlanders. There was more organization about them, more discipline. The borderers came with large wheeled chariots and sometimes six horses to a team. Oceanians had never had much use for the wheel, which they knew only in the form of the rolling log, but they saw its worth in those chariots.

The Oceanians watched in amazement as the charioteers, one man in a canoe on wheels, came hurtling at their battle line clutching a bunch of spears. When the charioteer was a certain distance from the line he leapt over the front of his chariot, ran down the centre pole between the six horses, threw two or three of his spears into the mob of Oceanians, then ran back up the pole and into his place again, just in time to turn his horses. It was an awesome feat of control and judgement, not to forget the skill and balance required to run up and down the pole.

'Those men are as quick and nimble on their feet as any Oceanian,' said Craig to Kieto. 'No wonder my father admired horsemen so much.'

'If they had two hundred of them, we would be done for,' agreed Kieto. 'We're lucky they can only muster a dozen or so of those war machines.'

The battles were exhausting for both sides, but especially for the Oceanians not used to the chill weather. There was disease in both camps too, taking its toll on lives. Then, as spring turned to early summer, the Oceanians saw the true colours of this land. Some blue skies, some white clouds, and a green landscape with foamy tops to the distant mountains.

Wild flowers and herbs came out in profusion: such dainty alpine flowers with delicate colours. The sun showed itself three days in a row, albeit a rather more fragile sun than the islanders were familiar with. Nevertheless it produced hot days on the moors and in the foothills, with midges in their millions, biting the unprotected and ignorant Oceanians. In the dusk the irritating insects arrived in such thick clouds men and women could hardly breathe without filling their lungs with them.

'What mad god invented these?' cried Hupa to Craig as she was being bitten on her face, breasts and thighs one evening, and tried to keep them out of her hair with a flaming brand. 'What cruel deity would dream up such an insanity?'

The midges got into every piece of clothing, past every fishnet-covered doorway, into every room. Nowhere was safe from them. When the midges and their cousins the mosquitoes were not around there were the clegs, huge things that Craig's father had called 'horse flies', which had almost as nasty a bite as a flying shark. The Oceanians tried burning all sorts of materials and produced a variety of perfumes to get rid of the insects, but every one of them failed, if not wholly then in part.

With the early summer the deer emerged from the forests to add more meat to the baskets.

Fighting in the oppressive hinterland heat became a chore and more often than not the Oceanians preferred to remain inside their wooden walls, while the Scots and Picts drifted away back to their homes in the highlands and lowlands, leaving only the diehards to man the watch platforms and call names from the plains below. Sea raiders summoned by the Celts came in from the ocean side, to try to attack the Oceanians from the rear, but by this time the invaders had completed their pa and waggled their fingers at the men from the wild sea.

Kieto sent a clutch of canoes homewards, to the islands, with instructions to recruit more men. These duly arrived to fill the places of those who had died in battle or of sickness. Of the gods nothing was heard, but the thunder storms and wind storms and sea storms were many, testifying to the fact that the battles amongst supernatural lords and ladies was still raging. Kikamana and the other kahuna and tohunga tried to reach the gods through their atua, but were not successful.

During a great lull in the fighting, Craig took a message to the chiefs amongst the Celts, suggesting that the two sides swap entertainers for an evening. It was one of those gestures which occur in the middle of a war, which helps to form a better understanding between opponents. Craig, through his gift from Uetonga, was able to understand the Gaelic language, the nuances of Alban-nach culture, but his fellow warriors could not.

He persuaded Kieto that it would be good for both sides to have a truce, during which they could entertain one another, much like fighting stopped for the Arioi in Oceania when they arrived during a war between two islands.

Craig confronted Cormac.

'You send your best people to us one evening, and the following evening we will come to you.'

Cormac viewed this scheme with great suspicion, as he did everything proposed by the Oceanians.

'What? Will ye fall on us to a man, after getting us drunk on that rotgut ye call *kava*? Will ye murder us in our seats, while we watch ye dancing like pretty wee fairies in the firelight, eh? Damn ye – you come to *us* for the first evening – then we'll come to you.'

Craig shrugged his shoulders.

'Fair enough. It doesn't matter to us which way round we do it. You can get us drunk on that stomach poison you call *wiskie*, and then chop us to pieces with your iron swords while we watch two oily Celts wrestling in the firelight and pretending they aren't enjoying touching each other's bodies.'

'They *don't* enjoy it, damn your eyes and liver,' roared the one-eyed Scot. 'It's a manly sport of strength and skill.'

'So you say,' sniffed Craig. 'We'll reserve judgement.'

When Prince Daggan heard about the entertainment, he called his wife Siko to his side.

'This is our chance,' he said. 'Tell me what I should do.'

'I have been sending my spies amongst the Celts, to learn of things which might be advantageous to us. There is a Scot who is not in tune with his nation at this present time. His name is Douglass son of Douglass. It was his father who was killed by Seumas and he thus bears a grudge against Craig, being the son of his father's killer.

'He and his clan have been banished by the war chief, Cormac, but they have sympathizers amongst others in the Celtic camp. We must contact one of these people and arrange something for tonight, or tomorrow night, when Kieto is vulnerable. Leave it to me. There must be no suspicion attached to you. You must be untainted when they come to you and ask you to take the dead Kieto's place as chief of chiefs.'

'I'm happy to leave things in your hands, my wife – but tell me – these agents, these spies of yours – are they human?'

Siko gave her husband a tight smile. 'Of course they aren't – I conjured them from other regions. Have you not seen the balepa, floating above the hills at night? Have you not felt the coldness of the kabu, lurking in the shadows? Or the marks in the dust of the putuperereko's great bollocks, where he's been dragging them around the battle plains? You should watch for these signs more closely, my husband.'

'Ah,' replied Daggan, shuddering, 'I thought so.'

Daggan left his wife, going off into the night. He had a meeting with Kapu, who was assisting the prince with his plans to become leader of the expedition. It was not that Kapu hated his father, or wanted his downfall, but he was frustrated by his father's lack of faith in him. He wanted to be made a chief, to lead Rarotongans into battle, himself at their head. Kieto would have none of it. He told his son he was too inexperienced to be made a general: that he would have to wait some years.

Kapu was impatient. He needed recognition *now*. He was fed up with being second to his sister, who though not lifted up by her father grasped the thing she wanted with both hands. She led her Whakatane, albeit unsanctioned by her father, while Kapu could not raise more than two or three men under his command. The older warriors laughed at his efforts to organize a secret society with him at the head. The younger ones were too impressed by his dismissal by the veterans to follow Kapu. Unlike the young women, they were afraid of losing their mana by following an unseasoned warrior.

So he had thrown his lot in with Daggan, who promised that the whole Rarotongan contingent would be given to Kapu, should Daggan ever become war chief.

PART SIX

Island of the Wondrous Beast

1

It occurred to Craig, through knowledge of his father's ways, that one aspect of their two separate cultures was the love of island stories. Seumas had often told his son that though the Celts were not a great sea-going nation, they were just as fascinated by individual voyages out on the ocean as were the Oceanians themselves. As with all nations there was amongst the Alban-nachs those men who built boats and went out to explore the unknown.

'Why have none come this far?' Craig had asked his father. 'How is it they have not washed up on the shores of our islands?'

'The boats they build are not like your ocean-going voyagers,' Seumas had replied. 'They are small one-man craft – little reed boats, or even a thing we call a coracle, a small round framework covered in animal skin barely large enough to contain a man – and they would not be able to make the distances to these islands. Our exploring mariners tended to leave from the far shores of Albainn, on the other side. They visit nearer islands in colder seas than these ...'

But there was this love of island stories amongst both peoples and Craig informed Boy-girl, who was to be the tale teller for the evening, of this fact. She caused a bit of a sensation amongst the rough Scots and Picts, when she stepped into the firelight to do her act. The word was passed to them, by Craig, that Boy-girl was a man brought up as a woman. He knew this would both shock and fascinate them, help to ensure and hold their attention, while Boy-girl related the tale.

Craig, for the most part, translated the words for the benefit of the Celts. However, many of the kahuna and tohunga had begun to learn the language of the Celts, through captured warriors, and being people of magic they were progressing at a rapid rate. Thus people like the Farseeing-virgin Kikamana were able to assist Craig in his endeavours to make the stories available to the ears of the Scots and Picts.

'This is the story of the Island of the Poukai Bird and involves two people – Pungarehu, an Oceanian warrior, and Seumas-the-Black, a Celt like yourselves. These two between them, with equal merit, helped to slay the monstrous Poukai Bird which had attacked, killed and eaten so many unfortunate cast-aways on its strange and magical island ...'

The Celtic audience stared at Boy-girl with wide eyes, taking in the shells and ribbons with which she decorated her long greying hair, noting the flamboyant and colourful dress she wore, observing her tall graceful figure and her complexion kept smooth over the years by sweet-smelling ointments, aware of the perfumes she exuded and her fragrant breath. Not one of them dare look at another, for fear they would reveal something about themselves which would forever be used to ridicule them.

They were held, too, by her strange words, for Boy-girl was like most Oceanian, and indeed Celtic, storytellers – she was a priest of that profession – and her words were sacred no matter what the language or understanding.

When she had finished her tale the Celts turned to one another and nodded gravely, mentioning that it was good that one of themselves was involved in such an heroic incident. They studiously avoided any reference to Boy-girl's gender, preferring instead to switch the subject of conversation to hunting, while giving each other hearty thumps on the shoulder.

Next Craig himself entertained them with a magnificent display of talent on the drums. At the end of this they cheered wildly and called for more wiskie. After Craig came acrobats, archery displays, poets, wrestling and dancing. The Oceanians avoided doing the hura, knowing it would offend their audience in the extreme to see two dancers actually copulating, albeit through grass skirts.

Craig remarked to Kieto that there was in both races this ambiguity. The Celts would come into battle naked, but they would have regarded the hura as distasteful. The Oceanians were prudish about nudity, but allowed themselves to be carried off by the sexuality of a dance.

The haka was a different thing and the Celts had seen the Oceanians do this before a battle. They witnessed it now at close quarters, finding the lolling tongues, the rolling eyes, and the strutting tattooed legs and jutting jaws just as awesome, just as intimidating, as they had been on the battlefield. Some of the younger men wanted to join in at the end.

Finally, when the show was almost over, one burly young crofter with sandy hair jumped into the circle and challenged any Oceanian wrestler to take him on. His comrades cheered and spat into the flames of the fire. The young man wore just his breeks and nothing else, stomping around the ring, yelling for an opponent to dare to step forward out of the 'brown-skins'.

Craig translated all this for the Oceanians.

Boy-girl stepped into the ring, removed her top and stared pointedly at the bulge in the front of the young man's breeks.

'Sorry I've been so long,' she said, 'I've been smearing my body with coconut oil and powdering my naughty bits. You need to do that before wrestling, you know. Look how my arms gleam in the firelight. Exciting, isn't it? I'm ready now.'

She stood languidly waiting for the young man to understand her words as Kikamana repeated all this in Gaelic.

The lad gawped at her, shifted his feet awkwardly, stared at his now quiet comrades, then mumbled an excuse before rushing off into the night.

At first the silence continued, then a sudden roar of laughter from both Oceanians and Celts ripped into the night air, while Boy-girl smiled sweetly and pranced around the ring, offering a fresh challenge to the Celts.

No one took her up on the proposal.

Before the Oceanians left the Celtic encampment, Craig asked Cormac-the-Venomous a question.

'When you first came to us there was a man called Douglass Barelegs, son of Douglass, who wanted to kill me. I know why he wishes to do so and my father charged me to make my peace with him. Where is the man now?'

Cormac said, 'Banished. He would have struck ye down the next time he saw you. He hates you and your family and would slaughter you to a man – or woman. I've no love for you, ye wee bastard, but you're too valuable to us as a go-between – there is no one else. I exiled him.'

Cormac folded his arms and looked out into the night.

'He's gone to join the Angles, damn his hide. It would have been better for him to go to the Bride Isles, but he's gone to seek the assistance of our traditional enemies. I would stay well clear of that one, Craig-the-Black, for he'll have your testicles drying on the end of his cromach stick else.'

'I've heard of the Angles, and another people, the Jutes.'

'Aye, well, the Angles and us don't see eye to eye – we make very poor neighbours if you get my meaning. The Jutes, well, there's not so many of them – just a wee area right up the top end of this place ye call Land-o'-Mists. The Angles steal Jute babies and raise them as if they were dogs. If ye go into battle against the Angles, ye'll see these naked men on the end o' leashes – savage, mindless creatures brought up without the meaning of language, kept like dogs, fed like dogs, running on all fours and snarling and snapping. They'll tear your head off if they catch you, those Jute curs …'

The following night the entertainment was returned when the Celts came to the campfires outside the pa. As the Oceanians had the night before, they brought with them their women and children, to enjoy the fun. There was much chatter in both languages which took some time for the clan chiefs on both sides to quell.

Finally, Kieto stepped into the area ringed by torches on posts, to welcome the enemy to the Oceanian night fires.

'… we know you will match, and probably even surpass, our attempts at entertainment yesterday evening,' he told the Celts politely, 'and as for wrestling …' he got no further than these words, however, for suddenly one of Cormac's bodyguards leapt from his seat on a log beside the great chieftain.

'ASSASSIN!' he yelled.

Before anyone knew what was happening this man had thrown a double-bladed battle-axe towards Kieto.

There was a shocked silence amongst the crowd as the axe swished through the air.

The weapon went spinning over Kieto's left shoulder, into a crowd of Celts on the far side. The blade buried itself in the chest of a slim blond warrior, who was at that moment drawing a bow. The loosed arrow went skimming erratically across the ground to bury itself in one of the campfires, kicking up clouds of sparks.

As he fell forwards, blood spurted like mountainside spring water from the chest of the mortally wounded Scot, his heart split in twain.

There was pandemonium, with Celtic clansmen leaping into the ring with drawn swords, and Oceanians instantly forming a guard around Kieto, waving their clubs and brandishing daggers. Warriors from both sides were yelling and snatching flaming brands from their holders. They were all looking to their leaders for guidance. Should they fight? Should they begin striking down the enemy? Who should make the first move?

Fortunately, the crush of people was such that few of the hotheads amongst both armies had room to use their weapons. They were hemmed in on all sides by those warriors at the rear pushing forwards, trying to find out what was happening. Many had no idea what was going on at all, being too far at the back to see what had occurred, and merely excited by the noise and movement around them. On top of all this, children were crying, caught up in the milling confusion of bodies.

Craig called for calm in both languages. Cormac took up his cry, as did Kieto. After a period of jostling and threatening, peace was finally restored. Celt had killed Celt and the truce had not actually been broken.

'One of Douglass's men,' growled Cormac, when the dead archer's body was brought to him. He kicked the corpse savagely and looked around the faces of his warriors. 'Who let thon bastard into my camp?'

Whichever clan was responsible, they were not saying.

Cormac had his enemies within as well as outside his camp. He had bonded together all clansmen for a common purpose, but that did not make him the idol of all. There were still those who would disrupt Cormac's efforts to unite the clans.

'Well,' said Kieto, 'I have to thank your bodyguard for his sharp eyes and the quickness of his hands. If it had not been for him I would probably be dead.'

'My people know better than to break the sanctity of a truce,' replied Cormac through the interpreters. 'I gave express orders to kill any man who looked like doing so. Ye have my deepest apology for this outrage. I'll not have ye thinking we are uncivilized barbarians who can't keep their word, nor have any sense of honour.'

'The thought never crossed my mind. There are always rotten fruit amongst the good. Your apology is unnecessary. The deed was not yours.'

Cormac looked down at the archer.

'I doubt this stupid *luch* would have killed ye though. Douglass's archers couldna hit a mountain if they were climbing up the sides ...'

While the chiefs were talking thus, helping to pacify their separate peoples, Hupa had gone to the fire and retrieved the arrowhead, the haft having burned away. She had discovered what she feared, that this was one of Lioumere's teeth. Had the assassin been allowed to fire his arrow at Kieto, the Oceanian chieftain would be lying dead on the ground instead of the archer.

'Where did the Celts get this?' she asked Craig, when he came to her side. 'And how did they know its power?'

'Obviously we have a traitor in our midst.'

'Or traitors,' replied Hupa. 'I'll speak to my father after the night's entertainment.'

With some semblance of calm restored, the evening's entertainments were allowed to begin.

There were feats of strength, with men lifting great stones and throwing them over a high wooden bar; tree trunks were tossed around as if they were kindling; there was horsemanship, bagpipe playing and running. For the most part the Celtic entertainment consisted of showing feats of prowess. There were sweet flute players though and drummers and others of a musical turn.

There was poetry too – a strong lilting poetry which spoke of heroic deeds – which Craig tried to do justice to in his translation.

Then came the storyteller for the Celts, who was a pugfaced, short, stocky man with deep blue eyes and flaxen hair. He stamped about the ground in front of the listeners, not only re-enacting the scene, playing several roles, but speaking as if he were actually there, witnessing what had taken place.

'As you all know,' said the storyteller, 'the voyager in this story is called Maeldune, who built himself a coracle of animal skins and set out one blustery day. He found many magical islands on his travels, but the one I am going to tell you about is the Island of the Wondrous Beast.

'There came a day when Maeldune needed to replenish his stores and he came to an island which was nothing but bare rock and sparse vegetation. Around this island was built a stone barrier, constructed either to keep people out, or to keep something else inside. Maeldune knew immediately, when he saw the sluggish water swilling around the island, and the sombre aspect of the gloomy landscape, that this was a magical island. He knew he should not go ashore.

'Unfortunately, Maeldune's fresh water was so low he could not continue without taking on more. He beached his coracle and climbed the stone wall. Once on the other side he took his goatskins to the nearest burn and began to fill them. All the while he kept his eyes peeled for anything unusual.

'Sure enough, when he was halfway through his task, he saw a strange creature emerge from the rocks. When the creature noticed Maeldune it went as mad as a loon and began running around the landscape, pausing occasionally to make sure the handsome Maeldune was still watching it.

'Every so often the beast would turn in its own skin, so that its hide remained still and the body inside reversed itself. Then on other occasions its body would remain still, but its skin would flow around it like water over a stone.

'Once Maeldune had filled his water bags, he ran back down to his coracle. The beast appeared to be annoyed that he was leaving and began to launch sharp stones at him. One of these missiles hit the coracle, sending it spinning around in circles on the surface of the sea. It spun right out into the ocean, with Maeldune feeling sick to his stomach, but having escaped the beast by the creature's own hand.'

There were sounds of appreciation from the Oceanian audience at the end of this story. It was true, they said to each other, the Albannachs had some similarities with themselves. They both enjoyed the same type of magical island story.

What happened next, however, perturbed the Oceanians.

The storyteller began strutting around the circle, making rude gestures with his fingers at the Oceanians. He called them old women and said they were not fit to scrub under the arms of his vest, let alone share the same air. He said their penises were the size of bone needles, their balls were like apple pips and their arseholes the size of bear caves, through frequent misuse by their fellow warriors. Craig decided to translate the storyteller's obscenities and insults, just as he had related the story the man had told.

This incensed Kieto and his men, who looked askance at each other wondering what it was all about.

Finally the storyteller told them he was not just a teller of tales, but also a famous barefist fighter from the border country, where the land raiders came from. Did the Oceanians know anything about barefist fighting? He doubted it. They all looked like pansy-faced wrestlers to him! Barefist fighting was the sport of *real* men. Let one of the brown-skins step into the circle and he would knock them down in an instant.

All the Celts cheered and stamped their feet at these words, adding their own insults to those of the pugfaced storyteller's. The hounds which had accompanied many of the Celts came up on their muscled haunches and howled into the night air. Foxes in the mountains around the plain took up the cry and began singing too. For a moment the whole world seemed to be in discord, with humans, dogs and foxes in full cry.

Now the Oceanians looked up at the moon, down at their own feet, and everywhere except into each other's eyes. They had never heard of boxing and thought it a strange thing to do. Were they actually expected to ball their hands into a fist, then strike another man's face with it? It did not seem right. It was a barbaric, grotesque, and unwholesome sport.

'What, are ye babies that ye can't fight with your fists?' cried Cormac. 'Is my man here expected to go home unchallenged by these brave brown-skinned warriors?'

As this was translated by Craig at last one of the Oceanians had had enough of the taunts. He stepped forward and removed his cloak, to bare his upper body. There was a great cheer from his own people, followed by one from the Albannachs. Watching out of the corner of his eye the Oceanian saw his opponent practising punches on the air in front of him.

So the Oceanian did the same, much to the mirth of the Scots and Picts, who cried out in amusement that he looked like a fairy picking blossoms from the branches of a cherry tree.

Finally, when the shadow boxing was over, the Celt removed his cloak to face his would-be opponent.

At this the Oceanian gave out a cry of surprise, for his Celtic adversary was clearly a woman, with large flattish breasts which had been hidden by the thick sheepskin cloak. She faced him with a grin on her broad features, her muscular shoulders gleaming palely in the firelight. She swung a right hook at his jaw which he managed to avoid only by leaping back with all the agility of a frightened deer.

Coming stolidly forward she threw a straight left which grazed past his startled nose, just nicking the end of it and causing his eyes to water. Then another right, this time to his stomach taking all the wind out of him. Finally he let out a cry and went running off into the night, with the jeers of the Albannachs loud in his ears.

The barefist-fighting-storyteller put on her cloak and with a great smirk on her face left the circle.

The Celts all rose to go, gathering up their hounds and their children, laughing quietly to themselves. As they went off into the night, Cormac turned and called to Craig, 'Tit for tat, ye bastards. Tit for bloody tat! And that's the truth of the matter, eh? In fact *two* bloody tits for one skinny tat. Ye don't get the better of an Albannach that easily!'

After the evening's entertainment was over and the Celts had all but gone, the Oceanians began to drift back to their several pa. Kieto had deliberately not let the Albannachs inside the pa, or they would have noted the weak spots and used the knowledge to advantage. The following day the truce would be over, they would be at war again, and men would be out on the plains battling for supremacy over their adversaries.

Since the war had reached such a stalemate, it was mostly a case of Celtic champions walking up to one pa or another and throwing down a challenge. Eventually someone would go out to meet the challenger and single combat would take place under the eyes of those on the fighting platforms of the pa, and those of the enemy standing on the slopes which formed a natural amphitheatre for the Albannachs.

One or the other combatant would eventually triumph, and someone's body would get dragged through the dust by its heels; there would be cheers and jeers from one side or the other, and by that time everyone would be hungry and the morning's conflict would cease in favour of eating and drinking.

In the afternoon there would be a repeat of the morning's action, with different protagonists.

There was one warrior from the Celts, a giant of a man called Guirk, who advanced to the walls of the pa every day and called for Kieto to come out and fight him. This Guirk, who had a bright sword and shield of metal, would fight no other opponents, rejecting anyone else who answered his challenge. When Kieto did not emerge after three challenges, Guirk would call the Oceanian general a coward, a whining cur, and many other insults, before trudging back to his own camp and leaving the field free for others.

The one-armed Kieto was not so stupid as to allow this to anger him to the point of accepting the challenge. He guessed it to be a Celtic ploy. While he did not consider himself entirely irreplaceable, this was his war and he was the spirit of the invasion. Without him he knew the Oceanians would lose heart and return to their canoes. They would sail back home to their islands, then sometime in the future the Albannachs, or the Angles, or both, would form their own fleet and follow the Oceanians to their islands, and subjugate them.

Kieto was not going to risk all this simply for the sake of vanity and pride.

'Let him yell all he likes,' he told his advisers, some of whom were for and some against answering the challenge. 'I am a symbol to my people and I am not going to get drawn or sidetracked into a petty brawl with some bone-headed warrior out to make a name for himself.'

Though his son Kapu was incensed at this decision by his father, saying all men and women would call him and his family cowards, his daughter Hupa approved. She believed the Celt had been sent by the chiefs on the other side, in order to disrupt the Oceanians and get them arguing amongst themselves.

Once, she had waited on a fighting platform of the pa, until Guirk came to within archer distance to shout his dare. She let loose an arrow at the man and was astonished when it was deflected by his black metal shield.

Guirk removed himself from range and Kieto admonished his daughter, telling her the rules of single combat did not allow intervention by third parties.

'You are impugning the honour of all Oceanians by employing such sneak action,' he had told her. 'It is fortunate the man was not struck – you must not do such a thing again.'

Hupa had begged her father's forgiveness and was left wondering how she had missed with her magic arrow.

'There must be other magical forces at work,' she told Craig. 'Lioumere's teeth *never* miss.'

Kieto had sent a message of regret to Guirk, apologizing for the incident and saying it would not occur again.

The following day the giant Guirk had come back again, daring Kieto to meet him face to face in single combat.

Craig had thought about all this, after the incident with the Celtic archer earlier in the evening, and wondered whether the two occurrences had anything to do with one another.

Now it was dark, with the cold distant stars fixed in their places on the roof of voyaging. These frozen stars seemed to Craig to be further away than they had been on Rarotonga, and the heavens less fluid. The face of Marama, God of the Moon, husband of Hine-keha, appeared sterner here. Or was it indeed Marama, who peered down on the landscape of Albainn? Perhaps it was the moon god of the Celts? Was it because the two opposing gods were locked in immortal combat, that the face on the moonscape appeared so severe and forbidding?

Craig had begun to walk back to the pa when Kieto called him over.

'Craig,' said Kieto, 'I have come to a decision. The Farseeing-virgin, high priestess Kikamana, has been looking into the future. She tells me that it is not the Celts we have to fear, but the Angles and other tribes from above the border. *These* are the warriors who will one day build ships of war and sail to Oceania, to try to destroy our peoples. It is the Angles who must be taught a lesson in warfare – who must be discouraged from ever attempting such an invasion on Oceania.

'Therefore I have decided to sue for peace with the Celts, so that we might concentrate our forces on the Angles. It would seem the Celts have no love for them either. But you must be the mediator between ourselves and the Celts. Cormac would listen to no other. It is essential you make yourself available tomorrow. You will go to Cormac and put the proposal to him, so that we might not waste the summer in this futile fighting between two peoples who need have no fear of one another.'

Craig was elated. His father's work was bearing fruit. If the Celts and Oceanians could join forces, one swift battle might be enough to subdue the Angles. Then they could go home before this terrible thing called 'winter' was upon the land.

'I'll go to Cormac at first light,' said Craig. 'He trusts me. We'll have peace before the sun warms the soil.'

'Good.'

Kieto left Craig then, the war chief going back with his bodyguard towards the pa.

Craig stood for a few moments, thinking about what had been said, obviously delighted with Kieto's decision. It was while he was thus engaged in thought that suddenly Kapu appeared out of the darkness. He seemed to be in an agitated state.

'Quickly, Craig,' said the boy. 'Someone has abducted my sister Hupa. Two Celts. I saw them drag her off into that clump of trees over there ...'

'What?' cried Craig, peering in the direction of a dark patch just definable as a spinney in the starlight. 'We must get some more men.'

'No, there isn't time,' said the young man, plucking at Craig's arm. 'We must rescue her – you and I. Everyone else has gone back to the pa.'

Craig stared around him. There was enough starlight to make out shapes in the gloom. The youth was right. The two of them were now alone. Valuable time would be wasted by running back to the pa. He turned to Kapu.

'Right – let's go,' he said. 'You get behind me. I don't want to take you back to your father with a broken skull.'

For once Kapu did not argue. He slipped behind Craig and followed him up to the treeline.

At the edge of the copse, Craig paused, but he heard a strange noise. A low whistling was coming from the centre of the clump of trees.

'I can hear something,' he told Kapu. 'You keep a few paces to the rear. If I'm attacked, you must come up swiftly behind my attackers and deal with them best you can. Between the two of us we should be able to cope with them.'

Craig began to creep forward. He followed the sound with his ear. It seemed to get lower and less distinct the nearer he got to it.

Brambles snatched at his clothing. Roots tried to trip him. The undergrowth became denser and less easy to navigate nearer the middle of the wood. Finally he reached a spot from which he was positive the sound originated. Parting the leaves of a tall shrub, he stared down to see a man. The fellow was squatting on his haunches. He had a blade of grass between cupped hands and was busy blowing through it, making the sound Craig had heard. On sensing someone's presence the man looked up into Craig's face – and then smiled broadly.

'Got you!' he said.

At that moment Craig felt a thump on the back of the neck as if from a club. Those stars he had believed so distant were now swimming immediately around his head. He staggered forward a couple of paces. Then a second blow landed right where a lump was already forming. Craig son of Seumas slipped quietly to the woodland floor and lost consciousness.

The man who had struck Craig with a heavy cudgel stood over his body for a moment, looking down on his work with some satisfaction. His aide and brother nodded at a good job done between the two of them. Then the brown-skin, the minion of Daggan, Douglass Barelegs's spy, came out of the bushes to stare down on the body of his father's friend. Also, out of the far side of the copse came Prince Daggan.

'He's not dead, is he?' whispered Kapu in a frightened voice. 'You haven't killed him?'

'No, he's just sleeping,' said Daggan. 'You did well, Kapu – we will soon have you raised above your sister. Once I am war chief your status will be that of my right hand man. How does that sound?'

Kapu seemed to be having a change of heart, now that the deed had been done. His worried expression did not change. He continued to fret over Craig's body.

'I wish it didn't have to be like this. You promised we would avoid bloodshed. You said Craig would be taken without undue force and sold into slavery in the north. I wouldn't want to be responsible for his death. I mean, as a slave he would at least be alive, and maybe one day set free again. He looks dead to me. Are you sure you didn't kill him …?'

'He's not dead,' growled Daggan. 'Stop chattering, boy.'

But Kapu's voice was becoming shriller and he was wringing his hands now.

'We shouldn't have done this thing. My father will be absolutely furious. Look, can't we find some other way of making you war chief? Perhaps if I persuaded my father to retire from the position …?'

Daggan shook his head slowly, looking at the trembling youth with tight lips. Then he nodded sharply to the two rough-looking characters who had felled Craig. A knife was produced and instantly plunged into the unsuspecting Kapu's throat, thus quenching any cry of alarm.

The boy fell to his knees, gargling, his hands trying to staunch the blood. Two swift and savage blows with the club on the back of his neck broke his spinal cord. Kapu fell dead at the feet of the three men.

Without anything further being said, the brother of the man with the cudgel lifted the body and carried it to a spot further in the trees. There was a prepared grave. He tossed Kapu's corpse into the hole and immediately filled it in. Afterwards dead leaves and fallen branches disguised the fresh earth. Then the man walked back to his two companions. He made a gesture of affirmation. Prince Daggan left the spinney.

Punga had been in the middle of a great battle when he heard Craig's silent call for help. The Oceanian gods had joined in battle with the Celtic gods, at much the same time that Kieto's army had first confronted Cormac's. Since then Punga had been wounded in a thousand places, but gods are not like men, they can withstand such injuries and still find the strength to fight.

Punga's thick feathered helmet had been split, his shield cracked, but he still wielded his club with energy. Several Celtic deities had felt its blows on their backs and heads, and respected the strength of the god behind those strikes.

Leaving the battlefield for a moment, the God of Ugly Creatures looked upon the scene below and witnessed Craig's abduction. Seeing the girl Hupa nearby he directed her attention to the scene and was satisfied to see that she followed the men who had Craig in their hands. It was the best Punga could do for the time being. He went back into the fray, avoiding a blow from a savage Celtic mountain god, and attempting to deliver one of his own.

All around him was fire and flood – mayhem – as the rival gods fought for space in the minds of men.

When Craig came to he found he was bound hand and foot. He was in some sort of cart drawn by an animal very much like a horse, except that this creature was smaller, stockier and not quite so handsome. Sitting up on the cart with him was the man he had seen blowing on the blade of grass. On foot, holding a strap on the jaws of the beast of burden, was another man. Craig did not recall seeing either one before this night.

These were rough-looking fellows in wolfskin cloaks, with leggings held on by long, criss-crossed leather sandal straps. Both men had shaven scalps around a hairy patch from which hung single long plaits. When they saw he was awake, they began speaking a guttural language which Craig did not understand. One of them said something to Craig but he remained silent, not knowing in the slightest what was going on.

'Ah,' said the one on the cart, in Gaelic now, 'don't understand our tongue, eh?'

'Who are you?' asked Craig. 'Why am I here?'

'Why, as to that, me and my companion here are what they call Jutes, so called because we hail from a piece of land which juts out into the sea. Not on this island, but in another great place, far away across the cold sea to the south-east.'

'South-east? What does that mean?'

The man grinned at him through a charcoal beard.

'Bottom end, right hand side, keep on going.'

Craig did not understand but let it drop.

'Where are you taking me?'

'There's a man wants to see you, down below the border. Says he's going to hang you, then draw you, and then have you quartered by four sturdy cart horses. That means they'll dangle you by your neck from a rope until you're half dead, cut open your stomach to let out your entrails, then have your limbs torn out of your torso. How does that sound?'

'Painful,' replied Craig.

The man grinned again, savagely, revealing several broken teeth behind a scarred lip.

'I've heard it's that all right. It's painful. They say you never forget the screaming of a hung, drawn and quartered man. They say it haunts you to the death ...'

The man leading the peculiar-looking horse said something in his own tongue and got a sharp reply from the one on the cart.

'Wants to know what we're saying to each other,' said broken-teeth. 'Doesn't trust either of us.'

'Does he not speak Gaelic?' asked Craig, thinking everyone in the Land-of-Mists spoke the language of the Celts.

'Naw, he only speaks Anglish – he's an ignorant man. He's not as bright as that donkey he's guiding. You got to make allowances for him though, for he helped his brother murder his mother and father when he was ten. Sort of sticks the brain together that kind of experience – hasn't moved on much since that time.' The man gave Craig another lopsided grin. 'I ought to know – I'm his brother, see.'

Whether this man was telling the truth or not, Craig knew he was in the hands of two evil characters.

'Who is this person who wishes to have me at his mercy – let me guess – Douglass Barelegs?'

'Ow, you're a clever one and no mistake,' cried his delighted companion. 'The very man. He's prepared to be generous too. Paying us well, he is. And you'd never guess it, he's got a couple of you invaders helping him. A man and his wife. A very pompous fellow they call Prince Daggan. And the woman's called Siko. Wouldn't mind humping that dark ewe, don't mind saying so, even to a man who's about to die.'

'Daggan and Siko are with Douglass?'

'Shouldn't have told you that, should I? Still, even if we can't deliver you for some reason, we've been ordered not to let you go. I think a red-hot iron poker up the arsehole was mentioned in dispatches? Ow! Makes you clench your buttocks when you think of it, don't it? Nasty way to die. Almost as bad as the triple-torture I mentioned – not quite – almost. Now you get some sleep, build your strength up for the big day ahead of you – we've got a long way to go yet, my lad.'

'Glad to hear it,' replied Craig, determined not to slip into a state of despair. His main concern was that, until he was able to escape, the war between the Oceanians and the Celts would continue. Cormac would not listen to any other messenger from the Oceanians. Craig had to get back, so that peace talks could start between the two peoples. In the meantime things might deteriorate between the Celts and Oceanians, to the point where reparations would not be possible. A great wave of despair and frustration swept through Craig. He had to get back, or all his father's work would come to nothing.

They hurried past a single great tree, from which dangled bleached rags and ribbons which fluttered in the dawn breezes. The tree's bole was thick, hollowed in places, and reminiscent of a human face. The two men glanced nervously at this shrine to some unknown cluster of spirits. Clearly they were not a couple who could laugh away the superstitions of others, nor tread easily over landscapes upon which they trespassed.

2

Seven days and seven nights the abductors carried Craig across country. Craig might have despaired did he not believe some god or other was watching over him. He felt, deep in his heart, that some deity was caring for his welfare. Thus the hope of release did not die in his breast.

For the most part they kept to lonely highways, mere tracks such as an animal might make, through moor and weald, through forest and field, over beck and gushing torrent, around hills and hollows. Until on the eighth day they came to a wide lake, where Broken-teeth told his brother, whom Craig had now named Big-nose, that they should rest. They settled on the grass at the edge of the lake with a dark wood to their back and the shining waters to their front.

For the past week it had been raining. They had trudged through muck and mire until all three men were sick of being wet and plastered with mud. Broken-teeth said it was good for him and his brother, for it meant that not many people were abroad. As Jutes they had to avoid coming into contact with both highland and lowland clans while in Albainn. Now that they were in border country, he told Craig, there were still bands of thieves, cut-throats and raiders roaming around.

'If we see any I shall yell for assistance,' Craig told his captors. 'Then perhaps the red-hot poker for you too, eh?'

Broken-teeth, tending a peat fire on which he was boiling pigeon's eggs, gave a little shudder.

'In this part of the world they use starving rats,' said Broken-teeth. 'They strap them in a cage to your stomach, so the only way out for the hungry beasts is to gnaw their way through your belly and past your back-bone. If you're going to yell, you might think on that before you open your mouth.'

Craig did not think there was a great deal to choose between any of the forms of death he was being offered, so he reserved his decision until the time came when he had the opportunity to use it. As it was the two brothers seemed expert at avoiding company, so there was not much point in worrying about it. In the meantime his bonds were cutting into his limbs, chafing his skin, and his immediate concern was the use of his legs.

'Can I be allowed to walk around?' asked Craig. 'My legs feel like someone else's.'

Broken-teeth said something to Big-nose and the other brother came and undid Craig's feet. He left his hands bound tightly behind his back, but tied another long rope in a noose around his throat, the end of which he attached to his wrist.

Broken-teeth said, 'My brother will strangle you if you try to run – he's not too fussy about things like that.'

'I'm sure he's not,' said Craig.

Craig tried to climb to his feet, but his legs were like dead eels. There was no strength in them and hardly any feeling. He fell over several times, much to the merriment of the two brothers. Their sense of humour was extraordinarily rich and bountiful. Finally, he asked them if they would untie his hands, so that he could rub his legs and feet.

'Oh, yes, we're likely to do that, aren't we?' replied Broken-teeth.

'I give you my word I will not try to escape on this occasion.'

'Your word? You a man of honour then? Are we supposed to trust your word?'

'Yes.'

Broken-teeth surprised him then by shrugging and saying, 'All right, but if you do run, remember we know the country, you don't.'

Once his hands had been untied Craig set to massaging his ankles and calves. When the blood came back into his limbs it was excruciatingly painful. This was cause for another few guffaws from the brothers. Finally, Craig managed to get to his feet and totter around the campsite, crashing into the bivouac Big-nose had built. After a while he regained use of his legs and was able to stagger down to the lake, on the end of the long leash, to drink the cool waters.

On the way down the bank he fell once again, on to ground extraordinarily soft. He looked down, expecting to see moss, but instead found a patch of flattened thistles. This surprised him but before he could discover what was going on, he was jerked to his feet by Broken-teeth, tugging on the other end of the rope.

'Are you going to lie there, or go down for a drink?' demanded his captor.

'Drink,' replied Craig, staring at the spot in front of his feet.

'Well, get on with it then.'

With a shrug of his shoulders Craig did as he was told, staggering the last few yards down to the edge of the lake.

It was as he was drinking, looking down into the clear waters, that he saw the horse. His first wild thought was that he could use the creature to escape. He had seen them ridden by the Celts and it did not look too difficult to him. You simply sat on the beast's back and gripped its mane with your right hand, slapping its rump with your left. The horse always seemed to do as it was told without too much fuss.

But then Craig suddenly realized that this horse was actually on the bottom of the lake, racing through a forest of green waving fronds. He jerked upright. Horses were quite new and magical creatures to him, but this did not seem right at all. No one had told him they were aquatic beasts. So far as he knew they were air-breathing creatures fit only for the land.

Yet here was this wild magnificent beast charging through the weeds on the bed of a lake, looking like a demon with its blazing eyes.

'Hey!' he called excitedly to Broken-teeth. 'Come over here, quickly.'

Now the creature below wheeled, stopped and then stared at the sound of the voice. Craig could see its flaxen mane floating in the currents, its beautiful tail drifting out behind it. It curled back its lips and revealed its teeth. Its eyes were like bright suns which burned in its head. Its nostrils flared and blew plumes of tiny bubbles. One hoof began scraping the muddy bottom, raising swirling clouds of mud. Craig tried to tear his gaze from that of the creature's, but found it impossible to turn away. Craig felt a growing urge to join the beast on the bottom of the lake.

'What is it?' snapped Broken-teeth, testily, not moving from his place at the fire. 'Your legs gone again?'

'No, come here – there's a horse on the bottom of the lake. It's looking at me. I think it wants me to dive down to it. I've never seen a creature like it. It seems to have stars for eyes ...'

Broken-teeth went pale and came hurrying over to where Craig was kneeling. He looked once down into the waters of the lake, saw the horse, and immediately looked away. Then without a second glance, he grabbed Craig by the rope around his neck and dragged him quickly from the bank.

Broken-teeth's breath was coming out in short, sharp gasps. When he had brought Craig back to the fireside, he stared at the edge of the lake for a long time, finally giving out a quick shudder before saying something to his brother. The two men were clearly ill at ease. Without saying anything more they bound Craig's hands behind his back again.

'What is it? What was that creature?'

'A bloody kelpie, you fool. If you'd have kept looking at it, you would have jumped in and drown yourself. Don't ask me why, because I don't know. All I know is let one of those creatures latch on to you, and you're done for.' He stared about him with a look of concern on his features, before adding, 'This must be a magical place. We'd better move on quickly. There'll be other creatures like that kelpie about, that's certain enough.'

The two brothers began to pack up camp swiftly, but before they were ready to leave a group of very short, stocky people came out of the forest.

The strangers had small square bodies fitted with large square heads. They wore hard serious expressions on their weatherbeaten faces. Their eyes were tiny glittering jewels pushed deep into clay-coloured complexions. Each of them was armed with a sword, stuck sheathless into a wide leather belt with a huge buckle. The buckles had various designs, but all involved beasts of the forest in their patterns.

Golden ornaments dripped from their chunky necks and wrists, were fixed to their cloaks: bracelets, torcs, brooches, pins, clasps. Several of them had golden teeth which flashed in the sunlight. Others had mouths of black rotten molars and incisors. On their heads they wore colourful floppy caps which fell to forked points at waist level on one side of their bodies. A big sweeping feather decorated each one of these marvellous hats. Most wore red or blue jerkins, with white and black striped pantaloons. On their feet were equally colourful slippers, the toes of which curled exotically up and over to touch their kneecaps.

Broken-teeth immediately went pale and he nudged Big-nose energetically. One of the little people came marching directly up to Broken-teeth and stood before him, arms akimbo, and stared him directly in the face.

'You know who I am?'

Broken-teeth gave out a nervous laugh.

'Why, sir, I do believe you're Laurin, King of the Dwarves.'

'I am indeed Laurin. What are you people doing here? Do you not know this is a sacred place? Sacred to me and my kind? Are you trying to provoke us into doing something rash? This lake is ours, this grove is ours. You trespass.'

Broken-teeth made an attempt at a smile.

'I've only just realized that, Laurin. As soon as my slave here saw the kelpie, I knew we shouldn't be here. You see, we've packed up camp already. We were just about to leave when you came out of the trees. I'm sorry.'

The small square Laurin studied the three humans carefully, muttering,

'A slave, eh?' Then he proceeded to look beyond Broken-teeth and Big-nose, as if searching for something, either on the ground or hanging in a tree.

'Did you feel something like a cobweb brushing your face as you walked under any trees?' asked Laurin, sharply. 'Come on, out with it now.'

Broken-teeth looked genuinely surprised.

'No, Laurin. What would that be?'

'Why, it would be Hel Keplein, my mantle of invisibility of course. I put it down somewhere and now I've lost it.' He looked with suspicion at Craig. 'Your slave hasn't stolen it, has he?'

By this time the other dwarves were walking through grass with large bare feet. They had removed their slippers and were feeling with their toes. Others were marching under trees waving their hands about. Others still were thrusting their arms down rabbit holes.

'If he has, I don't know anything about it.'

Craig said to the king, 'It must be very difficult to find an invisible cloak once you've forgotten where you've placed it.'

For a moment the king looked quite miserable.

'Well nigh impossible. You have to come across it by accident,' he sighed. He was now staring about him in despair. 'I'm sure I had it when I was last here. Now my enemies will be gathering in the hills. How shall I avoid them without Hel Keplein?'

The dwarf-king looked so upset that Craig felt he had to reveal something he had been holding back for the appropriate moment.

'King Laurin – I know where the mantle is.'

All the dwarves stopped their search and began murmuring like a swarm of bees. The king looked quickly at Craig's face. He stared hard into his eyes. Craig knew that Laurin was searching in them for the truth. He held his head high, staring back at the king.

'Where is it then?' demanded Laurin.

'First we must bargain,' replied Craig. 'Do you promise to make these men set me free if I show you where to find your Hel Keplein?'

'Set you free? It will be done in an instant.'

Broken-teeth looked upset at these words and glanced away over his right shoulder, as if forcing back some comment.

'In that case, you'll find the mantle down by the lake. There's a patch of thistles which appeared to have been flattened by some heavy weight. I suspect it's Hel Keplein that's pressing them down. I knelt on it when I fell over a short while ago. I'm sure that's where you'll find it.'

Dwarves rushed down to the lake, yelling excitedly. Eventually, after scouring the bank for a short while, one of them let out a yell and held up his arm.

'It's here, my liege. I have it in my hand. Your own Hel Keplein.'

A look of great relief came over Laurin's wide features. His body seemed to slump for a moment and tears came to his eyes. Reaching out he grasped Craig's arm for a moment in a gesture of gratefulness. Then the cloak was restored to him by the finder.

He draped it over his shoulders. The effect was startling: only his head was now visible, seemingly floating at waist-height to Craig, off the ground. The king nodded gravely.

'How can I ever thank you?' Laurin said to Craig.

'Why,' said Craig, 'by keeping your promise.'

Craig, on hearing a stifled laugh behind him, turned to find Broken-teeth sniggering to himself.

'What are you looking so pleased about?' asked Craig, surprised.

'You'll see.'

A feeling of alarm flooded through Craig. He turned back to face the king.

'Will you have your dwarves cut me loose now? You promised to set me free, if you remember, as a reward for finding the mantle. I should like to be on my way ...'

'Alas,' cried the king, a small stubby-fingered disembodied hand appearing out of nowhere and grasping Craig's arm again. 'How I wish I could do that.'

'But you promised,' cried the astonished Craig. 'Have you dwarves no honour?'

'Honour is not what we lack,' replied Laurin, sadly, 'but the means. We cannot meddle in human affairs. It is against our laws. If a human does something wrong, such as you three trespassing, why, then we can kill them stone dead. But we cannot interfere between the three of you. You are a slave, my friend – be satisfied with your station in life. Your master here looks like a kindly man. Be happy with your lot.'

'I can't believe you're doing this,' Craig cried. 'You *promised* to help me.'

Broken-teeth laughed and pulled on the rope, tightening the noose around Craig's neck.

'Come on, you. Let's not bother the king with our little problems. We'll be on our way then, Laurin. You watch that kelpie.' Broken-teeth nodded towards the lake. 'I hear it's a savage one. Tore the throat out of one of my friends with its teeth. Almost took his head off in one bite. Well, look after that mantle of yours – we'll be off.'

Craig was dragged away on the end of the line. Broken-teeth and Big-nose now took it in turns to ride the donkey, while Craig was forced to trot behind, his feet becoming bloody and raw in the process. They travelled over dark rough country, stopping occasionally at villages now they were over that wide stretch of land of border country. Up here in the 'north' it seemed Broken-teeth and Big-nose were made welcome, no questions asked about the man on the end of the rope. They simply paid their way, sleeping in houses made of timber plugged with clay.

Deeper and deeper they went above the border, until at last Craig asked the question, 'Where are you taking me? You said Douglass was waiting just beyond the land of the Celts. We are now in the country of the Angles.'

Broken-teeth looked at his brother Big-nose and then sniffed loudly.

'Well, as to that, we decided to hold on to you for a bit longer. Douglass is a mean bastard. He thought to get away with giving us just a few of his scrawny sheep, but now we're in a position to bargain with him. We've got the goods he wants. I'm sure he'll pay us a tidy bit more for you, once we let him know that you're for sale at a higher price.'

Craig fell into an even more weighty state of despair. Even should he manage to escape now he would have the greatest difficulty in getting back to his people alive. He was on a huge island full of savages – the tribes of Angles seemed even less civilized than the Celts – and he would have to pass through or around them. His memory maps were good, but he realized that sometimes he would have to deviate from them, in order to skirt a village or travel through the territory of a less hostile tribe. It would be easy to become lost in an unknown land.

Broken-teeth was smiling at him.

'What's the matter?' said that man. 'You missing someone?'

'You pig's arse,' replied Craig, releasing some venom, 'you have bird shit for brains ...'

This earned him a cuff around the head, which set his ears ringing. Over the past few days Craig had been kicked and punched, not just by his two captors, but by anyone who felt the need to rid themselves of spleen. Often tied to a post in the middle of the village as he was, all sorts of tough men and women, and children, had given him the benefit of their strength. He now felt thoroughly abandoned and abused.

That night they camped by a river. Craig could smell a damp mustiness carried on the cool wind. He could see the ruffling of the water on the river, from which came the occasional 'plop' of a fish breaking the surface of the water. The trout were after the storm flies which heralded rain. Otherwise the night was quiet.

Big-nose made a fire by striking flints together. Yellow flames were soon licking at the darkness around them. Big-nose sat hunched over a hearth made with smooth river stones, staring out into the blackness. He looked uneasy and from the tone of his brother's voice, Broken-teeth was trying to console him. It seemed the dim one of the two was not happy with something.

'What's the matter with your brother?' asked Craig. 'Conscience bothering him?'

'Conscience? What's that?' said Broken-teeth, looking in his brother's direction, 'a wasp or something?'

Craig realized that Broken-teeth was genuinely ignorant regarding any feelings of guilt or remorse he was supposed to be having concerning Craig's abduction. The Oceanian saw then just how dangerous was this man. He was an intrinsically bad man – born not made – who simply did not know the difference between good and evil, only between poverty and riches.

At that moment Big-nose threw some woodshavings from his whittling on the fire, which flared brightly, lighting up the faces of the men. There was a very small sound out in the darkness which attracted Craig's attention. Broken-teeth was saying, 'You shadow-skins, you don't know a dwarf from a horse's arse. Why I – gaaahhhhhhh …'

Craig sensed that Broken-teeth was now partially standing. The Oceanian prisoner turned back to see that his main captor's face was ugly with contortion, his eyes staring wildly at Craig. The strange crouch gave the impression he had been halfway through a crap when he had been interrupted. There was something wrong with his throat and his hands scrabbled at a projection which had appeared there, as if it had grown out of the sides of his thick neck.

It was a good second or two before Craig realized that what Broken-teeth was trying to remove from his neck was in fact an arrow. The mysterious missile had pierced from one side and gone right though.

The arrow must have smashed through Broken-teeth's spinal column, where it met his head. At the next moment the fatally wounded man fell on the floor with his body twitching and jerking, his tongue lolling out. His brother was now yelling and trying to wrench the arrow from flesh and bone. Broken-teeth's feet kicked spasmodically at the fire, scattering bits of flaming wood and bark in all directions.

Just as Broken-teeth's breath bubbled its last in a strangled effort to force air down a severed windpipe, Big-nose fell backwards with a stunned look on his features. A second arrow had come out of the darkness and now protruded from the big man's chest, just left of the breastbone. Big-nose coughed once and a great gobbet of blood came from his mouth to flop in the embers of the fire where it sizzled. Then he too fell backwards, to lie with his great foot rammed in his brother's open mouth, neither man being conscious of the indignity of the position.

'Who's there?' cried Craig, concerned that he would be next on the archer's list of victims. 'Do you speak Gaelic?'

'Cut that demon tongue,' replied a familiar, cheerful female voice, as Hupa stepped out of the shadows on the edge of the forest. 'I hate to hear you talk like a goblin.'

'Hupa? Thank the gods!' cried Craig, feeling the fear drain from him. 'Where are the others?'

Hupa knelt down beside him and cut his bonds with an obsidian knife. She rubbed the red, raw places where the ropes had chafed him. Craig climbed unsteadily to his feet, having to place a hand on her shoulder to steady himself. He wanted to hug her for her timely entrance. All his reserve had gone from him and the spark of his spirit had been about to go out.

While he was thus attempting to gain his balance she told him something he had not wanted to hear.

'I'm alone, Craig. No one came with me. I noticed you go into the copse after the entertainments. When you didn't come out again, I went in to look for you, thinking you might have had an accident. I found signs of a struggle and some tracks. I hoped to reach you quickly, so I didn't go back to the pa for help, I simply tracked you.

'But it was difficult following spoor in the darkness, and I lost a lot of time. Since then I've been tracking you night and day, over the landscape, sometimes losing the trail and having to patiently search for signs again. Finally, tonight, I caught up with you – and there you see the result.'

They both stared at the dead men, lying on the mossy bank of the river, and it was hard for Craig to feel sorry for them.

PART SEVEN

The Celtic Otherworld

1

When his two agents did not meet him at the agreed point in the southern hills of Umberland, Douglass knew that they had betrayed him. The only balm for his wrath over the next few days was devising ways of killing them both when they did surface. He had no doubt they would contact him with a demand for more payment. That would be typical of those two Jutes.

Douglass was a man rich in cattle, sheep and horses, but he was not one to squander his wealth. It would be a pleasure to make a bargain, then break it and grab the pair of them. Douglass knew a torturer, an artist of pain, amongst the Angles. This expert's particular genius was to turn men inside out while the body remained alive – almost alive – enough to feel agony and distress, which was enough for Douglass.

'I'll get him to reverse one of them, then I'll hang the carcass for a day or so from a tree, before cooking him like a hare.' He smiled to himself. *Jugged human*. 'Then I'll force the other brother to eat him. That will be a suitable end for one of them at least.'

There was a third brother, a much younger man, who was now Douglass's hostage. Some satisfaction had been gained by cutting off two of the fingers of the youth's left hand, at the second knuckle, when those pair of renegades out on the trail had failed to appear at the meeting place. These had been used to plug the boy's nose while Douglass clamped a broad palm over his mouth, demanding to know the whereabouts of his kin.

However, since the young man had not talked, even after passing out several times with the pain wracking his chest, it had to be assumed their non-appearance had not been planned beforehand, but was a spontaneous action.

In the meantime he had to attempt to find them. He was at the moment a guest of the Wuffingas tribe – the 'wolf people' – but only because he was paying their chief a tribute. The Wuffingas were a clan within the greater tribe of the Angles, who lived in Albainn. The Angles and the Jutes had come originally from a huge land mass in the cold seas to the south-east of Albainn.

It seemed invasions from this place never ceased. Already there was another people beginning to make tentative forays into Albainn and what was now called Engaland. They too came from this cold vast land to the south-east. They were the sea raiders now on the small outer islands and they called themselves Saxons.

In truth Douglass was more concerned about the Saxons than he was the

Oceanians. He did not believe the brown-skins would stay. He had heard they came from a place of warm seas, vertical suns, lush vegetation and colourful wildlife. Why would they want to stay in a climate which pissed rain and snow alternately from the skies for half the year? One winter in Albainn would send them scuttling back to Oceania, and it would be as if they had never come at all.

The Oceanians would leave and all trace of their ever having been there would be gone. The Celts would burn their wooden fortresses and no one would ever know they had set foot on this sacred land of Albainn.

This was what the witch had told him and he believed her – she had been right about everything so far. She had also told him that the Celtic gods were at war above, under and around the island, with those who had accompanied the Oceanians. She did not know who was winning this ethereal war, but some of the terrible storms attested to the struggle going on.

The victors will be *our* gods, thought Douglass, for they are warriors of great might. They will crush these invaders with lightning and thunderbolts, strangle them with their bare hands, stamp them into oblivion with their feet. These foreign gods will follow their people back to Oceania, with their tails between their legs like the curs they be.

He paused in his thoughts as he saw two of his sub-chiefs talking with local women.

'Dunan, Conall, get ye here by me.'

The two men in deer-skin cloaks came running at his call.

'Aye, Douglass, what will you have of us?'

'Take some men and post them in the hills around. There'll be a messenger arriving for me soon. I want to know which direction he comes from. I'll have those two Jute bastards as well as the half-breed, Craig, or whatever he calls himself. They may think they'll get the better of Douglass Barelegs, but they're as wrong as they could ever be. Get to it.'

'Aye, Douglass.'

'And the pick of my sheep for the man who first spots the messenger.'

Dunan grinned. 'Would it be the pretty ewe, the one with the glossy fleece, Douglass?'

'Get out of here, ye debauched man,' laughed Conall. 'Are ye no satisfied with the Wuffingas women?'

'They're too ugly. They all look like sows.'

Douglass did not have a great sense of humour and he roared at his men to get on with what they were supposed to be about, then stomped back into the village through a gate in the thorn-bush defences, already changing his mind about jugging one of the brothers, thinking instead he might cut off their testicles and have them sewn inside their mouths ...

*

Punga, having lost his weapons, had been locked in a wrestling embrace with a god named Oenghus mac in Og, who was a worthy opponent for the profusely bleeding God of Ugly Creatures. Now he had escaped the clutches of Oenghus and was going to the assistance of Tangaroa, the Great Sea God, who was being flailed by Manannan mac Lir, the Celtic God of the Sea. Nearby, Tawhaki, the God of Thunder, was battling with lightning lances against Taranis, his opposite number.

While he staggered across the battlefield, where many gods lay wounded and dying, Punga had time to glance down to see that his charge, Craig, was now safe from the hands of his abductors. Punga had guided Hupa, the archer, to the site where Craig was being held by the two Jutes, and now she had performed her task of freeing the young man. All was well there, though Craig had to be returned to the pa of his people.

'Punga, you ugly creature!' roared Tangaroa, in his pain and suffering. 'Why so slow? Leap upon the back of this Taranis, Lord of the Cold Seas, while I take his flail ...'

The loyal Punga did as he was bid, suffering some savage blows which stripped the skin from his shoulders in so doing.

Like many of the gods he was gradually being torn to pieces and those pieces were being scattered about the earth. He wondered for how much longer he could keep going ...

That night Hupa and Craig buried the bodies of the two Jutes under a great tree with spreading boughs. The leaves of the tree had scalloped edges and the nuts were like small coconuts in shape, but protruding from a half-husk. Hupa said she sensed tree spirits in this place and the souls of the men would have company on their journey to the land of the dead, wherever that was for people of their kind.

'We have triumphed over the evil of these men,' said Hupa, 'and whoever sent them.'

Craig, however, felt there was someone else who should be thanked for their deliverance. An ancestor perhaps? Or a god? Some supernatural being was taking time out to watch over the whereabouts of the son of Seumas. He could feel it in the very wind which blew across this cursed land.

Craig said to Hupa, 'I must get back to the pa as quickly as possible. The night I was abducted, Kieto told me he wanted to sue for peace with the Celts and concentrate on a war with the Angles. It can't happen without me. Cormac-the-Venomous will trust no other Oceanian.'

'Now we must get some rest,' she told Craig. 'In the morning we'll retrace our journey as best we can. Although, it's as you said, we'll need to go around villages. Perhaps there's a river we can follow? It might be easier to travel by water than over land?'

'We'll see,' replied Craig. 'In the meantime, I am so weary I could drop. Is this a safe place to sleep, do you think?'

'We'll have to risk it,' replied Hupa. 'I sense rock spirits, river spirits and tree spirits all round us, but they seem harmless creatures.'

'How come you sense them and I don't?'

'Because you're a man. Women have a greater sensitivity to such things.'

Before either of them could fall asleep, however, there was a howling in the night around them. Both sat bolt upright and stared out into the darkness. Hupa took up her bow and quiver of arrows. The howling was a haunting sound which it might seem came from the mouths of the dead. It was mournful, it was cold and distant, and it chilled one to the marrow.

'I think that is a messenger from the world of the dead,' Hupa said, shivering. 'Come to collect the souls of those two Jutes I killed.'

'Sensitive female!' snorted Craig, putting more dead branches on the fire to build up the flames. 'That's an animal they call a wolf. The two Jutes spoke about it all the time. It roams in packs. You've seen their skins – the Celts make cloaks out of them. Coarse grey pelts. A wolf is like a dog only much fiercer in aspect and in behaviour.'

'Foxes, dogs, deer, horses, badgers, otters – I even saw a creature much like a rat only longer and sleeker, with very sharp teeth – killing one of those rats with long ears they call hares. A baby hare, it looked like. There are so many more animals here than on our own islands.'

Some pictures came into Craig's mind: descriptions from his father when he was alive.

'What you saw was either a weasel, stoat, polecat or tree marten – something of that kind. There are many variations on a theme here. Let's get some sleep. The fire will keep the wolves away. I hope.'

Craig did at last manage to fall asleep, but he seemed to wake in the middle of the night. The fire had gone cold and the wolves were calling all around. He climbed to his feet and looked about him, sensing something different about the landscape in the emerging light of the coming dawn. There was a chill breeze from somewhere, like a draught from an open door, and on it was the whisper of his father's voice.

Come to me, Craig – bring a weapon with you – an iron sword if you can – if not, even a stone axe will do.

An intense-looking hunched bird, a white owl, suddenly appeared on the branch of a nearby tree and hooted at Craig and stared hard at him. When Craig approached the owl, its head swivelled round back to front. It seemed to be telling him to follow where it went. Then it took off, silently flying towards some foothills, and Craig proceeded to go in the same direction, pausing only to pick up one of the daggers left by the Jutes.

Craig found he was walking in the direction from which the cold wind was coming. Hupa remained asleep by the remnants of the fire as he strode away from their camp in the wake of the night-hunting owl. His journey across the country, which he seemed to cover remarkably quickly, was through forested foothills, and once he passed between some wolves.

The wolf pack regarded both him and the owl but casually, as if they were only half there, letting him weave his way through their midst without a murmur. One of their number was on a crag, calling in hollow tones as if to a listener on the moon. Looking into their strange hazel-coloured eyes, he saw other distant places, other lands, stranger even than the misty regions of the island which he now traversed.

Finally, he and the owl came to a cave, whereupon the owl disappeared inside it. Craig entered without a second thought, as his father's voice became stronger in his head. Within the cave it was quite cold and he wished he had brought a thicker cloak with him. Finally, after many hours walking in the darkness, he saw a grey light in the distance. It seemed he was coming to the end of his journey. When he drew nearer, there was a creature guarding the exit, a monster with three heads.

'I have come to see my father,' said Craig.

These seemed to be the right words, for the monster remained unmoving as Craig passed between it and one wall of the cave, then out into a swirling, hazy world of half-light. If he thought he had been cold before, he was wrong. In this place there were the substances called ice and snow, which his father had told him about. There was also a wind which carried sharp invisible shark's-teeth in its jaws. Craig felt as if his flesh were being stripped from his bones.

Never in his life had he experienced such a feeling of coldness. His lungs hurt him when he drew in oxygen. Freezing air made his mouth numb as he tried to suck it down. His nose, ears, indeed all his extremities, felt as if they were about to snap away from his body. The channels within him – his nostrils, his windpipe – had shrivelled.

'The sun god has abandoned this place,' he told no one in particular. 'Here the light comes from within this ice.'

He wrapped his cloak around himself and walked out into the crashing whirlwind blizzard which raged around him. It was like a tempest out in the ocean, a typhoon, which turned the world upside down and whipped its whiteness from the foaming mouths of waves. Except here was not wetness but solid light, battering his body with tiny chips of translucent gravel, stinging his eyes and cheeks with their sharpness.

And here the snow his father had told him about was not just of one whiteness, but many different shades, even down to a kind of blueness. Everything seemed impenetrable. There was no clear sight to the centre of things. All was opaque, frosted, cracked and veined. Everything had a layer of solid wind upon its surface, almost thick enough to cut with an axe.

Just as his eyes were becoming used to the white darkness, a hideous monster rose out of the snow in front of him. It was twice as tall as Craig, and covered in white fur. Standing on its hind legs it opened its mouth to reveal two terrible rows of teeth which could tear raw flesh from bone. Its eyes blazed in fury, as if Craig had trespassed on some holy place, and its forelegs, tipped with long claws, opened wide as if about to enfold the Oceanian in a embrace of death.

The monster roared and stumbled forwards, but out of the vortex of snow came another shape, which hurled itself at the monster and gripped it by the throat. This creature was in the shape of a naked man whose powerful arms began to strangle the giant. Craig could see ridges of muscle and sinew standing proud on those large forearms. The man's legs were wrapped around the beast's chest, attempting to crush its ribs.

The creature bellowed and thrashed around, trying to get those claws to rip open its assailant, but the man, almost buried beneath the thick fur, was protected by the beast's pelt, and their points were ineffectual. Its slavering jaws with those dreadful teeth were utterly useless to it, so long as the man was locked around its throat choking the life from it.

Gradually the moaning beast sank to the ground, yet still the naked man remained fastened to its head, strangling the life from its body. Eventually, after a very long time, the struggle ceased, and the creature lay still. It was dead.

'Thank you,' said Craig, stepping forward. 'You saved my life.'

'Only your dream-life, Craig,' replied the man, getting to his feet, 'for you are not really here in body.'

Now Craig recognized his saviour and it was his own father, Seumas, though much younger, in perfect form.

'Father?' he cried. 'You're still alive!'

He went forward to embrace Seumas, only to be warned away by a thrusting hand.

'No, my son – here you cannot. This is Ifurin, the Otherworld of the Celts, which has me in its thrall. I asked you to come to me because I neglected to bring a weapon with which to defend myself. Had I not been years in Oceania I would have remembered to die with a weapon in my hand. There are many monsters in this place, some of which cannot be killed by these two hands, strong as they may now be. I have been reborn in the best condition I owned when in the world of the living, but I must have something with which to defend myself.

'Did you bring your father a sword, Craig? I must have some metal about me. I must fend off the dark creatures of this world until I can find your step-mother.'

Craig shrugged his shoulders, feeling he had failed his father.

'Only this iron dagger. The Jutes who abducted me had no swords. You may have the knife, Father.'

'A dagger will do for now,' replied Seumas, 'thank you, my son – but when you are able, you must find a sword and cast it into the depths of the nearest loch. I will retrieve it from there, though it be locked under thick ice, for the Otherworld is but a reflection of the one you now inhabit.'

'Not for long,' replied Craig, hugging himself. 'After this, I shall wish to go home to the islands. Is the Otherworld of the Celts always so cold and brittle?'

'Winter in Albainn is not much warmer,' replied his father, with a phantom of a smile. 'I told you your mother's people were soft and womanish.'

'Dorcha's people?'

'Your real mother.'

Craig studied the ghost of his father before him, seeing something substantial yet sensing there was but a shadow there. He had never seen Seumas as a young man and he was astonished how much he looked like the man Craig saw when he looked into a reflecting surface. He was his father's son, there could be no doubt about that. Perhaps one day there might be an opportunity for him to visit the Otherworld of the Oceanians, and meet his mother for the first time? If one had happened, then why not the other?

Seumas said to him, 'What of Douglass's son?'

'Douglass Barelegs? He tries to kill me, Father. I am told he will not rest until the death of his father has been avenged.'

'You *must* try to make your peace with him,' Seumas insisted. 'He has been wronged.'

Craig replied, 'I have promised to try, Father, but this is a thing of *your* making, not mine. I will risk my life, but I will not throw it away because you could not control your temper as a young man. That would be a foolish thing to do. I will attempt to repair the damage you caused, but I can't be held responsible for it. You understand?'

The ghost of his father stared at him for a long time, before saying, 'You have grown wiser, my son.'

'What of the other Douglass, the one you killed for his sword? He must be here too.'

'Why, he is long gone, his soul eaten by a supernatural creature similar to the Shark-God, Dakuwanga. He had no weapon with which to defend himself, and so he was taken, as I will be eventually if you do not send me a sword.'

'Why did he not send for his son, as you have done, to bring him a weapon?'

Seumas shook his head. 'He did, but Douglass son of Douglass panicked when he saw the three-headed creature guarding the entrance to this world. He ran back. It was not long after that his father met one of the largest and fiercest of the monsters in Ifurin, the Icharacha, a creature like a lobster with a thousand legs, each leg bristling with sharp pincers large enough to snip a man's limbs from his body. Douglass could not defend himself. He was first pruned and then eaten.'

'Now I must go.'

'Now you must go. Go quickly. We cannot embrace in this place.'

'Will you be here for ever, Father?'

'I think not, for the spiritual world is changing. The old gods, the Other-worlds, these seem to be fading. There is a place where Dorcha has gone, not yet open to a heathen like me. I hope to join her when this is settled.'

Craig nodded, then turned and hurried towards the cave. He looked back once, to see a swirling shape of mist and snow, which might have been his father's ghost, then entered the cave. The three-headed monster was still there. Craig slipped past it and down the long passage to the real world. When he arrived back at the campsite, Hupa was still asleep.

He lay down on the other side of the fire, conscious that she was a beautiful young woman and he a married man.

2

On waking the following morning, Hupa went to the river to wash. Unused to the dirt and squalor which seemed part of the Land-of-Mists, she stripped and entered the water to bathe all over, wearing only the shark's-tooth necklace which proclaimed her ariki rank. Since she had been on this foreign island she had never felt physically clean. The Celts themselves were often covered in mud, smelled of oily peatbog-water and animal dung, and carried about them various foodstuffs that either dripped, or mouldered, or rotted in some way.

She tried to imagine what it would be like to be married to a Pict or Scot, and shuddered as she splashed water between her legs, getting in those crevices which harboured the odours of young womanhood. It was her time of month and having no tapa bark pads with her she was having to use an awkward combination of dry moss and grasses. Still, she prided herself on being inventive enough to overcome these inconveniences.

No, to be married to *anyone* from this island would be quite horrible. She was an Oceanian ariki, a virgin of noble rank, and her husband should be likewise. He should be noble, a great warrior, a man of learning, good, kind and gentle, with a dry sense of humour. In short, he should be quite perfect, for she knew herself to be a prize to be treasured. The idea of being attached to a stinking lump of lard in a poorly cured wolfskin was quite abhorrent to her.

Yet – yet – she would like to be married to one who carried Pictish blood in his veins. She glanced guiltily towards the spot where the red-haired man who was her companion slept. Hupa had loved Craig since she was fourteen, when she first realized he was not such an old man as she had always thought. Now she was eighteen and ready for a man, yet the one person she wanted was not available, was already married.

'I shall stay a virgin all my life,' she told the trees, the river, the grassy banks dotted with wild flowers. 'I shall be like Kikamana, pure in body and spirit.'

Yes, but her heart ached, for she thought Craig perfect in every way for her. True, he was not a virgin, but that was of small account. Hupa hated it when pictures of Craig making love to Linloa, his wife, entered her mind, but she usually managed to change faces with Linloa before any great hurt was felt.

She imagined that tattooed limb, the painted leg, nestling between hers after making love, while he whispered wonderful words into her ear, telling her how beautiful she was, how much he adored her, how he would die for her.

A silver fish came near as she bathed, darting through the green weeds at the bottom of the clear water. Her bow and quiver were on the bank. She wondered if she could get to the weapon before the fish went away, but it shot off along the gravelled bed into a nest of fronds in the next moment. It had been frightened by a shadow falling on the surface.

She looked up, startled to see Craig had awoken and come down to the riverside. He stood there, staring at her nude body, his eyes soft and blue. Troubled a little by his quietness, she covered her small breasts with her hands.

He turned away, quickly.

'I'm sorry,' he said, 'that was unforgivable of me – but you looked so – so pretty. My thoughts were innocent. It was like catching a young faun unawares. It will not happen again – I'll – I'll go and stir the ashes of the fire ...'

He walked away and she found herself wishing he would not go, catching the words in her throat. The look in his eyes told her his thoughts had not been entirely innocent, as he had maintained. It would have taken but a word or a gesture, to have encouraged him. When it came to it though, Hupa could not rid her mind of Linloa, that quiet modest woman who had stayed at home to raise his children.

Next time though, thought Hupa fiercely as she dressed, I will not hold back. I deserve the man I love as much as anyone else. Why should she have him just because she saw him first? It is about who loves the most, not about who grabs who before anyone else can get to them. Watch out, Linloa, I will not let a second opportunity pass me by.

Once dressed she took her bow and went wading again, searching for that large silver fish. She found it, or its twin, in the shallows further up. Her aim was true and very soon she returned to the fire, which was now in a state for cooking her catch. Craig stared in admiration.

'By the gods,' he said, 'you're a fine hunter, Hupa – you'll make some great hero a fine partner in life, if that's what you choose.'

You, she thought, the pit of her stomach aching. *You*.

They roasted and ate the fish, then started on their journey south. Since the river must have been flowing towards the sea, they decided to follow it. Once they reached the coast it would simply be a matter of following that, too, until they reached the pa which they knew to have the sea at its back.

'So long as the river goes to the right side of the island,' replied Hupa. 'Are you sure it does?'

'It must do. We have never been that far from the sea, wherever we were. I can smell the salt air. Besides, I took the direction from the sun.'

Their progress was slow, due to the nature of the braided river, which meandered over a vast area, causing them to make deviations to previous dry rocky beds which were difficult to walk across. Towards the first evening it was obvious by the blackness above that a storm was coming in. There was already a growling in the throat of the sky. Almost simultaneously, they saw some smoke curling above a patch of woodland.

It was only one column, which meant a single dwelling rather than a village.

'Let's go and see,' said Hupa. 'We can remain hidden if it looks dangerous.'

In a clearing, in the middle of the wood, they saw a huge green mound like a grave. It was from a hole in the top of this mound that the smoke drifted. There were two other squarish holes in the turf which seemed to serve as windows. These were close to the ground and framed by thick wooden logs. Thin dirty rags covered the windows, preventing anyone from peering inside. Up against one sloping turf wall – or roof, for it served as both – was a stack of broken branches and kindling, but no axe. In a pen made of wands, were some birds with flattish beaks that made a monotonous kind of *quak-quak-quak* sound.

Beyond this ugly little hovel stood an earthen well, lined with stones. Not long after the pair had ventured into the glade and had hidden themselves in bushes, someone came out of the stone, timber and turf dwelling to draw water at this well. It was a child, hunched, with wild black hair and smoke-darkened, wrinkled skin: a child with an old man's face.

She was accompanied by a small animal. A tame creature, much like the wild one Hupa had earlier described as sucking the blood of a baby hare. It flowed in, around and between the child's legs as she walked. It seemed to be caressing her ankles with its soft-looking, furry, serpentine form.

While she was at the well, Craig hurried over to one of the windows, lifted the covering rag and peered inside. Then he crept back to where Hupa was hidden.

'No one else there,' he whispered.

The child-with-the-old-man's-face was on her way back to her hovel. She suddenly stopped and stiffened, putting down her obviously heavy wooden bucket for a moment. She stared hard at where the two were lying. Her pet immediately went up on its hind legs, staring in the same direction, but whether it was doing so because it had heard, seen or smelled something, or whether it was just copying the child, was not really evident.

But then the child-with-the-old-man's-face took up the bucket again, her pet now back on all fours and weaving its strange patterns through her legs, and the two of them went back into her dwelling. At that moment large drops of rain began to fall, splattering on the leaves above Hupa's head. Somewhere in the distance a sharp crack sounded and there was a flash.

'The storm,' she said, looking up.

'She's alone in that dwelling,' whispered Craig. 'We could spend the night here. One small child can't hurt us. What do you think?'

'I agree there's no need to fear a person of her stature.'

'Let's do it then.'

They went down to the thick wooden door of the hovel and Craig yelled to the child in Gaelic, hoping she spoke the tongue of the Celts.

'Hallo in there!'

To his relief she replied in kind. 'What do you want?' Her voice was low and rasping, like that of an elderly woman racked with some respiratory disease.

'We are two weary strangers. May we spend the night under your roof? A heavy storm is coming up. We'll be caught out here and may be killed by a struck tree. There's already squalling rain, which is soaking us to the roots of our hair.'

'How can I trust ye?'

'There's nothing to fear. We are ...' Craig looked pointedly at Hupa, 'we are a man and his wife. We are travelling south to the land of the Celts. You sound like a Celt yourself ...'

'I am,' said the child-with-the-old-man's-face, beginning to open the door now, 'they're not all south of the border.' Once she laid eyes on them, however, she started backwards in alarm, crying, 'But look at you! Ye have the skins of demons. And strange stripes across your face! What's this? Are you from some Otherworld? Do I need magic to send ye hence?'

'We are – castaways,' replied Craig. 'We come from another land. Our skins are dark because we live always in the sun. And these bars across my face are only tattoos, such as those Picts decorate themselves with. But have no fear, we are not supernatural. If we were, why would we be afraid of a storm? Why would we need to call to you to open your door? If we were demons we would come down your chimney, or slide under your window rags.'

'These things are true,' replied the child, peering hard into his face. 'Ye do not look like a demon. Ye look like something born of man, but with a strange darkness to you.'

When Craig translated this for Hupa, the girl became incensed.

'Better than having skin the colour of the belly of a fish,' she snapped.

The child-with-the-old-man's-face clearly knew an insult had been flung, even though she did not understand the language. Instead of shutting the door in their faces, the child smiled.

'Fiery strumpet, ain't she? What kind of tongue is that? It sounds like the speech of bogles, hobgoblins, boggarts and other such creatures of an unnatural stamp. Are ye from the world of such beings? Come on, speak up. Tell me the truth.'

'I have no idea what you mean.'

'Have ye not, then,' she said, peering into his eyes. 'What a pity. What a pity. I always hope for visitors from such regions. Once they might have clustered at my window, but I killed an elf you see, it drowned in a pail of milk, and now they won't come any more, except to plague me. Today I am a child, tomorrow an old man, then next a young woman – sometimes even betwixt and between, when they feel at their most cruel.'

'Today you are between,' said Craig.

'Am I?' shrieked the child, running her hands over her face and head, looking down at her body. 'Damn those fairies!'

'I don't know what an elf is,' confessed Craig. 'Is it some kind of a butterfly or moth?'

Her face changed again and she laughed and leaned on the doorpost.

'Butterflies and moths – some folks see them as such ...'

Craig studied the child's face as she spoke, unable to determine her age. Her skin was careworn and dry, with deep wrinkles, but the eyes were young and very alive. They flicked from feature to feature, quickly, taking in everything about these visitors at her door. They were so bright those eyes, and the blue in them washed to such a fascinating hue, that he found it hard to look into them.

'Well, are ye coming in, or do you stand in the doorway and gawp at me?'

She stood aside, letting them enter.

The inside of the hovel was not much different from the outside. There was a hard dirt floor, a ring of stones in the middle of the one room which served as a hearth, a bed of straw in a far corner, and thick logs to sit on. In a pile on one side were rotting cabbage stalks, bits of offal and other remnants of past meals. Flies covered this heap and were evident in most other parts of the room too.

From the beamed ceiling, plugged with clay, hung bunches of dried herbs, dried animal parts and smoked fish. She took down one of the fish, which looked as brittle as bark, and broke it into pieces, offering the pair a piece each. Craig took his and began chewing on it. Hupa did likewise. The child dipped hers in the bucket of water for a time, before sucking on it.

'My teeth are loose,' she explained. 'One falls out every day or so. It's some sickness of the gums.'

Just as the three of them sat down on thick, up-ended logs, around the fire, the thunderstorm broke outside. Rain came hissing down onto the turf roof above. There were almost deafening explosions as thunder punched the belly out of the sky, right above their heads. Lightning blasted through the clouds as if it were splitting giant trees, making Hupa jump.

'Frightened, strumpet?' laughed the child-with-the-old-man's-face. 'Frightened *and* fiery – there's a combination.'

Outside, the downpour increased in fury, smacking into the hovel like a flood. Water began to run under the door and down the walls on either sides of the windows. There was dampness in the air. Just then, Craig himself started, but not with the thunder and lightning, for things began to move in various parts of the room. Something snaked out of a woodpile, something else crept from the darkness of a corner, yet another creature appeared from out of the straw of the bed.

'What? What is it?' cried the child, sensing his discomfort. 'Oh, my *beasties*. They'll not hurt you, boy. They're my children, my precious ones.'

There was a weasel, and some kind of a rat, and a short, slim snake. They were clearly disturbed by the storm and went to the child. She lifted the hem of her ragged shift and they went under her skirts, hiding there. Hupa shuddered, making the child laugh huskily, before throwing a log on the fire.

'Fiery, frightened and fussy!'

The storm outside built itself to a terrible fury, crashing and blundering about in the woods like an insane giant. Inside the hovel the group were at least safe from being struck by lightning. Craig went into a doze, swaying on his log seat as he sat by the fire looking into the flames. Hupa too was lolling on his shoulder. Some time later the child and her pets went to her bed in the corner and Craig, finding Hupa asleep on his arm, lifted her up and carried her to a dry spot to lay her down.

Then he himself found another suitable patch on the earthen floor and slept fitfully as the storm continued.

In the middle of the night they were all woken suddenly by a crashing sound. Beams on the ceiling fractured and the whole structure bulged inwards. A huge broken branch, still attached to a trunk, speared the roof and buried its point in the dirt floor. It was this branch which saved their lives and prevented the tree to which it was joined from smashing through the roof. Had the branch not been there a massive trunk would have crushed the hovel and possibly those in it. As it was the water came pouring in, through the hole in the roof and down the branch, causing Hupa to move her position.

'Ferret's shit!' swore the child from the corner. 'My little home ...'

But there was clearly nothing to be done until the morning, so everyone went back to sleep.

When daybreak came, Craig woke to find a child-with-a-child's-face examining Hupa's bow and quiver of arrows. She seemed to find the points of the arrows particularly interesting, running a finger over one of them, murmuring to herself.

'What are you doing?' asked Craig, and at that moment Hupa woke and, seeing what was happening, snatched her arrow from the child's grasp.

'Manners!' murmured the child.

'I asked you what you were doing,' Craig said again. 'Why did you take that arrow without permission?'

'Don't fash yourself, boy,' she snapped back. 'I was just looking. Can't a person look at something in her own home, without being treated like a thief? You carry too much on yourself. Here, I'll break our fast with some cooked food, while you see what is to be done about the roof.'

It seemed it was an order, rather than a request.

Craig decided it was best to let the matter drop. It seemed a harmless enough piece of curiosity. He then set about examining the structure of the hovel. The beams were fractured all right and clay and stones had been dislodged, but the tree that had fallen, breaking the back of the roof, could not be moved. It would have taken an army of strong people to lift that wooden giant out of its present position.

'You'd best patch round it, leave the tree where it is,' he advised. 'It's quite secure now, resting on that broken bough. Over the next year or so I should build yourself a new place, because eventually the branch will rot and the tree will sink lower and lower into the room.'

'That's your advice, is it?'

'You asked me for it.'

She nodded, thoughtfully, and continued with her cooking.

After the meal, as they were preparing to leave, the child asked them for payment for a night's lodging and food.

'Payment?' said Craig. 'What do you mean?'

'Night's lodgings. You owe me.'

Hupa said, 'What does she want?'

'She wants to be paid, for giving us shelter and food.'

Hupa expressed her repugnance of such behaviour. In Oceania, you shared what you had with neighbours and strangers alike. It was not unknown for a childless couple to ask parents of a large family for one of their offspring and expect to be offered a baby or an infant. Certainly if you had food and someone asked for some, you gave it without question. If a person asked for hospitality, you gave it willingly and would not dream of requesting payment for it.

Craig turned to the child. 'It is not in our nature to pay for such services.'

Her face twisted and she went back on her heels.

'Ho, I see, it's not in your nature to pay for such services, is it? Well, I'm not asking you to act natural. Treat it as a peculiar request if ye will. Think on me as quirky and unusual. Because in this part of this great island we expect to be paid when we hand over hard-earned food and open up our homes to passing outlanders. Now give up.'

'I refuse,' replied Craig, annoyed. 'In any case, what would we give you? We have nothing.'

The child's eyes narrowed. 'Ye got them bow and arrows. Them there arrowheads is magic, I can tell. I can *feel* the magic flowing from 'em. Give me one. Or better still, give me them all. What do you want in exchange? I'll do anything for arrows with such magical properties.'

'We don't need anything. All we want is to get back to our people.'

'I can do that for you too,' said the child-with-a-child's-face. 'I can help you get back to 'em quicker than that.'

'How?'

'I'm what ye might call an enchantress. I can change you into a deer, fleet of foot, for one whole day. So long as you are willing. So long as ye give me such permissions as I ask. Or a wolf? Ye could cross the country twice as fast if you were a deer or wolf. But I can't do it against your nature – it must be with ye, not against ye – what say ye, eh?'

'A shapechanger?'

'D'ye not see the weasel?' sniggered the child. 'He used to be a man, a woodcutter. And the others my distant neighbour's sons. I change 'em back when I need something only they can give me, but they're less of a nuisance this way. Later they can move the tree from my little house. I can keep 'em better in hand in the form of beasts.'

Craig raised his eyebrows at this.

'They *let* you turn them into animals?'

'In this way they don't have to serve any clan chief. Such great bullies are always coming through here, looking for men to do their killin' for them, to recover some lost fief or other. My man stays with me – and my boys too – they stay with their cook and bedmaker. They recognize no fealty to this one or that one, so-called lords who march through the land looking for vassals.'

'Is this approved, by the clans?'

She laughed. 'See how I trust you, stranger? They would burn me if they knew of my powers. Yet, I confess it to you, because I want those arrows so much. What would ye have me change you into? Come on, speak.'

'Birds,' said Craig, as he saw the possibilities. 'What about birds?'

'Aye – pigeons then? They have a good sense of direction. Pigeons I can recommend.'

'No, we'd be killed by the first hawk. What about those large black birds, I've seen hereabouts. No hawk would attack one of *them*.'

'Crows, ye mean? Twa corbies? I could do that.'

Craig turned to Hupa. 'Give the child your weapon – the bow and quiver.'

Hupa clutched her bow tighter. 'What? What's going on? I'm not surrendering my weapon to anyone. Are you mad?'

'Just give them to her. She's promised to change us into birds – those black creatures – she calls them crows. We can get back to the pa more quickly that way. You have to give up your bow and quiver of arrows. Another bow can be made and there are still a few more of Lioumere's teeth, in your father's possession, back at the pa.'

Hupa was quiet for a moment, then she argued with Craig.

'If she can change us into birds or beasts, I would rather be a wolf. I don't like the look of those crow birds. They look shifty and mean. Tell her to change us into wolves and I'll agree to let her have the bow and quiver.'

Craig saw a certain amount of sense in what Hupa was suggesting. As wolves they could follow their own scent, back to the pa. Such creatures could travel across the countryside swiftly, fearing nothing but meeting men. These they could avoid, as wolves can, using their superior instincts, camouflage and wild-country skills. It was probably better to be a wolf than a crow, since neither he nor Hupa knew what it was like to fly and how things looked from a bird's perspective.

'All right then,' he agreed, and told the child-with-the-child's-face of the change of choice.

She said that changing them into wolves would be just as easy as transfiguring them into crows.

Still suspicious, Hupa removed the string from her bow and tied it around her own waist.

Turning to Craig, she said, 'Tell her she can string the bow again later. I have no wish to be shot by my own weapon, as a running wolf.'

The child seemed to understand why Hupa had done as she had and scowled at her.

Craig said in Gaelic, 'I'm placing the bow and quiver at your feet – don't touch them until you've changed us into wolves – you may begin.'

'Tell the girl to stare into my eyes. You too. Both of ye look deeply into my eyes ...'

3

They were not wolves but wild dogs. Afraid of the child-with-the-child's-face now that they were undomesticated beasts, animals of field and woodland, they ran off in panic. Somehow they managed to stay together, by scent and sound more than by sight, and paused in the high grasses of an open stretch of land to get their breath. Unable to communicate with the use of spoken language, Craig managed to convey to Hupa that he would still remain friendly towards her, so long as she remained submissive to him. He nipped her rump and shouldered her.

Hupa retaliated immediately, not at all sure that the hierarchy had been established. She bit his jaw, making him back off with his eyes watering. In fact it was clear to Craig that his female companion was not prepared to roll over, belly-up, in submissive pose just because he was a male. It was bulk which counted here and Hupa's size as a bitch was not much different to that of Craig's as a dog.

All this was quite frustrating to Craig, who felt they were wasting time by trying to establish the dominant animal, especially when there were only two of them. However, he was not going to assume that position without a contest. It was not in his animal nature to do so.

The pair of them began a mock fight, which turned serious occasionally. After much rolling in the dust, side attacks at hairy flanks, chewing of tails, and growling, snapping and snarling, Hupa's canine spirit overcame that of Craig's, and she assumed the role of leader. Craig flipped over onto his back, exposing his vulnerable throat and belly. He rolled his eyes showing the whites and twisted his jaw to give it a lopsided look.

In effect he was saying: *I give in – you can be the dominant member of our small pack – until I make another challenge against your authority. Then we'll have to go through all this again, perhaps with the same result, but hopefully with me taking responsibility for the pack.*

Once she had established her superiority, Hupa went off in search of food, her prime consideration as a wild dog. Craig had some vague idea they should be following a scent trail, but having given way to her as the master, he trotted obediently behind, stopping to sniff things occasionally – grass clumps, trees roots, river banks, the genitals of his companion – finding each interesting in its way but not satisfying any of the primal drives which now ruled his canine life.

Suddenly, as they approached a wooded area, Hupa stopped and stiffened. The hackles rose on her neck. She began growling softly and menacingly in the back of her throat. A few moments later another wild dog came out of the grasses in front and stopped to stare curiously at the pair. Craig sniffed the air and immediately scented bitch on heat. He went bounding off towards the female in front, only to come to a skidding halt when yet another dog, and another, came out of the tall weeds.

There was a pack of six or seven, including a puppy. One big male came up from behind the pack and made straight for Hupa and Craig, his hair bristling and his mouth a snarling red cavern of teeth. They both hunched in the grass for a moment, watching to see if he would swerve away, then when he looked like coming on they bolted for the nearest hill. The big dark male followed them for some way, then turned and joined his pack, who were waiting either for his victory or his retreat.

After that incident the pair moved more warily onwards, not really knowing where they were heading except that their nostrils were tuned to smells of fresh meat. Occasionally they stopped to drink in a puddle, or sniff some interesting animal's urine marking its territorial border, but for the most part it was a kind of meandering progress across country, towards some distant mountainous region. These mountains seemed to be pulling Craig towards them, urging him to enter their domain.

Once, they saw a herd of deer and both animals, inexperienced as they were, set off in pursuit. They did not stand an earthly chance of catching the beasts, which sprang away like lightning and sped across the plains powered by long athletic legs. Another time they actually saw some wolves – the creatures they had wanted to be – and wisely kept a great distance between themselves and the large grey beasts. Even the scent of these creatures from a long way away was enough to strike a terrible fear in the heart of Craig.

Towards evening they heard a great noise and at last smelled the fresh meat for which they had been searching. Coming to the top of a ridge they looked down to see clusters of humans running and clashing together, yelling from their mouths, the shiny things in their hands making high clinking sounds as they came together. There were humans on the ground, some lying still, others moving but making groaning sounds. Here and there were severed limbs and broken heads, eyes that stared from dead skulls, blood seeping into the grasses. Yet still the humans screamed at each other and swished through the air with strips of something which flashed like the sun on a fast-flowing stream.

One man came running towards the two dogs, as they hunched in the grasses, watching this carnage. He managed to get halfway up the embankment, when a straight piece of wood struck him in the back, the point coming through and out of his chest. He looked down and gave a great cry of dismay and despair, then fell to the ground, his legs twitching and jerking.

Still the dogs remained where they were, knowing that if they went down amongst those blood-crazy humans, they themselves might be cut to pieces. When the twilight drained from the sky and the darkness began moving in, the human activity gradually ceased, until there were men strolling away from the scene in bloody rags, or carrying a broken comrade, or simply staggering dazed and blind in the direction of the rising moon.

Food, Craig sensed Hupa saying with her canine gestures. *Fresh meat.*

Once the darkness folded over the plain, they went down and began feeding on the bodies. Other creatures came out of their hidden holes and secret places, also to feed on the fresh meat. Weasels, stoats, polecats, martens, foxes, wolves, rats, mice. Birds came too – carrion. There was plenty to be had. A kind of truce existed between the creatures, now that there was ample food to be had, all in one place. Occasionally a larger beast would move a smaller creature on, to some other feeding ground, or warning growls would ripple from a throat or two, but for the most part they were equal. Even the birds.

Craig gorged on the soft lights of a man whose belly had been sliced open and whose innards were exposed.

When he was glutted he went looking for Hupa, finding her gnawing on the shoulder of another fallen man. He waited patiently for her to finish, then the pair of them went away into the night, to find a place to rest until the morning. Craig was conscious of the thought that the food would still be there the next day. They could eat again, once the sun came up. Unless the humans returned to fight each other again.

When the sun came up, the pair went down again to feed. Again there were others there, but everyone scattered when the humans returned to carry off their dead. The humans carried clubs with them and began to beat off the wild beasts, shouting in anger. Hupa and Craig left the field again, running through some marshland, to stop on the other side.

Craig lay down on his back, exhausted, staring at the sky. There were small storm flies coming from the oily marsh water, settling on his sweaty skin. He swatted them, then scratched the places where they had bitten him with his nails. When the lethargy left him a little, he rolled over on to his side, to stare at Hupa. She was kneeling, looking down at her hands, her nails thick with dried blood and mud.

'We're back,' he said, suddenly realizing he was no longer covered in fur. 'We've changed back.'

'If we ever went away,' replied Hupa, wiping the blood away from her mouth. She seemed to find a bit of gristle between her teeth and hooked it out with a fingernail. Then she turned away and began heaving and retching, being sick on the grass. Craig, realizing she was having a reaction against what they had eaten, sat and watched her, feeling sympathetic.

When she had finished, she looked at him.

'How is it that you're not sick?' she asked. 'Do you have a tough constitution?'

'You mean because of what we ate? Why, you Rarotongans haven't fought many enemies in the past, have you? Don't forget I was raised a Hivan. There were wars between the islands all the time. We ate our foes for breakfast after the battle.'

Hupa looked at him and was then sick again.

He continued, saying, 'Your father has probably done the same in his time.'

'I don't *care,*' she said. 'I haven't. I found it disgusting. We ate those people because we were *hungry,* not because we wanted their mana. Not because we wanted to debase and humiliate them, prevent their atua from receiving reward after death ...'

Craig shrugged. Except that the meat had been raw, he did not see what to get in a fuss about. Nowadays, he would not eat his enemies, because those rituals were slightly out of fashion with Rarotongans, but he saw nothing disgusting about it. The Hivans, Fijians and Tongans still did it. He felt that Hupa was making a bother about nothing.

'What did you mean – *if we ever went away?*' he asked her, when he felt she was able to reply.

'I meant that perhaps we only thought we were dogs.'

Craig considered this very carefully. Hypnotism, he knew, was a very powerful tool. Boy-girl could hypnotize. It was always better, he had been told, if the victim is willing and allows the hypnotist inside his or her head. Well, they had done that, with the sorceress. Perhaps it was true? Maybe they had been running on their knuckles and toes? After all, they were still wearing clothes, which were now covered in the blood of a people he assumed were two Angle tribes, who had been battling over some quarrel or other.

He inspected his hands and feet.

'I still think we were really transformed into wild dogs,' he said at last.

'It doesn't really matter now, does it? We're well and truly lost. If I ever get my hands on that child again, I'll strangle her with my bow. Now we have no weapons and we're deep in the hinterland of a vast foreign land. What shall we do now? Fall on our knees and beg our ancestors to guide us out?'

'I am a navigator. I can never be thoroughly lost. The sun will go down behind those mountains,' said Craig. 'That's the way we have to point our chins. I agree it's not a very accurate way to navigate, but it's better than heading in the wrong direction altogether. Come on. Pick yourself up. You can wash off that blood and gore at the next stream, but for now just lick your chops and get your feet moving.'

What he had not told Hupa was the fact that he felt an overwhelming attraction coming from the mountains. It was as if they were pulling him into their heart. He was now, and had been since first laying eyes on them, vaguely conscious that some destiny awaited him in those mountains. Somehow this whole episode, including being abducted and finding the home of the child-with-the-old-man's-face, had a feeling of a manipulative power behind it, as if unseen forces were directing his movements, urging him gently along a prepared path.

Perhaps there was a task for him to perform, for which he alone was suitable?

PART EIGHT

Over the Magic Mountains

1

Before the two companions went up into the mountains, Craig had an urge to go back to the battlefield below. Given a few moments in the early morning, Craig had said his usual prayers to Punga, the God of Ugly Creatures, and had heard something in the wind as it blew through the trees. He had been *told* by Punga to return to the site of the bloody fight. Punga was his household deity and Craig could no more have ignored the faint call of this god than he could have rejected a plea from his own mother.

The Angles had gathered their dead and had gone. After searching a long time amongst the blood-soaked long grasses he found what he was looking for: an iron broadsword. This was the weapon which his father desired in order to be able to defend himself in Ifurin.

However, there was no loch in this part of the country, in which to fling the sword as instructed, so Craig stuck the weapon in his waistband and went back to Hupa. She grumbled at him, saying that it was all right for him, he had a weapon now, but she felt naked without her bow and quiver.

'We'll make you a bow as soon as we find a suitable kind of tree,' he said. 'And some arrows.'

He felt uncomfortable. She had chosen the wrong words to describe her state. Her talk of feeling naked made him come over hot and embarrassed. Such words from her mouth filled his head with forbidden pictures. He hoped that nothing had happened between them, while they had been dogs – or worse – if they had not been dogs. Certainly the animal lust had been upon him during that time. She was (he hoped *still*) a virgin of high rank and he was married to a woman who loved him deeply. Violation would be unforgivable.

'How do you feel?' he asked her casually. 'In yourself I mean?'

Hupa stared back as he gazed at her. She was small, neatly proportioned, and youthful. An athlete. There were no feminine wiles, no frilly edges. What he saw was plain and simple Hupa: without artifice. Her gender was secondary to most people who knew her. Yet to him she seemed totally desirable.

'Me? I feel sick. I've never eaten raw people before – what do you expect? But I'll get over it.'

'That wasn't what I meant. You see, we spent time as wild dogs – or at least, *thought* we were dogs. Something – something could have happened which we might regret later.'

715

Hupa looked him directly in the eyes. She might have been wholly inex-perienced sexually, but she was not naive. She knew immediately what he was talking about.

'Fat chance,' she muttered. 'You've made it plain how you feel about – about us.'

'I may have done that,' he said, frustrated and angry with himself and her, 'but did the bloody dog in me remember to respect this vow of celibacy?'

'I remember everything,' replied Hupa. 'Don't you?'

He was miserable. 'No, not all of it. There are bits caught up in the heat of hunting – bits which are not clear. There's a kind of hot blood haze over some of it. How come you have such clarity of memory?'

'Because I was cool,' she said, smiling in a superior way at him. 'I was cool and calm, while you were hot and bothered. Perhaps you're not the holy man you pretend to be? Perhaps you do have strong feelings for me? If I was better at being a woman I could probably get you easily, couldn't I? If I was good at those alluring little tricks which some women use to capture a man, I could have you just like that.'

'I don't know what you're talking about,' he replied, huffily. 'I think you've got a strong imagination.'

She laughed.

Disconcerted, he began to stride out, into the foothills of the mountains, knowing she would follow.

'Don't leave me behind,' she called. 'I've nothing with which to defend myself.'

'Keep up then,' he replied, uncharitably.

They began to climb, first up gradients which were easily scaled, and then into the mountains proper. Craig found trails, not well worn, but certainly more than goat trails. Up and up they went, past the vegetation line, through tall stacks and onto steeper paths beyond.

The air grew colder and the pair realized they should have gathered more clothing from the battlefield below.

When they were well into the crags and sheer walls of the mountains, they met a traveller coming the other way. This was a man of middle age with a huge hooked nose. On his back was a framework of sticks with an animal skin pack.

Craig gripped his sword as the man approached, but then with head down the stranger passed them by, not even glancing up, let alone offering a greeting. This surprised both Craig and Hupa, who had been expecting acknowledgement of their presence.

They caught a strong whiff of animal fat from the man's clothing, which were not much more than partially cured skins tied together. His feet were bound in hide, as was his head. He appeared to be dressed in no particular clannish style and Craig wondered if he were an outcast.

'Hey, you!' cried Craig in Gaelic. 'Stop a minute.'

For a short while it appeared the man might run on, rather than obey the summons, but in the end he turned round. His face was as brown as those of the two Oceanians. There were places where a blue dye had stained his skin. Above the great eagle-beak nose brown eyes regarded the pair with suspicion.

'Are you real?' he asked. 'Or is it the loneliness of these mountains? I often see things. I sometimes hear things. True the two do not usually come together, but I'm sure the solitude of the mountains can arrange anything it wishes.'

'We're real, and we're not mountain goblins or anything of that sort,' replied Craig, walking up to the man. 'Take no notice of these tattoos on my face, they make me look fiercer than I am. We're strangers from another land. Castaways. Now we're lost in these mountains. Can you help us?'

The man continued to regard the pair for a few more moments, then he removed his heavy pack. There were creases where the straps had cut into his shoulders. His weathered features cracked into a smile which produced crow's-feet in the corners of his eyes and his mouth.

'You don't look fierce. I thought you was a player – a travelling performer. That's an interesting leg you have there, friend – I've never seen one so heavily tattooed. Looks almost black from a distance. Now I'm close up though, I can see the patterns. It must have hurt. Oh, yes – who am I? Hookey Walker at your service.' He touched his nose to show where his first name had come from. 'How can I help you?' he asked. 'Do you wish to buy?'

'Buy? Buy what?'

'Goods. I'm a pedlar.'

'What's a pedlar?'

The man laughed and sat on his pack.

'You really are strangers, aren't you? I'm a traveller, I go between villages and towns, selling my wares.'

'Are you not murdered for your goods?' said Craig, surprised. 'I would not trust the people hereabouts.'

'A pedlar has some protection, at least from those who are not out-and-out robbers and thieves. If I am attacked and killed, then villages will have no go-between to carry their news to each other, to bring them goods they cannot make themselves. Of course,' he stared up at the crags, 'there are those who respect no common laws and who would slit my throat in a moment, but I can protect myself. I have been a warrior.'

He pointed to a faded patch of blue dye on his forearm, which looked as if it had resisted attempts to wash it off.

'This attests to my former occupation. Woad. I fought for the Fraser clan in the south, and for a Cymru tribe in the north-east, though I am an Angle born. Old Hookey was a paid warrior, fighting for the side which fed him best. No, no, my friend, I have greater fear of wild beasts than I do of any man I might meet on the road.'

Craig translated all this briefly for Hupa's sake.

'He fights for material rewards? Oceanians fight for honour!' she said, emphatically.

Craig told Hookey what she had said.

He smiled and shook his head. 'We both fight for what we have not got,' he replied.

Craig decided not to translate this, or Hupa would probably leap on the man and scratch out his eyes.

'What have you in your pack?' asked Craig.

The man glanced at his huge deerskin bundle.

'Clay pots, wooden spoons, daggers, hand axes, spearheads, arrowheads ...'

'Arrowheads? Made of what?'

'Of metal of course. Not iron, but bronze. Magic works better with bronze. Would you like to see some?'

Craig indicated that they would like to see them, though privately he wondered how he would pay for them, if Hupa wanted them.

'You say they are magic?' said Craig.

The pedlar nodded and began sorting through his pack.

'They have been dipped in the Tarn-of-the-neverlost, a high lake in the mountains of Ud. A witch sold them to me for a bag of dried blackthorn sloes. Witches in those high places never get anything to eat, which is why they're so scrawny.'

'If they don't eat, they should die.'

'And so they would, if they weren't witches and stuffed full of magic. It's a known fact that witches are never hungry, yet this one liked to chew on something. She said it was a habit with her and that it helped her to think. She also put dried grasses in her mouth, lit them and sucked down the smoke. Witches are unfathomable creatures, my friend.'

Finally the pedlar took a small soft-leather pouch from his pack and undid it to reveal the arrowheads. Hupa predictably gave a shout and picked one up to inspect it.

'Nicely made,' she said. 'Good balance. With these and some eagle's feathers to fletch the hafts, I could have my weapon back.'

When this was translated, Hookey Walker said he would throw in a couple of golden eagle feathers and some cord.

Craig told Hupa the history of the arrowheads and she asked, 'What's the significance of them being dipped in this pool, this Tarn-of-the-neverlost?'

The pedlar smiled at the enquiry, when it was passed on by Craig.

'Why, I'll show you.'

He picked up one of the bronze arrowheads and skimmed it away from him like a child will fling a stone into the ocean. It fell on a slope of scree amongst thousands of stone shards, instantly lost to their eyes.

'Go and look for it,' he said to Craig.

Craig, thinking there was not a hope in earth and sky of finding the arrow-head amongst the scree, found it immediately he reached the general area. He had not been guided by anything shiny, for the arrowhead was dull, almost black in appearance, not having been polished after leaving its mould. It had simply been a case of walking right up to it.

'You'll never lose another arrow in the trees or grasses – not with these heads,' said the pedlar, grinning.

Hupa tried it next, two or three throws, and it worked every time.

'Once dipped in the magic tarn,' said the pedlar, 'it is never lost.'

'I like these arrowheads,' Hupa said.

'With a very different kind of magic,' reminded Craig. 'You may not hit the target now.'

'My archery does not *need* that kind of magic – it's helpful but it's not necessary. I am accurate enough without it.'

'Such a modest maiden,' sighed Craig. 'Now, how do we pay for these. How many do you want? Four? Six?'

'Six would be better than four. Offer him this necklace of shark's-teeth,' she said, removing the ornament from around her slim throat.

Craig was a little concerned by this. 'But the necklace warns others of your rank, as an ariki. How will they know not to touch you? Your mana, your tapu – these may be harmful to tutua who do not know you are of noble rank.'

'If being high-born means I cannot have you,' she pouted, 'then I'd rather not be one anyway. Look, Craig, how many tutua will we meet on this trail? As soon as I see my father again, he will give me another such badge of rank. In the meantime, give this pedlar fellow the necklace. Tell him they're magic teeth, that the wearer will experience good health for the rest of his life.'

'That's a good one,' said the pedlar, inspecting the necklace. 'If the wearer does fall into poor health, he thinks he is going to die – and most people when they're convinced they are dying, they usually do.'

'Well, what about the trade?'

'The necklace is unusual. Two arrowheads.'

'Five.'

'Three.'

'Four.'

'A bargain,' finished the pedlar. 'Four arrowheads.'

He began to sort four out when Hupa pounced and chose her own, to much sighing from the pedlar. Then Hookey Walker fastened his deerskin pack, lifted the frame onto his back, and gave them a farewell wave.

'Be careful, my friends,' he called. 'There are distractions on your route. Leave them be, is Old Hookey's advice. These mountains are not as ordinary as they appear – they have their secrets which are best left uncovered. Go without curiosity and you may get to the other side unharmed.'

'What sort of distractions?'

The pedlar walked on, hidden behind his load, calling back that this was for him to keep and for them to find out, for if he told them of one thing, they might come across another and think it harmless.

'Be wary of *everything*,' he warned. 'Let no one thing lure you from the path. And be especially careful not to tarry near a tower if you see one.'

Craig's heart began to beat faster for no explicable reason on hearing the last sentence.

'What tower?'

'You'll see – or not.'

'Where?'

'Who knows?' said Hookey, enigmatically. 'It appears – sometimes here, sometimes there. On a moor, in the mountains, down by a bleak seashore. No one knows why, but I've learned one thing in my life – keep clear of towers that appear like mushrooms overnight. They can only lead to trouble.'

They had to be satisfied with this and went on up into the coldness of the mountains. The wind had an edge like that of a lei-o-mano and howled in their faces. Clouds were almost within touching distance as they swirled about the peaks like mad atua. There were strange gods up here, in the crags and buttresses of the high mountains. Craig could sense their incomprehensible forms lurking amongst the tall stones, in the crevices and caves, around the sheer drops. Craig wanted to be over the pass and down amongst the green valleys again. They were not his valleys, but they were preferable to alien mountains.

Towards the top of one saddle they came to a huge pile of stones. This Craig knew from his father's tales of the mountains to be called a cairn. Not far from the cairn was a sight which both Oceanians gawped at: a tall circular tower made of drystones with what appeared to be a room made of solid chalk blocks right at its head. There were no windows to this structure, nor any doors that Craig could see, once he had walked around it. Simply a hollow tower of roughly hewn blocks of granite with the top third of dazzling white chalk.

'What is this place?' he asked, more of himself than Hupa. 'Why would anyone build a tower up here?'

'The pedlar said not to give way to curiosity.'

'True – he did warn us.'

At that moment the voice of a woman came floating down from the white room. It filled Craig's head. With a sudden chill Craig recognized the voice. It was that of his dead step-mother, Dorcha. She was giving him an order.

'Open the tower, Craig. It is time. The world is ready for the creature within. The old gods are destroying one another. The beast in the chalk room will bring about the final change. Hereafter women and men will make their own destiny, without interference from supernatural beings or forces. The fate of humankind will be in the hands of humankind.'

'Did you hear that?' asked Craig of Hupa, looking up. 'There's someone in there.'

'I heard nothing …'

'They were asking for assistance,' Craig interrupted her. 'It was – it sounded like Dorcha. Dorcha's spirit is trapped in this tower. We have to let her out.'

He realized he was talking feverishly and frightening Hupa, but he could not control his words.

'We have to ignore it,' argued Hupa. 'The pedlar warned us against things like this. Do not get involved. These are magical mountains, much like those we have on islands like Moorea, near Tahiti. Would you go climbing up into the heights on Moorea? And if you did, would you interfere with what you might find there?'

Craig insisted, 'This is different. Listen, I hear her call again.'

'Open the tower, Craig. You promised your father you would look after his people. His people were the Oceanians and the Albannachs. Open the tower to help them both.'

'I have to do this thing. I have to let her out. Dorcha's soul is imprisoned in this stone tower without windows on the cold hillside of this barren land-scape. I tell you, we have to do something, Hupa. That could be your soul trapped in there.'

The force of his words were such that Hupa knew he could not be turned from this task. She watched as he carefully scaled the outside of the round wall, choosing handholds in which to insert his fingers and toes. It did not appear an impossible task, for though Craig was not an especially good climber, the stones appeared to have been cut and shaped by maladroit giants, and there were plenty of gaps.

When he reached the chalk room at the top, there were no more hand-holds. It had been weathered smooth by the rain and wind, the gaps sealing together to form one solid hollow cap of chalk. He moved around the tower carefully, in frustration, trying to find some chink in the wall of chalk, and all the time the woman within pleaded with him to release her.

Craig climbed down again, to where Hupa waited.

'Well,' she said, 'are you satisfied?'

Craig shook his head and again inspected the base of the tower. There he found something he had not previously noticed, because it was indistinct, weathered. At first he thought they were symbols, but then realized that it was an inscription which encircled the granite tower. It was in a stylized form of Hiro's writing, the letters linking each other like fishhooks to form a complete circle around the stone structure. The writing was so faint and so swirlingly curlicued he had great difficulty in reading it, but finally the words came to him:

}{In time the Natural laws of the world must triumph over Preternatural forces just as Good will eventually subdue Evil}{It takes but one man to break the chain and release from bondage the Agent within}{You Stranger standing before this tower}{Banish the element of Chaos and give mankind a natural Order}{

Craig did not really understand the meaning of these words, but he saw the significance in the way they had been written. They formed a chain around the tower. Chains, he knew from his father, were metal ropes used to keep men fettered, hold them captive, so that they might never escape. If one broke the chain, then the imprisoned might go free. What he had to do was make a break in this chain which encircled the tower.

'Stand back,' he said to Hupa, 'I'm going to try something.'

He took his sword from his waistband and struck the granite where it projected slightly, chipping out a single piece which carried but one word. The word, which was Chaos, went spinning away into the scree, leaving a gap in the chain. Immediately the stones began to crumble at the base. The chalk room dropped as the mighty granite blocks slipped from under each other, tumbling away from their places. It was as if Craig had removed the keystone. With no mortar to bind them together, once the blocks began to fall they came down in a landslide.

'RUN!' cried Craig, and he and Hupa raced away from the tower as it came crashing down upon the mountain top. Fortunately they reached a safe distance and turned to see the chalk room perched on a pile of rubble. Still this white structure which had sat on the top of the tower remained whole and complete, without a crack or fissure.

Now a wind, a natural agent of the weather, came up from nowhere out of the valleys and passes below. It brought with it a fine grit, a sand, which cut into the skins of the two watchers. They fell to the ground and crawled into a nearby cave, there burying their heads in their arms, while the wind howled and screamed around the entrance. The duststorm continued for half a day before it abated.

When the pair finally emerged from the cave, the chalk room had been worn away, leaving but an open shell like a molar which has been hollowed and scoured.

Out of this shell emerged not Dorcha's soul, but a strange dark cloud of dust as fine as woodfire smoke.

This cloud drifted here and there, shaping and reshaping itself into nebulous beasts, creatures neither Craig nor Hupa could recognize. There was one with eagle's claws for its feet and a dog's head with pointed ears. There was another with thick, lithe and supple legs attached to a muscled torso and a face with strange flattened features. One like a horse with a straight horn from its forehead.

Fuzzy, drifting contours floated over the mountainside, forming, re-forming, growing almost imperceptibly as it rolled away like a thundercloud with a purpose.

'What was that?' cried Hupa. 'What have you let out of the tower?'

Craig was upset. 'I don't know.'

'You were warned not to interfere, Craig. That – that *thing* could be something terrible. You may have released Plague, or Famine, or something equally as bad. What have you sent out into the world, Craig?'

'I don't know,' he confessed, 'but it is an agent of order, not chaos, so it won't be either of those you mentioned. It – it must be something for the common good. Look at us! We are not struck down by some deadly disease, are we?'

Hupa admitted this was true.

'Well then, let's not fret over something from which the world may benefit. Come on, let's make our way down now. Look, there are green valleys below. We can make you a bow and some hafts for your arrowheads. Let's not dwell on what can't be changed ...'

He strode off, down the mountain track, appearing light-hearted to Hupa, but within he was fearful of what he had done, wondering if she was right and that he had released something awful on the unsuspecting world.

2

Every day at noon, rain or sun, wind or calm, Guirk came down to the walls of the pa and called for Kieto to meet him in single combat. When no one appeared for the period over which he waited, Guirk did not seem too disappointed. He shouted his taunts – someone had taught him insults in Oceanian – then turned and trudged back to the Celt encampment. There was always tomorrow. He would be there whatever the weather. It had become a habit – a ritual.

The day came when Kieto's elder brother, Totua, could stand it no longer. He called a tohunga and asked the priest to accompany him outside the pa. The priest looked worried, but Totua told the man he was only needed as an interpreter. The young man looked relieved and nodded his assent.

'Must I listen to my family being maligned,' cried the elderly Totua, aggrieved, as Guirk's ringing tones penetrated the noon air of the pa. 'Do I have to stand here while our mother is called ugly names and our father's honour is impugned? I will kill this Guirk with my own hands.'

With the priest at his heels Totua, already wearing his helmet of scarlet feathers and his dogskin war cloak, snatched a war club, one made of ironwood and obsidian, and went out to meet the challenge from Guirk. Totua swept the cloak away from his shoulders to reveal the tattoos on his chest: badges of his manhood and courage cut into his dark wrinkled skin.

Family pride was at stake and he could take no more from this upstart.

Totua's son, idling by the gate, was surprised to see his elderly father go striding past on his way out of the pa.

'Where are you going, Papa Totua?' asked the youth, surprised. 'Have you been called to a challenge?'

'I am going to smash the skull of that mouth they call Guirk,' snarled his father. 'Our family has stood enough insults. If my brother can't go out because he's too precious to the nation, then I must silence the liar.'

The boy snatched at Totua's arm.

'Don't go out there, Papa Totua,' he hissed. 'They say that Guirk has a magic shield and sword. You can't kill him while he has those ...'

'Who says?' asked his father, his eyes narrowing.

'Why – why Daggan and Siko. They say the Celt has weapons made from Lioumere's iron teeth. That's what they say, my father. Go back, now. Don't go out to fight this man.'

'Where would a Celt get such iron?'

'I – I don't know – it's what they say. I'm sure it's true. Please stay here.'

Totua snorted in contempt and marched past the youth, the priest trotting behind.

He stood in front of the Celt, who was stripped to the skin except for a thick leather belt and copper arm braces. As always Guirk bore his shield and sword. He looked Totua up and down in disgust. It was clear that the Celt did not think much of his opponent. Totua was no mean warrior and this further incensed him, causing his blood to burn in his veins.

'I am Kieto,' he told thick-set Guirk, using the interpreter. 'I have come to silence your lying tongue.'

'Seems to me,' said Guirk, staring at Totua's magnificent tall helmet, 'that the liar here is wearing a chicken on his head.'

'A chicken?' cried Totua.

'You wouldn't catch me wearing one of those things – they crap all over you, don't they? Look, yours has shit blue turds onto your chest.'

Guirk pointed with his sword at Totua's tattoos.

'*I-am-Kieto,*' shrieked Totua.

'Not unless you grew an arm overnight,' smirked the Celt. 'I saw this Kieto at the campfire entertainments. You are not he. You are some old fart with an addled brain. Go home to grandma and get her to tuck you into bed with a nice warm glass of milk, grandpa.'

When this was translated by the priest, who had been told by the high priestess always faithfully to reproduce the Gaelic in his mother tongue, Totua cried that he was Kieto's older brother and therefore entitled to take up challenges on his behalf.

With these words he took a swing with his two-handed club at the head of Guirk.

Guirk held up his shield and the nokonoko club with the stone edge glanced away swiftly, not even touching the shield, as if there was a buffer of air between it and the metal. Totua shook his head in anger and tried again, only to see and feel the club bounce away as it struck an invisible barrier. Several more blows, serving to exhaust the old man, were treated with the same contempt by Guirk and his magic shield.

Then the Celt began to ridicule the old man further, telling him he was as weak as a puppy, that he should be back on weaning milk again, for he was but a baby. Guirk belittled him by knocking off his helmet with the flat of his sword, then obscenely waggling his testicles at the old man when Totua began weeping in frustration. When Totua bent to pick up his headgear, Guirk farted in his face.

Totua stood up straight again and gathered a gob of spit in his mouth. This he launched accurately into his adversary's face, satisfied at seeing it splatter in Guirk's eyes and drip from his nose and chin.

'Magic shields don't ward off a good slab of phlegm,' laughed the old man. 'You'll probably get some nasty disease from that ...'

Guirk's eyes opened wide with fury. In that moment he forgot his instructions from Cormac-the-Venomous, which was to fight only Kieto and no other warrior. Guirk swept down with his sword at Totua's head. The old man had lost little of his swiftness in battle over the years. Instantly the club was held up like a staff, protecting his head. To no avail. Incredibly the sword cut through the ironwood without a pause. It continued in its descent to split the old man's head in two, and on down to the middle of his chest.

The priest gave out a strangled cry of horror and turned and ran back to the pa like a chicken with a dog behind it.

Even Guirk was amazed at what he had done. The Celt had put the minimum of strength behind the blow. Now he could see the Oceanian's heart still beating inside his chest. There were lungs exposed like pulsating grey balloons. Totua fell to the floor, his brains and other matter spilling over the dust. His precious helmet fell into two neat halves like the split husk of a coconut.

'Now look at what you've made me do, you fucking old sheep-shagger,' cried Guirk. 'You made me kill you.'

He shook his head in annoyance at the leaking body, as if Totua could still hear and see him.

Guirk decided he had to make a show of it. Now the deed was done some use might be made of it. He signalled for a horse from one of his clansmen. A man came riding up. Guirk cut off the two halves of Totua's head at the neck, spooned out the brains, scraped the inside of the hemi-skulls clean and then tied them one either side of the horse's mane by the hair. They dangled there in the company of other heads, dead clansmen from another war. Then Guirk fastened the feet of the headless corpse to the horse's tail and swung himself up onto the beast's back.

Guirk next galloped the horse three times around the pa, dragging Totua's remains behind in the dirt, yelling for Kieto to come out and avenge his older brother.

Oceanians flocked to the walls to see what the noises were about and were appalled by what they saw. This was worse than eating your enemy. To treat a corpse with such disrespect was something only uncivilized people would do, people who in their ignorance knew no better. When the Oceanians ate their foe it was to ingest their mana, their courage, their skill at warfare, and even then whatever remained of the body would be placed on an ahu, a sacrificial platform, as an offering to the gods.

Kieto had at the time of Totua's death been in the temple with Kikamana the Farseeing-virgin. He had been communing with his atua, through the high priestess, when suddenly his ancestral spirits screamed in his head. Never had this happened before and both the priestess and Kieto went white with fear.

'What are they saying?' asked Kieto, putting his hands over his ears but finding it impossible to block out the voices in his head. 'I can't understand what they're saying.'

Kikamana, more familiar with the language of the spirit world, answered him.

'They say that a great offence has occurred. They say they have been humiliated. They say that at this moment someone is causing them great insult outside the walls of the pa ...'

Kieto rushed outside the temple to hear the moans and shouts of his people on the platforms above, as they witnessed that which was offending Kieto's ancestors.

When Kieto himself saw what Guirk was doing with his brother's body, he was enraged beyond reason. He ran to his quarters and found three throwing spears. Running back up onto the battlements of the pa, he stood out over the walls on a projecting platform. When Guirk next came thundering past him, the corpse of Totua bouncing and jerking on the end of the rope, he threw all three spears in quick succession.

Guirk did not even bother with the shield, but held up his magic sword instead. The spears were parried by some unseen force, skimming away before they reached within a body-length of the Celtic warrior. Guirk laughed, waving his sword at Kieto.

'Come out and fight, you weakling,' he called. 'I'll give you a taste of what I gave your brother.'

Indeed, Kieto would have answered the challenge there and then, by jumping down from the platform to the ground outside the pa, but Kikamana anticipated his rashness. She ordered some priests to take him and hold him down, which they did while he kicked and struggled, crying that he had to avenge his family, his ancestors, and slay the barbarian.

'When the time is ready,' said Kikamana, 'but not now. You would be cut down out there, leaving the army leaderless. You must look to your responsibilities.'

Kieto knew what she meant and indeed did calm down. With Guirk's taunts in his ears he went back to the temple. There he fell on the floor and wept bitter tears, assuring his atua that he would one day even the score.

'Justice will be mine,' he whispered hoarsely. 'I will have it. I will have the head of Guirk. But I will not consume his eyes and liver, nor devour his heart, for he is not fit even to be eaten. He is a man without honour.'

Kieto's ancestors had to be satisfied with promises.

A steady drizzle fell on Hupa and Craig as they made their way through the mountains. Mist swirled in the passes around the peaks through which they travelled. They were cold and hungry, following in the wake of the strange force that Craig had released from the chalk room in the high tower. He wondered now if it had been an accident that he had passed the tower. Surely some force had taken him there, for why else would he have been encouraged in his act by the voice of Dorcha?

When they finally came down out of the mountains they were in a lush green valley, with orchards all around. Here there were natural hedgerows bursting with flowers. Birds flitted from bush to bush, singing beautiful songs. Animals with red fur and bushy tails leaped from branch to branch. There were pools with clear water. The air was pleasantly warm, with seeds floating on it like small canoes.

They found a type of tree with a small dark green leaf, a sapling of which seemed suitable for a bow. The sapling bent without snapping and sprang back into its former straightness when released. Craig cut one of these flexible rods with his sword and gave it to Hupa. She still had the cord from her old bow and set about fitting it to the rod. Then Craig went off to look for some suitable hafts, while Hupa rested on a mossy bank beneath a great oak, enjoying the smell of wild herbs.

A brief spell of sunshine came out and she fell asleep on the damp ground.

She was woken, not by Craig, but by the hand of a beautiful youth. She smiled sweetly at him. He was dressed in a flimsy garment which was blown against his body by the breeze, emphasizing his delightful shape. Around his head he wore a halo of blossoms. Similarly around his ankles and wrists were delicate alpine flowers. His smile was enchanting, revealing strong white teeth. Flaxen hair flowed behind him like a swept-back veil. His eyes were of a purple hue, speckled with golden flecks. His step was so light he seemed almost to float like a white tropic bird.

Hupa had never seen anything like him. Perhaps some local person might have suspected he was not all he seemed, but she was an Oceanian. There were many strange people in this country of Land-of-Mists. She looked up, startled, as he bent down and kissed her cheek. Then he stroked her neck with a slim soft hand. He seemed to be carrying something down by his side and on looking hard she saw it was an earthenware jar.

He offered her a drink.

'Would you partake of some refreshment with me, beauteous lady?' he asked. 'I have been so lonely these past days ...'

His voice was like the ringing of delicate wooden bells. He sat down beside her and she could feel the warmth of his thigh against hers. She wanted to enfold him within her arms, caress him, kiss those sweet lips. Instead she just stared at him dumbfounded. Finally, she took the jar from his strong hands.

'What kind of drink is it?' she asked.

Her voice sounded peculiar to her own ears, sort of thick and husky, but she was too interested in the young man to worry about the oncomings of a sore throat.

'Mead, made from the honey of bees, mixed with fermented elderberry juice,' he said, flashing her a wonderful smile. 'Summer wine we call it. It is so cool and tasteful. Try it.'

He held it up to her lips and she took a sip, finding it lighter than she thought it would be, considering the rich fruity aroma. It slipped away on the palate leaving but a tingle behind. It was difficult not to gulp it down, it was so refreshing. There was an underlying hint of alcohol, but nothing more than that. Certainly it was sweeter and more delicious than kava, with the same effect.

She was embarrassed to find she was dribbling out of the sides of her mouth, like an old woman.

'What are you doing here?' she asked the youth, as she wiped away the wine with the back of her hand. 'Do you live in these parts?'

He pouted divinely. 'I have been abandoned. It is good that you came along. Perhaps you will give me some of your interesting company, just for a short while? I am so starved of mortal affection ...'

He placed a hand upon her arm and looked into her eyes entreatingly.

Mortal affection? That was a funny way of putting it.

'Well, I'm not sure I can stay *too* long. My friend is out looking for arrows for my bow. Once he returns we must be on our way. But while I'm here I'm willing to talk.'

He smiled. 'Have some more summer wine.' He held the jar up to her lips again.

She found herself drinking, talking, laughing with the youth, until things became less lighthearted. They lay in the grasses together, the wind-blown seeds tangled in their hair, the soft breeze stroking their naked bodies. Why she was naked she did not know. She did not remember removing her clothes, but it felt natural enough.

The youth told her he had been waiting for her all his life, that she was the answer to his dreams. Words came from his mouth more intoxicating than the summer wine.

'You were sent to be my ash tree,' he told her, stroking her brow. 'You will be my tall and stately support. Do you think you could love me?' he asked her coquettishly. 'Could you stay with me?'

Hupa looked into those purple eyes with the golden flecks. A sensation of drowning overcame her. She fought for air, speaking thickly, her head spinning. 'I think I love you already – I've – I've never known anyone like you. I want to stay here in this valley with you for the rest of my life.'

More summer wine went down her throat.

Her mind began to spin in a dizzy fashion and her limbs grew lethargic. She felt as if she were slipping away, down a long black shaft. He filled her head with nonsense, chattering like a thousand sparrows. At the same time a lightness of spirit entered her, making it all feel quite unreal to her. Hupa would not have been surprised had he vanished before her eyes and she discovered it was all some trick of the light and shadow.

His face was like a small white delicate shell, a *precious wentletrap*, drifting in and out of her vision. Finally, he took her hand and began to lead her away. Hupa found him impossible to resist. She was walking very awkwardly, stumbling along like a two-year-old child, and she put it down to the drink. In fact she felt peculiar all over, as if there was something wrong with her arms and legs, though she was not given any time to decide what that might be, for the youth trilled away in a voice like a flute. She would have fallen over, several times, had he not prevented it with his strong arm.

They entered a copse, a ring of trees in the middle of which was a circle of fawn-coloured toadstools. Somehow they both found themselves standing inside this circle and when they stepped out of it the scene had changed. The trees were much smaller, the flowers quite tiny and the grass spread like a closely woven blanket over the gentle hills and pastures between.

'What's that perfume?' she asked, thickly.

The youth said, 'Flowers and tree blossoms. It is always spring here. We don't have winter or high summer …'

We don't have winter. Hupa was vaguely aware that this was a strange thing to say, but she could not put her finger on why that was so. *Here.* Where were they then, that he should say they were *here?* Perhaps she had missed something with the passing of time? Did it matter? She thought not, so long as she could have some more of that summer wine.

Small, delicate-looking people began to gather round them. Hupa was not sure where they had come from: they seemed to appear out of the ground, or from behind trees, some of them perhaps even from the sky. They clustered around her like children with sticky fingers, touching her face and hands, everywhere. Where they touched they left a residue which stained her clothes and skin peat brown. It was as if their fingers were horse chestnut buds, oozing brown sap. She noticed many of them had storm flies stuck to the tips of their fingers, which they licked absentmindedly every so often.

'Who are these creatures?' she asked, mildly alarmed. 'Are these your people?'

The youth nodded. He seemed to have lost a lot of his stature now and was smaller than before. When Hupa stared into his face she decided it was not so startlingly handsome as she had first imagined. Now his features seemed sharper and more shrewish, like the faces of the other little people around them. Though they were smooth and without lines there were centuries of experience in those countenances.

They appeared to have lived a long time, without gathering the signs of age. They had an unnatural smoothness of complexion, which was like mother-of-pearl. Their bones were angular and showed through their waxy skin. The depth of their magenta eyes when Hupa stared into them seemed fathomless. These were ancients, beings who had been alive when one of Hupa's great-great-grandmothers had been a young girl walking the hills of Raiatea, picking fruits and wild mushrooms.

'Have I been here before?' she asked, finding a feeling of familiarity creeping into her sobering mind. 'Do I know you – do you know me?'

'Dance!' cried one of the creatures, ignoring her question. 'Let us dance!'

Immediately reed flutes appeared from within folds of clothing. Logs were found to use as percussion instruments. A musical instrument like Hupa's bow was drawn across the strings of a heart-shaped hollow implement to produce a high sweet sound which thrilled her from her hair to her toes.

A lively tune was struck and the creatures began leaping up and down, twirling, flying through the air in graceful arcs to land neatly on one pointed toe. Soon Hupa found herself dancing too, without restraint, though her movements were the clumping steps of a disorientated giant. She kept falling over, much to the amusement of the little people. Normally quite supple and quick on her feet, she found this lack of co-ordination and balance irritating. Yet the harder she tried, the more she made mistakes and ended up on her back.

When she had grown weary of dancing however, she began to feel concern about Craig. He would be waiting for her at the spot where she had left him. There was something about this whole episode which was uncomfortably familiar. In the back of her mind was the thought that these creatures would not let her go, unless she did something to please them, something to put them in a compliant frame of mind.

'Shall I sing for you?' she asked. 'Shall I sing some old songs to aid your dancing?'

Her lilting voice floated out over the glade in which they were dancing.

The little people stopped dancing immediately and put their small hands over their ears.

'Stop that noise,' they yelled impolitely. 'Stop her making that awful racket.'

Clearly they did not appreciate her gift for sweet music, her genius as a songster, in this part of the world. They scowled at her and kicked oak mast in her face. One of them grabbed her ankle and tried to topple her over. Hupa stood there helplessly, wondering how she had managed to upset these creatures.

'Play for us!' they ordered. 'Let us have one of your best tunes.'

Someone put a flute into her hands. Now Hupa had a fairly mediocre talent for playing an instrument. Like most Oceanians she enjoyed the flute, but had given up lessons halfway through childhood. Her rendering of a seafaring tune was not exceptional, though it might have nestled quite happily in the full sound of a orchestra. She was not used to playing solo and was shy to start. However, once she did she was astounded to find her notes high and sweet, not at all like her normal playing tone, and she delighted the little people with her rendering of a traditional Oceanian song.

They certainly seemed to prefer her playing to her singing.

They flocked around her, looking at her rather disconcertingly straight in the eyes as she played.

'*My* mortal,' cried the youth who had brought her to this place, with admiration and possessiveness in his tones. 'She belongs to me. She's mine, mine, mine. She shall remain with me for ever ...'

'Dusky maiden!' chanted others. 'Dusky maiden. Dusky maiden. She can play like an angel.'

Hupa's flute drew other creatures, of a different aspect, from out of the foliage and woodlands around them. They came with pointed ears and sharp noses. They came with long fingers and knobbed joints. They came with dewdrop eyes and skins encrusted with algae. Of human shape, but not of human mind, they emerged from recesses in the landscape, to watch and wonder at this person who had brought such music to their region.

Animals and birds came too: deer stood alongside wolves, ducks by foxes, to listen to her flute.

When she had finished, the little people asked her questions, some of which she could not answer.

'Have you been taken from your village by any dragons?'

'Are there giants where you live?'

'Where is your kingdom?'

She answered those she could and said she did not understand the others.

The dancing began again, and the quaffing of the wine, and night seemed never to come. They fed her and gave her wine, since she could not seem to get her hands in the right position to do it herself. When they were tired, when she was tired, they lay on the grass and slept.

During one dancing session, Craig suddenly appeared at her side, looking angry. He confronted her, saying, 'Why did you come here? I followed your tracks. Don't you recognize where you are?'

'No,' she replied, helplessly. 'Where am I?'

'It doesn't matter now,' he said, looking down at his feet with a puzzled expression on his face, 'we have to get away. I can't think properly at the moment. Not with this damned music playing. I have to think of a way to get them to let you go.'

She was not given the opportunity of speaking with Craig again for a while because the youth who had brought her there became jealous and drew her away from him. Even when they stopped dancing, the creature stayed with her, resting by her side, his eyes on Craig.

Whenever she lay her head on the grass it felt heavy and swollen – a big-domed thing – but since she had not stopped drinking wine from the moment she had set eyes on the youth it did not seem at all surprising to her. She was drunk. She knew she was drunk. She was so drunk that most of what was happening was a blur. That was why she could not stay on her feet, or sing properly, and why her head felt twice its normal size.

On waking they began cavorting again, sometimes pausing to eat mushrooms, or nuts, or small berries from the bushes, but the cycle of merry dancing and rest seemed never to end. Hupa, continually asked to play the flute and dance, grew weary of spirit.

She began to feel hollow and spent, and wished it would all end. When she looked at Craig, lying on a grassy hillock not far away, he seemed to have changed. He did not look himself. During one rest period someone went up to Craig, who lay not far away. He was a square, chunky creature. They were whispering, but loud enough for Hupa to hear them both. Hupa looked quickly into the face of her possessive youth and saw that he was mercifully fast asleep. She listened intently to what passed between the chunky creature and Craig.

'What are you doing in fairyland?'

'Who are you?' asked Craig. 'Your face is familiar, but I can't recall where ...'

'King Laurin,' whispered the other quickly. 'You remember me? I am King of the Dwarves. You found my mantle for me. I owe you a favour. I ask you again, what are you doing in fairyland? Do you not know if you remain here much longer, you will never be able to depart?

'Your lady has been taken,' said the dwarf-king, 'no doubt by that fairy youth who sleeps beside her – they who are without mercy have her in thrall. You two mortals will be danced to death, if you stay. They will make you play until your heart bursts in your breast. You must depart from here as quickly as possible. Don't look back. Simply walk away, towards that light that shimmers in the east.'

'How will I get away?' asked Craig, distressed. 'My feet won't do what I want them to without support.'

'Your head is on back to front, that's why, you idiot.'

Craig's hands went up to his face. Hupa looked down at her own body. It was true. Her vision was slightly fogged but she could now see that her feet were facing the wrong way. She could see her buttocks and the small of her back when she pressed her chin against her shoulder blades.

'Oh, what fiendish creatures these little people are,' Craig croaked. 'And what's wrong with my head, it feels swollen and bruised – and,' he ran his hands over his face and chin, 'and my nose feels thick and bristly!'

'Someone has given you the head of a pig. Probably that youth.'

It took a few seconds for these words to sink in, but when they did Craig was appalled. He felt over his head with his hands again, finding that Laurin had spoken the truth. Despair filled his heart.

'Hoghead? Pigface? Me? Oh, you cruel gods ...' wailed Craig, though it came out more of squeal than a howl.

'Quiet, you fool,' hissed the dwarf-king, looking round, 'do you want to wake everyone? We must get you away from them.' He became rather severe, staring at Craig as if he were very disappointed with him. 'If they find out you're the one who set the beast free, then they'll kill you anyway.'

'Set the beast free?' repeated Craig, weakly.

'You let the beast out of the tower, didn't you? One of my mountain dwarves saw you. Don't you know what you've done? I'm not at all pleased with you myself, though I know it had to happen *sometime*. The world must change over the course of time and you are one of its instruments of progress. If not you, then some other chosen man or woman.'

'What is the beast?'

'No time for that now. Get going now, take your lady with you, while they're all fast asleep. You'll have to look over your shoulder as you walk.'

'What if they wake and see us,' Craig asked, fearfully.

'You must borrow Hel Keplein, my mantle,' replied Laurin. 'While it is about your shoulders, you will be invisible. I'll follow your trail out of here later, when the furore has died down.'

'Can you do that?'

King Laurin snorted in humour. 'A wild pig running away from the hunters leaves a trail like the wake of a hurricane.'

'That's not funny.'

'Leave it hanging from some young oak tree. Leave a marker to show me which tree.'

'I shall snap one of the branches to show you which tree to look under.'

Laurin looked horrified. 'You will do no such thing. To cause such agony to the tree is not necessary. Would you have it weeping in pain? You will leave a white stone as large as your fist an arm's length from the tree. We'll find it easily if you leave such a marker. Now quickly, put this on …'

The dwarf-king waved his arms around Craig's shoulders and suddenly Hupa's friend disappeared. A few moments later she felt herself being lifted up and enfolded in something soft. Craig was carrying her, the cloak about them both.

They turned their back on the dozing fairies and walked eastward, towards a brightness in the sky. Craig found if he glanced over his shoulder, every so often, he could remain going in the right direction. He walked for a very long time, until finally they discovered themselves back in the place where Hupa had met the devious youth.

'We've made it,' she groaned, as he placed her on the grass, noticing their bodies were now normal.

'What a stupid thing to do,' remonstrated Craig, as he draped the cloak on a young sapling he obviously believed to be an oak. 'To go off with a man like that.'

'You can talk,' she protested, vehemently, as he took a large white stone from a stream and placed it at the base of the sapling. 'I seem to remember you did the same with a maiden once. Have you forgotten King Uetonga's people?'

That shut him up, though he still looked annoyed.

The pair of them then fell into a proper sleep, one from which they knew they would awaken refreshed. While they were dozing Hupa dreamed that a strange dark cloud in the shape of a beast came floating through their camp. It drifted over them like smoke and wound through the trees, over the stones and grass, touching everything with its paws.

When the couple woke they saw that King Laurin's mantle, Hel Keplein, was now completely visible. It was a voluminous silver cloak which flashed in the sun. Now anyone could see it, steal it if they wished. Hupa wondered if they should hide it, but Craig was of the opinion that Laurin would be by soon to collect it and Craig felt he had to obey the king's instructions to the letter.

'We'll just leave it there,' he said.

They vacated the place, quickly, with troubled minds. On the way, Craig collected his sword, which he had hidden in a cave not far away from their camp.

He had not wanted to be robbed of the weapon by Hupa's abductors, and there had been too many of them for it to be of any use in a fight, so he had taken the wise precaution of secreting it in a crevice before following her tracks.

It felt good to have it back in his possession.

3

The rain came down as a drifting mizzle, finding its way into every crease of the body, irritating in its persistence, impossible to ignore.

'Call this rain?' Craig said, obviously irked by the weather. 'Can't the skies do better than this? When it rains in Oceania, at least it does so *thoroughly*. This is just a fine seaspray, only we're not out on the ocean. And it never stops. Where does it come from, this more-than-mist-but-not-quite-rain? At least when it rains out on the islands, it comes down in a recognizable flood – and then when everything is wet, it stops.'

'I wasn't talking about the rain – you changed the subject – I was speaking of your foolishness,' Hupa said.

'My foolishness? You're the one who went off with a pretty young boy.'

'Have you forgotten Princess Niwareka so quickly? You were beguiled by her in just the same way. You're supposed to be a sensible married man, yet it's all right for you to go off with any feminine creature who blinks and smiles at you. You are so wanton.'

'I am not wanton – I am loyal and true.'

Hupa was prepared to keep up her tirade the whole day long, being contrarily incensed at Craig for her own fickleness. However, as they were talking Hupa heard a small sound in the trees behind them. She quietly fitted an arrow to her bow.

'Come out, whoever you are, or I'll ...'

She was never able to finish the sentence, because a figure wearing a blue smock stepped out of the trees. It was a hideous dwarf with strange ears. Hupa gave out a gasp and took a step backwards. Craig stared hard, but was less impressed, having seen many such creatures recently.

'Who are you?' said Craig. 'Did you follow us out of fairyland?'

'I am Urgan,' the creature replied. 'You see the form of an elf, but I am actually a mortal like you. I was taken from my cradle as an infant and raised in elf-land. Now I wish to go home to my real people. I did indeed follow you out of fairyland and was grateful to be shown the way. I saw King Laurin speak to you and knew he had given you instructions on how to leave that world. I followed the tracks you left. You have enabled me to escape from that prison bounded by the power of fairy will. May I travel with you further, until I am in my own country?'

'Why are you so ugly?' asked Hupa, with a shudder.

Craig gave her a look of censure, but Urgan shook his head and gave her a sad smile.

'I'm sure I was not intended to be thus, but when one lives in elf-land one takes on the camouflage of an elf in order to survive. Too long there and the disguise becomes permanent. I fear I shall remain ugly, even though I have left the creatures who stole me from my mother's breast while she slept.'

'Oh, you poor man,' cried Hupa, her naturally sympathetic instincts rushing to the fore. 'Perhaps you will change back again one day? Don't give up hope.'

'I shall try not to.'

Craig said, 'Of course you must travel with us. We are going to the south, to where a great battle is being fought between Oceanians and Celts.'

'Oceanians? Are they some kind of fairy folk?'

'No, they're foreigners, from islands far across the ocean. We are members of that invasion force. This young woman is an Oceanian. I am half-Celt. If you feel you still want to travel with us, after learning who we are, you're most welcome, but I shall understand if you wish to withdraw.'

Urgan shrugged his elfin shoulders. 'It matters nought to me, whether you are spotted snakes or windhovers. I am lost in this world, never having known it, and need the company of mortals who know its paths.'

'Then you'd better find somebody else,' muttered Hupa, 'because we're just as lost.'

'Ah,' replied the elf. 'Then we shall be lost together. At least you are company.'

Hupa said in a puzzled tone, 'How is it that you and I understand one another – do you speak the Oceanian language?'

Urgan smiled. 'I am fairy. How did you understand the youth who beguiled you? Fairy people learn things from nature. I can imbibe your thoughts. I am told your innermost desires, simply by listening to what the wind has to say about them. Your secrets, the secrets of the wind, flow into me. The wind has been everywhere, knows everything.'

After they had eaten a hare shot by Hupa and roasted over a small fire, she said to Craig, 'By the way, I lost an arrow when I was hunting.'

Craig raised his eyebrows. 'So?'

'So the pedlar Hookey Walker told us the arrowheads were magic and I *couldn't* lose them.'

Craig nodded, thoughtfully. 'That's true, he even proved it to us.'

'Perhaps it was a trick?' said Urgan. 'These pedlars, you cannot trust them. They have all sorts of tricks up their sleeves. They wish to sell their wares and will do anything to get you to buy them. Some of them claim to sell such things as love potions, elixirs, drinks which will render the user invincible in battle, drinks which will make a man or woman immortal – all these are the province of fairies and witches, not travelling salesmen.'

'You think he lied?' asked Hupa.

'I have no doubt about it. If they were magic when he sold them to you, they would be magic now. Magic is not a thing which fades or wears off.'

'That's true,' said Hupa. 'If I ever see Hookey Walker again I'll pin his ears to a tree with my last two arrows.'

'You have *three* arrows,' Urgan pointed out.

'Perhaps the final arrow will be for his nose.'

The three companions then set out, walking through the foothills. As the evening came on they came to a great loch of shining water. Craig remembered his father's wish and took the sword from his waistband. He sighed. He would be loath to lose the weapon, to which he had now become strangely attached. Yet a promise was a promise.

'I must cast the broadsword into the waters,' he told Hupa.

Urgan said nothing, but watched as Craig drew back his arm and sent the blade skimming over the surface of the loch. It did not fall in with a splash as expected, however, but went spinning in a curved sweep, to come hurtling back towards Craig. It buried itself point-first at the young man's feet.

'What an extraordinary thing,' said Craig, plucking the sword from the turf. 'It was almost as if the sword was reluctant to enter the water. Was that some of your doing, Urgan? Some magic you learned in elf-land?'

'Not I,' said the elf. 'I am as puzzled as you are.'

Craig tried throwing it again, and once more it went spinning in a wide flat arc, horizontal to the shining waters, and returned to plant itself at Craig's feet once again, this time up to the hilt. Several more throws produced the same effect, until finally Craig said he was giving up.

'It's clear I'm not going to be successful with this – perhaps the waters themselves are magic?'

With the sword continually burying itself in the earth, the broadsword had taken on a silver sheen. The earth had the effect of polishing the weapon, so that the blade was now shiny. Urgan reached over and gently took the sword from Craig's hand, to inspect it more closely. He pointed to something on the blade: some words etched into the metal.

'What's this?' he said. 'Did you know this weapon had been specially forged for someone? The weapon itself has been named, as well as bearing the name of its owner. This is only done when a sword is of great worth. The craftsmanship which goes into such a sword will have come from a great weapon-maker. Look, there is an egret etched on the crown of the hilt. This is the mark of Walberwicke, one of the divine blacksmiths.'

Craig took back the weapon and stared at the writing on the blade.

The words said: *Onsang's Stele Sweord* – SUNDERER

Urgan read the words as Craig's finger traced their course along the bloodgroove of the blade.

'Steel?' mused Urgan. 'I have heard the fairies speak of this metal with disapproval. It is said to be tougher than iron – an unnatural metal fashioned mistakenly by the alchemists, as they searched for ways of turning base metals into gold. Fairies cannot work magic on things which are not natural. This is why they would hold it in disfavour.'

'Tough, is it?' said Craig.

He walked over to a rock and swung at it. The blade struck the granite with its sharp edge, sending out a high ringing note. It split the stone in two halves. On inspecting the honed edge of the weapon, Craig found it was still sharp. The granite had not chipped or scored the metal in any way. This was truly a strong weapon: stronger than any Craig had held. He felt the power in it, as it nestled comfortably in his grip, as if it were moulding itself to the contours of his hand.

'If that had been an iron sword,' said Urgan, 'it would have shattered.'

'Magic, is it?' Hupa asked.

Urgan shook his head. 'Not magic, for I have already told you, the blade is steel. Even fairies have difficulty with steel. I would say it does not need magic. It is, in itself, a perfectly balanced weapon with an unbreakable blade – what could magic do to improve on this?'

'Why didn't it fall in the loch?'

'Perhaps your father wishes you to use the sword for some purpose, before passing it to him? I would say that a spirit sent the weapon flying back to you. Keep it for a while. You may have need of it,' said Urgan.

Craig saw the truth in this and decided the ugly elf-man was right. Besides, there was no way the loch was going to accept the sword. He could not stand on its banks for ever, throwing a sword which whirled back to him every time.

'I shall keep it until I have used it,' Craig said, 'and then send it to my father.'

*

Douglass Barelegs visited the witch on the mountain at great risk to his safety. He was inside Albainn, from which he had been banished by Cormac, and if discovered he would be hanged. Cormac had declared Douglass an outlaw and there were plenty who would enjoy taking advantage of such a proclamation. Once the war was over Cormac would no longer be war chief and go back to being just another clan head. Then Douglass Barelegs could return and take his revenge on those who had wronged him.

She was huddled against the stone needle, staring down into the glen beyond with a sharp expression.

'Well, hag? What news have you of the son of my father's murtherer?'

'How do I know? He is lost,' she said, tracing idly in the dust with a child's thighbone. 'Lost in Engaland or lost in Albainn. Causing all kinds of havoc and mayhem. Never should he have been let loose in our countryside. Ye muckle-headed doety-brain. Tis yer ain fault this mither o' disaster is roamin' free, interferin' wi' the natural ways of the world.'

'Don't talk to me that way, woman,' growled Douglass, 'or I'll cut out your spleen and feed it to my dogs.'

She turned on him fiercely at these words.

'Dinnae mention food to me,' she snarled. 'D'ye no ken what that furriner has done? He has let out the beast! He has set the beast upon the likes o' me and my kind. Ask yer questions, Douglass son of Douglass, for the time has gaen when I could answer them.'

'What are you talking about, woman?'

'I'm talking of magic. He has set loose the beast who will destroy us.'

'How do you know this?'

She stared at him with malice in her expression.

'Because I'm *hungry*, damn you. D'ye not ken that witches are *never* hungry. What d'ye think it means then, if I feel ravenous?'

'I don't know,' said Douglass, helplessly.

'Why, ye brainless loon – it means I'm no longer a witch – I've lost the means to work my magic.'

Douglass was not sure whether the crone was telling the truth, or whether she simply wanted more for her information. They all used tricks, pretending it was too difficult to peer into the lives of others, telling you the auguries were not right, that the portents were not good, pointing to a dark sky or a strange flock of birds. All this was to nudge the price a little higher.

'You greedy bitch,' cried Douglass. 'Tell me exactly where the bastard murtherer is, or I'll lift your head.'

'Go to hell, ye blackhearted dog,' she spat back at him. 'Here, cut it off – what have I got to live for now?'

She stuck her neck out like a viper poking its head from a hole in the ground.

What could he do? Douglass had to be a man of his word or he would get no discipline. He whipped out his sword and decapitated the hag: one swift slice through gristle and bone. She had begun shrieking before the blade had struck. The head continued to scream as it rolled down the mountainside, bouncing like a loose rock from crag to crag, until it disappeared still wailing over the edge of a precipice.

The remains of the body shrivelled before his eyes, making him start back in horror. Before very long it looked like a dried black lizard draped over the scree. Douglass booted the husk and it broke into pieces, discharging a foul khaki-coloured powder into the atmosphere. The wind took the powder, blowing it into his eyes and up his nose.

'Filthy old termagant,' he coughed. 'Had to get in the last word, eh, whut? The end of magic, is it? Will the sun go out? Will the sea swallow the land? Will the mountains roll into the glens? I think not, ye crimped pig's crinkum. I bid you an unfond farewell and hope ye end up a turd travelling through the gut of the hound of the Otherworld.'

With that he made his way back along the blustery ridge, being thankful at least that this was the last time he need make this climb through the high cold winds.

PART NINE

Briar Wood

1

Once more Punga had left the battle of the giants to see to the welfare of his charge, Craig, son of Seumas. It was Punga who had pointed the elf-man in the direction of the real world, so that he could act as a guide to Craig and Hupa. Now Punga had to attend to himself again.

He looked about him at the utter devastation and destruction amongst the mighty supernaturals. Many were the fallen. Eagles picked at their entrails on the mountain-tops. Their hearts had fallen amongst wolves in high places, to be devoured like the offal of deer. Their livers were in the mouths of wild-cats, hurrying home to feed their young.

Most of the more formidable gods had already gone.

Maomao was now nothing more than a wind without will: only the anguish of the Great Wind-God's dying cry was in its howl. A goddess called The Morrigan, Phantom Queen of Death, Sexuality and Conflict, was but a smudge on the face of the sky. Tawhiri-atea, Storm-God, wave-whipper, leveller of forests, had himself been levelled to the ground. Many, many more.

But Punga was just managing to survive obliteration. Because he was a minor god, he often went unnoticed by the Great Gods roaming the battlefield, looking for worthy opponents. He slipped here and there, managing to hold his own against gods of similar stature, and escaped the attention of the great.

Still, he was sorely wounded. The blood from his cuts and holes stained the clouds. It seeped into the evening heavens and dripped from the moon and stars. Blood was everywhere, draining from gods and goddesses on every side. There were red rivers flowing through the canyons of the sky. There were scarlet streams gushing between towers of cumulus. The bright hues of death and oblivion were ubiquitous …

'What a beautiful sunset,' said Hupa. 'How pretty the sky looks when it turns that colour.'

'Yes,' replied Urgan, 'but I am listening to Craig. The sunset can wait. There will be others.'

After Craig had described the region of the country where the Oceanians were at war with the Celts, Urgan explained that he knew where it was and how to get there.

'I thought you had never been out of fairyland,' said Hupa. 'How do you know the ways outside?'

'Fairyland is not a completely separate place – it is this country and yet it is *another* country. They exist as one, yet you cannot be in both at the same time. How can I explain it? You are people of the sea, are you not?' said the ugly elf. 'Consider this, you have a beautiful scallop shell, hinged at its foot, two perfect halves which fit exactly together. An insect cannot be on one half and on the other at the same time, yet it can be said to be crawling over *one* whole shell.

'This is somewhat like the land of the fairies and the land of the mortals – they exist together, as one, but yet inhabit two different portions of space. I have been to the region you describe, but to the exact same fairyland one, not to the one inhabited by mortals.'

The two Oceanians digested this piece of information with no real difficulty, since they came from a place where spirits and ancestors lived alongside the living, there being only one land, one sea, one earth for all.

Hupa said, 'I believe things are the way you say they are, but tell me how is it that we have been running into people of magic all the while?'

'Because this Craig is special, being kinsman to many in this land, yet coming from another …'

Craig listened intently as Urgan explained his origins to Hupa, who stood amazed at what she heard.

'… and his father Seumas-from-the-Blackwater did not spring from earth without relatives – he too had a father, a mother, brothers, sisters, cousins, ancestors. One of those forebears was a fairy, way back in the mists of time, when mortals and supernatural folk commonly met and loved one another in the morning mists of a spring day, amongst the primroses and forget-me-nots, protected oft-times by the dog-rose briar.

'Also his mission here is empowered with Goodness, which gives him special privilege. You pair have been drifting in and out of fairyland the whole time you have been on your travels.'

'Did my father really have brothers and sisters?'

'His clan is a small one,' explained the elf, 'but yet there are those who carry his blood. No true brother or sister exists, for Seumas was the only one to survive the cliffs until he was past his manhood. All his siblings fell to their deaths before they reached their fifteenth year. The Picts from the Blackwater are in the main poor estuary and coastal dwellers, who live by that which the shoreline has to offer. They exist on a diet of crabs, seabirds' eggs, shellfish and the like.'

'It's true, my father gathered the oil from the stomachs of fulmar birds. He climbed cliffs to snatch the fulmars from their nest and strangled them before the birds could disgorge their precious load.'

'A hard way to earn a living,' said Urgan, 'but if one has nimble feet and does not fall easily, then the rewards are better than if one spends one's time collecting cockles and mussels from the estuary mud.'

Craig said, 'How do you know all this?'

'An elf from elf-land knows more than he needs to know, if he or she holds an interest in human affairs.'

Craig nodded. 'And what of my father's name? How did he come to be called "Seumas". It's not a name I have heard amongst the other Celts. What does it mean?'

'Your father was named after a monk-errant, a holy-man who came over the seas, from a distant kingdom out of which has sprung a belief new to this part of the world. This "monk" also touched your adopted mother, Dorcha, on the brow with his hallowed fingertips when she was but an infant.

'Seumas-the-monk drifted to this land by coracle and tried to preach against the local gods in favour of a One-God, tried to change the ways of the people, and was burned to death inside a straw dog for his trouble. This monk-errant was before his time – many people were not ready for change. The druids especially, for it was they who ordered his live cremation.'

Hupa shivered. 'A dog made of straw? Like a wicker shark, I suppose – but we do not burn people in wicker sharks – they are merely signs of tapu. But have the people been changed at all by what the errant-monk Seumas told them? I know Dorcha believed that such change was coming. And Seumas-the-Black's mother must have thought so too, or she would not have called her child after the monk.'

'Why yes, many have, and this One-God religion is spreading throughout the land, though very slowly. Even now there are monks on the outer Fame Islands, who plan to come here despite the dangers. The time of the many-gods is ending. The time of magic is passing. The One-God and a practice called "science" to which several wizards and sorcerers are now turning, will eventually replace these two beliefs.'

Craig said, 'We understand about the One-God, for we have a Supreme Being, the Old One called Io, who is so superior to the other gods that he lives alone above the Twelfth Level, neither seen, nor touched, nor heard, even by other gods. He communicates by means of his Mareikura – spirits of light who are his messengers and servants.'

'That sounds like him. That sounds like the One-God.'

'Has Io grown so powerful then, that he has no need of the other gods at all?' asked Hupa.

'If he is the One-God.'

Craig nodded, thoughtfully, then asked, 'This thing called "science" – do you believe it is good?'

'Inherently evil,' replied Urgan without hesitation. 'I would not trust it a thumbnail's length.'

While this discussion had been interesting and threw a great deal of light on the confused and confusing world, Craig felt it was time to move on.

'You said you knew a short-cut to the battlefields?'

'Yes, but it is through Briar Wood.'

Hupa commented, 'You make it sound a dangerous place.'

'Not so much dangerous in that it threatens life, although many have lost theirs in it through stupidity, but it can delay travellers for years. On the other hand, if you pass through unhampered, it might save you days on your journey.'

'The chance of years against days does not sound much like a bargain to me,' Craig said. 'And why have people lost their lives if it is not dangerous?'

'They panicked and lost themselves.'

'But we have you to guide us,' said Hupa, 'so we shall not lose ourselves.'

Urgan nodded, smiling. 'This maiden with the bow, a huntress of the dawn if ever I saw one, has brains as well as skill with a weapon. Can she shoot true?'

'She could hit a sparrow on the wing,' replied Craig with a grin, 'if she wanted to, which she doesn't, because she kills only to preserve life.'

'A maiden after my own heart,' said Urgan, 'and is she spoken for?'

'In marriage? No. There isn't a warrior who would dare ask her. None can match her skill and our warriors are notoriously concerned about their manhood. They would hate being put to shame by their own wife. Also, she has a reputation for being bad-tempered.'

'I have not,' replied Hupa, hotly.

'Would it bother you?' asked Urgan. 'To have a wife who could beat you at a man's game?'

'Not at all, but I'm already married, otherwise ...' Craig paused, then finished what he was going to say '... otherwise I would ask her to be my wife this very moment.'

Hupa gave a little gasp and stared at him, misty-eyed. Craig had known that his words were unwise, but he wanted to say it once – just once – to have the truth out in the open. However, he had no intention of carrying any of it further. He had his wife, whom he loved, and his children whom he adored. To put those at risk was madness. He could not hurt those he loved in order to indulge an immediate passion.

'Well, if you don't want her,' cried the hideous dwarf, 'then I don't mind having her.'

'I am not a bundle of sticks!' cried Hupa. 'I wouldn't have either of you if you came to me as gods with flowers growing out of your orifices. I hate men.'

'Then you love women?' said Urgan, his ugly face dropping in disappointment.

'Not in the sense you mean, though I prefer their company to that of crass males,' replied the spirited maiden. 'I just think men are boors. They love themselves too much. They have this air of superiority which is not matched by their wits or their talents. Men live a myth. Give me women every time.'

'Except when they chatter like roosting starlings,' said the elf.

'Even then,' muttered Hupa. 'Even then. Better than the grunting of men. Better than that.'

'I *like* this maiden,' said Urgan. 'I will marry her if the chance ever comes. She has such a way with her. I love her to distraction already. I could bide awhile with her.'

'Could you now?' said the young woman. 'Well, I doubt a creature as ugly as a toad gets many chances ...'

Craig made a noise of disapproval, but Urgan laughed. 'No, no, Craig – that's her spirit – that's what I love about her – she puts such *feeling* into her words. Cruel words, but true. I *am* as ugly as a toad. Uglier, even. Now, let us get down to making decisions – do you wish to go through Briar Wood, despite all that I have told you about it?'

Craig said, 'I must get back to the pa as quickly as possible – we must take the chance.'

'Then let us to it.'

They followed a winding dusty path through granite foothills, between forests, over burns, around chalk pits, until finally they were faced by a massive tangle of rose briars as tall as a forest of oaks and elms. On entering they found the brambles were as thick as a man's leg and went sweeping from the ground in huge barbed vaults whose apexes were high above their heads. The monstrous stems, some green and succulent, some brown and brittle, were covered with thorns the size of women's thumbs. A person might stumble and be stabbed to death before he or she was able to rise.

The floor of Briar Wood was covered in petals from the huge dog roses which grew on the vines. Their colours ranged from white to purple-black. Those that had lain on the ground for a long time, forming a soft mattress beneath the travellers' feet, were brown with age. They were so thick that sometimes the three sank down to their knees in dying blossoms. Any daylight which managed to penetrate the tangle of dense briars, drifting down through great shooting arches of wicked thorns from above, turned to a russet hue before falling on the still floor.

'This is a magic place,' whispered Hupa, as she picked her way beneath the arcing vines with their talons ready to pierce her unblemished skin. 'Is this a magic place, Urgan?'

'Of course,' replied the elf. 'Briar Wood holds many secrets and any place with secrets is magic.'

Carefully and cautiously, they threaded their way through the sepia forest, tinged with green on its canopy above, until they came to a place where the briars were even more numerous and impossible to get through without cutting them.

Craig took out *Sunderer* and began to slice a path through the twists of barbed vines. On the way they passed a place where pale-skinned figures in iron apparel – *armour* Urgan called it – had been trapped by the monstrous snaking, hooked brambles, caught there like birds, perhaps to flutter and die. The tangle of burnt sienna vines formed a cage so secure that it would have taken the three companions over a day to release the men.

There were five together, their metal exoskeletons rusting to a reddish-brown which melted into the ochre hues of the forest around them. One or two still had on their helmets, their faces half hidden from view. Yet one, a youth of great beauty, still had his sword in hand and was standing upright, the sturdy rose briars holding him fast in his position. They wound around his limbs and torso like giant serpents, locking him.

The youth's blue eyes stared out in blindness at Hupa. Though his skin was wan, his lips were cherry red in the raw umber light. Slim fingers, fashioned for more delicate work than wielding a weapon, were wrapped around the hilt of his sword, as if he had but grasped it just a moment ago. It almost seemed as if he breathed shallow breaths beneath his metal breast.

'Are they really dead?' asked Hupa in a quiet voice. 'Or just asleep?'

'Perhaps between the two,' replied Urgan. 'This is a magic woodland after all. Best not to try to wake them though, for then they would surely die. If they are at rest, then there is a purpose for them being so. See, their garments are torn, but there is not one spot of blood, though the thorns prick their pale flesh with sharp points. Look how their shields are trapped high above the brambles, as if they were taken from their hands and carried upwards by the growth of decades.'

'Their swords look better than the one I have,' said Craig.

Urgan replied, 'Do not even consider exchanging yours for one of theirs. Would you rob these poor trapped creatures of their weapons? If they are not dead and eventually wake, then think how they would feel. And do not imagine you found your own blade by chance young man – *Sunderer* found its way into your hand – not the other way around. Onsang was a warrior saved from the sea by your great-grandfather. He sent his weapon from Ifurin to help you through troubled times ahead.'

'What troubled times?' asked Craig, staring at the sword in his hand. 'When will I have need of such a weapon?'

'Sooner than you think,' grunted the elf, but would go no further with his explanation. Urgan hesitated before adding, 'Also it is the sword your father killed Douglass for – it is, in a sense, responsible for your existence and your presence here now. Without the sword Dorcha would never have fallen from the cliff, your father would not therefore have attempted to save her, thus landing both of them in Kupe's hands. The Oceanians would not have learned of the whereabouts of Albainn and Engaland, and you would never have been born.'

'How do you know all this?' asked Craig, looking wonderingly at the instrument responsible for a whole history. 'Do you know all things?'

'Not *all* things,' replied Urgan, 'but the more I am near you the more secrets I am told by the wind.'

They left the men in armour to their fate.

Urgan knew that if the three companions were to survive Briar Wood, nothing must be touched, everything must be left the way it was. It was unfortunate that they had to cut their way through the brambles, slicing through the succulent vines, but this was necessary. To attempt to wake the waxen men who lingered under the flying briars, caught in the tresses of climbing roses, soft petals for their sheets – or, if they were lifeless, for their shrouds – would surely bring misfortune on the small group struggling to reach the other side.

Later they came to a place where above their heads were hundreds of dead birds, pierced through the heart by thorns. They were magpies, cuckoos, and all those birds which perpetrated evil acts on their own kind – nest-robbers, chick-killers and the like. The living briars dispensed rough justice to such creatures for its own dark reasons. It was judge and executioner in one and afterwards became the gibbet, displaying the robber-killer birds to others, perhaps as some kind of warning, or perhaps simply to promote its own power.

Further on still, deeper in Briar Wood, they passed under a hundred or so human corpses, skeletons with the flesh still dripping from the bones. Weapons too, caught in the briars, had been borne up. Some kind of battle had taken place before the brambles had grown in this area and the bodies and their trappings had been carried aloft as on the crest of sea waves, and were now like flotsam and jetsam on the heaving swell of brambles above.

As they struggled through Briar Wood there were many animals and birds, running, flying through the brambles as if it were not dangerous in the least. These creatures seemed to have an unerring sense of judgement which made Craig feel like an awkward lumbering creature trespassing on the earth, in a place quite unfitted for his size and cumbersome nature.

'We're lost,' said Urgan, looking upwards. 'I knew this would happen. I can't see the sun any longer.'

It was true, the canopy above had folded over to obscure the light. It was almost dark inside the brambles now. A chill went through Craig. If they got lost in this place they were dead. There was nothing to eat, nothing to drink. They would soon wilt and fall on that springy mat of petals, perhaps to sink down to the roots and become food for the briars.

'How can you be lost? You were brought up by the fairies, weren't you? Aren't you supposed to be a part of all this, a part of the natural world? How can you become lost in something of which you are a part?'

It was a hot-tempered and frustrated Hupa that spoke these words.

'My kind of elf, which is closer to a gnome or a goblin than a pixie, doesn't have all those attributes you mortals consider fairies ought to have. I couldn't find my way out of a badger sett, if I didn't know the way. I was all right when I could see the direction of the sun through the briars – I knew which way to go then. I'm lost now.'

Hupa said, 'What about you, Craig?'

'How would I know where we are?'

'Then it's up to me,' growled Hupa, sniffing the air. 'Fortunately I still have enough of the dog in me to follow an animal trail ...'

'You were a dog?' said Urgan.

'A bitch. Craig and I met some kind of sorcerer in a hut who changed us into dogs – we think. I still retain some of the canine instincts.' She sniffed again. 'See that track,' she said, pointing. 'That's an animal path. Follow it. I'm sure it'll lead us to the edge of Briar Wood. After all, what beast could live in here? This wood is a dead place.'

During their journey Craig also noticed that something was happening to Urgan. By degrees he seemed to be growing taller, losing his squatness. At the same time the lumps and wrinkles on the elf's face were smoothing themselves out. The change was almost imperceptible and at times Craig wondered whether it was merely a trick of the light, rather than an actual occurrence, so he said nothing to either Urgan or Hupa. Now, as Urgan was caught in a shaft of light, he saw that he had indeed been transformed into a handsome young man.

Craig was unable to comment on this, however, for a new emergency arose.

Suddenly he was trapped in something which required his whole attention. The briars were no longer static, but had begun to quicken in their growth, springing from the earth around the companions, as if trying to separate them, trying to trap them like the armoured thanes they had seen earlier. Thorns sprang out like claws from a cat's paw. The three companions had to continually jerk their heads from side to side, to avoid a spike in the eye or throat.

'What's happening?' cried Craig, hacking like mad at the snaking vines which twisted and curled in their flight from the earth to the sky. 'It's growing too fast!'

'Cut! Cut!' yelled Urgan.

Craig did as he was bid, his sword arm working like mad, chopping, slicing, slashing at the undergrowth and overgrowth which vomited from the earth. Very soon his arm became tired and he had to change hands. Finally, exhausted with having to keep up with the growth, he threw the sword to Hupa and told her to carry on the fight.

Two-handed, the slim young maiden did her best to keep the foliage at bay, but soon her arms began to tire too. She passed the weapon to Urgan.

Urgan set to with a fury, hewing a path for them all through the briars, until eventually there was light on the other side of the russet woodland. Verdant hills could be seen and a blue sky. Urgan continued to hack away, until at last the three companions emerged from the thorny cage.

'Out,' breathed Hupa. 'We're safe.'

Urgan lay on his back on the grass, exhausted. Craig fell down beside him. All three felt as if they had narrowly escaped a living death.

'You said it wasn't dangerous,' Craig grumbled. 'I think we were lucky to get out.'

'I lied,' said Urgan. 'You don't expect elves to tell the truth, do you?' He laughed. 'It was highly dangerous. It was the most dangerous thing I've ever done. I feel lightheaded. We got away with it. And we saved three days of walking.'

'You mean we could have ended up like those poor men in iron cloaks?' Hupa said.

'Highly probable,' Urgan replied. 'We could be stuck in there – at least until the soft-nosed beast Craig released from the tower came by.'

'Why? What would that do?' asked Craig.

'You'll find out.'

Suddenly, Hupa let out a cry. 'You've changed,' she said, almost accusingly. 'You're different.'

Craig rolled over and looked at Urgan. There he was, now a youthful man, tall and quite handsome – for a pallid-skinned native of the Land-of-Mists. His shoulders were broad, his chest deep. Urgan's complexion was turning a healthy, ruddy colour. His clothes, which had burst at the seams, hung from him in tatters, revealing everything he owned in the way of manhood.

Hupa turned away, blushing furiously.

'Why have you changed?' she asked. 'What happened to you?'

'I told you. I was taken from my cradle as a baby …'

'You said you were torn from your mother's breast as an infant,' she corrected.

'Poetic licence. The fairies took me, leaving a changeling, which died shortly afterwards – a sickly elf that would not have lived anyway. My mother saw only me in the cot, the fairies having left an aura on the elf.'

'How did you manage to change back again, after being an elf for so long?' asked Hupa. 'Is it because you are now out of elf-land and amongst mortals?'

Urgan winked at Craig, before replying, 'It was love that did it. If you hadn't fallen in love with me, Hupa, I should still be a hideous dwarf, not the handsome young man who stands behind you now …'

She turned, crying, 'I don't love …' then spun round again. 'Will you cover yourself?' she demanded.

'With what?' he asked, reasonably.

She took off her tapa bark skirt, her shift being long enough to fall down past her hips and thighs.

'Put this on,' she said, holding it behind her. 'And don't stare at my legs.'

Urgan wrapped the skirt around his waist.

'I'm not used to wearing women's clothing,' he said, 'but I think this suits me, don't you?'

She turned now and stared at him, a grimace on her face.

'You look like Boy-girl on a bad-taste day.'

The three companions continued their journey through a wilderness consisting of marshy bogs and dreary flatlands. The sky was black with dark clouds, through which only a little light filtered, making the scenery around them even more sombre. To make matters worse there were gallows on every rise from which hanged men and women dangled in various stages of decomposition. Grim faces stared down at the travellers as they passed beneath: cracked skulls with eye-sockets picked clean by crows.

'We are coming to the country which harbours your enemy, Douglass Barelegs,' Urgan told Craig. 'You must soon confront the son of the man your father killed.'

'The lord of this region must be a cruel ruler,' replied Craig, 'to want to display death in this manner.'

'He is indeed a man whose spirit is in need of some cleansing,' said Urgan, generously. 'His name is Skaan and he gives sanctuary to murderers and cut-throats, fleeing from justice. Those people who hang there on those gallows are men and women who made the mistake of refusing to bend to the will of Skaan, or who tried to organize a rebellion against him.'

After the fields of the hanged people they followed a dark river to a wind-swept moor upon which stood great slabs of stone, like doorways from around which the dwellings had collapsed and rotted into the earth. These structures were decorated with twigs, feathers, red-clay shapes and figures and, grotesquely, human heads along the lintel and human hands at the ends. There were feet at the base of the uprights. There were also symbols and motifs painted on the stone uprights in blue woad.

The fleshly appendages were in most cases rotting, though some were fresh. Again the birds were at work, gorging on the soft parts, pecking between fingers and toes.

'Scarefolks,' said Urgan.

'What?'

'Those caricatures, they're meant to frighten people away. Like scarecrows frighten birds. These are scarefolks. We're getting near Skaan's castle now. It's called Eagal Keep.'

Craig knew that 'eagal' meant 'fear' in Gaelic.

'Well, they certainly frighten me,' said Hupa, shuddering. 'What are they meant to be?'

Urgan shrugged. 'Stone men with human heads? Some people say they walk the moors at night and eat those who are lost abroad. You can believe it if you wish. Soon there will be no more of such things, when Craig's beast gets to work.'

'You keep calling it *my* beast,' said Craig with some irritation. 'It does not belong to me.'

'You set it free – therefore it is your beast.'

It was coming on evening as they approached Eagal Keep. Craig had never seen anything like this fortified dwelling. It consisted of unhewn blocks of granite built in the fashion of drystone walls. Each stone fitted in with those around it and formed an uneven structure held together by its own weight. There was little symmetry about the design: it was as if the building had formed during a terrible gale in which blocks were blown together in no ordered fashion. It sprawled over the undulating ground like some over-weight crustacean, not more than twice the height of an ordinary man.

Yet it looked formidable, with uneven slits through which arrows could be fired. It had ramparts and standing stones behind which the keep's occupants could hide while throwing spears. Whole trees sprouted from one or two places, obviously used to support the weak areas. Rooks still roosted at the top of these trees and were even now quarrelling noisily, as those birds always seemed to do. Some of them were pecking at animal hides, which had been draped over the walls to dry in the sun. Smoke rose from several fires in various places inside the structure. There were no sentries visible.

Neither was there a strong door. A deerskin had been draped over a hole in the side of the keep. This pelt hanging from a beam served as an entrance. It was so small, however, that only a single man could pass through while crouched low, so that the defenders could immediately chop any intruders down one by one and stomp them into the dust.

Urgan gestured towards the castle.

'There you are, my friend – inside you will find Skaan and his guest, Douglass, feasting or fornicating – their two main pleasures in life apart from chopping pieces from live human beings for use as decoration.'

'Why don't they ever kill each other, these evil men?' asked Hupa.

'Everyone needs allies,' replied Urgan, 'but you can be sure if there was any profit in it, these two would not hesitate for a moment before destroying one another.'

'Look,' said Craig, 'the curtain's moving – someone's coming out to meet us.'

2

It was a tall thin man who came out of the keep and confronted the three companions. The sun had now gone down behind the horizon and night's shadow was moving across the land. The man stood before them as someone with obvious authority might stand before peasants, looking them up and down with distaste in his expression. Finally he spoke to them.

'You will get no food or shelter here. This is Eagal Keep, the castle of Lord Skaan. If you don't want to be hanging from a gibbet by the morning you'd best show us your backs.'

'Who are you?' asked Craig. 'Are you a priest?'

The man leaned forward, peering at this stranger with keen eyes that tried to penetrate the darkness. Suddenly, seeing something he did not like, he jumped backwards. He went from arrogance to pitiful terror in a moment. His features were twisted in fear and his arms and legs shook violently.

'You have the mark of the devil on your face!' he cried. 'Help, ho! Here are demons!'

Despite the man's shouts no one came to his assistance. Whether men came to the rugged arrowloops in the walls to see what was the matter, Craig did not know. They were merely slits of darkness to his eyes. He only knew he had to get his message across and leave this place. 'I am no demon. I am Craig, son of Seumas-the-Black. Half-Pict, half-Hivan. Tell Douglass Barelegs that I will meet him out on the moor at daybreak. I wish to speak to him alone. If he is accompanied, he will find me gone.'

'Help, help! My master's enemy! Come quickly.'

Urgan stepped forward and slapped the man around the face, to bring him to his senses.

'Did you get the message – on the moor at dawn.'

With that the elf-man who had come out of fairyland gripped Craig by the arm and urged him to get away. Hupa followed quickly behind, seeing flaming torches appear on the battlements of the crude castle behind them, flickering as figures passed behind narrow windows. There were shouts then, the sound of a drum beating, followed by that of a gong. Shouts of 'Where foe? Where foe?' pierced the night's shielding cloak.

Once safe in the darkness of the moor, the three rested under one of the stone scarefolks. Hupa was too exhausted to be frightened by the massive figures around them. A lapwing's feather once dipped in blood, now dangling from a cord, actually caressed her brow as she drifted off into sleep.

Craig was too agitated to sleep soundly and kept waking, the sound of foxes barking coldly on the moor making him start up from time to time, thinking his father was calling him again from the depths of freezing Ifurin. Urgan kept the watch.

At daybreak the blare of horns and the baying of hounds could be heard from the south. All across the moor from the direction of the castle clumps of birds flew up as if startled by an approach. Someone was racing along the edge of the dawn. Urgan went to a rise and watched from there.

Black shapes of tors emerged from the darkness to float on the morning mists of the undulating moor, some flattish and long like boats, others tall and peaked with thrusting towers. Birds shot from the heather like stones from a sling, to alight on gorse and begin their songs. Wild horses galloped away to the east, manes and tails flying. Peat hags hunched against the oncoming day, as if affronted by its approach.

Finally Urgan called to Craig, 'He comes.'

'Is he alone?'

'Quite alone. The dogs you hear must be still in the keep. Douglass wants you very badly.'

Urgan retired, taking the sleepy but concerned Hupa with him, moving off to a distance.

'This is between them,' he told Hupa. 'It began before you were born.'

'And it will end before I die,' she murmured, 'but if he harms my country-man he will suffer.'

Craig heard these words but he was in no position to debate with his female companion. He waited, sword in hand, watching carefully as a big warrior approached at a quick walk. There was wrath in the man's bearing, and a certain pleasure at having his prayers fulfilled. There was revenge printed in his stride as surely as if it were written in blood on his forehead. On his head was a wooden helmet, a mask of oakwood, which he pulled down over his face as he drew nigh. In his fists was a double-handed, double-edged sword of great weight.

He stopped in front of Craig and regarded him for a moment.

'At *last!*' he said. 'Now ye will feel the cleansing touch of my sword. I will cut out your heart, ye damned whelp, and in so doing expunge this dishon-our from my own. Your fether killed mine – now the sons stand one against the other. I will avenge the wrong or die in the attempt.'

'Let me see your face,' ordered Craig.

Douglass took a step back. 'What?'

'I cannot fight a man who hides his face from me. Are you a coward that you dare not let me see whether there is truth or whether there are lies in your features? What is it that you have to keep secret from my eyes?'

Douglass whipped off the helmet, his eyes blazing.

'There – damn ye, damn all your kinsmen, damn the earth ye stand on, damn your mother and most especially, damn your fether – may the whole pack of ye be driven from the face of the earth and herded up some loathsome god's arsehole, to rot there amongst the shite for all eternity ...'

'We must speak,' said Craig, now that he had the man face to face. 'My father ...'

'Damn his polluted soul!'

'My father told me to make my peace with you. He bitterly regrets the killing of your father and is willing to acknowledge the injury he has caused you as that man's son. I cannot fight you, even if I wanted to – I made a deathbed promise to Seumas-the-Black that I would make my peace with you. Nothing on this earth would make me kill you, so I am asking ...'

Craig got no further. The blade of the great battle sword flashed in the early morning sun. It whistled through the air and would have taken off his head if he had not been agile enough to dance out of its way. Douglass seemed to be expecting to miss with the first blow, for he instantly twisted the blade and brought it up from under, skimming Craig's right shoulder. Craig felt a sting as the honed edge of the great sword took a small slice from his upper arm.

'I don't want to do this,' Craig yelled at his adversary. 'I have no wish to kill you – I can't go back on my promise to my father.'

'More fool you,' snapped Douglass, preparing for another blow. 'Whatever barbarian gods ye pray to, do it now.'

The sun was above the horizon now: a great blinding disc of light. Craig parried the next two blows with *Sunderer*. He worked his way round so that he had the sun behind him. Douglass was then staring directly into the glare. The Scot had to squint to see his opponent. Craig kept himself in this position, dancing agilely out of reach of the unwieldy weapon that Douglass swung at him with wild, terrible blows.

If it had not been for *Sunderer*, Craig would have been struck down within the first few moments. The steel broadsword had five times the strength of the iron sword of Douglass. It swallowed blows from the heavier weapon, taking bites out of the great iron blade. Soon the once-honed bright edge of Douglass's weapon was blunted and chipped in many places. The big Scot could not understand why his sword was so ineffective. He renewed his attacks with vigour and strength, his great swinging strokes hissing past Craig's head, while the Oceanian skipped and leapt, his own strokes a flurry of quick slices, the flashes from the blade serving to further confuse his foe.

It was heavy work for the Scot. His weapon was weighty. Finally Douglass stopped for breath, leaning on his sword for support. Craig stepped forward quickly. He chopped at Douglass's iron sword with his own much tougher steel blade. There was a *crack* and the double-bladed weapon snapped off about a third of a length from its point. Douglass fell on the turf looking stunned. Then his arms went up around his head, to ward off any blow at his skull.

Craig reached down and offered the Scot his hand.

'Come on, man – we can talk about this. It wasn't me who killed your father after all. Surely the sons need not make the same mistake as their elders?'

Douglass spat on the hand and jumped to his feet. He snatched up his broken blade and thrust with it. The jagged end pierced Craig's side, leaving a gaping uneven wound. Craig heard a cry from Hupa as he sank to his knees clutching his side. He could feel the warm blood oozing through his fingers. Standing above him, Douglass was wielding his broken but still effective weapon two-handed. A blow was directed at Craig's skull, intended to split it.

Craig rolled sideways. Douglass's sword struck a flint in the turf, giving out a ringing note, sending up sparks. The Scot shouted in frustration, swinging sideways. The sideswipe missed Craig's head by the thickness of a fingernail. Craig had had enough. He was never going to convince Douglass to lay down his arms and talk peace. Craig swung up and down, one stroke, and chopped the left foot of Douglass in half.

Douglass crashed to the ground. He gave out a grunt of disbelief. He sat up quickly and looked down at his foot, staring at the appendage, sliced as cleanly as bacon. The other sandalled half with its toes lay a yard away.

'Ye bastard!' cried the Scot. 'Can ye no fight fair?'

Craig staggered to his feet, clutching his wounded side, to stand over his adversary.

'I told you I didn't want to fight at all.'

'Go shag a wasps' nest, ye tattooed bastard.'

Craig raised *Sunderer* over the man's head. Douglass sneered up into his face. Craig brought the blade down with a swish. At the last moment he turned it from the Scotsman's neck. Instead the sharp steel snicked through the wrist of Douglass Barelegs, severing his right hand. Douglass stared in horror at the stump, just inches from his eyes.

'Ye bluddy bastard,' he yelled. 'Ma hand!'

He picked up his own hand by the fingers and stared at it, knowing it could not be reunited with his wrist. Then he flung it from himself like a piece of useless meat. He stared up into the face of his enemy.

'Kill me!' he roared.

'No,' said Craig, as the other two came to stand by the pair. 'I promised my father I would not.'

Urgan said, 'You're finished as a warrior, Douglass. You brought this on yourself. Take up sheep-rearing, some gentle occupation. You'll never fight again …'

Douglass stared with visible hatred into the faces around him, then keeled over as the weakness caused by loss of blood overcame him.

Urgan first tended to Craig's wounds, finding some yarrow and binding it into his cut side with strips of cloth.

'What is the herb?' asked Hupa.

'We call it "staunch grass" or sometimes "thousand leaf"', replied Urgan. 'It will help the blood to clot.'

Hupa insisted on tidying up the binding herself, though there was really nothing wrong with it. She helped Craig to his feet, telling him to lean on her. Giddy from blood-loss he was willing to use her as a crutch.

In the meantime Urgan bound up Douglass's wounds, as he lay unconscious on the grass. Even if he lived – for men often died of such wounds if they went black and rotten – the big Scot's fighting days were indeed over. With only half a foot and no right hand he would not even be a match for a six-year-old with a sharpened stick.

The sound of a horn came from not far away. Warriors in wolfskins pinned with bird-bones at the collar came running across the moor with hounds at their heels. They reached the place where the three were standing. One fellow with a great black beard and wild staring eyes stepped forward. He glanced at Douglass lying motionless in the grass.

'I am Skaan. Is this man dead?'

'Crippled,' replied Urgan.

Skaan looked hard at him. 'I know who these two are, but who are you?'

'I am Urgan of Umberland, taken from my mother's breast at birth and raised by the fairies.'

At these words the group of warriors backed away from Urgan quickly, pulling on the leashes of their hounds. Skaan stared, looking Urgan up and down. He too looked nervous and uncomfortable.

'Did you do this?' he said, eventually, pointing to Douglass's wounds.

'No,' replied Urgan, 'this was between the stranger and Douglass – I had no part in it. I am merely their guide. But,' he smiled, 'you know the ways of the fairies. I have things at my fingertips which would make you borderers sweat in your bed at night just to think of them.'

'Such as?'

'Would you like to see your dead mother, wizened and dwarfish, popping up and down from the reeds as you hurry across the moors at night?'

'That I would not.'

'Or your headless father – whom you decapitated yourself – roll his talking skull into the room where you sleep?'

'Nor that either.'

'Then you will know we must part as friends.'

Skaan stared at Urgan for a very long time, his black beard glistening with dried spittle, then he nodded.

'Be on your way before I turn you into tripe, the three of you. And be warned, brown-skins,' he told Hupa and Craig, 'there's an army of Angles coming down from the north. They have heard of your landing. They'll destroy every last one of you. You had better get in your little boats and go home.'

'You know this for certain?' asked Craig.

Skaan grinned a mouthful of blackened teeth. 'I know this because I shall be joining with them.'

Craig nodded. They left the warriors to carry Douglass back to Eagal Keep. Urgan went on the other side of Craig and helped to take his weight. Together the three of them left the border country and went down into Albainn.

On coming to a loch which they had to cross, Urgan fashioned a coracle from reeds caulked with clay. It was not the most lake-worthy of craft, but it would do for a single journey over the shining water.

'Are you sure this will carry us?' asked Craig, dubiously, staring at the flimsy-looking vessel. 'It doesn't seem as if it'll take much to sink it.'

'It'll be fine so long as we keep it balanced. Don't stand up suddenly. In fact, don't stand up at all. Just sit upright, back to the wall, with your legs pointing to the middle of the coracle. Let me do the work.'

The three companions settled into the boat, which was a cramped craft to the two Oceanians: even fishing canoes used in local island waters had more room than this tiny coracle. Urgan paddled them out onto the glistening waters of the loch, purple in the evening light as it reflected heather on the surrounding mountains. It was a calm and tranquil end to the day, with nothing but the plash of the oar to break the silence. Not even the sound of birds, out on the still waters.

Only the midges caused any annoyance and these were not as bad as they had been earlier in the season. Overhead a fish eagle wheeled about above the surface, but it abruptly glided away quickly on the edge of a breeze as if it had seen something it did not like in the deeps.

When they were halfway across a monstrous scaly head, dripping mud and weed, suddenly broke the surface not far from the coracle. Parts of a body also appeared behind the head: a body ridged with spikes and spines. Water streamed from the creature's back, as the head rose ever higher out of the loch. Hupa gave a shout of alarm as the monster's mouth opened to reveal rows of savage-looking teeth. Two fleshy horns protruded from the monster's head, giving it the look of a sea dragon.

'A taniwha!' cried Craig.

Instantly and instinctively Hupa fitted an arrow to her bow. Before Urgan could stop her she stood up and fired at the beast. The arrow struck the creature behind the ear. Its huge mouth opened to cavernous proportions and the wounded beast let out a bellow of pain and anger which echoed around the mountains and glens with a deafening sound. Its eyes turned hot and red as it regarded the puny little being which had wounded it.

Hupa stared in alarm at the beast as she fought to keep her balance in the unstable coracle.

A quick flick of some previously hidden fin or tail removed the offending dart from behind the monster's ear. Then the great green creature dived below the waters causing a shock wave to wash towards the coracle. Hupa overbalanced even before the wave hit the craft, toppling into the water. The two men clung to the coracle, trying to keep it steady. If it overturned they would have a long hard swim to the far shore.

'Wait until the waves have settled before we pull her back in,' said Urgan.

'Don't tell me how to manage a boat,' grumbled Craig. 'Our people are raised with them.'

Finally the waters calmed, while Hupa trod water, anxiously peering around her for signs of the taniwha.

'What was that?' she asked, as they dragged her back into the coracle. 'Did I kill it?'

'You gave it a mosquito sting,' snorted Urgan. 'What a foolish thing to do. Did you believe you could destroy the loch monster with a little arrow?'

'We have rid the world of monsters in our time,' replied Hupa, haughtily.

'Monsters as large as that?'

'Well, no,' she admitted, 'but I'm sure I gave it more than a sting.'

'We'd better get out of here,' Urgan said, paddling in earnest. 'If the monster decides to come back, we'll end up as fish meal.'

They took turns to paddle now, as Urgan grew weary, and gradually made their way to the far darkening shore. Luckily the monster did not return to take its revenge on Hupa. She was inclined to think she had taught it a lesson, but Urgan shook his head and said the monster had been in the loch since the beginning of time and would be there at the end of time, and no maiden from far isles was going to change that.

Before they reached the bank, Craig threw his father's sword into the deep loch. This time the water took the blade, swallowing it. Craig watched its silver shape as it slipped down to the seemingly fathomless bottom like a diving fish.

'Now my father will be able to defend himself against the monsters of Ifurin,' he said. 'If he has not been devoured already.'

'Seumas will still be whole,' Hupa persuaded him. 'He was a resourceful man in life – and so in death. He will have found some way to survive while you used the sword. Otherwise he would not have rejected it the first time, giving you the opportunity to use it in your fight with Douglass Barelegs.'

'I hope you are right,' said Craig.

Craig's wound was healing quite rapidly, but whether that was due to the herb or to fairy magic was a matter for speculation amongst the two Oceanians. By the time they finally came to the country where the Celts and Oceanians were still executing the war, there were but hard white scars on his shoulder and side to show where Douglass's sword had struck.

Urgan told the other two that they were still many days walk from where they wanted to be and that they would have to do something to speed up their journey time.

'What can we do, grow wings?' asked Craig. 'I can't believe how far we are away from the pa.'

'When you travelled with the two Jutes, and as dogs, you were always heading north. You went deep into fairy country. Of course you ended up a long way from home. What did you expect? But I have a solution.'

Both Hupa and Craig looked at Urgan expectantly.

'What are we to do?' asked Hupa.

Urgan pointed to some mystical shapes out on the moor ahead of them. They were largish creatures with tails like flails and necks with soft, floating manes. They moved like gods across the landscape, incredibly fleet of foot. Magnificent in form and movement, they were muscled beasts of beauty, whose very presence on the earth seemed to have been conjured by supernature. If the strength was flowing out of the gods, it was surely flowing into these splendid animals of which Seumas had been proud.

'Horses,' said Craig. 'What of them?'

'We catch three of them and ride them to your pa.'

Hupa laughed, a little hysterically. 'You must be crazy – we can't ride *those*. They'd kill us.'

'Nonsense,' replied Urgan. 'Horses and humans are made for each other. You wait and see ...'

Urgan had them build a corral of staves with reed-leaf lashings, with a gate through which they could herd the horses. Then the elf-man went and stood on a crag at the back of the corral and whinnied just as those creatures out on the moor whinnied, causing several horses to stop in mid-canter and stare at the corral. Urgan continued calling, until a small herd of mares headed his way, answering his call with their own. Urgan was the stallion whose females were coming to their master, while the hidden Oceanians prepared to rush out and shut the gate behind the unsuspecting creatures of the wind.

They were of course wary of the open gateway, but Urgan kept up his pretence of being a stallion and eventually the mares entered the corral.

Hupa and Craig ran out and slammed the gate shut on the creatures, who immediately went absolutely berserk, kicking and screaming, lashing out with their hind hooves, biting the air savagely with their teeth, whipping their heads back and forth, and trying to jump the fence which surrounded them. Only when night fell did they give up in exhaustion.

'I will break three of the horses,' said Urgan, the next early morning, 'but once I've broken them in, you two will have to ride one each. I want no faint hearts.'

The Oceanians said nothing, but watched in rising panic as Urgan lassoed the first mare and climbed on top of this kicking, bucking creature. He was thrown almost immediately, somersaulting several times through the air before hitting the soft peaty ground. To the amazement of the other two he immediately scrambled back on the horse, wrapped his legs around its girth, clung on hard to the mane hair, and continued in his attempts to break the spirit of the animal under him.

Although Urgan was thrown off the horse's back several times, he always climbed back on again immediately. Gradually he wore the beast down, until finally it gave in. It stood there allowing him to mount and dismount. Urgan rode it around the corral, growing in confidence all the time. When he got off the beast the last time, he tied a rope around its neck and handed the other end of the rope to Hupa.

'This little brown horse – a chestnut we call it – is yours, Hupa.'

'Do I want it?' she asked, trembling.

'Don't be such a baby. It's tame now. Take the rein.'

She did as she was told, not taking her eyes from the horse's face, wondering when it was going to try to bite her.

'ARRRGGHHH!' Craig yelled suddenly, his face suffused with pain.

'What is it?' cried Hupa.

Craig sat down and held his foot. He pointed dramatically at the mare.

'That sneaky – mare – stood on my foot,' he complained. 'Urgan – do you call that tame?'

'A horse is never *completely* tame. You always have to be the master of it and they'll always have a go at those they feel are inferior to them. You have to look them in the eye and not flinch. They can smell fear. I never saw such a pair of cowards as you two. Hupa, get on the mare's back, now. If you hesitate any longer you'll never be able to ride.'

Urgan cupped his hands like a stirrup and told her to use it for her foot. Once her toe was in his hands he tossed her up on to the horse before she could complain or back away again. She sat there looking tense and terrified. She felt she was sitting on a treetop, high off the ground in a strong wind, on something completely unstable. Between her slim thighs was this monstrous living, breathing volcano which might erupt at any moment – and without any decent warning.

She waited for it to bolt, her heart racing ahead of her. She could feel the sweaty back on her bottom – could *smell* the sweat – and this did nothing to calm her fears. Gingerly she reached out to pat its neck, the way she had seen Urgan do.

The horse snorted and shook its head impatiently.

'That's right. Hold on – yes, even that tightly – to the mane,' said Urgan, 'I'll trot you round.'

He took the woven-grass rein and led her round the corral, first at a walk, then at a trot, finally at a mild canter. Initially she was rigid with fear and complained that it was hurting her bottom. Then she began to relax when nothing untoward happened. She began to get the rhythm of the trot and canter, using her knees to rise and fall with the movement of the mare. Gradually a smile appeared on Hupa's face. She clung on to the horse like a little girl, delighted with her first ride.

'I shall call her Brownie,' said Hupa. 'My little Brownie.'

'How original,' muttered Urgan, drily. 'But I suppose there are other meanings of the word – especially to one who came out of fairyland. Brownie it is.'

When he felt she had been on the horse for a good while, Urgan gave Craig a turn. Craig, on seeing that Hupa had done so well, was less apprehensive. He too was soon enjoying a slow trot around the ring, his arms wrapped around the horse's neck. Once he had been on her for a while Hupa became a little jealous and reminded everyone that Brownie was her horse and she thought Craig had been on *her* horse long enough.

Urgan did not bother to break in two more horses. Instead he selected the mares he wanted, then took some shiny dust out of his pocket for them to sniff. Once they had inhaled the fairyland snuff, they became docile enough to ride. In effect he had tamed them by using magic. Craig and Hupa were perplexed by this. They confronted him with the subject.

'Why did you physically break in that first horse, if you could do it using magic?' asked Hupa.

'I wanted to see if I could,' replied Urgan, simply. 'Why do things the easy way, when you can do them just as well the hard way?'

'Now I know he's mad,' Hupa said to Craig. 'And this is the man I'm supposed to be in love with?'

But there was a light in her eyes when she said it, as she watched the elf-man moving amongst the horses he had tamed.

The time came for them to mount up.

Craig got on his mare, a big roan one with a white flash on her forehead. He gripped the grass rein and gave the horse a little nudge in the ribs with his heels. The roan trotted out through the gateway obediently. Craig was exhilarated. Hupa rode up beside him. They glanced at each other and then laughed, both full of the spirit of riding. Here they were, high on a horse's back, feeling like royalty. There was nothing like it. And so far they had only trotted or cantered.

'Time to gallop,' cried Urgan, nudging his mare through the pair of them. 'We must ride like the wind!'

Urgan set the pace, flying out in front. Once Craig's mare saw the other pair building up to the gallop, she too took off. The wind rushed past Craig's face and for a moment the colour drained from his complexion. He had never moved so fast in his life before. No matter what Urgan had said, this was a terrifying experience.

Perhaps a canoe had skipped over the waves almost as swiftly, but that was different. The ground rushed under him like a fast-flowing river, and the drumming of the roan's hooves on the hard earth reminded Craig of his own expertise and how his hands flew with the sticks in them as they pounded a log drum.

'This is wonderful!' he cried, breathlessly, as he caught up to the others. 'I'm scared to death!'

'So am I,' laughed Hupa.

They thundered over moor and meadow, through brake and past stone, three riders on strong young mounts. Craig could feel the hard-packed mus-cled body moving beneath him. He could hear the snorts of air rushing in and out of the roan's nostrils. Flecks of foam came up from the beast's mouth and splattered his face. Clearly the creature itself, with its eyes white and wide, was enjoying this as much as the person on its back. The world flashed by them at a wonderfully alarming rate. No wonder the man on the horse was king. No wonder Seumas had warned them of such creatures. One of these creatures was worth half a man's life to own.

'What a joy there is in this,' Craig shouted above the noise of the rushing wind. 'I could ride for ever!'

'So could I,' yelled Hupa.

'Unfortunately,' answered Urgan, 'we don't have for ever.'

They knew he was right.

3

The death of Totua had wounded Kieto badly. This had come on top of other bereavements: the murder of his son whose grave had eventually been found in a wood. And the disappearance and suspected death of his daughter. Kieto was sick of death: his kin were vanishing before his eyes. He would have to go home to his wife without his children. These losses had piled themselves on his head and were weighing him down.

There were days when he paced his hut inside the pa, railing at Guirk. There were nights when he prayed quietly to his ancestors, begging their forgiveness for not answering the barbarian's call. Every noon Guirk still came up to the walls of the pa and demanded single combat with Kieto. Every evening the Celt trudged back into the hills, disappointed by the non-appearance of the Oceanian chief. Finally, the taunts and jeers, underlined by Guirk's abuse of Totua's corpse, got deep enough beneath Kieto's skin to make him respond.

Kikamana came into Kieto's hut to find him strapping on his feathered helmet.

'What are you doing?' the elderly high priestess asked him. 'Are you going out there?'

'I have to,' he sighed. 'I can stand it no longer. It's a matter of personal and national honour. We are at a stalemate. We go out to battle with the Celts, but neither side wins any great victory. What we have at the moment amounts to a siege. We are hemmed inside our trenches and stockades and the Celts cannot go to their homes, but have to camp in the surrounding hills. Perhaps my death, if it must be so, will break this deadlock in some way. Another war chief will be found and he will have fresh ideas, new thoughts.'

'You don't have to go out there and commit suicide in order to find fresh ideas. You know Guirk has a magic shield, made from iron bands fashioned from the teeth of the ogress Lioumere. And a magic sword, forged from the same enchanted metal. You will be slaughtered in the same way as Totua – cut down without mercy. Your head will decorate a Celt's horse. Your body will be dragged headless in the dust. Where is the honour in that? It would be as well to seek your revenge through other minds, rather than waste yourself in this foolish venture.'

'I know – but I can't rely on my advisors to find an answer – the best of them has gone missing. My son is dead, my daughter has disappeared, most likely she is dead too, and my brother has been killed by a thick-skulled thug. What else is left for me but to fight this loudmouthed barbarian?'

Kikamana knew that by 'advisors' Kieto meant Craig, who had disappeared the night of the last entertainment, along with Hupa his daughter. There were ugly rumours that the two had become lovers and had run away together.

Kieto did not believe this – nor did Kikamana.

It was believed by right-thinking Oceanians that Craig and Hupa had been murdered by the Celts, their bodies disposed of in some way. There was mourning amongst the women of the Whakatane, for their leader. And many of the other chiefs missed Craig's calming influence, his quiet reasoning. Some were calling for a change in leadership. The foremost of the contenders for the place of chief-of-chiefs was Prince Daggan, who was also the loudest in demanding that Kieto step down.

Perhaps, thought Kieto, we do need someone like Daggan at the head of the army? Someone without morals, someone without mercy, someone without principles?

The grating voice of Guirk penetrated the still afternoon air making Kikamana wince.

'I must go,' Kieto said. 'Help me on with my war cloak.'

Kikamana, the Farseeing-virgin, assisted Kieto with his splendid warrior-chief's mantle made of dogskin and parrot feathers. Then Kieto took down a heavy wahaika club from its hooks on the wall, its edges rimmed with shark's teeth. Kieto carried no other weapons, except for a lei-o-mano in his maro. However, Kikamana excused herself and left the hut for a short while, returning from her temple with another weapon.

'A greenstone club,' said Kieto, admiring the precious weapon his high priestess offered him. 'I shall carry this with great pride.'

He laid aside his wahaika club and took the smooth, beautiful and heavy greenstone mace.

'This is the weapon of a king,' he said.

'It once belonged to a king and has been blessed by the gods. It will increase your mana. Now I must place a tapu on you, to give you the best chance of victory. You will need all the help you can get out there.'

Kikamana performed the rituals and prepared her leader for the oncoming fight. Once he was ready he stood tall and proud, his expression arrogant. A warrior did not go out to fight looking like a bedraggled dog hiding from the rain.

'*Only war can make a real man and a real man must have the war he loves,*' said Kieto, quoting an old saying. 'The only path to glory is across the battlefield, for one man, or for a nation. There is nothing else worthwhile. A man's soul will not shine like a beacon in the afterlife without great deeds on the field of battle. To be remembered in songs, to be part of one's island history, this is all that matters.'

'Not everyone believes in such ideas,' said Kikamana. 'There are deeds greater than those performed by warriors.'

Kieto shook his head. He was too upset to argue. It was the wrong frame of mind in which to go out into battle. A warrior needed joy in his heart to beat the enemy. Weariness and despair were the worst of allies in a fight, especially one of single combat. Kieto wondered whether his time had indeed come, whether his mission to the Land-of-Mists was abortive and should never have taken place. Perhaps he should have ignored the inner calling and remained a fisherman's son?

Yet events had conspired against him throughout his life, to ensure his presence on this island. The moment that giant octopus had taken Kupe's bait and had fled with it, an enraged Kupe in pursuit, Kieto's fate had been sealed. One could not ignore a land as great as this, for such a huge island would not ignore others for very long. To explore, to seek new lands to conquer, that was in the basic nature of man. If not Kieto and his people, then some future Cormac and his Celts, or some king of the Angles, thirsting for power.

Kikamana, as if reading his thoughts, said, 'Some go out after knowledge, rather than to conquer. This is the true nature of the search for mankind.'

'Like Hiro, you mean?'

'Yes, like Hiro.'

Kieto said, petulantly, 'We can't all be Hiros.'

With that he swept from the room, his magnificent cloak lifting as he walked. Those who saw him coming from the walls cried out in excitement to others.

'Kieto! It's Kieto. He is going to fight Guirk!'

There was relief in the sound, as if at last a drought had been broken by the coming of rain.

The colours, red and green and yellow, of Kieto's tall feathered helmet sparkled in the sunlight. He held his greenstone club aloft, to salute his men, his ancestors, his gods. Then he strode towards the gates of the pa, the black mood at last lifting from his shoulders. He was going to avenge his brother. If that meant death, so be it, then let death come, the quicker the better.

Outside the pa, the word was going back into the hills, Kieto was coming out to fight Guirk.

Celts began to pour down from their encampments in their dull rough garments. Cormac came with his retinue of clan chiefs. Camp followers from the countryside swept towards the place where Guirk stood waiting, nervously, knowing that at last his wish was going to be answered. Despite the reassurance that he could not lose, that the magic in his weapons ensured his victory, the Celt was tense. This was the moment for which he had been waiting and the world was looking on.

Out of the various stockades, over the ditches and dykes, came the Oceanians, also eager to see what would be the outcome of this single combat, mano-a-mano, two warriors battling to the death, each carrying the pride of his people. There had been too many listless days, too many ragged battles neither won nor lost had been fought in the mud and grit of this strange land, and the coming duel signalled a change. Whatever happened in this contest, things were not going to be the same afterwards.

A fresh breeze was blowing in from the mountains.

Once the decision had been made, Kieto put everything into his bearing and demeanour. The figure that strode towards Guirk was tall and straight, proud, defiant, confident. Guirk shuffled in his sandals, bolstered only by the knowledge that he could not lose, that the magic of his weapons were so powerful that even men like Kieto could not defeat him.

When Kieto was not far from his adversary, he did his dance, the haka, learned from the Maori. In the bent-knee position, he stamped forward, gesturing with his weapon, his tongue out and spread over his chin, his eyes rolling. He uttered a karakia as he did so, his voice deep and menacing. The feathers on his tall helmet and long cloak fluffed and flapped in the wind, making him seem larger than an ordinary man.

Guirk, on seeing this frightening display, called forth a bagpiper and, when the wailing began, proceeded to do a sword dance, his eyes contemptuously on his enemy. Guirk had added to his protective trappings a silver helmet and chain-mail shoulder guards. These flashed in the sun while he danced, giving rise to a great cheer from the Celts.

When both men had ceased their posturing, they stood before one another, their weapons at the ready.

Around them, on the terraces of the hills, outside the walls of the pa, stood the spectators. There was not a man or woman left in the Celtic camps, nor anyone but the sentries on the walls of the pa. This single combat was about to be witnessed by the complete armies of two great peoples.

'Come on then,' said Guirk, swishing his magic blade, 'come to meet your death, you overdressed jay.'

Kieto was not one to waste time circling, bluffing or feinting; he went straight in. He brought the greenstone club down towards the shield, only to find it rebuffed by a cushion of air. He tried again. The same thing happened. His heart sank as he proved to himself that what they said about the shield and sword of Guirk was true. They had magical powers. They must indeed have been fashioned from Lioumere's teeth.

'What's the matter?' crowed Guirk. 'Lost your strength? All that prancing and dancing, no doubt. You banana-eaters will have to do better than this. You're the second old man whose ambitions have been higher than his skills.'

Kieto had no idea what Guirk was saying to him, but he guessed it was to do with his brother.

The Oceanian stepped forward again, swiping at the Celt's head. Guirk flicked out his sword arm. The point of the sword nicked Kieto's brow, a slit right across from one temple to the other. Blood trickled down into Kieto's eyes, making it difficult for him to see. Celtic warriors let out their breath as if they had been holding it in for such a moment. The Oceanians were quiet, knowing that Guirk was playing with their leader, like a cat plays with its kill.

'Finish him, Guirk,' came the voice of Cormac from the midst of the Celts. 'Finish him *now*.'

This was spoken as an act of kindness. The Celtic leader did not like to see a man made to look foolish, especially a leader like Kieto whom he secretly admired.

Guirk looked sullen but he raised his sword to strike the man before him. A sudden breeze riffled Kieto's feathers as the Oceanian stood there ready to receive the blow. Then someone shouted from the Celt side in such a strange voice that both the combatants turned to look. Over the plain, from the direction of the mountains, came a dark cloud in the shape of a feline creature, moving rapidly, expanding over the whole region. Soon the people were in its blackness, which wrapped around them like a soft cloak, destroying all visibility.

Then the insubstantial giant beast had passed over, was now bigger than before, running soft-footed towards the north.

'What was that?' cried a Celt from the crowd, as men shuddered and women shivered. 'Was that a *god*?'

'That?' said a stranger to their camp, making his way through the throng on horseback. 'That was the beast-who-eats-magic.'

Guirk blinked, then turned back to his opponent.

'Time to die, you pig's orphan,' he said, aiming a blow with his sword. 'Now!'

Kieto instinctively held up his greenstone club.

To the astonishment of the crowds, though Guirk's sword struck the green obsidian weapon squarely in the middle, it slid along it and glanced off, singing out a metal note.

'What?' cried Guirk in surprise.

He had expected his sword to cleft the stone in two.

Kieto was swift to reply, swinging his club at Guirk. Guirk protected his head. This time the stone struck the shield, severely denting it, causing Guirk to yell out in pain as his shield arm took the force of the blow.

No magic sword, no magic shield.

Kieto went in, battering his opponent with the greenstone club, not letting up for an instant. Guirk was caught completely on the defensive. He backed towards his own people, holding the battered shield over his head. One or two ineffective swipes with his sword told him he was not going to be successful with it. He dropped the weapon altogether and concentrated on preventing his head from being crushed.

His efforts were to no avail. Finally his arm was too tired to parry a blow. The greenstone club came crashing down on his conical silver helmet, driving it down to cut off his ears, nose and upper lip with its studded edge. There was a dent in the top which had crushed his brain inside his skull. His legs collapsed underneath him. Guirk fell to the dust as dead as a nail. Kieto stood over him, panting and heaving with the effort, realizing he was the unexpected victor.

A great yell of triumph went up from the Oceanian side, followed by a low moan of misery from the Celts. Kieto took Guirk by the legs and began to drag him face-down in the mud, towards the pa. A shout from a friend stopped him short.

'Leave the body, Kieto. Leave the remains for his kin.'

Kieto stared up at the speaker who had ridden through the ranks of warriors on a horse.

It was Craig. With him was Hupa, also on one of those terrible animals. And the stranger who seemed to know about the dark beast. These three came towards Kieto. They dismounted and stood holding the reins of their mounts.

Kieto dropped the feet of his defeated antagonist.

The young man everyone thought was dead rubbed noses with the Oceanian leader. This exhibition brought nervous laughter from the Celtic camp. Despite the defeat of their champion the Celts seemed not unduly despondent. The two friends took no notice of this ignorance of their culture, knowing that it would be misunderstood. They stood before one another, holding each other's forearms.

'Where have you been?' asked Kieto, the sound of relief mingling with joy in his voice. Then nodding at Urgan, he cried, 'And who is this who brings my daughter back to me, with all her limbs and her heart intact?'

'I cannot speak for her heart,' said Urgan, smiling, 'but her arms and legs are all there.'

'This is Urgan,' said Craig, and not willing to go into the business of the fairies added, 'he is from the borderlands.'

Kieto clasped Urgan's forearms. 'Welcome,' said the Oceanian chief-of-chiefs. 'I take it you have been their guide and I am most grateful. I thought my daughter was dead,' his eyes misted over, 'but here she is, alive and well.'

Hupa did not go too close in case her father smothered her with too much love in front of her Whakatane.

'Very much alive and well, Father.'

Once the reunion was over, there was still a serious situation lying before Kieto. His warriors were all outside the pa. Facing them were the Celtic hordes, most of them armed. One battle here, hand-to-hand, might finish the war. Yet the risks for both sides were high. There would be a slaughter, perhaps even a massacre, and many would die in both armies. In the extreme it would be reduced to the last man standing. Cormac knew this, Kieto knew it. Even if the Oceanians tried their trick of running, they would be cut down by so near a foe.

'Well?' said Cormac, reading the situation accurately himself, 'D'we fight or no?'

The interpreters shouted out the question even before it was fully out of Cormac's mouth. Everyone was wary. Everyone was edgy. Swords were gripped tightly. Spears were balanced. Clubs were hefted through practice swings. There was a tautness to the air. Once the hacking began, it would be every man for himself. The women, all except those who were armed for a fight, began to lead their children away.

'Let us fight!' cried the voice of Prince Daggan of Raiatea, from behind Kieto. 'Rally around me, warriors! I shall lead you to victory over the barbarian hordes!'

Fortunately the tension at that time had not gathered to breaking point. Warriors shuffled and stared at each other, but none went to the side of Daggan. The prince let out a snort of disgust.

'Are you *all* cowards now? Have you fallen into the ways of this fisherman's son?' He pointed with his club at Kieto. 'It has taken him many days and nights to gather the courage to fight this thick-headed creature he has now clubbed to the ground. I would have done it at the first challenge. Let us now waste no more time, but drive into the Celts with our weapons.'

Still no one moved; all stood watching warily.

'There will be many deaths,' Kieto said, 'on both sides.'

The interpreters gave voice and once Cormac understood the words he spoke.

'Aye, that's true enough,' replied Cormac, 'but it's better than rotting in camps and stockades.'

Kieto nodded. 'That's true also.'

There was utter silence over the plain for a few moments, save for the sound of birds and insects.

A highly strung warrior let out a sharp exhalation of air and thousands of heads turned sharply to stare at him.

Then the faces turned back to the chiefs again, watching intently for the signal to begin the slaughter.

Urgan stepped forward, no longer the wizened elf he was when he had walked out of fairyland and joined the Oceanians in their quest. Now a tall handsome man of thirty years, with broad shoulders and sturdy limbs, he stood firmly between the two armies, holding up his arms for attention.

When he felt all eyes were on him, he spoke in the most dramatic voice he could muster.

'The Angles are coming!'

There was a stunned look on the faces around him – the first to break the silence was the leader of the Celts.

'What?' cried Cormac, his eyes brightening, his attention completely captured by this news. 'When?'

'It's true,' Craig said, 'they're on their way down here now. They said they were going to join …'

'Join forces at the border and come down here to destroy the Celts and the brown-skin invaders, both in one breath,' Urgan interrupted quickly.

Craig had been about to say 'join forces with Celts' but now saw what Urgan was doing.

'Destroy us, is it?' cried Cormac, the interpreters working with him excitedly, three of them translating the same words at once. 'Aye, well, we'll see about that.'

'It's said they have a mighty army,' Craig said, 'but what if the Celts and Oceanians were to fight together, side by side, to defeat the invading Angles?'

Urgan gave him a look as if to say, you may have spoken too soon, my friend, for the Celts were all muttering about not needing any brown-skins to help them defeat the Angles, they could do it on their own. It was their land which was being invaded after all. The Oceanians could run away to their boats and go back to wherever they came from in the first place.

But Cormac was a wise chief-of-chiefs, being from a small clan, which needed guile and cunning to survive.

'When did we last beat an army out of Engaland?' he said. 'Once – just once the Scots and Picts have hammered those bastards from the north. And then they outnumbered us two to one. But what a shock they would get to find an army to *match* them in numbers, eh? What a bloody nose we could give the buggers this time! There'd be a clutch o' widows up there on top o' the border after such a fight.'

'We'd give them such a thrashing, they'd stay up there for more than a wee while,' cried another clan chief. 'But would these painted demons join with us?'

These words were translated by Craig.

Kieto said, 'We came here to strike a hard blow, a warning blow, to dissuade any future would-be invaders of our islands. We have shown the Celts that we are not lacking in skill at warfare. Now it is time to impress upon the Angles that if they come to our part of the world with war in mind, they can expect a fiery reception from Oceanian island warriors.'

'It's settled then,' cried Cormac, 'the war between the Celts and Oceanians is at an end. We are allies against the Angles and their Jute dogs. If ye leave this land after we thrash the bastards, then there need be no more strife between us.'

A great cheer went up when this was translated by the interpreters and the whole Oceanian army surged forward to begin hugging the reluctant Scots and Picts. The hairy Celts detached themselves as soon as possible from this unseemly show of affection. They dusted themselves off subconsciously, and nodded grim-faced, as if to say, enough's enough, no more touching of bodies if you please, for we're not that way inclined down here in the cold southern climes.

Guirk's corpse was taken away by his clan for burial, while Kikamana and Boy-girl came to speak with Craig and Urgan.

'What was it you said?' Kikamana asked of Urgan. 'You spoke about a beast-that-eats-magic.'

'It's true,' replied the man brought up by elves, whose hybrid status made him the focus for knowledge found only in the ether, making of him a universal messenger. 'Craig let the beast out of the tower. This was his destiny, the reason for his being here in Albainn. The One-God has decided it is time to end the rule of magic in the land. At this moment all our greater and lesser gods – those of the Celts and those of the Oceanians – are in their last throes of existence. They are a spent force. They have fought a great battle in their divine domains and have destroyed each other. Nought but a handful of kitchen gods survive, without power, without any force beyond that which can be found in nature, among natural things ...'

'How do you know all this?' asked Kikamana.

'It comes to my tongue.'

'Just like that? From nowhere?'

'From *everywhere*,' he corrected. 'It is my destiny to speak the word, as it was Craig's to release the beast. We are both creatures of two worlds, children of a third culture. We have special duties on this earth.'

'Tell us more,' said Kikamana.

'Now will begin a time of discovery, slow at first, about all the natural wonders around us.'

'No more magic,' repeated Boy-girl with sadness in her voice. 'Won't that make the world a dull place?'

'Not necessarily,' replied Urgan, 'for the earth has many secrets and we know but a handful of them yet. There will be revelations to make us gasp in amazement.'

'But everything will be boringly predictable!' she said.

At that moment it began to drizzle, the fine summer rain sweeping in from the sea. A few moments previously it had been bright sunshine. Now the light was dimming above them, as the sun was swallowed by high clouds.

'There's always the weather,' said Urgan, 'if you're looking for unpredictability. No one will ever be able to cure the weather of its spontaneous character. If you want change, look to the skies.'

A distant rumble of thunder came from some black clouds over the mountains. There was a flash of light, a brightness deep within the dark folds of the heavens. A faraway thunderstorm was in progress, muted by the miles between. Were these the last dying gasps of the now feeble gods? Were they stumbling over each other, flailing blindly with weak arms, falling to oblivion as each cancelled the other out? Or were these natural phenomena, simply a change in the weather?

And was the One-God looking down at the fading light of lesser deities as he handed over responsibility for the world to ordinary mortals?

PART TEN

In the wake of the great whale

1

The evening before the battle an Angle envoy arrived in the Celt camp asking if they would ally themselves with the northerners to fight the Oceanians.

The envoy was sent away with a flea in his ear.

Later in the night, as was the custom, the Celts sent three messengers asking for earth, fire and water. If these three were given it meant the Angles were prepared to negotiate a peace settlement on equal terms with the allies. The envoy had been returned unharmed to his people, so the Celts believed their messengers would be treated with the same courtesy. They were mistaken. Normally it would have been so, but unfortunately the present chief-of-chiefs of the Angles was a man to whom integrity and honour meant very little.

The first messenger was thrown into a pit of starving wolves and told to take his earth from there.

The second messenger was thrown down a well and was left there to drown.

The third was cast into a blazing bonfire.

When Cormac-the-Venomous heard of this violation of an unwritten code, for messengers were supposed to be ambassadors and immune, he vowed at all costs to kill the leader of the Angles, one Drathvarn from a region known as Merkia, a man known for his cruelty even amongst his own people.

The next morning a great army of the Angles came down from the north, the dawn spread behind them like a vast cloak.

On long leashes before them, six to one burly handler, ran the human dogs of war. Several hundred. These were the Jutes, naked and covered in woad symbols, running on all fours, snapping and snarling, their long blond manes hanging down over their shoulders. Every so often one of them would rise up on its back legs and let out a terrible scream of fury, only to be whipped down again into the animal position by the handlers' assistants. These human dogs with their long nails, their dirty teeth, and their insane appearance, were indeed a frightening vanguard of the huge army.

Next came the drummers and shrill-whistlers, and the men whirling bullroarers, and the horn-blowers and trumpet-blarers, marching under a variety of banners which represented the many different clans of Angles and Celts from all over the near and far north. This was a pageant, which the northerners loved. They enjoyed spectacle. Their bagpipes, smaller and different from the southern Celtic pipes, squealed and wailed along the line.

Some of the banners and streamers had seen better times, were merely flying in tatters, but it added to the colour of the second line, and the standards with their horse skulls, goat skulls and even human skulls, providing a touch of white grimness amongst the many-hued flags.

Behind the banners came the foot-warriors, on a wide front which stretched across the valley from wall to wall. Amongst them were the lesser chiefs, with their bodyguards and companions, their cloaks pinned to their shoulders with burnished bronze brooches that gleamed in the sun. These foot-warriors were armed with pikes and spears, swords and maces, bows and slingshots. The clatter of their iron weapons, and odd bits of armour, added an eerie undernote to the cries of the Jute dogs and the sound of martial music.

To the right and left were the horsemen, too undisciplined to be called even irregular cavalry. These were mainly noblemen – thanes with their sons and grandsons – the only warriors rich enough to own horses. Here and there was a wealthy crop-grower on a plough-horse, sitting several hands higher than the frisky mounts of the thanes, looking awkward and rustic. In the main the horses were protected with thick blankets and sacking, held on by leather straps, around their heads and flanks. Some wore wooden masks, with holes through which to see. Many of the horses were painted in the same way as the Jute dogs.

At the back of this enormous army of Angles came a wave of men dragging monstrous wicker and straw animals on wheeled platforms. These were the druids in their hooded habits of unbleached wool. Their faces were hidden as they pulled in their harnesses, tugging giant representations of pigs, goats, dogs, sheep, horses and men. It was the sight of these beast-shaped pyres, fashioned for burning clutches of live prisoners after the battle, which sent a chill through the waiting Celts and Oceanians. Many were the warriors who swore an oath to themselves that they would rather die on the battlefield than be taken alive and roasted in a wicker basket.

'Steady,' said Cormac to his warriors on the right of the field, 'remember we have a plan.'

It was the first time the Celts had sat down the night before a battle and actually discussed strategy and tactics. Normally they just found a piece of good ground and threw themselves into the enemy from there, hacking and chopping until it was evident which side was winning. The Angles were much the same, though they were more organized in their hierarchy and ranks: their men fought in columns, rather than as individuals, but without any set goal except to annihilate the foe.

In fact, the allies had been working all night, digging a wide shallow trench across the battleground. The trench had now been laid with a bed of grasses and kindling, on top of which was strewn a layer of charcoal. When the Angles had first been sighted, Celtic brand-carriers lit the grasses in the trench.

The enemy approached. Charcoal glowed red hot between the two armies. A swathe of blistering embers five strides in width crossed the broad valley.

The many tribes of Angles and their allies, which included two tribes of the northern Celts, stopped dead three hundred paces away. Their martial music drifted away into silence. They stood stock-still and stared at the enemy they had come to fight. For a time all that could be heard was the champing of the horses. The only movement to be seen that of the fluttering banners. The southern Celts and their Oceanian allies stood and waited, equally calm. Now was the time for a few moments of quiet reflection, for studying the ground and the foe, before the bloody battle began in earnest.

Craig tried to imagine what the Angles were thinking: what could be going through their heads at the scene before them.

They would see their old enemies, the vast majority of Celtic tribes, waiting to settle ancient scores.

But they would also see a dark-skinned multitude, hosts of brown bodies, tens of thousands of strangers from who knew where? Some of these defiant-looking strangers had tattooed faces, all had painted bodies. The brown-skinned men carried strange weapons in their hands – black iron-wood clubs of twisted and gnarled design – swords with jagged-toothed edges from sawfish – bows of another shape – tall spears and short spears with glittering mother-of-pearl points – shark-toothed daggers, stingray-backbone daggers, daggers of every description – shields of some curious matting and uncommon-looking wood – all wielded by broad and savage-looking warriors of an unknown region, some with black woolly hair, some with black straight hair.

The Angles would study the unusual clothes, would see dogskin cloaks of white and brown, tall elaborately feathered helmets of fantastic colours. Over there stood some men with bones through their noses, with grass skirts around their waists. Over here grinning warriors with teeth filed to points for eating human flesh. At the back, tall and lean men with fierce blazing eyes. At the front, short stocky men with wild expressions.

And these dark warriors, it was said, had travelled thousands of miles by canoe simply to fight! Here were peoples the like of which the Angles had never seen. A people who appeared to the pale-skinned warriors of Engaland like demons from a terrifying nightmare. All their most dreadful imaginings stood there waiting to do battle: creatures from hell.

The word ran along the lines of Angles.

'*Yfelnyss!*'

Wickedness!

The Celts had conjured up demons from the underworld to assist them in their fight.

Craig could imagine the ripple of terror which ran through the Angle army like fear through a herd of deer on seeing a pack of starving wolves for the first time.

Yet they stood their ground, unflinching. Not one man turned and ran before this awful sight. If there were demons to fight, so be it. They would fight demons. Send in the giants, the dragons and hobgoblins too, if needs must. A fight was a fight and glory waited for a warrior, whether he lived or died, so long as he did not *run*.

Yet there were more surprises in store for the Angles.

Suddenly a cry went up from one of the brown-skinned demons. There was movement amongst the newcomers. They began to dance, but such a dance had never before been witnessed by any Angle or Jute. There was a stamping of the ground as dark warriors moved in unison, crouching, marching forward slowly, threateningly. Then they showed their tongues, flat against their chins, and their eyes rolled most horribly. They chanted loudly in ugly voices as they made their vile gestures. They jabbed with their spears, killing an invisible enemy. They enacted the defeat of the foe before the battle even began.

This time the Angles wavered, glanced at each other along the lines, found it hard to hold their places.

Fortunately at that moment the order was given to advance again and the music wailed back to life, the earth shuddered with the stamp of tens of thousands of feet, of thousands of hooves, of hundreds of wheels.

Fifty strides from the trench the dog-handlers let loose the savage, mindless Jutes. These human beasts came hurtling forward now they were off their leashes. They howled and snarled like a pack of wolves, their great manes flying in the wind, their eyes blazing. When they reached the trench they ran straight on to the coals, only to scream in agony and limp back with burned hands and feet towards their masters. The handlers, ready with their whips, urged the Jutes back over the coals. It was while they were so engaged that allied archers began to pick them off, one by one, thus ending a lifetime of misery.

The Jute dogs stood no chance; caught on the coals, or between their handlers and the trench, they were cut down swiftly by accurate fire from the allies. Both Craig and Hupa felt for the poor creatures. They recalled their own time as wild dogs and considered themselves lucky they were not among these canine Jutes now being slaughtered in a rain of arrows.

Hupa and Craig were not riding their horses in the battle, but had loaned them to some Celts. They were not proficient enough to fight on horseback yet. Once they had seen how a Celt rode the same beast, picking up a small nut on the point of a sword while hanging from the side of the horse, they realized how inexperienced they were at riding. There were Celts who could ride standing on the horse's rump, or under its belly, or sliding behind on their heels in the dust while holding its tail.

No, the two Oceanians were still rank amateurs.

At a signal from Kieto, Fijian and Samoan firewalkers then crossed the coals on their bare feet. Once on the other side they attacked the dog-handlers and the first line of Angles, engaging them with ironwood double-handed clubs. Shark-toothed weapons ripped horrible wounds into the shoulders and faces of the Angles, who fought back with pike and spear. However, no sooner had the Fijians and Samoans struck, than they had raced back over the coals again, leaving the dead behind them.

'That'll make 'em wail,' cried a delighted Cormac. 'They're not used to this kind of warfare.'

And indeed the Angle front let up a great cry of anger and disbelief on finding their enemy had wafted away like smoke to safety on the other side of the blazing trench. Some of the Angles tried running over the coals, but the rags and skins with which they bound their feet caught fire. Any that did make it across, crippled of foot, were instantly attacked by the waiting Celts. While they were in disarray the Fijians and Samoans made one or two more forays across the river of fire, reducing the numbers in the front ranks by several score.

The Angles were not used to these kind of losses so early in the battle. The chiefs in the second line called to one another for advice. Drathvarn, their war chief, who had placed himself amongst the horsemen on the left flank, screamed at his warriors to get off their fat arses and wade into the Celts and their dark allies. For a while there was some confusion in the ranks of the Angles, as men from the rear pushed those in front forward onto the hot coals, and these unfortunates turned and like wounded bulls began to bore their way back through the mass of people bringing up the rear.

Eventually men in armour and on horseback began to surge forwards, kicking the live coals out of the trench and scattering them abroad. At another signal from Kieto, Rarotongan warriors rushed forward and threw coconut shells full of vegetable and shark oil, commodities of which the Oceanians had plenty, covering the men in armour. The live coals did the rest, setting light to the oil. Soon there were thanes staggering around like burning torches, screaming as they cooked inside their metal suits. Those on horseback found their mounts bolting in blind panic. Some galloped into the Celts who pulled the riders from their saddles and gleefully cut them down.

Now that the Angles were confused, Cormac gave a signal and the ranks of the allies parted to let through horsemen dragging wet reed mats. These were raced forward and cut loose over the trench of hot charcoal. Once in place Celts and Oceanians began to stream over the mats to engage the dazed Angles. The Celts went for the mass of men to fight iron with iron, while the Oceanians, who had been briefed by the Celt clan chiefs, went for the leaders amongst the Angles. Like the Celts in their earlier battles with the Oceanians, the Angle chiefs were incensed to find themselves the sole targets of the Oceanians, who clubbed them mercilessly to the ground.

Craig found himself in the thick of the fight, using an obsidian canoe breaker to smash wooden shields aside, allowing his men to rush in and finish off the foe. Urgan was not in the fight. He had told a disgusted Hupa that he could not fight in case he killed his own father or brother, whose names and titles he did not know. Hupa was upset, though realizing that Urgan was an Angle, albeit from just above the border. She was commanding her archers, her Whakatane, who were on the right flank, firing arrows into the oncoming horsemen.

Once the Angles had rallied, however, some fierce fighting took place in the centre line. Spears were used to drive back the Celts and Oceanians, where they overlapped on the battlefront, and there was a threat of the allies being overrun at that point, of the Angles breaking through in a great wedge. The front centre line of the allies began to crack and crumble. Cormac's and Kieto's warriors were being rolled aside as the wedge of veteran Angles drove through the gap, forcing the allies to part like water falling either side of a canoe.

At this point Kieto himself brought forward a new wave of prepared warriors. These consisted of a mix of Tongans, Hivans and Celts. The Celts were placed so that they each had an Oceanian on their right, bearing a gata waka club. The Oceanian with the club would smash aside an Angle's shield and the Celt next to him would then make a thrust with his sword at the unguarded midriff of the Angle.

The gata waka clubs were wielded with great skill. The Tongans and Hivans had practised with such weapons all their lives. Sometimes the club stroke was so hard and accurate it would spin the enemy soldier completely round, so that his back was exposed to the sword thrust. Soon the Angles began to fall back under these tactics, not ever having experienced such fighting methods before. Finally, first one, then another broke from the pack and began running. Before long they were streaming away like a comet's tail, fleeing to the far end of the valley where it funnelled them out into open country.

The enemy horsemen then tried to outflank the allied army, but Cormac had chosen his ground well. The walls of the u-shaped valley assisted in preventing any pincer movement by these riders. This natural defence had been reinforced on both sides of the glen, where the allies had placed tree trunks horizontally, their ends supported by shoulder-high rocks. Sharpened stakes had been driven into the ground between the barriers to close any gaps.

Knots of archers fired from behind these barriers, which were effective in preventing the horsemen from sweeping round the flanks of the allies. Unwilling to risk their precious mounts over such formidable terrain, some horsemen tried to chop their way through the throng of foot-warriors, only to be dragged off their saddles and clubbed to death.

Drathvarn and his bodyguards were attacked by Celt horsemen, hand-picked men who knew how to use a mace or broadsword from the saddle. Soon the best of Drathvarn's companions had been whittled away, leaving the way open to the chief himself. Many of them had fought bravely, but they were battling on a narrow front, the bulk of their army behind them. The spearpoint cavalry tactics of Cormac ensured that they only engaged two or three foes at a time and this frustrated them.

When he saw that he was being defeated, the Merkian chief, Drathvarn, turned his horse. He tried to ride at full gallop to the end of the valley, mindless of his own fallen men over whom his mount's hooves were trampling. Cormac on his own mount saw the chief-of-chiefs of the Angles defecting. Bareback on his charger, he gave chase, the hair on the heads of former enemies flying as he rode after his hated adversary. Cormac's sturdy little steed caught the fleeing chief. There was the quick flash of a broadsword and Drathvarn's head bounced in the dust. Another trophy to decorate the mane of a Celt's horse.

Drathvarn's steed went riding on, a headless corpse at the reins, blood founts spurting from the open neck.

Now the advancing allied warriors, the front ranks at a run, had reached the wicker figures at the end of the valley. The druids had gone, fled when they saw the first of the deserters pass them in a panic. Their wicker cages, built to hold dozens of prisoners, were dragged back down the valley, towards the allied encampment. Later they were used to burn the bodies of the Angle dead, including the remains of Drathvarn, which were found slammed against a tree at the head of the valley. His horse had gone. Either it had run off or had been taken by one of Drathvarn's own men as transport to the north.

At the end of the day the Angles had been routed. They drifted up to their homeland in knots. In truth, many of them had not wanted to fight at all, but being serfs had had little choice in the matter. Now that it was all over they were anxious to get back to their families, to the little plots of land they worked, to their hunting and fishing. For once the Celts had won the day. It smarted, but it could be borne.

Cormac was ecstatic. 'By the Mossy Stone of Drummock Moor, we gave them a whupping today, eh, lads? They won't forget that one in a hurry.' Then he turned to Kieto and added bluntly, 'When are ye leaving?'

Kieto, when he heard this, laughed gravely. 'These Celts are curt people, aren't they?' he said to Craig. 'No standing on ceremony. Just out with it.'

Kieto affirmed that they would be gone very soon. They had one more duty to perform. Once that was done, then the Oceanians would sail away from the Land-of-Mists and hopefully never have to return.

'What duty?' asked Cormac, suspiciously.

'A funeral,' replied the one-handed Kieto, enigmatically. 'A funeral for a friend.'

This sounded rather strange, since there were many funerals to perform – or rather one great funeral for those who had fallen on the field of battle. However, Kieto told the Celt that the funeral he had in mind was one which would take place after the burial of the war dead.

'This is for the death of a great hero.'

There was much feasting and dancing in the camps of the Celts. The Oceanians had their own celebrations. The Hivans and Fijians, and some from other islands, had roasted a few of the Angle chiefs. Somehow they did not think the Celts would approve of cannibalism, even if it was ritualized and done for a very good reason. Only chieftains who had fought hard and courageously were cooked and eaten. No one was interested in weaklings and cowards. The idea was to increase one's manna, not dilute it. Brave men only were worth eating.

Once the battle was over of course, the Oceanians had to have their tapu removed by the priests, otherwise they might damage themselves and others by carrying an unnecessary burden. This having been done, some Oceanians went off to the camps of the Celts, to seek out men they had fought with that day, and give them thanks for timely interventions on their behalf. Celts were drifting into the pa, also on the same errand. Lives had been saved on both sides, often at great risk.

Even though they had been allies in a great battle, one which would be retold as part of both their histories, the Celts and the Oceanians still did not fully trust each other. Kieto had sent for the ocean-going canoes, which had spent the summer moored in the harbour of a small island some way off from the mainland. It was time to return to the islands in the sun. Most Oceanians were by now very homesick.

The joy of battle was one thing: the feeling of bliss on being told they were going home was quite another.

The day following the battle, when all was quiet and people in the pa were recovering from the effects of last night's kava, Urgan went looking for Craig. He found him sitting with Hupa outside a hut. Instead of approaching the pair, he caught Craig's eye and motioned with his head. Craig raised his eyebrows in surprise, but then got up and went to where Urgan was standing, in order to listen to him.

Urgan seemed a little embarrassed, especially with Hupa's eyes on him. But he spoke up bravely.

'Is – is Hupa married, or betrothed at all? We haven't spoken about such things a great deal. I mean, if you yourself have some interest in her ...'

Craig shook his head in bewilderment. 'I've told you she's a maiden. I myself am married with children. Why are you going over all this again?'

'Well, we were travelling companions before,' replied the nervous man. 'Things are different when you are wandering together. Sometimes things are said to impress, rather than to reveal truths. So – so she is free, is she?'

'Why would you think otherwise, if you've been told so?'

'In fairyland no one tells the truth. The whole place is buzzing with lies. Fairies are like that. They love to boast, they like to make things up – creativity they call it – and they love embellishing things. A fairy will never tell the truth when the lie is more colourful. It's difficult for me to get out of that frame of mind. I have been an elf for most of my life, after all. It's difficult to change.'

'You're a man now. A man has his honour to think of. You should throw off these fairy ways.'

Urgan looked shame-faced. 'I know.'

Craig did not take his eyes off the tall, handsome young man before him, but called to Hupa.

'Come over here a minute,' he said. 'Someone has something to say to you.'

Hupa, scrubbed and shining, her bow over her shoulder and her quiver of arrows at her hip, looked every part the huntress, the fleet-of-foot maiden who runs through the forest, her boyish beauty enchanting any watchers.

'What?' she said, coming up to the men. 'Yes, Urgan?'

'I – er – I wondered – that is – what is it like in Oceania – the thing is see ...'

'He wants to marry you,' said Craig, bluntly.

'He does?' cried Hupa, her eyebrows shooting up. She went bright scarlet, then added a soft, 'Oh.'

Urgan was also as red as an island sunset. 'Well?'

Hupa smiled and looked bashful. 'All right then.'

'You will marry me?' yelled Urgan, triumphantly.

'If my father allows it.'

'Ah,' said the young man, 'I knew there would be a catch – of course, you're Kieto's daughter. Only the most important man amongst the Oceanians at this time. Only the warlord, the leader of the expedition ...'

'I think I can speak to him for you,' said Craig, 'and I'm sure he'll give his consent. In the meantime, I congratulate both of you.' Craig looked at Hupa – a long lingering look – then gravely kissed her cheek. 'You're getting a prize here, Urgan. One of the most coveted maidens on this earth. Treat her well. And you, Hupa, do the same with him. The time for your tantrums is over. Time to become a woman.'

'I'm not giving up my Whakatane,' she said, firmly.

'Wouldn't expect you to,' replied Urgan. 'I don't want a wife who does nothing but cook and raise children.'

'Good,' she said, 'because you wouldn't be getting one of those. And I couldn't live here.' She shivered. 'The summers are bad enough – the winters would kill me.'

'Have no concern. I want to come with you. I wish to be the first Angle to live amongst the Oceanians. I want to be the Seumas of the northern tribes.'

She smiled, taking his hand. 'It's settled then.'

Craig went off to find Kieto and persuade him that his new prospective son-in-law was a good man to have in the family. On the way he collected Boy-girl to assist him, and the pair of them shared Kieto's basket late that afternoon.

Kieto was resistant to the idea at first. Urgan was not even a Celt. He was an Angle. Kieto felt he knew the Celts, through his long association with Seumas and Dorcha, but he knew nothing of the Angles. Perhaps they had certain practices which were not savoury? What did they do with their dead? How did they treat their relatives? How did they raise their babies? All these questions needed answering.

'People are much the same everywhere,' said Craig. 'They have cultural differences, but love can overcome such things. So long as they are basically good people in their heart – and I believe Urgan would pass in that respect. He's a brave man, and sound of limb and mind, and what's more he was not raised amongst the Angles, but amongst fairies.'

'I think you should trust your daughter to choose,' said Boy-girl. 'Let's face it, Kieto, she is not a typical young woman. Whoever she chooses will be out of the ordinary. This Urgan has proved himself a sensible man and was a good friend to Craig and Hupa when they were lost in this Land-of-Mists. I think you could do much worse. Some wild Hawaiian, or a Rapanuian who lives far from Rarotonga.'

In the end, Kieto gave his consent and Boy-girl went off to tell the lovers the good news, while Craig went to seek out Kikamana, to make the wedding arrangements.

Hupa was after all an ariki.

The young maiden later expressed only one sadness – that her brother Kapu was not there to see her married to this lovely young man.

Once the arrangements were settled with the high priestess, Craig asked the Farseeing-virgin, 'Is magic really gone? Are the gods really dead?'

'Yes.'

'Did I do that?' he said, feeling guilty. 'Did I rob the world of magic?'

'You had no choice in the matter – you were merely Io's instrument,' said Kikamana. 'We'll learn to do without magic – besides, there will always be little pockets, small secret places which the beast has missed – and we can certainly do without the petty squabblings of the old gods.'

'Do you know any more about this land? Do they have an Io who has survived?'

'I am told so, by a Celt woman who knows. She says the One-God religion is spreading rapidly. There have been people called monks who travelled through, but now one of them has come to settle in the land of the Celts. His name is Columba. Another, by the name of Cedd, has landed in Engaland. He has built a meeting house out of stones from an ancient wall on the mouth of the Blackwater River. The name of this house escapes me, but be assured the Angles and Celts are well served.'

Craig said he hoped so, but it was going to take some getting used to, living without gods of thunder, lightning, sea, earth and sky.

'They are still there, only now absorbed into one form, into the single creator we call Io.'

'And what of our ancestors, our atua?' asked Craig.

'They have accepted the change, just as we must.'

That evening a group of painted Picts arrived at the pa and asked for Craig. They said they were his cousins. Craig went out to meet them, men and women from the Blackwater clan. He grasped their shoulders as he greeted them, one by one, and placed his cheek next to theirs. They were as shy with him as he was with them. These were his father's relations – *his* relations – and though the meeting was awkward it was rewarding for both him and the people he met. Common blood flowed in their veins and obviously this created a bond between them. They saw Blackwater clan likenesses in him and he was amazed how familiar they appeared to him.

When they left he gave them gifts – scrimshaws carved by Seumas – and they handed him presents in return. One bright-eyed young woman who had Seumas's eyes, nose and chin, gave him a special hug and was reprimanded by her father for showing too much affection. The girl made a face behind her father's back and then smiled at Craig as if to say, 'These old people and their conventions, they don't understand, do they?'

The whole episode was a marvellous experience for Craig, who had known but one member of his family until now.

2

Before the Oceanians left the mountain country of Land-of-Mists, that place where water drops in veils from high places and no matter where a person stands he can hear water running, they had one more duty to perform. The burial of the heart of Seumas was the funeral about which Kieto had spoken to Cormac. It was a ceremony Kieto was determined to carry out with all the rites due to a great hero: one such as Kupe himself had been given.

A spot was chosen on top of the cliffs where Seumas had first been seen climbing by a seven-year-old Kieto those many years ago. It was a grassy knoll with a natural quartz headstone upon which the first rays of the morning sun fell with a sparkling lustre. This rock would be the only marker to the grave. It overlooked the wild grey-green seas into which Seumas and Dorcha had fallen, to be plucked from the tall waves by Kupe and carried off to Oceania. It was a place where the mist hung continually around the crags and the smell of salt-spray, the sound of seabirds, were ever present.

'Will he not want his marker to be next to Dorcha's, on Rarotonga?' asked a worried Craig. 'Should they not be together?'

'This is merely the home of the heart, which is an earthly relic,' said Kieto. 'You can be sure that wherever the essence of Seumas finally rests, it will be with Dorcha's. If he is not already with her, you can be sure his spirit is planning the journey which will bring them together.'

Next, Kikamana, Boy-girl, Polahiki, Craig and Kieto blackened their faces, cut off their hair and gashed their bodies with sharks' teeth. These five were the chief mourners. They donned a tapa-bark garment known as a pakoko, made of cloth which had been dyed red with the sap of candle-nut trees, then dipped in the black mud of taro-growing soil. The pakoko gave off an obnoxious smell, symbolic of the decaying state of the dead person. Finally they wore crowns made of fern, which had been singed by fire at the edges to produce a reddish look.

On the first day of the funeral the mourning dances began and traditionally no cloth-beating took place during such a time. The goddess Mueu, who gave cloth-beating to the world, had a cloth-flail the strokes of which normally dispensed death to mortals at the end of their natural lifespan. Mueu was present at the funeral of every great person and to beat ordinary cloth in her presence would have caused offence. Old habits died hard.

The Celts in the surrounding countryside watched these funeral games with great interest, wondering who it was that was to be buried, for it seemed that all the peoples of Oceania, to a man, woman and child, were taking part. There was sadness and grief in the air, like a tangible thing, pervading every corner of the land of the Albannachs.

When the Celts learned it was one of themselves, a man of little significance being a bird-strangler and an egg-collector, nothing more, they were astonished. Why, the Blackwater clan to which the man had belonged, was a small inferior cliff-top tribe, pinched and worn by poverty. They had few notable deeds to their credit, nor heroes to the clan's name. Traditionally they lived by plundering the tidal reaches, the shoreline with its meagre offerings. It was a mystery to the Celts that such a man would be given so great an honour. Why, it amounted to raising up a beachcomber or a crab-fisher and making him a god!

On the fifth day the embalmed heart wrapped in pandanus leaves was carried on a litter and placed for a time on a stone ahu built specially for the purpose, while the Oceanians crowded round in their thousands, passing the ahu and touching its stone uprights, wailing and tearing on their hair in a show of terrible grief. The Blackwater clan, who came to see this extraordinary interment of one of their number, got so caught up in the general hysteria that they too began sorrowing and lamenting for a man they had actually forgotten a few days after he had disappeared.

The other Celtic tribes gathered on the surrounding hills, absolutely astounded by the spectacle. That a scruffy cliff-climber whom no one had heard of before now should warrant such a ceremony of mourning was incredible. What had this man done to gain such adoration from the brown-skinned nations of Oceania?

'He was brought to us by a hero,' they were told, 'and he became such himself.'

But how? What did he do? What were his deeds?

'Manifold heroic deeds were his – battles against Hivans – the slaying of the Poukai bird – the slaying of a terrible taniwha – the tricking of Matuku the demi-god – voyages of renown – many, many deeds.'

An *egg-collector* did all this?

'This and much more. He was beloved. He is missed.'

Well, it just showed you, you could be born a nothing-man in a nothing-clan and still get to the top.

The heart was then carried with great ceremony, accompanied by songs and dances specially composed for this occasion alone, over the landscape to the grave. Once the heart of Seumas had been interred, the chief mourners remained behind, exhausted by their grief, to sleep in a rugged cave overlooking the sea. There Kieto, Kikamana and Craig sang the final song to Seumas-the-Black, to the sound of flutes played by Boy-girl and Polahiki.

Solo	This is a day for mourning, he has gone out, never to return to his house again.
Chorus	A new house will be built for him on Rarotonga, a house of fine stone, small, a house for spirits, where he may live with Dorcha for ever.
Solo	Whence came this great man?
Chorus	He came from the Land-of-Mists, found by sailing just left of the setting sun. He fell from his cliff into the arms of Kupe, who bore him to our islands, skimming the seas on voyager barks, over Tangaroa's wide ocean.
Solo	Where has he gone?
Chorus	He has gone to the place of dazzling light.
Solo	Where is his netherland?
Chorus	No man or woman knows, for it is in the land of ghosts, but he is well and happy.

When the dawn rays struck the cave from the south-east, the mourners prepared to leave the last burial place of Seumas-the-Black's heart. Just as they began to drift away a mad horseman came galloping out of the mist. He had a wounded foot and his right hand was missing. In his left he wielded a broadsword. With a terrible scream of fury he bore down on Craig, who stood not far from his father's resting stone.

'It's Douglass Barelegs,' cried a voice from the crowd.

Others took up the cry of the Scotsman's name as he swept through an aisle of mourners and Celt spectators, bearing down on Craig. Divots flew from his mount's unshod hooves, as the pair drummed over the peaty ground, weaving occasionally to avoid standing rocks. The wicked edge of the warrior's honed sword flashed blindingly in the sunlight. On Douglass's face was a look of determination. He was going to destroy his father's enemy, come what may.

'Kill him!' came the voice of Cormac, out of the crowds. 'A whole sheep for the man who kills Barelegs.'

Archers from amongst both the Celts and Oceanians began firing arrows at the fierce horseman who charged down through the avenue of watchers. Arrows began to skim past the grim rider, but none hit him. Closer and closer he came to his target, who stood helpless and unarmed by the quartz stone.

'Die, Blackwater bastard!' came the cry from Douglass Barelegs' lips. Triumph was in his eyes as he swished the iron blade, making ready to decapitate his foe. Mist swirled around him like a white cloak billowing in the wind. 'Flee, ye craven son of a sow's runt – flee!'

But Craig stood his ground, having nowhere to run.

Punga, on seeing the certain death of his charge, Craig, struggled to remain in the light for just one last act. He was fading to darkness quickly, but he managed with one last great effort to rouse the spirit of the father, Seumas, from his grave.

'*Help your son!*' cried the God of Ugly Creatures. '*Leap up, destroy the enemy!*'

Once the call had been made, Punga became as fine mist on the moorland, as night darkness on a hill, as spume on the great ocean. Like the other gods, great and small, he was now only a part of this world in natural form. Supernature was lost.

Seumas, on hearing Punga's call, woke and thrust himself into the world of the living. Fierce and terrible now that his strength had been restored to him in death, he rose from his grave sword in hand, with a mighty roar. The old warrior was three times the size he had been as a mortal man and his fury three times that which it had been on earth. There he stood before Douglass Barelegs, his visage awesome to behold, his fearsome anger unquenchable.

Douglass Barelegs saw and recognized his immortal foe and knew great terror as his own death rushed into his face.

Something happened which was unaccountable to the watchers. Some said a dark shape rose up swiftly out of the turf in front of the gravestone to loom menacingly over horse and rider. Others maintained they saw nothing but a thickening of the mist around the craggy rock. Something strange did happen to be sure but whether it was supernatural or commonplace was a matter for argument amongst the watchers. It was certain that Craig saw nothing at all, because his eyes were on the rider and horse and not on the headstone beside him.

Whatever the cause, the result was that the horse checked abruptly and swerved. Douglass Barelegs went hurtling from the beast's back. Had both his legs been sound he might have been able to grip the flanks of his steed and remain on the horse's back. But Craig had robbed him of a foot.

His neck then somehow became entangled in the reins. When the weight of his flying body had stretched the leathers to their full length, he was curtly strangled. A sound came from his throat not unlike that made by a fulmar bird being throttled by the hands of a Pict. It was a harsh guttural noise which was stemmed abruptly when the body reached full stretch.

As the body was whipped back – jerked violently on the end of the reins – all heard the snapping of a neckbone.

The sound was loud in the morning's silence.

Then the frightened horse thundered off into the mist, weaving amongst the crags. The corpse of Douglass Barelegs was dragged, bouncing, over the uneven ground. Finally, all was still again. The silence was broken aptly by a Pict.

'Good bloody riddance,' cried the voice of Cormac-the-Venomous. 'May the bastard freeze his balls off on the bleak wastes of Ifurin.'

The show over, the mourners and spectators continued on their journeys homewards, reflecting on the supernatural laws of justice which reached out from beyond the grave. Douglass had not been well liked and his loss meant little to the Celts who had seen him die. It had simply been an exciting performance which had ended reasonably satisfactorily.

The Oceanians, Craig included, left the scene and went back to the pa, walking through the mist-covered heather, seeing the deer start from coverts, watching the eagles soar overhead, hearing the foxes go to ground. Some things they would miss about this land: the huge variety of wildlife, the differentness of the vegetation, the strange vastness of the rugged landscape. Other things they would be pleased to leave behind: the chill air, the coming winter, the greyness and the misty regions.

It had been a great adventure.

Exactly one week later the ocean-going canoes put out to sea, bearing the Oceanians, a man who used to be an elf, and three horses. One craft remained beached until the others were well out on the waves. This was the canoe of Kieto, who along with others – Craig, Boy-girl, Kikamana, Hupa, Urgan, Prince Daggan and his wife Siko – were the last to leave the foreign shore. When the canoe was ready to go, Kieto turned to Cormac, who had come with a band of warriors to watch the Oceanians leave.

'Come to make sure we go?' asked Kieto, through Craig.

'Something like that,' grunted Cormac. 'One can never be certain of a thing unless one sees it happen.'

Kieto nodded and went to rub noses with the Celt chieftain, who backed away in horror.

'None o' that,' cried Cormac. 'Would ye make a woman of me?'

Kieto smiled in understanding.

Boy-girl said privately to her companions, 'It would take more than a nose-rub to turn that heap of dung and hair into a divine creature like myself.'

Kikamana laughed for the first time in years.

The Oceanians then boarded their vessel. At the last minute, Kieto went into the deck-hut and brought out the greenstone club with which he had slain Guirk. He handed it to Prince Daggan.

'You and your wife take this to Cormac, as a parting gift for joining with us in battle against the Angles.'

Daggan looked surprised. 'Why us?'

'It is appropriate,' said Kieto. 'A royal family, a man and his wife, together. Bear it between you. Give it a sense of occasion. You know how to do these things. There is no one else on board of real noble lineage. I myself am not an ariki born, not like the two of you. I lack the breeding.'

'Quite so,' said Prince Daggan. 'My dear?'

'As Kieto says, it was a fishwife who gave him birth,' she replied, with a smile on her lips. 'Beautiful gifts should be given by those who appreciate such things.'

The pair then stepped into the shallows and were solemnly handed the greenstone club. They bore it with an air of ceremonious pomp towards the Celts. Cormac stepped forward as if he had been expecting this present and waited for them to reach him. He took the club and then turned to hold it aloft, while his men cheered. Then he turned to face the sea again and raised his fist in a salute to the departing canoe. Daggan and Siko, on turning around, gave out a yell of despair.

The tipairua was now well out on the waves, sailing around the headland.

'They've left us behind!' he shrieked. 'Siko, they're abandoning us.'

The unfortunate Oceanian couple left the grinning Celts and raced to the top of the cliff, hoping to catch the canoe on the other side of the headland, but when they reached the heights, they stood there breathless, watching in helpless frustrated agony as the tipairua headed out to sea.

'Why?' screamed Siko, into the wind, her voice sounding little different from the gulls which swooped over the waves. 'Why?'

'Treachery!' came back the answer. 'Murder!'

Daggan sank to the floor, staring in disbelief as the twin crab-claw sailed craft dipped and rose on its way to meet the rest of the fleet out on the ocean. Siko stood there, however, with the wind whipping through her tangled locks. There was a defiant look on her face. As always, she was the strong one.

'They found out, somehow,' she said. 'Cormac probably told them. And having found out we were traitors, they guessed we were responsible for Kapu's death. Well, we've been banished, for life it seems. Unless you want to make a canoe and do the journey on our own ...'

She looked down at her pitiful partner, who was weeping tears into the Albainn turf.

'No, I don't think so. You're no Kupe, my husband. I guess we're stuck here for the rest of our natural lives.'

'Where will we live?' he wailed. 'How will we survive the winter? I hear it's cold enough to make water go hard.'

'We'll fashion a croft, like these damn natives,' she replied, 'and you'll dig peat to make our fires to keep us warm. You'll learn to hunt deer, fight marauders, and make wolfskin coats for the both of us. We'll survive.'

'I don't think I want to survive – not in a place like this – it'll be utter misery.'

She stared at this pathetic man of hers and then made a decision.

'Let's die then,' she said, shrugging. 'I'll go first.'

With that she stepped over the edge of the cliff and fell head-first onto the rugged rocks below. Her body lay there for a while, as the waves lashed it, and was then dragged out into the maw of the sea. There it floated, carried by the currents and tides, perhaps bound for the distant islands of Oceania.

Daggan was left on top of the cliff, afraid to live, yet afraid to die. He was still there, a hunched motionless figure, when the Celts walked back to their crofts from the beach. They stared but made no move to aid him. He was not one they would wish to assist. No one likes a traitor – even those on whose behalf the man has carried out his treachery.

Kieto's tipairua caught up with the rest of the fleet. They were island bound. Their hearts were light, but they travelled homeward with a sense of loss in their hearts. The news from the priests was that the old gods were no more – that they were going home accompanied by only one god – the Great One, Io, who dwelt above the Twelfth Level of the roof of voyaging.

Craig especially felt the death of the god Punga deeply. Would Io have time for them all: every individual whose problems and troubles sometimes seemed infinite? Each god had been responsible for one or at most a few aspects of life. Now Io was responsible for *everything*.

Punga himself had watched personally over all ugly creatures: had had time for a little girl, a middle child, who had been not been born as pretty as her brother and sister. Would Io be as assiduous in his attentions to a small child with great worries? Who would love the stonefish, now that Punga was gone? Who would take time to shape each individual cloud, now that Ao was no more? Who would save the drowning infant now that Pere was but a cold silent star in the roof of voyaging? Who was there to blame for a capsized canoe, now that Aremata-popoa had been destroyed and his divine presence scattered and lost?

Craig feared this new world was more impersonal than the old. Like others, he felt a great sadness fall upon him, like a cold dark cloak. The deities had gone, the magic had gone, the wonderful heroes would become mere distant figures in stories of the past. Soon they would not be part of real life at all, but merely names on the tongues of storytellers. All the great voyages were over: the oceans had been sailed and there were no new journeys to make.

All the weight of earthly cares was now on the shoulders of humankind. The responsibility was bearable, but nevertheless it was hard to bear. A new seriousness had entered their lives, which had driven out the innocence of yesterday. It might be the *right* course for the world to take, but was it the *best?* The old gods with their petty squabbles had at least made things interesting.

While Craig mused on these important thoughts, the fleet passed some landfalls. In the straits between a clutch of islands they met a great whale. They followed the creature, as Kupe had followed the giant octopus in the opposite direction, which was heading towards their beloved Oceania. Thus they travelled in the wake of this huge mammal, as on a track across the open ocean.

On the way they passed a half-dozen longships manned by sea-raiders. Both sides watched each other warily. The Hawaiians, the best of the naval forces, were fortunately on the far side of the Oceanian flotilla, or they might have been tempted to have a go at these arrogant-looking long-ships. No doubt the Tahitians, who also liked a sea-battle, would have joined them. As it was, the two fleets passed each other without incident.

Craig thought he saw something in the hard light-blue eyes of the sea-raiders, as they almost brushed vessels: some hint of a future engagement.

But that was pure speculation on his part.

At the front of each canoe, Tiki sat impassive, ready to guide his people home. His place in this changed world was not dependent on the presence of the old gods. He had not been a part of their terrible struggle. After all, he was not a god himself but the First Man, the divine ancestor of all Oceanians: as revered as the gods had been, but not of their number.

Tiki's birth as a mortal would ensure his survival.

GLOSSARY

Adaro: Malevolent sea-spirit in the shape of a fish-man.

Ahu: Sacrificial platform, sometimes of stone or planks, sometimes of raised bark cloth.

Airo fai: Dagger made of a stingray's back-bone.

Akiaki: Fairy tern.

Aotearoa: Land of the Long White Cloud, New Zealand.

Ariki: High-born noble.

Arioi: Magnificent dance and song company formed in ancient Tahiti which cruised between the islands and dispensed entertainment to the masses.

Atoro: Fifth rank Arioi, one small stripe on left side.

Avae Parai: Painted Leg, top rank of Arioi, equal to a king.

Balepa: Corpse still wrapped in its burial mat which flies above villages at night.

Ei: Halo of flowers.

Fanakenga star: Zenith star.

Fangu: Magic spell for various general uses.

Gata waka club: Fijian war club made from a thick curved branch with a stubby forked end.

Haka: Maori war dance.

Harotea: Third rank Arioi, both sides of the body marked with stain from armpits downwards.

Hawaiki: The mythical island birthplace of the Polynesian peoples, called the Sacred Isle.

Hivan Islands: Marquesas group.

Hoki: Group of wandering musicians, poets and dancers based in the Marquesas.

Hotu Matua: Legendary Polynesian discoverer of Easter Island and its people's first king.

Hua: Fourth rank Arioi, two or three figures tattooed on shoulders.

Hura: Erotic Tahitian dance.

Icharacha: Huge supernatural beast which roams an Otherworld of the Celts, a crustacean with a dozen horns and many legs, each leg armed with several pincers.

Ifurin: One of the Celtic Otherworlds.

I Ula: Light Fijian throwing club.

I Wau: Heavy Fijian warclub.

Kabu: Soul with a visible shape, though not necessarily human form.

Kahuna: Priest, wise person, versed in the arts of black magic. (Hawaiian word, but used here to distinguish between a 'high priest or priestess' and a tohunga, a specialist in something, e.g. funeral rites, tattooing.)

Kapuku: Art of raising the dead.

Karakia: Magic chant to use against aggressors, as protection or as a weapon. It will also drive out the demons which cause illness.

Kava: Intoxicating drink made by chewing the root of a *Piper methysticum* shrub and mixing the subsequent paste with water.

Kaveinga: Paths of stars which follow each other up from one spot on the horizon. Polynesian sailors used these natural paths as a navigational aid.

Kopu: Morning Star.

Kopuwai: Dog-headed man of savage disposition.

Kotiate club: Hand club shaped like a stunted paddle with a bite out of one side.

Kotuku: Very rare white heron.

Kukui: Candlenut tree.

Kurangai-tuku: New Zealand ogress who used her lips like a spear, shooting them out to impale the prey.

Lei-o-mano: Dagger made of hardwood rimmed with shark's teeth.

Lipsipsip: Dwarves who live in old trees and ancient rocks.

Lotophagoi: Islands of Eternal Souls, where there is no day or night, the sun always shines, and no one is unhappy.

Luch: Gaelic for 'mouse'.

Mana: Magical or supernatural powers, the grace and favour of the divinities, conferred by them. A chief has great mana naturally, but another man must build his mana (carried in the head) by doing great deeds, by becoming a famous warrior or priest.

Manu's Body: Sirius.

Marae: Courtyard in front of a temple or king's house, a sacred place where sacrificial victims are prepared.

Mareikura: Heavenly angels, servants of Io.

Maro: Waist belt.

Maru-ura: The sacred red girdle of kingship on Raiatea, made of scarlet feathers sewn into tapa cloth to form a history of the royal line.

Matatoa: 'Birdman', an Easter Island death cult which evolved during the period of the island's clan wars.

Ngaro: The food of the dead.

Niwareka: Daughter of Uetonga, King of the fair-haired fairies of Rarohenga, a land below the earth.

Nokonoko, or aito: Ironwood tree, used for making weapons.

Omemara: Sixth rank Arioi, a small circle on each ankle.

Otiore: Second rank (one from the top) member of the Arioi, tattooed from fingers to shoulders.

Pa: Fortified Maori village.

Pahi: Large, double-hulled ocean-going canoe with a flat deck between the hulls, able to carry seventy or more passengers and ten crew for a month-long voyage without touching land.

Pahi Tamai: Double-hulled paddled war canoes.

Pakoko: Mourning dress worn at the funeral of a great person.

Patu club: Hand club shaped like a stunted paddle.

Pia: Arrowroot, which when scraped is white like snow.

Ponaturi: Sea-fairies, vicious and aggressive, often staging pitched battles with heroes of Oceania.

Poo: Seventh rank Arioi, 'pleasure-making class', known as *flappers*.

Puata: Living monster conceived out of wood and clay, a boar-like creature but much larger than a real boar. A puata talks, and walks on its hind legs, but is stupid.

Puhi: High-born virgin, a maiden princess.

Putuperereko: Evil spirit with huge testicles.

Rapanui: Easter Island.

Sau: Spiritual puissance of a man or woman.

Sobesila: Fijian club.

Sokilaki: Fijian multi-barbed fighting spear.

Tai-moana: Long drum carried on board a double-hulled ocean-going canoe – 'Threnody of the Seas'.

Taniwha: Monster of some kind, perhaps a giant lizard or a fish, or a creature which assumes the shape of someone's worst fears.

Tapa: Bark-cloth made from the inner bark of the paper mulberry tree.

Tapu: Taboo, sacred or consecrated, forbidden – it applies not only to the person or thing prohibited, but also to the prohibition and any person breaking the prohibition.

Tapu-tapu atia: Most Sacred, Most Feared.

Tapua: Goblin-like creature with a white skin.

Targolo: Evil spirit which seduces people of both sexes and cuts up their genitals to kill them.

Te lapa: Underwater streaks of light from active volcanoes beneath the surface of the sea.

Te Reinga: Land of the Dead.

Tekoteko: Carving above the gate of a Maori pa, either of human, animal or demon. A tekoteko has magical properties.

Ti: Cabbage-tree.

Ti'i: Wooden images used by magicians to assist them in their spells.

Tipairu: Race of fairies who love dancing and who descend on moonlit nights to take part in celebrations, always disappearing back into the forest at dawn.

Tipairua: Double-hulled ocean-going canoe similar to the pahi but closely resembling a war canoe.

Tipua: Goblins.

Tohua: Marquesan temple.

Tohunga: Priest who specializes in tapu, funeral rites and communing with the spirits of air, sea and earth.

Tu'i Tonga: Title of Ruler of Tonga.

Turehu: Fairies from the land of Rarohenga, an Underworld.

Tutua: Low-born people, peasants.

Uetonga: King of the Turehu fairies and grandson of Ruau Moko, God of Earthquakes.

Umu: Earth oven lined with stones to retain the heat.

Váa: Small paddled outriggerless canoe.

Váa motu: Outrigger sailing canoe.

Vis: Blood-drinking succubus.

Wahaika club: Hand club shaped like a violin.

If you've enjoyed these books and would like to read more, you'll find literally thousands of classic Science Fiction & Fantasy titles through the **SF Gateway**

✳

For the new home of
Science Fiction & Fantasy . . .

✳

For the most comprehensive collection
of classic SF on the internet . . .

✳

Visit the SF Gateway

www.sfgateway.com

Garry Kilworth (1941–)

Garry Douglas Kilworth was born in York in 1941 and travelled widely as a child, his father being a serviceman. After seventeen years in the RAF and eight working for Cable and Wireless, he attended King's College, London University, where he obtained an honours degree in English. Garry Kilworth has published novels under a number of pseudonyms in the fields of Science Fiction, Fantasy, Historical Fiction and Children's Fiction, winning the British and World Fantasy Awards and being twice shortlisted for the prestigious Carnegie Award for Children's Literature.